RISE
OF THE ANCIENT
SEA KINGS

BY

KYLE CLAYTON

1

THE FUGITIVE

The snow before him broke as the sea in a storm, chopped and frozen that a tired god might probe its surface for an eternity in the moment before the next wave fell. Here was a heel, or the deep knuckle of a toe where he passed once amid the turmoil. Over that, the dimple of knees pressed the sharp ice into peaks, and the furrows of a shin scraped through. Now a hand pressed its mark near the end of his slow spiral out from the center, the third journey against the sun. His knees ached from the cold. His fingers ached from the cold. Tunguk brushed aside a bit of slush where he thought he saw a dark spot, and blinked it clear. The late morning light began to give up its shadows so at last he could see his work. The spray of color lifted. It shone white against the blemishes, now easy to spot.

A quarter circle behind, he heard the ice crunch in his wake. She insisted on it. His efforts alone were not trusted. To his right lay the smooth snow, unmarred by travel. It lapped against the ragged seam of the circle, tamped by the footprint of their tukit the night before. He switched the hand that held the front tail of his tunic against his chest now that the other settled its throbbing. Though they had taken much of the dark snow, he knew that he would find more. As many times as they cared to pass. A grin crossed his lips as he considered how much trouble even the gods must have to find a man who goes over the side in a storm—even though they might scour the span of the sea for eternity in the moment before the next wave falls.

He closed his eyes for some time to let the dark relieve them against the glare long before they protested. Kjartke would have to cut masks for them soon. When he opened them, the familiar pain in his head returned, and he allowed it to beat with his heart, then proceeded before he wanted to. The sound of her pace urged him on as a hunter does a seal over the pack. His knees shuffled forward, then the one hand came down for support, and he scanned the next patch. The snow was sharp, and he pored his effort over the six hundred ridges between the broken prints. It was here he would find what had not yet been forced into the hollows where it might disappear.

Three journeys from the center to the edge against the sun: First they tore it up by the armload. Then the handful. Yet there were still so many proud ridges that had not fallen beneath their weight. Wild, and defiant. There would not be time to see to them all. Tunguk hoped only that he had done enough that it would take a great patience to find what he overlooked, and few would have it.

He broke once more into the song that occupied him in bursts this last round. It was not a song for finding things that were lost, or escaping one's enemies, nor a song to hide in plain sight. Tunguk sang in the farri's tongue, for it was not even a song of the Mattaka. Its purpose was to help men raise the anchor, and to torment Kjartke.

"I go nowhere but here,
for the sea, it turns beneath me.
I but lift me foot
and the bottom, she would leave me.
One! Two!
Three! Four!
Drag me not.
Shore! Shore!
One! Two!
Three! Four!
Two and twenty
I've gone before!
Two and twenty
I've gone before!"

His eyes narrowed in a smile she could not see. Only then, in the blur of a moment's distraction, did it catch him. Tunguk scooted forward. Plain against the sharp white ice stood a speck of rust. He leaned in so as not to disturb it, and extended his long fingers to pinch it off at the base. Clean snow stuck to it but it was unmistakable when he held it before his nose. With care, Tunguk opened the tail of his tunic and deposited it in the growing wet pile.

He finished his course, "Four and thirty I've gone before!" Then rose to his feet, careful not to step over the edge into the perfect field until he came to the place their tracks exited. A few yards away, he opened the sleeping bag, stuffed thick over halfway full. Inside, the reds warmed to brown, or mixed with the whites to settle in pink clumps. There seemed enough blood in the snow to fill a new man. All of it had to go. Brother had many enemies now. They could not learn of his wound, and it would be unwise to let them gather some part of him that they might use for a curse.

Tunguk let his tail fall and brushed the contents free. He looked back over the circle. Kjartke crawled the last of her passage. From this distance, he could see none of the colors in his bag. But no eye could mistake the chaos of the place against the youthful plain around it. Heavy ruts of movement carved deep wrinkles to where he stood and beyond. The dark had not brought the winds and the drift they prayed for, and the air stood calm. Now if the breeze stirred, it would come from the water, where there was no snow to ride upon it. On the far side, even his "ancestor eyes," she called them, could make out the trail of footprints that led away to Drummoc where many boots passed before the dawn.

His heart caught like a mooring line against a bobbing ship. An early verse from the Song of Vitjukvattajuk returned to him—the one about how the sea remembers every wake. He watched his own stretch down from the foot of Urkuk, through the winding town; to the harbor where a ship left with Foster, or it did not; and to the open water beyond. Kjartke finished her work and brushed past him through the same channel. The water, as unblemished as the snow plain. It would not remain so. Men and ships alike traveled few courses. It would be vain to hope otherwise. Soon they would follow once more along this way, and he wondered only who: a friendly sled, or a column of boots.

It was good to see the *Gairhle* off. The sail ran up the mast as she pitched through a distant haze. Oars almost too small to make out stretched their tired arms over the water and drew in to rest. The ship herself seemed to let go a breath she had held for some time. It was a light, fair wind, and Haraket thought the *Gairhle* should enjoy it, because there would be few traveling her way from here on. He longed for the same breath. Perhaps only the Navy boiled his heart more, and too often the difference between sailor and whaler was but the season. Yet some part of him that found kin in suffering soared for those vanishing now on the benches. He had taken to sleeping open at the harbor instead of with his family. His charge was as precious, and the accidents of mood that could grant a man permission to launch were so fleeting that he dared not sacrifice a moment to comfort.

The whalers' torches across the harbor had given him solace at night. Though he slept alone, there was another crew, just as eager and at odds with Costig that he often felt there were fifty souls on watch for him. It did not matter that of late, Palqua slept among them. Twice, he nearly got off due to the distraction they caused. There was little time for concern with a supply run to Camne Drumlag when the dread of a loose-tongued whaler hung above the admiral.

Now, the difficulty grew. He imagined that this Leopard Seal would take their place. A new distraction, and as much of an excuse to tie him down. He wished to see the admiral lashed for his insolence. The parade of lies astonished him. They would only dare be so bold with a Mattaka. He could feel their laughter bubbling out of their cheeks as they told him with somber faces that he had the wrong ship, the wrong crew, or risked a stowaway in a vessel they loaded themselves and that could be searched at a glance.

The only grace of the Navy's grip on Drummoc was their senility. It would be too firm a hand to live under if the hand could often remember what it was doing, and expect help from the other hand. Haraket recalled that his cousin, upon being arrested for the serious offense of stabbing a man, was given over to another unit in such clumsy fashion that he manged to convince them he was, in fact, a blacksmith who arrived for work drunk and whose master asked that he be detained until sunset without pay as punishment.

The jailer released Muk as soon as the shift changed, saying that he would perform, "no errands for squains." No man would do what another should have done, and if a word must be passed, it would be gnawed to scraps by the kaim before it found the proper ears. Their sloth and stupidity made a fine salve for their brutal oversight.

This is how Haraket had a darraig fully loaded and searched to ensure that no fugitives were curled among the casks before the whaler ever got pinned. There was even a navy crew that, for the moment, thought they were assigned to carry him to Camne Drumlag as soon as the harbor was clear to launch. Only the harbormaster's sniveling held him for want of an admiralty letter. He'd heard about the ship that sailed without one a few days ago by charging that a navy crew destined for the mines needn't observe the pointless formality. That crew belonged to a halot. A man with a single lowly power would never yield it to a squain.

It was as close as he ever came to leaving, and still Haraket was almost certain he would spend another night huddled beside his people's supplies. No one would ask on his behalf. Costig was already barking orders at the men beside him and brushing off the hand-waving ministers. Haraket set his jaw and marched toward the navy hall, anticipating the admiral's path. He forced himself to stare at his feet as he closed—he could ill-afford a look of pride. Better to be so near invisible that he could be halfway to Camne Drumlag with a letter before Costig remembered granting the request.

The admiral's departure was the bird that scattered the flock. Hardly a man in Drummoc was missing from the *Gairhle*'s send-off. Now a current of them flowed after the officer while clusters of Mattaka or navy crews broke off to their obligations. Haraket dodged between bodies. It had the effect of shielding his approach while his eyes steered, fixed on the stout head like a line thrown between ships. With care, he fell in alongside to avoid inflicting the slightest stutter on the admiral's pace.

"Sir! The crew stands ready and the ship is prepared to launch according to orders. It is only the harbormaster who asks your letter." He cut through the voices begging attention.

"Who the fuck are you, again?"

"Haraket, sir."

The admiral stopped to take in the agitator, and the column behind collapsed into itself. His brow narrowed. The ruddy cheeks rose in an uneven grin.

"Camne Drumlag." He started up again. Haraket nearly leapt to keep astride. "You're persistent. I'll be sure to tell the assistant viceroy."

"*Sir!*" Haraket frightened himself with the emphasis. The line halted once more behind the surprised officer. Haraket hurried to recover his cultivated patience. "Admiral Costig," his voice softened. Amusement flickered across the admiral's fair eyes. He waited for the young man to muster his courage. With effort, Haraket pressed back the cursed pride of the Mennegur family to remind himself he had come to secure the needs of his fellows across the channel, and no more.

"Your men have taken pains to load a darraig that is not used for drills. The captain himself recounted the supplies, and saw that no man found his way aboard. It is my privilege to report to the assistant viceroy that you have spared us all that you could, at the earliest time possible."

The two Amposi idlers who accompanied the admiral everywhere made no secret of their disdain. Costig looked back over the platoon of morning beggars, then again at Haraket. The cheer on his face was a sharp wound to the envoy's hopes.

"Then you've done just as I've asked, lad. Not a beam to level?"

"Aye, sir."

"I'll need to see her, of course. Would you have me inspect her now?"

Haraket felt it was a challenge to his gall. If he said no, he would not see the admiral until he found the courage to ask the same of him the following morning. But to demand the officer of colony change course for his meager errand would ensure he was well-remembered for the duration of what could be a lengthy dockside stay.

"If it isn't too much trouble for the admiral, we might still arrive before dark."

"No trouble at all, me son." He turned to his beggar flock. "You heard him, lads! Back to the dock! The sooner we inspect his ship, the sooner we can see to your affairs!"

Haraket's stomach dropped out as it became clear the tack Costig was taking. He hurried to keep at the admiral's heels so he would not have to face the bitter looks of the men who now found themselves in tow to his concerns. By the gods' favor, the crew he conjured had not yet wandered off, though a good half slept against their stuffed bags. The little darraig—the lowest in the patchwork fleet—groaned against the quay in the lapping waters. Already, the middle benches stood claimed. Most of the men, however, loafed on shore with as little optimism as Haraket that she would sail.

Costig squared his feet and planted his hands on his hips. He drew no closer. His eyes did the accounting, while his ample mustache pursed out over his lips in consideration.

"She floats." He almost sounded surprised.

"Aye, sir," Haraket said enthusiastically. "I would not trouble her with the waters of the Attavaik, but she has many good runs over the channel in her."

Costig nodded in agreement. "And many she'll make. Perhaps as soon as tomorrow." It was a gut punch, and it hurt no less that he saw it coming. Haraket did not respond. "This your crew?"

He nodded.

Costig waved two fingers at the captain to approach. "Amachar! Who assigned you to this run?"

The newly-arrived Amposi took a moment to work over the question. "Figured it was you, admiral."

"I've forgotten half of what I did yesterday, and half again the day before. But I'm square on what I didn't. Who passed along the order?" Amachar tilted his head toward Haraket. A brief panic flared before he gathered himself.

"What of it, me son? Who told you to pass along the order?" He feared that Costig knew Haraket's scheme all too well. There was nothing to be gained by admitting it, though.

"Perhaps it was told poorly. I understood the crew that was assigned yesterday would see her over. But the captain told me his men were to march on Urkuk today. He said the roster would pass to those who held the watch."

"No one's goin' to Urkuk today. All hands were to muster at the harbor to see the *Gairhle* off. Perhaps he lied to you to save himself the trouble." Haraket nodded. "Who was the captain? I can't have me man lyin' to squains to shirk his duty." This was not Palqua, and he was farther yet from Turrha. Haraket weighed whether the admiral would bother to track down Barrow Jak and confront him with the story.

"I do not recall his name, sir," he lied. "But I would know his face." It was the only bluff he dared. If Costig meant to gather all his captains for Haraket to pick him out, he trembled to imagine the consequences. The way the admiral studied him, he was certain they both knew it.

"Amachar's men stood watch last night. It's a cruel bastard who'd send tired dogs over the sound."

Turrha would, Haraket thought. Palqua. This one, too, if he saw fit.

"Fear not, me son. *Polc!*" He shouted. It was the captain of Tolba's messenger who appeared from the throng.

"Aye, Admiral!"

"You're just back from Camne Drumlag. You remember the way?"

"If she'll have me again."

"Take this lad's kit over to the assistant viceroy."

"Aye, sir. The men'll be glad to hear they've escaped Rixtan another day."

Costig raised a hand. "Hang on. Were you on for drills today?"

Polc looked baffled for a moment. "Aye, sir. Accordin' to yourself."

Costig made a show of rolling his eyes and shaking his head. "Apologies, lad! It's like I said: somethin' about forgettin' half of what I said." He turned to Haraket. "These men are fresh enlistments and need their paces. Can't have them flounderin' before Donnab's bastards come Spring. Report to Rixtan," he ordered Polc. "And tomorrow, to this squain. What was your name, lad?" Costig's eyes shone right to the back of his skull.

"Haraket. Sir." He choked.

"I'll not forget it."

A high shout broke their attention. There panted a boy, barely able to keep up with his own steps as he sprinted across the harbor from somewhere up the peninsula. Every few pumps of his arms, he swung them wide at his trousers as a young bird trying to take flight. It was not the sky he wanted, but the eyes of those assembled. The shout came again, and it was the admiral's name—no title, rude and familiar. What seemed a youth grew smaller as he stumbled up and transformed into a child of perhaps eight. His collapse seemed imminent—or his collision with Costig. He whirled his arms to propel him. It was too baffling to be an attack. Even the marines who should have stepped between them frowned where they stood.

"Costig!" the youth cried once more. Haraket thought he would stop at last, but he crumpled into the stout officer and clawed at his clothing for balance. Costig took his armpits to steady him on his feet. Horror washed over the onlookers—the Mattaka, especially. A man in his place would have been cut down. The admiral pried him loose with a fatherly hand while he gathered his lungs. This boy had trespassed beyond even Haraket's mistake. He should have trembled for his life. The island was already astir over one prisoner who tried to fall upon the officer in an aggressive manner, and he, one of the admiral's own kind. But the boy grinned up as wide as his mouth would part.

"Costig," he huffed.

"What of it, lad?"

The boy settled himself on his feet and straightened his grease-stained tunic. "I come for the reward." Costig folded his arms to wait. "Grandfather," he took another deep breath, "send for you. We have Leopard Seal."

Three piles of sleds. This was the boys' bounty after more than a day of digging out the overflow mounds. Sifting through every forlorn tukit, yanking with all their might to free the impossible tangles that the runners wove in winter's privacy. Sawi kept them until the sun made a shadow of the bowl where the dog camp rippled out of the snow. He pried them from sleep in anticipation of its return. It was the first time Norwet had felt such action. The place seemed in a slumber when he arrived—one that began long before the last season ended, and threatened to wallow under a stiff blanket until nothing stirred.

Now the surface broke and flashed like a clear fjord under the first oars of the morning. The sunrise dripped warmth into the upper layer, calling to that beneath it, stretching out in a wake. The dogs kept a nervous vigil. He did not know why—it could only mean work for them, and theirs was the hardest. But all the creatures wanted was to lean into leather, and run.

Glittering to one side stood three rows of sleds that survived the neglectful night in pristine condition. Every strap on them would still need to be tightened or replaced; every runner planed and iced; a missing cross brace substituted. There was little to fault.

To the other, those in need of repair. Where the first lot would pull this evening if they must, these begged a skilled hand. Old wood cracked under hasty storage, or pieces vanished altogether. It was not clear which ones limped this last season, or sat wanting for much longer. The boys also excavated Sawi's wood pile, and it was a pitiful assortment. A fair portion was not even new sled wood from Ampos, but split from irreparable hulls or masts that would never leave Drummoc. Far too little to put all of them back on the trail. Perhaps there was more for sale in Drummoc, and Sawi would pay for it once he saw the condition of things. Norwet knew that no more ships would arrive this season, so if the Navy lacked the materials or Sawi the coin, the fate of these sleds fell upon the third pile.

And this one, a true pile. No care was needed with the bones of these fallen laborers. Most no longer looked like sleds to any but the trained eye. It was custom to call the sled wood "bones," because in the past it *was* bone, and they made the skeleton of the body that bore the firestone behind the thumping legs of the dogs. In this case, it was often true. Whale bones and even seal, smoothed and darkened, crossed one another with ragged bits of strap rotting from the ends. Many of them were shattered and unusable. Nothing was ever discarded. There were too many things the family may need that could come of it. Too many surprising births of necessity. Little of it would be in his father's scrap pile, though. Norwet thought it fit for beads, or dolls at best. He shook loose a promising strip of wood.

"Cross brace." Senadak, the father of his two cousins, examined it. He bent it back and forth a few times before eliciting a snap. "Cracked."

He handed it back to Norwet, who tossed it into a fourth pile that he hoped to separate from Sawi's fancies once and for all. Across the scraps, Ferrakut caught his gaze. Norwet could already see the bulge under his brother's tunic.

"Senadak! What of this one?" He blurted before he had a piece in mind. The first thing he grasped was a shameful chunk of seal bone, charred at one end—hopeless in any capacity. His cousin scowled and snatched it away.

"You would use this at Nunoc?" He flung it aside. Norwet tensed. It was a Seleku scrap, he thought. Vjarku had no such refuse among their sleds. Senadak noticed Ferrakut's hesitation across the pile.

"What are you doing? It is too early to fuck around. Come here!" Ferrakut froze, then turned his back, his lower half concealed by the mound. A quick squatting motion, and he faced them to slink around to Senadak. The reproach continued on his arrival, but now freed of the attention, Norwet meandered to where his brother had squatted. In the snow, just apart from the rest, lay a stout length of whale bone that could only have been used as a cross brace at one time. The notches where the strap would bind it were rounded and in need of a blade, but it was a fine bit. He glanced over. Sawi and a grown cousin, Umatbarak, took account of the modest rows of working sleds with Sawi's sons—Milak, Ravitak, and Arnake. The other man of the bunch, Sawi's younger brother Onag, had his face buried in the pile that required repairs, with Saunlauk and Siguvik. The latter noticed Norwet's look, and turned to speak to his uncle.

Norwet bent down and slipped the bone under his tunic. He took a step, then hesitated and backed diagonally to the discarded bits. One knee found the snow, and he gathered the cracked length of wood that Senadak abandoned. They burned cold against his belly as he shuffled beyond the scrap pile to a small, empty drift where they had dug up much of what they now sorted. One more look, then he knelt and plunged his hand in to find the corner of the leather blanket. Norwet raised it as little as he could to slide the two pieces under, atop the ill-matched collection of strap and slat. He smoothed the leather back down, and swept at the snow until once more it was a seamless white drift.

Costig winced as the hard edge of one of the gold coins in his boot dug into his hurried step. He jerked his foot and quickened his pace to disguise the movement, stifling the urge to limp. The boy led with a tired jog. Behind him, whatever hangers-on were present hustled dutifully after their admiral. He had no time to summon marines. It would be moments before the rest of the Mattaka realized what was going on. Already, a few sprinted ahead among the huts in a disorganized effort. Young blood, with their own purposes for trying to reach the lad's grandfather first. Whether they intended to free the fugitive, or collect the argots that bore into Costig's foot, they would not be kind to the old man. Besides the usual complement of pestering officials, he had Wendell, and Polc's crew. Gerachay went for reinforcements, but they wouldn't know where to go. He'd no notion of how Tolba's hire would fare if the population pressed them, but it would have to do.

No matter who got there first, there remained the problem in his boot. He wondered how long it would be until he had a moment to himself to move the two pieces of gold. When he set out to meet Foster and Parks, he did not expect to return with the coins, and now was glad he did. They hardly seemed likely to help, now.

The boy led them toward the north coast, well away from the place he last saw what was left of the fugitive. It couldn't be Parks, he thought. A trick, or a mistake. Another speculative guess. But he regretted using the reward as an excuse to lighten the treasury of the coin he needed to pay his dagger men. It was too much. The frenzy it whipped up among the people from the moment he announced it made him want to crack himself. Nor had he a plan to account for the missing coin, hoping that something would occur to him over the course of the siege.

This was the last place he'd expect to find the idiot, but if he arrived to a dismembered lad and the outstretched hand of a squain, there was still the third argot to explain—the one he sent off on the whaler. He should have waited for Willakuy's count of the treasury, then blamed the missing money on the assistant viceroy instead of recording his withdrawal as a reward. The coin stabbed him again on his behalf.

Rather than a right turn to enter the town as he expected, the lad veered hard toward the coast. Almost immediately, they could make out a gray head crouched on the rock beside his skin boat with a spear clenched at the ready. As yet, there was no one else in sight. Costig sprung ahead in unadmiral-like excitement. His wind made itself known by the time he stopped at the grandfather. The old man trembled with relief as the column arrived. Tears welled in his eyes, and he embraced his grandson with pride. He knew the stakes as well as Costig did.

"Polc! Form up your men to the town. Two lines abreast, staggered to gap."

"Aye, sir! You heard him, cunts!"

The crew stumbled into a undisciplined wall. This was not their trade, but they looked keen enough for a fight, and there was at least a knife to each of them.

"Is there a marine among us?" He said to the audience-seekers. Three men hurried to the front. Two of them weren't even in leathers, and he recognized one as a lad who last season had begged transfer to the Navy, which he'd granted. The other was like to have the same story, but they knew Costig would prefer a bluecoat loafer who used to know a thing to the rest of the grassbenders and whalers in the fleet.

"Palchar," Costig recalled the Marine's name. "Run back for Gerachay and see that the men know where to find us."

"Aye, sir!"

"You two, on me."

Wendell found his way to Costig's side. "Better to have you," Costig greeted him in the custom of a man on the line before battle. He could tell Wendell thought it an indulgent jest, and he grinned to downplay it. "Make these scullions look purposeful," He said of the dozen or so officials and naval officers who'd come to ask some idiotic question of him that morning.

A shout from the town caught his ear, and a squain lad on the far side of Polc's men was joined by several companions. They held their ground, and soon more voices rose. The people poured from their huts—the very old and very young who were not occupied in the mines. Women drew out in their curiosity, and a thick band of young men in sooted leathers formed up across from Polc. Blacksmiths. Not a forge going to redden his steel, by the looks of it. Gangs of the younger ones, too small for the mines or yet claiming it until the right boat should appear. If the lot of Mattaka had been an army, it already overwhelmed his own scant line, with more trickling in. How they knew so fast, he could never say. As though the streets sent word ahead of the mouths. He considered addressing them to stand clear, or perhaps to disperse. It wouldn't go. Better to tend his affairs as if the crowd were gawkers of no concern.

The old man and his grandson fixed upon him, full of anticipation. They thought themselves safe, behind four dozen blades. Costig knew it was a hope.

"Well?" Was all he said. The man hurried toward the little boat. Costig nodded his two marines into service. His stomach lurched. He doubted with great conviction that he would see the face of the vaunted Leopard Seal, but it would be enough of a disaster that he could not settle his bile. They wrestled with something in the boat. An object, more than a person. Even the line of mercenaries turned to have a look, while the crowd strained over their shoulders from as close as they dared. It was apparent before the vaguest of features that the man they lay on the rock was quite dead.

Costig bent over the wet corpse with an eye on the Mattaka. A wave of relief drew back as he took in the two bloated legs, near bursting. The whole of his skin was bruised and smashed by the surf. The birds had not found him, so he must have been fresh. It was a halot. That much, and only that, he was sure of. The wet leathers were worth no description. The face, ground to meal by the pestle of the sea. The argot curled under his toes as he gripped and released it. A dead fugitive earned but three silvers, and that, he could spare.

When he looked again, it was as though the crowd had given birth—larger again by half. The front pressed toward the line against its will by those pushing in from the back. Its span now stretched far enough to flank Polc on both sides. Fingers curled and feet shifted among the unsteadier of those men. He snatched Polc by the collar and growled in his ear.

"Hold your stabbin'. They don't take it well."

It was a certain kind of gift. This one had too many limbs, and only Costig knew it. Dead, too. He needn't worry about a rush to free the man. It could remain a curiosity if they held their liver. Moreover, he saw the pretense it could spare him: more doomed searches to conduct; messages to run; all under the nose of men like Wendell, who paid attention. He considered bringing him in. By Euskus, he could tell the whole island how he seeded the *Gairhle* without consequence now that she was off. But it would give them cause to watch him closer. And there was yet the problem across the channel. Better to brag of deeds when they were done. This could still be his Leopard Seal, if he pleased. Three silvers to an old man, and then the problem of failing to return the argots to the treasury. That would be forgiven with praise at the end of the siege if his infiltrators did their work.

He bent over the corpse to feign examination. The lie would be easier. Declare it the Leopard Seal, pay the man, and be done. There was another Costig, though: the marine-turned-admiral who sought a criminal in earnest. The man who once turned out a ship over a broken seal on a cask. And who, finding no sweet breath, plumbed the bottom to raise a bundle of fresh steel, liberated from the forge. Nor did he take the officers' story of squains smuggling forbidden blades to their kin at Drummoc. He parted them and put them on the ice until their stories broke, and the captain himself confessed with every officer but the coxswain. The Costig that squared the load if he had to load it thrice—that's the one these men expected to see. None would be taken aback to see him wither in admiral's boots, as they all did. Most would lose confidence with a shrug, and go about their affairs. It would be himself whose disapproval harried him most. That was still the Costig all of them needed to see.

"Found him like this, did you?" The old man nodded reassuringly. "Then how do you know it's the Leopard Seal?" The face turned, as he sensed an official who intended to deprive him of his just compensation.

"It is him. Who else?"

Costig felt the murmur of the crowd grow. If they could not have their man, they would want the thrill of the silver falling into the hands of one of their own. It was an admiral's way to promise much and give nothing.

He lowered himself beside the body with a groan. "Wendell. Are we missin' a man?"

"I'll ask about."

Costig nodded. He scooted forward so that the heel of his golden boot was even with the cracked, bare feet. Costig lay back, inches away, and folded his hands over his chest to squint at the sky. His head rolled to his left where he studied the remains of an ear. The baffled concern of the officials nearby stirred him with amusement.

"Tough cast, mate," he said to the corpse. "Did you have the pleasure to meet the Leopard Seal, Wendell?"

"'Fraid not, Costig."

"He was a fine-lookin' fellow. Shame what Hawe's done to him. Even stole his boots, and made him shorter by a head."

"*Ha*!" Wayranapan cried in jubilation. "It is not him! The admiral stood but to his neck, and this man, only to the admiral's brow!"

The old Mattaka poured out his protest, but it was drowned by the breaking roar of the crowd. Costig worked back to his feet. To a soul, they sprung and whooped at the proclamation. Polc's lads tensed, fearing a rush, but there was nothing this side of the line they could have wanted. The admiral beamed to his men, then back over the people, who had turned their shouting on each other. It was not clear what their grievance was, but he was glad to have it aimed elsewhere. Most of them seemed to taunt a group of boys who responded with obscene gestures even for the old women, which only roused them more.

A different youth of perhaps twelve separated himself from the throng and set in on his own histrionics, directed at Costig. He thumped his chest and waved in lazy deference. It was the boasting of a warrior seeking acknowledgment.

"You wait!" He shouted over the line of mercenaries. "You wait! I will come! I bring him to you. Gold hand, you wait!"

The taunted lads striped him in Mattakatan, and he returned it. Two more came to his aid, as the five drifted towards him. Once the hands loosed overhead, Costig knew there was little room for retreat.

"Back to your huts!" He shouted to disperse the crowd. "Back to your huts!" Polc's men took up his chorus. The lads could hear none but each other. The offended group fell back a step, and he believed in a blink it was over. Then another word, and one of them lunged forward with a swipe of his arm that seemed to miss. It did not. The boaster's eyebrow hung down in a flap from a clean gash that poured over his face. His own blade came out, and the center of the crowd circled back to escape the flurry. The two mates of the bloody face fled into the throng, and straight away he found himself encircled by the five lads, knives slashing the air in blind arcs. They lunged in and out, probing for contact, and he swung with fury in all directions, stumbling in a dizzy rage.

"Part 'em!" Costig implored his men. None rushed forward to insert himself. Costig couldn't fault them. If they riled the rest of the crowd, they would be the ones facing the knives. He broke through the shoulders of the line and exhorted once more: "Stop! Back to your huts!"

When it had exactly the effect he supposed, he plunged ahead and grabbed the outermost from behind and slung him down. Two of his men were happy to pounce upon him, and Costig leapt back into the melee. The next of the bunch saw him, and had the sense not to swing at an admiral. He surrendered his knife, and Costig threw him into the line, as well. The others were more intent. A flash turned his eye, ready to defend—Polc darted past and went two arms to the one, then dragged the next lad out. Now the crew took fire. Several of the men bashed him until the little body fell limp under their kicks. Costig side-stepped an opening and wrapped up the lone defender to shield him. The other two boys shouted threats as he led the bloody mess toward the safety of his men. The last two gave up as Polc set upon them.

"Enough!" He shouted at Polc's crew where they pummeled the thin bodies. He yanked one by the tunic and dropped him with a fist across the chin. "Enough!" He repeated before Polc joined the order and the men held their fists. They drug the lads away from the crowd, who were now reunited in their contempt for the Navy of Ampos. It seethed once more at his ranks. Every man near him had someone's blood on him.

"Back to your huts!" He tried once more. Most of those who waved at him and cast their oaths were women, and grandfathers. He was certain that had the miners been home for winter, it would have sufficed for a riot. This lot in itself was on the verge when the voices of a marine platoon boomed from the west behind Gerachay. They sprinted into the dismal line and held without needing to be told. The Mattaka still outnumbered them by several fold, but this would be a different affair if they cared to make it one.

As a wave that finds the high cliff and foams back into the surf, the crowd turned its enthusiasm toward the town. They spilled in rivulets between the huts, shouting in joy, protest, or threat. Costig found no relief in it. He knew it would not simply die. A froth sought a collision.

"Wayranapan. All hands not on maneuvers, report to the harbor. Post half at the shipyard, and the rest split between the two halls. Brothel privileges suspended. No man enters the town without me personal order. No man shits alone. What's the word on the masons?"

"Those who can fix the walls are at the mines, sir."

"Wendell, where are the seven squains you arrested?"

"Got 'em in a barracks. Couple marines posted."

"Let 'em go. I'll not give their temper a glint to seize upon." He turned back to Wayranapan. "And take the carved fellow to the poye." He indicated the boy that somehow, despite a half dozen ragged gashes, stood defiant under guard in better shape than most of his attackers, after Polc's men got hold of them.

"Release these," he swept a hand over the five boys. One of them looked up with concern. He knew as well as Costig he and his mates were unpopular just now, and safer in custody. But Costig wouldn't have navy men or masonry between the Mattaka and their grievances.

"Put the dead man back to sea with rites. And Wendell—"

"I'll have his name by end of day."

"Good man." Costig knew by the silence around him he must have been in one of his red faces that paralyzed the most presumptuous of marines. He could well storm off to clean the blood from his tunic and spare himself the mendicants. But the fight had restored him in a way neither sleep nor command could. For the first time in over a week, there was something of himself to give.

"What of it?" He barked to the column.

Costig spent the walk back to the harbor under an earful of problems that either should have been done without a thought from the complainant, or else were altogether insoluble. These last had a common word on the tongue: Camne Drumlag. There had been no late season auxiliary run this year, so there was bound to already be a pile on the shores. And that meant there were no coal ships stuck here for the winter. Nothing worth the name to carry out his order to Lamachar that all the coal brought down this season should be ferried to Drummoc before the ice. The coal minister was unable to grasp that a bushel would, in fact, sit on any ship where it was placed, though it would have to be done in a painstaking number of loads among the two dog ships and a handful of warships. The very notion of any coal at all piled on the shores of Drummoc seemed to rock the man between bewilderment and despair.

The workers he needed for everything from prison repair, to laying up meat, to erecting fortifications in case of a land battle were stuck at the mines. Foster's admonition rung: "If you think a whaler headin' the other way is your biggest problem, you're gonna want a 'mate' across the way." It had been a blessing that Alexicus sailed when he did. Last thing Costig could afford was every man on the island trying to work out whose orders he had to follow. Now he wondered if it weren't better to have the man where he could see him. No doubt, the lad exaggerated on behalf of his one-legged conspirator. If there was any truth to it, though, he wanted to know. It was within his right to take charge under a siege as the ranking officer—and in any other case, as far as he was concerned. But he needed to know his leeway. Show up and arrest the bastard? Strand him? Or tread with care under a favored son of a new viceroy of whom he knew nothing?

It was his luck that Foster was not the only pair of eyes who had seen it, and there were more ways of learning than to pray the Leopard Seal found his feet again.

"A word, lad!" Costig separated Polc from his crew where they prepared to join maneuvers under Rixtan. They drifted clear to watch the Navy form up in confusion across the harbor. "Were you pleased?"

"Pardon, sir?"

"Your men, back there."

Polc offered a wry grin. "Not worse than I expected. Give me a winter and there might be somethin' for you."

"I'll take it. Men rise or fall to their captain, and yours was the first ugly face I saw in the thick of it."

"After yours."

"Somethin' tells me you'll get another crack." Costig said. Polc nodded. "And what of your run? Were you able to get your message off?"

"I delivered it to the commander of the colony some weeks ago," he deferred. "But aye, I gave it as well to the chief official."

"Tolba chose his man well. What news of Camne Drumlag?"

Polc shrugged. "I don't know the old of it, but it's like to be the same, or more of a shithole than it always was."

"And the men. The sailors? The miners?"

"All in good spirits, sir. Though I can't divine why that coxcomb takes to their company."

"Hm!" Costig laughed. "No word for meself, then? When I might expect him, or me twenty-six lads?"

Polc shook his head, "Not to the likes of me."

Costig hid whatever he was thinking behind his stout whiskers.

With that, he left him to Rixtan. It was no more than he would have expected. Alexicus on parade where people might be impressed. Foster on a bluff. And himself, nothing to go on. He could have pressed the lad, but he didn't care to sound desperate. There was no advantage in giving his men cause to think him concerned with the affairs of a petty official. In part, he didn't care to give himself the impression, either. As it stood, he might send his boats at his leisure and get his coal. If the bureaucrat objected, he could politely wrest command over all the affairs of Drummoc on grounds of war.

Foster was off, and would never know what became of his partner. That would be the light of the load for Costig. He could even march his men right to the spot, arrest the nuisance, and keep the reward since navy weren't eligible. Then there was just the problem of how to explain to the dead man how an Amposi argot floated away on a whaler.

The feeling of something unaccounted nagged him. Before the navy hall, a group of Mattaka women rallied behind the oldest, who lit into one of the captains like a sergeant-at-arms into a marine late on deck. Anger welled behind his round cheeks at the thought of one going after his man like that, then it shifted to the captain, who stood there listening while his men loafed about, waiting for someone to come by and explain which foot they should step with next.

The harbor in chaos, a directionless navy, and the wretched spirits of Donnab poised at the Sun Gate with sails furled, awaiting the open jaw of Omera in the spring. He longed for the day when he had few enough men under his command that he could lash every ear that failed him. Now they stretched before him and beyond his sight. Not just the stiff leathers of the Marines, but the patches of blue, the idle sailors, the timid sons of Ampos who could secure no better post than this. The gray-faced Mattaka, the pallid lad across the channel, prancing like a northern stag under his crown. The one sweating his last feverish days in a hut on the foothills of Urkuk. They were all his now. Too many hateful stumblers to curse them by name. If there were but one he could descend upon—sort him, or ship him—he would feel himself again.

Near the entire force had mustered, and there might have been a dozen not fucking up something. He could have his pick, if he thought it would help. It was as though they were a single body, loose of thread and slack of jaw. Feet pointed aside and head scanning for help. He could see the lad he wanted to light into: his leathers not once scrubbed of grease. His spearhead wobbling on the shaft. Newly arrived and huddled against the chill, nose full-drip, already dreaming of his great battles before he managed to form up in his first line. Eager to show his mates what a bright blade their luck had brung them—and they didn't even know it yet.

The face came clear, as when the water of a pool stills. It was the same one he always saw. The man who thought he could do better alone, sneaking behind his brothers. The man who lost a prisoner, and loosed a ship with news he couldn't afford whispered outside these distant waters;

who didn't stand tall enough before a challenger because he was too fresh to believe in his footing. The man who dangled gold before so many eyes, until they had no choice but to go mad for it, and now turned out the town and their slashing blades, and the lost souls who knew not how to contain them but couldn't dare admit it. The whole mess of it lay not with Turrha, or Palqua, or Alexicus. Nor was it boastful Tolba. Costig knew the man who had failed him, and who now begged for the fiery brand of his temper. There was nothing more to say of it.

At least Polc thought something of him, if he was being honest. Costig could still turn out in a scuffle. Now he had to wonder who else had seen his fumbling. For all he was wise of, he could have lost the trust of every man but Foster and Parks, whose trust was conscripted by circumstance.

He circled back over Polc's report. Costig no longer needed the big lad, if it was true. What if it wasn't? Polc couldn't know he'd spoken to Foster, and that their tales were at odds. What cause could he have to ease the admiral's fears if the place deserved them?

He found a man, and sent for Wendell. Costig set on the quarrel and drew both voices with his presence.

"Get her back," he said to a sailor who roped off the women with his arms.

"Hoy," Captain Ithir spat in a manner he didn't care for. "The squains say there's young blades turnin' folk out of their huts. Searchin' after the Leopard Seal."

He let it go unacknowledged, then put his shoulder toward the officer to face the women. "How many?"

"Many."

"Nothin' for it."

"We do law. Where is law now? They are not invited!"

She referred to the sacred way by which none could enter a Mattaka dwelling without being asked by he who erected it, or the head of the family dwelling there. It was a great geiss to violate—taken almost daily by thieves, and cousins, and himself.

"Bring 'em to me and I'll square 'em." Her mouth closed tight and she sank back in defiance. They would get no help from the Navy, and it troubled him. He was helpless to move into the town in force under these winds. It was only a matter of when the squains started stabbing one another. They would not find the man. But Costig wondered if he ought to.

"I've not got you the dead man yet," Wendell interrupted.

"Fair enough." Costig pulled him away from the others. He located Polc, hustling his crew across the harbor grounds. "I've got a live one I need you to look after."

Milak knew he was too late when his father signaled him to keep his distance. He let the armful of hunting spears tumble to the snow at his frustrated feet. Sawipelagannapuk was right. The men made haste down the rim of the bowl and would reach the others before he did. They must have seen him run to the tukits and sensed his purpose. There was nothing that need concern them about a group of Mattaka approaching the camp. It was common to conduct trade, and at this season, to inquire of work with the teams. Something about the men upset Sawi, though. Perhaps he recognized them, or knew more than Milak of why visitors may choose this moment to come. And there were twelve of them.

In all matters of importance, the Mattaka took pains to act in groups of sixes. Of his own family, there were also twelve. Beside Sawi was their aunt's father-in-law, their uncle, and their two cousins. Then there were the seven boys. None had more than a small knife, and he could see the guests carried knives and hammers, and even a few spears. Blacksmiths. He recognized Sewadkut, and some of the men. The younger ones were apprentices. Few strong men remained in Drummoc during the mining season, and these were them. If he returned, he would add to the arms, and his family would gain the numbers. But the number would be thirteen. Better to face twelve with twelve, Sawi knew. Milak could not guess what they wanted, but if it did not matter, Sawi would not have sent for spears, nor prevented his oldest son from standing at his side.

Milak planted the butt of the first spear in the snow, then raised the other five in a defiant line. Some of the boys, just older than himself, studied him through the fence as he slipped back among the tukits.

Norwet watched him go. If they split to sixes, he might be expected to go with the five men, as the oldest. But he could also see that Sawi may prefer to split the men, and the boys among them. There was no opportunity to say before the blacksmiths joined them. He would wait, and watch for his answer.

The men paused some yards away out of respect. Sawi did not call out his greeting. They were not guests. When it was clear, they gave up their courtesy with a shrug and came forward to greet Sawi.

"We do not wish to interrupt your work," one of the older smiths said. "I see you have much to prepare."

"Then go," Sawi replied.

Sewadkut, the oldest smith, ignored the remark. "A man broke the prison. The Navy cannot find him in Drummoc, and the people have not seen him."

"If he passed here, I would collect the reward myself."

"I think so. I saw you at the navy hall before. It is magnificent, eh?" Sawi hardened, and Norwet wondered what the smith meant. "But you have many tukits. Maybe we help you look."

"You think I am fool enough to hide a man the Navy seeks? Or fool enough that I don't know who passes my camp?"

"I think it is one of those." A master smith, younger than Sewadkut and more frequent on the anvil by appearance, spoke to spare his elder the insult. "If it is the first, bring him out and we will share the reward." He paused while Sawi held his tongue. "If a man is not in town, there are few places for him. All must pass the dogs." He said it in a way that left it up to them whether he meant the animals, or their handlers, too.

"The Navy does not sort the faces of the people, but many saw what boys were jailed for fighting. It was good of the Leopard Seal to free you." Now his gaze fell on Norwet. "I wonder if you saw which way he went."

Norwet's toes curled. He should have known they would be seen, but he had not considered the people would care.

"My uncle speaks the truth." That he did not know where the prisoner was, and that he was a fool, thought Norwet.

The blacksmiths split into two groups, and swept calmly to either side of the family. Sawi spun in anger and stalked after the man who had insulted him.

"I demand that you leave!" The other men followed him, and Baldrakut, the stooped old man whose late son Senadak replaced when he married Sawi's sister, looked back for him. Norwet felt the pull of bodies drawing him after. He avoided the old man's eyes, and shoved a reluctant Arnake in their direction while he drifted among the boys, who formed around him. There was no time for protest from either Arnake or Baldrakut. The men trailed after the first bunch of smiths, while the boys under Norwet took the wake of the other. The searchers ignored the line of spears erected by Milak. Norwet's group was closest, and could have armed without resistance. That was all. Every man of the intruders was of fighting age, and they couldn't count on Baldrakut, or any of the boys besides he and Milak, who was out of sight and odd man out. There wasn't a swinging hope against the hammer men. The smiths were so sure of it, they let Sawi's sharp tongue fall upon them like a wife after her husband as he works. Perhaps the men knew they had earned it, and felt it was their price for the search.

The women assembled out of the tukits and kept their distance from all of the men. The group Norwet followed took their place, and made a short circle through each of the four dwellings out of duty. They knew there would be no fugitive. Among the boys, there was almost a spirit of humor, and they stole glances at the oldest for a crack of a smile that would give them permission to have a secret laugh among themselves. Let them run like dogs and dig out every windbreak, they would find no Leopard Seal.. Norwet withheld approval.

Sawi knew as well as the rest of the town who was in those walls with the prisoner, if not their role. Maybe the way he forced them to turn out the gear was his way of searching his own camp without saying, but if so, it was casual. Many of the piles never earned a look, but were trusted entirely to the boys. That's what allowed them to amass most of a sled, including a fine runner, under a lump that he hoped the searchers would not turn out in front of Sawi. If his uncle were in doubt, he would have taken more care. So he believed their story, even though Milak admitted he was forced to change it under the rod.

If the wind did not bring down fresh snow, they could follow sled tracks to their reward in less time than it would take to make a thorough search of the camp. Norwet looked up at the sun, near as high as it would be. Tunguk made it clear: they were to bring a sled before dark. But if the smiths left with light to spare, it would be they who arrived first. He could find a way to delay them. They didn't know as he did how close it was, and they would fear being caught on the snow after dark. But if he took their light, he took his own, as well, and no two joints of his sled were lashed. They were short on lashings altogether. Those came from the women, and the tukits, now unguarded. He hoped Milak had the sense to get them while the rest of the camp was occupied.

Ostuk laughed to himself that it was Lamachar who came for him. For weeks before they made land, he dreamed of it many times, in many worlds. It was Marines who came for him. Navy. At times, Turrha himself, and soon Costig, once he arrived to correct the vision. Torn away from his supper, or hunted in the home of a family member who was taken, as well. They caught him in the snow, as he collapsed from exhaustion. Climbing aboard a ship in a cloak. There were occasions when he fought, and even met the spear, but most often he went without a word, as he did now. His mother, his sister and her children, their cousins waited in the crowd somewhere. They did not know why he preferred to remain estranged, sleeping once in the tukit of any man from whom he could beg a kindness before moving on. But they understood that something had changed.

Lamachar slowed his pace with every step beyond the line of marines in front of the foundry. Half the town gathered in the open—the timid half. Now that the yelling had tired their lungs, they clustered in little groups among a greater one, and at times sent emissaries to nearby families for news or pleasantries. The other half, he imagined, stood watch at their doors to repel the bands of people who howled through the town looking for Brother. Or they *were* the bands.

At first, this bunch had fled to the refuge of the open, unable to resist an intrusion. Some thought to take their valuables. Most were women, or the very old and young, but some tradesmen milled among them, including his former crew. Then they raised a cry of their own. The Navy refused to intervene. They would not send a spear into the maze to protect the Mattaka or their homes. What the people did to one another, they did freely. The crowd lay its anger at the feet of the bluecoats, and it appeared he had escaped one fight for another, but the sailors hemmed them loosely on either side—away from the ships, and the public row. A crew of salted whalers had been unable to bring them to blood, and the practice paid them well. They did nothing to incite the grandmothers.

The crowd rustled and stilled. Their ill-wishes hung in the air, but they waited now for the danger to pass, content at least that there was no resolution they could affect.

Thus, Lamachar. If anyone was to be torn to bits, it would be the Minister of Coal, to the mourning of neither Costig nor the people. His jaw trembled with the awareness. Someone nearby pointed him over. He whispered in Ostuk's ear, and parted. The eyes of the Mattaka followed him to the line of marines, who stood aside then closed behind him. He dreamed it would be the navy hall, or the prison. It was never the foundry. A peace welled over him as he forfeited his clumsy visions. It was true of Ralte that it spared a sailor whatever he could anticipate. His death may come anyway, but at least he wouldn't guess it.

The inside was dimmer than he expected with the forges cold. A number of lamps had been commissioned to give the Navy their eyes as they fussed over materials with a pair of Mattaka. Costig finished a heated order and sent his attendants away when Ostuk appeared.

"I fucked up, mate." He greeted the former captain cordially. "Tell me, you didn't see a load of steel hurryin' the other direction, did you?"

Ostuk frowned. "No."

"Not a smith turned up for his wage with the reward on. Not a one to swing me hammers. There's no need to post a guard on the buildin' when someone's at the forges, but now I'm missin' spearheads. Don't know if it's an armful or a boatload, but it's gone, and no one's makin' more."

The candor took him aback. He doubted the admiral summoned him to report a theft.

"And you. How's your family? Alright, then?"

Ostuk hesitated. He'd taken pains to separate himself from his ship and his kin, but to his knowledge, word had not yet reached the admiral that the *Juhketappat* was without a captain. If he lay a claim, the consequences for all would be severe when the Navy learned of the sinking of the abiama.

"I hear they are well." His stomach took a bow at the words.

"You hear?"

He nodded. The tale was thin, and he meant to make Costig pry it from him. The admiral narrowed his eye, but let it stand.

"Well if you haven't got me thieves, I'll take your repairs."

"Repairs?"

"Aye, what do you need to sail? And don't say, 'mast!'"

"The *Juhketappat* has a cracked amu."

"Can it be joined?"

"Aye, for now. But it will soon need to be replaced."

"Next season."

"She also requires small wood and pitch. New ropes. And a new steering oar."

"Fuck's sake. I'll have to see what I can do. How long do you make until the ice can get the dogs up?"

Ostuk mulled it over. "It's warm, yet. I think two weeks, three weeks late this year. Perhaps more."

"Get her ready now. Walk out that door, and do not shit, eat, or smile until you've settled your crew and made ready to receive supplies. Cut and splice anything you can before you get them. You're gonna have a busy season."

"Do you mean to address the captain of the *Juhketappat*, Admiral?"

Costig could hardly hide his annoyance. "Do I not?"

"I can inquire with my family, if you wish."

"Come off it, me son. I haven't the leisure to torture you."

"I was unable to resolve the debt I owed my family for the ship. The ownership has gone back."

"I don't care who owns it. We've only got the two dog ships, and we've a siege, which means she's a coal ship, now, perhaps a warship by Spring. You'll have the beasts over as soon as the ice comes down to greet her, and then it's bushels back to Drummoc until the sea freezes. I can't pay much, but I'll cover your expenses, and your men will get their wage."

"Admiral—"

"No more. You know the lanes. If your family takes cross over it, send 'em to me with their new captain. Otherwise, prepare to sail. That'll be, 'Aye, sir.'"

"Aye. Sir." Ostuk sank. He had managed to lose his ship and chain himself to the deck in the same breath. Would he really walk out of this building a free man? Not a word of the Leopard Seal, or the abiama. Just a repair bill and a berth.

"Oh." Costig stopped him. "You were just there, weren't you?"

"Sir?"

"Camne Drumlag. What's the look of it?"

Ostuk recalled the voyage with Foster and Polc, the confrontation with the man at the empty camp. "Warm."

"And how fares our mate the assistant viceroy?"

Another one he didn't care to mingle with his name. "I sailed as a pilot," Ostuk lowered his eyes. "It was not for me to have audience with such a man."

"And the camp?"

He wondered what the admiral may have heard. There was no use burying himself in more lies. If he dismissed it, and the supply ship found anything to report, the admiral would wonder of his motives. "It is best to ask Captain Polc."

The six boys followed like noon shadows after the smiths, who breached every tukit to harassment. "He is not there," nipped at their heels, and, "See? I told you a fool searches for nothing," greeted them when they emerged. It was impossible to step back without bumping into a vulgar pup who reminded them of their violation, warned them this one would collapse on their heads, or openly prayed failure. One or two of the group had to occupy himself with watching to see they weren't attacked from behind. Norwet caused a storm when he accused them of using the search as a pretense to steal from them, and demanded they lift their tunics. He thought one of the hammers would find his skull until the oldest smith quenched the tempers. It was a welcome diversion to sorting sleds.

Across the camp, Sawi and the men hung back in somber attendance. They made no such efforts to harry the other group. It was best for them to have their fill and be gone. Not so for the boys. Norwet knew that these men dreamed of gold in their palm with every flap of leather turned and every stack probed. He and his brothers, his cousins, reveled in their disappointment. They knew right where the Leopard Seal would be found, until and unless they removed him themselves. He asked himself if the others had thought the same: it could be them who took the reward. They were probably too young to care. It was only a flicker in the spirit world. Norwet did not know why the admiral sent messages to Tunguk—a key in the latest one. But there was perhaps less fortune in it than claimed.

Their gold was the empty hand. The knowledge of what every man sought and none could find. He could not think of what it would bring them, but the feeling that there was a wild creature who no hunter could spear filled him with more rich cargo than any ship could hold. That creature would not remain free for long, though.

The blacksmiths moved fast. It was their fortune that the boys had cleared most of the storage tukits already in order to prepare for the season. Some took no more than a quick glance. The waning sun still had enough oil to see them through and back twice if they chose to move deeper into the wilds beneath Urkuk. He scanned for Milak, and did not see his cousin.

When the group ducked into the last of the storage, he backed off with the younger boys and formed a line between the smiths and the mounds they used for overflow.

"You have seen it all. Now go to your work. When we finish, we will be by to search your forges." His cousins chuckled.

The sudden reposition gave them pause, and the leader of the blacksmiths lifted his neck around them.

"What's in there?" He pointed to the dozen or more snow-covered lumps behind them.

Norwet exaggerated a dismissive look. "Broken sleds. Trail tukits." He asked himself what he would say if there were a man there, and he wanted to rid himself of the curious. The Navy didn't bother to search them when they came through. If the smiths didn't either, there were plenty of sled tracks and footprints for them up the trail.

The apprentices started toward the other group. Norwet tensed. When he was sure the master was watching, he risked a quick glance back over his shoulder. It was enough.

"Hold." The master smith who insulted Sawi approached. "The snow is turned fresh."

"We put it in order after we pulled the sleds." He wanted to add a warning not to touch it, but it seemed too heavy.

"Then we will find them empty."

"Will you put the snow back? It took much work. We will not do it again."

"Who works less of the year than a dog driver? You might find you like it."

Norwet moved into his path. "No."

One of the apprentices stepped forward. "Move."

"For what? A man cannot live under snow."

"Not for long," the master smith said. "If he is there, we should dig him out before gold turns to silver," he joked.

"Move," the older boy repeated.

"Fuck you, orphan."

The boy snapped his palms into Norwet's chest, thumping him back a step. He looked to Saunlauk in disbelief, then turned with a fist that cracked the lip of the youth. The smith glowered and raised his hammer. Norwet caught the forearm to divert the blow as he fell back. The boy tried to reposition himself for another swing, but five little pairs of hands collapsed around him and drug him to the ground with Norwet. Ulwet flew over the bigger cousins to pound the smith's face with a thin and furious fist. Two more smith boys leapt into the fray. Norwet got his feet, and caught the next punch. He grasped for the body that threw it and came back with air. In the edge of his eye, he saw a boy twice Ulwet's age land a heavy punch that crumpled his little brother like a sack. It was all a distraction. He knew it. But he felt the rage of Tanset rise in him, and he wished he had taken the spears so that he could plunge them in all of these men. The hand that pulled his knife did not feel like his own. One of the grown smiths wrapped him from the side and slung him down, he thought for the last time. Then the oldest did the same with the young hammerer who poised to crush his skull. Shouts from across the camp grew. In a mad panic, he tried to free himself.

Sawi's voice cut through, and Norwet waited for the blow or the slash that would end him. The men had more sense. Smith and dog driver joined to part the young ones. His uncle took over the hold, and wrestled the knife from his grasp. He came up panting, bleeding, held from behind in an embrace that felt it would crush his ribs.

"He is mad!" The master smith said.

"You pushed him!" Ferrakut protested.

"He called me 'orphan.'" The apprentice said from the hold of one of his fellows.

"You insult us with your intrusion!" Sawi fired back. "Do you come to kill us? Look at my nephew! Look at my nephew!" He jerked his head to Ulwet.

The master smith stepped over to where the one who pushed Norwet was held. His fist crashed across the apprentice's jaw, sending him into the snow.

"We come for the fugitive. You let us search, and we will be done. What of it? Do you think it the last time? The Navy has been here. They will come again. When a man is nowhere in Drummoc, where else can he be? I don't think you hide him. I think he hides. Maybe he has help," the smith looked at Norwet.

"It is best for the people that we find him. He brings the admiral into our homes, our shops. The Marines treat us roughly. Whoever doesn't search for him is thought to aid him. There is no good to come of this man, who is not our man. There will be misery for the people while he lives. Hear me, Sawi. We will go now if you ask. I am ashamed to bring this to your home." He waved over the scene. "Or let us search. If your nephews have deceived you, the admiral will think it is your doing. We will say you helped us. You will have one of the three argots. Let us into the mounds."

It had not been so many years since he left, yet the memory of Drummoc gaped in Haraket like the revered bones of an ancestor, its ribs bare of the irksome flesh that once sat beside him for a dark winter and drove him to stretch his toes into the first crack of sun. What stood before him now was different. Haraket had never witnessed this crowd, pulsating as it did. Nervous families cordoned on the open rock while every navy man on the island clumped around the public buildings and the ships. Splashing in the harbor. A fugitive, loose as none in his lifetime had managed. Siege, reward. These were not the familiar things. It was undeniable that Drummoc had changed as a young relative after seasons away at sail. Only the flesh, though.

In the bones he recognized the work and the quarrels, the way their deaths unfolded. He recognized the men who held her to task. In truth, few of them would have been the same. He recalled vaguely the face of the admiral—perhaps it was true, rather than something he carved from recent experience. The others were passing birds who neither nested here nor hunted. But he recognized the way that every one of them could muster as if occupied, yet have no purpose. Their presence was to them a fulfillment of their duty.

In the people, he saw the same anxious quiet, and felt the restless hum within the town. They sat, or shouted among the tukits, and this told the Navy that it guarded the valuable holdings of the King of Ampos. The Navy stood about in the thin sliver of this place that it could occupy, and in turn told the people how their work and their quarrels and their deaths should unfold.

There were hundreds of men who could row his ship, still moored and loaded. None of them would be bothered, and this ritual of unrest was sufficient that it would be some time before anyone would be forced to resume their normal duties. To his benefit, they would also not bother to unload his ship again while they could play at something more important. Haraket watched the crew he was supposed to have the next morning run their paces. They were better than most of the others, he admitted. This bunch had rowed down together, while the rest of the men may row beside another who they knew only as a face from the hall. He would not ask Costig the next morning. It would be too soon to press, and he anticipated the excuse the admiral prepared for himself— too wasted from drills under the blistering Rixtan. Wait another day.

There were things that could change here, and things that could not. His voyages were short by many standards. His name would have been noted when he jumped, and circulated among men who struggled with the sound of it. That was when the rest of the world was the thing he revered. No sooner than he was able to put flesh and form to it did he feel the pull change places with his home. The miserable details faded from old Drummoc and followed him to the trade route, until what was left of his island held the distant, blurry beauty that drew a man who still wanted something. He came ashore in plain sight, nothing demanded of him but a name. He gave them one, and then it was to the mines. If not the sea, then the mines. The things that could be different were unrecognizable and would never return. The rest was Drummoc.

Few of his family roosted among the bunch at the harbor, so he needn't ask what they thought of all this. One could guess where a Mennegur stood by the name alone. He still had it, among the people, at least. And yet his absence let him stand apart. A few seasons at sea, and a man became a foreigner, envied beyond his actual experience. They knew the old one, and had a wild notion of the new. It was the discrepancy that occupied Haraket's boots.

He shuffled an indirect path to one he knew before as a sailor of dogs, and now as a man who lost his berth on the *Juhketappat*, due to one of many red rumors. The man stood beside his nephew, one of the few hardy men of Autumn. Haraket could not know who it was he now approached. He had never spoken to the man before—only knew him as one does all men on Drummoc. Between the rumors and the dog work, there would be one like himself. It was that one who Haraket sought.

"Kurrhatet drives his children hard this season," he said of the dog god. "It is a shame about the ship." Haraket did not specify if it were the one that stood dry without captain or crew, or the one that never arrived at all.

The man shrugged. "It is not for us to know where he heads, or how fast he must get there."

"I am Haraket. Of the mines."

"I know."

"There will have to be a new captain. I am sure the Navy won't rest the dogs. Whoever sails will need a crew." The man waited for Haraket to arrive at his point. "It's likely you will be hired to the very same boat. Who else knows more of how she turns? Or the harbor at Camne Drumlag? You have been there many times, haven't you?"

He nodded.

"You know where to head, and how fast you must get there?"

The man chuckled.

"If you wait, you are sure to be hired back." He leaned in and quieted his voice only a little. "I have sailed," he said with a gleam as if confessing a crime. "Only a fool would take a fresh crew when a salted one stands ready."

"Have you come to reassure us?"

"I have come because the one who hires me pays me to. You will make your wage soon at Camne Drumlag, as will I. Does it matter who pays it?"

"I know what you ask."

"Good! Then I don't have to ask it."

"I do not think the admiral would be pleased."

"What is your name, uncle?" He used the general term of respect for one slightly older.

"Arwoset."

"Do you recall mine?" Arwoset shook his head. "Nor I. Since I have returned, the people to call me 'Haraket.'"

Milak's father stalked toward town before the last of the blacksmiths cleared the rim above the camp. He wanted them to know their insolence would reach many ears before they returned. Maybe the same navy that just tore apart the dog camp would take offense to it when Mattaka did it, or maybe the people would speak of them in low tones. The men looked back at Sawi before they hurried in the wilds beyond the camp. If it worried them, it was not enough to stop them.

Now there was one less—an odd number. Old Baldrakut waved him over to restore them to twelve. Milak shifted his legs and curled his toes as he walked. Ice-pricks shot through his legs, and he knew the straps were too tight. He'd made a point to wrap them loosely under his trousers. It was not loose enough. The blood pooled below and made his steps tender. There would be no opportunity to adjust them now. Norwet and the boys stood in for a tongue lashing as he approached, and he slowed to spare himself the blustering. Whatever they had done, it caused the smiths to tear up every snow-topped mound in their search, and it was no surprise they had not put them back in order.

"Milak. Help them." Senadak and the men parted, probably for the day. There was light left, and work to do, but the excitement would turn them to hasqa and bellowing in a warm tukit. It was boys' work to restore the mounds.

The moment they vanished, he flung himself to the ground and tore off his bottoms, then writhed and shook his bared legs to his cousins' laughter while he uncoiled the leathers so the color could return to his gray flesh.

"What about a runner?" Norwet did not bother to praise him for the leather, and he was ready for it with a grin for an answer.

One pair at a time, young eyes turned to the rim, near the spot where the smiths first appeared. Milak froze with fear until he was sure it was only one who plodded down the slope toward them, and then remembered to pull up his pants. They must have been watching for some time, waiting for the others to depart. He considered running for the spears again. The man wore his hood up. He slipped and struggled under the load of a sack on his shoulder. As he approached, he failed to gain stature, until he came level with them and they saw it was a boy. Milak checked for prying auntie eyes, then hurried over with the others.

The visitor slung the sack at his feet.

"For the Leopard Seal." It was a girl's voice.

"We don't know where he is."

She pulled back her hood. "Do you know me?"

"You are kin to Mennetsatletaluk."

"Tell him it is from my family."

"Tunguk."

The sound stirred him from the spirit world. Her eyes held the thing that bid her to call him. Her sight was young, and it took his some effort when he joined her. It was dogs he hoped to see. Even then he must be cautious—other men knew how to drive. He tried hard to make a team of the black flecks that began to separate themselves from the terrain. It was no use. They insisted otherwise. No rolling backs fanned before a swift body. No eager yelps carried across the plain. Just a slow, narrow line that traveled in its own prints. He waited for the snow to turn white behind the tail, and settled them at twelve. Mattaka, then.

He left her and plunged into the packed circle, hugged the right side, and emerged opposite where he started after the pile of tukit ribs. Tunguk had been careful to avoid thinking of this before. To prepare a plan he did not want to follow was to invite it in. But he did not send it away, either, and now it waited for him eager to speak of its journey. He knelt, and ran his fingers over the curve of the whale bones, careful to trace each one even when he thought he found his choice. His hands settled around a pair, then lay them a few feet apart. He took a second pair—the straightest of the bunch, except where they curved upward at the ends—and lay them the opposite way across the first. The third pair crossed this one again. He spilled Kjartke's bag and whipped the tangles from the binding leather they used to erect the tukit. Now she joined him, perhaps curious, or distrustful of his work.

Tunguk lashed the joints where the top four bones crossed—the other pair propped them clear of the snow so he could make the turns. The runners were wider than usual, to accommodate the load, and because the crossbraces were far too long, themselves. The woman saw his intent. She lifted the front so he could remove one of the props and turn it into the third crossbrace. They added the last one, stood back. It looked like a fat man who walked with his legs and arms stretched to the side. Tunguk gave it a shake, and already the bindings were loose. He and Kjartke started at opposite ends, freed them one by one and retightened.

"Sit." He instructed her. She eased herself down on one end and stretched her legs over the frame. Tunguk tied off a long strap to the front crossbrace so that it forked off in two strands. He hiked both over his shoulder, and gave it a tug. The bindings creaked, and the clumsy sled lurched then jammed to a stop. One of the sides of the crossbraces stuck in the snow of the slope. Kjartke kicked it free, and used her legs to help propel them another few feet before the same bone stuck again. Too much hung over. It would always do so unless the ground was level, and there was no place that was level.

Tunguk looked back where their tukit had stood. He could not see the men approaching from here, but even the modest weight of Kjartke wore on him. To cross the plain was uphill. To climb Urkuk was uphill. These were the ways they may find a new site. It would take several strong men to drag their load and free it every time it tipped. The only way an old man and a woman could move it was downhill. Downhill led on one side to the men approaching, on the other, to the sea. Every foot they moved was sacrificed. It could not be retaken. Without dogs, they would wind down the slope until they were pinned to the cliffs to await what followed in their tracks.

If they pulled until their toes hung over the sea, there would be daylight left and plenty of time for the men to reach them. But one who follows a track does not know if it leads around the next rock or many miles. He was not sure what could happen in their favor, but with more trail between them, the kaim might intervene. At the least, he had to show he still tried.

"Off."

Kjartke swung her feet onto the snow and helped him wrangle the sled beside the dark pile of tukit covers. The lump had not protested for a while. He thought it wise to see if there was a purpose to it before straining with the lift. Tunguk bent and peeled back the edge of the cover. A single foot bound loosely in fur greeted him. He'd forgotten which end was which. They fought with the sled to point it the other way, then he bent again and threw back the sheet.

A pair of closed eyes shut harder in the gray glare and a moan seeped through a dry throat. The face was a shade darker than the snow beneath them, the beard still ripe with his own vomit. Tunguk dropped the cover back into place. He gathered the two corners of the bottom sheet in his fists and waited for Kjartke to do the same on her end. The first pull ended when his feet slipped from beneath him. It may as well have been a rock he tried to pry from the mountain's grip. He repositioned, and felt the strain shoot hot through his body. His legs quivered, but it moved. They tried to sidestep to bring it over the sled, but the crossbraces were too wide. The sagging body bumped into one, and they got it only as far as the nearest runner before it fell onto the bones. The sled tipped so that every crossbrace planted its head in the ground on the right side.

Brother moaned much louder this time, and twisted in agony under the cover. They hurried to regain a grip, and with one foot on the hovering part of the sled, Tunguk managed to slide the man into the center of the runners. Kjartke jerked twice more before her end came along, and Tunguk had to fall on Brother's chest to keep him from writhing off in his agony. Kjartke caught the foot with firm hands.

"Be still," she said in his language. There was no form to the deck other than the four braces, and he sagged through every opening. Kjartke hurried around to cradle the head where it hung free. Tunguk fashioned a sling out of bindings for it to rest on, then did the same for the stump that could not reach the last brace. Brother twisted in pain. The sled groaned beneath him in sympathy. It had taken many hours for him to find sleep, and sleep was the only thing that eased the fever. He would have to feel everything, now.

Kjartke dumped the rest of their things on Brother's chest. Tunguk took up the line, and motioned her alongside to tend their load and free the wide crossbraces. He spun and gave a yank. The nose agreed to his direction and whipped around. With a few more yanks, the sled pointed down the steep slope that led soon to the cliffs. Tunguk glanced back with hesitation. If it started down with vigor, there was no way to stop it, and he was in the path. He removed himself to the side and pulled once at an angle, then crossed the center and pulled once more from the other side. It was a miserable tack. It was his fortune that it did not last long.

On the next pull, the crossbrace stuck in the snow. Kjartke kicked at it to free it, and when he jerked the line the other way, he felt a new resistance. Brother's bottom sagged between the braces to scrape along the snow. Tunguk did not see a way to stretch him back out. He hoped this would at least prevent the sled from careening. Another pull, another stick and a kick to free them. He felt the thin air in his chest, and his rising heart. The sled refused to budge. Kjartke took the butt of a spear and chipped at the snow in front of the wide bone while Tunguk leaned against the line and slipped for footing. The pile of tukit coverings twisted side to side and rattled an awful cry. At last, the bone broke free and the sled lurched forward with promise, before the lower bindings wrenched apart and it collapsed in the snow like a carcass.

The old woman came upon Costig in a frenzy. She gnashed and wailed, folded over the arms of the marines, her toes at times kicking above the ground. Ostuk approached because he knew they would not understand her. By now, many of the people had ventured back to their tukits to take stock of the trouble. Others remained, hoping their presence would force the timid Navy into the town. The harbor still crackled, as a fire that glitters among the last coals. But it faded with the daylight. It was to his reputation that the fever of the morning had run its course. Costig would not fight them, or let them fight. He kept formation. No more raids. The people were upset when the Navy violated their doors. Now they were upset the Navy refused to come when their neighbors did the same. It was mad, and Ostuk believed all saw it. That was why a wild kaim that looked as though it would sweep the island now barked half-heartedly and paced against its lead. The people were accustomed to finding cause to be angry. This admiral had so far searched for a criminal, and offered gold for help. Their blame was in much the state of the old woman—desperate, grasping, tiring itself against calm arms.

Several older men followed him, and a group of marines broke off to block Ostuk. It was close enough.

"What's she on about?" Costig demanded of him.

He listened for something he could recognize in the bleating Mattakatan. "'They are killing them.'"

"Who?"

Ostuk shrugged. "She wants you to send men."

"None of these lads will attend to you or anyone else, until your people go home in good order," Costig raised his voice over her cries. She gurgled her response.

"Is it far?" Ostuk asked in their tongue.

She took a few gasps to compose herself. "I will show."

Costig said nothing in consent when Ostuk followed her with two others into the bending lanes. Within the first tukits he felt a world apart. The clear masses of the harbor and the safe stillness dispersed like water racing through the streets. Lone shouts bounded over the tops of the homes in anger, celebration, something he could not place. He kept his hand on the woman's back and struggled to match her surprising pace. Bodies flitted across the path ahead—one and two and three boys in a sprint. A woman cursed from within a tukit. The jumble of noise made familiar stone feel strange, as it had when he was a boy and the Navy pressed into the town against the miners after a pair of coal ships were lost in a gale. It was as though everything were sharpened and slick with ice. Unsettled. His mother insisted he stay inside, but he couldn't help stand in front of their door and listen for meaning and distance in the terrible sounds.

They slammed to a halt as their path contradicted a woman and her son. The boy nearly dropped the armful of spears he carried. She scolded him and hurried him along, two full sacks of their neighbors' belongings on her shoulders.

Ostuk bent his ears around the turns. Now and then, he glanced back to be sure the feet behind him were the two who started with him. If they carried nothing and entered no homes, they should pass unmolested, he told himself. Until they got to whoever sent the woman screaming to the harbor. He carried a knife, as he knew the old men did without having to look. Even when he first saw the smear of blood on the stone wall, he left it on his belt. It was a hand reaching for balance. She proceeded from memory, but he collected each new stain. Drops underfoot, like a seal wounded by an arrow and scampering for his hole.

At last she paused, and peered around a tukit with caution. There was no one. The woman seemed not to know how to proceed, so Ostuk pushed past her. At the foot of the home was a large smear on the ground where a wounded creature fell before fighting to stand again. He did not go far. A grandfather—her husband—slumped against a wall with a knife clenched in his fist. His eyes were so clear, it couldn't have been long since his breath ceased. She did not behave as Ostuk thought she should, but begged them past, as though looking for something she lost. The men were as perplexed as Ostuk. They fanned into several streets, and he thought she was mad with grief until he saw another trail, red feathers in intervals along the walls. They sank, as if floating side-to-side down to Ajatse's breast from a departed bird. Ostuk knew before he leaned through the next turn what he would find.

The dog man was irate over something, and Costig wished he could tend it himself. Sure bet it had to do with argots and Leopard Seals. It was fine for them to speak in the hall, among the endless stream. To hear him now would make others interested in what he had to say, and Costig preferred to keep him at a spear's distance.

Gerachay stood in consolation. Through as many corner-eyes are he dared, the admiral watched them battle, slashing gesture for parrying nod. He'd made no promises. No cause to weigh his word more than others'. He could only hope Gerachay thought so, as well.

It was absurd. When the official rejoined him, his stomach felt like a young marine found by his sergeant. I'm the fuckin' admiral, he had to remind himself.

"Blacksmiths interrupted his work to search the camp. Uninvited." Costig made a show of his reaction. The squains bristled at the distinction, and Sawi would be watching. "They were rough with his things."

"Sooted cunts," Costig needn't exaggerate now. "I stood watch over their forge meself to see that looters had no more of it, and where are they? Lootin' the dog man!" Gerachay was becoming comfortable enough with him to grin. "Well, his luck is with him. I won't send a man into town when they're on one like this." He scanned the slackening crowd. "But he's the only grievin' bastard keeps his beasts beyond it. Make it twelve, so they know I mean it. I want those cunts back on their anvils if they have one swing of daylight left."

Gerachay hesitated. "They are no longer at the camp."

"Then what of it?"

"The men believe he hides beneath Urkuk. They have gone to search."

Costig's chest lurched like a prow slapping into a wave. He'd given the old man the day to move. It would be a wonder if he'd done it.

"Would have been there meself by now if I hadn't me hands full." He wasn't sure if it was meant for Gerachay, or him.

"Shall I send the men to bring them back?"

Costig shook his head. "Too far." It was too desperate. Too late. He found it alone, in the dark. "If they bring him in, so be it. Whose crew's set to march Urkuk in the mornin'?"

"All hands on deck here."

"Resume the trainin' marches. It'll show we aren't bothered about this mess. When Polc gets in, tell him it's his bunch. No mention of a search. Don't want no more amateurs headin' us off. We clear the wilds tomorrow. With a fair luck, we'll save Tolba three argots."

"Sir, you scheduled Polc's crew to take the supply darraig to Camne Drumlag."

"Couldn't have planned it better if I planned it." Costig and Gerachay laughed.

A stir from the edge of the buildings drew their eye. A loose crowd of Mattaka bounded at the heels of several men. They made for the admiral. More joined as they noticed. The marines stepped between to block their path, but Costig waved the dog captain through. The two old men behind them carried a third, dangling arms and legs between them without ceremony. Ostuk took more care to cradle the smaller form to his chest. He knelt and lay the boy at the admiral's feet. Had he slept, he may have forgotten the lad who stormed him that morning, eyes full of silver. The two folded like bloody rags torn by stone.

A woman's angry shout sailed from the crowd, answered by another. They came from the periphery to get a look. They came back from the town. The whole of the wide body that moments before threatened to break for home now lingered and swirled around the navy men. Voices skittered through them with news, or a cry of sympathy.

"I'll have the man who did it," Costig made himself heard. It was not like to be a man, at all. There were few enough here, and he could keep them down if needed, but it was better to comport himself to them. "Bring the woman!" He motioned for the grandmother. "Who was it?"

She wailed at him in Mattakatan, and whatever it was, he was sure it was not a name. Costig snagged a marine.

"Keep her here." He meant it for her protection. When the lad dragged her within the sailors, she kicked and reached for her grandson's body. Two more came to help, and it was all the Mattaka needed to go off the leads with their shouting.

"Tell her it's for her own good," he pleaded with Ostuk. The Mattakatan fell on the deaf ears of grief. He didn't blame her, and he would have been happy to let her give him the worst of it. There was at least sense to her madness. It was the shifting crowd who lost sense. Some brave lad waved a hand overhead, and when Costig didn't answer it—couldn't answer it—there came another. These beggars would have him post a man at each door so they didn't butcher one another, and he'd lose a fair dozen of his own in the melee, and load of squains, beside. It wasn't Costig who tried to pass a drowned drunk for the Leopard Seal, nor he who put them to the knife. By the gods' and his own grace, these were the only two casualties. They didn't square it that way.

The air hissed as something flew by his ear and thudded against a marine. His answer had to be swift. Before the next hand had a thought to do the same.

"Who saw it?" He bellowed. A sailor pointed into the crowd. Costig nodded. He'd no notion if it was true. He wasn't sure anyone did. Four men rushed the old man and flung him on his face. They hauled him up into the navy lines, that swelled and sagged into more of a cluster. A sharp rock cut the arm of one of the arresting lads. Another glided over the formation like a browsing gull from the opposite quarter.

He snagged the first blaze of bluecoat he saw: "Run to the harbor. Signal Rixtan to bring the crews in." He shoved the man off. Most of his contingent were scattered between the ships and the hall, with less than a third attending to himself. The Mattaka were just as disorganized, though the ruckus lured them from afar.

He salvaged the old man from the beating and drug him to his feet, then steered him beyond the line and gave him a push back to his people.

"Disperse! Back to your homes! Back to your homes! Or it'll be a peltast's courtesy for you!" His officers echoed his cry. The nearest of the squains melted from the surge of bodies that ushered them toward the town. But they merely fled to the flanks, and a new group formed between the admiral and the men down the way. It was all boys and women and the stubborn aged. Nothing they couldn't stand. It was his own that worried him. Most of this lot had never calmed a squain fit before. Stray rocks sung past them, and curses stung their ears. It wasn't a fight—they wouldn't know that.

The first of his sailors cracked a spit-screaming woman, and brandished his spear when the crowd came to her aid. He collared the lad and hurled him toward his own.

"Form up!" Now he turned his attention to his side. There was space-enough to sail through in his lines, with terrified ministers and bead men wandering the van.

"Form up!" He may as well order the squains to disperse, Costig thought. Now the waving hands ebbed back their direction. He didn't care for the ground he gave, but the fresher lads took it to heart. They spilled around to flank, pushing anyone they could reach toward their huts. There was nothing doing to resist a strong sailor, but faceless shades sent rocks into the confusion without concern for which side they found.

By now, the rest of the harbor had noticed. Most of the people pressed on his group to surround them on three sides. They could fight through to the others easily enough. What he needed was for every pitch-scraper and knot-cincher to stay exactly where he put them. There was no need for reinforcements, because it wasn't a fight. He'd men on the foundry and the hall; near enough the warehouses between; on the shipyard, and on the quay. If they'd but stay put, he'd be happy to let the whole of Drummoc sputter and flail to exhaustion. Not a man would have rushed to the aid of a Marine sergeant-at-arms, come in for a dusting. It was the luck of a tender admiral that led them to stream to his position as if to the aid of a drowning man.

The crowd scattered before them in terror, though not as far as their homes. They parted to either side, allowing the Navy to connect in a thin rivulet that Costig hurried to meet. He didn't even know who was in charge. He caught an officer coming his way.

"Get your fuckin' sogers back where I had you!" The man recoiled to watch those same "sogers" mix hopelessly with Costig's own, with more on the way. Now the Mattaka indignation turned to the terror of a raid. Many of them fled toward the shipyard, while the detail posted to guard it bled off every which way. The rest of the town packed in as he only wished his own would, their backs to the huts that stood as retreat or reinforcement.

His center gaped with a lethargic bewilderment. The edges foamed with the fists of sailors and coal sons. He saw as many trickle into the huts as out: to flee, give word, or return at arms.

They now stood between him and the foundry, where every sharp scrap he ordered for the impending siege lay unprotected. Costig found Etan, one of his captains.

"Take twenty men—don't give a fuck which—and anchor yourself in that foundry. Do not leave without me orders if the roof burns above you." Etan nodded. "I'll hear an 'aye!'"

"Aye, sir!" He sounded off, then watched in disgust as the captain attempted to net his crew one at a time. A glance at the harbor granted him a pair of masts headed for the landing. At least someone did as they were told, and he'd have the drill crews in soon.

"Back to your posts!" He shouted in every ear that passed before him. "Back to posts!" Every third man obeyed. He gave up trying to find an officer he liked. Instead, Costig harnessed a barrel of a navy lad he knew from the hall—fresh as the first frost, but with a voice that carried and a presence to match.

"Take a crew to the hall and stay there, or I'll execute you, meself." He started to protest, but Costig turned away and soon heard his lungs threatening the lives of all around him if they didn't ship out.

It was better rocks that harried them, now. He noticed that no one moved to cover him with their bodies the way he'd often done for admirals and ministers. No projectiles found him, though, nor would they have troubled him if they did. It was still a trickle, but someone had gotten into his pile from the prison. There were too many to be strays plucked from the ground.

Costig didn't care to think what he'd do if one more of his orders were ignored, so he stopped barking. For all their floundering about, they did well enough converging on him, so he stomped across the grounds toward Rixtan's bunch.

The first ship was already driving up the landing. Most of the lads probably thought this a riot. He knew it would only come to that if the squains were provoked, and even then, with the men at the mines, it may not be possible. His men did their best, though. They clung to him in fear, or brawled on the fringes. Some tried to take charge, shouting advice that conflicted with one another and good judgment. In such times, he knew the first thing to have them do was anything different. If a man moved, he should stand, and if he stood, switch places. Costig marched, and his men came along—ahead or behind or bowing to the sides, but they moved as fish toward the harbor. There was little of value at the harbor, but hundreds of sailors stood between the two groups of Mattaka, and the mother began to worry for its young. All he cared to do was remove himself so they could rejoin.

Two marines trotted along with the old woman still suspended between them. She clawed and twisted to no effect.

"Set her down." Costig paused in their path and addressed the grandmother. "I advise you to stay with us. For your safety." He nodded for the men to release their hold. She gave a defiant lip and pushed through the sailors toward her people. It was enough that none could blame him. They would, of course.

Rixtan stood off in disgust when they arrived, a knotted root of a man. He'd look as sour if he just finished drilling the crew of the standard-ship in the farri's fleet, and Costig suspected this one came a bit wide of that mark. He'd given the first ship's crew their earful. Now he hungered for a go at the second. Fair chance he hadn't even noticed the mass of squains that sent them Drummoc wages—what they called it when the bastards started chucking coal.

Polc backed water, dutifully awaiting them to clear the landing. The low sun sent a wake of light glittering across the harbor. A shadow broke it, pitched hard to port headed west. It was enough of a surprise that Costig did not immediately recall that he had only two ships out for drills. He peeled back sailors to get an unobstructed view. The sheet hung full of the evening breeze off of Urkuk, and he saw but three oars to the side giving it their all to bring them clear of the harbor into the wind.

"Rixtan!" He gripped the coxswain's shoulder. "Who the fuck is that?" Rixtan was not one to speak what he didn't know, and he didn't speak. Costig gathered the shape. It was a darraig. Couldn't make the crew. The briefest panic set him scouring the horizon for the rest of Donnab's fleet, half a year early behind their scout. It was impossible, but if Polc made it through—

As with some sleight of hand the frightful miracle changed places with perplexity, and gave to fury when he realized something was missing. It came as rough consolation: he was not besieged. He would live another day as a fool. Haraket's familiar ship, full and empty, crewed and abandoned, now abiama, now darraig, had vanished from her berth to reappear beating toward Camne Drumlag.

The blacksmiths stood in the packed circle surveying the dizzy herd of prints on all sides. Behind them, Fire King's harem—the bright pinks and oranges—danced across the snow, following their chief to Drummoc. The young ones wished to press on. The wide sled tracks that led away to the sea were clear. The rest of the prints were the furrows of chores. None left the camp. It was pulled by hand, they decided. No dog tracks. A single pair of feet. Perhaps they could catch it before dark. But the old ones were not sure how long ago the traveler set out, and the ladies of the harem made a good pace.

The snow turned gray again beneath a deepening blue that shone only from one quarter. If Sawi were to share in the reward, he would let them stay at his camp overnight. No others knew. They could return in the morning. To spend the night exposed could exact a heavier share. There was talk that they need not pay Sawi, either. He must have known they would find no one in his camp. Two apprentices volunteered to remain until dawn, but the masters did not trust them, or cared for them as fathers. The group traced the sled until the first hump of land, and when they saw nothing beyond, they turned back through the tamped circle toward the town.

Tunguk recalled the feeling. To stand within reach of a dream so wild it was shameful to tell another, and to know it was yours—soon. He listened until he heard them no more, and remained until the shadows were thick with secrets. He did not think them clever enough to wait for him to return, but he stole in silence to the lookout and peered over. The thin moon shone on the snow but it was too dim. He would have to take his guests at their word.

The familiar cold of a night in the foothills raced through his skin as he rose from the ground and brushed his coat. He gave thanks without knowing who he addressed that the men had no light to search. A steep outcrop cradled the camp on two sides. Two pairs of prints, easy to overlook among the prominent sled tracks pleading for attention, led in another direction past one outcrop then another. A few yards more and Tunguk felt his way into a nook that protruded only feet from the main wall of rock.

There he rejoined the black bundle of leather swaddled around the blue lips his hand covered during their visit. Each time he peeled back the sheet to find a dead man, he was disheartened. There had been no words for some time, but there must be something of the man left. When Tunguk silenced him for their guests, the moans did not try to force their way through his fingers. Now that the hand was gone, they rose with enthusiasm, as though greeting family they had not seen for some time.

He settled down beside Brother to watch the clouds of breath puff and disappear. As long as they continued, he was a ship at anchor. The dog boys failed to arrive. Even if Kjartke returned, the two of them had moved him as far as they could. This was where he would greet the party. None could miss them in the light. A stillness found him in the rhythm of steam that vented like the mouth of Urkuk himself, far above them. At every interval, he knew that if the vapor ceased, he might rise and slip away. It would be easy, but he did not pray for it. He felt the anticipation of one who in exhaustion at his oar spots land, and wells up with a spirit than can suffer any torment in these last paces before his voyage is done. It was dark, and he had no bone, but he knew the bead he would carve if he could.

At last, the roar of the surf against the cliffs separated itself from the scrape of whale bone over snow. The terrain was steep now. If she went any farther, it would be difficult to manage the sled. Kjartke dropped the lead and gathered the sack from the deck. Anything heavier would have mangled the bindings long ago. For a moment she thought Tunguk clever when he first lashed the tukit ribs, but it was the cleverness of a boy whose vision collapses in its first steps beyond the spirit world. She did not think much more of this one, either. If someone was to stay and care for Brother, she was better suited. He needed no protection—there was no fight the old man could win. And if one was to drag the crippled frame that maneuvered with the grace of a tukit, and find their way back by a different route as instructed, it should fall to Tunguk.

She cradled the bundle to her chest and leaned back, at times sliding on her seat toward the break of the water. Dense cloud off the coast took her stars and her light. Toward the sound, she thought, but not too close. It was difficult to see where the edge might appear. Perhaps he feared this part. Not likely, though. He often avoided things because he thought them unwise, or because he was lazy, but not out of fear.

Kjartke paused to let her eyes adjust. She inched on by digging her heels into the snow to break her slide until she thought she saw the line of horizon in the distance contrasted against the sky. A few more timid steps and her heart fluttered as she realized it was not the sea miles away but the end of land a few feet in front of her. Now a third sliver of color appeared where the water intervened. Somewhere beyond, she heard that a wall of ice rose out of the bay, tall and barren—Pautatse, they called her. One of the daughters of Ajatse. When the cold came, she gave birth and her children traveled all the way to the rock below. The sea bristled with ice and the waves she heard became the home of the clan until Ketklemak returned to drive them to their ancestral grounds.

It was a fool's errand—little more than a rite to demonstrate that Tunguk thought the man might live. Why else hide the scraps of Brother as if they could be used against a corpse? Once, he sent her to Drummoc to fetch the poye and assumed she would return. Kjartke felt some embarrassment that he was right. Now he made the same mistake. How many times would she forgive his error? She knew nothing of coin, but she had seen silver and gold. Foster's gold, which the admiral promised to use in their care if they were wise enough to avoid being caught. She did not know what lies these men traded in, but if at least this was true, she would not need the poye's help. She would have meat, and a place to sleep. Perhaps hides to work, flint and bone to busy her hands.

She was by no means certain that was what she would do as she unwrapped the tie on the swollen sack. Kjartke held it firmly in the middle and shook it to free the first of the bloody ice over the cliffs, black as the snow beneath her, black as the dust of firestone. The core was firm, and that, she kept in a sure grip until most every flake and crystal that surrounded it was freed. Now she rose as tall as she dared.

He stood beside her, silent as the dead, his hair lifted around his cheekbones as he searched the waters. She did not care to look below his waist. Kjartke thought it an ill omen that he came at all, but soon enough she was alone again. In a single movement she drew the limb and flicked the sack and the rest of its careful collection over the edge. The frozen hair and dried blood made her palms feel gritty as she sang in a half-whisper of disinterest, rather than discretion.

It would be difficult to find the camp again. Much easier to follow the slope up to the plain, then down again to Drummoc, where they could ask no more of her.

Kjartke raised the leg. It felt small—too small to support the man. If he woke before they found him, she wondered, would he know it was gone? Again she saw them, not as they were now, but as before: the tukit in the gray light, whipped by blowing snow. She felt him with the old man, and felt the absence of the Leopard Seal and his taunts. Only Brother, and no Foster to aid him. It was a bleak place that tempted no visitor. Rather, it seemed to push her around and away like the curves of the tukit did the unwelcome gale. The frail warmth inside grew colder as she stared. At last, she understood why Tunguk sent her: the old fool did not mean for her to find her way back. He meant to free her.

With a heave, she threw the icy leg into the sea.

2

THE WHALER

The stern rose on a gentle roller that leaned him back for a better view of the cloudless sky. The second hands of the sea—it glided under the hull like a fingertip that beckoned her gently on, then lifted Foster so the square sail slipped out of the way to reveal the petrel. Even with a full sail they seemed motionless beneath the still wings as it closed. Everything passed them. The men spoke of speed—a swift run if it held. Sixty days for the hopeful, though the old salts swore it impossible, and warned that a guess is never granted. Eighty was likelier, except it had been said aloud. He wondered how many it would be for the feathered fellow streaking in off their starboard beam.

He shifted as much as he dared on the rocky load. The moment they sighted the bird, Corm offered to unload some of the ballast the men griped about if any of them flinched from "grievous wound," which Foster at last understood to mean if anyone scared it off he'd be thrown overboard.

Maybe their friend came from Drummoc. He could be soaring after them with news of the Leopard Seal. It had been at least a week. A long blur of wet and cold and fair wind, and those second hands, counting down the hours until the sickness left him. He was already worlds better.

Parks was dead. Or he had the Navy chasing their tails. The more Foster imagined it, the less likely it seemed. Whatever happened had happened by now. If someone offered to tell him, he wasn't sure he would take it. Nor did he give a drowned rat's ass to see the petrel land on the ship. He thought the feather thing before departure was sufficient, but this was the second-luckiest bird. Better to have the whole animal, the crew reckoned.

It was clear enough that his hopes and his crewmates' were not the same. They weren't headed the same place, they wouldn't get there in the same time. Until then, his friend lay in a black wigwam under the endless night awaiting judgment. And in his head, he probably saw Foster bobbing on an open deck atop a clock that circled the southern globe, never arriving, never sinking, until the moment he stepped off the gangplank in Drummoc. It would take at least that long before Parks could stand, if he ever did. If the two of them didn't vanish from memory in a dim picture of a hut and a boat. He squinted back at the omen that craned its neck to consider them.

"Don't look at the bird, cunt!" Came a sharp whisper.

"Who's lookin' at the bird?" Someone down the way protested. Gionn shushed him with a hiss.

Foster buried his chin in his collar and folded his hands inside the sleeves of his oilskin. Out of the corner of his eye, he tracked the visitor and shivered. His pants and tunic were permanently soaked through. He couldn't tell if his oilskin kept water out, in, or had lost all repellent properties at this point. The one thing it was good for was attracting torment. Every man aft of him—which was every man on the ship but the blacksmith's boys—was stripped to bare arms at least, and many bare chest and worse. Their clothes stretched over every flat surface or hung tied off of stays according to strict rules of what articles can dry on what objects without incurring the wrath of whatever neurotic gods kept track of such things. None of it changed the fact that it was fucking cold. The full sun seemed to lie to his face. It was an impostor in a faded disguise who never came quite high enough to be exposed as a fraud. None of the blistering autumn breezes or the mythical ice made an appearance. This was probably as good as it would ever get, and yet he shivered every second with a feverish headache and a nose that both swole shut and leaked nonstop. If someone touched the tip of it, he was certain he'd cry like a little girl.

At least the bird earned him a reprieve from the hazing. Foster had often wondered why the weirdos in the Navy didn't just stop acting so weird. To be the nail that sticks out on a ship was to crave misery. Now it made a little more sense. Where he could help it, he just didn't care.

The petrel swung low and Foster felt the collective breath of the crew draw in and hold. He wasn't sure what they expected. If it didn't light on the pitching mast, there wasn't a spot more than a foot from the nearest filthy criminal. Maybe the tall curve of wood that loomed aft over the little section of raised deck. It was higher than the one fore by several feet, and together, they closed the crew in their parentheses.

Or the tarp. As soon as they got under sail, Corm erected a covering that spanned the full beam over the last few thwarts so that some part of the seas that came over the back might roll out again instead of filling the bilge. Of course, the big bastard reclined under it, but the bird didn't know that.

He only knew the fate of the Leopard Seal, and whether this ship would arrive thousands of miles across open water in a few months time.

Foster shifted. A rock jabbed his right kidney. The thwart gave his spine a sudden curve. He could stretch out one of his legs in the space beside the man in front of him. In the past week, this was as close as he'd been to comfy. It was quiet enough to hear the snap of the sail in a moment's lull of the wind. If he closed his eyes, the sickness calmed and the dip of the prow with each tick of the sea felt more like a rocking cradle. He could still see the bird—the image on the back of his eyelids, descending over the *Gairhle* to deliberate. When he peeked again the real one was browner, and indeterminably farther off. *Shoo, bitch*, he thought. He shut them and felt the hollow beat of his sinuses.

Foster dreamed an old crone. She bent over his feet and squeezed at his calf and his arch with a snaggled grin.

"We must keep the left." Tunguk advised. He and Kjartke attended at either side. "The other has the right." A little wave of loss sloshed through him, but it felt like a tough call that had to be made, and he couldn't fault them. It just unsettled him how eager she seemed to have the thing.

"Bucket!" The cry woke him in the last minutes of twilight. It was the longest continuous stretch of sleep since Drummoc. He gathered the vague hulk of Gionn rearranging a bit of ballast near his outstretched leg. The whole thing tingled numb. He had to manually bend his knee with his hands, and winced against the needles that shot down to his foot.

"It's not in there," he said.

"What's that?"

"You know. Not in my boot." Mischief glimmered in his smile. "Not that one, anyway."

"Wake yourself before you talk nonsense, cunt."

"*Bucket!*" Someone repeated. Foster struggled to sit up, and caught himself looking around for the long-gone petrel. He pried himself up until his ass rode the thwart, dead leg still trailing behind as it refilled with blood. Between there, the foremost seat, and the short deck of the forward quarter, he reached down to peel back the top of the blanket. Even in the distorted light, the thin face was the wrong color for a Mattaka. Or "Mattakan"? He'd have to ask. Foster replaced it, and checked inside his sleeping bag. This other one was a little farther from death. Neither of the boys had ever been to sea. Maybe not even toodling the coast in a hunting boat.

"Yo, they're still fucked. Use one of the buckets up there."

"I'll use your mouth if you open it again when I'm talkin' to Bucket!"

He couldn't yet tell who it was by the voice, and he didn't know most of them yet, anyway. It wasn't Captain Corm, though.

"This as smooth as it gets, brother. You afraid to fall in? Use one up there, or hang your ass over the side."

"I want the good bucket! Bring it yourself. I won't stab you nowhere important."

"Who's that, Wife Seal?" Another boomed. *That* one was Corm.

"Aye."

"Send Bucket with the bucket or bring it yourself," The captain issued.

He clenched his lips. "Aye, aye." He heard a muffled fit of laughter aft.

Foster grabbed each end of the sleeping bag and shimmied it below the boy's shoulders. He squirmed to recover it, but Foster grabbed his shirt and yanked.

"Come on. Up." He shook his head. "Up. I need my bag back. You done had a week. Ain't gonna get no better if you don't haul your ass up and start actin' alive." An arm swatted at him. He swung to the far side of the thwart and slapped him in a quarter-nelson. The nameless kid twisted and tried to pry free. Foster knelt on one edge of the bag and drug him halfway out.

"*Listen.*" He spat. "You're one of two motherfuckers on this ship I can kill. Don't tempt me." The fight leaked out of the kid.

"I'm not Bucket."

"I know that. But none of them do, and they wouldn't give a shit if they did. Your boy can't move. Take one for the team." Foster let him go, and carefully lifted the bucket between his fingertips from its resting place between the boys' heads. He couldn't see inside it in the dark, but it made him gag thinking about it. In the handful of hours before the Mattaka became completely incapacitated with seasickness, they were subject to a chorus of enthusiasm from every man who could force something out. It was Gionn who took the honor of the maiden voyage, and only the boys' willingness to try the crew's death threats earned them a temporary peace.

The littler one took it from Foster by the rope handle.

"Wife Seal!" Corm shouted.

"He's comin'!" Foster replied. The boy glared at him—as if he could expect better from anyone else. Foster felt no pity. There were things to learn, and no polite way to come about them. It was probably how the others felt when they called him "Wife Seal" for his permanent oilskin and famous companion, thanks to a certain clever sailor. That was just boats—everything was going to hurt, until you could pass it to someone lower.

"There goes your keenest mate," Gionn muttered.

"Sour grapes."

"Filthy cod. Are we sayin' things we don't care to eat?"

"It means something you wish you could reach, so you pretend not to want it."

"Can't think of a single example. All tits, me life. No disappointments yet."

Foster rapped his knuckles on the gunwale.

"What's that?" Concern passed over Gionn's face.

"Knock on wood. Or the thing you said comes true."

"It wouldn't dare!" He tried to grin it off, but his eyes narrowed on Foster. He tapped on the opposite gunwale. "Twice enough?"

"Better add one to be sure." Gionn begrudged the last knock.

The United States Navy had its share of superstitions, and they only increased at sea. But the captain and fifty-three men of the *Gairhle* turned the practice into a goddamn Baroque masterpiece. There was no rowing, and for him, no sailing either. He was kept dizzy day and night by a whirling mess of rules that had no basis in reason, history, or good hygiene. Worse, the crew could only agree on about half, while the others brought grown men near to murder on regional variation and at least a few things drawn from the bucket-end of a doubtful intellect.

One of the most frightful men aboard was reduced to tears by his imminent death when Tawatu—the "caskip," (a perversion of "cask-keep," according to Gionn, and the sole individual entrusted with rationing out food and water) absentmindedly served him the last portion from the slop pail instead of refilling it before continuing down the line. A whaler under sail reminded him of nothing more than an asylum full of lunatics twitching compulsively at their own delusions.

"A lousy copper." Foster rolled his eyes as Gionn started in. "A poor debt to lay between yourself and the best mate a man could hope for."

"You think I'd rather have you than Cap'n?"

"What makes you think he'll have *you*? I was mates with a captain once. Complicates matters."

"For starters, I'm the only one who don't make him richer by fallin' overboard." Foster referred to his status as the only member of the crew who had no share of any payout.

"You, the clever cunt who suggested he forfeit three of his shares to settle the count? A wonder he put you in the bow!"

Gionn had a point that he didn't dare concede. As glad as they were to have a number man aboard, they spent the first day of the voyage going over the accounting in great detail. Foster knotted at the memory of when he had to explain to the captain that his numbers were wonkier than a drunk on a pitching deck. He'd lost count of shares and men alike, and by the time Foster squared everything, the whole ship looked at him side-eyed. It struck them as a devilish magic trick, the way he made numbers vanish. They would no more name a quantity within his hearing than leave a wallet unattended.

"Bow's the best seat in the house," Foster insisted.

"Ha!" Gionn laughed hysterically.

"I'm dead serious. Back there, you got seas comin' in. And midship's got too much shit piled up."

"Do you not feel the spray hittin' us this very moment? Oh right," he tugged on Foster's sleeve. "You haven't ventured out of your foreskin.

Take me word of it, we'll never dry out. And he may not fatten up from it, but he certainly put you where you'd have the shortest trip overboard. If I were the cunt, and the first three shares to find a natural death returned to me account, I'd fill me bow with a couple of useless half-share squains, you, and *Palqua*!"

A tense ripple of laughter ran forward a few benches to remind Foster that no word on the ship was in confidence.

"Half and half and two is three. See? I can count, too. I'll do it for two shares when you go over," he announced to more noncommittal laughs. "But that would be too obvious. So he put me here, instead."

"You are last on," offered Chirim, an Amposi voice from the bench in front of Gionn. "The seats are promised."

"Last after the carpenters, and they're midship," countered Bentos, the man in front of Foster.

"What's that say about you cunts?" Gionn fired back.

"You got the bow because he's not afraid of you." Foster couldn't see the man in the dark, but it sounded like it came from Hogue, another two spots aft. As long as he'd been on the ship now, he'd never ventured past the man, and Hogue marked the line of those he knew directly. Beyond, most of the names were a mystery, and his only contact was the rare shout over something like a bucket.

Hogue went on. "I been with him long enough to tell you if there's a row that worries him, it won't be so far from his blade as this."

"Too loose. I do not like this talk. Your tongue, most of all, Gionn." Now it was the Amposi in front of Chirim. He was quieter. Foster hadn't caught his name.

"Me tongue is a model of discretion, you leather cunt. This is row talk, not side talk. You'll thank me for all the reasons I *haven't* mentioned that a man might end up in the bow. Now bury your ears. Me mate's a stranger to the rosters." Gionn's tone shifted so that it was clear he now addressed Foster. "There's a lot to know if you're to survive a season on a whaler, and at this point, most of it can't be said aloud. Take me word: if your only mate isn't the cunt beside you, you don't have one. It would be unwise to give it up on such a pittance as a little copper."

"Do you have the copper?" Chirim asked.

"Aye, he does." Gionn answered.

"You should pay him. Very bad to sail in debt to a crewmate."

The Navy man was right: Gionn played it too loose for Foster's liking. "Doesn't count as a debt if you ain't yet done the thing you were supposed to do."

"It is true," Chirim said. "What did you ask of him?"

Foster hesitated and realized he had cornered himself without a story. "I'm a little lost, in case yall hadn't noticed." The men snorted at the remark. "Gionn promised to get me to where I can find a ship home."

"For a *copper*?" Bentos nearly choked in disbelief.

"Sew it, cunt. I wouldn't do that for an argot! Wife's inside out, but he's gentle enough not to embarrass his mates. I will indeed see him home, if he likes, but not for any pitiful sum. I was out of graces in Nunoc when he found me. Had a spot of blood on me knife. Not a soul had cause to help me or saw sense in doin' so, but he ran afoul of the viceroy for me—why do you think he keeps that oilskin on? Besides bein' a twat? Striped like a fish! They took me in and got me out, him and the arse-cunt Leopard Seal. I swore I'd get the lad a ship if I had to stretch a squain boat out of me own hide.

"If there's a fault in him—other than the ones I've mentioned—he's boiled stiff. Didn't trust a big, strong lad like meself with a wet blade. I handed in me arms, but it was a courtesy, not a surrender, and you know as well as I that to gift a blade uncompensated is to sever the bonds between two men. We'd part ways at best, and go to war if we didn't. So I sold it to him for a pittance. Which he didn't have, and therefore entered me debt.

"I got me sword back after I earned his trust. I insisted he keep the knife to honor our arrangement. Had I taken it, it would have been a surrender, or a severance. Now I happen to know he's come upon a copper. And unless it crosses me palm, I'm afraid I've gifted him a knife, uncompensated. With all the geiss that carries. Now the Wife Seal finds himself on a strange whaler, very far from home, sharin' a row with a grateful mate, or an unwilling enemy, as he would have it."

Foster blinked in admiration. Little as he wanted to tangle with Gionn in a fight, facing him in a battle of lies was the scarier prospect. Just as at Nunoc, he was the first to unsheathe his bullshit, and the advantage was his.

"Take it." He pressed the handle of the knife to Gionn's chest.

"What's this? Are you giftin' me a knife? I got nothin' to pay you, cunt."

"I'm returnin' it so you'll quit your bitchin'."

"Not that simple. It's yours. I don't think our relationship can bear another gift."

Foster pulled his hand back. "I don't know the exchange rates around here, but maybe I'll just put it out there: would any man here care to buy a knife?"

Bentos sat up. "I'll give you one copper for it." The others nearby laughed at what was apparently a bargain.

"And if I give that coin straight to you," he spoke to the dark shape beside him, "we're even? I'll get no more grief from you?"

Gionn hesitated. "Aye. When you've paid me the *sum you owe*, that will be the case," he growled, and there was no doubt on Foster's part which one he meant. "But then what will you do when a rope you never saw comin' snatches you up and aims to carry you over?"

"Get yanked over I reckon. Same as you, if you don't accept it."

"I'm not the kind to get caught up in me ropes."

A low chatter of Amposi in front of them broke their rhythm when the words "Wife Seal" and "Gionn" sprung from the nonsense.

"Hoy! I'll not hear me name in monkey-tongue! Farri's tongue on the whaler. Out with it, or I'll cut it out!"

"Farri's tongue is soon Amposi!" Chirim cackled.

"Tolba can't even keep his own admirals from profitin' off his ruin. It'll be Atlantean, or I'll nip your toes til they number ten, you raft-foot monsters."

"Settle, lad. They're just takin' bets," Bentos explained. "Which of you's first for a swim."

A rustle and a string of curses rolled their way from midship. "Get the fuck off of me!" Someone protested, followed by a dull thud, and bigger crash, and a fit of laughter. Another voice raised in fury.

"Is that shit?" He stuttered in disbelief. "I kill you!"

"Run, Bucket!" Someone else yelped, and the middle benches erupted in uncontrollable laughter, with one man still cutting above the others.

"You pour shit? *You pour shit?* I fuckin' kill you!" Foster heard the slap of feet as silhouettes ducked out of the way to avoid the swinging latrine as it fled forward. A small foot dug hard into Foster's thigh then tumbled over his row and landed on the other boy.

"Yo, you gotta toss it before you try to walk half a boat in the dark," Foster reproached him. The uproar of mostly amusement spread through the whole ship in a dozen side conversations yelling over one another, while one man howled with indignity. Foster couldn't see, but it sounded like it turned into a scuffle. Corm boomed into the throng, and it took some moments before they settled the man enough to return to their ridicule. It mingled with the spray then spread out in the silence of waning moonlight on the water.

"Cunt, cunt, cunt, cunt cunt." Gionn *tsk*-ed him. "There's more ways home than you think. I'm pointin' you to one that might actually work. All I ask is a token of faith."

"I got plenty faith in you, brother. It's trust I'm strugglin' with."

"I suppose you'll explain to a poor ignorant whaler the fuckin' difference."

"Didn't know myself til recently. But it makes sense now. Faith means I can expect you to follow your nature. Trust means I can expect you to follow your word."

A thick hand wrapped around his shoulder.

"Me coin." The sharp whisper stung his ear. "Or I stand when you sit, and sit when you stand. You don't know whalers. Can't be done without me."

"You have my word: you'll get it when you earn it."

"Or some other way. Sweet dreams, sweet prince." Gionn leaned closer. "It's in your arse, isn't it?"

Foster drew his hood over his head and stretched out his leg as he settled to his sharp cranny, unable to sleep.

Morning found him as it always did: shivering a prayer for the dawn. In these hours, he was alone atop a sea beast who snorted puffs of air and dipped its creaking joints in lazy undulation. Its scales shifted as darker shadows that reared up to block the stars for a moment. There were no crew. The voices never ceased, of course, though they moved from here to there, but to Foster they were imps and orcs at some kind of mischief. While he was still blind came the call: "Eager on the watch!" Cormdran was the overzealous rooster who announced the shift change—how he knew what time it was, Foster hadn't a notion. Only the third watch did so much as unroll an eyelid. As the last of the watches, they would sit out breakfast. Theirs were the first human sounds, and the sign that the *Gairhle* was transforming back into a ship. Most went back to sleep. Foster begrudged overdue daylight. At last, the burst of deep blue appeared on the horizon and bled outward like a wound. Each day it came later and later. He wasn't sure if he felt the cold minutes piling up, or if he just knew it to be true.

Scarcely more than a week, and he knew the ritual like a Psalm. At the first light and well before the stars faded, the captain took a bearing. This, too, was a mystery to Foster, since he had no instruments. It must have had something to do with the heavens. He probably had a fair idea of their position, but then he retired under his canopy, and was joined by Eckerd, the first mate and officer of the third watch, whose orders kept the ship on course from the time he inherited their position from the officer of the second watch, and so forth. Corm would return a little later and give the first sailing orders of the day before the Sun crested the following sea. Most of the time it was "hold course," usually with a colorful prediction of the weather or some omen, and a word of encouragement in the form of a threat. That day: "If she keeps this fair, lads, I'll have to toss over the stillest of you to get me shares before Taclann!"

No one jumped to action. There was nothing to do, except for the real sailors, which was not Foster. The watch only had to keep their eyes open until after breakfast. They would eat theirs late, but Foster wasn't even trusted with that much responsibility. It was an honor to miss meals or sleep to watch for ice and weather—one he was glad to be denied.

The rest of the men were stirred by the sound of the first cask being pried. Foster sat up, which was inaccurate. There was no way to sit, stand, or lie in the precise definitions of the words, but there were relative approximations into which you could conform your body. He gathered his water bladder and cast an eye across the "bench," which was not flat like the pine one in baseball, but widely rounded, more like the head of the bat. He wanted badly to check on the argot, but there wouldn't be an opportunity soon.

"Warm of the mornin', mate!" Gionn greeted him a little too cheerfully. Foster looked back at the Mattaka boys. Every dawn he told himself this would be the last he suffered without his sleeping bag. By the noon sun, he'd forget it, but his soft heart felt particularly frosted on this occasion.

A man already sat atop the boom to tighten up the ropes that the generous wind had eased. The slop pail went first to Corm, then worked its way in an egalitarian fashion forward from the stern. No one had told him he needed to bring his own bowl. Some men had theirs ready, and would fill it with water on the next pass. The well-appointed ones had a bowl *and* a bladder.

The caskip dropped a hunk of dried seal and a four-inch strip of whale blubber in his palms. The only way he could stomach either was to rip a shred of the lean jerky, hold it on his tongue, then chew and suck loose some of the gasoline fat to grind together. Every morning he came up with clever complaints about the food that he would make to Parks one day. Comparisons to the mess on the carrier, or the slimy flesh they rode on in Tunguk's boat. As he grimaced through a swallow, he crafted others that would get a laugh from his mom and uncles, or some girl on a third date when he finally worked up the courage to suggest he was once lost in a bizarre version of Antarctica. Despite it, the two meals— breakfast and supper—were by far the highlight of his day, and he shook like wet pup when the pail came around.

"Stand by, the watch!"

The last half dozen finally got a portion that grew more frugal each time the caskip reached down. The same man made another pass with the slop pail, this time filled with water that he dipped out with a stone cup that had a single scrolled handle big enough for a finger, and a triangular spout. Foster learned early that Tawatu was a busy man. He couldn't take the care the aim a delicate stream into the small opening of a leather water bladder, which was made for submerging in pools, or catching a meltwater trickle. A nonrefundable portion would end up on his lap if he didn't roll a scrap of leather into a funnel and spread the top to corral the pour. As loosey-goosey as he played it with each sailor's share, Tawatu had a priestly reverence for the water itself. He doled out about a pint, three times a day. The nine barrels of fresh looked like a lot, but the pained expression every time the caskip parted with a little suggested they'd go fast. He carried the pail like a mother, her newborn, and guarded against confusion with the other buckets. Refills stopped well-short of the brim. More trips meant less spilled, and even an unexpected pitch that threatened a slosh buoyed the men's hearts into their throats.

Before the last man could gulp his water, Foster leapt into action. The end of breakfast marked the work day. It took him the first one to realize that. His mistake on the second was to ask what he could do to help. That added "dumb cunt" and "arse-tickler" to his reputation for laziness. There was only one day on the whaler, though. It repeated with minor variations upon a cruel memory, but at least it repeated. Each time, he came one closer to getting it right. There was not "nothing to do." He wasn't trusted to sail of course, or keep watch by night, and there was no thought of prying open a cask. If anything, it meant more was expected of him. The deference of Polc's men, the ambivalence of the crew on the *Juhketappat*, Kjartke's needle and grease—none of it taught him a damn thing.

There were no orders. Corm retired to his canopy, or joked with men in the stern. He adjusted the course or the sail from time to time, and spent the entire first week smoothing the ballast—micromanaging the men as they played a mighty game of Tetris to rearrange the rocks and the cargo until she rode to her captain's liking—but nothing like the checklists and client services he fielded every minute, bunk-to-bunk, on the *Qarapara*. Yet the number of things that had to be done to keep men alive at sea on an open wooden vessel staggered him.

As soon as the bowls were away, every bucket aboard was employed in returning the night's water to where it came from. He snatched the prize from the curled boys and scrambled forward. No one had spoken it, but the ship was much smaller for him. There seemed to be secret laws about how far a man might venture from his own seat. Foster never even had to be corrected. He had a strong suspicion that this—Hogue's seat— was his limit. The range seemed to vary by stature of the man.

There were few enough places that were open to get a bucket down into the bilge, and this was the nearest. He got there before anyone else could do it, or tell him he ought to. When a man worked near your bench, he learned from an earful on the third day, you take the man's seat. In practice, if that man had come from far enough, someone else took his, and you occupied the musical chair nearest your station. That sent Hogue forward without a word of acknowledgment. Words of acknowledgment never seemed to go Foster's way.

He plunged his hands into the icy pool in the bilge that never quite disappeared. Each morning was the same, and a new exercise to see how long he could go without abuse. He learned on the fifth day that a man slapping you up and down with enough force to rattle your brain is not usually an act of aggression on a whaler, and he was ridiculed for losing his temper to the point of being restrained by Gionn. By the time the first bucketful hit the sea, he was already strategizing what he'd do next.

The men behind him unrolled the "third quarter"—that was the name for their section of the spare leather mainsail, stored in three portions throughout the ship. He had never seen a fourth quarter, and was assured the three sections were the whole of it. Every morning, the stiff rolls were laid out and the ice hammered from the edges by fist, after which they were wet and brushed with something beyond the most frazzled bristles he'd ever laid toothpaste to, then spread across the width of the ship to dry. If someone needed to pass, he had to crawl under, on account of some forgotten doom. Others uncoiled rope and wound it again clockwise, always "with the sun", to keep it pliable. There were frays to trim and splice, hot spots to grease, and endless pitch-picking. Whatever black gunk they slathered her with to waterproof her ran with a life of its own. It oozed from every seam and boiled up beneath them even though it was rock solid to the touch. He never saw it move, but each day its boundaries crept on. Any rivulet or drop that wasn't actively engaged in sealing the crack between two pieces of wood was scraped up and harvested for stuffing leaks. Leak hunting was its own labor, and there was no day without plugging one.

Beyond that, it was pinching or hammering—the former, splinters; and the latter, nails. The smallest shard of wood that might catch an arm of a foot would be blamed on the nearest seat. They weren't just ripped off and tossed over, either. Wood in these parts was a precious gem. If you squeezed a shard out of your finger, it went into a little sack full of cousins that could be used for kindling if they needed to get a flame going. He hadn't seen one yet, but it sure wouldn't be wasted on a hot meal for the crew.

When the waterline receded below concern, and some but not all of the other bailers bailed on the job, Foster stowed his bucket and hurried forward to retrieve his favorite rock. He always hid it in a new location and tried to be slick about it, not because he was afraid someone would take it, but because he knew Gionn was watching. Let the bastard take the time to rifle through ballast for his fucking argot. All he would find was Foster's rock: small enough to half-close a fist with a near-right angle on one of the facets that did a number on any nail with a deserter's disposition. The wave action hammered them out as fast as they could put them back. Anything above flush got a good crack, and he came to know the usual suspects. Some were so consistent, he could push them back in with a fingertip. In good weather like this, they were even expected to hang over the side to tap anything above the sea level. On the sixth day, Corm bored him a new asshole for it, with the punchline being that he wasn't giving the captain a fair chance to earn his pay back by falling over without a share to his name. Today, he decided to risk it again on the wager that it was a compliment.

He nailed what he could with an easy reach, then noticed a pair that stood a few millimeters proud, disappearing under the surface with every short roller. No rational thought would have driven him to care. He could pretend he hadn't seen them. That's probably what most of the men did. But a deeper terror gripped him. He felt it the first time he helped his uncle bale hay; when the forklift ran out of butane at his new nursery job and the grown men made a sophomore climb the leaning tower of empty pallets to throw down what they needed; with every fresh set of bodies the Navy sent him to. It wasn't injury or death that held his chest to the gunwale as he leaned over the side, but the fear of looking like a little bitch who didn't know what the hell he was doing.

Inch-by-inch, he worked outward until his stomach braced him. Blood pooled in his face and his gut ached. His full reach was still a good four inches away.

"Leg over!" Someone from midships shouted. Foster exhaled and gasped as he returned aboard in confusion. "Get your leg over! You wanna go for a tumble? Idiot cunt!"

"Hell, I was doin' that the other day. Yuray-what's-his-face told me not to."

"Fuckin' die, then." It was a sinew-woven fellow, diminutive and gray though hardly old, knotted in the permanent curve of a rower. His bottom jaw jutted forward with an angry Amish beard and he sawed his teeth back and forth over his upper lip while he took in Foster's insolence.

"Do not listen to the madman." Yuray, the Amposi in front of Chirim, spoke. "Where your leg go, you follow."

"Lies!" The first man screamed. "You'd see Gionn to Manhas!"

Yuray laughed. "That is the Wife Seal!"

"The bead lad?"

"He does not use beads."

"I know that! You lob! He got no beads but he beads. You're the fuckin' idiot! Not I!"

"You thought that was Gionn."

"Aye? Fresh smells fresh."

"Gionn's the big red cunt, Fergo," Pitras clarified.

"You think you're a bright fuckin' blade, do you?" Fergo turned on Foster.

"Me?" He clutched his chest. "I didn't say shit!"

"Jump, then! On with you!" Fergo waved them off and returned to the pile of fiber he braided each day until noon, and only that long.

Everyone in the vicinity had an awkward chuckle at the man. Foster leaned back over the side, hoping to conceal himself in his work. He feared the same as every New Guy. Same as himself every time he stumbled in under that banner. At least the blows and insults were honest. The cruelest abuse was advice. Again he edged himself out, but a moment of weightlessness stopped him. It was almost imagined. He felt the turning momentum Fergo described that would simply lift his feet over his head with the effort of a child.

"Leg over!" This time, it was Pitras. "Better yet, have the *other* Gionn do it."

The fingers on his left hand white-knuckled the edge, and the side of his foot pinched hard against the inner hull. Foster lowered his hips over and let his right leg hang for balance. The water welled up to his calf, and down again as he reached further. Twice he pulled his hammer back to keep it out of the brimming sea that gulped at the nails. The third time it receded, he struck hard, twice on each, and rolled gasping back into the boat.

It took until that day for him to learn when to quit. The carrier and the *Qarapara* taught him there was always something else. If you can lean, you can clean. One more act of groveling at a baseboard, or counting and stowing something inane for the first time in human history. The bastards on the *Gairhle* knocked off when they were done. Initially, he took their insults as confirmation that he did the right thing by assigning himself ever-more marginal tasks. Once they began offering his busy hands things to polish, he got the message that they didn't believe in work for work's sake—straight blasphemy in his world. A man who kept at it was an arse-tickler, then a madman. Finally Bentos had to buckle his knee with a kick, sending him sprawling onto sharp ballast with a threat of dismemberment if he crossed the man's bench again. Everything he could do was wrong. They teased him when he stopped working at a reasonable time, and three of the six men he passed on the way back to his seat offered him conflicting recommendations for how— and how important it was—to return to the good graces of Fergo.

Foster slumped. It was his best effort yet. No one believed a thing he said or did. He couldn't even piss off the side with conviction at this point.

"The next time that worm pulls the rag out his twat to speak to you, I say count up the teeth you remove from his jaw. You're the number man. You'll take no peltin' from him!" Gionn encouraged. That made four. All night and all morning he choked back dread of how his partner would respond to their argument. Foster could hardly sleep for fear of a pat down. The only thing worse than the tension he expected was the sudden kindness he received, instead.

"Mornin', cunt!" Was one of the few times he got his usual title. What Foster felt as a wedge slowly tapped between them vanished so completely that he now wondered if he had been sensitive to imagine it. Gionn joked about the squain boys, complained about the rations, and gave him warning when a sailor came stomping over thwarts where Foster's hand rested during a hammering. If he hadn't known better, he'd assume the scumbag found his coin during the night. It unnerved him. But he couldn't come up with a reason to remain bitter.

He tongued the gap in his bottom jaw. "I lost it." He looked up at Gionn. "Speakin' of teeth." His companion forced an uneasy smile.

"The one Moipa knocked out?"

"What other one is there?" Gionn's eyebrow peaked, and Foster realized what his companion thought he was talking about. He pulled his lip back and pointed to the hole. "This one. Had it rolled in the top of my boot, but I forgot all about it until this mornin'. Can't even you tell you what day it was. Hell, I only kept it cause you told me to. It ain't like it's goin' back in."

Gionn relaxed his smile. "May you find it before your enemies."

It was noon. Foster knew before he checked the sun when Cormdran rose on a cask near the stern. There was no attention-on-deck for the whalers. The men who still worked at something kept on it. The imposing figure steadied himself on a rope as he stepped to the next wood top, or rock. There wasn't an inch of open board for the captain's walk. No one who saw him on shore would have guessed his grace as he swung his leg to an uneven landing on a pitching ship. At six-foot-six, the man was taller than Parks and bigger around. Foster was no fool to think that size made a man a fighter, but nor was he fool enough to think it didn't matter. Maybe at some point the crew saw this dude set down a thick skull or two. It was equally possible that they were in awe of a giant. Plenty of threats issued from his mouth, but they were all the kind that served to emphasize an order. Corm's orders were few, and always followed. There had been no reason for him to demonstrate any of the fury that men liked to imagine into a mighty frame. Foster considered that others knew him a lot better, and they chose to stay on his good side.

If he ruled by fear, it was not by violence. His daily inspection hardly warranted the name. If anything was out of order, Eckerd would have ear-fucked it into shape before Corm had a chance to venture forward. No one made a pretense of straightening up. Some men exchanged a few words. No complaints or requests. Passing remarks of no consequence seemed like the standard. Some men took an insult, others made one— nothing sharper than a poke, he noticed. The majority turned their casual attention but didn't delay him with a word. Every day Corm made it as far as the mast. The mast seemed an extension of himself: towering over with the sail, puffed out to an easy pride. Here, he paused for a longer yarn with the first mate. Some days, that would be it. He'd turn aft, and enjoy the the sun from his own bench, or invite a man or two under his canopy. Others, he would continue forward as far as his interest took him. He could spend an hour shooting the shit, or be done and back in minutes. Foster only saw the captain venture as far as his own bench on one occasion. The second day at sea, when both he and the blacksmith's apprentices took ill, Corm arrived under the pretense of belittling them, but his was the patronizing tone of a father giving his sons a rough welcome to the family trade.

They'd hardly exchanged a word since. All his instincts told Foster to snap-to, look busy, salute, greet the man with deference. With an act of will, he limited himself to a brief glance and a smile, then averted his eyes to the sea. The thick legs stopped on the thwart in front of him. If the captain wanted to speak to him, he'd do it, Foster convinced himself. He didn't know what to say that wouldn't come off as ass-kissing or disrespectful. Silence was the safe bet.

But the boots didn't move. He felt the bore of those deep-set eyes upon him, and worried that now he might be snubbing his captain. Foster looked up again, and Corm's glare had not left. Gionn was wordless. That should mean something to him, but he didn't know what. The weight of the gaze felt like the man himself leaned on Foster.

"Bet you're lovin' this weather, Cap'n." He wanted to punch himself as soon as the panicked statement fell out. Corm held on to him a little longer, then leaned out over the final bench. Behind it, the Mattaka boys lay curled around their stomachs.

"You got until sundown to finish your dyin'," he belted. "If you can't manage it, I'll find you up and about. Or I'll unload some of the ballast these sogers complain of." He got no response, and didn't wait for one. "How rides the bow?" He shielded off Foster with his back to ask Gionn.

"Heavy and wet. But your oars are locked. Least, these four."

Corm frowned over Gionn in disbelief. "Hear there was a bit of loose talk this way."

"Aye, must have been meself. Can't think who else would do it."

Now the captain looked behind him with a half-cocked grin as though to see if anyone else shared his amusement. The crew remained disengaged, but their side chatter faded and Foster could tell all ears were on them.

"Well? Out with it! I love good scuttle."

"I know what you're thinkin'. No need to lose sleep over your bow, Corm. Chirim and Bentos get one in the back if they stand too fast for a piss."

"Fuck *off*," Bentos groaned. "Corm, is there a loud son of a bitch aft you're sick of? I'm a fair trade."

"Not sure I've ever heard a man talk openly of mutiny to his captain."

Foster cringed. At least his bitch-ass weather comment didn't seem so bad anymore.

"Have you ever seen one?"

"A mutiny? Aye. Several," Corm swayed forward and back over Gionn.

"Exactly!" Gionn slapped his thigh. He let the crew work over their confusion a second. "You've never seen a man talk loose of mutiny on a ship where there was a mutiny. Nor have I, and I've seen me share. Who of sound constitution would abuse his mates if there were any thought of an arse leavin' his seat? It's only a problem when you can't joke about it." Corm squinted. Gionn continued.

"Every cunt aboard knows the lay of it." He looked to Foster. "Almost. What captain needs an admiral underfoot? Better yet: what admiral humbles himself to a captain? Everyone's thinkin' it. And on any other ship, I'd stitch me lips. Too many shares danglin' from every yard and sheet. As it happens, we've a luck with us that'll make every man here richer than a squain whore in winter. All we have to do is get to Taclann.

"I say 'all.' You lot know we won't do that without every oar before me. Not if we're squabblin' and whisperin' and guessin' and countin' who might stand and when. Besides, Foster's shown a mockery of your dumb cunt counts. Shall we limp in with eight wounded sailors and expect Tolba's lads to politely help us load? There's more work than can be done in a season, and we need every man for it. Even the bucket lads. But if we can keep our heads up and our arses down, every last one of us will be captain of his own ship, paid in full, three years from now."

A murmur of approval spread over the benches, but Gionn interrupted it. "But if you don't let us talk, what will we think? There may be nothin' to it, but every man will dream it bubblin' beneath us. He'll dream rifts, and shares, and spears in every low voice and short look, until he's forced to side for his own good." He paused. "Mutiny!" The crew recoiled. "*Mutiny!*" Gionn laughed. "There, I said it! Do you know the Numians believe that to name a fate is to avoid it? Let it carry on like a spy, though, and your ruin's secured. I hate Numians. They're a shiftless bunch, and their women are hideous. I'd almost rather marry an Amposi. But the gods aren't so cruel they won't let every group of mongrels be right about one thing."

Cormdran wrinkled his nose and took in the whole of the crew. Not a man betrayed his reaction, and they could no longer feign disinterest. The boat rested on her captain.

"A fine speech, lad. You must think you've got me well-marked to brave it."

"I don't brave anything. Ask Foster. I'm a jumper through-and-through, as much as you're a barrel. I just hope those Amposi deserters share your sense of humor."

Corm's face flushed red and his eyes widened. He appeared to tremble. But he couldn't hold it. The captain burst into a fit of laughter that the crew joined with glee. Foster hadn't even noticed it: a stiff and brittle film that hung in the air cracked and fell away. He thought it part of the whaler, if he ever thought of it at all. Now, it was as though someone had rolled down the window of a musty car and let the breeze whip through with scents of salt and clean mineral. A dozen conversations erupted as Corm turned for his seat. Gionn called after him.

"Don't worry mate! I've always been a shore-putter, anyway! Give a man a chance, I say. Never know when someone might happen along for a rescue." Corm grabbed his sack and shook it at Gionn with a grin.

Relief flooded Foster. He knew nothing about the ship, her crew, or the trade, but some part of him felt the tension of the rowers strung taut. Shoulders fell, and voices lost their edge. Even their cheerful departure felt guarded by comparison. Their constant vigilance on Drummoc had worn on them, but it also brought them together. Now they were among themselves again. Snatches of conversation with Costig drifted back to him. He knew one of the admirals had joined up with a slew of his friends, but it was a meaningless fact at the time. The name came to him soon enough, and that was trivia, too: So-and-So made treaty with King Whoever the fourth in 1460. It was history to memorize.

Gionn mentioned there was a lot he needed to know about whalers if he meant to live. All of this hummed along right under his nose, and any act he'd taken to undermine the ship would have been carried out in complete ignorance of the basic currents within the crew. Foster wondered if the show wasn't Gionn's way of getting him as much information as he could.

They hated whispers here. Even two men engaged in the same work had to speak up loud enough that a few others could hear them. No one told him that, except the clear voices that rang at him from a bench away. If they were going to conspire together—and he was far from confident that was the case—he and Gionn would have to offer every word of it up to the crew. The way he and Parks had tried when Ostuk arrested them for suspicion of mutiny. Their "code" didn't even fool the old Mattaka who guarded them. At the time, he was sure of his ally, and shared a world of common experiences.

But Gionn's rant seemed like a risk, even for him. Foster didn't understand the fine social cues he needed to do the same. Or the heedless balls, for that matter.

Chirim laughed at something Gionn said—they seemed to be plotting their reigns once the fortune of the ship was cashed out.

"And would King Chirim swear to Tolba? Or Young Donnab?"

"Already you start another mutiny!"

"Ha! Wait and see who shows up first, eh? I like it. Ecuba's a fair call for either. Whichever it is, don't take their first offer!"

"Of course not!" Chirim slapped Gionn's knee. "And where will I find me mate's fleet?"

"Halfway between yours and your best trade." They cackled together.

There were few moments during the day when Foster remembered why he sat on this bench. Parks came to mind, and Kjartke. Behind a wall of hide, frozen in time, unsettled. But that wasn't it, either. From there, another leap returned him to his purpose. A quiet disaster had been at least temporarily abated. The relief he felt was the crew's. It couldn't be his own. Every man here was at odds with his mission. He'd missed his chance to take advantage of their rift because he hadn't noticed it. Gionn saw it, but if he couldn't have his argot, there was no reason to help Foster. And if he did have it, well—there was no reason to help Foster.

Less often now than his mission, which he could only name in terms like, "Costig's plan," or "get her to Nunoc," Foster thought of another purpose that ran deeper and sank farther into obscurity every day behind the wind, the water, the crew in front of him. It was an abstraction. He couldn't even imagine how, or when it might happen. There were too many things in between here and there. But he felt its grip and the gentle tug that guided him through all of it—most of all, when he forgot. At some point, he promised a friend, they would go home.

His benchmate didn't need to scheme and manipulate. He didn't even need to be a jerk. If the crew got along, he won. If that was his angle, the opening round was his. Foster's starting advantage was lost before he even understood the rules. All he knew was there were fifty-two other men on this ship, and Gionn just drafted every last one of them to his team.

Almost. Foster wheeled forward to face the raised deck.

"You heard the cap'n." He ripped the blanket off of pale Bucket. The boy squirmed away from the light, pressing his cheek into the thin pool of bile. Foster kicked his own sleeping bag to rouse the other one, the nameless stunt double.

"Come on. Help me get your boy up." The smaller one tried to twist away, but now all Foster had to do was start for him, and he scowled his way to a seated position.

"Trust me, I been in your shoes. All the way down from Nunoc. I was sick as a dog every day, with no signs of lettin' up. You know what I did?" Bucket opened the top eye a slit. "I got my ass up. I walked that deck and I fed dogs, even though I wanted to puke. I couldn't see straight. I gagged and dry-heaved and barely took down water. I fell on my goddamn face. But I stood up, and I worked. And by the end of the day, I felt like some tiny part of me was human again. Then I woke up and did it the next day, and the next. You think this is bad? Bitch, I was toppin' out water halfway up the mast of a dog ship!"

Bucket closed his eye and buried his forehead in his arm.

"Come on. We're gonna stand up, and I'll show you how to splinter-pick. Each of yall gonna get me one splinter. *One!* That's all I'm askin'. Then you walk up toward the mast, put it in the splinter sack, and get on back. They may ask you for a bucket. If so, get it. That's what you signed on for. That's your ship, and you gotta ride it. What do you say? Can we do that?"

"You trick us," Bucket moaned.

"What?"

The other boy pointed at the bucket. "You give it to us. You know what will happen."

Foster started to deny it, then hesitated. "Yeah. I knew. I knew if you showed up empty-handed, your asses would be in Drummoc wavin' goodbye. Do you know how to count? You know how to sail? You a carpenter? A caskip? A spinnaker? A navigator? A rower? I don't see a forge on this ship, and yall don't look like you had that job very long, either. You know what else I know? Drummoc's a shithole. If I had to choose between catchin' turds in a bucket for a few months and spendin' the rest of my life starvin' to death in a dark, frozen ghetto while the Navy hassled my people, and my kids could choose between dyin' of black lung in the mines or on the anvil, I would pick the goddamn bucket."

Both of the boys looked to him, and waited.

"However any of us got here, here we are. Here we fuckin' are. No one likes yall. They call you Bucket, and they don't even know you're not the same kid, so they call you Bucket, too. If it's any consolation, I got pegged with Wife Seal." The boys giggled. "Better'n the last one I had. I promise, the nicknames improve with every ship. *If* you stand up."

Bucket nodded. He pushed himself off the rocks and winced from the deep bruises in his side. Foster and the other boy eased him to sitting.

"What's your name, son?"

"Atalkut."

"And you?"

The smaller boy paused, then looked at his knees. "Tunguk."

Foster split open ear-to-ear. "One of my best buds is named Tunguk." The boy perked up a little. "Is that a common name among your people?"

"Aye, it is common," Atalkut said the word in a way that suggested to Foster it meant something other than what he'd intended. "When one of the Mattaka is orphaned or cast out so that the living don't know his name, he must call himself *Tunguk*—Wanderer. It is a bad fate." The boy looked upon his friend with pity.

But Foster could afford him no such luxury.

"On three." They seemed confused. "I'll count to three. That's what I do. One, two, three, and we stand Got it?" He extended his arms and took each thin hand, then leaned back for momentum.

"One…two…"

The *Gairhle* stood a few hundred yards off the dock in the Drummoc harbor. Cormdran locked his oar, which sufficed for the order. The daille was only now being hauled out. Whether it took them that long to spot her or to wake from their sloth didn't concern him. He was going to need a moment if he meant to do anything other than wheeze in this ninny's face.

The mountains to the west glowed like a forge. There was an unbelievable quiet to this place. Not a cry could reach her. Far away, squain folk paused to have a look offshore, but few yet took an interest in their arrival. He supposed that meant it wouldn't be consummated for some time. The men faced forward. How many thousands of miles lay behind them! Yet here was the stretch of water that made the journey. Eckerd, tireless Eckerd, rummaged out the pennant and with nothing to run it up, stood upon the side of the mast where she rested in her berth along the length of the vessel. He waved it at the daille until he was certain she saw.

Corm gathered his feet and stood most of the way before his back turned wooden. Better no orders at all than to leak one from tired lungs and have it ignored. The Navy sculled toward them under two pairs of oars, and an officer idle in the bow. In that one stroke, whatever grudges and hopes and reservations he had for the remaining twenty-seven men evaporated. At last, he saw them again as a single crew, and was no prouder of any vigorous act or fate-loving sacrifice carried out thus far than he was now: every one of them sitting tall at his damnedest when the bluecoat came within a cast.

Eckerd caught the line and Corm waded amidships to meet them. The daille drew alongside until she bumped the hull. The rowers held her steady while the officer rose from the bow and extended a hand for help to clear the higher side of the *Gairhle*. Corm placed a boot on the gunwale where the man planned to come over, and leaned down to regard this latest assailant. Amposi brown, and vain enough to wear the blue. The effort to conceal his distaste when he realized he would not be lifted up put some blood in Corm's haunches. Here began the dance. No graceful bend of oar to gain the weather-gage before it went to rams could compare to a full whaler angling her approach to port. The officer withdrew his hand to calculate the cost of the insult. He did not speak, and Corm had already decided to see for how long. He knew the wait, and had been away from land long enough that he felt he could stand it better than the rocking daille. That, and he was fucking tired.

The officer sensed defeat and decided a quick one was preferred. He looked over the stowed mast.

"How long have you been under oars?"

"Half a day." He wondered if this captain was the Amposi preener variety—the appointed kind—or the one who'd see the truth in the men's faces. "Will this be long?" Corm knew the answer. The show of impatience was his concession for the slight. The officer's smirk showed it had done its job.

"Oh, I doubt very much. Dismasted?" He indicated the port bow, where the rail was gone entirely, and several boards beneath it cut out in a gaping wound. Corm shook his head.

"Wave ran us into a rock landin' for water a few weeks back."

"And the mast?"

"Too much play against the wedge for me likin'. Took her down this mornin' when a tern circled twice and flew back to shore."

The captain nodded. "Merchant?"

"Serves me," Corm shrugged. They shared what was almost a smile.

"Admiralty letter?"

"Fell overboard. Slippery things."

"Do not worry, Captain. It happens often. We will accommodate you until we can send to Nunoc for another on your behalf. In the spring."

"Will you give us all three rooms, or crowd us into the one?" He recalled the lay of the prison.

The officer laughed. "Have you been to Drummoc before?"

"Aye. And I think once Admiral Galichar sees our wares, we'll be able to work somethin' out."

"Admiral *Turrha's* standing orders are that any ship seeking harbor must have an admiralty letter, or be seized, along with her cargo and men, until one can be supplied." Corm didn't remember this captain, but it had been three years. The man betrayed no pleasure in the proclamation. Something near regret, in fact. He couldn't have been entirely fresh. "Of course, you could always turn around."

Corm chewed it over like a piece of gristle he knew his teeth would meet at some point.

"Think I'd rather stay here and get to know the man who'll be rowin' me first, and probably not me last, counter to this Turrha cunt."

The officer smiled. "It would have to be most impressive for the admiral to reconsider his position. But it shall be rowed all the same by Captain Palqua." He gave a modest salute.

Foster considered the filet before sinking in his teeth. It was raw—skin and all, and he could already taste the way the scales would flake off on his tongue and lodge in his gums. The fish was a mystery, but the men in the stern had been pulling them in all day from one of the frequent entourages that took up following the *Gairhle* for a few hours, or a few days. Tawatu didn't even need to pop a cask that evening. Now he watched the boat at their meal with the downcast stare of a new freshman in the lunch room.

Corm was out of sight, eating under the tarp with his two-share men. It was the first time Foster could recall all of them having supper together, but he wanted to kick himself for being unsure. As the sole mutineer, he ate alone. *It doesn't have to be mutiny*, he reminded himself. *You just have to get the boat in at Nunoc.* It was a rock dropped into a bottomless well. Nothing echoed to tell him what was true, or possible. He should be plotting and scheming. Chatting with the boys, sowing discontent. Whatever he had to do, it hung over the ship like a fog on a windless morning. He could hardly know the world two feet away. Gionn's warning was as friendly as the son of a bitch could have made it, but it festered in him. He couldn't move, because he didn't have the faintest motion where to start.

Foster ripped a jagged bite from the rubbery skin. He was a newborn, not much better than the two boys behind him. Ripped from the warm womb of solid ground into a world he was naive-enough to hope he could understand. Once he was done flailing and carrying on, he started in to relate these things to those he already knew. Anything that reminded him of the Navy, a TV show, traveling with Tunguk, became an anchor. From that security, he ventured into imitation. For days, he worked how he saw them work, ate how he saw them eat. Some part of him was sure that if he could only get a foothold, the incomprehensible rituals of life on the whaler would unfold for him, one by one. That he would soon crawl, then walk.

It took, what—seven, eight days now?—to realize his error.

Sometime after noon, a high, flat cloud cover enveloped the sun. No one asked Fergo what it meant. Though the man seemed hardly able to string together two intelligible thoughts, he was for some reason regarded as a master of the "signs". Every nautical superstition launched a bitter debate, but a good many were settled in the eyes of most of the crew by getting the final word from a man who thought that Foster's name was "Gionn." Not so with the clouds. Some of the crew spent minutes straining into the distance, then declared it was a "sea-sky." Their course took them through ice-free waters. It was as though a uniform expanse of gray clearly demarcated a border between the world of Fergo, and that of someone like Eckerd, whose pronouncement went unquestioned.

When Foster threw a leg over the side to hammer a few loose nails, he thought he did it because Pitras confirmed the technique, and Pitras would know—he was a two-share man. And maybe there was a touch of guilt that made him go with Fergo's advice after the confused argument he started. Foster knew it felt more like logic and less like superstition to have a second vote.

But under a sea-sky, heading into one more future chosen by a bunch of illiterate scoundrels, it dawned on him at last. There was nothing here that came from a Foster world. No one tacked, or put a leg over, or ate with a certain somebody for any reason he could fathom by logic or hoodoo. He may as well have been hard at work discovering new species, only to carry them home to die in a plastic zoo of his own creation. There were no anchors. He couldn't even sound the bottom.

And so Foster resolved to be the newborn. Every sight and smell was a blur that had nothing to do with anything he'd experienced before. To relate it to the carrier or the mess hall could only assure he would lose himself before he even began. Gionn knew this world. So did Corm, the two-share men under that tarp, even the Mattaka boys. At least, they had a purchase on it. To this very minute, when the word "whaler" popped into his head, he thought of some ship he probably saw in a movie about 18th century cannon battles muddled with summaries of *Moby Dick*, which he never bothered to read. The beached calf they killed in the channel. Oil lamps and perfume. It took vigorous mental effort to brush it all aside and actually look-the-hell around him.

Foster wasn't ready to orchestrate a mutiny. He knew a good part of that sentiment was his own doubt that he could even pull it off, but there was a deeper truth to it. His world right now was as wide as his bench, and his only job was to notice it.

It took him this long just to see the *Gairhle*, and himself on it. That time was gone. All he could do was now was notice who the captain had over for supper. Not why—no guesses—just who. Who he spoke to when he went on his walks. Who spoke to each other when the captain was aft. Eckerd called out an adjustment, and a pair of men jumped up to the ropes without being named. Foster realized he didn't know their names, though he'd seen them at the sail plenty of times. There was another man, Baghar, who was often called on for the same work, but these and a few others just did it. Not every name came to him at once, and when it did, there was a reason for it. No, not a reason. An event. Something coaxed it from the lungs of another.

The sailor on Gionn's side reached across his body to steady himself on one of the sheets with his left hand. Suddenly, every hand on the ship leapt out at Foster, mending a tear, taking a drink, gesturing. He could look at certain men and hear the sound of their voices in his head. Others, especially farther back, Foster couldn't imagine. He was sure every last one of them would come eventually. But to a man, he had to build them. He would notice whether they put a foot up on the side to piss. Who made them laugh, or grimace. Their accent, how they reacted when a little wave came over their bench. How far from their bench they dared to stray during work and leisure, and how far they shouted beyond that. If he ate alone, like Foster, or turned to others. It was too soon to call them allies, enemies, seasoned veterans, badasses, whiners, idiots, or even something as meaningless to him as "Amposi". Those were the ways he would prefer to arrange them, because they made him feel like he understood. Just as a certain sky gave a man faith in the sea ahead. Maybe their superstitions were right sometimes, he thought. Maybe they deserved more credit. But if so, it was because at some point in the past, men noticed something in their naivete. Something happened, and they told themselves the two were part of the same thing.

Was he any better? Foster had spent the past week—a lot longer, if he had the stomach to admit it—telling himself what would happen soon. Someone would rally to him, or betray him. A ship would sail with him on it. If only he spoke a certain way, worked hard, kept his head down, he would conjure exactly the thing he wanted from people he called friends, conspirators, threats, insignificant. Now he wondered what he'd find if he bothered to count up how many times his superstitions came true. Were old Tunguk and Kjartke what he thought they were at first glance? Or even when he said goodbye? And what about Parks, who he knew as well as anything outside his own skin? What signs did he miss that left his friend mutilated on a snow-capped volcano? Did he dare imagine what he'd find if he could break this ship off and return?

He looked beside him to the redhead drinking the last fish juice and flakes from his wrist, where he cupped his hands into a bowl. A thousand stories flashed by. Images of the man pulling a knife across a boy's throat. A joke he made. His silhouette in the poorman's quarters, or Ingputka. That broad back fleeing, then rowing on the skin boat. Foster saw Gionn defiant on the deck of the dog ship, then handing him his tooth. He closed his eyes and shook it all clear. His benchmate saw him, gave an easy smile, and turned away again. Foster forced himself to look.

Again, he had to cast aside his notions of the man, which were something like memories, and what he felt about them. He set his gaze on the damp hair, the square jaw and pink-white flesh. The thick hands wiped themselves clean on filthy trousers. He saw the knife flash again— the one in his belt—and pushed it away. It was just some incomprehensible creature resting on a thwart.

Foster didn't know if he loved it or hated it. The legs stretched out. The torso wrenched one way, then the other in a groaning stretch. At his waist, the bronze-pommeled sword twisted as the guard touched a rock. A wave of disorientation washed over Foster. For a second, he couldn't remember where he was, and he didn't care. Every piece of ballast stood proud before him in their separate lines. The slosh of the hidden bilge rushed under in contrast to the rolling swell. The sea curled matte gray in a breeze that stuttered as over a washboard. He saw the tip of the mast sway between the edge of one cloud and another, and the quilt that yawned over the darkening sky that before he thought was a single smoky mass. A line went taut again as a sailor tied it off. Voices rippled forward over the benches between the buffeting of the leather sail, itself quilted from smaller rectangles. He watched a crest break over the stern and send two little streams of water over the tarp to cross one another and run off again. It reminded him of the feeling of the cloak that Tunguk once lay over his shoulders on a cold night at sea.

Foster looked over the starboard beam in the direction of land. He couldn't see it. Thoughts intruded of searching for little islands of fresh water, pebbles on a map speckling the coast. He swept them aside again to stare at the featureless surface until it erupted in features: the main swell, long and steady. A million smaller ripples from the wind and the clash of water that broke facets and textured the sea like a cloth dropped haphazardly and pressed into a surface of soft clay.

A white plume burst in the air, followed by a quick flash of pitch black. He watched for some time before it came again from an unexpected position. Then a second one too far ahead to be the same. Soon they came like lightning bugs at dusk. More plumes, then a long black back sailing under a dorsal fin. Someone sounded off from midship:

"Whale, ho!"

The men on the port side rose for a better look. Foster's attention wavered between the pod that veered their direction and the faces of the whalers, solemn and curious. Even in the short voyage, they'd seen spouts several times, but always far off or in isolation. The familiar thoughts he'd worked so hard to set aside rushed back with the same force as he proudly recognized the white eyes and chin of the killer whales. It might have been the only animal species in Antarctica that he could name with confidence.

"Angotaks!" Bucket shouted. *Atalkut*, he reminded himself.

The crew turned on the boy with glares of resentment he hardly seemed to have earned. Foster knew the word. He tied it to a half-remembered story from Ostuk—some myth of them chasing the Mattaka for some reason. Massive as they were, he felt no fear when they drew within a hundred yards of the ship. The *Gairhle* was too big, he was sure, and they seemed playful, interested.

"We'll be stopped before the Sun Gate," someone said as if admitting to something painful.

"Only if they approach. If they turn, we'll slip past, or be ignored." Pitras corrected. The crew broke into local murmurs of varying levels of concern.

"We drop sail and let 'em pass!" Someone else suggested.

"Are you captain now?" Corm growled. "Steady on!"

"Aye, you can hardly cross the Attavaik without seein' 'em a dozen times," Bentos dismissed the worriers. "Do you suppose every ship runs into the Angotaks?"

"It's not the seein' 'em, but if the herd bears on the ship," Pitras repeated.

"The damn herd can do as it like!" Fergo spat.

"If they breach first behind, it is escape. If ahead, it is a fight," Tawatu said. "Amposi know this. Between ship and land, they will block our route but we may escape. Out to sea, we will be trapped."

"Who saw first breach?" Chirim asked. A number of the men scanned the benches for an answer.

"I saw 'em landward," the first man to raise a cry said. "Did any of you cunts see 'em before?"

"Don't fuckin' matter," Fergo said.

"Shut up, and let Fergo say it!" Cormdran stalked forward toward the mast.

"The jumper's right," Fergo said of Bentos. "Can't go south without seein' 'em. It's not the herd, it's the bull. If he takes keen to us, we'll be met, and if he ignores us, we go past. But if he crosses the ship to the other side, it's Manhas for us."

Foster leaned over to Gionn quietly. "Which one' s the bull?"

"Dunno, mate. Haven't had a chance to flip 'em over and check."

Chirim heard them, and repeated Foster's question for the ship. Fergo pointed to one near the lead, and only his finger transformed it from another whale into a hulk that loomed over the others, and broke the surface with more zeal. The big male positioned himself closest to the ship, but still fifty yards off the starboard beam.

"Don't let him cross!" Several men in the back took up spears, ready to jab.

"Hold your cocks!" Corm shouted. "You'll just provoke him."

The crew held its breath in its vigil. Foster recalled the commotion over the petrel that either landed or didn't. Again, he wanted to laugh and sneer it away. It should have been a source of amusement. At the least, disinterest. But there was something else there: in the pod, the creaking wooden beast, the very atmosphere. It was the animal he knew best, but aside from a movie or a documentary, had never seen. There was more to it than the whale.

Angotaks. Another inside joke he wasn't privy to. He doubted they thought the actual whales would harm them. It meant something else to the crew. An omen of enemy ships, probably, but who, and why? And like that, he felt his old habit reemerge to taunt him. It wasn't Sea World swimming off the beam. Hell, maybe it *was* the whales, themselves, that would be the death of them. Who was he to say? Foster was only sure that he had no inkling what connection a group of marine mammals had to the fates of the men in this ship. And though he could hardly think it for the abyss it tore in his stomach, no amount of confusion or terror that the orcas could instill would compare to what he felt when he returned his senses to a wooden vessel, square-rigged full of ancient mariners, plowing the waters off a continent no longer called Antarctica.

He felt beads of sweat form under his hood. Cold as he was, it brought his attention to his arms and his thighs, now as clammy as his neck. For the first time since they left Drummoc, Foster peeled off his oilskin. The cool air sent shivers over his flesh. His wet tunic clung to his chest, and he shed that, too. Goosebumps rose over his body. The bone chill shuddered through him and breached the surface, and in a few minutes passed with the dry breeze. It felt like a fever breaking.

His eyes turned to the killer whales. The angotaks. Voices settled without an order. For half an hour, he watched the pod keep pace, and did his damnedest to care just as much as the crew. Corm made no effort to steer away, as if the slightest intent to interfere with some process of fate would bring it down with twice the force. At last, the whales bent toward the coast and fell behind. There were a few minutes of disbelief where no one wanted to say it, but the pregnant glances gave in to a raucous cheer that shook the ship. Foster whooped and hollered as loud as any of them. In his carrying-on, he found himself confronted with the red hulk across the way, and out of pure instinct, raised a palm before he realized the gesture wouldn't translate, and awkwardly returned it to his side. But Gionn offered his up.

"High five, mate?"

Now Foster recalled Parks laying one on their hostage to celebrate his near-abandoning them on Nunoc. He slapped the hand, and they smiled like old friends. A foot away on his thwart, he saw the Foster who rode out here, sulking and rolling his eyes in condescension. A few orcas and a high five didn't mean shit. The ship was going down, and Gionn would betray him. But as his bare flesh crackled in the cool air that snapped the sail, it was worlds better where he stood, a participant.

Cormdran strode the barrels and benches with the grace of a cat, pausing to gather his momentum before letting the ship take the next step for him. For only the second time on the journey and that day, he came to rest in front of their bench. Foster's shit-eating grin lacked the calculation to look away, and the captain's lip curled in amicable dismissal. He found the Mattaka boys, both "arse-to-bench" for the first time. They still looked like day-old butthole to Foster—especially Bucket—but there they were.

"Right. With me, lads. And bring your bucket." The men had a cackle at the boys while Corm turned for his place at the stern. Pleading eyes fell on Foster as if there was a damn thing he could do.

"Make sure yall empty it before you try to walk back."

He settled to his seat again in a satisfied daze. It never dawned on him how much he relied on people like Tunguk. The word "rely" didn't even cut it. Foster lived through them. He never had to understand a thing about the world beyond the first few hours. An old man walked before him, spoke to people, steered him away from danger like a watchful parent more times than he probably realized. It was as though he stumbled along in some parallel fantasy, full of old dreams that he tethered to Parks so he might never wander too far from a place he recognized. Inside jokes and high fives. Dimming memories of ships that gave them passage. It was by the grace of good advice that it wasn't him holding that bucket. How naive had he been to think he could steal a coal ship? Piss off a viceroy? Earn a bench on a whaler? Only by somebody else's miracle was he still drawing air.

There were no more friendly Injun guides here. They weren't enemies, either, though. It was a crew, each from his own place, here for his own reason, and heading somewhere only he could dream of, on the kindness of every marine animal and passing cloud. If Chirim thought he would be some petty king of…where was it, Ecuba? Was that any more ridiculous than retiring to a double-wide on the eastern slope of the Blue Ridge Mountains? Every man of them bore the cold better and knew the ropes and rules of an open boat. Most carried steel to his stone. Not a one needed another to captain his ship.

Rising now from his disgust was a core of admiration. The helpless kind he felt as a boy for his mama, who could do anything, bring anything into the world if only she meant it. A mystery and a wonder and a power. And at the leading edge of it, a secret sense that one day, he would inherit the same.

The crew fluttered back to their roosts, the handful of feet they would occupy for thousands of miles. Voices still boomed in exhilaration. Absent was Gionn's. Maybe he was reeling from his outburst to Corm, and felt the need to balance it with uncharacteristic modesty. It was tempting to think he was just plotting. But Foster always thought that, and never wondered if it were true. Whatever his ends, the bastard was as alone on this ship as he was. Probably on every ship. Coming from a place forbidden to ask, bound somewhere he didn't dare tell. You could probably say that about all of them, but there was a melancholy to the man that may have just been Foster's own, projected out of the desire to relate to something he couldn't yet understand.

It was still loud enough. He figured he should say something while there was noise to drown it out. Nothing too bold. A smart-ass remark, or an innocent question that would mean more to his conspirator, and maybe even gauge where they stood. But that felt trivial. The bare clatter of talk and the creak of wood rising and falling, the whip of rope and of clothing coming down from the sheets to find a shoulder in the cold evening—it defied all his attempts at wit to stand unanswerable to his plans and definitions. There was nothing to say that could comfort him. When he resigned himself to silence, he spoke before he knew he meant to.

"I know what we are."

Gionn waited with amusement.

"'Whalers.' I'm embarrassed it took me so long." Foster scanned the horizon where he knew there was coast as if searching for something he set down before he walked off. "Reckon part of me always knew. I just didn't expect to be here long enough to think about it."

Gionn laughed, and there was nothing patronizing in his tone. It was a laugh of consideration, as though something plain had been called to his attention.

"When I look around, I see many such cunts, mate." He fixed on Foster. "When I look at you, no such cunt." There must have been a moment of sting on Foster's face. Gionn followed, "I mean it as a compliment." He slung his cloak on, a garment that Foster had never seen in his possession before they left Drummoc, and it failed by several sizes to close in the front.

"Behave yourself, sweet prince."

3

TEMPLE OF OMERA

The first time the dogs woke Sawipelagannapuk, he thought little of it. Hasqa still warmed his blood—the same that softened him to the blacksmiths the night before. He had not forgotten their offense when they returned at dark begging a place to camp. But they assured him they would be gone before he woke. Sawi didn't think they would come to harm if he sent them on, so it was within the bounds of hospitality to refuse them quarter, but their passing into the back country after the melee with the boys left him feeling absolved: the fugitive was not in his camp. The absurd fear that anyone might think otherwise still heckled him, so that he felt a shift—a kinship with the invaders—when it wasn't so. Besides, they promised him his share of the reward if they found the one they hunted. These men didn't know of his other arrangement. He would be much wealthier if he delayed them until others could do the work. But the escape harried his preparations, and distracted the boys. He worried if it took too long, they would become tangled in a way no longer possible to conceal.

Sawi supposed the din was the opinion of the pack regarding the hateful blacksmiths as they trudged past the tethers on their way out. They must have found something promising. Smiths did not tread often in snow.

Sleep took him soon. The second time the dogs woke Sawi, the howls perplexed him. A Seleku man needn't leave his tukit to know what alerted his animals. He could tell by the short and the long, by the pitch and how many joined whether it was a fight, a feeding, a familiar visitor. Now they sounded in chaos. It was as though many people tried to speak at once of many different things. He sat up and saw that the other men were also roused to curiosity. They slept in the boys' dwelling, nearest the pack in order to offer the finest tukit to the guests. Perhaps he wasn't used to the way the sound came through these walls, but it seemed to come from uncommon quarters.

His head throbbed and he had to lean his hands on his thighs for a moment when he first stood to steady the ground beneath him. There was yet no glow of sunrise when he threw back the flap and stepped into the chill. The moon was dim, and afforded him only vague outlines. Something moved fast in front of him and stopped. His eyes carved out the shape of an angular head, ears turned toward him at attention.

"*Bauu!*" The dog gave a short cry as if to mention Sawi's presence to the others, then darted off after his affairs.

It was lost among the others. The entire pack yipped and howled in exasperation. Each time he thought he picked out a fight, or the joy of being tethered to a sled, something else rose up to contradict it. Sawi stomped around the hut toward the tethers and saw another short figure race past. It didn't seem as if it could have been the same one.

"*Hoy!*" He shouted after it. "Fuck." A team had chewed itself loose. No wonder the rest were beside themselves with jealousy. He found the outline of the hasty trail tukit they raised for the boys to share. "My sons!" Sawi cupped his hands. "Up! Dogs are loose!" They must have heard. He tested his sight, but could only make out general movement among the pack. Were Gilak and Eurak here, he would not have to rouse them. They would be among the animals already, Sawi fumed. The arrival of the Vjarku boys had only made his own sons more troublesome.

He threw back the cover. "What the fuck are you doing? Get up and help me!"

"Father!" the voice came from far away. He listened to the sound of crunching snow as two distinct sets of feet approached.

"Who's there?"

"Arnake," his youngest replied. "And Ulwet."

"Where are your brothers?"

He jogged after the boys toward the dogs. A wispy cloud passed from before the moon. Sawi blinked, and his eyes adjusted to a horror. Everywhere he glanced, dogs ran free. Those still bound foamed with rage at the ones who bounced and turned as if to taunt them. He strained into the distance, and saw the back of a sled disappear over the ridge toward Urkuk.

"Who is that?"

"They are after the dogs."

"With my best sleds?" Sawi glowered though he understood. "Milak?"

"Milak and Norwet. Saunlauk and Siguvik, and also Ravitak and Ferrakut." There was something strange about the way Arnake listed them out. "They told us to capture the ones who don't run off."

"*Three sleds*? Why did you not wake me?"

Arnake hesitated.

"We tried!" Ulwet protested. Sawi wondered how hard.

He swore at the top of his lungs and threw his cloak to the ground. He was too angry to be cold, and the carnage burned off the last of the hasqa daze. "Get your uncles. And the smiths! They ask our hospitality, they must help us!"

"They are gone. The smiths are gone." Ulwet took charge now. He let it sink in. "We don't know how so many got loose."

"This was not the work of teeth."

"Do you think it was tricksters?" Arnake said.

Sawi set his gaze upon his son hot enough to smelt iron from the boy. He hoped it was the blacksmiths. They would suffer greatly when the town heard of their crass violation of hospitality. But he knew there was at least one other who hid behind the feet of Urkuk. He had denied the old man dogs once before. And he wasn't sure the blacksmiths had the courage to wade among the pack. Arnake turned and shouted a halt, then ran after a dog, tether trailing. Ulwet wasted no time in joining.

Tricksters, Sawi thought. It fanned his rage to think that men he quartered would harm him. Or that someone in his employ, who worked his animals on the difficult passage from Nunoc, would betray his trust, even after he was lent a sled. How stupid was he to take pity on them! Tunguk returned what he borrowed, but none of this would follow had Sawi denied him the thing to begin with. As furious as it made him, either of these possibilities did him little harm compared to the third one he had in mind.

"Stop chasing dogs like fools!" He called to the remaining boys. "Harness me a sled." They were unusually clumsy. Sawi felt a pull from the ridge where he saw the last of the older boys disappear. He meant to catch the dogs, to be sure, but above all, he wanted to *see*.

"Fetch a team and drive it to me!" He left them to their fumbling and ran as fast as he dared up the slope until it was a slow plod, and he came gasping to the rim. The first deep shades of a hidden sun showed themselves in the east, but the moon was still his torch. He squinted where he thought the sleds vanished, but saw nothing.

Sawi turned impatiently to check the boys' progress. Parallel to the camp, movement called to him. A serpent wound its way past along the route the Navy had used lately for training marches. But it was too early for that. His heart soared. There was no way to see a face, but he could tell by the time and the cadence it was a vigorous spirit who led his platoon into the wilds.

The tide queen flees the king's return, Tunguk reminded himself of the way the Mattaka looked upon the lightening sky. She grew bolder, and her reigns longer now. It was with disdain that she retreated to wait out the bright kingdom, and sooner each time she would steal back, for it was the part of the day when she stretched her cloak over the whole of Ajatse.

From his lookout, Tunguk watched the black snow turn purple and betray the men who wound over familiar tracks. He allowed himself to be startled. It was unexpected that they travel so far before the sun. Down the slope a few yards, he noted the footprints that led to the tamped circle. There would be even more of a trail this time to lead from the fray to the rocky prominence where he and Brother shivered through the night. When Tunguk told the elders he meant to go hunting, and walked away from the Kapadak camp, he thought he would feel powerful currents underfoot, and the sweep of inevitability. That the spirits of the land would sing out to him, and paint the mountains and the waves below as he had yet to see. Perhaps he would be lifted with excitement, or weighed by longing. Or that his fear would pull him with equal strength in two directions, and he would have to make a choice. Instead, it felt like a walk.

There were other times, especially in his youth, when he sensed the presence of the gods in audience—even leaning around a prow beside him, or armored astride his path. It was not always the occasions he anticipated, but it filled him with purpose and strung him between the things that mattered. Less and less, he came upon them, until he wondered whether he had grown too old to spot them, or they had turned to more interesting affairs. No man was his father, he recalled. Not for many days. He convinced himself that it was the young who needed such guides. That his travels were up to him, now. Nevertheless, he thought he would be stirred to his spirit once more. Perhaps this, too, was not it. The moment he anticipated lay farther along.

Tunguk stood, and chose his footing down the slope to the circle, landing as best he could in the prints of the blacksmiths. He fell to his knees, and crawled around the outside of the circle to avoid leaving new traces, then joined his own prints, though never precisely enough to fool a keen eye. He felt like an old man with cold feet, stumbling in the snow as the horizon swelled the blue of the sea, ready to give birth. The rocks and the ice kept to themselves. Nothing betrayed significance, or curiosity. Even the craving for relief grew distant. Whatever came of it would happen in due course, remote to the world in a place too quiet for a song. The only thing that moved him now was not of the gods. Like a dim lamp, it was the same fluttering presence that guided his wanderings for many years, and more brightly since he encountered a pair of impossible creatures while on a walk of no importance. There, around the corner where the remainder of a man lay, burned the small fear that he had not yet done enough.

Ba-doom! A metallic thunk echoed through the hull of the ship, fainter and farther away each time. The engine. That's what Parks called any sound he didn't understand. It galloped through again, piercing his head with each iteration. He clenched his eyes and faded between sleep and waking. He would have guessed he was hungover, except there was no alcohol on duty, and they were always on duty. Without opening his eyes, the walls seemed to shift inward and out, though it was probably the rocking of the hull. The only constant was his body, which was bizarre and pressure-bound. His head, his lips, his hands, his feet felt three times their normal size, while his torso and limbs were that of a midget.

"Get up, bro!" Parks cringed at the noise. "We've got work to do."

He awoke on the bottom bunk in the belly of the *Qarapara*. Carabiner loomed over him wearing his naval uniform. Parks tried to swallow, and it felt like crumbled rust poured down a dry throat.

"We've been boarded," Carabiner added in a low, dramatic tone.

"Where's Foster?" He coughed.

"He's on the deck. Turns out he was a double agent."

"Fuck."

"I told them you were down here. Had to. The King of the Mermen wants to speak with you. He has a trident and a fish tail."

Parks nodded with the kind of resignation that had long expected the inevitable. "Like *The Little Mermaid*."

"Like *The Little Mermaid*."

"What about?"

"He wants to cut off your legs and give you a fin, so he can marry you to his daughter."

A pair of figures flashed across the open door, and the little girl paused to look in. Parks met her gaze. Her mother, indistinct in the shadows, grabbed her by the hand and pulled her on.

"Joe?" Parks called as much as he asked.

"No luck, bro. Captain's dead. Dead. Dead. They're all dead."

"I just saw some. Some people."

"Shh!" Carabiner whispered. "He can hear everything underwater." His voice returned to volume. "Just you and me, now."

Parks felt the bottom drop out of his stomach, as if he were consigned to the Navy once again and realized he was late to report for duty. His attention shifted to the large map on the wall, a place he'd never seen. Beneath it, a ship's compass spun, the face tilting on its axis in three dimensions. He looked at the thin wool blanket that covered his body, and was filled with dread at the thought of throwing it off. His headache seized up so that his ears rang. It felt like great ages swept past as he contorted his fingers in pain, but when he looked up Carabiner was still there.

"There's only one way off this ship. Follow my lead."

Carabiner turned and slid out of the room like a snail on the lower body of a fish. Parks sighed. He felt something sharp jab him under the covers, and dug out the source: a flint arrow. He held it to his chest, tip just short of his chin.

"Joe," he said, and heard his voice echo over the intercom throughout the ship. Panic gripped him as he realized the King of the Mermen would hear, too. He decided he didn't care. There were no more secrets. It was just a race. "Joe!" He paged.

A cover flung back and icy air fell across his face. There was a sharp pull as his frozen eyelashes held fast. Something rose like the need to sneeze, then a violent chill cascaded through his body, rippling off his soles and washing back through his skull. It left a warmth in its wake that clung to his skin like thin fog. Beneath, his nerves lit up like a grid sputtering to life, half the bulbs burnt since the switch was last thrown. His heart beat hard followed by a stutter, a few regular efforts, and then fumbled again in indecision.

This was not the first time he woke. It had been a day, or a month. He fluttered in and out between fevered dreams and the cold world. That was all he could make of it. Parks had no sense of where he was. What went on. There were visits, though. Voices called his name, or sung. Joe, Kjartke, Foster, Carabiner, his mom. He remembered water being poured down his throat and coughing. There was no way to tell the dreams apart. The only indication that he was conscious now was the pain that radiated up his thigh, through his crotch to his spine. Every joint ached with the cold, and his back felt like any sudden movement would leave him paralyzed. There may have been a dagger, or a large needle embedded where his neck held a toppled head, stuck to one side on the uneven blanket, water seeping through to his hair. This was the longest and clearest bout yet. It must have been the sky above him. The blackness wasn't as absolute.

"You have returned." Joe sounded mildly amused. Parks tried to move his hands to wipe his eyes, but his arms weren't taking requests. The old Reverse-Eskimo appeared to him as a double, made of blown glass and filled with dark strips of color. He turned to something in the distance. "You, and one more."

"Did we make it off the ship?" Parks faded again, and snapped to, as on a long drive. Now the cold seeped into to his clammy flesh and he shook. His teeth clattered so hard he thought he chipped one. Parks tried to draw his knees inward toward his center. A thousand tiny darts rained over his left leg. He cried in agony, and the muscles in his calf and thigh cramped so hard it made him nauseous. His neck bulged as he tried to wriggle for relief, but it gripped his heart and threatened to lock his throat. Parks gurgled. He passed out, and woke just as soon. All he wanted was to bend the cramping leg toward his heart. To ask Joe to raise his leg. It was basic sports medicine, and he couldn't form a word, much less hope to explain. Once more, he tried to sit up, but his hip flexor slammed tight and arched his lower back until he thought it would snap. A hand touched his chest. He gave up then and there as tears and snot bubbles erupted against the background of his pleading moan. That was all. His shoulders slumped back and he let out a whine so high he could barely hear it over the dry sobs convulsing from his lungs. After a few seconds, the whistle fell to a lowering tone that ended as a nasal growl at the bottom of his register, sustained over a single breath. Parks gave himself over to the death rattle, and resigned himself that when the noise ended, he would, too.

Instead, his back let go, and his inner thigh spasmed with lessening tension. The cramp felt like it would twist apart the ligaments of his knee even while it retreated. He took a short gasp and prolonged his moan, now as cracked as his lips.

"Do you want to live?" Joe's voice was ethereal.

Parks rifled through his brain for a clever response, but Joe cut him off. "Do not answer so fast. Many men think they know. They think it is asked by one who knows, too. If I say this, it is not for you to say, 'yes,' thinking that I wish to hear it. We do not have long, but hold this to yourself while you can."

Hard pass. That's what he would've said. Or, *define "live."* The jokes rang hollow as he uttered them to himself, then quieted altogether. His raspy breath puffed skyward. Nothing moved. No bird called. The gentlest wind brushed over the edge of something above him. He nearly slipped into sleep again, and Foster's voice woke him: "...drag your cripple ass through."

A wave of guilt surged over him. He lay like a rusted anchor in the surf. Eskimo Joe was here. Maybe Kjartke, too. Foster was coming. Coming all the way back, just for him. He thought there were others, but it was too much to dredge them up. He saw Barzos' grinning face, and couldn't quite picture Grom and Blowhole. Too many. The wave passed. If he just subsided into the earth, a hundred lines would be cut free. He wanted to hang in due to some sense of obligation, but this was not a pain anyone could describe to him. There was no one he owed this much. His eyes welled up again with a sense of departure. His cheerful songs in the skin boat, the fading dock at Nunoc, all were as lost to the implacable past as his home, and the deuces he slung overhead when he left his parents outside the terminal bound for Chile.

Joe was right. It wasn't a question he cared to consider. Parks had always figured that no matter how bad things got, the only thing that made sense was to claw and fight until the life was torn from you. He crossed that point briefly in the water when he washed from the *Qarapara*, and again as he fled the man sitting next to him. Maybe a few more times, but now he was sure it was a lie people tell themselves to feel tough when they're watching another survival documentary. There was no refuge left for doubt in his broken corpse. At some point, the body simply refuses. And before that, maybe a good while before, it no longer feels that staving off the relentless, patient beast one more time is worth the effort. There can't be much more pain—probably only a change in kind.

Then relief.

A sigh escaped that seemed to empty his lungs. The phantoms of allies, with all their expectations, ceased to plead with him.

"Can I get back to you?" This time, it was his own voice he heard, as loud as if his lips moved but so small it should have been imperceptible.

"No," Joe replied. "You may choose, but it affects many. It is a different act."

Joe folded back the blanket in a neat rectangle until Parks' chest was exposed, then smoothed it with a tender stroke. The swing of the sheath against Joe's hip caught his attention, with the nub of a bone handle protruding from the top. Parks didn't need to be told that Joe would not just leave him exposed. He would be with him until the last ragged breath, no matter what the decision. If it came to that, he imagined the blade would slide across with the same tenderness. A sound pricked him. Boots, crunching his way.

His skin curled in a kind of terror. It wasn't of the present, or what approached them now. He understood that since he hit the water for the first time, he had always been pursued. If it wasn't a man or a ship, it was a wave, a gnawing hunger, a nightmare, an unseen force devouring all that hesitated. If he survived this day, he would feel it pressing on his heels tomorrow, and the next day. It was a shapeshifter that never tired. His dread was not for death. It was for all he would have to do to cling to life.

Parks realized that his hand gripped Joe's wrist with crushing force. He let it go with embarrassment, and felt the fears separate like a sack of marbles burst across a wood floor. His mind returned to the bare stars, the sound of footsteps, and the old man waiting. Nothing was binding. What he chose here today wouldn't damn him to a life of misery. If he wanted that, he'd have to choose it again tomorrow, and the next day. He tilted his head to look at the blanket that covered two-thirds of his body, then let it collapse onto the snow, his eyelids clamped tight enough to wring moisture from the icy corners.

"Live."

"Then we must be swift." Joe threaded a hand under his upper back and grasped his elbow with the other. The weak pressure did little to move him.

"What are you doing?"

"It is not enough to say. You must do."

"What, sit up?" Parks pushed his left hand into the blanket to pry himself onto his right hip, but as soon as his pelvis shifted, his body erupted in pain that sent him to his back again. "Can't."

"No. Stand."

The thing he knew but couldn't think settled its weight onto his ribs. His breath shortened to little gasps.

"Fuck off."

"Do you want to?"

"*Stand?* No!" Tunguk again positioned his hands to help Parks to a seat, but Parks burrowed in. "You've fucking lost it."

"The men are near."

Parks sobered. "How many?"

"Enough."

"What do we do?"

"We will see."

The old man's motionless calm did little to soothe Parks. Shouldn't *he* be the one who stands? His knife remained in its sheath. What were the two of them supposed to do? Parks instinctively slowed his breathing to tiny sips, and held as still as a rock. Joe should cover him—that's what. It was still dark. They might pass right by, he bargained. Or at least give him a spear. He could poke someone's ankles for the assist. The snow shallowed and the feet quickened. The anxiety invigorated him. Having accepted the more painful prospect, he felt almost like he was cheating to be killed so soon after.

Any thought he had of going unnoticed vanished when Eskimo Joe turned toward the approaching boots, who paused just beyond the feet of Parks' lump of blankets. It was hard to see the old lines on the face in the dark, but Parks sensed something wavering between disappointment and gratitude in his compadre.

"Help me get him up," Joe said.

There was a confused silence, then a nasty string of Reverse-Eskimo. Kjartke moved around to take a look at the sailor.

"He's trying to make me stand," he pleaded as if his mother just came home to catch his dad at one of his forbidden rituals. She scolded the old man again. He responded in a cool sentence that took her aback. She knelt on the other side, and peered over Parks like a suspicious nurse. He wanted her to confirm his helplessness, and at the same time, was overcome with embarrassment.

"Only for a moment," she spoke to him, now. Her warm fog swept across his chin.

"What?" He was perplexed, until she joined the old man under his back and gripped his other elbow. "Hang on!" He protested too late. They hoisted in unison, and he cried out in agony, stiffening his legs to prevent it.

Kjartke shushed him. "They will hear."

"Can't. I'm injured," he said as though they must have forgotten. "I'm legit injured." Where was Foster to criticize their medical credentials? What they asked of him was insane.

"Do you want our help?" Joe said.

"Yes. I mean, no. Not up! Help me other ways."

"You ask much of us. Perhaps we will die soon," Joe softened his grip and let Parks catch his breath.

"Please. Please help. I want to do it. But. Too fucked."

"You want to live."

"Yes, please."

"How will you live on your back?"

Parks hesitated. "Temporarily?"

"If we are to believe you, show us. Show *you*."

"Please. I don't think you know." All the excitement had turned up the burner. Now his leg bubbled with pressure. Scalding liquid ran inside of the frozen exterior, causing it to swell more and pulse to the contrast. Parks writhed for a better position, but found none. "You've never had this. You don't know how bad it hurts."

"Then you must go," Joe said to Kjartke.

"No, no no. Hang on, hang on. What if I sit up?"

"You must stand." Joe's tone was sympathetic, more patient than it should have been.

Parks shut his eyes and took deep breaths, which he exhaled sharply. "Not for long, right?"

"Not long," Kjartke assured him.

"OK, OK. But we go on my count." He offered up his forearms. Before Parks could utter the first number, they yanked him to his butt. The sudden movement shifted his leg hard and the cramp gripped him. It felt like a shark had taken hold of his thigh and was gnawing for a better bite. He collapsed to his right elbow to take weight off that side and cringed in agony. Something prevented him from screaming, but a high moan reverberated through his body as he clutched the leg with his left hand. Half of his muscles pinched or seized while the others seemed to stretch and snap like threads. Kjartke immediately moved behind him to block his retreat to his back. She clasped her arms over his stomach, pressing her chest into his back. Parks shut his eyes as tight as he could and gritted his teeth. Wave after wave crashed through the rest of his body. The mere pressure of the blanket on his frostbitten toes was unbearable. His neck contorted. The shoulder on his support side trembled with weakness. Parks' balls and asshole felt like someone twisted them in opposite directions. Now he started to cough in dry, iron-flecked hacks that ended in him hyperventilating.

He settled his weight back into her, determined to go no farther.

"Look," Joe said.

Parks raised his eyes, confused. Joe pointed at his lower half. Out of instinct, Parks turned half away. Joe tore the end of the blanket out from under his hip then threw it aside in a single motion.

"Look!" He demanded.

Parks couldn't see shit. Everything spun. He lost consciousness briefly, then blinked to. He felt nauseous, and his vision fizzed with TV static that sank to shreds of silver foil, like confetti thrown into the air, settling until only a few strands remained aloft. From the primeval dark, he saw the outline where the black blankets met the near-black snow that spread before him.

"Look." Joe lifted Parks' chin with his fingers. A lump extended before him, barely visible in relief on top of the hide he lay on. It seemed to belong not to him but the landscape. At first, there was nothing familiar. Then a line in the middle came into focus, and he saw the separation between his legs. The right led to a bulbous mass: his foot, boot removed, bound in a leather strip and what he realized was the mangled parchment of his map. To the other side the pant leg flared past his knee and twisted on itself. Eskimo Joe crouch-walked over and peeled back the strips. Parks went light. Not dizzy, not unconscious. His vision hovered and danced like dust in a beam of day, detached from all around it. The details remained obscure in the pre-dawn smear. He closed his lids to gather himself, and Joe repeated: "Look."

These weren't even his, he thought. Where were the thick thighs of a lumbering tight end? The trousers sunk as though someone let the air out, to rest on a slender pair of bones, one longer than the other. For a second, he couldn't think at all, or even remember. There was the sight before him, stripped of meaning, and the fire that coiled like a snake inside his skin. This was not him. There was nothing of himself present. Just a throbbing dream of sensation. A feeling of dozens of tiny hands tugging at a ragged cloth. His edges flared and collapsed in rhythm like a jellyfish. A faint song rattled through his head in the tongue of Joe and Kjartke, but it didn't come from them, and he knew it was gibberish. The skeleton of something he'd heard, somewhere, sometime, reassembled in vague tones. He felt the snake move in response to it. The cold raised a few icy stars out of the mire of his fever. Toes and the side of a foot, knees, hands, ears, nose. A crawling numbness alerted him to his right arm, up through the shoulder where it drifted to sleep on a bed of nails. The notion hit him that he could get up and leave before anyone realized it. While they were all distracted. There was no evidence he'd ever been here. He would have to act now, before these shifting points settled into something solid.

His back appeared to him in a narrow patch of pressure. He felt a tap, distant and dull—the muffled drumbeat of her heart. He felt the expansion that radiated from the center of the patch, then eased with the brush of air over his neck, and knew that it was the ribs of the woman pushing into his own as she breathed. A thirst for air overtook him, and he gasped as he realized he'd been holding his breath. Now the two tides interposed, and he felt the shape of her arms around the front resisting the swell of his abdomen. A scent that wasn't pleasant entered his nostrils, but it was sharp and pleasing in that it stood out from the sterile snow. He shifted, and hair brushed the ridge of his ear. His cheeks flushed. The weight of his clothes clung to his flesh and the cold infiltrated his lungs.

Parks found himself gazing up at the brighter constellations that resisted the encroaching glare that had already claimed the weaker stars. A bony hand tilted his head forward. He reemerged, every scrap of him, miserably solid. The pain had been terrible enough to hold him out of consciousness this long, and if it lessened enough that he could experience it, at the same time it grew unbearable. Though he still shivered involuntarily, sweat beaded on his face and froze to a gritty film. He snatched his right elbow up, numb from support, and shook the blood back in while his friends used the opening to shift him completely to a sitting position. That set off his leg even more, and if he were in a hospital, he would have screamed and abused the nurses until they unhanded him. It was malpractice to move him in his condition. He should be on a ketamine drip.

Parks winced and doubled forward, clutching his stomach as his leg tried to spasm him down again. He blinked hard to avoid passing out.

"Look. What do you see?"

Parks followed Eskimo Joe's line. "Leg." He said contemptuously.

"Where?"

He saw the thigh shift inward above the tattered pennants. "Nowhere."

Joe repositioned himself to take hold of Parks' arm. "Come."

"I can't fuckin' walk."

"Up. Then you sit again."

"How's that gonna help?"

"I do not know yet."

Parks rolled his eyes. He felt a raw tension in his breast. It reminded him of some humiliating camp ritual, or even his line crossing ceremony, with the crew cursing him forward into the absurd. But this felt graver, its main relation being the sense that to go back—to simply lie down again—would be the easiest thing in the world, yet it was a way as closed to him as the past, just a second before. As impossible as turning around in the moment he felt the rise of the surfboard and the feeling that he would find his feet or go over the falls.

He nodded in submission.

Parks felt himself lift and transfer weight into his front heel. His knee bent, and his butt hovered over the ground.

"Wait, wait, wait! Put me down." They ignored him, but he felt the futility. There was no way these two had the strength to hoist him forward, even in his depleted form.

"Stop, stop, stop!" Their leverage slid out. Joe fell to a knee, Parks's tailbone slammed down, and Kjartke caved on top of him. He gritted his teeth to muffle the scream. As the other two extracted themselves from the tangle, Parks rolled to his side. He felt a hand try to pull him, but he thrust it off.

"My way," he pleaded. "We go my way." Their grip slackened, and millimeter by millimeter he shifted until he lay curled in a fetal position on his right, with the opposite thigh resting against the inside of his knee. That fractional pressure was enough to ignite the wound, and he knew if it hit the ground he wouldn't be able to bear it.

"Grab the pants and hold it up," he mumbled into the blanket. "Don't let it touch the ground." There was a short debate in their language as to what he meant, then Kjartke gathered the loose ends with one hand, twisted them, and lifted to gain separation.

"Gentle!" He warned. Now Parks eased himself up on his elbows, and rolled toward his stomach. He dug his right knee and forehead into the ground to prop himself. Kjartke did her best to hold his injured side clear, but as it rolled past to the other side the pressure of the cloth pulling back caused him to jerk his leg. She found herself reaching across unexpectedly, and when she tried to adjust her grip, the entire leg slammed into the snow. A white hot flash sent his ears ringing. He moaned through his nose in a pitiful sound that descended like the cry of a coyote. Kjartke tried to gather it again, but he shooed her.

"Forget it. Get my arm." She took up his right armpit, and Joe his left. He wiggled his hands, and they took them with their free arms. At last, Parks felt he had something firm. He pushed his knee in, lifted his chest, and squeezed down on their arms. The wide torso rose and his head left the ground. But he realized he had no further leverage to get himself off his knee and to his foot. Parks dug in his toe, and shifted back. His knee raised a hair, but he underestimated the condition of his right foot. The second he lay pressure, it felt as though someone ran a serrated knife under his toes and across the arch. Parks collapsed to his knee again. He let out a whimper of despair. They were not strong enough to lift him without significant help. What he needed was Foster. And Gionn.

His stomach turned in anxiety at the names. As long as he was fantasizing, he might as well wish to wake up at home in his bed in Santa Cruz. It would be a miracle if he saw the first again, and if the saw the second, he'd rather stab him than accept help. This was what he had to work with. These were the ones who stayed.

Once more, Parks planted his toe, and the shredding pain started early in anticipation. He pressed into their arms, taking them by surprise, but they offered enough resistance that the blanket retreated beneath him. Parks threw his butt back and sent all his weight into the frozen foot. Just as he was sure the arch would snap under the searing pain, it rolled back and the heel found the ground as his chest nearly touched his thigh. The thick bindings made it hard to stabilize in the uneven snow, but his friends saw their chance and lifted with all their might. His arms thrust around their shoulders and he went weightless for a second, then felt the spring as they bore him to a bent over position. There was no way he could straighten. The tightness of his hip and abs made it clear he would spill his entrails over the snow before he would reach his full height, but his head rose near as high as the other two. He teetered side-to-side. Weight settled into the single column, and he felt the muscles engage all the way up to his lower spine. Blood rushed like sand into the bottom of his leg and a warm sensation flowed where the parts of him held fast to the earth now released and welcomed the return of life. Parks panted. They came up so fast that now his head spun. His sinuses rang. He squeezed his companions close under his great wings.

For no telling how long, he had no idea where he was. He recalled the bumping sled ride. The dark wigwam. The dreams. Whether he was awake or not, they were dreams. Movement, stillness, adjustments, low voices. The slope, always a pull to one side. Light and dark. Almost entirely dark. Was it days or weeks? Hours, for all he knew. Now he stood, and he saw to his right a black outcrop, to his left, a long rock extending from their backs, dusted in snow. A slope tugged them forward into a field whose curves were indistinguishable from its shadows—snow and slope for as many yards as his vision allowed. It was so little to go on, but so definite.

There was sound again. The scrape of snow that had become so familiar to him as the mark of ghosts shifting just out of sight. It was louder, though, and he understood his mistake to confuse the crunch of Kjartke's little feet for Joe's "men". This was something more. The "engine"? Or a monster, dragging its tail while it scurried along on a hundred pincers.

There was a pause, and a command in Reverse-Eskimo. The terrible rattle started up, faded along the rock, then burst around the outcrop as a beast of many heads.

Even before the first glow of dawn found the high places, the sky lightened like shallowing water to reveal a band of shadows a few hundred yards off their course. It was a veritable king's road: the snow was marked by more boots than Costig could discern, crossed in places by sled tracks. Polc seemed amused at the find. At the least, his men were glad to be free of the riot that sputtered through the dark hours and promised to renew itself with the sun. The admiral knew he'd face talk for leaving the ordeal in another's charge to hunt down the Leopard Seal. None of it would reach him, but it would occupy the Navy and Mattaka, alike. A small price to reach the camp first, but given these tracks, that was no longer possible. One of these pairs of prints was his own, he thought, from his cloaked visit by dark. If he intended to confuse his men and lead them astray, the advantage was lost. But Costig wasn't sure that was his purpose, anymore. There were other ways to learn of the assistant viceroy. It would serve him just as well to happen into the old man's camp and arrest the poor lot of them to save the gold before that ship, too, had departed.

Behind him, he heard Polc chide his slower lads. Ones who had probably never set heel in the white. There were too many tales now of what went on at Camne Drumlag, and few agreed with anything other than an instinct that rendered his innards. Nothing to report, if the messenger was to be believed. What, then, gave a squain the courage to steal away from the harbor in an admiral's ship?

A distant shape bounded over the plain. Costig paused the column to pick out the loose dog. It glanced back now and then to check the progress of the team and the sled in pursuit, keeping effortlessly ahead of a pair of boys and six envious mates.

When the trail sloped up, he halted again to let the line take in the slack before the short climb. Costig had to stay himself from ordering them to "ready arms." The tip from the dog man that led them here was imprecise as to how far they'd travel, and though he knew the answer exactly, he couldn't admit it to the others. More than one kind of disaster could wait, and Costig grasped in vain for what could possibly please him.

Half his men topped the ridge before the Mattaka happened to turn their way. The little group froze in the circle where a skin hut once held a notorious guest. Costig kept the same casual pace as they filed into the tamped crater, arms stowed or hanging loose at their sides.

"Are you not as glad to see me as I am, you?" Costig called cheerfully. He recognized an older face. "He wasn't in the latrine. Did you forget to mention this place? What was it again?"

"Sewadkut."

"Aye. Sewadkut. These days I'm learnin' more squain names than I care to drill, and none for the joy they bring me."

"Admiral," he gave a gesture of respect. "It is a place we just find."

"Is this all of you?"

The old man hesitated, then shook his head. "The others follow tracks up the trail."

"Call 'em back."

Sewadkut pressed two fingers to the corners of his mouth and gave a series of whistles. Costig's bunch fanned out around the circle, and Polc led a pair out the other side along another trail thick with tracks to watch for the returning smiths. The admiral paced the site, then returned to the master.

"Think they were here?"

"Aye," he nodded with cautious enthusiasm. "See?" He pointed at the sweeping curves of sled runners cutting the site several times in different directions. "Not here last night. Fresh. Not far."

"You were here last night, then?" Costig grinned in surprise. "Didn't think to report it?"

Sewadkut grew nervous. "We found it late. Made camp with Sawipelagannapuk. We want to bring you Leopard Seal himself! No more guesses!" He laughed.

"So you think he escaped in the direction I'll see your men return from. If they return."

"They come." Sewadkut repeated his whistle with more insistence.

"Right. I recall a certain order I placed with your forge. Is that done already?"

"Soon," Sewadkut tilted his head in deference. "We help you find Leopard Seal."

"Fancy the reward, then?" Sewadkut and the boys grinned in agreement. "Three argots. I must have been mad! That's enough that none of you would ever need to swing a hammer again."

"Oh! No! No, we work. We work hard," they all nodded in agreement.

"Noble of you. I can replace miners and rowers easier than planks. Blacksmiths, you lot are different. It would pain the colony to lose you. For any reason."

"No, no! No lose. We help search, then we work!"

"Well I'll hardly need your help now, will I?"

Sewadkut drew his lips aside in a pathetic show of humor that did little to hide a sense that things had turned on him, and he didn't understand how. "We help."

"You hammer. I'll take it from here."

The master's companions stiffened. They had the look of lads as the sea infiltrates faster than they can bail. "More men is better. We find him faster."

"No."

"Of course. Good men!" He remarked of the platoon. "They will find him. I'm sure of it. We will have for you the finest spears. Soon! Every man will work with the strength of six to know he has his reward."

"Reward for what?" Sewadkut melted. "You never told me to search here. I found it meself. Unless one of your lads rounds that corner with the fugitive in hand, I'd say it'll be me who finds him. And seein' as I'm the dumb bastard who lost him to begin with, I don't think I should be eligible for the reward."

"We find this place! We show you the trail! Please. You honor us."

"Aye, you found it, and I found you. A couple of searchers with the same bright notion. At least, that's the look of it. I suppose the only men I'd expect to find here are those who search for the fugitive, or those who aid him." Sewadkut staggered at the suggestion as if gut-stabbed.

Costig held off his protests. "If your men don't return with my prisoner, and I walk the way they came and find him, I suppose your reward will be the luck of a smith: were you a miner, I'd haul you in for helpin' a prisoner escape. A smith, though? Can't live without 'em, as long as they're workin', that is. A smith, I'd say, was on about his search in support of the admiralty, and came just short."

Sewadkut trembled white as the snow. Behind him, Polc hurried aside in time to avoid a scampering flash of fur that raced through the frightened men into the center of the circle, where the passenger leapt off as the driver overturned it to stop the animals short of Costig. Three more dogs trailed behind it, tethered to to the back. The lad who hopped off strode to the center, one more squain whose name hung in Costig's roster.

"Have you seen any dogs?" Norwet challenged. "We chase some through here, but they are gone."

"No, lad. We have not."

"Many teams escaped," the driver, a year or so less than Norwet, joined in. "It is strange. They were well-tied when we prepared a tukit for the blacksmiths. But when we woke, the men were gone, and six-hundred leads were cut."

"Your beasts slept when we left!" Sewadkut turned on him. The team took offense to the older man's posture and snarled in defense of their handlers. Polc's men backed away with no less enthusiasm than the hammer-lads.

"Don't suppose you came across the Leopard Seal gatherin' your dogs?"

Norwet's eyes blazed like a forge the way they met Costig's. "No. But we saw *his* dogs." He indicated Sewadkut. Six more blacksmiths appeared at last before Polc, who led them toward the circle. Costig waited for the fervor of barking to fade to a mere nuisance, then raised his voice that all could hear.

"Since none of you've been down Drummoc-way since yesterday, it's fair I warn you: a lad and his grandfather were cut down by your people for the great crime of turnin' in a drowned man they thought to be the fugitive, and despite that I declared him otherwise. For the mere act of seekin' not gold but silver at the misfortune of an enemy of the king. Dog lads are as hard to restore as blacksmiths. I pray you leave the search to me spears so long as the reward for catchin' the blaggard is the same as the one for aidin' him."

An oil lamp lit the parchments laid across the top of a chest. The gentle face poked at a mat of beads of every shape, and all the colors that could be reliably sent south. His other finger held a spot on the parchment, and keen gray eyes darted between the two. There were additional carvings, he knew, not found in Ampos but serving the Hiade scribes as convenient substitutes for rare dyes. The position and number of the knots meant something, and so did the bare vertical strips tying the lines into a grid. Small strands—Amposi versions of admiralty letters, important messages, or personal references—dangled loose from appropriate places. There was no element that didn't modify the meaning in some way. Even the braided borders qualified the record, and it was rumored that the scribes employed ciphers and tiny imperfections that alerted their own to a hidden quality.

It was a strange place to find a marine. Only the dress marked Wendell, with his thin stooping frame, receding hair, sagging neck. Nor was his cheerful temperance any clue to the trade he took for himself so many years ago. He lacked the stirring popularity of a Costig, but offended no man—spear or quill—and enjoyed the civil confidence of those who wore the stiff leather. Though none could fault his service and it had been commended often enough, there were few posts in the kingdom that a man of his disposition could serve. And serve, he had, with a quiet pride. Wendell left the judgment to other men, and hadn't worried a day at what it might be.

The storeroom door opened to the navy hall, offering a brief rumble of the proceedings outside.

"You sent for me?" Willakuy, the bead man, closed it behind him. Wendell had mustered to find Costig off hunting a particular seal, and the garrison in the hands of Captain Bruco of the Navy. A different marine may have taken it as a sleight. Wendell felt embarrassed at the initial sting, and moments later smiled when he realized that it was both a deference to the Navy and a safeguard. Bruco being one of the more prim captains, there was little chance of the riot turning memorable. He'd posture nervously while the Mattaka steamed, and was hardly like to install himself as the fourth admiral in as many weeks. Wendell soon remembered he had his orders, too, and they spared him the noise and the fray, as he himself would choose.

"Gods be thanked, lad!" Wendell greeted him in fluent Amposi, with a lilting accent that struggled on those syllables that natives drug across the back of the throat like a corpse over gravel. "Thought I'd use the riot as a chance to sort out me beads, but I've run up the pennant."

Willakuy laughed and answered in the common tongue. "I heard they broke the tavern in the night and commandeered every cask of hasqa, so you may yet have your chance." He leaned over the chest, then pulled back with delight. "I see you already have your letters."

"Rubbish! I can see when two shapes look alike, aye. It's the damn beads that turn me over."

"You have managed to find two of the rosters for the *Gairhle*—an arrival, and another one without a departure. Looks like it was compiled under Admiral Turrha. And this mat," he scanned it, then switched the two parchment rosters so the other lay beside the beads. "This is the same as this one. Arrival." He grinned at Wendell. "Not bad for one who sees shapes."

"If only I can convince one of you lot to apprentice me. What's the initiation on that?"

"I saw seven years while I mastered the beads. Another half a year for the letters," he added vainly.

"Perhaps I'll just have you read 'em to me."

"There should be another for the departure." Willakuy rummaged in a nearby chest.

"There isn't. Not in letters."

"No, but here is the mat," he drew one from the tangled pile. "Are you sure? They are required to copy all records into the farri's script."

"Aye, required. And if they do, it's as like to be as little as a head count and the kind of ship."

Willakuy sighed. "I am afraid the beads are often no better. Here," he lifted a short strand tied to the mat on one end. "This is an admiralty letter from the spring. Not even a count. They just tied it on! I will bring this up with Tuilapoy on your behalf."

"No need, me son. If you can just find the manifests for the *Juhketappat* and the ships belonging to the assistant viceroy, and to Captain Polc, as well."

The men spent the next hours calling off names and checking them between the two records, where two existed. The beads had no more to say about the assistant viceroy. A visitor with any sort of privilege who wasn't a merchant or a navy charge could get by with a cursory note of its name and captain, and number of crew. Assistant Viceroy Alexicus was also mentioned by name, but his wife and three Mattaka passengers were not. Polc, too, was the only name of his bunch, but his came with a rare curiosity: a strand of beads from Tolba, himself, that declared a royal message bound from Ampos to be treated as from the King's own lips.

The dog ship was a mess, and it centered around the Navy crew that somehow joined mid-voyage. At first, they were taken as a number like the passengers. Then some heroic conserver of parchment undertook to add their names in the margins at several occasions, apparently tracking them down a few at a time under threat from Tuilapoy or Costig, and finding most but not all. Also appended were the non-Mattaka passengers: Foster, Parks, and Gionn. Only the beads contained a note that they were examined by the admiral for potential service in the Navy, and found wanting.

The *Gairhle*, being of pressing interest, was the most complete of all. Wendell had personally missed the latter half of the saga while off attending to the hunting camp. He recalled the arrival, and the events it launched, but those were minor compared to the storm that broke with Polc's news. Between the initial misfortunes, and the great reversal a few weeks prior, all but nine of the original twenty-eight men found other prospects. He knew it was nine, despite twenty names carrying over to the departure, because the beads marked twelve of the repeats as Navy. Turned blue, and right back, Wendell thought.

Missing was one of the nine loyal lads, an Oterec. There was one man stabbed, and another arrested, Wendell recalled, but both were listed elsewhere as coming from Palqua's bunch. No Oterec ever graced the Navy lists, and those, at least, were somewhat reliable. It puzzled Wendell. With the pitch of hostilities between the whalers and the Navy, he could hardly imagine a member of the crew could vanish without Corm's lads raising a cry. The names who could have replaced him offered no help: a pair he knew to be Polc's carpenters, Foster, Gionn, and "two squains." Of course, it was policy to take the names of all Mattaka, especially those leaving, so that if they bothered to return in five years and weren't clever enough to give a new name, they could be summarily executed. A luck, or rather a kaim, had found these two, if dying on a whaler qualified as good fortune.

Yet no hint of Oterec. Wendell tossed it without a word, for it was none of Willakuy's affairs, but came to only a pair of conclusions: the man was killed by Corm's order, or otherwise vanished so near their departure that they didn't bother to fuss. He did recall reports that Foster slipped their grasp and joined the whaler only that very morning. Perhaps the fugitive's mate cleared a seat for himself, first.

So there it was. A single soul unaccounted for in all of Drummoc. Wendell couldn't tell the admiral why the man left the company of the whalers, but he knew where the poor bastard arrived.

The endless chatter of names and numbers wore on Wendell. They echoed in his head like rocks in an empty barrel. Willakuy, though, seemed renewed. As if he'd plunged into cold water and emerged sanctified, while his blood steamed the very air around him. There was a stroke of disappointment on his face when Wendell thanked him.

"Back to the treasury, then?"

"No," Willakuy said with regret. "I have finished the count and await the admiral."

"Good on you. How much ballast did Alexicus carry to Camne Drumlag?"

"Ballast? Oh, I wouldn't know, sir. My apologies, is it 'Captain?'"

"Sergeant, and you'll forgive a poor joke. It's none of me affairs to ask what the viceroy's man may have spared the treasury."

"Spared?"

"Stole with his filthy halot hands, if you prefer."

Willakuy reeled from the remark, and Wendell had to settle for a note that the man's humor was not as sharp as his beadwork.

The bead man nodded. "Very good, sir."

Wendell paused to see if silence would trouble the official to wag his tongue. When discretion held, he steered the topic from his speculative thrust. "Well, if I know Costig, you'll need deduct neither argots nor decairs on his return." Willakuy seemed vexed by the notion of altering his careful sum. Wendell clarified: "The reward. I'd bet me pay for a season Costig finds him before any squain."

"Ah, very good! Then I will merely have to add it back in." Now it was Wendell's turn to be confused. "The admiral withdrew it for his keeping."

Wendell frowned. "Wouldn't it be less trouble to keep it in the treasury? He'll not need to pay for both a living *and* a dead man."

"Aye, the admiral was worried to have the sum on hand." Concern came over Willakuy's face. "There are those who suggest he doesn't think so highly of the king's appointees."

"*No!* Oh, I wouldn't say that!" Wendell saw the bead man relax a share. But it hadn't the power to convince.

"I cannot think why else he would trust the coin to a marine rather than myself." Willakuy froze in fear at his mistake. "I am sorry! Of course, I meant—"

"I've been called worse." Wendell flashed that fair smile of his that so often put doomed men at ease.

"It is just that..." Willakuy paused to choose his words more carefully. "Those who are unaccustomed to handling such sums, at times don't understand the weight, if you will permit me to speak in the conjurations of poets."

"You refer, of course, to the moanin' outside."

Willakuy avoided confirmation. "It is hard to imagine that a reward of perhaps three decairs for the man, and three coppers for his corpse, would arouse such passion, or be any less motivating in the eyes of the Mattaka."

"It makes a fine bounty for a king, or a king from a fine bounty," Wendell conceded.

"It is mad."

The Marine stood and placed a hand on the treasurer's shoulder. "Perhaps we've privileged ourselves too much of a wag. We'll thank the beads for deafness, and leave such talk to the rumormongers." Wendell started for the door. "In fact, I'd be surprised if the thing weren't already done."

The sight of the daille skimming leisurely across the harbor no longer pleased Corm. They'd made him wait overnight at anchor for the first reply, and two more nights before this appearance. Yet he didn't share the crew's anticipation. The first concession the admiral sent was so foul, it gave him back the crew for a moment. He could have talked them into sacking the town sooner than accepting the offer. This one was not bound to be much better.

Of course, the lads knew the dance. Every trip out was a chance to glean something of their cargo (Corm refused to declare it), and how fresh they were. A full crew of bristling barrels riding on top a load of hasqa, or wood—the gold of Drummoc—would have been escorted dockside with a song. But to know it was not to like it. It was near impious to keep men at sea after coming so far, and the only thing the captain could do to stop it was concede. He sorted them over in his head. No one complained. Not a man. It was their pay, too, and none had less than a double share by then. He'd heard of captains stripped bare just hundreds of yards from the dock, though, and it was here that the threat of mutiny ran highest. No longer did his spear and his seamanship, his audacity, the secrets of his piloting keep him in esteem. Any cunt could heave her in.

This Palqua would be a sharp one. The runner had to have an eye for dissent in the crew, and the state of the ship. Corm knew they didn't believe him about the damage. He hoped he was able to at least cast doubt as to its severity. A few planks wouldn't hurt him much, but to learn of the condition of the wedge would scrap them. It was a weak move to withhold the cargo, too. A fine one would shout it from the mast. His success sailed on the hope that they were desperate-enough for something that they would dream it into his hold, bulging beneath the careful tarps.

The captain gave no orders. At this stage, the men were tired of hearing them, and it was better for him to see who jumped to what without being told. Eckerd made ready the line. Uldred and Bale did their best to straighten the covers over the hold. Corm paid a visit aft to Gaspar. His wounds had sickened under the sweat and toil of the row, and his was a longer wait than any. The lad lay coiled under a damp cloak, white as a pumiced board. At sea, he said little of it. The rigor of the journey was enough to stay the illness. But now arrived three days, and how close to going ashore none could guess, the fight had gone out of him.

"Runner's come, me son. If he's wise, for the last time." Corm didn't order him to sit up, and Gaspar didn't offer. A concerned look from the captain was enough to get a few sailors clustered before him to block the view from the daille. Most of the men moved forward and to port as much as they could without seeming too eager to hear the proceedings. Pitras stood as Cormdran passed.

"You asked me to mention the water, Old Cunt."

"Aye. Mentioned." They were a week yet from trouble, but no port no matter how callus the negotiations would let a ship die of thirst while they sat out for fair terms. It was a tactic to ensure the next visit from the runner would be expedient, best not used too soon.

If the call to accept this new offer came from anywhere, it would be Pitras. Maybe Ordacles or Arthas. No one else could carry it but Eckerd, and Corm couldn't bear to think he'd try. Then it would be relent, if they gave him the chance. He was certain he could get more for them—all of them. But it wouldn't be this round. He already knew his next offer, and had only to hope it was close enough to what he was about to hear. They were still on the "ribs"—the large bones of contention. Once it turned to the "scales," it was a sign both parties were ready to move on. It was then he could grant little whims, like the right for the Navy to deny quarter to any crew on their fugitive roster; an oath that none would sign to any other ship not belonging to the king for one year; forfeiture of a bowl, a cloak, even a fine knife to the admiral, though it likely never made it beyond the runner.

"Please forgive the delay," Palqua called as the men towed them abeam.

"A fine tactic, to kill us of thirst," Corm let slip his play.

"Admiral Turrha is very busy this time of year finalizing the northbound traffic and the winter rosters."

"And he'll be done tomorrow, no more spots on either, I'm sure." Corm sneered. His barb hooked back to his side whatever men would've gone for the lie.

"I told him you were no tender one, but he insisted we weaken our position with a clumsy ploy."

"Too bad you've no power have a go of it yourself."

"It is. I'd be done with this daille and hearing your tales over a hasqa. But I am a luckless mediary for one who knows before he sees, and does not care if a man flings a spear into his poor captain."

"That bad?"

"I have to face you. It would shame me if I did not remind you that you may always accept the most recent offer up until the new one is spoken."

The crew held their disgust but the air aboard the *Gairhle* stiffened. Corm parted out his adversary. Another child's trick the admiral insisted he try? It didn't matter. The last offer would never do, and though he'd never seen one get worse, he didn't have to take this one, either. Tired as they were, no man was eager for it. The only favorable bit was the right of quarter for all aboard. The rest of the terms were the kind of insult that would have them row all the way to Taclann. In truth, Corm was grateful for such a blunder. The real negotiation was for the will of the crew. Where they stood, the way was clear.

"Go ahead with it, I'll ready me spear."

Palqua nodded with regret. "Admiral Turrha respectfully refuses your counteroffer. From our previous position, it is thus the same: no right to repair, and the right to sell your ship or her parts with no fee imposed."

"Turn around, cunt." Someone barked, and Corm didn't reproach the laughs that made the Navy man wait.

"We have generously decided," Palqua continued, "to continue to offer the right to sell your wares without an admiralty letter. Again, it is the Navy who will sell them on your behalf." More grumbling coursed the benches. "But! We have agreed to reduce the fee." Palqua let the suspense build. "From four of five, down to three of five."

Even Corm had to scoff now. "I'm no number man, but I budged from one of ten to one of five. That's a spread-fuckin'-arse compared to your move."

"Our number men are very good, and they assure me ours is the more deferential."

"Then send those cunts out so I can chuck at the one who thinks me an idiot."

"Fuck off!" Another shouted—it sounded like Fergo's voice was coming back.

"You've yet to even warrant me to call the lads to stand. Here's what you can tell your Turrha—"

"Do you not wish to hear the remainder?" Palqua interrupted.

The crew rattled to a bewildered stop. Those were the only terms worth discussing until they were set. Cormdran could hardly deny the hearing, though. Another obvious maneuver could only seal the Navy's desperation in the eyes of the oars.

"We are still prepared to extend quarter to the crew. But I'm afraid the admiral has withdrawn his offer to quarter the captain." The announcement met with silence. Corm indeed considered his spear for the moment it took to remember that the only thing this changed was that the men would be forced to divide the remainder of his shares while he awaited impaling. "That is, unless the ship discloses her full cargo. Then we will return with a new offer."

"Counter," Corm blurted before there could be any notion of consideration. "Since your latest is an offense to the labors of the fine men of the *Gairhle*, I'll prove meself the nobler that while your terms have rotted through, mine will remain as they were: Quarter! For all board. The right to seek repair. The right to sell our wares, and sell them ourselves, at our own prices. The bluecocks will have one of five as their fee. We're too fuckin' tired to turn around, and you know it. But if you insist on making a landing so desperate a prospect, I'm sure we can find it in us to sail for Camne Drumlag, put a ram in every coal ship at anchor, and the first two Navy barges that try us. Do you think we rode down on good looks and a followin' sea? I know your lot. You'll win, aye, at the same cost as the Battle of Arhaid. Good Tolba will ask what petty fee you kept for the price of his ore and his ships."

Cormdran's face swelled red and his throat burned raw with hot ash. Palqua took his portion and looked only at the crew. He dipped his chin, then at last made contact with the captain.

"You may think you are the first to threaten us with a raid. By a single ship! Hm!" He laughed. "How embarrassing for us! Do you know why it hasn't worked yet?" Corm withheld response, and Palqua, the explanation. "Very good. Would you have me convey only the offer, or the threat as well?"

"As you see fit," Corm growled.

The daille turned for shore, and its captain called as the men sculled off, "I will send your water!"

The men leaned hard which way they could to clear a path for the fuming giant. Corm stomped the length of the cargo, and cast aside the concerned approach of the first mate. His toe snagged in a fold of tarp, sending him into a big, desperate step that clattered off the side of a wayward bucket before he miraculously found a foothold that stopped his fall. The captain seethed as if it were a hand that reached out to trip him. He steadied himself and kicked the bucket in a low arc into the sea.

"That's no way to treat a loyal companion," Hogue launched a dart to lighten the mood. A rage he couldn't place welled up in Corm, and he caught it just before it found the brim. He spun on the mariner, and the rest of the crew froze before the spear-wielding man. The remark itself felt like a betrayal, and though he prized the man, Corm wanted little more than to bury his point in that breast. But there was no place for tender souls on a whaler. He sensed a landmass well up in his course, now faced with a sudden choice of which side to steer. His clenched grip and stinging bile begged him one way, where he stood unchallenged in his power. It was this way the current of his rage pulled. He felt the men going the other way, and through the fog, he saw who it was that set them apart.

"Stand, you stone-hearted cunts!" He demanded. Now even Hogue was confused. "The man is right." They shifted nervously, and the corners of their sight measured the distance to a blade. Corm placed a foot on the gunwale and stared out at the last curve of the vanquished bucket as it gulped once more, then filled with brine. His spear clattered down, and his right arm crossed his chest to rest his fingertips on his left shoulder as his chin dip solemnly.

"Hear me, Uinab! Fouler! Shifter! Thief! Lift him from the thirsting sea! Bless the lad, that he weren't me!" Corm extended his arms before him as if he bore a body—as if they were the ribs of a ship. "A boat! A boat! To bear him up! A boat! A boat! To bear to him up!"

A fit of laughter cascaded through the men. Hogue was first to join his captain in the position, and their right arms crossed their chests again while a few more hurried to their sides. It was the crew's turn, and Hogue led them in the second round of the "shipwright," one of the favorite send-offs for those lost overboard.

"Lift him from the thirsting sea! Bless the lad, that he weren't me! A boat! A boat! To bear him up! A boat! A boat! To bear to him up!" Most of the men chanted.

They took it up a third time, now with the captain and all the stragglers. The deep voices carried over the water to the vanishing bucket. Then Corm added the last line, the luck—that carved daemon that rode the prow of most ships and watched over her crew. "Terror of Manhas!" He consecrated the tool.

The men fell over themselves with glee.

"If anyone needs to have a shit, call for Hogue to open his mouth," he declared.

"Good to see you're still with us, Corm," Pitras clapped him.

"Fuck that knobber," Gewar started in on Palqua. "'Send your water.' How many more days for that?"

"He'll send it tomorrow," Ordacles insisted. "Just that he won't be out himself with an offer for a few more."

Jonn stood, the youngest and a grassbender, yet thick as any. He'd won over the men on this, his first sail. "They'll come faster if we turn for Camne Drumlag."

"Are you the negotiator now? Arse down, lad!" Eckerd did his job.

"You cunts see his face?" Fergo's voice rasped like two ships scraping sides. He'd taken the sea cough, and though it was behind him, he couldn't speak for many days, and now when men couldn't understand him took to shouting louder and losing it again at intervals. "I said, 'he knows it'll be him they send first into battle!'" He repeated.

"Easy, lads. Corm's no fool. Keep your rams in your trousers." Pitras declared.

"Aye, and only a fool would take that offer. Do you think I make idle threats?" Cormdran blustered. "We land on our terms, or die on 'em!" Pitras was able to hide his disappointment, but Corm felt it in his silence as he let the odd cheers pass over. A nagging sense of incompleteness led him to add to his comment, as if one more thing would salvage it. "I've never seen a bastard try to pass a worse offer than the one before!" The same voices jeered with indignation.

"Only for you," Arthas spoke from where he reclined against the mast.

"What's that?"

"Only worse for you."

The excitement of the ship quenched like a flame under a breaking wave. Corm moved to tower over the sailor.

"Then you would take it, would you?" With that, the prevailing tension returned to brush aside the conciliatory joy that had only for a moment glittered over the ship in the evening sun. It was the first mate's unspoken task to turn the paler insolences from the captain's path, and when it wasn't done, all men suffered that it fell to Corm—him, the most.

"I never said I'd take it. And I wouldn't. But at some point, we got to stand for it." Arthas begrudged the explanation.

Now Eckerd flanked the retreating remark. "It was no quarter for the captain. To stand for that is to stand for mutiny."

That thrust Arthas to his feet, breath-to-breath with Eckerd. "You accusin' me of unrest? I've fuckin' pulled as much as any man here—"

"Hoy! Leave it!" Pitras and a few others gently threaded themselves between the two men and turned Arthas for a bench as he cursed Eckerd over his shoulder.

"I never said that! Fuckin' whelp! The man said himself we'd have a new offer if we declared the cargo. Is that not worth a chat over?"

"Nothin' about that offer was worth a chat. It's a damned wedge! More for the crew, less for the captain. You're blind not to see it. Meant to get cunts like you thinkin' you know more than him who got us here." Eckerd shouted back.

"Shut your flappin' arses, you both!" Corm cut them off. Eckerd knew his extra share bought him the abuse of both sides to spare the direct friction of captain and crew.

"You think I staunch me crew? How many times have I let you stand for one pittance or another all the way down? You want to have your say in declarin' the cargo, because you think I'm mistaken to cover it? Call for it! Call for it right now."

"You know I won't, Corm."

"Then what's your fuss?"

"You let us stand, aye, when you're the one asks for it. I won't call for it 'cause Eckerd's right. He's a cunt, but he's right—that's callin' for mutiny. Do you see an 'M' on me arm? Don't put those words upon me.

I want to set me feet on rock, as we all do. The offer's shit, but there's no talk of what we'd take. If you know, you're not sayin'. I pulled for you, and I'll land with you—don't you fuckin' doubt it. But I need to know what you're after. I'm fuckin' tired! And I'll take a shit offer before I wage war on a coal ship to drown beneath Ampos' rams."

Arthas settled beside the wounded Gaspar. There were a hundred replies, all of them as true as they were futile. A mere stone's cast away, the daille met the dock they'd sought for thousands of miles. Corm knotted around the thought of Arthas as a tree around a wound, and wondered if the sea yet demanded blood before they set foot on that rock—and whose.

Gionn slammed a half-rusted hook into hollow ice and slipped once before his foot found a hold. He thrust his chest over the lip, sank his hook again, and hauled himself to all fours. Beyond the outer wall that held off the vulgar, there sprawled before him a glaring plateau. Ahead lay a tapered dome that rose to shame even the Dedications—those colossal monuments to the faces of Uinab that hailed sailors across the northern coast from Vequitan to Tsaba. The homage of rough stone paled to this, the impossible blues, fogged white and clear for yards through the walls themselves, dusted on the outside by stray snow pressed to the surface in the gentle breeze. It gnarled in places like old roots that grew skyward, vining around the mirrors and sharp lines that caught the dimmest light that seeped through the clouds and shattered it like gems spilled across a marble floor. High as he was, there stood wave-carved grottoes that looked to weave the ice like catacombs, their entrances humming with the fear and curiosity that a place only feels when it encounters a man for the first time, though it be very old.

Beyond the shrine a wall thrust into a mountain of ice, half a mile long, that climbed ever higher until at last, it met the gray clouds hundreds of feet above. Ice. All of it, ice—underfoot, before, and above.

Gionn uttered in a low tone before he took his feet: "Omera, don't fuck me now, and I'll drown any cunt you name."

He shuffled to the edge and gazed out over the sea, empty as it was unruly. The waves tossed like maiden's hair, shallow and careless in a lighter field of water that stretched its silver raiment much farther than he expected before it met the smooth seas beyond her influence. A brief panic that defied his surest memory seized him until he bent his knees, dipped his torso over, and again saw the *Gairhle* bobbing where he left her below. Another chinking sound followed, and the next man entered into the sublime terror he'd just extricated himself from.

Gionn closed his eyes and peered dripping wet across a narrow channel at the island on the other side, where the brothers of Oduy reigned. His hand went to the little pouch of fish that hung from his belt, a single ration. Vast as it was, this place closed around him and cleaved his world into something even smaller than the narrow hull of a ship. There was no counting the awful places he'd made land and dreamed of leaving before his second foot came down. This was new. Ice, of course, but something else. His breath shortened, and he blinked himself steady.

They're right there, cunt. They're right there, he repeated. It gripped him from the moment he went over the side, but there were too many watching, and he urged himself on. Now he backed away and went to Bentos. Another look over, and he saw the other two more than a dozen feet below, negotiating their approach from the low shelf where the water barrel sat, the ship and all her crew in full view beyond. It was enough to drive off that unwelcome spirit, but he knew it had not left entirely— rather, hid among the inhuman grottoes to wait out his task.

"Hoy, lads! Have you ever seen somethin' so grand?" he shouted. "And the best of it's that the old fat cunt can't hear us plottin' on him! I thought I'd go mad, bein' so damn quiet on that ship, with that dumb bastard farting in me ear every time he passed. Ugly end of a cock, that one!" He capped his sarcastic barb.

Cormdran cupped his hands and shouted back. "Full sail!" The crew cackled, and the joke unsettled Gionn more than he liked.

"Oh, sorry Corm! Didn't realize me voice carried! Don't bother with anything you mishear. Loads of echoes about!"

The *Gairhle* stood off a few hundred yards. She ran a bare pole, now that a light sea breeze chilled Gionn's nose. They'd felt the wind shudder as though it would back, and made in toward the coast. He'd never sailed this season, but the signs were known even to the buckets: if you felt a shift to landward, you'd best run for the coast into the lull because the worst gales would turn into your face. Close enough in and you might find the following breeze again, but once it shifted to the northern quarter and turned again, you'd pick up the westerlies.

Then they'd seen it. For the first time he could remember, Foster spotted a thing before anyone else. They'd only just opened the second barrel of fresh water since Drummoc, but Corm decided to use the calm to fill what he could without having to row all the way to the coast and have his scouts fail to find a trickle.

"Never seen anything like it," Bentos breathed frost.

"Course not, you're Drummoc Navy. Why would you know the first thing about the Attavaik?"

Bentos scoffed. "It's your third time here, is it?"

"My last time. I've at least seen one off the beam."

"We all have. Even Foster. What'd he call it?"

"'Iceberg.' Sounds like a noise he made up for gullible cunts. Foster's never seen a woman on her back, much less a temple of Omera."

Both men regarded the third as he struggled up to the plateau without a twitch of concern. A lad of eighteen or twenty, well-hewed, stood and was followed by another man from the aft benches. Gionn knew only their faces, and he thought the younger one was called Jonn. These last two carried the short axes they'd use to fill the barrel.

"Which of you lads got sent in case we manage to cut ice before they strand us?"

The one who spoke was Gionn's age, shorter and a steak thinner than the other but with a good look about him. "I've cut ice, but that's not why *I* was sent."

"Favored sons, all of us," Gionn quipped. "Here I thought Corm appreciated me sense of humor, but he's put me out with three of Palqua's lads. I'll stay here to signal when they leave us."

"Oh, he'll get on fine with you," Jonn said.

"Aye, you're just his sort. You'll be here for your ears. Always a spy in a shore party," the ice man concurred.

"I'm no filthy spy. I'm under honest orders to kill all of you. Lighten up a few shares along the way." They grinned. "Got cozy with him under that tarp, then?"

"Me and Arthas pulled for him since Lau," Jonn failed to disguise the pride in his voice.

Gionn considered them. "Ha! Turned bluecoat, and turned again! Nothin' a small fortune won't smooth over."

"If you'll spare me toes," Bentos wiggled his boots, "it'll be a fine tale to pass the time while you cut."

Jonn looked to the other, who bent where they stood and hacked a few strokes into the ice. Shards flew, and he watched for their reaction. It was a demonstration rather than a test. "See that?" Arthas indicated the largest grotto. "Used to be underwater. Probably birthed from a bigger one that held her down. The soft bits'll be up a ways."

They found a suitable cleft, and stood in a line of deliberation.

"Gionn?" Bentos suggested. "First up should do it."

"Not me, soger. I hate prayin' to gods I don't know. Besides, I've already begged her for me life, and I'm afraid if I add you cunts, it'll be askin' too much."

"What, do your people not have a miserable ice goddess, Bentos?" Jonn wondered.

"No decent people do. He should've sent an Amposi." Bentos took the lump of coal from Jonn and placed it at the junction. With his fingers upon it and the other hand pressed to the frozen wall, he made the offering: "Omera, bright upon the waves, grant us water, and our ship again."

"But if not, remember that mine was first and better spoken," Gionn added.

They ribbed Bentos the rest of the way—by that wording, his prayer might be granted through a lungful of saltwater and a corpse recovered face down by the crew. Soon the ice they sought gave underfoot to mark the transition to what had always remained above the sea. The axe men set in, and there was great satisfaction in the way the blades crunched through so deep a cut that all but the hand and handle disappeared with the smallest effort. Soon two blocks came free. Gionn wrapped the first in his cloak and braced against the cold that stung his chest while he carried it back to the edge of the plateau.

The *Gairhle* put no trust in the fates. She'd backed off so far now that he wouldn't waste his voice to curse Corm. The sea breeze remained as mild as could be noticed. That and a refill of a single barrel was a more thorough endorsement of a captain than fifty-three wagging tongues could give. It came as a surprise, but no displeasure that his man was more cautious than he reckoned. Nor was Corm an iron grip of insecurity. Still, Gionn measured with care the intervals between his best remarks. It was fine to tease mutiny, given that only one so obviously inferior could get away with prodding a captain. On the other hand, he'd yet to hear more than a reassuring word from Palqua.

Gionn heaved the block a dozen feet down to break on the shelf where it landed. It was a kindness to find such an hospitable landing—it spared them the danger of mooring to a temple of Omera while trying to hack away at salty ice.

He crossed Bentos without a word on the way back, and his appearance brought a cheerful tenor to whatever Jonn and Arthas discussed by the time he came within hearing. On the third trip, he braced his arms in irritation.

"Come on, cunts! That one's half the barrel."

"It's the same as the others," Jonn defended the size of the block.

"It's sure fuckin' grown by the same as the others. Half it."

"The sooner we fill up, the sooner we're off," Arthas reminded him.

"Then hand me the axe, and *you* hug it."

Arthas shook his head in annoyance and split the block with a swing.

Gionn weathered a chill now that his tunic was his only garment, and the wind puffed a moment longer in his face. It was to court a terrible luck to be the first to complain of the cold in a new place, so he bit it off. There was no Bentos on the way back, and he felt a flutter when he came to the edge and saw no one. But a peek found the Navy man below on the shelf, fitting the fragments into the barrel. It was a lazy cunt tactic, and one he'd meant to adopt soon himself. Gionn made sure the crashing block was near enough to earn him a foul warning from the man. When Bentos remained after the next trip, Gionn returned with his hook and made the precarious descent—much more exhilarating than the way up—to speed up the process. With every bit clear, and at less than half-full, they both had to return for more. The loosest of flakes hurried past their feet.

"I'll let you take the first one back," Gionn offered.

"How kind of you."

"Aye, it is. That way you can escort her down and call for me throw, then take as long as you like to organize it while I get the rest." Bentos grinned. "Course, then I'll be back with one of the axes, that I've said I need to fit more in the barrel, and send you to carry the remainder with the cunt whose axe I got."

"Maybe I'll let you take the first back, then."

"That's what I was hopin' for." Bentos looked crosswise at him. "Then I'll pack the barrel, and you'll have no luck talkin' an axe out of a lazy hand."

"And you would?"

"The grassbender'll spread for me if I say. You've got the charm of..." he gave it thought. "Foster. So which is it? Show your oars, and I'll ram you either way."

"One like you on every ship." Bentos couldn't help but laugh.

"How much does it bother you that I'm already your favorite?"

Bentos shook his head and relented. "More than you can know."

Gionn slapped him on the back, and secretly longed to wrap his cloak around himself. "You're not Navy, proper." He saw Bentos warm to the compliment. "How many angotaks you have kill on your way down?"

"None. Once we showed our letter."

"Ah! You shirker!" Gionn wrapped an arm and ground his ribs with his knuckles.

"And yourself?"

"The same. Sailed right up with a very clever forgery."

Bentos' eyes widened. "I'll grant you silver bollocks beneath your thick head." He walked a few more paces before he spoke again. "Jonn and Arthas, though..." Bentos shuddered at some unspoken knowledge.

"They're still here," Gionn shrugged. So they hadn't made the run unscathed. "Bad?" He pressed.

"I've yet to hear Corm's lads speak of it."

"Fair lot of hard bastards we got then. Those two, the mate, Pitras, Ordacles, Moipa..."

Bentos shook his head. "No, no. Not Moipa."

"You sure? I swore he was a *Gairhle* lad." Gionn smiled inwardly as another hit teased out the benches for him.

"Oh, no. Few enough of those left."

"Half?"

Bentos searched his memory. "Of Corm's original whalers? Eight. Seven," he corrected. "Then the lads we brought back."

Jonn and Arthas appeared, and the talk died at the sight. It was Gionn who took the first load, and in view of Bentos, threw it down onto the shelf and started back for another. His benchmate followed in turn. When they had a fair pile, Gionn told him to, "go and fetch the axe." It was Jonn himself who arrived. They set the larger pieces in the barrel, then had a chop at it to fill as much free space as possible before the next. Exposed as it was on the shelf, it wasn't half as frigid as the wind on the plateau a few yards above, but the adventure had worn thin by the time Arthas and Bentos came with the last load. Gionn signaled the *Gairhle* while the others filled the barrel short of the brim, that the lid would not freeze to it.

After a second call, there was no sign of oars. He gathered his hook and made the short scramble one more for the vantage of the plateau. An icy blast buffeted him as soon as he crested, and he wasn't sure if it was the elevation. A peek below showed none of the others had put their cloaks back on yet, so his would have to remain off for the moment. It was soaked and frozen, but no less of a temptation.

Finally, those long arms extended from the ship, and he hoped Foster had got the hang of it by now. She made an inelegant turn, then battled the crossing swell. He scurried down to the shelf again to watch the waves that now leaped up the edge when they timed it right. With a growing wind behind them, the ship made good on their approach, though they were out of rhythm. That would have to be fixed, or they wouldn't need Foster to swamp them.

The barrel brimmed, and the others joined him in waiting.

"All at once?" Gionn showed his cloak, and they nodded. Arthas made to drop his, and fumbled it on just after the others. Now the *Gairhle* turned back west. It unsettled them, but Corm wanted no part of a direct approach with the gusts behind. He fought around the temple and turned east at a wide distance. After a bit of a maneuver that still left them hundreds of yards off, someone from the midship signaled them "coming round." They soon learned it was for lack of a more accurate signal, for the *Gairhle* put her prow to sea, stood well off, and stowed oars. The four men ashore erupted in a barrage of curses that would have compelled the biggest jumper in the Amposi fleet into battle rather than face another awful word.

But the crew never even regained their original distance. The gale picked up with such ferocity that neither oath nor prayer could reach the ship. The old man was right: they'd have been smashed had he tried to moor.

The shelf offered no shelter except the barrel, and that, little enough. No grudge could keep a freezing sailor from pressing crotch to his mate as they huddled with their hoods pulled high. None had brought his sleeping bag, but the failing light meant that even if the gale lifted in a few hours there was no hope of embarking before the morning.

Just before they lost the sun entirely, Gionn urged them upward. No one protested the climb to the plateau, where the wind drove them along until they reached a large grotto, and hesitated.

"Might be sacred," Bentos feared.

"We offered," said Jonn with less confidence.

"Coal," Bentos pointed out.

"They all like coal," Jonn retorted.

"Aye, when it's burned."

"Blubber has to burn, too. On coal, at that." Arthas made no move for the shimmering cavern.

"Aye blubber's the best," Gionn confirmed. "Just look at all the wonderful blessings the squains have received from their gods."

Bentos had no answer, but none of the men would move to cross the threshold. They found the place at the back of the temple where their lump still sat shielded from the north wind, and huddled for the night. It was a bitter cold trade between fitful dreams and the sleepless dread that the temple of Omera would like them to remain. Several times, Gionn thought he saw Parks visit him, and was relieved that the imbecile had finally gone on from his torment. If it were so, there could be no guilt from seeing the ship through. They'd spurned him—both of them—over a light denouncement and a lack of enthusiasm for betrayal. That, despite all his help.

By the last of the stars, the gale had softened its abuse. They ventured out as soon as they could see their toes. The persistent breeze raised concern that Corm would refuse another try until later in the day, but it was at least possible now. Gionn led the party to the edge of the plateau and let his eyes adjust. The water stretched calm before them. No wave or ripple marred the perfect surface. There lie the *Gairhle* where they left her, fast upon the frozen sea.

A fleet of fingers still combed through the snow of the site when Costig returned from his vigil on the ridge. Blacksmiths sifted alongside Polc's lads in the circle and beyond through every footprint. The admiral had offered them three coppers for help that wasn't needed, except to soothe their bruised pride and tired feet. One of the apprentices beamed when he showed off the few kernels of brown ice he thought to be blood. Costig dismissed it with a grunt. There'd be nothing of it by the time they reached anyone who could use it to inconvenience the owner. But for a speck, the place was barren, and the colors of evening warned of their departure.

Polc and his squad returned from the tracks to report they'd reached the end of the smiths' explorations and much more. Nothing but a pair of sleds, he announced where all could hear. It was the same pair they could trace all the way to Sawi's camp, and no sign of anything more than runners after a muddle of paws.

Most of the men took the reunion of the party as permission to stand, stretch, feign a last effort with a probing toe. Others persisted with a more reckless course, choosing spots with neither rhyme nor divination in search of a late artifact that would endear them to the admiral.

Mentewat, alone, held his path against the sun, turning over even the piles of twice-dredged snow, probing every knee dent and finger rut. It was near the outer edge that something separated itself from the grease and the snow. He glanced to see the admiral occupied, the rest of the searchers given up or buried in a final effort, before he took it in his hand: brown at the root of a yellowed body, with a strange black mark in the center, as if some ore waited to smelted free. Without urgency, he straightened the top of his boot, and the tooth disappeared from his hand before he resumed his search.

4

THE STRANGER

The dogs at last pulled together when the old man disappeared over the ridge that split the peninsula and ran like a tail inland to the spine of Urkuk. Kjartke did not understand why they were driving once again up that hateful mountain, but Tunguk did not privilege her with his plans. She looked back as she had six hundred times on the empty trail, and smelled the damp leather and salted wood of the *Juhketappat,* when she strained to pick the ship that pursued them from the stormy distance.

A lurch threw her back into the foothills. The sled stuck, as it had every fifteen or thirty feet, and it took ever more of a grunt to jerk free.

"*Unnh*!" Brother moaned. The structure beneath him flexed and twisted more like a net than a frame of wood. She had seen few sleds, but the dog boys' gift struck her as its cobblers: a flimsy dream of a thing not yet jarred apart by the right mistake. The whole platform tilted left, where the leather-thin runner flexed like a stream over bumps. Near all of the bindings were loose, and that after several stops to tighten them. It seemed it would not do to use a single piece of wood where two mismatched sections could be braced together with a third. Worst was the way it stuck to the snow as if the bottoms of the runners had been painted with cold pitch. The six whale ribs that formed the tukit had to be discarded soon after they left, for it would not hold both their weight and that of Brother.

At first, she pitied him the ride. It was with guilt that she shook the sled free at every interval. Perhaps Tunguk was wise to make him stand. She was not convinced. But it cost him the comfort of his travels in the spirit world. Now nothing could bring sleep to the man, his vigor gone, and every ripple in the snow a source of pain. His cries never ceased. They ran high and low; at times, matched the rhythm of the trail; others, the desperate gasps of his soul. Kjartke had never heard a man carry on as such. Her pity turned to resentment, and now almost a pleasure when one of her quick shifts raised a howl.

The runners stuck again, and she went to a knee. Her breath heaved cold and she struggled with urgency to loose it before the dogs stopped pulling. "They will not search long for these two," Milak had assured them of the animals. She knew he spoke the truth. Never had she known a pair so reluctant to do the only task before them. Perhaps it was too much to ask of any two creatures to tow such a clumsy thing laden with the heaviest man in Drummoc. There should be six, she knew that, but she did not think any of the dogs she had seen would complain more than their passenger.

And what of the driver? Something taunted her in the voice of Tunguk. Kjartke shrugged it aside. The old man could do it himself if he faulted her. But she knew these two would not pull unless there was a frontrunner, nor would they follow if she led. Dog driver, Kjartke sneered at herself. Was there no dignified life for her in Drummoc? Tunguk thought himself involved in something noble, she had no doubt. The town was in riot over a name that filled them with visions of gold or heroism. Kjartke could hardly believe that she did anything other than push a corpse uphill.

A jolt sent the dogs to their bellies as it stuck again near the ridge. Brother screamed.

"Quiet!" She snarled at him. Kjartke threw her shoulders side-to-side as she had so many times, but it was stuck fast. "Tunguk!" She called over the ridge with irritation. Within a few more attempts, she felt the tension of the leads relax but was too invested in her runners to scold the animals for not pulling. Now with slack, she tried to back it out downhill to loosen it. A few yanks, and Brother began to moan louder.

"Quiet!"

His protest only grew as she struggled with the sled, so she stopped to catch her breath. But he did not. Now his voice reached a panic.

"*Ah!* Stop! Wolf! Wolf!"

She looked up find the male dog with his front paws up on the sled, teeth fastened hungrily to the map that bound Brother's right foot.

"Let go!" Kjartke charged over to the animal. He gnawed on the leather and tried to wrench it free from the limb it held. "Tunguk!" She yelled again. Kjartke started to reach for the head, but hesitated. She grabbed the foot instead, trying to tug it free, but the beast bit down harder and backed the other way. Kjartke raised a hand as if to strike him, and he growled without releasing. Brother kept on like a child. Now she went to the sled and unlashed her spear. Kjartke leveled the stone point at the dog, which only aggravated it. She gingerly poked toward his gums to threaten his grip, and he lunged at her and barked. Kjartke staggered back, and the dog took the map again, whipped its head to free a piece, and swallowed it with a few snaps. He sank in for more when the old man finally hobbled back over the ridge.

Tunguk hissed at the dog, which gave him the same growl as Kjartke. "You do not need that," he scolded her for the spear and stepped between them. The heel of his palm crashed down on the dog's snout. The animal let go, and lunged at Tunguk with a bark. But the old man held his ground, and the dog paused to consider this new challenge, then seized hold of the map. Tunguk brought a fist into the muzzle once, twice, three times. The dog seemed to relinquish his grip out of annoyance rather than pain. Tunguk lifted him by the harness and threw him off.

Together, they freed the sled, and at length coaxed the dogs over the ridge, where Tunguk halted the party again. It seemed a terribly exposed place to stop, but the wind was calm, and after removing Brother from the sled and turning it on the side, she knew Tunguk sought the vantage. Here, he could make his repairs, while she could see in all directions if a party approached from many miles away.

After a short walk to find the right rock, Tunguk scoured the caked ice on the bottoms of the runners, breaking away most of the knotted, frozen spurs that forever snagged in the trail. They were far from smooth. Once more, he praised the boys for doing what they could even as he fixed their oversights. Tunguk took a sip of water and sprayed it onto his sleeve over his palm, then brushed the runners with the water so that it froze into the thinnest of strips. This, he repeated many times while Kjartke collapsed panting on the slope next to Brother. The female dog sought their company. She had no affection for her teammate, and though she was a wilted spirit, when he put his nose too often under her tail her fire returned.

Kjartke eyed the dog with some suspicion. She no longer felt the old fear at its closeness. Perhaps it was the memory of this one curled beneath

Foster on the deck, and his favoritism for her. She did not seem a bad dog, but Milak told them that because she tasted her master's flesh, her puppies were taken to be weaned by another. Where the male was beyond control of even the sternest driver, she could hardly be urged to action, so that awful as he was, it was he who did the pulling. The animal caught her watching, and withdrew its tongue. Her ears lifted and a wet nose raised Kjartke's way. She had seen on many occasions how Foster stroked her coat and spoke to her. Brother had the same habit when he was well. If that's what she expected, it was too bizarre for Kjartke. They regarded one another until the dog lay its chin on the snow and closed its eyes.

Tunguk resettled the sled and joined them.

"We have some distance to go before we rest."

"It will go?" She asked.

"We will sleep once more, maybe twice, before it falls apart."

"You mean to put distance between us and our enemies before then."

Tunguk grinned. "I mean to put us among them."

Brother cried out, and they leapt to their feet. The male dog thrashed his head, ripping free the bundled map and strips of leather to expose the swollen foot. Kjartke caught the other end and sat back in the snow as he kicked out snow with all his might to pry it from her. Tunguk hurried to the sled, and she smiled when he returned with a spear and swung the back down hard on the animal's shoulders.

Foster manhandled a chunk of rock up to his chest, took aim, and thrust it over the side where it cracked through the thin lip of ice that rose to touch the hull and receded in turn.

"Lighten, lads! Before she bites!" Cormdran implored the crew. Every man scrambled for ballast, so carefully lain, to unleash on the encroaching floes like cannonade. Now Foster seized the piece he'd been avoiding—an oblong section as big as a gravestone near the empty bench where Gionn once sat. With no clean footing, he couldn't even square himself to it, and the rock hovered a second before tumbling into a new position. He tossed his head at Tunguk and Bucket, and the three of them set around it. Their little arms were the same diameter from wrist to shoulder, so it surprised him when it moved sooner than he thought. One heave at a time, they scooted it to the port bow, opposite Foster's bench, then up to the gunwale, on wood much fresher than that around it.

The rock hit a floe and pushed the end under before it bobbed back, split, and let the monster slip between the seam into the waves. Breaking up the ice was as satisfying as it was futile. As with most work on the ship, Foster undertook it without the slightest notion why. It started as an uncanny shift in the way the boat rocked beneath him in the margins of sleep. The water quieted. There was a weak hiss, intermittent and like someone sucking spit at the sides of their tongue. Then a knock, as if an oar reached out to touch the hull from beyond. A debate of voices carried over the slumbering benches until half the boat was awake, squinting into the black. No moon came to their aid, but soon it was light enough to see the pale reflection on top the water. They bloomed like huge jellyfish, ghosts come to the surface to haunt the living. It was not yet solid, but it stretched as far as anyone could see in bright patches that clicked against once another, rode over and under, stuck, and separated.

The panicked rush was all Foster needed to know of the seriousness.

"Damn you, Pitras! If you hadn't insisted I carry so much ballast!" Corm stomped past the two-share man. Even in their frenzy the crew laughed.

"Don't bother yourselves, lads, we'll be in the Orin any moment and you'll thank me," Pitras replied. Foster grinned. Of course, it was Corm's ballast, and now he knew who was chief among the bitchers. The captain made his way past the Mattaka boys onto the little forward deck, where he could examine the ice.

"Faster, buckets!" He called to the boys, and maybe Foster. "You're lookin' heavy, yourselves." He raised his voice to the entire crew. "Gimme every second bench! Turn into the ice, and hold her."

"North, or south?" Hogue wondered aloud, and by the way it gave Corm pause, Foster knew it meant something. The captain looked him in the eye, and he did his best not to show his bewilderment.

"You two weren't close, were you?" Corm asked. Foster followed his gaze across the waters where the first glimpse of the berg shone beyond a mile of thickening ice.

Gionn was first down to the shelf. It was a useless act as far as salvation was concerned, but he was overcome by the desire to be far from the others. Behind him, he could hear the clink of hooks and knew they followed out of habit, so he hadn't long to collect himself. Already the young sheets pressed a hummock into the edge of the temple, and the wind promised more to follow. He sunk to his knees and felt the familiar pressure of invisible boundaries, treacherous to the eye.

For the eye told him of a wide place, and waters to take him anywhere. But the feet would not affirm it. He could close his eyes and see a hundred ports, variously welcoming; open them, and behold the ship that would take him there. The lie of it was that this edge of upturned ice before him was the border of his world. Another island, though this one a fair measure colder than the last place he was stranded. Without having to see the rest of it he felt all sides at once, everywhere that land ended, and damn the view. His breath shortened. When he tried to fill his lungs all he got was a dry gasp that made him try another, with the same result. There was no change to the air he'd breathed for the past day, except now it was the only air he was permitted to dream of, and so it staled to hopeless inadequacy.

The crushing confines of an open ship, mates' elbows and heels and the same few feet of space—even the ship had its boundaries as transparent as the clear of his eye. None of them gripped his ribs and filled him with the panic of an island. A ship, for all its limitations, may as well be any place in the world, and in the darkest nights it was all of them. None of them very likely, of course he knew, but even the most remote possibility was enough to unfurl every strip of sea and beckoning coast between the two places as though they were already assured to him. It hardly mattered that he could go for a stroll here if it meant all those fair ports were blockaded and razed, and at last swallowed by pilfering Uinab.

A sharp exhale, then another quick gasp, and he found the bottom of his lungs, and used it to calm his shallow breath while he heard the others come up behind him.

"It's loose!" Jonn declared. "They can still row it!" It was true enough. The little floes piled up at the foot of the temple, but they slid readily in the swell, and there were lanes of water filled with splintered ice webbing through them not many yards beyond.

"If they can row it, they can fuck off," Gionn pointed out.

"They're peelin' ballast. We saw 'em." Arthas didn't offer an interpretation, and it felt like he preferred to represent a hope than be so dumb as to state it.

"What idiot cunt rows into the pack to be crushed?" Gionn almost prayed for a sensible answer.

"Corm wouldn't even try a bit of wind," Bentos reminded them.

"Aye, he's no idiot, but I've not seen him leave a man could be got." Jonn looked to Arthas for confirmation, and got none.

"*Fuck*!" Gionn kicked a piece of ice. "The fuck did we need water for? One filthy barrel. He knew this would happen. Bastard saw it would ice over, and took the lane to unload four shares."

"Nah," Bentos waved a dismissal. "Too soon for that. It's a cross luck, but we're fucked the same."

"He'll try for us," Jonn insisted.

"You know him well, lad. I pray better than us," Bentos said.

Arthas scoffed. "You think Corm wants the two of us back?"

"He took us once."

"Aye, and do you know for certain he chose it?"

"Fair enough. Fingers out me arse for a moment: say Bentos is right. He didn't mean to strand us. But he did choose his shore party. Suppose he fancied a stout lad and a break from me mouth. Now: why'd he send *you* cunts?"

Bentos shrugged. "I'm no one. One of Palqua's lads. Could as well have been any."

"Aye, you're here because landin' on ice is a risk, and it don't matter which of Palqua's takes it," Arthas offered.

"And you two are his. *Were*," Gionn corrected himself. "Are again. Think carefully, cunts. You came down with the man. If there's anything deliberate, it's meant for the two of you. Is there any cause under the wide fetch of Hadalis that, given a difficult circumstance of great inconvenience, he might not want you back?"

Eckerd climbed the aft deck while the wind snapped at his tunic under a darkening sky. Every man who could still hold an oar sat at the ready and craned his neck after the first mate. They were already under way, fleeing for deeper waters against the first tendrils of the gale when the pennants came up on shore. Now the sharp eyes bounded down to the captain.

"Closer look won't hurt." The mate scampered past to the foredeck in anticipation of the turn. She reversed course, and it was soon enough that the two signals came clear for all: one to land, and one that promised neutral quarter—a concession that guaranteed their safety without committing to terms.

Corm's surprise unnerved him. He was prepared to ride out a miserable existence for as many days as it took. Nothing of the negotiations prepared him for any kind of mercy. It was as strange as a besieged port embracing her blockade, until he reminded himself that he was a merchant who sought only fair commerce. The men, too, held their joy. They waited dutifully for something to cheer, and it was no less plain in their faces. He hesitated.

Their last offer held no quarter for the captain. It was the most contentious port bargain he'd ever faced, and it would hardly surprise him if he were seized and the crew held to the last offer from the admiral. But it was the fear of a lad often struck, upon seeing the sudden flinch of a hand. A treachery would harm the Navy far more than it benefited them. Word would get out—forget that most of their number once sat in his own position—and they'd starve themselves of resources that could strike a better bargain at a warmer port. If anything, the storm had forced them prematurely. They'd sent the water with the regards of Captain Palqua, and when they saw that Corm still stalked the deck, they knew their mutinous offer had missed its mark.

It wasn't the break he expected. But if they managed to ride out the storm at all, they wouldn't have the strength to sail against Camne Drumlag. His threat was sunk. He wasn't even sure if he meant it, now. The rage was there. He would happily spear Turrha until there was more of him open than closed. The pennants softened him, though. There came to him something like the respect of a victor for a valiant opponent.

"Up the ramp, lads! With a will!" None had the heart to celebrate, but he felt the whole ship breathe again, and a man's last pull never faltered. The keel scraped stone before the winds could find their pace and the *Gairhle* herself seemed to slump in relief.

Palqua waited with a pair of officers while they stowed without the help of the Navy, cowering away in some warm hole. It was a storm job—enough to be done with it. She wouldn't sink where they sat her, anyhow. Not a man set off for shelter or hung back in the lee of the ship when the officers approached. They crowded round Corm and bent an ear against the screaming gusts.

"Admiral Turrha is not like to come out in the weather," Captain Palqua shouted. "It will be a kindness if you do not draw attention. There's lodging for those who would pay, and you will also find the poorman's quarters has good walls."

"And the offer?"

Palqua cringed in deliberation. "He asked that you not receive it until after the storm. But then he also would have me leave you in the harbor to ride the gale. It is the curse of the man who carries orders to seem cruel. But I say to myself, I must face these same men again some day."

"I'll hold me thanks til I hear it."

"If it is not to your favor, of course you may stay for the storm, but you must put out soon after until we have an agreement." Cormdran nodded assent. "I'm pleased to tell you his temper has waned. The admiral extends quarter once more to the captain." Corm buried his reaction. Palqua went on. "And it will please you that he allows your men to sell their own wares, be they what they may, at their own prices. But I cannot offer you the right to repair your vessel."

"And the fee?"

"It remains three of five."

Corm permitted himself a turn to Eckerd. The lads held their tongues. Had the offer sculled over in a daille, he would have sent it back with a spear through it. Of course, he'd refuse to put out again. He'd seen it as being to his advantage. They forfeited the one term his men wanted more than anything—land. Now looking back at the foaming sea, he felt through his own denial that he hadn't the heart for it himself. Maybe a few days behind a wall would refresh them, if he remained captain that long. If he kept them together, and in spirits, they may well take up the oars again for another round and a lower fee.

But he saw the error, as well. In the narrow beam of a ship his men were his own. They were one body by necessity, and it moved with the measured stride of all those men who carved themselves at sea for long ages, century after century, sleeping and rowing and fighting by a custom as strong as the Greater Fahaile current. A current that moved nothing and no one who stood ashore.

He'd long tired of counting the roster of potential mutineers in his head. And if he ordered them out, they would have to go, or lose their shares. But no one would begrudge a crew to strand a greedy captain, already ashore, when the bastard tried to force them out to sea for a lower fee. Were he once again scrabbling for shares at an oar, he might do the thing, himself. There would be enough opportunity for it, in low tones at a tavern, a brothel, meandering the lanes.

Worse to Corm was the thought of this bunch who served so cheerfully under peril, through the worst gauntlet of lucks he'd ever sailed, who pooled their blood as brothers and carried her home as bench after bench fell around them—that these, his proud sons, would forsake him in the final hour. There were times he thought the morning would see them all stand against him. But they were keen enough to know the hand that guided them, and it was no small trust that kept him at the helm. There was nothing else for it. He had asked of them all they could give, and got it. There was no fair share they could receive given what the men of the *Gairhle* had done, but it belonged to all of them, and he could ask no more.

"Does your admiral give so little rope to a capable man that he can't grant a concession?"

Palqua glowed in the acknowledgment, and perhaps the intuition that his task neared its end. "He is a firm man. But as you see with this last offer, I can at times be persuasive."

"Right to repair. The rest stands." Nothing from the crew rose above the wind, but Corm felt a stir of anticipation behind him. Palqua narrowed, as if to first determine whether he'd been outmaneuvered, and then how far his own latitude extended. Corm already knew that if the Navy man sought to bring the offer to his superior, he would withdraw it for more generous terms. It was a brief set of terms, a mad one, for the captain alone.

"I will of course let you discuss it with your crew," Palqua nodded with deference.

"No need." Corm bent his elbow and held it before his chest. Palqua smiled and hooked his own so that their forearms crossed beneath their fists.

"May Pallaia-Akanoa welcome you to Drummoc." He leaned off into the gale with his mates for the navy hall.

Corm watched them go as long as he could, aware that when he faced his men it was under a different standard. They were still his—or rather, he was theirs—until the cargo was paid out. But his role had changed from spitting master of ship, bright spear, gold-sower; now he became the fatherly merchant, the careful dole who must charm enough arses to once again polish his thwarts north. To his great relief, he stood before them as captain, no different than the day they left. It was with humility and some regret that he spun to look upon his salted bastards. None would pretend it was the haul they hoped for, though it was better than what the fates offered them along the way. But Drummoc at a profit was no small feat. There were captains who made it once and back, and never let an ear pass without mentioning it. Thrice now Cormdran, son of Gerig, stood here. Only Eckerd could boast more, and none of those occasions as a captain.

It was clear there would be no song, and no whoop for it. There were too many missing, too much wind, and the fee was high. He didn't expect it, but he felt a pang of disappointment as one who does the deed, and just that. The groaning part of his burden gone, he wanted nothing but the tavern. It was his ship, though, and the first watch would belong to the captain.

"I'll have six hardy spears who'll give half a day to beat back the peekers and the thieves." No volunteer stepped forward. It would have earned them a tongue-lashing on the ship. Instead, Corm waited for the cold to scatter the tender ones to the walls. The wind would carve his watch if the men couldn't.

"Navy oughta do it," Arthas glowered. "The hold's more theirs than ours." A few brave laughs confirmed the sentiment. "*Three of five!*" He added in disbelief.

"Nothin' like port to make a man bold again," Corm snorted.

"Or soft."

"What's that, lad? I've no patience for riddles. Thrust if you mean to."

"Three of five!" Arthas repeated. Eckerd glared his disapproval but otherwise stood off. Shore had a way of shifting a man—unfurling one, trimming another—that it was necessary to learn one's mates all over again. Corm didn't blame him. This was his deed to answer.

"Aye, and none's poorer for it than me. Did you think you sailed into the Perides under the farri's standard? This is Drummoc, me son.

We got no letter, no wedge, and nothin' they want. If you think you can talk the crew into puttin' her back out for a few days, I'll be the first to admit you got more charm than I."

"A blistered arse has more charm than you, Corm, and I'd have never took her in."

"You'd stay out, would you? Tell me, *Captain*, do you think Gaspar would be alive after tossin' a few days in this blow?

"Gaspar's fuckin' dead anyway. Are you sure it was him you were worried wouldn't make it in?"

Corm seethed. A hush of dread passed over the sailors. "I don't think I've ever seen a mutiny on shore after the terms are brokered."

"And stow your shit! You think you'll shut us up every time you mention the word. It's a fuckin' dodge. No one said a damned thing about it. You can't stand to hear an honest word against you. I never thought you were the preenin' sort, crossin' your legs every time someone looks your way a moment too long."

"Call it what you will. You'll call it with me spear in your mouth." Corm spat. Eckerd and several others pushed between the two and dragged Arthas back behind neutral shoulders.

"Get the fuck off me," he shrugged.

"Every piss-saver on a ship thinks he could've done better," Corm hollered over the crew between them. "You've your luck to thank you're ashore at all!"

"You want a mutiny? Look to yourself! I never seen a captain strand his lads like that."

"Strand you? With pay and a ship home—for the ones who know when to shut the fuck up?"

"Aye! What did you get by comin' in? You act as though it's a better deal. That monkey bastard had us at three of five and your head. We fuckin' sat with you, mate! Not a man called for it. Sat two more days because you got us here, and not much more, but it was no small feat. No small feat. How many crews would be thrilled to divide the captain's shares? We sat with you, and a good many was ready to make war on Ampos."

"Not you!"

"No. Not me, but I'd have gone if it was the will of the crew. And what did you do? Stranded us on the worst fuckin' fee I've heard from any lyin' sailor. Only one whose terms improved was yours. A captain would have stood with his men, weathered the storm, and offered one of five or sharp steel."

Corm neared boiling, and sailors who looked to topple in exhaustion moments before forgot the wind and their agony as they did their best to wall off the two. An uncommitted cheer erupted from a few mouths in support of Arthas, and he recognized Fergo's rasp.

The captain leaned his considerable weight into the arms that held him. "No improvement? Do you have a fuckin' notion what our pay would be if the Navy set their own prices? Better four of five and we sell, than no fee and a handful of coppers for the whole load."

"A cheap trick! That was never gonna stand."

"Right to repair! How many seasons do you think you'd serve the bluecoats before you got hired north? One? Two? You had a ship and a seat for Spring before you tongued your way out of it."

"There'll be a dozen or more ships in the spring. Only one who cares to ride back on the *Gairhle* is yourself."

Arthas broke free of the arms and stomped off toward the town. Pitras called after him, then trotted off as if to console him, though it was just as likely an excuse to get off first watch. A few more followed without a word, then the whole of the gathered collapsed. Man after man turned for shelter. Corm's rage warmed all but the end of his nose as he shouted after Arthas.

"You fuckin' dead cunt! Show your face once if you've a man in you! Fuckin' blaggard!" Eckered gave him a look of what he hoped was regret, and feared was pity, then trudged off. The mate had to go, he told himself. He'd keep second watch. But no reassurance could take the sting from what was likely no sleight at all. Half of the six he called for stayed, and one was Gaspar, unable to move himself. Corm followed the white heights of Urkuk to where they disappeared in the racing clouds above the town. Arthas' words came to him again, and were choked off with blood as the captain buried his spear in the insolent shade time and again.

The *Gairhle* lay dry. He had to remind himself of it. There was no choosing how. That was not a captain's privilege. Nor was it to second-guess every trim and every tack that led them here. It was the tender lads who could afford an imagination.

"Get him to a fuckin' poye!" He snapped at the two who cared for Gaspar—Nemas and Muir—and marked them the last to leave, as he marked those who went first. Corm clutched his spear and sank into the lee of the Gairhle, able to shiver at last on solitary watch. He leaned against her, solid, damp, pregnant with his labors. She made Drummoc. He swore now she would make Taclann, if he were the only man aboard.

Parks' body hit the slope with a thunk and a groan, then rotated so that his head was uphill. Blood rushed to clear his left side where it pooled against the straps. There wasn't an inch of ground that didn't tilt him this way or that. Stillness spread over him like a blanket. His vessels rattled with the residual motion of hours on the sled, and the tingling faded in places to a low burn. He prayed he wouldn't be forced to stand again. Beyond the cruelty of it, the act had the effect of tearing him from his merciful delirium. Now he felt everything. Jagged skin, seizing muscles, and a bone ache that radiated clear up to his pelvis. Somehow, he must have found a sort of sleep. But even that was delicate, as if he still had a foot in the waking world, tethered to the loud pain.

The jolt woke him fully, and the intensity climbed until it seared between his temples and his eyelids clenched to wring fluid from the corners. When he opened them, he somehow knew he'd fled again to his dreams. Joe and Kjartke were gone, but he still reclined on a vast white plain. It didn't hurt to sit up, or rather, it felt like it hurt someone other than him.

The creature appeared far off and to his right. It took some time to recognize that it was hopping. A little leap, a pause, and a leap. The bizarre movement and swirling form soon separated itself from his imagination as a long cloak fluttering around a large man. Parks had no sense of it as a threat or a friend. He only knew its coming carried a throbbing dread.

The closer it got, the more pathetic its effort seemed. Eager, and undignified. He wrinkled his nose when it came to rest on a single boot protruding beneath the tail of the garment. From a low hood, the man spoke.

"My turn yet?"

"What?" Parks shuddered. "Who are you?"

"You know. Say it."

Parks looked around for anyone else—anything at all. He felt at his waist for his map, so he could pretend to stare at it like a cell phone in unwanted company. Nothing presented itself. He collapsed onto his back in defeat to squint at the sky. There was a heavy crunch, crunch, crunch. The hooded man leaned over him.

"I'm going to tell you a story that won't make sense. It never will. But it'll work just the same."

"'Kay."

"The gates in the two worlds don't always align." Parks rose to his elbow to listen. "In the familiar world, you might be on a ship. Let's say it's your line crossing. Everyone's in costume. There's a lot of activity, and it feels important. Someone pours water over your head. They lead you through a doorway and take you below, and speak strange rites. Everyone you know is there. Foster, too. The captain. There's decorations, and shit. You get a card that says you're forever changed. Meanwhile in the secret world, you sit on a board in the ocean, and it's flat. No waves." He paused.

"Other times, in the familiar world, you're lying still. But in the secret one, you're on a sled racing through a narrowing channel. There's a lot to do. Don't fuck it up."

Parks scrunched his face. "Is that how we get back?"

"I told you it's not supposed to make sense. Oh, and you're gonna need a weapon. Something badass."

"I have an arrow."

"Nah. That's a singing arrow. Let me finish."

"Sorry."

"Actually, that was all I had to say."

Parks coughed himself awake and felt something wet and gritty cross his lips. He tried to swallow and choked.

"Chew," Kjartke's voice insisted. She put a bladder to his mouth. He swished and washed down what tasted suspiciously like the same dried seal. Her hand took his jaw, and two fingers wiped a glob of paste off on the back of his bottom teeth.

"Chew." This time, she clamped his mouth shut and waited until a lump passed his throat. Parks shook his head when she offered more, but she gripped his chin.

"You must find your strength."

He worked the substance around until he felt brave enough to swallow, then saw Kjartke spit a mouthful of something into her hand. Parks gagged, but he couldn't stop her. There was little force to it. The certainty of her touch alone gained compliance.

"Are we there yet?" He gulped.

"Better to ask one who know."

He lifted his head and followed the noise to Joe where he knelt downslope, fussing with the sled turned over on its side.

"Do they ask you to go with them?" Kjartke's question surprised him.

"Hm? Who?"

"The one you talk to." He must have been muttering in his sleep. Parks shook his head. "Good."

She swung a knee over him as if to sit astride him, but the other followed and put her on his other side. Her fingertips touched his knee, and Parks recoiled in a pain that was more expected than elicited. Kjartke left her hand resting on him until the tension released, then she rolled back the two sides of his split trouser with care. He closed his eyes hard again as if he could force himself back into a nightmare that would hurt any less than what coursed his body. No such mercy came. Kjartke startled when instead he pushed himself up just enough to see what she was doing. There lay a bruised root, gnarled and swollen, snaked with blue veins and pools of dark purple flesh. When she took the end in her palms he slammed back with a cry but did all in his power not to jerk away.

"Be still. I must clean it."

Parks glanced up to watch her squeeze and press downward as if coaxing toothpaste from an opening. "Easy!" He shouted when she passed over the folds of stitched flesh. This time, she listened, and the tearing sensation of raw skin being pulled apart dialed back just enough that she made it to the end of a thick wad that felt like a baseball in his leg. Kjartke moved back to the top and repeated the stroke, this time inflicting marginally less pain—a margin that improved with each subsequent pass. It was still enough to make him sob helplessly even as he felt fluid moving into thirsty corners.

Finally, she took a handful of snow and touched it to the bottom. The cold was at once welcome and shocking. Parks realized when her fingers slid along the inner edge that his skin was open to the interior. The scrape of the ice make him jerk and cry out.

"Easy," she repeated his own admonition back to him.

Parks whimpered, then before he realized it, began to sing to himself in soft mumbling tones. "Say my name, say my name. When no one is around me, say baby I love you if you ain't runnin' game." He felt a confidence flood into her touch as she dabbed the ice into the blistering edges of his pain. Parks surrendered so that all of him was motionless, except what moved in another's hands.

The ice blunted the main swell that reminded them of its stubborn presence with a lateral pitch that lifted port, then starboard. The *Gairhle* took the north wind in the face. By seat, it should have been him and the boys up on the foredeck with oars, staving off the floes that crowded past them like a highway of maniacs without lanes, jammed up and crashing off one another at a walking pace. It was important-enough work that they weren't trusted.

He didn't need to be much of a sailor to realize the iceberg was in their rearview. The sail was down. The ice grew by the hour as it fused, spun, scraped, and cracked in a steady advance that threatened to pave over the last slushy patches of open water. But they were poised for a breakout the moment they had a shot. Four men stood over them, prying the nose this way or that clear of the ice, everyone of them plus Corm and Eckerd barking their expert opinions of where to push and how urgently.

The rest of the crew jabbed at the wet edges that tried to cling to the hull like a hand digging in its fingernails as it drifted past. The Mattaka boys were forced back into Gionn and Bentos' benches, where they did everything they could just to hold on to the oars. Foster cringed when the ship lurched with a gut-wrenching howl from Bucket's side. Men scrambled to separate a scraping commuter from the hull. Nothing unfortunate could happen without the nearest bystander being cussed seven ways from Sunday as if it was his plot all along.

At least a brief contact with good ice gave them a respite from their tossing. He almost prayed they would be hemmed in to stop the battle with the oars. The thick white banks seemed like a herd of pale monsters pinballing off one another as they thundered by, oblivious to the whaler's presence.

He wondered if Gionn could see them. Nothing that looked like a man distinguished itself from the enormous fortress of ice, but the shore party must have noticed that the ship that turned from broadside to seaward, and it couldn't have been a welcome sight. Long weeks of having his fate rattling around in the same cup pulled his chest taut at first. They rode all the same boats, fled the same folks. By sheer association he'd come to think of the man as an ally. Maybe he was. Whatever you could say about Gionn's intentions, his loyalties, his integrity, he did always seem to act on Foster's behalf in the end. And he was the only one on the ship that knew why Foster was there.

But for the moment, Gionn did everything in his power to undermine that effort. He wouldn't help unless he was paid, and if he was paid, he wouldn't help. Now Foster wondered whether the same bad habit of association had managed to creep into Gionn's brain. How long did he say he crewed for Oduy? It was years, that was for sure.

"Lead!" Came Hogue's voice from the foredeck. The crew echoed it at intervals along the length of the ship. Foster followed their twisting necks to a dark line about 300 yards off the starboard bow. It looked like a thin mountain stream snaking through the spring snow, north to south and widening under the incalculable influence of wind and swell and freezing chaos.

"Is she clear?" Someone asked.

"Clear past the eye," Hogue reported.

"It'll be a current," said Aldan, one of Polc's defected carpenter's. "Like rowin' upriver."

"Upriver's better then rowin' on the ice!" Ordacles challenged.

"Will we fly like a bird to get there?" Yuray scoffed.

"It's loose yet, if we go now." Ordacles by now had stowed his oar and hung off the mast for a look. The crew burst into the familiar cacophony of counter-arguments and side conversations that reminded Foster of an unruly classroom. It wasn't Cormdran's way to inject himself into these melees. It was no small surprise, but one he was learning to see on its own terms, that the scum of a whaler were granted more leeway than a room of eighth graders, and that contrary to every cinematic notion of his, he had yet to encounter anything like a dictatorship wherever the hell he was. There were no equals, that was for sure, but even the hardest of hands slackened for debate, or let a consequence slide that no petty lieutenant of the United States Navy would have suffered. That wasn't to say he would dream of pissing off the captain. But the old man seemed to sail on a tossing sea of personality, taking the winds he could find, as opposed to rolling down a seamless highway straight into the interminable distance.

"What say you, Corm?" Ordacles called. The captain waited on his perch until the fist-shakers settled. He waited for the straggling word to die before he addressed them.

"What say I? It's a good lead, and we can make it." A pair of distinct roars greeted the proclamation. When they passed, he went on. "Good lead. May not take us out the pack, but it'll be close, and a better chance the next time. If it weren't so, I wouldn't need to remind you four of your mates sail with Omera. One of 'em thinks we should stand for it every time we tack." A few laughs slipped from some of the senior crew. "But I got shares to recoup. Let no man say Cormdran, son of Gerig, stranded his lads to weight his purse. I put it to the crew."

They let out a cheer to a man except Foster, who could never be sure he followed what they were talking about, even with the simplest of issues. The Mattaka boys must have felt likewise, because they watched him for his reaction and held their own to imitate it.

"Number cunt! Where's the wife of the Leopard Seal?" He called superfluously. Foster sat only yards away where he always did.

"Aye!" He answered begrudgingly.

"We'll not have a repeat of Drummoc. It's no mutiny, so count's by shares, not arses. Give us a tally before we stand."

"Just to be clear: you want me to count the two share men as two, the one-point-fives as one-point-five, ones as one, et cetera, et cetera?" They looked at him as if he just insulted them in a foreign tongue.

"No, thick fuck!" Corm's words almost felt like a blow. "Do you think you can cut a man in half and make another? Twos are two. Everyone else is one. You and the squains are yet to earn your say."

He nodded, unnerved at the simple twist. Foster could do math. He was confident of that. He also knew he could fuck up the most basic of problems with great confidence. While he was sure no one would know, the lingering doubt surrounding his one function on the ship filled him with dread of an error that would make him no better than ballast.

"You got six men at two shares, right? And we had fifty-four aboard includin' you. Do I count the ones on the berg? The big ice thing," he clarified.

"Are they here to stand? What kind of a number man has to ask his captain how to count?"

Foster gathered himself. "We had fifty-four," he spoke aloud for his own benefit, since he didn't have pencil and paper, but hoped the crew would take it as transparency. "Um. So minus four on the berg, and the captain and us no-shares, that's forty-six of yall in play. Six got double shares. Fifty-two. It's fifty-two votes. Stands. Whatever you call 'em. That means twenty-seven to win it. Unless it's a two-thirds to win situation, which based on yall's countin' ability, I can't imagine is likely."

"That sounds a fuck-up to me!" Fergo protested.

"You lose count when you tally your toes," Pitras sniped.

"I get nine every time!" Fergo put the crew into fits.

"Bicker until the lead closes!" Corm shut them up. "We'll have one for go, one for stay, and once you're counted, you're up. Who'll argue we row? Ordacles?" Enough men cheered him on that it was settled.

This was Foster's champion, he realized. He flushed with regret. Most all of him wanted to see the ginger son of a bitch seated across from him. It was the wish of that part of him that brought the boat ashore on Gionn's island in the first place, desperate for someone familiar. How miserable would he be if they'd actually found someone from that raft? What kind of impossible nuisance would they cause for him now? Gionn was by far better to have—maybe because he was easier to let go.

It came also from that part of him that ended sentences with "sir"; that treated Kjartke with a Southern chivalry even Parks couldn't unerstand; that wanted to be right at all costs: about his friends, about his count, and that one day not too far from this one, he would stand atop a long driveway in North Carolina. It was only by wading through a mire of guilt that he now admitted he needed them to die.

The Gionn he wanted was one made of hopes and prunings from memory. He didn't like Bentos, and the other two were no more than recognizable faces. Ordacles seemed to forgive him as he made point after point about the condition of the ice. If it slackened, it wouldn't be for long. And if it didn't, they would winter here. Lose whatever promise the word "Taclann" held for them, even if they somehow avoided starvation and broke free in the spring melt. Those men knew the risks. Every man aboard knew he would have a turn, and couldn't expect the crew to treat them as an anchor. There was no hope of rowing in, he said, and if the ice was solid enough to walk, they were already fucked. By the end of it, Foster felt absolved, at least from the outside. He was more worried about losing a water barrel than four men.

But the inconsolable angel woke to patrol his shoulder when Palqua himself stood. It was the first time he was certain he heard the man speak, and it was that glimmering, pretentious Amposi tone that sounded of plucked strings in a hollow gourd. Despite the accent, his English was better than most of the native speakers on the ship. Than Foster himself, if he was honest. It was a studied grasp, and every word as careful as it was permissive. There was no bark. Every danger understated, every contention fluffed and smoothed. The only man of that nation Foster knew well was Barzos, and though Palqua commanded more of a presence, he saw in the two men the whole of the people. They were a bunch of dandies compared to the crude "halots," of which he was considered a member. But he remembered Amachar and the men on the dog ship, what they endured. The fiery snap of the Viceroy's whip, too, reminded him that he might not want to read too much into a mannerism.

Palqua's argument carried a charm that flowed without pressure. Foster thought he'd lost it when he spent the first minute conceding every point Ordacles made.

"Close your eyes and stand at the foot of Omera's temple," he implored the crew. "Close your eyes…Close your eyes…" Palqua repeated until they were sure he wouldn't go on until they did. "What do you think moves on the ship? Who calls for oars, and who stalls for a luck to intervene? There will be more barrels to fill. Meat to harvest. Perhaps we collect more ballast," he said with a wry smile to Corm.

"Will your ship return for you? Those aboard will remember when you stood to abandon four men without the mildest effort to recover them. If we go so soon, it will be hard to name a shore party. Will we stand for that, as well? No man will set foot over the beam when his captain orders it. I ask you to open, now, and look upon the place where four of your mates tear at their garments and swear vows for rescue. See them, and recall that Gama-Nitl crossed three seas to recover Achallay from atop a wave. That Hadalis, when still a youth, braved Uinab's fury to reunite the lost sons of Ouros. Or Jarken when he traced his footprints over the Atlantic to free Arka from the Sea King of Razama."

"Or Raratuk when he came for his brother, Vitjukvattajuk," Tunguk leaned in to whisper, as if it meant something to Foster. Instead, the names tore away his attention even as they moved the others. Palqua laid out a litany of sailor's rules and vague references to times when men stood in noble defiance. Foster couldn't even tell if it was history or mythology, but all of it sounded impossible. Not just the feats, but the simple heroism that acted with unflinching virtue in the worst of peril.

Foster had been one of those men: when he was ashore, a beer in hand, or trading stories in a bunk. The company he met underwhelmed him wherever he went. In the Navy, the unconscionable city, and many times more the Amposi ports of Antarctica. He built himself, rib and plank, by the stubborn refusal to compromise anything he held dear. By the things he would never entertain, or would always issue forth in the direst moments as easy as the next breath. The few times he was tested to some degree, his action bore it out, and he came to believe them. It was as vivid and undeniable to him as any mythology that lifted the men of the *Gairhle*.

So he stood for things, when all it required was an idle boast or a bloody nose. A few more times, when the cost was great but his own arrogance blinded him to it. It was easy to be noble when your day began and ended in a bed. He couldn't remember the last time he was warm. If his ass weren't scraped by a bench he was contorted into an impossible shape against rock and wood and a thin strip of leather. With each mounting crisis, he sensed what he couldn't have recognized anywhere else: virtue was a death wish. It ran through his fingers the colder, the more emaciated they became, until he felt with just as much certainty as in his boasting that if it hurt just a little more, he couldn't afford to be so noble.

Something set around him and pressed on all sides like ice against a hull. He could only claim a high principle if he held it always. That meant there was nothing true of a man unless he was willing to die for it. Each measure he dared to claim was one more way to commit suicide. It was one more obligation to stare a danger in the face, and remain until it killed him. Suddenly, Gionn made a little more sense. He'd been cold enough to freeze, hungry enough to starve, and faced with his share of blades. There was no illusion in the man's mind about what he would do, which is to say, who he was. Foster always thought the scumbag survived in spite of his complete lack of redeemable qualities. In truth, it was because there were so few ways in which Gionn insisted on being killed.

His own irrepressible nature began to look a little threadbare. It held together where it hadn't been strained, but Foster sensed it fraying. The abstraction of death loosened at the seams as he felt the frigid water on his toes, the pangs for a handful of seal and a gulp of water. It was no longer a story about the future. He felt it as something that was present always. A gradient, like the temperature, that moved one way today and another tomorrow. There was a point of no return, and though it still felt like a rumor at times, he now believed as surely as in his honor that one day, he would cross it.

"The lead would close if he spoke any longer," Corm's jab brought Foster back to the ship as a fair number hooted their approval for Palqua. "Arses down! We'll stand first for 'go.' You've until the number cunt makes your bench to decide. Number cunt!" Corm beckoned Foster to stand. The men on the foredeck hurried back to their seats, except the captain.

Foster rose, and glanced at the Mattaka boys, seated with the luxury of no commitment. He reckoned he was supposed to walk the length as he tallied, and was afraid to ask. The first bench was Chirim's. Foster paused to give him a chance, but moved on when the Amposi held his seat. He wondered how many of the crew would "stand for go" if it were him. Didn't matter, he told himself. Not my crew.

When he reached his first man, Hogue, he braved an announcement: "If yall are two shares, raise your damn hand when I meet you or I'll count you as one."

"Aloud!" Corm bellowed as he passed in silence. Foster took a step back.

"One."

His thoughts turned to those he left in the wigwam. Maybe it didn't matter what he thought about Gionn, or any of these fools. His crew was at Drummoc, and if he seemed to lose his integrity, maybe it was because there wasn't yet any question of what would happen to the only people he really cared about—not here, anyway. He resolved that they were alive and in good health, and would remain that way until he confirmed otherwise. Get this ship to Nunoc. Find another. Go back for Parks. That was all he was beholden to. Maybe he wasn't as bad as he thought. Or none of it yet hinged on a death he could avoid.

Each step now carried him into new territory, a piece of the ship where he never had cause to set foot. His hand rested on the mast for the first time, and it filled his lungs with crisp air. A faintness came over him, and Foster struggled to count faces he had never seen so close since they embarked. There were more than he thought on their feet after Palqua's speech. Eckerd, Pitras, and Ordacles all raised hands for a second vote. But the crew was mixed, and for all his "numbers," he couldn't sort out which way it would go. No one part of the ship showed too heavily for either side. When he reached the tarp over the last few benches, he turned and raised his voice so Corm could hear at the other end.

"Twenty-six."

There came a smattering of cheers. "To oars!" Some ordered with urgency.

"Hang on. You need twenty-seven to win." Looks of confusion abounded, until he added: "It's a tie, dumbasses. Twenty-six apiece."

"How do you know? You haven't counted the 'stay' lads." Corm shouted back.

"I don't need to. Fifty-two votes, minus twenty-six, is twenty-six."

The crew turned on him, united again in their displeasure with what struck them as a scam. Corm ordered them down, and Foster shook his head as the "stays" stood, and he repeated the count in the other direction, arriving once more at the captain.

"Like I said. Twenty-six." There was another uproar of astonishment, and Fergo recoiled as if he had witnessed some dark magic, spitting something under his breath while he made strange gestures of protection.

Corm again waited for the furor to level off, then set on Foster. "And you?"

"Me?"

"Aye."

Foster staunched his terror. "Thought I didn't get counted."

"You don't. But you still have to declare. You and the squains. Do you think the crew'll row with no-bollocks cunts who don't say where they stand?"

Relief flooded over him. Foster looked at the empty seat beside and in front of him. His opinion didn't matter, except that even if they never saw Gionn again, the rest of the crew would know him as the man who stranded his neighbors.

"Stay." The contingent, heavy with Amposi Navy, sounded off their approval. Tunguk and Bucket made short consideration before joining Foster on their feet.

"Stay," they confirmed.

"Falls to the captain!" Gewar shouted.

Corm waited until every man took his bench, then strode barrel tops all the way to the mast. He spread a long glance across the face of the iceberg. Foster had no say, and it filled him with gratitude that he could claim loyalty if his old ally returned. But he lurched with an anxiety whose source he couldn't place. The *Gairhle* felt small to him, as if seen from a distance, undetermined.

Corm's head snapped around to the billowing lead.

Costig surveyed the town from the deck of the viceroy's barc. The tide of Mattaka had ebbed into the huts for the night, but he was sure it would come in again. Someone had a cache of hasqa now, and it was not like to quell them. At least he would know who the thieves were when they stumbled out.

The Navy held their posts at half strength, the other having retired for a rest. A few troublemakers arrived early to pace in anticipation. It was not over. He knew that. The excitement was too keen to settle without some satisfactory event. He could beat them back, of course, but he'd done so in the past, and cursed the admiral who put his marines in that fray and made them the focal point of cursing and violence for seasons to come. The tidal approach was better: wait for the next one to arrive, and wait again for it to disperse, each time weaker if he didn't aggravate it.

Such was his search, out by day, back by night, and out again to cover old miles in hopes of new inches. The Navy lacked the incentive. Each time they came back empty their spirits would shrug until an order became a formality to wander out of sight for most of a day. And if he let the squains after it, he'd have civil war. There was no way Parks could stay out long, if he were more than a well-concealed corpse at this point. But just as he knew he could outlast the town if he gave them no cause for fresh vigor, so the fugitives must have known they could retreat just far enough to keep their toes dry each day.

It both consoled him, and wounded his pride. The admiral in him would find his mark if he gave his men the nudge they needed to miss theirs. It was Sergeant-at-Arms Costig who suffered, prevented by his commander from the redeeming thrust of his spear.

The sound of boots on the hull returned him, and a pair of arms appeared over the side. With a grunt, Wendell rolled aboard and joined Costig at the rail.

"She's a fine one, isn't she?" Wendell greeted him.

The fleet of Drummoc reclined on the rock all around them—darraig and abiama and docogon, dog ship and overturned daille. Errant coal ships and merchant barcs in full repose. A fair sight if half of them could sail. They tilted like bird-picked corpses, swallowed more each year by their cannibal sisters who disappeared north.

"Correscu has taken the outrigger for her fleet, and the favored sons of Ampos strut the seas in the old Atlantean build," Wendell noted the irony. They stood higher than all but the worst benches of a docogon, beneath a pair of masts, and no unsightly outrigger—the barc refused to travel on her elbow. The hold was wasted by high, narrow walls and swelled to a merchant-style deck, her ample hips curved above the slender symmetry of her body.

"I understand he's got a darraig, now."

"Aye, a fair trade," Costig replied.

Wendell nodded with his customary grin. "Oterec."

"That his name?"

"Off the whaler, and the original crew, at that."

"Remind me next time some mangled bastard washes up to recognize the Leopard Seal."

Wendell extended a Mattaka-style bladder to Costig, who took it and gave the mouth a sniff. He smiled and warmed his stomach with a pull.

"Took it off a stumblin' lad overnight. Ten, I'd say. His father won't be pleased when he comes home from a hard season to find not a drop in the tavern for winter."

Costig passed it back. "Can't imagine he'd blame me."

The men watched the morning take shape over the decks of the dry fleet. Navy returned to duty, uncertain of the mounting crowd. Costig could probably unravel the riot in a stroke if he just arrested every male under fifteen. The future miners filled him with no enthusiasm. But the little gangs they roved in held more hatred for each other than the Marines. Were he to lump them together in the one cell, it would be a massacre. Easier to arrest a single fugitive.

"Easy": a word reserved for those who left the details to others. For starters, there was more than one fugitive, and they had both Costig's word and Foster's coin to look after them. If he wanted to pull the offer, he should have done it when he found them in the skin hut. Now he weighed whether he'd let Drummoc burn to preserve his honor.

They passed another sniff between them, then Wendell plugged it.

"You'll have to let me tell you sooner or later," he said. Costig felt an apprehension rise in the wake of the hasqa. "The huntin' camp," Wendell clarified. The admiral let out an airy belch that eased his distress. He nodded Wendell on.

"You'll recall from your humbler post that the shipments were light. The squains have their own tales, but I found a good number unaccounted."

"How many?"

"Not much of a counter meself. A third? It's hard to have an honest chat with those folk. They say the huntin' was poor. A group moved to a different ground they thought would fill their holds better. No one could quite say where."

"If you had the gift to divine it?"

"It's plain I don't. With all they took, couldn't be far in those leather dailles. But you know me curious nature…"

"Curious is the word."

"I had the captain swing by Neferwet's Foot on the way back. Seal are right where we left 'em, and thick as thieves."

"Maybe they went for whale."

"Could be."

Costig marked the lack of conviction in Wendell's voice. "I haven't yet checked if the squains broke into the stores, as well. I do know from rumors that food is a fine thing to have in a siege, and the more, the better. Set a ration. Let it be known how much they're expected to put away. Maybe a healthy fear of famine'll quell their tempers. And if they broke into the stores, we won't be replacin' it. Say that, anyway. Though if I got ships in me harbor and starvin' squains gatherin' rocks behind me, I don't think it'll matter much about Leopard Seals and assistant viceroys."

"Aye, I've seldom found a man undone by the problems that hold his eye," Wendell confirmed.

"A man. Not 'a Navy?'"

Wendell chuckled. "Ah, well, I meant it in the broader sense: all men. Navies, sea kings, farris, the one begets the other."

"It won't pain me if you think I've botched it, but it would if you thought I was the kind of arse you couldn't tell."

"Nooooo, Costig! Banish that! You got the vessel with more leaks than wood. It's to your reputation that it still floats."

"You'd have done the same?"

"Aye!" Wendell assured him.

"With the Leopard Seal, and all?"

"I'd have sent twenty fresh mercenaries sloggin' after him this very mornin'."

Costig rolled into a modest laugh, satisfying and genuine. "They were the ones knew where to pick up the track."

"I've had much less to concern me, and I still can't tell you a word about Polc. I just keep thinkin' of Turrha. What a mess we'd be in if he were at the helm. What his face must have looked like when you drove the spear!" They both gazed off affectionately.

"It's a good way, that. Nothin' else I try has the same effect."

"You're a Marine, through-and-through." Costig furrowed his brow. "What? It's a compliment!" Wendell insisted.

"Not to an admiral."

"What'll I call you, then? What does Costig say of himself?" The billowing mustache folded tight over his lip in deliberation. Wendell took a different tack. "Has he got a sled?"

Costig nodded.

"If you must hear it: one of Polc's lads. Four or five swift Marines. And a silver to the dog man if he guides them to success. There's nowhere to run. It's a matter of cuttin' off the track."

"Then the spear."

"Put me on him. I'll let you have that part, and it'll be one less to fuss with."

"No, you're right." Costig said. "About that, aye, and the rest. It's the problem we see," he tilted his chin over the first timid gestures of defiance as the Mattaka formed in loose groups in what was becoming their customary territory. "That might be the least of 'em. Find the missin' squains, and tell 'em all they'll fill me hold or starve."

"I'll send a darraig at first light tomorrow."

"Go yourself," Costig clapped him on the shoulder, then spread his hand over the assistant viceroy's ship. "I've a fine barc for you."

Gionn extended a pair of open palms, tilted to the shimmering facade that breached the sky. A few feet behind, the other three repeated in clumsy unison: "Hoy! Omera! A fine one, your temple. Just look at the colors. Freezin' me toes."

"Hoy! Omera!" Gionn shouted as if tryin to get the attention of a distant shipmate. "Queen of the South. Ample your bosom with penguins and seals." They echoed his call the next moment, and when they were done, he hesitated. His eyes fell on the crease where their original offering still rested. "Hoy! Omera! We gave you some coal. Take it and let us fuck off from your shores."

Bentos, Arthas, and Jonn repeated with waning investment and a few puzzled looks. Gionn continued, and they dogged close behind:

"Hoy! Omera! Spare us your teeth. Be a good lass. Bite somewhere else.

"Hoy! Omera! Spare us the ship. That's not your ship. Fuck off from the ship.

"Hoy! Omera! Finest of cunts! Hear me prayer! Omera! Omera!"

They hurried away more like lads who'd just thrown rocks at a rough party than a group of pious miracle-seekers.

"Were you makin' it up as you went?" Jonn complained.

"Plug it, cunt. You're the lot forced me to lead it. I told you how I feel about prayin' to strangers."

The sailors shuffled as fast as footing allowed to the north edge of the temple, where their vision danced in frantic effort to pick out the *Gairhle* among the ice. It was Jonn who spotted her, and even then, Gionn didn't believe it until he guided them to the dark shape silhouetted against the floes. She hadn't moved from where they left her, still pointed north, their hopes pinned to her by the ice.

Bentos let out an involuntary flutter of relief. Gionn reveled in his error—he knew with all his knowing that they'd return to find an empty sea—and just as soon, he told himself a new tale: it was no better. As bleak as before. Soon as the ice thinned, they were off, and the sailors without a morsel of food would bicker over small offenses, whatever resources they had; who held the axes, without admitting to themselves what they were afraid the other would do with them; and deeper still, wondering what he himself was capable of.

"We make a run. Over the ice." They looked at Gionn with an amusement grafted to underlying horror. "If it thins enough to sail, you see the way she points."

Arthas scowled over the sea. "There's open leads," he said.

"Where?" Jonn asked. Arthas pointed. "That's a crack! I could step that."

"If it don't move. And it only gets worse farther out. North winds are short here. It'll back to west, and the whole thing'll scatter."

"Then we drown instead of starve." Gionn started for the climb down to the shelf. Two men followed. He turned to Arthas. "There's no ship comin' to get us."

Arthas joined them at the bottom as they tried to survey the state of the pack over the little hummock forming against the base of the temple.

"Jump down, you're thickest," Jonn said. "If it holds you, we'll be grand."

"You're next thickest, and first dumbest, cunt. And still a lad! Nothin' done worth mournin'."

"What I done in me few years got me the same place as you in all of yours," Jonn parried.

Gionn planted his hook and eased himself over the honed bevels of young ice. He searched for each foothold before committing to a sharp edge that would slice his foot. Whole sections moved under his weight. Halfway down he had to kick everything until it packed in on itself enough to support him. The fingers on his free hand froze. The faces hovering over him looked more curious than supportive. With a yard to go, there was nothing but a smooth shard, flat as a broken table turned on its side. Below, wisps of powder blew across the ice into a little furrow at the base. It made the top look as solid as he hoped, but he had no way of knowing if the sea had frozen two feet or two inches. No chance for a tentative touch. Gionn closed his eyes and hopped backward.

His heels hit, and he felt a crunch before he rolled over his back and knocked his head as his legs somersaulted into a kneeling position. He held still as a sighted bird on its perch. His breath gathered, he lifted one hand from a clear impression. A fractional layer on the top gave to the slightest touch, but only enough to leave a mark. With the utmost care, he drug a foot forward and pressed himself upright. When he stood, he was sure he felt the whole thing move, but another step told him it was his own conjuration. The surface was pliable, but beneath, it was hard as rock. Gionn marched about, and added force to each step until he stomped with glee over the fresh crust.

Jonn didn't even wait for the word before he began his short descent. Meanwhile Gionn tramped farther out. He could just make out a shape that must have been the *Gairhle* by its bearing, but the low angle posed a navigational challenge. As long as it was clear, and the ice fair in all directions, they could make it for supper. Anything else, and it would be as easy to lose the way there as to Taclann.

A shout of delight revealed Jonn dancing on the surface and Bentos starting down after him. Gionn turned again into the wind and squinted through the tears it wrung from his eyes. A miserable walk, but let it rage all it liked if it held the pack, and the ship, in place. He came to the first seam worthy of the name, tested it with his boot, then stepped over to solid footing. It wasn't clear if he was proving the ice or leaving everyone behind. Arthas and Jonn were quiet about the way up, but the name "Corm" was enough to knot them with anxiety. He knew the look inside and out. There were names of his own that jarred him so, and none of them would retrieve him at any convenience from an icy death.

A hollow crunch snatched his leg from below. Gionn tumbled forward through the ice and felt the freezing water rush up to greet him.

He flailed and spun for anything to grip, landing on his arse and elbows before he realized his plunge had taken no more than a foot before another layer of solid ice caught him in a shoal beneath a slush of thin, clear chips. He scooted backward as fast as he could until he rested once more on firm ground, drenched and shivering in the wind.

The others saw his fall and hurried to the sound of swearing. With help, he righted himself, and then stamped along the edges. It broke through in half-solid imprints lapped by water, freezing again almost immediately under the influence of the breeze. The difference in this ice was as clear now as it was invisible a moment before. It spread before them like a garden pond to the north and the east.

"We'll be wadin' to the ship," Jonn proclaimed.

"Wade if you like. I'll be back to search me luck in the mornin'." Gionn took off a boot and emptied it with a splash.

"It's just a thin bit," Bentos assured them. "See? We can go around that way."

"Aye, for how long?" Arthas questioned.

"As far as we can. It'll freeze the same whether we're down here, or up there. I'd rather be ready to take the next step when it firms than wait for the whole thing to lay out the welcome." Bentos argued.

"Aye," Jonn agreed. "Might get worse rather than better."

"Can I have your share when I get to the ship in the mornin'?" Gionn asked.

"You're the one said we got no choice. Starve or drown."

"I said 'make a run,' not 'swim for it.' I'll starve a little longer."

"Do as you like," Jonn started around the thin ice, and Bentos with him.

"You'll freeze if you don't make it before the night!" Arthas warned them.

They paid no heed. Gionn's teeth chattered as he slapped and twisted his pant legs to free the water turning to ice.

"Be a mate and have a bash at me backside," he told Arthas. The sailor paused, but Gionn spread his arms and legs in offering, and soon he felt generous slaps breaking his cloak into folds once more. He dreaded the climb back up the temple, the huddled dark, which would be sleepless, and the waking nightmare as they walked back to the ice again in the morning with visions of open sea and missing ships.

"You're not the cunt I hoped to find meself agreein' with," Gionn thanked his companion. They watched the two men take step after firm step over the icy plain until they blurred in a light snow swept off the top of a distant sea, then turned for Omera's temple.

Tunguk spun the braided sling over his head and whipped another rock from his pile over the edge. There was a delay, then the sharp clunk of wood came back over the sound of the nearby surf. He loosed another, and another, the pause between stretching as his collection dwindled. It was not Kjartke whose presence he felt behind him. Tunguk became more self-conscious of his casts. Nothing about them changed, but he felt the subtle weight of an element of performance. He determined not to acknowledge the visitor, and for a while, aimed his rocks with a growing hope that the succession would bore the interloper away. His concentration returned to his task. The rhythm of the projectiles passing from his hand into the pouch, then sailing over the horizon captivated him, until soon he forgot for a moment, then another. The thought faded. It might well have left, or deceived him from the beginning. The motion seized him so that he separated from all that led him to this precipice, and all he dreamed of when he left. It became round as the floor of a tukit, an eddy just off the main current. Rock on distant rock— on occasion, the satisfying thump of wood.

It startled him when the boy spoke.

"This is what old men do?" The pest from town joined him, and considered the line of sea beyond the edge. "I will find a good death before I gather rocks."

The feeling of an audience returned to Tunguk. He put an extra snap on the next toss.

"What do you hate?" The boy leaned out over the edge. Tunguk slid closer and did the same. He threw another. It whistled through the air 200 feet below where it cracked off a wood launch ramp in the cove below. "A fine enemy," the pest sneered.

"It is a secret a young man must learn: choose those you can beat."

"That is why you are a peltast. Where are your friends? Someone should take you home."

"They are in trouble," Tunguk admitted.

The pest raised a scornful smile. "Do you tell yourself you are helping?"

"I am no peltast. I am rioting." The boy was unimpressed with the distinction. "A peltast hides where he cannot be reached. For a young warrior, eager to spill blood, he makes a hateful rain. There is nothing to do but curse his tormentor and wait for him to run out of stones. It is the worst storm to weather. You kill him six hundred ways before the last is thrown. Men are shredded like a tunic. Others hide well, then rush forward blind with anger to be slain. Other times, they do the worst to those they overtake. But a riot is different."

"Stones are stones. It is the work of those without courage."

"It is a different kind of courage. The peltast invites battle. The rioter cannot withstand it. The people speak as one with great consequence. The rocks are their words. I have traveled, but never have I joined the people's unrest. It is one more thing for an old man—for those who like to count."

Kjartke's head topped a rise. Her belly swelled and she held her tunic to herself with both arms.

"You will probably carve a bead for it." The pest looked at the woman with disdain. They both held their tongues as she neared. Kjartke bent her knees and let the tail of her tunic fall. Tunguk's pile toppled with fresh rocks. She looked at him with suspicion before she turned. It was the way she regarded him when she wondered if he faltered and did well to hide it. They waited for her to disappear.

"Your memory is good? I think there is a way down."

"There is."

"Once it is dark, they will not worry about being hit on the climb."

The pest's eyes widened. "There are men." He thought it over. "I can find it."

"Soon. There is light left." He held out a stone. "Will you join me?"

Tunguk watched as the disgust turned to amusement, where it remained for the boy while much deeper it passed to something else. His left hand closed around a stone. Two more arced over the cliff in unison.

The crash of the occasional missile rang out though they could no longer see them fall against the sky. They pressed their backs against the wall of the cove. An afternoon of work lost. It wouldn't have bothered the three navy carpenters but for the way they spent it. They'd been warned of the riot—that boys may test their vigilance around the piles of timber and baskets of nails that fed their work on the second effort to build a new temporary ramp for the Calm Harbor. They thought it would be many, or none, and nothing a steel point couldn't deter. The admiral didn't even bother to reinforce them.

So it came as a surprise when the first missile hurtled down with enough force to dent one of the main timbers to the thickness of two fingers. At that height, their bones would fare worse than the Amposi hardwood. Unay took it as more than mere inconvenience. He bore the insult when the first ramp failed Costig's eye—when a marine decided he knew more of a build than the one whose trade it was. Now he was confined to the site until it was done, while boys gathered now and then at the boat launch, pretending to wait for a craft while watching for slack in the men's attention so they could disappear with a handful of nails or a scrap of wood. This was the first direct harassment, though. There could be no call for it but to irritate him, and it had done that. Above all, the persistence of the one or two squains who dinged their build wore on him. It was as though the rioters had assigned a crew just as remote and forgotten as his to remind him of his importance.

Now he listened to the clatter and built the mouth of the route in his vision. He had climbed it many times—it was hard, but far shorter than the long trail back to the cliffs. By day, the hand-over-foot route would have exposed them to easy hurls. But now, it was a short dash beyond the ramp, and no blind toss would stop them. They gathered their spears, waited for one more to hit, then hurried past with ease before the next fell in their wake.

Short spears in hand, they probed for the trail, and moments later were ascending while sputtering rocks skipped below. A breeze swirled into the cove, and Unay halted the short column while it whistled through the outcrops like a swarm of feet scampering over the face of the cliffs. A gust so deep in the cove was rare, and usually signaled a turn in the weather, though not for some time yet. There were few stretches when every hand and foot was not simultaneously occupied. Climbing with a spear was fine during the day, but it was hard to see where to rest the butt to make it any use as a staff, so he tapped quietly for the next hold.

The heights and the darkness stirred the kaim. He was no admirer of the Mattaka spirits, and they grew more daring the farther one went from town. Twice, he halted and swore he heard a scrape of feet a little behind them, but an appeal to the night gleaned nothing. It would not surprise him for some iniquitous creature to try to trip an Amposi from the wall like an invader cast down while scaling a stronghold.

It was a relief when all three of them stood upright at the top, the winds no longer pretending they would cooperate for long. The faint tap of rocks striking below was still audible, so they proceeded with care along the cliff edge, several yards back and testing the way with the butt of a spear. Finally, Unay heard it: the faintest click of rocks. He inched ahead until a silhouette swung between him and an early star. Some time later, the arm passed again, and the rest of it became visible. A dark shape concealed in a hood crouched on the snow. He shook the spear of the man behind him, and the signal passed to the third. They readied themselves to relieve the nuisance. Unay had no thoughts of prisoners. He was close enough to the sea that Costig need not find out, and whoever sent this peltast couldn't protest if they missed him at all.

Unay fanned away, aiming to cut off retreat and pin the slinger to the edge. The rocks continued, and he simmered with excitement that their arrival would be announced with a spear point.

The night shattered with an inhuman howl, followed by a series of ferocious barks. A pair of eyes lit up ten yards away and danced side to side with a fury that froze his blood. The cloaked figure stood, and his beast lunged. Unay leveled his quaking spear and heard footsteps behind him scrambling back the way they came. The eyes jerked, and he realized the brute was tethered to its master. He needed no more encouragement. Unay slipped and fled toward the trail. He listened with great care for the sound of hideous feet scratching after him, but the baying grew in distance. He saw a flutter of movement at the entrance to the climb— one of the men sliding away for his life, he was sure. Unay stepped forward to follow.

The board struck him across the forehead. His vision spun though it was pitch black. The cold on his neck and head told him he was lying down in the snow. Unay's spear was inches away and might as well have been a league apart. He heard boots beside him, and awaited the last strike with some relief that it was not the monster, still howling its approval. He felt a hand at his belt. His adze slipped free of the knot. The cries of the beast faded into the distance. The blow never came. His eyes closed, and sleep washed over him.

Foster crouched on the gunwale and gauged the distance. No one slept the previous night. Like blind men, they stabbed their oars at the advancing crust to chip and pry free the fingers that clawed at the *Gairhle*. The morning proved the effort. Sometime after midnight the north wind, after a determined pounding, managed to fuse the pack. There was no lead, no loose shards to push through. The ice became one in all places except a narrow hollow around the ship itself—a pond of a few feet that froze shut by the minute against the pounding oars. The ship didn't bob. There was ice-enough beneath her to hold her, but slack that allowed a little twist to remind them they weren't yet stuck.

Overnight the north wind finally breathed its last, granting them calm for the first time in days. They awoke to a fog bleeding their way from land. The berg was gone altogether. Beyond a hundred yards landward, the wisps overlapped to swallow the visibility. Now a grimmer sign rose out of the west. The prevailing wind fluttered to life. To Foster, it meant no more than they took the wind broadside, but the saltier hands sprung into the kind of diligence that precedes a panic. Corm expected the pack to break—a temporary congregation that would soon scatter at the return of the westerlies.

"Fast to starboard!" Was the order, and like every other order, it made no sense to Foster until the others acted. One end of a rope spun and stretched over the ice, and two men followed. It was only a few feet down, but every part of the boat was slick with a frozen film, and with no way to gauge the thickness of the pack, the crew rejoiced when the men didn't just plunge through. A light anchor stone followed, and soon the boat was taut to the edge, and every hand on the starboard side poured over.

As Foster prepared to leap, someone from the stern slid out on the landing and smashed into his shoulder with a scream. The shape of the limb sickened Foster when the man sat up. Immediately, three others lifted him and hung on the arm, yanking and twisting in a way that

Foster couldn't watch. Most of the men were over. He felt the press of inevitability. Once more he had to do something he would never choose because the others had chosen for him.

He flung himself as far as he could and rolled through on ice as hard as concrete. Another rope followed him. He wasn't sure what to do with it, but he was nearest, so he grabbed it and pulled out the slack from the Mattaka boys who held the other end. Hogue side-stepped another anchor that seemed intended to crush his legs, then secured it to Foster's line.

"Away, the squain docogon!" Corm boomed to scattered laughter. The men aboard lifted the Mattaka skin boat, impossibly light for its size, and passed it down to those on the ice. The last time he saw it, just before sunset, it was a flaccid tent, unearthed from the depths of the hold where he never knew it resided. This was the whaler's equivalent of an inflatable life raft, Foster figured. A dim flash of a floating orange wigwam returned to him, shrinking into the massive seas behind the *Qarapara*. The spinnaker and two of the best sewers—no small compliment on a whaler, apparently—spent all afternoon and through the night lashing the bones and stitching the hide, so that it looked something like a seaworthy craft except for a few ends flapping here and there.

Eckerd tossed over a sack of pennants, and the men rummaged past the white ones for the various shades and fades of red. He knew little enough of the ropes and the ice that he put himself in line to receive one. The floe secured, they would fan out in sight of one another from the ship in a widening arc. The men on the iceberg had to know they wouldn't be getting a taxi. If they did the only thing they could, they should arrive through the fog at a red triangle funneling them to the ship. Foster was confident this was a job he could excel at.

Corm's enormous frame hurtled through the air and tucked into a soft roll that shamed Foster's own delicate landing. He walked straight to the injured sailor and clapped him on his newly-reinstalled shoulder. "You fly like a fuckin' penguin!" The man let out a hearty laugh that swallowed his pain like a rock beneath a stream, without a hint of self-pity.

The captain found the spinnaker. "How long?"

"Sooner'n your fat arse finds a way back on the ship."

"You'll have no qualms about sailin' in your own work?"

"A great many," Irilo replied.

"Hoy!" Corm called to all present. "This fine vessel requires a captain. Ordacles?" He joked.

"Fuck off! I'll swim before I sail a carcass."

"Right, then. Every captain has to start somewhere." No one flinched for fear of being volun-told. "With any luck, you'll carry it there and back. Come on, sogers. Don't make me choose who to send to their death. Half of you wanted it." None but the westerlies had anything to say. "I don't suppose any of you has experience on a squain boat."

Foster's eyes darted to Bucket and Tunguk.

Gionn waited for Arthas to finish his descent this time. The fog was thick enough that they couldn't see the shelf until their feet hit it, nor the ice on which they now stood. Little strands here and there began to set off with the new breeze, but the direction of the ship was a memory he lost confidence in by the moment. Were it land, he would head north, this way and that, and sure as a piss found the water, he'd be on the ship. But even a stuck ship moved with the pack. It may be where he saw it, or miles east by now.

"Told you it was wise to wait, cunt." Gionn boasted. "Now we can't see far enough to spit, and the westerlies'll make us our own rafts before midday. Nothin' I hate more than a dull walk."

"At least it'll be a dry one. If we hurry."

Gionn extended his arm and pointed with a bladed palm, then swiveled a little to his right. "I make that northwest."

"Agreed. She lies more north, I think. Wind's not been at it long."

"I think we all know whose blade is bigger. Let's compare ice experience. I got none, but I know the outside of the pack moves a lot faster than the bit we're on. Could be more west than you suppose."

"I've cut ice, and seen pack, but never fast in it. I did row with a lad who spent a winter under the ship tryin' to get free of Nunoc, though. Have you ever seen a mirror?"

Gionn thought it over. "No."

"It's like a polished boss of bronze—"

"I get the fuckin' notion."

Arthas collected himself. "The pack's the same: she bends the near to far, and far appears within reach. Whatever time we think we got, it'll be more if we rush, or less if we idle."

"Have you ever seen a stair step? It goes up, then right, then up, then right." Gionn drew the shape in the air.

"Fuck off. Aye, I take your point. More chance of seein' somethin'. But I say we split. You start west of me, just in sight. Always in sight. We make ten paces north, then ten west."

"Is that as high as you can count? Seems like a fuckin' nuisance."

"It was you I was worried about. Fifty then."

"Better that way. I'd hate to show up arm-in-arm with the captain's bane."

"If we lose sight, I won't be able to hear you against the wind. I'll stay put and call your name, you find me." Arthas voice already grew faint as Gionn drifted with the wind. He stopped.

"In case I never see you again: why does Corm fuckin' hate you?"

"He doesn't!" Arthas cupped his hands. "You never rubbed a captain wrong?"

"Me? I'm the unbedded love of all the fleets. It'd be an insufferable bastard who could find a cross word for Gionn! I'll teach you how to not be such a miserable shit when we get back to the *Gairhle*!"

Gionn spun as he walked, checking every few steps that Arthas remained in sight. The farther he dared, the better their chances, but only if they could keep sight. When his mate became a dull shade separated by wisps of fog, he stopped and signaled, and saw it returned. As they paced out the count, Gionn scanned the ice for signs of yesterday's swamp. Wide as it was, he had to be on it by now. Unless the whole pack had already turned around the temple like the field of stars around the spear that protruded from the head of Tair. It was a great temptation to recognize some whorl underfoot. His pulse quickened and he glanced at his only landmark, counting unheard paces far to his left. The looming temple vanished in the first fifty. He was adrift, boatless. The fog couldn't hold in the growing breeze, he expected, and so knew that it would, just to defy him. At a place in the formless void, he stopped, took the signal, and turned right. Arthas would have his back to follow, but Gionn could only look ahead into the mist.

"One, two..." he said aloud and hated himself for one of those idiots who couldn't make a figure with his mouth shut. The numbers climbed, and with it, his fear that he went too fast, or skipped one though he knew he heard them all. Now he grasped why Arthas wanted it at ten. He resisted the desire to slow, to make sure he didn't drift away while the other calculated or tripped. His doubts again found him and assured him he was lost, never to see another soul. "Thirty…" Walking west to find a ship he last saw north was a special kind of madness. Despair seized him and begged him to turn and run as fast as his feet could carry him north to the fleeing ship. He could leave Arthas to his mirrors and stairs. It climbed his spine in a tremble of dread. He braced as when a wave curls over the beam for another five paces, then turned.

Arthas pointed north again, and Gionn's breath shuddered with gratitude. He thought his was the better place: farther west, and always in earshot. Now he wondered how he would go as far as the *Gairhle* like this.

Twice more, they probed forward, and right. The old panics merely faded to a low taunt, trotting at his heels. He swore Arthas was fainter now. Somehow, one of them must have stepped too long or too short. It as well could have been the fog pouring in from the west. Gionn gathered himself on this half, the northern paces, saving his anxiety for when Arthas stood at his back. He buried his concentration into each number, and spoke loud despite a throat wearing in cold, dry air. It began to feel like there was an actual stair beneath him—something solid taking shape that guided him against the current of chattering spirits. Whether these resided with the ice, or were drug here by him to scamper upon the crystal sea, he couldn't be sure.

His footing slipped a little on twenty-three. It took two more to realize it was not his own shit balance. The top layer of ice sunk by an inch and he slid on a slurry that quickly refilled with water. "Fuck!" Gionn paused, then remembering the tether that the count held between him, forced himself on. "Arthas!" He called without looking up. "Arthas!" A glance confirmed his voice was lost to the wind. He shortened his step was much as he dared. All around him now the surface took on a sheen. It could only have frozen that morning to be so flawlessly smooth, and every step sunk a little deeper through the film.

It was all around him, and he wondered if his mate had the same. By the look of it, Arthas walked solid ice. He didn't look up at Gionn's frantic waving. The only way now was to make fifty. His boots soaked through. Gionn picked out lighter patches and told himself they wet him less. His prints behind him filled. "Forty-five." The water came to his ankles. There was nothing for it. He simply had to rejoin his mate and search for a better route together.

"Forty-*seven*!" Gionn shouted the second part faithfully as he lost his footing and plunged through a section on his hands and knees. Bits of ice swirled under his stomach. He righted himself as fast as he could and stumbled three more steps, fell again, then stood and turned into the wind.

Fog swept by him like a tide. "*Arthas*!" He shouted in futility. His mate had vanished in the haze.

Foster adjusted the rope higher on his shoulder. The weight was trivial, but the boat slung between them became a sail for every gust of the wind, now finding its stride. One moment, he could see two tiers of red pennants snapping behind him in the distance, and the next the fog would take them, return the outermost, and then blanket the group so he could just make out Bucket and Tunguk at the front, fighting with their own ropes to hold the Mattaka craft from whisking them off their feet.

An artillery report sounded behind them. Palqua must have taken his concern for superstition. "Do not worry. It is only the pack breaking." That was exactly what Foster feared, and the reason for the boat. The former officer shouted instructions to the boys up front, steering them a little west to compensate for their leeward drift. Foster didn't know whether to take it as a compliment that the three of them drew such esteemed company, or for a sign that Corm thought they weren't likely to return. The only thing they'd have to do if they were lucky is walk, and at worst, paddle across a few yards of water to the next floe if the ice gave. Anyone who knew how a boat worked could have figured that out, but it met with enthusiastic cat calls from the crew when they betrayed their familiarity. It was a joke to them to send the "bow cunts."

A gust caught the bottom of the hull and whipped it into Foster. Palqua slid behind the momentum. In front of him Tunguk lost the rope entirely, and the bow lifted like it would turn the whole thing over the beam. Bucket took a bone to the lip in front of Foster, and the four collapsed on the frame to secure it to the pack.

"Lower," Palqua ordered when they picked it up again. "And eyes wide, lads." Another set of cracks like two quick shots followed by a car sideswiping another reached them from upwind. It couldn't have been as distant as it seemed.

"How far we gonna go?" Foster made the first attempt to nail down something like a plan. The flag men followed a rough order suggested by their nearest neighbors, fanning out by one additional sailor each semicircle from the ship, but neither Corm nor Palqua had a word of advice for the boat crew. As if it were painfully obvious what they were supposed to do. Or impossible to say.

"Crew, temple, or open water," Palqua replied cheerfully. He must have meant the berg—the thing everyone called the "temple of Omera." For all the words he shared with these folks, it tempted Foster to say that they spoke the same language. It made for a fine delusion. Between the boat slang and the common terms that meant something else entirely, he wondered if he really knew what people were saying.

Sometimes he knew he didn't, but how many confident misunderstandings had he already stumbled through? His mind turned to the *old* Tunguk and Kjartke, and the greater struggle to convey meaning to the Mattaka—hell, even the ones in front of him. His gaze cast down at the polished ice. Memories of Parks across empty beers accused him of having "gone full Appalachia," incomprehensible in drawl and description. He knew he'd miss the bastard. What he didn't realize was *which* bastard. It wasn't his Navy friend. It was the fur-covered, two-legged, song-singing whiner who embarrassed him with how he couldn't see, or care, how alien he was. Who spoke to natives like they were millennial bros from Santa Cruz. As if by addressing the world like it was his own, he could prevent himself from having to learn the first thing about the place he ended up—or to accept it. That Parks held a line that kept him from sweeping out to sea, adrift in a madness with no point of reference, boatless on a spinning surface.

"*Taima*! There!" Tunguk shouted.

His finger seemed to disappear into the fog bank. The wind cleared a fold like blowing up the tail of a long coat. Foster felt a pang of terror at the first glimpse of a dim, inhuman figure, covered soon by another cloud. The boys doubled the pace without an order. In less than a minute, the misty shield passed in a wide swathe that tripled their field of vision. A man lumbered over the ice from their right in nearly the same direction as the wind. His southeast bearing would cross their path well ahead, and if he kept it, he wouldn't find berg or boat.

"It's not Gionn." Foster stated flatly. He knew that shape in any visibility.

"We will find your mate," Palqua reassured him, missing the point entirely. "Head him off!"

They worked up a quick trot, as fast as their load and the footing allowed. Once more, fog moved between them but it never fully obscured the sailor, and when it left Foster had the sense the wind would clear it entirely if they could stay out long enough.

"Hey! Stop!" He called out, and they all took their turn to no avail. The closer they drew, the less sure he was that it was even one of their party, though that seemed impossible. The man's gait felt absent of purpose. It was slow enough that four dudes carrying a boat overtook him. Palqua told the bucket boys to hold down the boat in his path. The man didn't notice them at all until Foster and the dinghy captain took him by the arms.

The face was wind-gnawed and crusted white on the nose and earlobes, lips blistered, lashes and nostrils caked with ice. His eyes seemed to both take them in and gaze right through them.

"Jonn! Where are the others?" Palqua guided him toward the boat. Jonn leaned heavily into the Amposi without reply. Foster got the sense they could point him any way they liked, let him go, and he would just keep walking. The boys greeted them with expressions of horror.

"What're we gonna do with this motherfucker while we look for the rest?" Foster asked. "He'll be lucky to make it straight back to the ship."

The word lit some dim fuel in the man. At the sight of the Mattaka boat, he stumbled free, put both hands on the gunwale, and threw himself in so hard, Foster was sure the bone frame would break and the leather tear on the ice beneath it. Jonn curled up and shook.

"Nah. Hey brother! You gotta get out. This ain't no stretcher."

"Jonn!" Palqua stepped in, Foster behind him, and tried to lift the sailor by his elbows. "We cannot carry you in this boat. Come on, lad. We will walk with you." Jonn flailed at their grips and broke free, his feet kicking hard against the ribs. They jumped out and begged him to stop, fearing the boat would come apart. Weak as he was, Jonn wore a solid

200 pounds, and stood a few inches taller than Foster's 5'9. With Palqua himself, at 5'5, and the Mattaka boys well-shorter, there was no one to overpower the muscled rower.

"Give him your cloak."

Foster looked at Palqua with disbelief. He met the stare, and didn't repeat the order, but an old habit of subordination peeled the precious layer from Foster's back and draped it over Jonn head-to-toe.

"Did you bring a knife?"

Foster nodded.

"If we try to carry him, the hull may rip. It is meant to hold men when there is water beneath."

"Then how do we find the others?"

"It is a good question, if there remain any others. I do not think it wise to split, or to go without a boat the way the wind sets on the ice. But the question I ask is how to do *we* return? Leave me now, I will think on it."

Foster panned over the expanse in every direction, less sure of which they might come from. Or, if they were anything like this, whether it was a good idea to find them.

"Aye, sir. What do I do with the knife?"

Palqua smiled apologetically. "If he is too much to remove all at once, we will have to do it in parts."

Furious barking snatched him from sleep. Parks awoke to the wigwam cover over his face, like a corpse awaiting removal from a battlefield. He swiped it away in irritation and coughed the stale air from his lungs with a dry wheeze. His sinuses flared at each hack under tension of his permanent headache. Precious sleep only came when the pain grew so intolerable and his body so exhausted that he passed out into a fitful nightmare in which he was still aware of too many things to rest. The dark sky refused to gauge the time. Minutes or hours lumbered past. Parks wanted no part of waking.

The wild baying belonged to the male, the crazy one. No one beat him or yelled at him to shut up, which meant they were gone. The jumping shape snapped against the leather rope. Parks wanted to scream at him, but the thought of more than a whisper made his head throb.

That, and he didn't want to remind the foot-eater that he was still around, not knowing how much slack they left in his leash.

Another voice answered with a howl, a little ways away. The response stoked the dog's vigor, and he struggled to commit between urgent barking and gnawing at the line that held him in frustration. It was like a smoke alarm Parks couldn't turn off, splitting his head and fraying his sanity to warn him of what he knew.

The dogs' exchange grew until they saw each other. The female shut up, but the one restrained tried to crash out of his skin with jealousy until Parks heard a thump and a yelp, and boots scraped the snow around him. The smaller dog led Kjartke on a leash and fought to sniff Parks' face. Another pair of voices bounded with excitement in Reverse-Eskimo. They could hardly speak without laughing. It rang, unsettling in his ears, and he realized it was more than his agony. Parks had never heard Kjartke laugh at all, except to mock some stupidity of his. Now she rolled with unbridled joy, and Joe returned it. A board plunked down beside him, and the old man knelt. He pulled a tool from his belt—hard to tell what, but maybe a hammer—and ran his other hand along the length of the wood, feeling the grain, testing the spring.

They joked in their language, for once unconcerned about drawing attention, or aggravating the sleeping man who wondered each time he drifted off if he would wake again. The glad sound passed over him, but not through.

"What's so funny?" He cleared the sticky phlegm from his throat.

"Tunguk," Kjartke said. Parks felt as isolated as when he awoke to the company of the dog, and remembered when Kjartke went off on him for his and Foster's incomprehensible speech and inside jokes.

His mind slipped to Foster and the coded babble they exchanged when they encountered the women from Kjartke's tribe. The sound of gentle scraping from Joe's tool called up the very different sound of the long knife slicing through whale flesh. Kjartke's forced silence during the encounter. He thought of all the ways he might know someone from his world—even a total stranger—without a word exchanged.

Foster had gone to find that place. Maybe he would come back himself, with a map, a "bird map" of the route. Or if he found the opening, send a team of Navy SEALs to do the deed, their rifles slung under their leather cloaks, rowing a skin boat in from their warship to avoid calling attention. What did Kjartke think when those chicks left without the slightest effort to rescue her?

The overwhelming sense of home swamped him like a wave from a foreign shore, someone else's dream crashing through his quiet beach, inundating his wigwams. It soaked with him guilt. He thought of his own people infiltrating Drummoc with earpieces under hoods to communicate with a destroyer that could annihilate any challenge from the brave Navy, rake the shores with artillery, shatter the simple ways of the Reverse-Eskimos all on his account.

It struck him as a violation of something sacred: an intrusion of a world that had no place here. His secret presence profaned this humble land. Even if no one noticed. Even if he fooled everyone, it felt like a sacrilege deserving of death. This was not that other world. He came here, and now he lay subject to Drummoc on its own terms. If it denied him entrance, or held him for eons, he had to respect the verdict.

He wondered if home would have him back. Would anyone remember him? Parks envisioned himself walking the streets of Santa Cruz, coated in leather and unshaven, and soon looked down to his leg, where the pants hung tied in a knot. He hopped the streets, a stranger, drifter, past the old convenience stores and bars where he once spent his time. Past his own home—occupied by some new family—the same as ever, but hardly recognizable. If there was something that Foster could bring him back to, who was it that would go?

The disheveled image of himself grayed. Its hair hung open like curtains on the shoulders of a fur seal coat. The close-set eyes of the old Eskimo stared back at him, apologetic and foreign. He once again felt an intruder, this time in his daydream. It was not his. It belonged to another. The rows of houses rounded to low wigwams. The trees froze into rock. Shrouded Drummoc stood behind Joe, who brushed over its surface with a nostalgic gaze. Parks felt the meaning of every bead on the story shirt, crying to be heard, impossible to understand for those who never left their coast to cross the tall seas.

The rhythm of the tool on the wood returned him to the peace of the slope. The dogs had long settled. He realized his pain left him for those minutes, and now that it was back, he was glad for it over the torment of the vision. Parks looked up at the silhouette that crouched beside him, a shadow against the heavens, as if a piece had gone missing.

"Joe," he said in a low rasp, then cleared his throat again.

"Brother."

"You're from *here*. Aren't you?"

The tool paused. Parks felt the stillness of Joe, of Kjartke, the dogs. In the dark he couldn't say, but he thought he felt a smile before the soothing scrape of wood resumed.

5

THE VOW

The admiral had only been back for the morning, and already Wendell exhaled at the sense of command that returned to the little station. He glanced over his shoulder at the figure who studied the harbor from the rail of the barc where he left him—the promised barc, and the next task now that he'd exhumed the dead whaler from the bickering lists.

To a man, they knew not to disturb the admiral while he helmed that dry fleet. He would be among them again when the spirit of the day required it. Wendell hoped not soon. Costig could drive like a dog as often as called upon, but like a dog, he couldn't pull with any less than full fury. It would be up to the one who called upon him to steer, and to know when to stop.

Most here answered to a man, but for a certain few, that deaf master was Drummoc. It was true, they also ran to the word of an admiral: a Galichar, a Turrha, at times. But it was a deference. They honored the orders even while they pricked an ear for that voice that commanded a deeper loyalty. He'd seen the tension in Costig when the voices crossed. How he strained to satisfy the loud one in a way that fulfilled only the word of it, while holding as close as was excusable to quiet insistence of the other.

As sergeant-at-arms, Costig once took the order to shake-out the returning miners for the contraband coal that served their offerings and Winter barter. Rather than meet them at the harbor, Costig sailed his marines to Camne Drumlag. He warned them that night they would have to muster for a search the following morning. When the marines found nothing, Costig lagged behind the coal ships that ferried the crews so that by the time he returned to a furious admiral, the miners had enjoyed a night among the bushels on the water, then dispersed to their huts with their trousers unusually heavy.

Wendell listened now to the east wind. It was from there that the weather came. The heads of the crews had ceased their swivel, and their chatter bore a joke that would have been out of place among the urgent shouts a day before. A few days of riot had baptized them, at least as far as they were concerned—those scavenged whalers and lads who still smelled of grass now fancied themselves salted barrels. They no longer crowded like fish. Whether by order or initiative, they spread in little groups to hall and tavern and warehouse, ignoring the mounting squains who sputtered like Urkuk as they passed.

The Mattaka, too, felt different. They had the hang of it now. No longer did they try those places the Navy denied them. Instead, they gathered in what pockets had become their custom in the preceding days, so that Wendell knew at a glance what contingent was where. The initial thrust of passion settled into the low, long pattern, while opportunists passed between them eager for a sign of renewal.

He found his way alone to the seam that took him one row into the buildings of Drummoc—a row no servant of Ampos dared cross except in strength the day before. A mill of sailors marked the huts that held the dry stock, just back of the prison and the waterhouse. Captain Amachar stood outside with his men fanned along the entryways in a slump that suited one assigned to "guard" the latrine. They'd not spoken since the initial interview. Wendell noted the life had seeped most of the way back in since their ride on the dog ship, despite long nights and a turn with Rixtan.

It was a loose word, "captain"—here more than anywhere. Even pared to its naval sense, it said little enough. Nothing to mark a true bluecoat from a winter roustabout with a bit of charm and a few rough mates. You could count that the man knew the lay of a ship, how to shove off and bring her in, and call the sails to those who could handle the particulars. The sails of what ship was another question. A good half of any crew could helm a darraig in known waters. Whether he were a leader of men was another matter. It wasn't the sea beneath their crews in Drummoc.

The longer they served, the less Wendell stood to think of them, so Amachar still enjoyed the praise of ignorance. Among those who stopped for a season or an exile, there were yet more kinds. Some men called captain knew the local waters. Others, like Amachar, could bring one in at Nunoc, or even Ampos. Or they knew the order of battle and how to sink a ram. Seldom were all the same man.

That Nunoc would think him worthy of a swift passage to Drummoc spoke something of Amachar, and that was enough to earn a hopeful admiration from Wendell. Still, it would have to be another he sought. Amachar was a stranger to Neferwet's Foot and the other hunting grounds. Nor could he ask Liam to take him again so soon. Wendell could fuss over the choice once he knew there were men loading his barc with food and water and ballast. When the ship creaked, she'd not fail to whisper the name of her master in his ear.

"Is it yourself I'll speak to about provisions?" Wendell greeted him cheerfully.

"Better to check with the squains," Captain Folmon ducked out of the nearest hut, tall and "stiff as a sailor," as they said of the forward curved posture and a certain stubbornness. He held the flap for Wendell to examine overturned jars and empty baskets, a few men scraping together what bits remained. "The others huts are the same."

"Was there no guard?" Wendell plead.

"Aye, after they looted the hasqa you'd expect one to be posted. Fuckin' Bruco. Dancin' in Costig's footprints while the lads traded their rocks for meat. At least the empty prison was safe behind a hundred spears." He thumbed toward the building a stone's throw away.

"Then it won't be much trouble to bring what's left to me barc."

"Maybe a barrel. Where to?"

"Huntin' camp, again. Wouldn't mind four or five more. Have we got water?"

"That, at least, he had the sense to post. But they got to the whole of the dry stock, and the colony stores, as well. None but the Navy meat left, and a few sides of blubber too heavy to haul off."

"Good the admiral's back from his hunt, then," Wendell brushed it aside.

Folmon accompanied him to the storefronts of the main row, where the sun hung back behind budding clouds.

"Fancy a blow?" Wendell asked.

Folmon considered the skies. "Should be enough to get you out of the harbor. It'd be kind of you to bring back a few spare carcasses."

"That'll be the order of the day for whoever I send."

Folsom blinked. "Then it's not you he sent?"

"It is, aye, but I've a nose that I'm needed here." They nodded past the guards into the main warehouse from which the Navy filled their bowls. Folmon waited until they passed the sailors.

"You've probably got enough leeway with the old man that you can skirt an order," Folmon seemed to admit the calculation. Wendell scanned the dim room in the shafts and spheres of light that played from the doorway and a few lamps along the wall. Much of it was "wet," meant to be taken fresh. Good enough for rations on land, but he didn't dare fill his barrels with what might sour at sea. It was other men who would sicken or starve, and though he wouldn't be going with them, he didn't care to waste a crew on a lazy order.

"Is there dry?"

"Some. Most of it for the poorman's quarters." Wendell recalled the charitable provisions were also housed under a Navy roof. Folmon probed his silence. "An ill omen, two runs to the huntin' camp in as many months. Should I chew me supper twice?"

Wendell chuckled. "I've faith it'll come through," he assured Folmon, if not himself.

They reemerged into the street, where a growing faction of Mattaka sat among piles of their things like refugees. Their lungs had long tired of beseeching the Navy. Individuals passed between relatives and smaller gatherings, into town and back out. It would have the early feel of a feast day but for the sullen faces.

Foster scowled at them. "Already sorted through their neighbors, and now it's on to us." Voices pitched as an argument broke out on the fringes between a woman and several older ones. The main group quickly turned against her. That would be the honest mothers, and those too weak for dishonest labors. A second woman pushed through to take her by the hair, and skipped after to swing and spit as she pulled away.

"Would be a blessin' if you could leave it to sort itself, wouldn't it?" Wendell probed hopefully.

Folmon laughed. "I'll load your barrels, and pass on your barc. Bruco suddenly finds himself with less to do, if you need a man."

"I need one who'll fill our stores."

Folmon nodded his admission. "There's one over there," he indicated Costig, set like a statue on the gunwale of the viceroy's ship. "Plenty of food left in Drummoc. We need only go door to door. A spear's the cure for a looter's hunger."

"Are you volunteerin'?"

Folmon held his tongue at the remark.

"Take it from the poorman's quarters," Wendell clapped him on the shoulder and left him.

"Arthas!"

Gionn stumbled and slid. His foot broke the surface anew, and he retreated from the slurry to the tangle of prints, winding around themselves over the floe. They arced from solid footing into the edge of the mush, swung out and tried again, and circled while strands of fog slipped between them. He damned himself for not just turning in his own tracks and braving the wet to reach his mate. He knew it would hold—it already had, just moments ago. Instead, his panic flung him north for firmer ice and not until he found it did he double back, now out of sight of his trail. Did he double back? The temple of Omera, the *Gairhle*, they were all gone. His reckoning faced him west, and the breeze confirmed it, but lost by a foot was lost by a mile.

He stopped and pricked his ears. Were the cunt half as concerned as he, his name would come on the wind. His own breath blew east and away, yet he still sent it at intervals, in case the sailor had already passed. There was nothing to the wind but a gathering momentum. Gionn couldn't feel it yet, but he knew the ice itself moved beneath his feet. A great hammer blow sang from somewhere north. A shorter series relayed from the west like quick steps coming his way. He paused, and when he started again, his wet boots, frozen to the surface, cracked free from a thin film.

Fuck Arthas, he thought. What's he but another boatless thing? Now Gionn was going the wrong way. What he needed was the *Gairhle*, if she hadn't already freed herself from the splintering perimeter. *Jonn. Bentos.* So much for a lump of coal and a shit prayer. They were cleaved, and the floes were soon to follow. Gionn swung around, north-by-northeast if he had any sense of it. There were no more prints or hand signs or loud cunts to guide him. Nothing but open water would break his pace now. *Fast and true*, he prayed to who might listen, and doubled his short steps while he concocted the stories he would tell Corm of how the others met their end. None of them were the simple truth: he'd claim they became separated, against sound advice; a fight over an axe, a desperate run to bring help for injured mates; a pact that none should come to harm on another's account. Even as he dreamed his salvation, he couldn't leave behind his lies.

Gionn had to remind himself to look down on occasion for the fissure a foul goddess lay for him. So fixed was he on the fog stirring past him, eyes skimming the distance for a silhouette to appear like a morsel in a soup, that he passed it before he noticed the bluer dimples against the bone-white floe. He scurried back and bent over at the shallow lip around the prints, not quite smoothed by the water that froze within. The surface may well have been rock again now. They couldn't be his, by place or time. Someone trod here when it was wet, and they followed a different course than Gionn.

Jonn or Bentos, he thought. To his death. As he turned to retake his line, doubt found him in the fog. Could they have known better than he? Perhaps in a clear moment under the moon they sighted a mast—just one of them, it seemed. Or he'd got himself spun around while he wandered out to drown. He cocked a head, and decided to follow for a few steps, his eyes still squinting in the direction he suspected he should have gone.

A howl of the wind that could have been a voice pricked him, but he held his course. It was as like to be the ice squealing itself apart. Another crack from the west assured him that what lie that way was lost. Too much east, though. That where this led him. His neck soon ached as the turn increased and he wondered if he still sighted the way. *Camne Drumlag*. The name reared within him. Could he not have bent his pride to sit a winter in careless vigil over some Amposi official for the same argot that Foster withheld? It was as though no sooner than he escaped the most awful place yet in all his wide travels, he would find a new contender to make him fond of the old.

Gionn scraped to a halt. He thought he stumbled to either side of the trail, and it took stillness to see that it was the other way around. That wasn't what stopped him. While this one disappeared ahead, another crossed it from the south and swerved west again, while he could make out a third a little north moving nearly parallel to his own. He'd fallen into the track of a drunken, circling fool.

He swore as he tossed aside the footprints like a shield in retreat and sprinted the way he knew—and knew he should have known—the ship lay.

"You fuck of a blind cunt, I told you not to go!" He screamed at—perhaps Jonn, Bentos. He hardly knew anything but that it made him feel very wise despite his imminent death. In his panic, he erupted in a foul argument, in which he could not identify speaker or respondent. "Foster would've killed you soon enough, impatient shit. Who walks the sea like a madman? Leopard Seal, me arse. Shows you to leave a mate. Fuck Costig! Fuck Corm! *Hoy! Gairhle!* Next time, let the bastards mutiny. I'll carve the 'M' meself. Fuckin' idiot, fuckin' idiot, fuckin' idiot! Hope you're fast beneath the ice of Manhas. *Hoy!* They'll never hear you, those deaf boot-scrapes. Piss, fuck, squain! *Foster! Hold up, me son!?* To Manhas with Foster! May he sink the lot of you for a pinch of gold, and in his dyin' breath—"

Gionn collided with something and tumbled forward, bracing to feel the ice shatter and the sea envelop him. Instead, it was a dull thud and a soft moan beneath. He pressed himself up and stared down at the snow-crusted beard he so despised.

"Get off me, bitch!"

He grinned as wide as the cold would allow and planted a dry kiss on Foster's forehead.

The blanket snapped back and Parks cinched his eyelids. Before he could issue a word of protest he already felt himself working onto an elbow, his newest habit. His leg hummed in anticipation of what would come: a rough nurse wringing the fluid out of the hole that the surgeon failed to close; the cruel Reverse-Eskimo physical therapist who forced him to sit up and chew regurgitated paste, maybe swallow some water, as often as he woke. But the tender hand didn't loop under his arm. No words of humiliation came. The sled creaked under his shift, and when he opened for look, a different dread filled him.

It was the dread of these relentless dreams. All around glowed a rough gray dome of sky, laid out in uneven grids of latitude and longitude, the sky of a child drawing squares to converge at an invisible pole overhead. It felt so close as to press in on him, to turn back his breath and the sound of his fidgeting. Being awake was agony enough, but the visions that imposed themselves going and coming from restless sleep seemed to delight in his torment. They didn't even care if he knew. A vague half-awareness hung in the air. Half the world around him, and half another, projected onto every convenient surface. He vacillated back and forth, one foot in reality and one—Parks caught himself and snorted at his own expense. He blushed at the thought of Joe's "spirits" mocking him. Soon one would appear to do something that felt cryptic and significant. He would pore over the clues when he awoke to prep for some exam that would come without announcement. But they never came twice. Each place gave to the next with no thread of connection, until the last one became a feeling without words. A pang. A throb, coursing in the background like those that gripped his body but never revealed their source or their cure.

He felt them as loss, or claustrophobia, or a sense of things starting without him. For now, he stared at the luminous sky. Something would pop out and speak to him any moment. A monster. If he was lucky, Foster, or an ex-girlfriend. The curdling in his stomach started up so he fixated on one of the crooked seams where north curved over west. *Wake up. If you can't wake up*, he bargained, *dream what you want*. Parks strained his forehead. *Foster*. He willed his friend to appear out of the gloom. He'd return with a boat. Parks held the surface with growing intensity, until he felt he had to pee, and if he tried any harder, it would end up down his leg. He let out a breath and closed his eyes. When he blinked open again, the grid was still there.

He refocused: surely the lines would disappear, and he would be under the stars. When they remained, he blurred his vision and they melted together. The dream persisted. Just him, trapped in a shoddy globe, longer than it was wide, featureless, a world of one. The shortness of breath returned. The blanket felt heavy on his chest, holding his lungs down. He flung it down past his waist and pivoted onto his good hip faster than he should have. His left side wailed, but the rest of his body followed through the new routine until he sat upright. Parks gazed at the sky in confusion while it alternated between very close and miles away. His hand rose and reached overhead. It stopped cold mere inches from his face.

"It is good?" Eskimo Joe appeared at his feet. "Kjartke feared it will bury us."

Parks yanked his freezing palm back. The man who spoke was as real as the roof. The room came into focus—it was a *room*, just wider than the sled and taller than his head.

"Igloo?"

Joe betrayed surprise. "*Aklu*—you know this word?"

"I know all the good words. Pretty sure it's '*igloo*.'"

Joe crouch-scooted to his side. "You must eat." The old man pulled a piece of dried seal from a sack and ripped off a hunk with his teeth.

"I have to pee. Where's Kjartke?"

"Glad to be rid of us."

Parks tensed. "She coming back?"

"No."

"Serious?"

Joe drooled a paste of meat into his fingers and held it out to Parks' wrinkled nose. "Eat."

"Dude, that's foul."

"It is the same you eat all along."

"Yeah, but Kjartke chews it." Joe didn't answer, as if he was still waiting for the explanation. Parks went on. "I mean, it's not like it's gay, but…it's like, not hot, either."

Joe wiped the meat back into his own mouth and extended the stiff chunk of seal. Parks considered it, then took the end in his mouth. The mere pressure of a bite on the leather jerky gave him a headache and sent waves of pain to his groin. He sawed his teeth gingerly until a piece came loose, then he worked it over in the tiniest bites he could produce.

"I have to pee," he announced again. "Sorry. I forget how we handle that. I feel like I haven't had to go since…" He nodded at his leg. "Is that a Kjartke thing? Please just say yes."

"You go many times."

"How?"

Eskimo Joe nodded at Parks' trousers, and he reddened. "When you are done, call to me. Quietly. We will clean the wound."

"Are people still chasing us?" Parks read his silence. "You think we'll get away?"

Tunguk crawled out the narrow opening, just large enough for a sled to slide through. The dogs hurried to their feet and pulled at their tethers, whimpering for any kind of change. He looked to the tracks that led here from the foothills beyond the Calm Harbor, sled and paw and foot extending in long curves into high country, unbroken to the camp where they rested, and before that, the home of Sawipelagannapuk if anyone cared to trace them. They chewed into one another where he came upon the right ice, and built the aklu. High above, the thin clouds spread like the skin of a fish, and beneath ran many figures: waves and ships and hunters who struggled after game, more numerous now than when he lay the first block. The light remained good. A calm gossiped of his excess. It said Tunguk was bold to raise something so permanent in fine weather, when others plowed his wake. He followed the tracks of Kjartke over the rise to look upon the town.

"You have often come upon me when I do not want it. Maybe I can trouble you?" He said aloud.

The boy appeared irked to leave his daydreams. He glanced at the aklu and snickered. "Do you think you will be here long?"

"Not if we are caught in a storm without shelter."

He searched the skies. "What storm? It is clear to the head of Urkuk."

"The storm that must fill our tracks if we will live. Do you see where it stops?" Tunguk pointed downhill where the snowline foamed at the bare rock like dying surf. Beyond it, so near they could see the curves of the tukits, lay Drummoc. "We can go no farther with the sled."

"Go where? To your death? You are pursued."

"Aye, they will not forget your stones at the Calm Harbor. If they look, they will find us."

The boy beamed with disdain. "*Your* stones. And they will take you sooner if your snow washes you into Drummoc."

"Maybe. What waits is less certain than what lies behind."

The youth's brow furrowed then domed in the middle as though to plead: "There must be *something* you can tell me. I can see it is no worthy end, but in between. Were there not deeds that many would speak of?"

"What end? I am still before you!" Tunguk grinned. "And you, you are here, too. Would you rather dream yourself upon some ship when your days have doubled? With no name for it, or the men of the crew, and robbed of all that brought you?"

"Aye! Do not speak to me of onik, old man. I know to make my steps small, but I cannot bear to move if I do not know they will lead me somewhere."

Tunguk nodded. "I do not speak of onik. A thread is one thing, and the one who sews it, another. Look." He pointed behind him. "I have many days behind me, and few ahead, whatever comes. But I have built an aklu. I cut the blocks, and laid them myself." The boy rolled his eyes as when an elder starts in on a suffocating tale.

"I could have laid this thread grimly, believing my greatness will come soon. Six hundred stitches, exact in their misery. I admit this is often what I have done. Then I arrive, and soon, I move on. But on this occasion, I was glad for each block, each cut. I did not dream of riding a three-legged dog into battle. To dream so far ahead is the relief of the young, and to hate each step along the way is the price for taking your spoils before they arrive. Maybe it will collapse and kill him—Kjartke thinks so. Or a storm may prolong us, but why wait?. Glory, no glory, I assure you if you build an aklu when you are my age, every block will be your joy."

"Then you have called on me to praise your wise words and your aklu. You want my blessing for your end."

"Perhaps. I tell myself I have called you for another purpose." The boy struggled to hide his anticipation lest it flatter Tunguk. "There are no wise words I can offer you. You will hate all that you do, and never arrive where you seek. I call because I like talking to you." The pest reacted with alarm. "When you are old, in some hateful land, maybe you will remember how you cursed every footfall, and it will bring a smile, that it was your curses that brought you here, no place you sought. That course was the only one that could have led you to cut a block, to build an aklu. And you will know then that each curse was your joy."

The boy stared at Drummoc—straight *through* Drummoc, until he found it: "If that is your end, you'll have no praise from me."

Tunguk looked to the high, thin clouds. "Then help me to ride a three-legged dog into battle. Pray for storm."

Gionn scrambled up and half-lifted, half-embraced his companion.

"Over here!" Foster called into the fog. Then lower, to Gionn: "Shout the whole fuckin' plan next time." A pair of silhouettes brightened into the bucket-bearers, and Foster swallowed whatever he was going to say.

A minute of peeling through the fog brought a pair of figures into view. Gionn shoved ahead.

"Arthas!" The sailor stood beside Palqua. Foster took some satisfaction in watching Gionn trot toward the man for what might have been an ecstatic reunion before he froze stiff when the little skin boat failed to grow into the *Gairhle*.

"*Cunt!*" He seemed to mean Foster. "Why did you make me kiss you when I'm still fucked?" Gionn leaned over the side to take in Jonn, quaking under Foster's cloak. He looked to Palqua, then the Mattaka boys. "They stranded us!"

"Chill, brother. They're right where we left 'em."

"Don't be a clodpoll. They wouldn't send you shits if they didn't plan to shove off the moment you were out of sight. What in Euskus' scrotum is this? Don't say 'squain boat,' I can see it's a squain boat with an arsehole inside. How did it appear on the ice to taunt us? I won't be ridin' in it, and if I must, I say we toss these three," he indicated Foster and the Mattaka.

"No one's ridin' in it unless the ice opens up. We just gotta figure out what to do with him." Foster indicated their passenger.

They instinctively looked to Palqua.

Jonn thudded onto the ice. They climbed out of the boat and surrounded him. He was heavy enough between the four of them for the moment they bore his weight. No one needed to say he wouldn't be carried.

"Jonn. Can you hear us lad?" Palqua asked in a fatherly tone. Foster wanted nothing more than to go. He danced from the cold of his missing cloak, and his impatience. Only the sense that everyone else shared his thoughts kept his mouth shut. A scream like ice sliding across itself threatened to well up out of his chest. "Can you walk?" The squad leader took his time pressing in around the issue.

Jonn looked up without a word. His eyes veered to his knees. He quaked and nodded off, snapped up and nodded again, a man falling asleep at the wheel. Foster would have voted to leave all of them if he had a say. Now confronted with the men, he pitied and hated the castaways in the same breath. The ice cracked now like the woods in deer season, all quarters under fire. If he was going to make it, Jonn would have to march the same as everyone.

"He's hypothermic. He ain't gonna talk." They looked to Foster. "Stand him up. If he walks, he walks."

"And if he don't?" Gionn said.

"We may have to cut his throat." Arthas answered with the weight of a confession.

"Isn't that your mate?" Gionn protested. "Fine cunt, you are!"

"Aye," he bent and looped his elbow under the trembling man's armpit. "It'll have to be him," he nodded to Foster.

"What you would do, do it fast," Palqua advised.

"Fuck's sake." Gionn took the other side, and while Foster held his breath, the two sailors lifted their companion between them and hooked his arms over their shoulders.

"Come on, lad," Arthas cheered. "Wife Seal's almost upon us," he lied. "I've seen you do a fair cast more than walk to get here. Look alive." They stumbled forward together and the suspended man's legs sank back. In another step it seemed they'd tumble to the ice in a tangle, but a foot shot forward and caught. Then another. Two more, and Jonn's corpse cooperated, if his head still wandered. Foster hurried to his rope at the back of the little boat, and the others lifted their corners. Palqua signaled them to hold.

"There is one other. Who stands to search for Bentos?" They stilled their feet and only risked the most peripheral of glances until Palqua spoke: "May he meet us at the ship."

The four-man crew settled on their tracks, young eyes in front. The trio limped in behind, and more than once, Foster checked over his shoulder that Jonn's feet moved, while the little knife banged against his thigh.

Norwet at first pretended confusion at Sawi's gestures. He frowned between his brothers, and caught the gaze of Milak nearby, but the hands repeated themselves until he could no longer deny who they beckoned across the camp where his uncle stood with six of the admiral's men.

"Ferrakut, take this binding," he handed the leather to his brother where he secured a crossbrace to the frame of the sled. "I will be right back." The questions he wished to ask tightened around him. Did the men call for him? His stomach cinched under the turns of doubt. There were too many possible charges to even cobble a story. They wanted to speak with him about the prison. The Leopard Seal. Someone had seen him running errands for Costig. Or Costig sent another. Could a hunter or a marching marine have noticed the circuit he took with Milak after the lost dogs, or how two sleds going out became one under a pair of drivers on its return? If his uncle was forced to sacrifice one of them, it would be a son of Alakset.

He trudged up with as much innocence as he could force. None wore the leather armor, but they had the look of Marines. Dressed for a march more than a fight, a spear to each. Sawi reeled him closer.

"This is the one you will want." They pored over him with eyes like leveled points. "Norwet. He is the oldest."

"But no man yet." An Amposi with longer hair than was the custom spoke for the group.

"The men, I cannot spare. Nor him! I should send a little brother. But he is a man. Made the Eye of the Needle, where we prove them. None but my brother and myself know the country better than Norwet." Sawi tilted his head toward Urkuk.

Norwet frowned. What he knew of the land beyond Drummoc was a few runs behind Milak. Sawi didn't wait for their approval. "Mentewat offers a silver from the admiral."

"For what?" He spat before he could feel the insolence of the remark.

Sawi smiled. "Leopard Seal." They seemed to gauge his reaction. "These men know the trail, but he is fast." Now Norwet took his turn to study their faces. Were they among the searchers he came upon at Tunguk's campsite? What had he told them that day? "You will take a fine team. Weather is clear. It is enough to run in his trail until you come upon him," Sawi assured.

Norwet hollowed at the truth of it. These were fleet of foot and too many to fight. Tunguk and Kjartke stood at the end of a rope, and the marines had come to trace it. Norwet gave no response. Nothing was asked. It would be as Sawi said. His uncle knew, as the marines did not, that the one sent to guide them knew better than anyone else the way to the Leopard Seal. That was what gripped him. It felt to a boy like a cruel justice: to make the one who aided the fugitive be the one to betray him. But Sawi was right: he was no boy. He had rounded the Eye of the Needle.

They didn't need him. The trail was enough. He would be expected only to advise on the condition of travel, where they should rest or even camp if needed, a shortcut. It would be his sled that bore the man back. If it was a silver his uncle sought, he should go himself. Anyone could be spared for a day. Milak knew the land beyond what Norwet could learn in many seasons.

"You wait," Sawi said to the men. "We will harness the team." He placed his arm over his nephew's shoulder as he'd never done before. His uncle spoke in Mattakatan with a casual cheer. "It is well if you bring me a silver. Stick to the trail and you will not be lost. But if you are delayed, it will be no great loss when I beat you home with three argots."

The navy hall rang hollow with the sound of Costig chewing. His mouth slapped open and closed over his second bowl of fish. Polc looked down the length of the table from his left—as long as a small ship—every bench empty but the one across and to Costig's right, where the minister of coal waited with pregnant patience over his empty dish.

"Are you sure you won't have another bowl?" The men shook their heads politely. "I don't usually eat so early," Costig explained. "Bad habit. Makes you slow of hand and wit." He whistled through his fingers, and the young cook scurried in with a heaping bowl and a jug of hasqa. "That'll do. Suppose these men weren't thirsty." The lad emptied their cups back into the jug.

"The admiral himself had no cup." Lamachar pointed out with deference.

"Was that it?" Costig's mustache pumped with laughter. "Toss me! I should've said somethin'. I'm not accustomed to men of such manners in the fleet" he nodded to Polc. "Had Turrha ever asked me to sit with him,

I'd have drained me glass before his arse hit the bench!" He grabbed the absconding lad by the arm. "Tell someone more important than yourself to fetch Wayranapan."

He smoothed a wet stain into his tunic and rested his chin on his fists. The captain and the minister took turns sneaking an amicable look. Costig lowered himself into the silence like a warm pool. He'd thought his room the only refuge, but that undermined his rank. All this time, he ate among the men. Low, loud men who banged the table and carried on with their mate across the hall. Was it his preference, or his custom? No one, and least himself, thought him the kind of admiral to clear a hall for a meal. It would take quite the preener, or a matter of grave importance, to call for it. But an admiral could call for most things, provided he could dream it up. Perhaps it was sergeant's thinking in an admiral's cloak that caused the mess outside to begin with. He blamed himself as too ambitious—maybe it was the opposite. He merely needed to clear a hall or two.

Costig belched. The minister of coal broke first.

"It is an honor to be invited to breakfast with the admiral," the rock nurse said.

"Aye," Costig confirmed.

"Is there—"

"Lamachar," the admiral interrupted. "Believe I've got a Nunoc lad by the name."

"Ah, very nearly true, sir. I believe you speak of Captain Amachar."

"Not your brother, then?"

"No, sir" he said with relief. "Tiril-Lama is he who took a wife from every shore, and so none would hold their child above the others, he put his seed in many canoes and sent them over the waves to arrive at once, that his progeny would never war upon themselves."

"I know a few bastards like that," Costig huffed.

"Ama," Lamachar went on absently, "was his twin sister."

"And you're the son."

Lamachar laughed as politely as he could through the offense. "Their son was of course Atxl, who you must know. My father also was Lamachar. I cannot speak for the good captain."

"Mine means 'twig,'" Polc cut in. "And I, too, am sure to be honored by the nature of your invitation."

"Did you know Captain Polc just returned from Camne Drumlag?" Costig asked the minister.

"Very good, captain. How did it impress you?" Lamachar pretended to hear the news for the first time.

Polc shrugged. "Good to learn why all the buildings are over here."

Wayranapan peered through the door and entered when he became certain he wasn't disturbing something important. Costig scraped back the bench and met him halfway for a whispered exchange before the official hurried back outside.

"Will you not walk out with me?" Costig called. The guests hurried to his side.

"Was there something you wanted to speak with us about?" Confusion rose above the concern in Lamachar's voice. An amused expression lifted the corners of the admiral's mustache.

"You two? Hm! None but the fine conversation." He held the door for the men and followed them out.

The Mattaka swirled in nervous anticipation. Far down by the public tavern, a, unusually large force of marines and sailors assembled in loose concert. The townsfolk set aside their fist fights and rivalries for the moment to float toward them with a veiled curiosity. Polc and Lamachar puzzled over it as well as they descended the steps to the jealous gaze of the sailors who'd been cleared of the building all morning. They'd be sure to note the favor shown these two by Costig, and if word ever got across the way to the assistant viceroy, as word was apt to do, two of Costig's most uncertain allies would be regarded with suspicion by the man most likely to turn their loyalties.

Costig sent off Lamachar with a familiar salute that he'd likely never received in all his years at Drummoc, then pulled Polc aside.

"Wayranapan tells me there were looters in the shipyard last night. Square your vessel, then wait for me at the public tavern. I've a job for you."

Ostuk marked their exit from the fringes of the crowd. Part of him wondered if the sudden and silent congregation hadn't another purpose. It was a strange pair: the minister of coal and the mercenary. If Costig had hoped for the meeting to go unnoticed by the people, it was in vain, but perhaps he sought only privacy. Ostuk hadn't spoken to Polc since the return from Camne Drumlag.

Camne Drumlag. Of that, at least, he'd told no lies.

He shuddered free of it. Over many shoulders, his mother's eyes longed for him. They gave him the distance he asked while they festered with worry over what could have compelled it. At least they were safe. No admiral took pains to treat the people with fairness, but at times sloth or inattention could spare one's family if they were unknown. His crew fated themselves otherwise. Ostuk made a show of their severance, only to watch them sign on to the renegade ship under Haraket. Had he kept them on, they would now be mates of the *Juhketappat*, sailing once more with the Navy's blessing. As it were, Ostuk stood chartered without a single hand on his crew. The riot gave him an excuse, but where he would find able seamen willing to work among dogs, he could not say.

Now a fearsome spirit aroused. The Navy had taken many rocks and curses, and suffered the looters with little more than idle violence. Ostuk studied the people like the surface of the sea. Their anger, crashing across one another. The people flooded in now from all camps to mix among the largest group, those like him who wanted no trouble. Squabbles that set the people against one another the day before seemed to have come to treaty under the concern of the growing company of men.

The Navy often gathered or dispersed. But it had been some days since so many collected in one place. First, a single crew joined the men guarding the tavern, already emptied by the looters. Through the morning, more arrived like boats that trickle in after a hunt. Nothing moved in force, and still they floated and joked among themselves. But it seemed each group had a captain, or some man of marked character among them—no loose stragglers. The Marines came as well, and their ease of manner contrasted to the days before when none knew his post or his task.

The rumor spread first among the women. More Navy donned what armor they owned, and though it was not strange in a riot, tempers had calmed of late, or turned inward on the people. Now Ostuk could not remember if there were so many helmets the evening before.

A serving boy, or a woman of the poye heard it. They planned to strike the tukits near the brothel suddenly, and in force. Some said it was a looter or the murderer of the old man and his grandson they sought, but most suspected the Leopard Seal. No matter that every home had been searched. He returned to aid the people, said one group, or an ally betrayed him for the reward. Ostuk knew the truth was always behind of such rumors, but never among them. He gathered as one who is tired, and longs for something to happen.

A hand fell on his shoulder. Wayranapan, one of the men who served the admiral, spoke in a low tone.

"Looters were able to steal into the shipyard last night. Costig wants every captain to check his ship." When Ostuk hesitated, he added: "Now."

Ostuk pried himself free of the group with regret. It was best to be far from such things when they happened. Far ahead, he saw Polc stride with purpose on the same errand. Any other season, he would have run to his ship, sick with anticipation. In his dreams, he'd already parted from her so many times, it felt like a falsehood to tend to her. Costig insisted there would be many more voyages between them, but in some recessed place, Ostuk prayed for circumstances to deliver him more swiftly to his fate. If only the looters could carry off the mast.

He found the hulk, propped and quiet, always so much smaller out of the water, where it felt like a world raised from the deep by Ajatse. The life seemed gone from the dry frame, a pair of eyes that barely lifted to acknowledge him before they sank again into a well-earned slumber. His boots clapped the false deck, and soon he dropped in amidship. There in the familiar embrace, the old tenderness returned to wound his breast at the sight of a hatch left open. A helpless anger whipped through him and fell into frustration. He'd battened it himself when they stowed. There was nothing down there for anyone to take, but it would be the wood they came for. He might well find her benchless. A fine excuse not to sail, but a painful violation no less.

He made the first few rungs when the voice boomed: "There's somethin' about speakin' suddenly in the dark when a man thinks himself alone," Ostuk spooked like a bird with nowhere to fly. "It's a joy I'll never tire of." He pressed his forehead to the side of the ladder to compose himself as Costig appeared in the shaft of light at the bottom.

"Take a moment. I've checked her for you."

Ostuk lowered himself opposite the admiral. "Good of the looter to allow us a visit."

"Had a nice chat with Captain Polc. Who knew Camne Drumlag could suddenly become so interestin'?" Ostuk held his tongue. "Curious if it fits your impressions."

Ostuk felt as though the deck tilted though he knew better. Many times, in many ways, his ship whispered to him to remain alert, though he didn't yet see why. "I stopped being impressed long ago. What did he think?"

"Your mother."

"Pardon?"

"How is she? And your family?" Costig shunted topics. "I mean it in all sincerity. You'll be hearin' it as a threat. I haven't the craft or the black hand for such tactics. If I want a man speared, I see to him meself, and if I want to show him I care, I ask about his mum, even if I don't know the look of her."

Ostuk nodded. "They are well, but we do not speak."

"Aye. The debt. You mentioned it. Does it extend to your home? The hut?"

It was a part of the story Ostuk failed to consider. He thought of those he lent it to, and decided they were no company for his mother. "No. I offer my hospitality to an old Mattaka who served passage, in place of wages."

"Right. Believe I met him when we searched. Travels with a young woman, marked on her chin?" Ostuk nodded. "And three halots, one goin' by the name Leopard Seal?" The dog captain decided to let the line run until the slack came out. "Me understandin' is the lot of 'em worked for yourself. Well-enough to be invited guests while you wander between mats."

"They worked the dogs. What these people do when they are ashore is no concern of mine."

"Signed on at Nunoc. Captain Amachar had fine words for the one called Foster. He helped you rescue them when they foundered, did he?" Costig waited, and Ostuk took the *Juhketappat*'s caution to remain silent. "Is that still your story? I ask, that you might show me what kind of man you are."

Ostuk felt the sea move beneath. The walls of the hold deadened as if they couldn't bear to hear anymore. Their talk in the forge returned to him. He'd dreaded his end far more on that occasion, and came away restored to duty. There were many things he couldn't say with so many ears around. Would he have said them elsewhere? It had a strange tenor to it, and he left feeling that something with quiet wings had fluttered past beneath notice. Perhaps it was a choice, going its own way unheeded. This one felt very different, and yet the thinnest lie damned him less than the truth.

"Aye."

Costig let out a breath of resignation. He waited some time, his bright eyes twinkling in the light from the hatch, though Ostuk felt the momentum of the talk, and the assurance that so far, it had gone precisely as the admiral expected. Perhaps he wished it hadn't.

"Before your clothes could dry—you're wonderin' when I found out. To Amachar's credit, he held up whatever bargain you had. Probably none too proud of bein' rammed by a dog ship." Costig's big cheeks rolled up in amusement. "Did you think forty sailors could hold a tongue? No, you're not that daft. That's why you severed your crew and turned their holdin's over to anyone you could. You sunk a Navy boat. But not before you boarded three fugitives from Nunoc, two of whom left on a whaler to ruin me supply chain, while the other lad has me colony tearin' itself apart on the eve of a siege."

The admiral's words leapt the bow like the first blast of cold water to anoint him underway. The passage remained unspeakable. The gods may blow and heave, but he, Ostuk, would have to make a distant shore if he made one at all. At last, he had his release. Yet he felt the swift current, clear and glimmering as only one who rode upon it could see.

"It is a strange place to arrest me."

"There he is!" Costig wagged his finger. "There's me lad! I knew you'd show me if I had the patience. You know as well as I that few men sail innocent to Drummoc. I admit, your boasts are better than most, but you're right: it's driftwood I've got to work with, and I'll find a purpose for every scrap."

"I have agreed to move your dogs and your coal. Again, it is a strange ruse to speak to me of something I know."

"Aye, I fucked up. There you have it," he tilted his head toward the opening above, the town outside. "Maybe you've done the same, and you

understand a man has to act—I won't call it desperate—*unexpectedly.*
Three argots!" Costig shook his head. "Should have given the lad a spear
for his troubles. I wonder what you thought when you saw that abiama
bearin' down of you."

Ostuk smiled in acknowledgment. For the first time, he considered
the crowd—they were the storm and the white sail behind the man in
his hold.

"I'm a marine, and you're a dog captain," Costig continued. "Men
like us shouldn't trade in such consequences. But havin' mourned that,
I'm an admiral, too, and I've already asked much of you to run me coal.
If what I say exceeds you, tell me. There'll be no justice—not from me.
Nunoc will do as it pleases, but you go as you see fit in Drummoc.
Nothin' for your mum, either. I find men are no good when they work
under a blade. But hear me treaty: your crime, and me problem, share
the name 'Leopard Seal.' Lead me to him, and I'll see you're forgiven
across the Attavaik."

"I do not know—"

"Aye, you don't know where he is. But you know those who aid him,
and if there's a man they can trust, it's the one who helped 'em here, at
great personal cost." The distress must have shown in Ostuk's face. Costig
hurried on: "I don't want the others. The old man. The woman. You've
me word they go free if they stand clear of me thrust. No one in
Drummoc will learn of your help. No knives waitin' for you."

"I would not know how to begin," Ostuk at last replied.

"I find that true of all beginnin's, and yet they have a way of sortin'
themselves once begun."

She hid as she had at first light, when the carpenter stomped toward
Drummoc shaking his spear. The sound of feet split until it became two,
then three. Voices of women at first. They snarled torments at one
another, cracking at the cusp of manhood. It was the farri's tongue, but
she heard the vestiges of a familiar accent, clicking together like flat rocks.

The boys stopped at the sight of a woman in their path. Their talk
fell away, then behind the tallest they approached with a bravery that
seemed bitter to have hesitated. Kjartke refused to yield the way. She
waited long enough to be certain they measured the insult.

"The carpenters will not be so patient with you today," she said in Mattakatan. "Go home."

One who stood just short of her and a season thicker than the rest took a sounding of her. His face wore dark lumps that only just began to yellow at the edges.

"Who are you to tell us, woman?" He replied in Atlantean.

Kjartke suspected he knew fouler words than that, and held his restraint against him. "I am your sister," she switched languages. "That is what we will say if the men see us returning. The only wood you get will follow steel." They snickered and sought council in one another's faces.

"You lie," a second challenged.

"For what purpose?"

"We come here often," the taller one said. "They don't give a fuck."

"You are eager for more beating?"

"This?" He swelled with pride. "It took many sailors to strike at Mennetarmenuk."

"Mennegur?"

"Who asks of my family, Jargadak?"

"One who wishes to speak with Mennetsatletaluk."

He scoffed with his friends. "Then swim to Camne Drumlag." They started around her, but Kjartke stepped to block them.

"There is a girl. Young. I wish to thank her."

"For what?"

She looked to the other two and narrowed. He considered her for a moment, then tossed his head.

The boys veered listlessly before her over the rock, and she could not help but see dogs in the spirit world, panting at their harnesses, ears pricked for a voice that did not believe itself, that they might defy it.

She saw them far enough, and the plain offered no cover: a group of men approached from town along the same path, the common way to the Calm Harbor. To flee or hide would invite attention. Nine, she counted, and no hope to escape, anyway. Instead, she set her tongue across the backs of the youth like a stinging whip. Kjartke swore and slapped and shoved them along. Her team bent to give the path to the sailors. The carpenter pressed in front with new vigor. He glared at the boys while she drove them on under the fury of a sibling who must retrieve her charges from their mayhem. The pause in his step assured her they would be stopped and questioned, but the men in tow lacked his thirst for vengeance, and amused themselves with the rough treatment she poured over the rounded shoulders.

Mennetarmenuk cried out with sincerity when her palm thudded against his ribs. His arm wrapped himself, and she feared he would collapse. Kjartke softened her blows as she caught him and held him up until they passed beyond the interest of the sailors, who turned sharply in the direction of the dog camp.

"Let me see." She pulled at his tunic. He jerked away. Kjartke persisted, and raised the leather to a storm-blue side.

"It is fine."

"Broke?" She said. He did not need to answer. With effort, she did not remind them of their fate had they ignored her warning, and though none spoke until they reached Drummoc, she felt their gratitude in the way their path straightened and their manner softened.

It was difficult to see to the harbor beyond the tukits, but they encountered no more sailors, so there must have been chores enough to busy them. As soon as they were safe within the round tops, the boy dismissed his friends: "I will find you in the crowd."

The streets wound them through with a sense of haste and expectation. They leaned away from an old woman who stood outside her home listening, but no others appeared, and the tukits felt hollow. Only now among the town did her bones speak to her of the cold and the long miles. They whimpered as dogs who felt the end of a journey that only the master knew had much more to go. The boy must have noticed her attention to each new doorway.

"They won't see you. The people are at the harbor."

Kjartke thought better than to acknowledge her concern. "Then who do you take me to?"

"Costig awaits us with the reward."

She stuck in her tracks, and he turned to laugh at her. "Come, woman. The harbor isn't safe for some. We stay to our own."

It was the fate of Kjartke that she often dragged along behind some boy. Their path took them from strange lanes she never traveled into the center, where at times it crossed a familiar track, and always she felt there was a place that knew her feet nearby. He had his own way of meandering. They were confident turns, born neither of habit or idle attention. Another day or two of wandering these streets and he would give himself over to the mines and the well-worn track.

A confluence leapt up to meet her, and she stopped. There remained no sign of it, but she stood at the place where Brother spit up before he nearly wandered off to Urkuk. The boy motioned his head impatiently, but Kjartke broke to another lane. She heard him join her when she paused before a tukit. The leather sheets that once covered the window and the door had vanished.

Kjartke ducked in, uncertain why. She knew that whatever she left inside was gone, as well. Mennetarmenuk stood framed in the doorway.

"The home of Ostuk, the dog captain," he declared.

Tunguk had left it up to her. Prepare a place, that was all he said— that, and to remind her of the girl who sent a gift with Milak. She could not think how they would meet her, or what could come of it. But even without knowing his intent, what kind of place, or the ways of Drummoc, not for a moment did she dream that they would come here. Yet to see it violated by thieves, laid bare for all who stood like her young guide to gawk upon its emptiness opened her with loss. The tukit sat in a wake of ruin, like the man who lent it, the town, many other things, because she passed through it. She saw Brother lying beside her, sweating and mumbling. Tunguk along the wall. All of them naked to the streets. *Prepare a place.* Kjartke wondered where she might settle, and how many more would fall behind her.

"Are you done, Jargadakne?"

Kjartke's face cinched with resentment. She moved deliberately from the tukit and made certain to stand close enough that he had to look up. "You call a mother like this? Look to yourself, Mennetarmenuk*ne*," she emphasized the final sound.

"I didn't know you were a mother." The boy averted his gaze in place of an apology. "I know who you are. But not your name." The swollen face set in defense. She noticed a stiffness to his words, and realized he pushed them out against the pain of a tender jaw. "Call me Armenuk. Or Nuk, if you think we will be mates."

"Armenuk," she tried it on, glad to drop the boastfulness of the family name. It was not her people's custom to have so many ways to be called, but so went the Kammatuk. "Kjartke."

It proved to be too much of a concession. They hardly took up the path again before the once-quiet boy set on her.

"What will you ask of my family?"

Her jaw clenched with regret, because she did not know, herself. "What I ask, I will ask of elders."

"I am the man of my family. Perhaps we don't need to go farther." Her laugh irked him. "I speak the truth. Satletaluk is at the mine."

"You have uncles?"

"Satletaluk is my uncle. My father is with him, my grandfather, many others."

"Your grandfather's father?"

"He doesn't speak for the family. I am the oldest of the young who remain."

"Cousins?"

"Younger. Or they are at the mine. Some are rowers on the firestone ships. The idiot ones. I will never be a rower. I would rather the mine, but we will see. I may be invited to apprentice in a better trade."

"You think to be asked while you steal wood? I see your trade. You wander streets with boys. Knives. This is no trade of a man who speak for family. It was a girl who bring food. Perhaps I speak to her."

"I would have!" He barked.

"You did not."

"I couldn't." She knew he wanted her to ask, so she didn't. He explained: "The men kicked me hard."

"What men?"

"That captain we passed earlier. His men. He didn't recognize me, but I don't forget him."

"So you fight Navy. This bring good to your family?"

He spun on her. "It brings good to you." Kjartke thought to strike him, as she would any younger relative who confronted a woman as such. But the split and lumpy face stayed her. "There was a loud boy. Bragging he would catch the Leopard Seal. After we saw to him, he was not so loud."

She clamped a hand over his mouth and whispered sharply, "Be careful what you speak."

He pulled it down and shouted, "*Leopard Seal!* It is fine. You are safe with me." She reached out and gently touched his ribs. He recoiled in pain from the demonstration. "There were many! Wait until the men come home. You will see. Wait until Leopard Seal returns. He stands a head higher than Costig! He will have his revenge. It is too bad, I like Costig. He pulled the Navy from me when they would beat a boy to death."

"Now you are boy, now again a man, as it please you. Tell me, who give the food to the girl?"

Frustration fell in a shadow over Armenuk. "Her mother. Vatjate. The wife of Satletaluk."

"Then I talk to your auntie."

He sulked ahead, but soon enough glanced back with a mischievous grin. Armenuk's stride took a bounce, and his voice belted like a crier with news for the people. "He is tall and strong and full of craft! Feared by all who hold a spear! Mate to the thieves of Tannawauk! The curse of Tolba's carrion crews!"

"Quiet!" She scolded him. His voice swelled.

"Smashed the prison, freed the Seleku! Who do I speak of? Costig, his dog, Costig, his fool! Who do I speak of? The tail-chasers circle, his laughter booms! He knows not the way to Urkuk! Tell me, Mattaka, who do I speak of?"

Kjartke collared him and he shrank beneath her grip. "Ay! Let me go!"

"You wish for ruin?"

"It is how we call the boys to fight us—my cousins and my mates. If they dare. If they are here, no one will come to lay eyes on you."

Her hand slackened, leaving a wad of stiffened leather. He smoothed it. "His woman is a great beauty! Who do I speak of?"

"Ha!" Kjartke sneered at the notion of herself as Brother's. Armenuk answered in his cries.

"It is true! She should not be so hard on herself!"

A burst of air cracked from her tight mouth in a single laugh that hurt her throat. Her face reddened that she could not dim her smile, and Armenuk gleamed when he saw it. Already, it weighed on her—the abandon she allowed with Tunguk, their rolling fits of joy all the way back from their trick. The sight of the carpenter breaking in terror at the sound of the barking mother dog fueled her. She indulged herself with the old man whose relation allowed no such intimacy, and now, so soon after, a wild boy returned her to that momentary passion. Her head throbbed, and her eyes watered under the strain of concealment.

"His woman is the fair daughter of Katillike! Maybe not right now, the trail is hard on beauty. But she cleans up good!" His tongue hung out the side of his mouth as he paused every few steps to delight in her contortions. "Who do I speak of?" Armenuk seemed to ask Kjartke.

"You, quiet! I kill you if I must," she barely managed with a straight face.

Armenuk switched to their native tongue: "Curse me in Mattakatan like my mother, if you wish."

"Flay your manhood! You drown in water where you might have stood!"

It was too much. They both collapsed into fits. Tears plowed bright wakes into the grime on her cheeks and she tasted them in the corner of her mouth. It felt too generous to let him think it was all for him. Even Tunguk could not account for it. She felt like a glacier in Spring. How she wished she could staunch his pleasure! But Armenuk basked in it, and it fed his own laughter, which she thought flowed from her insult, though wondered if it had not waited near as long as hers.

For many more bends, they could hardly share a word or a look that did not spark them afresh. If her father knew she laughed with boys on the streets of Drummoc! It sobered her in a slow tide that left her no less glowing from a secret place within, like a lump of firestone that still breathed beneath the ashes. Armenuk, too, faded and fixed on the way ahead. By this, she knew they neared the home of his auntie. There needed to be no agreement for them to understand that neither could invite the ecstatic kaim that found them on their walk into their respective camps.

"Tell him Nuk is first among his benches," Armenuk said as they stopped before a tukit that she placed deep in the rear of town, on the harbor-side. He leaned his voice toward the doorway, and the tone melted again to that of a boy. "Auntie! It is Nukne! We have a guest."

"Your auntie is away," an old woman's voice called. "Bring your guest in quick."

"Grandmother! Where is she? The guest is not for you!"

Kjartke cringed at the way he spoke. A shuffle from inside breached the flap, and a girl emerged, barely younger than Armenuk.

"Don't scream through the door, Nuk" she scolded in a low tone. "She visits Etsatep." The girl took in Kjartke without a word. "We will host her until mother returns," the girl addressed her cousin.

"My guest is busy," he took ownership of the hospitality. "We will go to Etsatep."

"Not now. Something stirs at the harbor. Linikut says a force readies to sweep the tukits near the brothel."

"Why?"

She shrugged. "They must think they will find him there."

Kjartke did not like the way both children looked to her for reassurance. It felt crude to acknowledge, but she knew it was too late to deceive them. "Let them search."

Armenuk's expression warmed with relief. "Etsatep is close. Let them search the shallow tukits all they wish."

The girl seemed to wait for Kjartke's word, and it was clear she stared at the marks on her chin. When Kjartke failed to protest, she slipped inside once more, leaving the two to their errands. It came as a relief. These were the people she sought, perhaps the only ones who might favor her, but the thought of entering their home, sitting among the strangers to beg what she could barely ask of herself—it unsettled her. If Vatjate, too, refused to see them Kjartke did not think she would be very upset. To her surprise, it was being alone again with Armenuk that eased her tension. She sensed the relief in him, as well. He probably longed to be the one to deliver this honored guest to his family. Perhaps it forgave him that a girl had to hike to the dog camp under peril because he writhed on a mat for his brashness. Or perhaps he hoped that Vatjate would be nowhere. That Mennetarmenuk, after all, would at last speak for his family.

Kjartke felt it as a welling up, swift and engulfing. As a girl, she stood in her father's boat watching the birds feast on the remains of seal they left scattered over the ice. Her brother pushed her, but she did not know until much later. It was too sudden and confusing. Salt burned in her nostrils. Overwhelming cold shook her, and her breath held itself before she realized she was underwater. She flailed then, and hissed to the surface, miserable and betrayed. Perhaps it was practice. This time, though she panicked and seethed, she was certain nothing on the face of Kjartke, daughter of Oljarbaruk, betrayed her.

Marines spilled from every lane. Armenuk slammed to the ground beneath a pair of bodies and she hurt for his ribs. A hand cast her aside into the sloped wall, and a spear leveled at her. "Fall on my point, bitch!" A foreigner invited her.

"Sergeant! Got one of the bashed lads!" Came the cry from atop Armenuk. Three more marines swept in, and Kjartke found her breath. They felt like a violent sea, but this was all. She counted ten. The girl stuck her head out of the door at the noise, and Kjartke shouted her back in.

"Help! I am seized! Help, brothers! There are not many!" Armenuk wailed to the tukits.

"Shut the fuck up!" A marine landed two solid punches, but Armenuk remained with himself better than Kjartke did.

"Help! Ten! To your knives, it is but ten!" He yelped as both of the men on top of him rained fists, and his calls turned to no more than the pitched whine of a dog. The other marines braced their spears toward every branching lane. The girl, finding her courage, came back out of the tukit.

"Let him go, jumpers! He is no one for you! You hit boys? Jumper dogs! Go to Camne Drumlag! See if you are brave enough to hit my father!"

Kjartke folded the girl in her arms and wrestled her against the tukit, her own back shielding the marines from the taunting—and she hoped, her face. The pitched cries faded to a low whimper that reminded Kjartke of nothing more than the one who waited with Tunguk for her hand to feed him.

"Up and out! On me!" The one called Sergeant hurried past toward the edge, the shortest path clear of the tukits and by her reckoning only a boatlength farther from where she and Armenuk had stopped. The boy dangled limp like a penguin between two hunters as the marines leaked away.

The girl felt it as an absence of pressure. When she looked up, the Jargadak woman was gone.

The bow lurched to a halt. Foster's momentum caused him to stumble and slide out. The boat they carried twisted in a way a boat never should, and rebounded to shape under a flurry of Mattakatan. *Down*, came the order from Palqua, and through the thinning fog they met their dread: lapping water cut the tracks that led to the *Gairhle*. The sea relished in the opportunity to well up where it could and pitch the two lips of ice, just parted. To the west and to the wind, a notch had shattered with the shards still bobbing in their places on the surface. With each pulse of water, the gap to the next floe yawned, then collapsed to click together again.

"Watch your toes, cunts, she bites!" Gionn and Arthas shuffled up with Jonn between them.

A chill distinct from the cold discharged through Foster's spine. It was a trivial gap. The ice still stuck when it smacked together, and a vigorous step would clear it. The fissure ran deeper. He knew he walked the sea, but this was the first axe-blow to the illusion of solidity. The litany of distant cracks shrank in intensity as they rose in number, until the entire sheet became a highway of heavy trucks jolting along just out of sight. The fog lent them confidence when they couldn't see an edge. Now there was no consolation—every step hereout came on a raft.

Little Tunguk measured the rhythm of the ice drawing out and snapping closed. Arthas took notice.

"Go with the wind," he ordered no one in particular. "She breaks first to the west and to the sea. Spins the floe. Go east and we'll have a clean step." It may have been the exposure that prevented Foster from imagining what he meant, but the party traced the crack without a word, and in short order the gap narrowed until it fused again with their own flow. Only then did he see how the western edge of the broken chunk was driven to the northeast, twisting the opposite side back into contact and driving it under their side so that it was a short step down onto the next piece. As simple as the jump might have been, Foster knew Arthas was right: better to skip the gymnastics.

It might have been the anxiety, but soon as his feet hit, Foster swore he felt thinness and separation. Not in the ice, which held firm, but in the bonds of the men beside him. In himself. A feeling that given time and time alone, everything would split in unexpected places and spin them out to sea.

"Captain Palqua! There!" Bucket pointed. All but the Mattaka boys seemed to squirm with discomfort at the mistaken title. The wind whipped up, and the fog ran in needles that pierced a hazy figure far ahead and moving away. It was the longest vantage the weather had allowed, and they held their breath for the ship. The wish faded behind a fresh bank, though not before Gionn announced it.

"Bentos."

No way to be sure, but Foster couldn't imagine who else would be out. A man from the ship scouting for them? Either way, there was no talk of going after him. They moved as one…for the moment.

Gionn strained into the fog, as though he could draw the *Gairhle* into being if he burst the blood in his eyes. Arthas was a clever mate to give him the lee side of the unburied sailor. Both their fat hulls leaned on the stiffening charade of his valor. Jonn hardly seemed to slow, which likely meant it was Gionn whose pace declined. His heart ached as for a woman when he thought Foster and the squain skippers gained their selfish yards on them. If Bentos made the ship while Omera devoured them, he'd be indignant. These were the worst of mates, quick with a cheerful word and a shared burden while they plotted their run the moment a mast appeared.

If he dropped his side and ran to catch up, Gionn wondered whether Arthas would do the same. There should be a way to swap with Foster. Only fair he took a shift as a crutch while Gionn bore the rear quarter of a feather. The back of his cloak rippled and stuck. It took a few more gusts for him to appreciate that the other two hobblers no longer broke the wind.

"Backed!" He shouted to catch Arthas' attention. "Wind's backed."

Arthas had a feel. "Doubt it. Westerlies run once they set."

"Then we're off! Fuckin' squain navigators couldn't hold a course to the bottom with an anchor around their legs!"

"Aye, they've lost the breeze, but we haven't changed course. The floe's spinnin'."

Gionn's knees softened as he saw that he still walked the length of a ship, while the bow had blown to starboard. "Then they've lost the *Gairhle*. Hoy! Cunts! Hard to port!" None of the four reacted. "*Hoy!*"

"Hoy! Arthas joined in. "Palqua! Wife! Bucket!" They carried on to no effect and a growing distance between the groups.

"Fair sail to you, takka-taks! Let 'em circle back to Drummoc, then. I'll take the wind in me left ear, mate, double your shit pace!"

Arthas failed to echo his enthusiasm. Gionn started to turn them back toward the north, the best of their finest guesses to the position of the *Gairhle*. But the line abreast refused to budge. Arthas stopped cold.

"No good, lad. If the floe can spin, we'll hit open water before the ship, sure as you're a red bastard." Before Gionn could answer, Jonn's weight sunk into him and he had to throw his arm around the man's far side to catch him. Arthas already bounded ahead. "Hold tight! I'll steer, and send one back to help you!" He jogged after the crew.

"Arthas! You shit! Get back here! Back, or I'll leave him!" If his words reached the man they thudded harmlessly off his skull. "If I have to run after you, I'll chew you up for Omera!" He swore volleys after his fading companions.

It was becoming a regular occurrence. The men who spilled over the rim of the dog camp numbered nine, and though there were ten who worked the sleds if he counted the runts like Ulwet and Arnake, only a fool would raise arms to greet the Navy at any strength.

Sawi and his brother Onagnutulauk, father of Saunlauk and Siguvik, had raced off soon after the marines summoned Norwet to what hateful deed. It was Senadak who held the camp, and he called the party of six—the two other men, and three oldest boys—to meet them. That he called the boys at all told Milak he did not know the intention of the visitors and chose to round out his group to bring them favor. Out of habit, Milak's chest surged that the youngest would be unsupervised for a moment, and could hide or steal what they may—before he remembered that there were no sleds to cobble, no fugitives to bury. So punctuated were their days now that he could barely enjoy the relief of having no schemes to perpetrate.

The one who marched ahead of the column wore a scowl and a lump on his head so big Milak thought it would sprout another eye. He stomped yards ahead of the rest, and seemed to have no kind words prepared, but when he came to the family, he folded his arms and stood aside to await the others without a word.

"As fine a Mattaka war party as I've seen!" One with little teeth called cheerfully. Senadak chose to keep his reply. "Where'll you have us?" He surveyed the camp. None of them quite understood, and the man took pleasure in it.

"Manners, cunt," one of his men teased.

"Ah, right. Polc, and they call me a captain. How shall I call me host?'

"Senadak." He begrudged.

"I see you're as delighted for us as we for you, but alas, mate, Admiral Costig bids us to impose upon your hospitality. Just this past night, the horned fellow to me right was attacked by rioters at the Calm Harbor, and I saw meself how the blacksmiths had a poke at you. Aye, but the good admiral does not forsake you. I'll have two of your warmest skin huts—one to post at the Calm Harbor, and one for meself and these other three. Between riots and murders and Leopard Seals, we can't have our dog lads comin' to harm." He smiled, and Milak could not look away from the gaps between his sharp teeth. The man noticed and closed his lips. "You wouldn't happen to be missin' a dog, would you?"

Norwet overturned the sled before the dogs trampled the marines. They trailed all morning in furious agitation at the pace of the frontrunners, and thrice now the man stopped them at a place where the tracks sprawled out to study every print . The signs were obvious. Norwet could have told him it was another rest, for the trail emerged clearly on the other side. He did not complain, though. Norwet snuck a look toward the coast while he pretended to untangle the dogs.

The two sleds he glimpsed shortly after they started had been careful to stay out of sight. There was no thought of reporting it to the leader, Mentewat. He knew it was Sawi. While the marines slogged through the long wake of Tunguk, his uncle meant to guess where the old man headed and cut off the route for his gold. Now they stood atop the crest of the ridgeline that led to Urkuk, and still nothing of the bounty seekers. Norwet hated the trick. Hated being sent for his lack of knowledge, and because Sawi knew he would act with treason if the opportunity came. Early on he considered turning the marines on his uncle. Though he knew little of the backcountry, he could see there were few places a rickety sled pulled by two worthless dogs could go, and Sawi would find them soon enough. But at least Tunguk stood a chance against two

Mattaka. Norwet heard tales on the *Juhketappat*. His uncle's mission disgusted him, but regardless of the outcome, it would be a heart-rending clash if those two met on the trail.

To involve the marines would assure destruction for one party or both. As hard as they pushed, it would take another day at least to catch Tunguk in thoughtless pursuit, and neither he nor Sawi advised them to bring a trail tukit. Now Norwet had only to weigh the timing of his insistence that they turn home before dark, so that it would be heeded without suspicion.

"Boy!" Mentewat called. Norwet noted he used the same word as Brother, rather than the "lad" that many halots preferred. He joined the marines, themselves impatient to move on. If the man were an officer, he was not a marine, and the way they argued at every stop, Norwet wondered if he were even in command. But so far, the will of the others folded to this stout Amposi. *Seven*, he grinned to himself again. He ruined the fortune of the party with his presence.

"What do you think of this?" Mentewat pointed at the flurry of prints. Norwet had already given his honest opinion that the sled they sought was damaged, and pulled by only two dogs and two pairs of feet. That, he suspected they could guess on their own and there was no cause yet to risk raising an eyebrow.

He knelt beneath the finger and lifted a scrap of leather from a well-stamped print. It bore a circle with a star of many points in the center, lines extending to all sides where they ran off the ragged edges marked by fangs. Norwet was no sailor, and he wondered why the man could not recognize a corner of a map himself. The same he saw bandaged around the foot of the Leopard Seal.

"They rest." The quality of his Atlantean fell apart for the marines' benefit. "Good view. See far here. Dogs need rest. Sled," he thought. "Runners—no good." He pointed to the jittery tracks. "Maybe fix."

"Not far, then?"

He shrugged. "This." He nodded to the sky.

"I see the light. I know as well as you we must turn soon."

Norwet shook his head. "No light. Cloud." The sky was clear enough, but the clouds looked like the body of a boy dragged behind a sled. In the east, the menacing east, something low and dark budded. It filled him with excitement. There was but one group out here with a tukit. "Bad. Storm come."

"Aye, you'd like us to fuck off, wouldn't you?" One of the marines challenged.

"He doesn't care what we do," Mentewat said. "He's got a team. If it starts to blow, won't be him who doesn't make it back."

"Fuck it," another said. "We can pick it up tomorrow, without all the weavin' and the sniffin' at prints."

"We stay on the trail," Mentewat insisted. "If it snows overnight, how will we find him out there?" He waved a hand at Urkuk.

The first marine shook his head. "You won't, because they aren't there." The others looked at the sled tracks, clearly leading up the mountain in contradiction. "Aye, I see 'em," he went on. "I been up there meself on march. If they went up, they're dead. And if this Leopard Cunt is half as clever as the squains think, he ran just far enough to make us chase for a day and turn around, thinkin' we'll never catch him. Then he headed for the coast and turned back for town. There's nothin' to hunt out there. Game's on the coast, and more than likely, he'll want to be close enough that his mates from Drummoc can deliver his meals." The marine glared at Norwet, as if daring him to contradict.

"We stay on the trail. The coast, we can search any time." Mentewat said.

"I say cut down to the coast. It's all downhill, lads. If we cross his tracks, we got him, and if not, it's back home for a sleep and another round. Just because you're Polc's lad fresh off the southern current don't make you sergeant-at-arms when I been five seasons under Costig himself."

"Sit if you're with Mentewat," the second marine said. No one moved. Norwet stole a line down the ridge again. Nothing moved in the old powder, and even the Amposi did not bother to lower himself. There would be tracks—that much he knew. Where they ended, and what he might do there, the oldest son of Alakset would learn before the moon took her throne.

It would *be the spears that came through, wouldn't it?* Costig thought. None noticed the little column of men before the admiral, so fixed were they on the small army who mustered just this side of the brothels. The Mattaka teemed at its edges, and ran between themselves and the town full of rumors and warnings. He'd many clever plans when he first took the helm, and perhaps this was one, but unlike the others, it rested in the end on a few sharp lads and their steel.

Costig could have cracked himself. Wendell should have been the damn admiral. This is what he would have done had he remained a sergeant-at-arms. The fast lads he sent after the Leopard Seal may turn up soon after these, a bigger quarry strung between them. That'd square half his problems, the ones born of Ingputka, and confirm his error lay in whispers at the well of the dead.

While the eyes scoured the main force, it took but ten good lads who knew their task to slip one-by-one into the town, hasten through the streets, and return now with what was more an offering than a culprit, though he may have been both. Navy and squain alike hardly regarded them as they hurried to their admiral's side and draped the lad at his feet, sputtering and twisting with disbelief. He had to wonder if he couldn't have found a way to handle the whaler in a similar manner. He'd taken two speculative throws, and his darts still hung in the air, when a blade from Corm may have undone the crew. No matter now. To regret is to march backwards into battle, he often reminded his men. Let Corm be the lesson that guided his hand in the coming fight.

He motioned a nearby crew to take up around them when the Mattaka began to notice. Even the sailors weren't sure of the fuss, but they felt the severity of it and hemmed their leader as a few shouts turned the fringes of the crowd to the budding scene. Ostuk stood among the first to sense it. The sight of the dog captain drew a pang from Costig— a reminder of his old self, speaking low in the bowels of ships. As old as that morning. These ten returning with their catch were all the marine needed to poke his head from the hold and breathe the spray. The body of the crowd now turned on them in confusion. Costig sent a runner to bring reinforcements from the considerable mass assembled on the edge of the town. The deception served, he wanted the stout body nearby in case he anticipated them wrong, and tempers flared.

In the stream of men changing places, he glimpsed a memory: Ostuk again, waving his admiralty letters with three ill-fated crew beside him the day they landed. He found a use for everyone. The more hopeless, the more satisfying. It was the nature of that mercy to bring the occasional disappointment. He'd done all he could, Costig insisted with hollow sincerity. It seemed such a casual problem at the time. A gold coin and a lad with a bad reputation should have done it. How was he to divine the big idiot's ability to trip over his own bollocks with such consistency? There was nothing for the indiscretion but to throw him in prison, and that should have lent him credibility at least. Had he just used the damn key! Costig couldn't have known they'd bash a guard and free every squain in the cells. He couldn't have thought a halot would captivate the locals so. Or land himself on the butcher's stone. Set the whole town against each other. Perhaps a better man would've known. Costig found himself out of clever notions to keep the Leopard Seal free.

The admission didn't bother him, nor did appearing a fool. His was a heart laden with lies. Every false operation he meant to fail; the way he sent off Wendell in fear of his diligence; fretted over Willakuy—pathetic Willakuy, waiting to count the coin that would never add up. The lies took on faces. They mustered at dawn, ate breakfast with him, turned in desperation to gnash at one another. He wanted nothing more than to confess his error to his laughing captains, but the assistant viceroy would be forewarned, and if he were smart, use it to remove a rival.

No, it would be lies who lay their mats beside his until he could sort Alexicus. He looked at the squain lad, bruised and re-bruised, fated over nonsense. The falsehood that clawed at him most was born in a skin hut on the snow, where he looked a fevered man over and let him think there would be a way through. It was a misjudgment, not a lie—not then, anyway.

Now the silence across the channel haunted him. There was no straight way out. It would be smaller lies, and smaller ones, until Alexicus stood before him and knew beyond a doubt what followed. Costig longed for an honest siege.

His forces rallied on him, and the Mattaka at last saw the ruse. One more deception slipped free like tight armor from his ribs. He drew in a long breath and belted for all to hear: "Drummoc, pay heed!" He summoned the last one who would play a part: the old woman whose husband and grandson set the town upon itself came forward.

"Did you see the blade who killed your men?"

She waited so long he feared a change of heart. Then the woman raised a crooked finger to the lad who lay at Costig's feet. The crowd whooped and foamed. At first, he could hardly tell in which way, but as they settled in, their frustrations found their voice. Most of the people wanted no part in any fugitives, reward or not. They wanted to see one of their own claim it for the joy it gave them to wonder what their own fortune might have looked like. But they festered at the looters, the rough sailors, the knives who roamed the streets. All riots ended because eventually, the people wanted to go home. This was no riot, Costig swore. It broke a day ago, and only loitered for want of an event. Their reaction was all the confirmation he required.

"The reward for a dead Leopard Seal stood at three silvers," they hushed as much as they could bear to follow his words. "Three silvers was all this woman's family asked. You seen what they got. What all of you got. Here's me consolation." He drew three decairs and dropped a pair, one at a time, into the old woman's palm. Then he searched the crowd for what he knew he would find. A young girl sobbed blood as a pair of older men restrained her from rushing the line of marines that shielded the captive boy—a relative, no doubt. Costig approached to her bewilderment and closed her fingers around the third coin. He was halfway back before it dawned on her what he meant to compensate, and her frenzy increased.

"I stand for no murders in Drummoc. You seen what I gave that whaler. Take me silver, and be restored, or else it be me steel."

He raised his spear, then buried it in the lad's chest to the song of the cheering crowd.

Jonn's shaking rippled through Gionn. There remained enough in the lad's legs not to go over, but he slumped into his only support and melted down the side. Gionn couldn't explain why he didn't just drop the cunt. The ice cracked like shields from the west. He squeezed and twisted them so the wind fell on his left cheek. He'd veer and spin his way back if he had to. If the footing didn't shatter beneath him like pot sherds. The only solid thing was the one who anchored him to the spot. Perhaps that's why he held on.

"Do you see that, Jonno? They mean to strand us! *Arthas!*" He pleaded with the fog. "Come on, I think I see the *Gairhle*. Few more steps. Boot-bottoms, lad." Gionn tried to haul forward, but his miserable cargo hardly got his toes off the ice before he crumpled to a knee. Gionn righted him with an effort that cost him more than it should have. He looked into those eyes like the surface of the pack, clouded and heaving.

Go, he told himself. The lump of coal they left her was shit. Maybe this is what she required. He recalled his words: *Omera, don't fuck me now, and I'll drown any cunt you say. Name him.* It was a sailor's jest. Not meant to be taken seriously. Leave it to an Amposi woman to botch his words. Not his fault if she took to the dumb bastard. Jonn wouldn't be his choice, were he a goddess, but then neither would the babbling prayers of a bunch of river monkeys who managed to pole their fortunes half the world over in the wake of finer men. There were better offerings than this lad, he was sure. But better this one than himself.

"Fair ship and a far shore, mate." Gionn eased him to his knees, where Jonn held under a strange balance, neither struggling for his feet nor tipping over. He seemed to gaze through the surface of the floe into the freezing sea. With a few clumsy pulls Gionn freed the axe from the sailor's belt. As he stood, a shadow broke the fog. Gionn secured the blade to his own belt and reached back for Jonn's armpit as if to raise him. He feigned surprise when a voice greeted him.

"You were 'bout leave his ass, weren't you?" Foster jogged up and threaded himself under Jonn's far side.

"What's it like to wake every day, suspectin' the worst of everyone?" They grunted together and by some miracle Jonn's legs held him upright again. "I was takin' a breath while you strolled over. That, and appointin' meself with a means of splittin' your skulls when I caught up to you."

"We're off course."

"Aye, I'm the one who said it."

"Keep the wind on your left."

"Tell me one more thing I know, and I'll lighten me load by one." He touched the hilt of the weapon.

Foster shook his head in disbelief. "'Thank you so much for comin' to rescue me, brother! I'm so grateful that you decided to die on a fuckin' ice cube rather than leave me behind!'" He mocked.

"Fuck off, would've been the ship that stood for it. I doubt Corm counted your shareless arse."

"There's the Gionn we all know and love! I figured the nice guy routine was bullshit."

"And your own tongue is innocent? Aye, you should have left us, you'd be two corpses closer to your scheme. At least I'm tryin' to hold the ship together."

Foster's eyes widened in silent reproof. He tilted his head at the man between them.

"This cunt?" Gionn gave Jonn a shake that swiveled his head as though it hung from a rope, to settle again in a forward lean. "Don't even know his own name. *Hoy!* Jonn! Care to hear what Foster has in store for you? You didn't think Costig would just let you sail away with a slap on the arse, did you?" Gionn delighted in Foster's squirming. Their charge tripped forward without a sign of presence.

"Hold the ship together?" Foster pained over the opportunity to speak in private, and the lingering fear that privacy was an illusion. He lowered his tone to a harsh whisper. "You just want the you-know-what so you can fuck off instead of earnin' it. I got bigger things ridin' on this, bitch. I don't give two shiny turds about pay if I can't show my face anywhere on the continent, and if you had a splinter of gratitude for the folks who got you where you are, you'd feel the same."

A fog bank cleared and gave them the rest of the crew, closer than they could have hoped. When they arrived, the boat already bobbed in an open lead beside the terminal edge of the floe. There lay hardly more than four strokes of water between them and the next sheet. A moment's row, and a sure death had they not brought the boat. Arthas held the launch while the other three bobbed.

"Wife Seal!" Palqua motioned him in.

"I'll go," Gionn offered. "Better on an oar."

"You're too fat!" Arthas teased. "Worried we won't come back twenty yards?"

"Hold firm, my sons!" Palqua called to Gionn and Jonn. Arthas steadied her for Foster, then slung one leg over and kicked off with the other.

Dumb cunt, he chided himself. Must he say his worst to Foster at every apparent deliverance? That wart always grew back, and his memory ran thick from the ladle. The squain boat never left sight, but it pulled the slack out from his chest until he thought his heart would tear free with it. His lip quivered, and he begged himself not to curse and threaten them. *Don't look needy. No one needs a needy shit.*

Palqua, Arthas, and one of the bucket twins disembarked. "Hoy! Less teeth, you dogs!" Gionn whispered an anxious warning when they scraped the hull clumsily against the far floe. He sputtered a ragged breath he didn't know he'd been holding when Foster and the other Bucket turned about and drug her back.

He'd spent more days at sea in a leather skiff than he thought possible, and still the narrow crossing filled him with dread. Jonn tumbled in violently despite their efforts, and she flattened and sloshed in protest. No way the boat would hold up to these idiots. If they made it across, they'd founder on the next one. It looked a lie that gray squains told themselves of the sea.

His foot found a rib and even then the frame twisted and sunk. Gionn fell as delicately as he could. Maybe the old man's vessel had stouter bones. Or whoever among the *Gairhle* wrought her hadn't the knack of the squains. This one felt as though they sailed a blanket that each held up on the sides with all his might. No bench and nothing beneath, the cold seeped through his arse and up his back.

But held, she did. It remained enough trouble to extract Jonn that he prayed it would be someone else who suggested the axe. None offered, and all soon made land. Gionn was glad to see the wet hull freeze stiff the moment she left the water. A little ice might bind her together for another lead or two.

The hollow thunder of the ice sheet splitting came to them in urgent succession. The wind sensed the imminent break up and redoubled its efforts. The others took up their ropes before there could be a debate, so he and Foster once more bore Jonn, who hadn't the wits to know or care if he moved at all. Gionn's thick legs felt swollen to twice their size and his feet registered his steps only with delay. Despite the torpor in his extremities, he sweated under the task, and longed to peel his cloak before it froze fast to his back. Any longer, and it would become less clear who supported who.

The crew ahead stalled, never out of sympathy. Their new floe proved shorter than the last, but their luck ran it into the one ahead. Foster counted three as if it meant something, then leapt, causing he and Jonn to stumble after. Only the squains ever looked back after them, he noticed.

She looked a wider raft, this one. Firm underfoot. His fear the ice wouldn't take them far enough gave way to a new one that after all their trudging, the *Gairhle* lay behind them. The indecision chopped at his steps. Palqua must have had some notion of where the ship lay, but then he was among the party that failed to note their drift. Gionn's search fanned out more and more to either side, and now and then he tossed an eye over his shoulder, hoping to be the one to see the mast. *Pity if the others were so far ahead they couldn't hear.* The crew carried a pace that confirmed it was every man for himself.

Soon as he wished it, the westerlies reared up and in a sweep through the battle line, routed the fog for a shining distance. Red blots welled up like wounds on the ice. Three, four, five. Pennants! Faded and fluttering in a line as at a harbor to mark the landing. One of the Buckets squealed so loud he heard it over the roar. His shadow sprung out for the first time that day, and just beyond, tall and black, the mast of the *Gairhle*.

No one needed to say it. They quickened until Jonn's feet only touched every other step. A snap sounded so loud he thought his own body had split. A line darted through the ice ahead between them and the squain boat. Foster and Gionn lifted their mate and charged over it before a lead could open to strand them. Now the pennants moved and danced, and more rows came into view between them. They were spotted!

Gionn practically whimpered. Now that the fog shredded in thin wisps the lay stood clear. Winter's early effort at a siege collapsed upon itself. From the west the ice either broke rank and scattered in pockets where widening leads raced between, or drove up on itself in twisting piles stitched by hummocks. A hundred yards to the ship, and the first line of pennants dropped. It seemed like they would make it dry, but the rest of the crew wasn't confident enough to wait on them. His every impulse begged him to sprint with all he had. Drop these two, if need be. But it was a bad look, and he'd learned recently enough that scorning his mates at the first sniff of safety had a way of coming back on him. Too far, yet. A run would kill them short of the mast, and none were like to test the ice again on his behalf.

Foster knew it, or was tired, which was as well as knowing. This far seaward and under bright sky, the floes gave up their pretense as land and began to shift like the deck of a sturdy ship. He felt first dizzy, then drunk, before he noticed their drift against the mast had increased, and their bodies made up the difference without a thought. The squain crew shuddered unnaturally well-ahead, and he hoped it was a fall. But a sharp bevel separated itself from the smooth field, and he saw their floe die beneath another than ran up over the top. A shallow lip drove up and the downhill tilt hurried their feet. It moved fast enough that he could see the creeping pack rotate. The others handled it clean enough, but Gionn saw the sea lick up onto their floe from the submerged end, and though he never set foot on pack, knew in his bones that any more weight from the hummock would snap the edge off beneath it and give them a lead to cross instead of a low dike. Foster noticed only the wet, and hesitated.

"It's cold toes, or a swim, cunt!" Gionn urged him on. They splashed ankle deep and Jonn's feet caught, sweeping back behind him so the two men nearly buckled under his full weight. The hummock stood barely shin high. They hove the frozen sailor up so that his torso crossed the barrier, then rolled over before collecting him again.

The squain boat reached the last line of pennants when they got Jonn underway again. Must have been something of him left, because his feet reached out again and again with a determination absent the rest of his body. Another little hummock—this one short enough to step over. Gionn's heart boiled and he thought he might vomit. A little puff of joy lifted him when the others made the ship. Now it was men, with faces and arms and names, who swarmed over the deck. Ropes struck free and flung aboard. Pennants scaled the side. Some sort of exchange between the ship and the squain boat stalled them from following. Every ache and frozen joint let up enough to confirm that he could bear it all along, truer now of the final steps. His chest rose in triumph and he bellowed steam when he and Foster tumbled up in a heap.

The *Gairhle* sat moored in her own lead, nothing but shattered pack before her to nudge aside. A pair of ropes fore and aft secured her to none but the men who held them.

"Always last aboard, these sogers!" Corm boomed. Hands, indistinct hands peeled Jonn from them, and only when unburdened did he feel the quaver of weak muscles. Gionn pressed his forehead to the ice and closed his eyes until the cold struck him like a hammer. He unfurled a grin for the captain, who directed the team of sailors fighting to stow Jonn.

"Did you not see us wave you down?"

Gionn looked at Foster, then back up. Corm pointed across the ice. There, a short distance away but separated from the ship by a pair of sparkling leads, stood Bentos. The floes were too thick to push through, the water too cold to swim. "Should have got him on your way up," Corm scolded. "Say the word if you don't have it in you. I've got soft and eager lads aplenty."

"I gave my word to bring them back," Palqua spoke before Gionn could collect himself. "Gionn, Wife, relieve the Buckets." Gionn sunk in horror. The squain lads scurried into the ship before anyone had a chance to second-guess the order. He'd saved just enough to make the ship with his dying effort, and these next would be his first steps in Manhas.

No one seemed willing to spare him a breath. He and Foster panted to the bow of the leather boat and took up their ropes. When they turned, the fog spun loose to reveal a glimpse of the distant temple of Omera. A short crystal, she glinted in the midday sun. It could hardly have been such a meager distance. The waves of doom and desperate efforts had done all their work in that short field, a stroll for any but a blind man. The water barrel they left may as well have sat in Drummoc for all that lie between them. It was a heavy cost to make her acquaintance, and a cost they may yet have to pay.

It went fair enough until they put in at the first lead.

"What're you doin'?" Arthas questioned his hesitation.

"Checkin' for leaks, arsehole. I don't care to drown four men for the amusement of one."

Foster pushed past him and climbed into the boat, and Gionn followed out of humiliation. As soon as the four shoved off into the quiet water, white chunks parting around them, the feeling returned. His chest clutched. Shallow gasps begged for the bottom of a lung they couldn't find. The freezing water against the skin hull reminded him of his plunge: the memory of a ship crackling aflame in his wake; the dull sound of blades smacking wet flesh; cries of the burned and the mutilated crews of Oduy Grassbender.

It was a swim of a quarter mile, as cold as he'd ever been. He begged his limbs to reach out once more, once more. The land refused to come until he gave up calling it. Gionn committed his face to the stinging sea until all at once the island stood over him, a pathetic wretch gasping with a change of heart. Sword weighing his side, leathers soaked. Gasping. He flailed and pulled his neck up to see the figure waiting for him on the beach.

The boat shook against the floe. Gionn was last to gather himself and find a way out. It felt as though he waded ashore, shivering until his teeth rang like a mason's chisel. He shook his head to remind himself he was dry but for a little sweat.

They hurried the length until they came to the next lead, not even wide enough to launch the boat. A few feet separated the crew from Bentos, who looked a king compared to Jonn.

"Hoy! Told you I'd make the ship before dark!" No one had a laugh for him.

"Can you not jump it, cunt?" Gionn hurried him.

"Lay the boat like a bridge," he suggested.

"It will chew up the hull," Palqua said. "We have another lead to cross." The Amposi measured it well. The edges were too sharp and unpredictable. What remained of Bentos' floe bobbed with his every movement.

"Well I'll be on the *Gairhle*, let me know what you decided when you turn up," Gionn threw down his rope.

"Aye, fine, you bastard."

"Come on, brother. We got you if you miss." Foster knelt on the edge with a hand extended. Gionn sighed and did the same a few feet away to bracket the landing.

"Are you a whaler? Will you ask every ship we meet to pull snug before you board her?"

Bentos waved off Gionn's remark and backed a few steps. He took a brief run and planted his foot for a leap. The edge collapsed. Bentos sprawled forward into the sea with a splash that wet Foster and Gionn. His arms flapped and Gionn caught one around the wrist. He could hear Arthas laughing behind him and meant to have his taunt ready the moment the head surfaced.

But the surge from the splash swept back and lifted the little floe, then sucked under again, causing it to lurch forward with terrifying force. Gionn tried to let go before he lost an arm. Bentos' grip locked him in place. He closed his eyes and braced himself for the agony of a severed wrist as the floe slammed into theirs with a snap like a jaw gnashing shut. It stuck fast as though pitch lined the edge, and Gionn thought the shock of amputation numbed him to the pain.

He opened his eyes to find his arm still gripping the other in the smallest open chip where Bentos' foot broke through. The rest of the man flapped beneath the ice. The gap offered just enough for a forearm. No head could fit to sip the air. The ice rocked again, and rather than loosening, the smaller floe pressed a ridge up between the two, taking another few inches from the hole.

"Axe!" Gionn screamed. Arthas slammed his blade on the edge so close and furious that Gionn expected it to slip through his arm the next stroke. He felt a tug at his waist, and Foster came up with his own axe. Shards stabbed his cheeks and eyelids as the two men smashed with all they had to widen the opening.

Bentos' other hand threaded through and clawed at Gionn's wrist, unable to come up with a hold. The pack seemed to rush in like a crowd behind. The ice creaked as it fused with an inhuman snarl. Any moment it would slip over and he would lose that hand, yet. His fingers wavered, weak from Jonn, wise to the danger. A chunk broke loose under Arthas' blade, and he tossed it free. The floe responded with a lurch that ran the thin pressure ridge another inch. Gionn turned his face from the flying ice and settled longingly on the skin boat.

"*Gionn!*" Foster scolded him like a caught child. "Don't let go, motherfucker. Do *not* let go!" He swung a knee across to straddle the seam and hack at the trailing edge.

Bentos faded. He felt it at the other end of his arm, like a fish who first considers giving up. There remained strength, movement. But he ceased his kicking to save what he had left, turning his fate to those above. If the ice didn't sever him, he'd drown soon.

The weight deadened, or his grip did. Gionn threw a second hand around the wrist and had to lean forward so that it was his hands underwater rather than Bentos' above. He felt another set of fingers grip his other wrist in weak reciprocation. The floe would take him at the elbows now—both elbows. Foster cleared another piece of ice. So many strokes for mere inches. Had they all day, and Omera willing, they could take him. It struck Gionn that with both hands beneath the surface, it'd be impossible for the others to tell who let go. He might even peel the fingers free.

He braved another look at the distant temple, appearing and disappearing behind Foster's axe. The site of his stranding. The panic of anchorage in so uncanny a place, gorgeous as it was inhospitable. It would have taken weeks to starve. The temple had another kind of severity. It glimmered around him like a thing that appears from another world to seduce a man to its shores. Had he stopped there, something stranger than death awaited. The allure overwhelmed him with a grace that demanded him in his entirety. That he be given up to something until no part of himself remained. A glinting shade, sailing the Attavaik while great ages of men passed, rising and melting like ice with the tide of a year.

He recalled his vow to drown anyone she could name. Here, granted the sight and touch of his ship, he wondered if she hadn't held up her end. One man dangled between him and his word. His arms shuddered.

"Hang on!" Foster implored.

Each time that imbecile told him something obvious, Gionn longed to find another way to spite him. How long could Bentos hold his breath, anyway? He wriggled his hands to see if anything might slip free, but it held. Gionn glanced up at the temple. She didn't strike him as forgiving and forgetful.

In the alternating shadow of the falling axe, he felt himself gasp as his hand slapped rock on the tiny island after his swim from the burning ship. His arms flung over, and he thought to rest a moment before he kicked up. With each breath he ignored the question of whether he had the last push in him at all. Perhaps he had it, but saw no use in the effort. Against the noon sun, a silhouette extended a hand.

Oduy.

A crack brought Gionn to the ice again. Foster's leg broke through, and he lifted it free with ease. He and Arthas tossed their axes and together, hurled a foot-long section onto the pack. Palqua wrapped his arms around Gionn and lifted his torso, a pair of white hands trailing behind. Foster and Arthas gripped the cloak and drug Bentos forward onto the ice where he coughed in disbelief.

By the time they helped him back to the lead, it had almost doubled. The others laughed and whooped with joy while the boat slipped across a sea brimming with new confidence. Bentos, too, found his voice, though every praise and slap of the back made Gionn wish more he had just let go. The ice yawned apart all around them, and the big floe that led to the *Gairhle* took a slight spin under quickening feet. The whole field seemed to lap on all sides, shattering even as its desperate claws tried to sink once more into their flesh. Gionn couldn't bear to look back at the temple of Omera, but he felt for all the world like her eyes had not strayed from him.

He wheezed hard for the shallowest air. Gionn's face tingled when they arrived at the ship in a blur. The men threw up a cheer, and he lay himself against Foster's back while the other got pulled in first. A swarm of rough hooks lifted him aboard and delivered him to his berth trembling, for all they knew, from the cold.

Two lamps glowed in the dark warehouse, and Wendell paused. "A door half-entered," and all that, though he knew oil burned for trouble. There flickered Folmon, as expected. The other lit Bayochar and Aymos, true blue Amposi lads. They seemed to enjoy the mild surprise they inflicted on a poor marine.

"I suppose if there must be a problem with me provisions, it's me fortune to have three of the finest captains the farri has to offer on the weather-gage."

"Slow-footed messenger," Folmon pleaded with a wry grin. "That's been sorted."

Wendell acceded his presence with a good-natured smile, and held off guessing what this lot meant to inflict.

"Did you find your captain for the hunting camp?" Bayochar asked.

"Aye, you're too late to volunteer!"

"Bruco, I hope," Folmon offered.

"Pity that, it's Etan."

Folmon shook his head with sarcastic disapproval. "What will Costig think when he sees you about town after that barc sails?"

They shared a guarded laugh. "May he trust me judgment."

"And may the reward for your arrest be quite small," Aymos joked to the others' delight. Wendell could hardly wipe a smile from his face, but it discomfited him—not that there stood any possibility, but that these men felt the courage to make sharp jokes under lamplight.

"I'd say your judgment is sound," Folmon consoled him. "Plenty here for a man like yourself, even if Costig has quieted the squains for a few days."

"And with minimal bloodshed," Wendell praised. "Do you not think it'll hold?"

The captains shared a patronizing look. "I will grant that the way he handled the boy was impressive—perhaps the finest moment of his command." Aymos declared.

"Aye, when I saw it, I thought, 'Costig has found his feet! We should be fortunate if it heralds the rest of his command.' Then he declares mourning!" Bayochar said with tempered exasperation. "Amposi mourning, for squains!"

"He meant to calm them. Feared they might retaliate." Folmon gauged Wendell. "Don't you think?"

Wendell saw the lay of it clear enough. It pained him to have to stand up between a mate, and his own thoughts from another's mouth.

"If you can't have clever, call for unexpected. They'll have themselves a weep and a sip, and in three days, I'll sail a dog's berth if six of 'em care to riot," Wendell offered sensibly, if not free of doubt.

"And meanwhile, every criminal may return to wail without fear of arrest. The reward's suspended. Leopard Seal can prance the streets if he please." Bayochar lamented. "Suspended! Not removed. Not reduced. That means it's back on once the mourning ends, and I think they may still find some passion for three argots." His huff of disbelief nearly sputtered out the flame of his lamp. A second lamp, Wendell noted. No call for two for a small chat. He saw two lights, and that meant at least as many who thought they should be the one who held it.

"I'm sure Costig would delight if our mate put in an appearance."

"He'd be mad to defile the mourning with an arrest! Leopard Seal or not!" Aymos became animated.

"May as well scuttle the ships for Donnab!" Bayochar added his concern.

"Lads!" Wendell laughed. "Costig knows your gods as well you. He's not fool-enough to violate it. But if we see the man and the state of him, who he speaks to, where he disappears, is it not to our benefit once it ends? Do you fear he'll raise an army of gold-hatin' squains in the meantime?"

Folmon placed a comforting hand on Aymos. "You'll forgive me mates their piety. As you said, it was...*unexpected.*"

"Aye, nor did I expect to find meself in such privileged company. And you'll forgive me if in turn I hasten you to your thrust. Is it the three of you who calls for it, or do you stand for others?"

Folmon forfeited the pretense with an admiring smile. "Those who care to be known choose to be present. But you cast us in a bad light, Wendell. We don't call for nothin' but your counsel."

"If it's that, you'll have it. But know I hold no command. No office. And no illusions. What could I have to offer?"

"You hold sway with the Marines."

"Not like Costig does."

"No, but enough. If you speak, enough'll listen."

His voice met in an edge that he never intended: "What is it you hope I ask of 'em?"

Folmon shook his head. "Not that, mate!" The captains laughed. "No one among the blues wants Costig to come to harm—I mean, *no one*. We need the rough bastard if we're to dream we might survive a landin'. He's a good fuckin' marine. Best sergeant-at-arms we got, and I've a blade for the first who says otherwise. What I've not seen, in any port of any kingdom, in any moment of desperation, is a marine in the admiral's quarters. And now that I've witnessed it, I know why."

It was fair, and meant for another, but Wendell felt the jab in his innards, and his gaze cast aside as if the humiliation were his own.

"I've never seen a flawless admiral." He lifted to stare softly at Folmon. "Nor one who cares as much as this one about his keep."

"He maintains a good order," Folmon acknowledged. "Among his men, anyway. The squains only riot for a light touch."

"Or one too firm." Wendell returned.

"It is beyond that," Bayochar said. "He's run afoul of the viceroy's fop. We have lost a ship to their bickering, and perhaps an ally in Nunoc. The man won't even set foot here as long as Costig has the helm."

Folmon nodded. "He's got me lads marchin' to death up that cursed mountain as though we're to meet Donnab at the summit. Now we're short on food, haven't slept, and the squains think we're a laugh. He's the first man in livin' memory to have watch over a prison break, and if that weren't easy enough to remedy, he built it into a riot. I like Costig in a fight. I'd have no one else on me deck when me ram sinks. But call me a bastard if it be so, Wendell: will the colony stand or fall on a man who couldn't stop a whaler from leavin' his harbor to set all of Taclann upon his support ships?"

Wendell allowed himself a ponderous silence that they mistook for disagreement.

"We ask you because you're his mate. If we meant to toss him, you wouldn't be here." Bayochar assured him.

"He'll listen to you," Aymos added.

"The one's true, and the other might be," Wendell admitted. He didn't bother to mention that if he went along, he'd be short a mate no matter how gracious Costig was—and grace was not the foremost of Costig's charms. "Which of you means to replace him?"

They exchanged sheepish grins. "Haven't got that far. Nor do we insist it be one of us," Folmon said.

"It is likely the Navy will stand for it," Aymos said.

"And not the Marines, as well?"

Aymos shrugged. "We saw the result when they had their say."

It had been a scent for Wendell's nose. He preferred a thing as a vague notion wafting on certain breezes. To be sure, it stung him to confirm he wasn't the only clever man at Drummoc. Errant as he thought some of Costig's ways, it seemed a fine command. Never had he considered the suggestion of replacement. Some corner of himself assumed Costig would hold sway for as many years as it took Tolba to find a new officer suitable for exile. Yet here were his suspicions given back to him in more certain words. Perhaps unfair, but not quite false.

The tales of Costig's reaction to the assignment split his side with laughter, and he knew the sergeant-at-arms would have preferred a lashing. In the end, he did his duty and despised it. But something told Wendell that no man of any character could be anything but offended by a request to step down.

"I'll need the terms if I'm to ask."

"He returns to his old command without penalty." Folmon said.

"He'll want to know more than that if he's gonna find a way to salvage his pride."

"Aye, we're workin' on it. Needed to know we had your support. Give us a few days to square the rest of the blues. Meantime, don't hop to his orders with much vigor if you can help it."

"I will speak to the officials. At the least, we will need Tuilapoy. And Willakuy must be told not to grant that mad reward." Bayochar cautioned.

Wendell raised a brow. "Won't be up to him, will it?" Confusion crossed their faces. "Costig's already withdrawn it. Used the silver to pay the blood-price to the squains."

Folmon surveyed the reactions, then said to Wendell: "Curious choice, that."

"Aye," Wendell said. It pained him before it crossed his lips, and crossed before he knew he'd ever thought it. "I'll be interested to see where the gold lands."

6

BATTLE OF THE AKLU

Tracks.

The eastern sky advanced on the last of their light retreating to the mountains of Camne Drumlag. They felt nothing yet in the shadow of Urkuk, but Norwet saw the speed of the clouds overhead. They spread like water seeping in to join in pools that swallowed the blue. A moonless dark would bury them sooner than expected. It vouched his earlier warning—no longer did they suggest he steered them off the trail of the Leopard Seal. No place would be safe from the galloping winds when Lanasep came to make her white bed. These tracks and all that told the wanderings of men in the wild would fall quiet. But it was too late for the Leopard Seal.

Norwet and the marines would hasten home one way or another. Now they could do it in their quarry's tracks. The dogs sensed the excitement in the six men ahead. They bounded at their harnesses. Tunguk steered a wise course, but there were too few places out here, and they had come to the last of them. He felt as though he swallowed a lump of firestone. Norwet considered the frontrunners. He told himself before they arrived that if they found the trail, he would race ahead to warn Tunguk while the men congratulated themselves. They wouldn't catch him, but as soon as they returned to Drummoc, a hundred men would march on his family's tukits.

Besides, if the marines found the trail, his uncles—Sawipelagann-apuk and Onagnutulauk—may already have arrived at the camp. There was little that an old man and a woman, running a broken sled with two broken dogs, could do to escape a strong team. Or even swift feet.

He prayed Tunguk had thrown the cobbled sled into the sea and put down the animals. If not, no lie would spare Norwet and his brothers.

Sawi—maybe Sawi would understand, and do it himself. He would be outraged, but he would not let the Navy tie a fugitive to his kin. They would have argots, Norwet consoled himself. New wood. Their own dog ship. He realized he was unsure what an argot could even buy. No Mattaka he knew had ever held one. The coins were blessed spirits who sailed with great men of Ampos, or Atlantis. Just as soon, he sickened to the thought. The frustrated faces, red with humiliation—he would give a ship full of argots to see the officials continue to sputter.

And Costig. He still didn't know what to make of the admiral. The one who should have wanted most to break them had some hand in the matter that Norwet couldn't understand. Perhaps—if there were nothing else he could do—he might run to Costig.

Brave thoughts parried one another as he set his team behind the pursuers. In the past weeks, Norwet had done many things he never believed he would. Up until the moment he moved, he often didn't know what his first step would be. His brothers, too. And his cousins. Captain Ostuk. Tunguk, so determined. And Kjartke, who sat behind him on the sled. It was true, what the old man said about the song of the Leopard Seal. It was the song of many, and perhaps more theirs than his. In his wavering courage, he wondered what they would lose if the man fell. Would it be much at all?

Something mighty may yet come of it. He would arrive, and only then see the way. For now, his stomach hummed with sickness. It was a fine name these men gave the fugitive. In some way, Norwet felt he wore it, too. But now, many tracks converged. Was it a name he would die for? How many would fall after him? These were the thoughts of a jumper, and he brushed them aside to watch the gray ice kick up behind the paws of his team. Still, he had seen Brother, standing on a single leg with two wretches under his arms, and he didn't look like one who could be called Leopard Seal.

Tunguk rested against the doorway of the aklu. The storm he anticipated spread its sail over the distant sky. He ran a lean hand under his tunic and brushed over many beads before he found the cluster. The brutal gale, the snow that would pile in a drift over the ice blocks—these joined with many other things that did not arrive in time. In the clouds, he saw three ships. A soapstone bowl and its contents. A man named Raratuk. Often, he waited with impatience. Hated a thing that never comes, or comes too late. He could not claim to be pleased now, but his days told him that it was not possible to be abandoned. Not a by a whisper in his ear full of promise, or a dream carved in his chest. A storm may hesitate, but something long-traveling would come instead.

"Almost." He said of the gathering sky.

Sawi nodded.

He and his brother stood off a respectful distance with their teams. They must have been relieved when he at last spoke. The two men flattered him to stand so quiet—he was old, and they had spears. It must have taken great will to keep themselves from the reward they sought beyond him. He also knew that when a desire came within reach it often made the hand that would grasp it heavy.

"Come, Tunguk. You can ride Onag's sled as far as the camp. It will be easier to walk home from there."

Tunguk wore a look that recalled something far off and pleasant.

"Come with us," Onag echoed. "I forget you, already."

The men shared a generous grin. No movement from Tunguk registered their words. Sawi and his brother gave him long enough before their eagerness stirred them.

"We are not the only ones who search for you. The Marines are close. If you are still here, they will not be so forgiving." When the old man again refused an answer, Sawi marched forward with quick steps. He stopped two spear-lengths away, his eyes darting to the long knife that still rested in Tunguk's sheath.

"Do you doubt what I say?"

"Why did you stop?" Sawi seemed taken by the question. "I thought you would be here by now."

Sawi ruffled. "I should! For corrupting my boys. Endangering my family."

"You have a grievance," Tunguk agreed. "But do you have a way?"

A perplexed look passed between Sawi and Onag. "Step aside, or I will show you."

"Then you've killed men with your spear. Good. I feared it would be only dogs and seals."

"It is the same thrust, grandfather."

"Maybe. I cannot remember. Only that it takes practice. I have not done it in so long, and it dulls even over a short sail."

Sawi weighed the spear in his hand against Tunguk's sheath. "What is this Leopard Seal to you?" He said in near-exasperation.

"Nuisance." Tunguk's eyelids lingered in a long blink. "I have waited for you many days," he said to Sawi. "I thought it was him." He nodded to the aklu. "And before, many others. Always, what I wait for arrives as something else. If it is you, you are too late! You should have come sooner, when it mattered." Tunguk laughed. Sawi turned to the two dogs in bewilderment. "Show me what I have anticipated, Sawipelagannapuk. Or we wait for marines."

Vatjate noticed the woman in the line of mourners outside the tukit of Nawalte. Every girl and grandmother of Drummoc who thought it decent took their turn with her sister. Many faces surprised her. Perhaps the Amposi mourning period brought out their curiosity, or the tension of the riot begged the release. It may have offered but a last chance to stand outside before the brooding autumn gale. Whatever moved them, she saw women she never expected. Some angered her. Days earlier they stole through the streets with sacks, or cursed her nephews. One, the mother of the boy gashed by knives at the first eruption of passions, filled her with humility, and drew a tear for a different reason. Vatjate was glad the child lived, and that the line was not for this woman.

Across town, another procession would draw many of the same for the old widow. Vatjate would not attend out of respect, but she sent Adelate and hoped it would not impose.

Though it was the Amposi gods who stood watch over the mourning, the people carried on in their own way. The only difference was the hum of excitement over a law they never enjoyed: that anyone might return to pay respect without fear of arrest. Some—including herself—doubted it. There were no enemies of Ampos here, anyway. Not unless Haraket returned from Camne Drumlag, but there was no way for word to reach him. Only one name surfaced. All guarded a secret desire to catch sight of the giant, loping the streets without fear. It would take a hateful courage for Costig to break his vow, but after what he did to Nukne, the Leopard Seal had better tread with care.

The first flurries of snow clung to her black hair. The Jargadak woman took Nawalte's hands and said as much as a stranger was required. Then she hurried into the heart of town.

Vatjate begged leave. She nearly lost the woman pushing through the oncoming mourners, but once free of the bodies, her paths were practiced and confident. The streets were again safe. A few guesses brought her into sight. Then around a short curve, the woman disappeared. Vatjate looped several times before she paused before the doorway of Ostuk's home, with its absurd windows. Light shone clear through where the leathers once hung. She slipped inside without asking, and earned the shock she hoped for as she took a seat opposite the Jargadak.

"You shouldn't use this tukit once the mourning ends," Vatjate offered in Mattakatan. "Many know who stayed here, and what company he kept." The woman raised her eyes without lifting her chin. "Forgive me," Vatjate said. "You sought me at my home. I forget you didn't know my face. I am Vatjate, aunt to Armenuk."

Kjartke considered whether she should apologize to Vatjate. She feared that some would think she contributed to the boy's arrest. If this woman and her sister were angry, or suspicious, they kept it within. It would not bother Kjartke. *She* felt anger and doubt for this visitor. For the boy, torn from her at the threshold where he stood on her behalf.

From the edge of the crowd she had watched the admiral drive his spear. It was far enough that it could have been any boy—Norwet, or Ferrakut, or little Ulwet. She hurried here where she gathered her knees and shook for all of them. It angered her that any of them had given her aid. One who slept in her care, in the very place Vatjate sat, wandered into the night and still had not returned. She did not understand the dreams of Brother, the acts of Costig, the instructions of Tunguk. Prison locks, or poye's medicine. The life had bled from this tukit, as with all she touched. It seemed a ghost who slid past the doorway. A ghost of Armenuk, where he stood earlier teasing her. But when she looked, she saw women file past in excited tones. Much light had gone, and when she swallowed her sickness, she had gone after them.

In the condolence line, she told herself she had violated their charity. They would turn her over to the men, and everyone with her. This is why she went. It was her turn to give her trust in trade for malice. When the mother took her hands and released them, her misery grew. She felt as though she defiled their mourning with her presence, which she gave not with consolation but out of a secret plea for forgiveness.

"There was something you wanted to ask of me," Vatjate interrupted.

"Yes. But you have given too much."

"Maybe. How do you know what you will end up giving me?"

"I know," Kjartke said.

Vatjate paused. "I can see who you blame. If you didn't, I would go. But set it in its place, child."

"I am a mother," Kjartke insisted.

"My apologies, sister. Tell me it was more than food you would ask."

She swallowed a lump into the deep hollow of her stomach. "He tells me to prepare a place." As soon as she said it Kjartke burned with regret. The corners of Vatjate's lip curled like a hair near a flame before she stuffed them down, and Kjartke knew who the woman thought she meant. She did not correct her.

"I don't know this man," Vatjate admitted. "But you think good of him. And the admiral is full of hate. If that's the measure of him, my family will do what we can."

"It is too much."

Vatjate searched for something. "What would you ask if it were my nephew who heard your favor?"

Kjartke struggled under the weight of the new proposition. She saw Armenuk in the spirit world, boasting in the foreign tongue, in words that garbled and burst. The voice took on a deep timbre. Brother's strange way of speech settled over it, and she could not separate the two.

"An army of boys with good steel. And a warship. No. We must raise a fleet, and sail to lands no Mattaka has ever seen. Nukne will be a captain." Her wager struck well. Vatjate sputtered with a wet smile. Tears ran the frame of her cheeks.

"You knew my nephew, then."

Kjartke blushed.

"I will say to you what I often said to him. 'What is the next-best thing?'"

"Tukit."

Vatjate nodded. "If I cannot find you a warship, we might see about that. Of course, the people know who sleeps in every tukit. Perhaps by then, feeling in the town will have changed. When does he mean to come?"

"Now."

Vatjate blinked her surprise away. "You are still speaking to Nukne. Now? Who will host him?" She seemed to grapple with it. "It is too much risk. Even the homes empty to the mines are filled on occasion with boys and drifters."

"Is your family large?"

"My family is large, and proud, and we don't slink before the admirals of Drummoc. But sister, no desire will keep him safe once the mourning ends. He should wait for the men to return. There is still the snow, the dogs, the firestone runs. You saw the liver of the Navy, how they breached every door. You and I cannot stop them. The boys are enthusiastic, but boys cannot fight marines."

They fell silent on the memory. Kjartke folded her arms over the crease of her hips in a cradle.

"He cannot wait."

"Then you are right. You ask too much." Vatjate tilted her ear as though she expected a retreat. When Kjartke held, she rose to leave, but thought better. "What will you do?"

Kjartke shrugged. "Prepare a place."

The mutiny on the *Gairhle* began the day she fled the ice. Corm walked the length of the ship near sundown to find Bentos and Gionn shivering in their cloaks over supper. It was their first moment of stillness.

In the hours after they crawled aboard, the entire crew locked in a vigorous fight to free themselves from the driving ice. Every oar swung to its own time, either to propel them or to push off some intruder. Twice, they seemed trapped again, but the merciless west wind shuffled the floes to give them a lane. After picking and scraping through minefield for what felt like a week but must have been hours, they reached a lead, shining and wide. Finally, the sail ran up and all Foster had to do was stay out of the way while the real sailors bent them through the lane until she broke into the open ocean with a cheer.

"Aft with you, lads! Warm your bones with Jonn and Arthas under me tarp."

"Aft cunts intimidate me," Gionn replied. "And as I don't find meself in need of a fat nurse, I'll enjoy the girls of the bow."

Bentos, already returning to form, gathered this bag and his bowl. "Come on Gionn. Don't be a cunt."

"What else would I be?"

"Would you deny your captain the tale?" Corm sang hopefully.

If Gionn ever meant to refuse him, he made no further effort. Foster stood with them, and the Mattaka boys when they saw Foster rise.

"Were you on the ice?" Corm said with indignation. They were, but Foster reckoned not long enough for the captain. "Think it's a fuckin' carnival?"

The captain cleared the bow with his chosen mates. The bench before and to Foster's side sat vacant. Out of instinct, his mind ran through the list of things he could do with a moment alone. Kick back, smoke, play a video game, think of a girl. It felt like an indulgence to have five or six feet of space, and only a couple of kids behind him. He settled for a piss. Foster didn't call for the bucket, an arm's length away. He took hold of one of the ropes running off the mast and planted a foot on the side, despite the new vigor of the breeze. The swell lifted the stern higher than he remembered and rolled under him. He checked the Mattaka, and found that a short hike on the ice gave them all an appreciation for a pitching deck that dampened any thoughts of sickness.

It looked like a damn carnival from where he stood. Jonn had been laid up under the tarp since they returned, and was apparently still alive. He couldn't see Corm or the rest of the water barrel bunch, but every bench aft not engaged in shaking out rope huddled at the opening, Palqua chief among them. The sound alone reached him—a boisterous scuffle without the clean outlines of words. Must have been a good story, and he had a hunch who told it. Little as he cared for those men, it annoyed him that anyone who never left the ship could join in where he was relegated to squain-status.

When he tied his pants and reclaimed his seat, he noticed most of the benches in front of him had turned to face the bow. They seeped into the vacant spots like a sprung leak. Juru, the next man up, took Bentos' spot and Hogue filled his. Chirim and Yuray collapsed on Gionn's side. Neighbors he'd never spoken to crowded forward, with benches as far as Fergo and Pitras shoving into the scrum.

"Why do I suddenly feel like the prettiest girl in the parkin' lot?"

"Out with it, Wife!" Fergo threatened.

He'd already found Gionn by the time he kicked himself. The loud, vile faces losing feature to the dark hovered rapt on every detail. The black tukit returned to him. He sat quiet while Rumit and Kullunuk told their versions of the fight with the strange wooden vessel. The whaler. He knew it now, as sure as the rise and fall of the *Gairhle*. Tunguk the elder, Parks the rapper. They all took their turns. Now he had only flashes left of the scene. Sensations of cold, fear, excitement. The feel of the wood when he scaled the deck. Most, he couldn't separate from the battles the others gave him. Even the version in Mattakatan that he couldn't understand clacked in his head.

They packed into a ship, months from anywhere, without a moment to themselves or a splinter to call their own. No wonder they foamed for a story. Every day turned on routine. It soaked the boards and circled around them on the relentless horizon, to the point that these men had fits over whale sightings. Everything was the same to them, and everything that wasn't was sacred.

Foster realized he left out how Palqua fretted over whether to just kill Jonn, and how that would change things for these men. There was still time to mention the silent vote to call off the search for Bentos, and he wondered if he should. Anything he said would be twisted and pruned, or stretched in the days to come for the men at the mast who couldn't hear. Maybe at some point, versions from Gionn and Bentos would reach their own seats. The two waves would cross and slosh back and forth like water in a foundering ship. Then it would belong to all of them, like the Mattaka said when they insisted he share his battle.

There must be a way, Foster pleaded with himself. There was a detail he could add, or omit. Not even a lie. A seed, if he wanted it. Or a slow poison that only does its work after the poisoner is gone. Gionn, above all, would appreciate that. Whatever rolled Foster's way through the crew would undo him. It would undo Parks. Tunguk. Kjartke. He had few enough allies on the ship, but he knew if he said the right thing, every mouth would work for him.

Foster shrank at the brutality of his honesty when he related his story to the hunters of Tunguk's clan. He hadn't a notion of what he wanted then. If his words were anything to go by, it was to be abandoned or killed. It was an act of surrender from a defeated man. Maybe if he gave these old boys his worst, all the way back to Costig, some miracle would come of it like before. But he couldn't afford to be defeated, now. He couldn't afford to be brave. Foster left out every cowardice and indecision. No one thought to act on his own behalf. Gionn waited with Jonn, Arthas guided them, and Palqua kept order and filled them with confidence. He downplayed his own role, and let Arthas hack most of the ice away from Bentos' grip. In the end, it was a different kind of concession. He didn't know their world yet, only that it was precarious, and too early to be wrong.

The crew drank up every detail, and pelted him with questions. By the time they reached the ship again he turned to the boys behind him.

"But I'm sure Atalkut and Tunguk saw it different."

"Who?" Fergo demanded. "The Buckets?"

"They were with you, weren't they?" Hogue waved them off. They took up their questions again, barking over each other until the commentary outpaced him. Soon, Foster couldn't get a word in between jokes and insults. The pennant men taunted the benches and the talk spread to old crews and ports in free association until very late, when Bentos and Gionn washed back to take their seats.

Sleep eluded Foster. Most of him throbbed with an interminable numbness. The new pitch of the ship and the heightened seas colluded to jolt him awake every time he came close to sleep. Most of their ballast spun its way to the ocean floor. The extra leg room made it easier to find a nook or a cranny to block some of the wind. The crew seemed to think Corm overdid it. But now he felt what the captain feared—the long drift of the gunwales toward the sea. Every disagreement between the sail and the waves pitched them beyond what he was used to, and every so often it took his stomach for a ride like a plane dropping in turbulence.

It'd be a while until they crossed the Drake Passage. And they never would if he did his job, he reminded himself. But until the one or the other, he settled at the end of a story to listen to the bilgewater whisper swift from stem to stem like a rumor.

No one sought Norwet's opinion when the tracks from two more teams joined the trail. Mentewat claimed to tire, and loaded himself on the sled. That the marines didn't taunt the man told Norwet where he stood: all assumed he would break to warn the enemy, or simply flee if he weren't burdened. Snow from Urkuk spun past them. He couldn't recall exactly how far they were from the dog camp, but he knew the Calm Harbor wasn't far, and they would come upon what made these prints beyond any corner, any ridge now. Tunguk could not run on bare rock.

Mentewat did him a favor. No longer did he burn with indecision about racing ahead. The other boys couldn't blame him. It would do no good unless he first cut the man's throat. Tunguk himself would never ask it.

Black hair bobbed in front of him and fell on the shoulders of Mentewat. The spear lay across his lap. It would be easy, if he didn't fumble. The Amposi never once turned around. It was a selfish desire, though. He hated to be bested. Though the dogs pulled with spirit and would outrun the marines, they would find their way to Drummoc, eventually. The lure of the songs held power, but he didn't think anyone would sing of a boy who was executed for helping a cripple live another day in defiance of—if not Costig, what?

Besides, Costig had sent these men, just as he sent the letters and the key. Maybe there was no call for concern, he persuaded himself.

A blade may as well have plunged into his breast when they rounded the outcrop to find his uncles standing across from a figure that he knew to be Tunguk. Dizziness took him, and it was only his grip on the sled and the dogs that kept them moving. He could hear the voices of Milak, Ferrakut, Ulwet curse him into bonemeal, and begged for some kaim to breathe through him with a redeeming blow.

The men beside the aklu watched them without reaction. Norwet steadied himself with thoughts that Sawi would have his argots. It would be good for the Seleku and the Vjarku. It had been a terrible season. Many of his kin were lost. This is what they needed, but it didn't stop him from hating his uncles, these marines. No thought of coin lifted him like the dream of a song yet to be sung, and for that, he hated himself.

The teams alerted at the sight of the approaching party. Tunguk's two scoundrel dogs rose to join the madness, and his own animals replied. The marines trotted up just short of the parties, where Mentewat hopped off the sled and overturned it to a stop. Norwet could not look at Sawi. His gaze briefly met Tunguk's, and then averted to the snow.

"Good of you to arrive before the storm," Sawi greeted them. "Come. Help me load him, and I will buy hasqa for each of you once Costig pays my reward."

Surprise and disappointment fell over Tunguk.

"Sawipelagannapuk! I thought better of you." The old man eased himself off the aklu. Sawi could only sneer. "These men are no fools. They see you help us. Give us dogs and sled. Make many promises to fight. And now, you would turn on your mates?"

Horror overcame Sawi and Onag. "What you say! I do not help this old vagabond!" He pleaded with the marines. "He lies to ruin honest men. I catch him for you."

Mentewat pointed his spear at Norwet's chin. "Do as I say, boy." Sawi started forward in protest, but the five marines brought their weapons to bear.

"No! He lies! We catch Leopard Seal. Wait for you to turn him in."

The marines fanned out in a thin line that stretched from Onag to the aklu, giving a fair berth to the thundering dogs. Their master verged on collapse. His quivering face could find no words for Tunguk or the marines.

"He in there?" The boldest marine nodded to the aklu. "Leopard Seal!" He shouted over the barking. "Surrender peacefully or we'll cut down the lot of you!"

"No! We—we capture him. He is ours," Sawi begged.

"Keep blubberin' and I'll grant me ears a mercy," another marine warned Sawi.

"Your fate is with us," Tunguk advised him. Sawi shrunk seething toward his team.

"Out with you, Leopard Seal! You won't like me if I have to come in." The marine faced off with Tunguk and raised his spear. "Aside, old cunt."

Tunguk drew his long knife and held it with two hands, vertical before his chest. The marine looked back at the others and shared a laugh. To the side of the entryway, the two dogs bounded against their leads in fury. The male choked and gasped between leaps as if he would strangle himself. The marine took a single step to give himself space.

"Last chance," he said to Tunguk.

Calmly in Mattakatan, Tunguk spoke. "Norwet, flee when they start on us."

Tunguk extended his arms low and to the side in submission. He crouched to lay his weapon on the snow, then regarded the marine and let out a wail of pain. The dogs renewed their threats. With a flick, the blade sliced through the lead that held the male. He fired as if from a bowstring. Teeth sunk into the marine's wrist. With a cry, and the spear fell as the dog whipped his head. Tunguk passed the knife under the man's ear. Blood spurted from his neck, and he hit the ground. The other dogs went mad with jealousy. Now the male latched onto the wound and growled at the flailing man.

The next marine bore down on them and raised his weapon over the animal. The point of a spear burst from the front of the man's neck, and when he fell, Tunguk was puzzled to see Mentewat standing over the body.

"Loose the dogs," Tunguk called to Sawi. He and Onag hurried to cut free their teams. Most of the animals surged to join the fight on the ground, but several danced at the end of the remaining marines' thrusts. With the dogs swirling after anything unfamiliar, Mentewat retreated to Norwet's sled, but he no longer held the weapon on the boy.

Two dogs slipped under the spear and took hold of a marine near Onag. He clubbed at them with his free hand until Onag's wounded him under his breastbone. Sawi prodded menacingly as the marine swiped to keep the dogs off. These were content to run around a wide perimeter barking until Onag urged them on. One took the heel of the marine, and the two brothers filled him with thrusts. Tunguk closed on a fourth marine who beat at a single pup. He called to the dogs engaged on the fallen men, but they were too furious to heed him. The pup took hold of the spear shaft and tugged against the marine. When he saw Tunguk, he let go and opened his hands in surrender. The dog darted off with his new prize. Tunguk slashed his knife across the belly of the marine. Entrails spilled onto the snow.

He spun to locate the fifth, and found him sprinting down the slope toward the town, well away from the attention of the teams.

Norwet stood transfixed through it all until a slap on the chest from Mentewat pointed him at the runner. There was no way to catch him on foot. Norwet jumped among his team, who snarled against their leads in jealousy while the other dogs seized on the marines. He beat them about the heads and yanked their scruffs to move their attention to the fleeing man. They ignored him until he righted the sled and called, "Up! Up!" Now the most vigorous dog startled in confusion. Norwet returned to the team and pointed him at the fleeing man. The dog howled, and at once the others set off with him. Norwet barely grabbed the sled and threw a foot on the runner as it passed.

The howl of the loose teams faded behind him to the silence of the trail—the rattle of wood and the scrape of ice. It could have been any hill they hurtled down. The dogs ran like an open sail, kicking up foam. He knew the rhythm from his earliest journeys to his turn around the Eye of the Needle at Nunoc. It was easy to forget the fight a moment past, and the man ahead. Norwet lost himself in the skip and the slide. Claws flung ice over the empty deck. He dreamt himself free of every beginning and end of a journey. It sank into the groove of every run. An exercise, an errand for Alakset. A peace came over him. There were no words he could think or speak.

The growing figure called him back vaguely, as if they'd encountered a stranger on the trail. The dogs swallowed the footprints of their frontrunner. One of them whined with excitement. Norwet had much time to examine the leather of the cloak and the swinging spear. Details emerged like the grain of a ship from the distance. A brown head of hair gripped him. At twenty yards, he saw a darker patch sewn over the elbow. Tongues wagged at an inevitable pace. He suddenly became aware that he would arrive somewhere foreign to him, and he did not know what he would do there.

The marine risked a glance back, panic on his face. He tried to quicken his step but it nearly tumbled him. The dogs bounded at his heels. Norwet felt sick. He could no sooner stop an arrow than what he had loosed.. The closer he came, the smaller he felt, until a terror filled him that could nevertheless do nothing to turn him aside. The dogs seemed to forget what set them out. They drew alongside, as if to pass. The nearest tossed a curious nose toward the man for a sniff while the others pulled with zeal as if to overtake a rival team. The marine looked again, this time at Norwet. It must have surprised them both that the animals chose to race him. There was no command for it. These were sled dogs, and they did the only thing they knew.

Norwet's lungs burned, though he'd done less than any of them. The marine veered hard to escape the team. In a single motion, Norwet overturned the sled and hit the ground in a headlong fall. Three quick steps launched him forward and he grasped with desperation. His hands wrapped the marine's shins, sending him face-first into the snow. Norwet scrambled onto his back and punched hard with the stone blade. The man felt like a giant who would rise and crumple him at any moment. He thrust again and again with uncertain desperation. The stout body bucked beneath him as though it felt nothing. The marine lurched forward a foot and Norwet hammered after him. He nearly crawled free once, twice more, gurgling under the blows, until he collapsed with exhaustion. Norwet blinded himself, plunging the knife again and again into the fear that any moment this man would turn and run him through, then his brothers in turn, his cousins, family, Tunguk, the Leopard Seal. He felt helpless to stop it, yet he thrust until he went dizzy.

Remembering to breathe, Norwet saw the faces of the team transfixed on him. They made no sound. The marine lay beneath him like a bloody stone. Shaking, he pushed himself to his feet. Norwet looked back at the way he'd come, far enough that he could see nothing of his uncles. Then the snow ahead, vanishing toward distant Drummoc.

It took much longer to return with the team. Sawi and Onag still worked to harness the last of the dogs they freed. Tunguk watched Menewat line the corpses before the aklu. A smirk crossed the Amposi's lips when he saw Norwet drive up with a fifth lashed to the deck. The boy's cheeks flushed. None of the men commented, and he was glad even though he knew there could be only praise. They knew the consequences of the marine reaching town, and must have had a worrisome wait. It was shame he felt when he unloaded the man, as though he revealed himself as different than they hoped, but he also felt pride like a bubble frozen into a block of ice. Perhaps that was the cause of his lowered gaze.

"I'm afraid I made a grave error," Mentewat addressed Tunguk over the corpses. "I thought five good marines could stand up to a single man, or I would have sent word to Costig when we found him. The Leopard Seal seized upon them like a beast of the wild upon children. Would have lent me a spear, too, if the boy had not put me on his sled and whipped us free. I trust you can see to these," he said of the dead. "It would not favor our mates if they are found with tooth marks." Mentewat smiled to Sawi and Onag.

"I do not know if the admiral will believe you," Tunguk said.

"No, he'll think me a jumper who fled at the first trouble. But if this one affirms it," he indicated Norwet, "he'll find it close enough to the truth when his men do not return."

Tunguk seemed unconsoled. "I fear for you if you tell this story. It is safer to say you saw the tide of battle. So you raised your spear against your own, to act as mate to the ones who aid the Leopard Seal. You convinced them, and when they freed you, you hurried to tell of the aklu, and the place where dogs war with men."

The old man spoke the words as advice, in a voice full of compassion. But even Norwet could see his course. If they spared the Amposi, his words could could undo them.

Mentewat grew somber. "If you think it, set your dogs. I won't resist. It must be hard to dream why I would help you when I was sent to capture the man. The truth is something I cannot say. But if you spare me, you will have a finer mate than you would know. Costig won't trouble you for long, and his enemies will soon find favor."

Norwet weighed Tunguk's reaction. He appeared to hold Mentewat as one did the side of a boat, placed in the water for the first time to test the stitch of the hull. No answer came, but something must have passed between them. Mentewat eased, and braved a remark.

"I would be glad to look on the man whose mates fight so ferociously for him," he regarded the aklu, then glanced at Norwet.

"You must leave now if you wish to beat the storm," Tunguk said. "All of you."

Norwet moved first, the least curious to see what lay within. He alone knew the state of the man, if nothing had gotten worse. Mentewat boarded his sled with flurries dusting their sleeves. His uncles, the black head before him—none suspected the truth of the fugitive, and how they crossed the admiral, himself. Even Norwet knew little more than there lay a crevasse field where these men tread. It made him wonder what lie beneath his own feet.

Sawi would be furious. Of that, he was certain. Norwet had feared the wrathful eye of his uncle every time he slunk through the camp, and every night he lie sleepless with worry. Now, with his presence a confession, the old feeling dulled like an overworked blade. The consequences of Norwet's crimes would be worse than Sawi could have dreamed, but it was a different Norwet who would face them.

"Up! Up!" He felt naked as he drove the dogs past his uncles, and sting though it did, there was a kinship in meeting one another as they never had. A shade fell over their brows, and Norwet realized it was their turn to fear.

Cormdran scowled at the two figures approaching from the navy hall. Behind him, a sullen sample of crew leaned or strew themselves about the ship. Tawatu hung from the mast and belted at a handful of bored sailors and a flock of squains.

"Hurry to the last and richest ship of the season! The knotting strands are nearly gone. The beads will follow. Nowhere in Hiade will you find such iqina tokens," the said of the Amposi gambling bits. "Reed grass, for plaiting and cushions! Fine garments fit for a princess of Ampos! Never seen in Drummoc! Win the love of your favorite toss. All will know to who she belong. Fighting men! Come near! I have a war club fit for Atxl! Blessed by the priests of Rampanatu! You are a man of peace? I have idols of the household! Geru, Ponotopl, Rugarapay! I have Mawena, and her frog, who is the holiest of creatures! No other figure will bring such blessing. He carries fortune and fertility in his jaw, and brings good visitors. Protects against shipwreck and rust, and holds a good luck for war or spoils or strong sons, any you desire!"

No one sung it better than Tawatu, but even Corm had to roll his eyes. The little charms were one of the few things selling these three days since the gale let up, but not even the most homesick Amposi cared for the fucking frog, of which they had more than all others combined.

An old woman tried to peer into the stock before Muir shook her off. "I look!" She claimed.

"Show your coin, I'll show you what it buys."

"No coin! I look! Trade!"

"Trade what, you old gull? We don't take your skins and bones. Coin, or fuck off!"

Coin had been hard coming. The beads and leather for stringing them had done well with the officials, but their visits had petered out. It was small cargo, useless to common sailors and locals. The Navy alone paid, and their bead dog Willakuy hovered over every transaction. Three of five would return to Turrha's coffers—if he gave a fair count. Corm had no faith in any number man of Drummoc. All captains knew ways to move stock to the locals beyond prying eyes, but few things in the hold were coveted by the Mattaka, and fewer still that they could afford. Only the pigments fared well with both Navy and squain, alike, but it forced him to price them so high that interest had retreated to wait for more desperate terms that all knew were in the offing.

"Captain! Good that I caught you in a lull," the Navy man greeted him with sarcasm.

"Where's Palqua?" Corm demanded the mediary who had shown himself less with each day.

"Where he chooses, and not with you. Captain Folmon, mate. Got your repair bill."

Corm had hardly expected it any earlier. Willakuy would have made a fair reckoning of what the hold could fetch so they would know what to carve out of him. "And a marine," Corm said of the stout little man with a proud mustache that arced down his jawline and connected to his cropped hair. "Brought him to carry the bronze lion you came to buy?"

"Me guess is to keep you from killin' him when you hear the sum," the marine answered.

"Should have brought more."

"You haven't met me, then. It's Costig. And he brought the right number."

Folmon interrupted. "You asked a wedge, and I'm glad to say we found one that'll fit your mast. Needs to be shaved down, but we got the carpenters for it. Your planks, as well," he thumbed at the shattered mess on the port side. "Basket of nails. Rope, main and lashin'. One halyard, six oars and as many oar locks. Two planes, thirty yards of tarp—"

"I asked fifteen."

"Then cut it yourself. Price is the same. Ten empty barrels. Love to hear the tale, by the way. Your pitch, your holystones—"

"I know what I asked." Corm snapped. "Stand behind your one marine, already."

Folmon took his time to demonstrate his enjoyment. "We'll have you under sail for eighty decairs."

"Eighty fuckin' decairs?"

"And you can use our carpenters at no cost."

"I've seen ships go for less! You know as well as I we haven't made twenty, yet."

"Is there no market for your women's garments and lion statue?" Folmon shared a laugh with the marine. "That cargo's worth an argot if I can count to ten."

"Aye, in Ampos." Corm protested.

"Then why'd you sail it to Drummoc?" Folmon waited for the reply he knew couldn't come. "Even Nunoc would have been better for an honest merchant like yourself, who merely lost his admiralty letter. Though we thank you heartily. No one expected a tiriloy so far south." Corm offered only a blank expression. "The tiriloy—surely you know of King Tolba's venture, if not the word. Men like yourself, carryin' proper wares to the far shores of the Amposi fetch. It's hard to get good lads here, and harder to keep 'em, cold and lonely as we are, and outnumbered by the squains. Wise Tolba realized if he wanted men, he needed women. So he sent his tiriloy out, last season and this, to fill the dark ports with the finery the gentle breed require. What us lesser men didn't understand is that the only thing stoppin' the noble daughters of Amposi from crossin' the Orin in an open boat and puppin' a hundred babes on the bare rock of Hiade to overwhelm the squains and secure the southern colonies, was the unavailability of jewelry and bead strands for their hair. I can hardly wait for the cunts to roll in. Maybe they'll bring something to burn in your excellent braziers."

Corm's face must have crackled enough that Pitras stepped in from the crew to buffer him. "Aye, we done you a service, so unless you come to buy a gift for your favorite whore, you can tell the admiral your insult landed, and come back with an honest fuckin' sum. The captain won't even stoop to counteroffer such madness."

"Good, it's not a negotiation. You've set your terms. You want Drummoc goods, you pay Drummoc prices."

Pitras instinctively stepped between Corm and the unfortunate captain, and the marine followed his example. But Corm held with a calm that he suspected unsettled his men, accustomed as they were to a certain wrath.

"How much of it's the wedge?" He said with precarious restraint.

"Eighty. Eighty for the lot, eighty for the wedge. Eighty for a brick of holystone. Can you guess what it'll cost you for a cup of hasqa?"

There were but eight of his men present. They came in shifts, but Corm hadn't failed to notice it was most of the same bodies. The fact that he got his number at all must have been the work of Eckerd. He must have kidded himself to think there would be any crew left once he paid out, but there'd be no voyage at all if he caved, and no spear beside him if he made war on this petty ferryman. With a will carved over his years at an oar, he waited for his rage to roll through his blood and settle futilely into his liver before he spoke in a measured tone.

"You don't want me coin. You're tryin' to pluck me ship."

"Now you're beyond me commission," Folmon said. "I repeat figures for wiser men. But if you decide to sell, I'll be happy to send for Palqua. Ships are more useful than ladies' garments, and a bit hard to come by here. You'll be in a much stronger position to bargain."

With that, he turned for the town. The marine lingered. "If it helps your cause, I'll have three mats of reed grass." Costig fumbled with small coin.

"For yourself?" Corm grinned. "Tell Turrha if he wants his cushion stuffed, it'll be eighty decairs."

The marine seemed almost pleased to be foiled, and left without a word.

"You see what they're doin'," Pitras guided the captain out of range of the ship-side market. "We'll never make that bill."

"I'll sail her to Camne Drumlag. You'll see what a parade of goods looks like to a miner with pay comin'. Who don't want a dress and a crock for his wife, and a toy for his lad?"

"Corm. I've got a whole barrel of virgin fuckin' soil for some cockheaded Amposi marriage ritual," Pitras pleaded.

"Then I'll load the mess of it and sail to Taclann! We won't be extorted. You men done too much for any but a full purse."

"You mean row? Can't sail if the mast don't stay up. If we could've made Taclann, we'd have done it when we first came on the whale."

"Aye, we were shorthanded. I'll fill the empty benches with Navy lads."

"Captain. Spare me if I'm the one to tell you, but you won't even fill 'em with the lads you brung."

Corm knew it was true, and he hated Pitras for saying it. "How many's gone?"

"Not sure. Haven't seen Arthas in two days, but I doubt he's fool enough to sign to the rosters without his pay. There's Gaspar…"

"How many captains run a tab with a poye for a man in that state?" Corm defended.

"I know, mate. I know. Believe me, the men notice. All I'm sayin'—"

"Aye, you came here to give me advice. Give it!"

Pitras collected himself. "You won't have the crew you hope. Don't ask me how many, but me bones tell me so. If you won't sell the ship, pay out what we've made so far."

"So half the men'll jump?"

"Aye! So they'll jump, have no claim on what we earn thereafter. So you'll know who's for you and who isn't. Then it's more coin for us, more for the bill. We make a winter of it. When the Spring ships arrive, that sum won't hold. Can't. We'll pick up escortin' coal."

"And if I pay, can you look me in the eye and say your name won't be among the Navy lists?" Pitras recoiled from the accusation, but Corm went on. "Do you know what a captain is without a crew here? If I haven't got a spear beside me, they'll charge me stowage and guard fees until I've no choice but to part with her for a handful of silver, if they don't just arrest me. I'll have nothin' but to scramble for a bench on the next northbound merchant, pullin' for pennies with the dregs of the seas."

"You mean like the rest of us?"

Corm bit down. "You'll have your pay when the hold is empty. Mark me, lad: the *Gairhle* sails north by Autumn."

The blast of air came welcome. There was no warning. The sled jerked, and then the noise enveloped PArks. It felt like some earth mover rained a load of sand and debris that poured over him without end. Any second, the blanket that cocooned him would strip free and he'd be buried alive. He folded back the top with his eyes clenched and drank of the air. Gusting snow stung his face, and pried at the seams of skin. He soaked the light in through his lids as long as he could tolerate before pulling the cover over his head and giving himself to the jostle of the sled.

For a length of time he couldn't sense in the dark of the igloo, locomotives rumbled past outside. He dreamed them when he slept, and when he woke, the storm snapped over him like a death shroud. He didn't even care if he died. That seemed too appealing to be plausible. He'd grown to fear above all else the maddening grip of claustrophobia. No light found him under a blanket, in a dim igloo, beneath a raging sky that shrouded a departing sun. No light meant no time, and the confines of the shelter didn't allow him to leave the sled. He crossed his feet for warmth out of habit and seethed impotently when he realized his mistake. Parks flailed for contact with anything at all, and sang for the sound. His hours—his only measure of time and chance to move—came when Joe forced him to sit and chew.

Not long before, he heard his name outside. Dogs went nuts. There were so many voices, most of them strange. He prayed someone would rip him from the igloo. But they faded, and Eskimo Joe returned quietly with no explanation. By the time the winds came, Parks began to forget things. Not certain things, but moments where he couldn't piece together where he was, or conjure a word to describe anything around him. He forgot what he regretted, and what he hoped would happen. Rather than put him at peace, it suffocated him with a feeling of permanence. He begged for a flash, a crack, any kind of punctuation. His own ruin, or a visit from a friend.

The slow jerk of the sled and the blistering wind delivered him. The agony in his leg and the cold drove away his confusion. He still couldn't remember if there were anyone else in all the world but him and Eskimo Joe, but he was freed from the burdensome desire to arrive anywhere in particular. Parks wanted only to move. A familiar numbness found his toes, and he imagined the curtain of white hair fluttering behind him as they climbed toward the top of the volcano.

Parks peeked out again. Snow piled on top of him and he had to close his right eye against the sharp flakes that blew in horizontally. He brushed a furrow clear from his stomach and it began to fill immediately. To either side, he could make only a few feet of terrain, but the angle of his body told him they were on a pitch, descending. He tilted to his right elbow and braced his opposite arm on his thigh. The blood in his hand stabbed like shards of glass where it rested against the powder collecting on his lap. Invigorated, Parks craned his neck back for a glimpse of his Reverse-Eskimo buddy until it cramped. He bent the kinks out, then in a stubborn embrace of the pain, pressed himself halfway up and twisted around.

Behind him, the handles of the sled danced unattended. He spun and squinted ahead, past the single lump of a foot in the blanket where no snow gathered. At the front of the sled, a pair of taut leather traces forked out from a hitch and disappeared into the blizzard.

The curtains and the door belonged to thieves. Ostuk must have had something to seal his damned windows for Winter, but it remained the secret of a roaming man. For the first day of the storm, Kjartke tried many ways to keep the snow out. It howled through the east window at the back of the tukit and carried a bitter chill that sent flakes through the open door and window opposite. She hung her emptied sewing sack as a curtain, but there was nothing to brace the bottom. The cloak held if she leaned against it, but snow collected in the hollow and settled between her shoulders and the wall.

At the height of the sun, she hunched out to take the span of it. Deep within the tukits, it was hard to say when the powder would coat the bare ground that led to Drummoc. The low tops did well to send it over, and what collected slid off in strands along the sides. The lanes still showed rock in places, but that meant little for the unprotected terrain to the east. She gathered a freezing coattail full, and tried to pack the window. Twice, the wind broke it when it reached half the height, and Kjartke slumped against the wall.

Tunguk was coming. He never said with certainty, but it was not his way. He did not know, himself. The storm must blow enough that there be snow, yet not so hard as to kill him. It was a narrow fold of opportunity between the two. When and where he appeared was hers to guess. A little girl's voice inside her insisted the two of them could not make the journey. She grew more sure when she wilted after two quick attempts to gather snow for the window. By night, it intensified. She recalled her father's stories of Ouretse, whose pale robe dragged behind and erased her footprints as soon as she stepped. There would be nothing left to lead men to Brother. Those who chose Winter to make their travel to Urkuk risked wandering the slopes without seeing the path of those who went before.

When the light returned—denuak—the storm slowed by half to catch her breath. Every moment Kjartke huddled in her cloak, she saw Tunguk faltering at the edge of town, searching for her, desperate for hospitality. With harsh words, she whipped herself to go out and meet him. She did not believe her excuse, that it was not enough time. Not enough snow, the trek too far. Kjartke hesitated until the storm gathered its courage. Now it ran like men from boats. There was no facing it. She must hide.

Her hollow preparations taunted her with the stray flurries that peeked through the open tukit. If he made the journey, Brother would be safe only until the blizzard ceased. There was no door to conceal him.

She startled at a flash before the west window. A moment later she swore she saw a gaunt figure in a cloak stagger past the doorway. It could not be. A fool would be out now, and even Tunguk would recognize the home of Ostuk a few feet away. She shook it loose as a dream. The spirit world, too, admonished her for hording her warmth, having done nothing she came to do. A vision of the old man called her outside to freeze from her guilt. She would not go, but knew now she must as soon as it slowed.

As surely as she convinced herself of the vision, doubt nipped at her. Kjartke flung herself to her feet. The cold current from the window urged her forward, and she peered around the way the spirit went. The lane curved away, empty. As she readied to duck back inside, an outline on the half-exposed ground called to her. There in the white dust lay the bite marks of a boot. She drew her hood over her face and plunged into the gale.

Overhead, the snow ran like crashing waves. Kjartke bent in half to keep the worst of it away. She shuffled after the prints that wobbled like a drunkard. In two turns, the man appeared ahead, leaning against a tukit for shelter and breath. He was short and slight, hunched as much as she. Like a mother who spots her wayward child, Kjartke stamped up and caught him by the shoulder. It was not Tunguk who turned.

The young sailor's eyes widened. His lips trembled blue and the tip of his nose and one of the mounds of his cheeks were already ashed with frost. He opened his mouth as if to conjure some explanation. Her hand clasped his face—he thought to silence him, but she pressed into the frozen skin, then rubbed it perhaps too hard until she saw the blood return. The boy—for it was no man—remained in a stupor. Kjartke could walk away now and leave him to his fate. She would have, but for embarrassment at having interrupted him. And perhaps some other purpose she could not explain.

He did not seem to understand her actions, but he gave no resistance, and when she drew back, there seemed some awareness that this woman was for his own good.

"B-b-b-," he stuttered. "B-brothel."

She realized he meant both his destination, and that her presence indicated to him he had arrived. Kjartke laughed. "You miss by much."

A weak hand grasped her forearm and seemed to plead with her. He needed to go inside. She considered her own tukit, so near, but worried that somehow Tunguk would be mad enough to try the storm. Instead, she allowed him to hook her arm.

"Come."

They could see nothing but the tukit in front of them. Kjartke marked her turns. She shook the boy awake when he leaned too much. That some wayward child on his first sail thought it wise to seek comfort in the brothel in a blizzard disgusted her. What woman would receive him? His mates no doubt encouraged the plan, laughing as he left. She told herself that at least it allowed her to look for Tunguk. It felt good to make a show of her obligation, and allowed her the warm feeling of resentment from suffering for another. Through every lane, she looked for prints. It did not seem a sled could fit within the town. There was too little snow, anyway. Was it any better beyond? For all its fury, it would be fitting that the storm failed to lay the faintest cover. That the Navy would find his stupid aklu the moment it cleared.

Kjartke knew she was near before she could see it, and woke the boy again. The frost bit his face once more. She took his far hand and pressed it to his nose, and he seemed to realize what she wanted from him. There was more cloak to him than bones, and only by this could she bear him to a door that she knew belonged to one of the women. The way the flap was sealed, there must have been someone inside.

"Hello!" She screamed in Mattakatan. It felt futile against the wind. Kjartke pried back the leather enough to put her face through. "A fool brings you coin."

Curses flew. "Close it! Get out!" Came the answer. A hand pushed her face. It roiled her so that she considered shoving the boy through and dusting her hands.

Instead, Kjartke pointed them toward the nearest of the barracks, a short walk that made impressive the sailor's feat of losing himself. Here, among the wider lanes between brothel and barrack, the snow lapped over their ankles. By his stiff strides she knew his toes would not last much longer. The boy slumped against the outer wall when she removed her support. She studied his features, and only now compared him to the faces that took Armenuk. This was no marine, but his relation to those who slew the boy wounded her. Had she a knife, she would have liked to use it on one so stupid. In her hatred, she saw also Nuk, and the arrogance of boys. Brother, and the helplessness.

The sailor said something lost to the wind. She leaned close, and he repeated in a shout: "I like it." Kjartke pulled away to dismiss his nonsense. But he touched a finger to her chin, and she realized he meant her setu. When she gave no reply, he melted bashfully through the door.

The harbor lay near, and while she was out, she may as well fear for Tunguk. Kjartke passed alongside the prison and hung in the shadow of the buildings. The snow ran in great currents overhead, washing the plain between town and sea. A blanket of white spread before her as far as she could tell, a few yards at best. The boneyard of ships and the water could have been a mile off if they were ten paces. She could not even see the far end of the prison. In a way, it favored them. Now she had no doubt the sled could pass into town. But where? She would have to trip over it to find it.

Kjartke retreated into the cover of buildings, which did not feel so cold anymore. She troubled to remember the sled. It could enter through any gap in the main row, but after that, the lanes were carved by Mattaka. Here and there she knew it would pass, but many places were too narrow. At certain junctures, she thought once that it would go, then another time that the runners were too wide. The sled swelled and shrunk in her memory. It must have fit Brother, but he, too, was now a giant, now a withered heap. Tunguk made no mention of it when he told her to make ready, and she cursed herself for not thinking it. The man couldn't walk two steps beyond the sled, and there was no hope of reaching Ostuk's tukit. Maybe Tunguk did know, and expected the same of her. It only made her angrier.

She did not care to walk exposed, so where there was a hope of passage, she went to the edge and peered around, then hurried back to cover. The snowfall in the little alleys was light-enough that prints would remain for some time, and here she searched for the twin lines of the runners, or the muddle of paws.

But the snow clung to her now. She slapped her cloak and pants. Her eyes fluttered awake like a bird. Kjartke felt the tug of sleep, and knew what it was that called to her. Soon she would return to her leaking sanctuary, or it would be her who was found. This walk must be made again, probably before dark, and as many times at next light as she dared. So far, she had not even covered the front of town. If he waited at any other side—she nodded off again. Where would he expect her to bring them?

If he understood the sled would not pass, and that it was too cold for her to march every border—and it was much to credit the old fool with that—he would think of her the way she now thought of him. He would recall her ways, and what he hated of her, he would assume of her actions. Perhaps he would know she did not consider the width of the sled, or failed to mark it, when she tried to find a place for Brother in a deep part of town. That much was true. Would he also suspect she would fail to find help? That the women would not risk much for her? She thought ill of him that he would think it of her. He dreamed her quick to give up, short of cleverness. Then she would be in the same tukit everyone knew they held, far from the edge, agonizing over whether to look a little longer or forfeit him to the storm.

Then he would lean on himself. Enter where he knew he could pass deepest. Tunguk withheld his choices until he'd gone as far as he could. He would be as foolish to wait for her as she would be to do the same.

Kjartke passed between the buildings once more, and found no tracks. She did not remember their number exactly, but felt there were few left before the neat stones of Ampos turned the corner, and nothing but Mattaka homes ran straight back toward Urkuk. There, the entries would be so narrow it would be a feat for an archer to fire the length of two tukits before he struck stone.

A song drifted to her from the spirit world where no storm could drown it. She muttered nonsense sounds, vaguely Mattakatan, to a rhythm that refused to leave. It was one of his. He must have babbled it among the many that he whimpered under her care. Now she could not be rid of it. Often, she had admonished him for holding his kaimatjuk—the arrow she made for him—to his chin while he hissed and hummed.

"No toy to drool on," she reproved him.

"It's my microphone," Brother insisted. Kjartke remembered the word because she did not know it, and liked the sound. "So you guys can hear me."

She started back into the tukits, and thought she could fire an arrow deeper here. Again, she rattled her head free of sleep, then looked over her shoulder into the thick of the snow. Kjartke pinched a few stray flakes from her lashes, and when the water cleared, a shadow struck her breast. Some yards out of the cover, it stopped, then altered its course for the opening. When the tight cloak emerged, she scoffed at herself for thinking the young sailor Tunguk. The difference was clear.

He held in either hand a rope. In a few paces, the low shades of two dogs appeared leaning into their harnesses. Not until he reached her between the warehouses did the sled show itself, laden black and piled with snow.

Kjartke beamed with a proud scorn at Tunguk's surprised expression.

"I forgot to think where the sled could pass," he admitted. "It is good that you remembered."

She led them in without response. With nowhere to go, there was little to do but bluff her way down the wide lane behind the buildings. When she turned to wait for them, the sight of the pathetic figure in his cloak sparked a low flame. She guarded this, her hope, until the sled passed as far as it could to where a cluster of tukits, set wider than the rest, marked the boundary of the sailors' world.

Tunguk grinned, and she gave it back with a confidence born of desperation.

"Oset forgive me," she begged as she pushed through the braced leather and fell into the tukit. A young girl cried out in protest as the snow swirled in. An older woman's voice joined, and bodies rustled toward her casting words in Mattakatan.

"Please," Kjartke said. The shouting stopped when they understood it was a Mattaka woman and not a lonely sailor who violated hospitality. "Look beyond your door."

The old woman hesitated, then Kjartke saw the glare as the flap peeled back. The poye flung it closed in disgust.

"You've had more than your silver from me. Best to be far when the storm lifts. The hunting camp. You can reach it by sled in not so many days."

"You know he will not make the journey."

"There is no more I can do."

Kjartke felt the rebuff against her collarbones as if the old woman physically pushed her toward the doorway. "You left the wound open to drain. It is drained."

"Can you not sew?"

"Leather," Kjartke answered. "Not flesh."

"It is the same."

"Then show us to our tukit, so I can start."

The poye erupted in a laugh of disbelief. "Go, child. Before you are seen."

"You offered me a place. I come to claim it."

"I offer you work! Not a sick bed for a criminal. Do you think you will go unseen for a single day?"

"I hope much longer. It will not be good if he is found with such a clean amputation. Only a skilled surgeon and a poye could made such cuts." The pressure within the pitch dark tukit collapsed as if struck away by a blow. Kjartke sat with the patience of a ship within a besieged harbor. A silence hung, then a whisper. She heard what she knew was the girl rise and pass through an interior curtain to the adjoined tukit.

"Where are you, child?" The poye's hands felt around until they rested in Kjartke's. The touch felt consoling. A grandmother offering advice in a time of need.

"You will bring death to the people of Drummoc," the poye said.

"I already have."

In the week after the rescue, the excitement on the *Gairhle* seemed to melt into the usual patterns. The watches returned to watch, the

Buckets emptied buckets. Foster once again prowled as far as he dared in search of work and circulation. He was still the Wife Seal, and he ranked "one arsehole above a bucket," as Gionn reminded him. Everything he did was as wrong as ever. No man went so far as to afford him respect. It was the tenor of their abuse that shifted.

He must have counted the mast as two shares, they teased him. Foster caught hell when any of the men they rescued got in the way, talked too much, or farted. "Watch this one," the bench aft of Yuray warned when Foster leaned too far over after one of his favorite nails. "He'll jump soon as there's somethin' hard enough to land on!"

If he looked idle, "he's still on the ice," and too busy, "an arse-tickler." Men asked loudly in his direction for "volunteers" for every lewd favor they could dream up. His friendship with the boys hadn't escaped attention. They were "Palqua's rats," having "a cuddle to thaw their bollocks," any time they and Foster exchanged a word.

For days, they swapped shifts of torment with Gionn, Arthas, and Bentos. When Jonn finally got the legs to emerge from the tarp and take his place, Foster earned a respite while the crew, himself included, lobbed insults to welcome the sailor back to life. None of it differed much from his own Navy, where the right kind of insult stood as the only acceptable form for expressing gratitude or compliment.

If anyone garnered praise for the event, it was Corm. Even that was never given without a dollop of scorn. Only Jonn thanked him publicly, quietly, without pretense, and he waved it off with a fatherly ho-hum. "Thought you were the captain, as much time as you spent under the tarp," he offered himself up for laughs. For the first time, the benches seemed united in a good humor, having all pitched together for a purpose, and no one needing to admit it.

Only when the fever began to fade did Foster sense that the wavering scales never quite settled to even. Squain Skipper surpassed Number Cunt for his second-most-popular nickname. He thought nothing of it—maybe beamed a little on the inside. A week passed. There was no way to be sure of such things, but it felt right. Aldan, one of Polc's carpenters, tried to refresh the joke by changing it to Squain's Mate. No one laughed, and when he explained that Palqua had been the skipper with sincere deference, the ship did what they could to ignore him.

There were a few pats for the former admiral when they first boarded, and that same day, Corm made a show of praise for the leader of the expedition. After that, the most generous words fell to the captain. It didn't bother Foster. He was used to brown-nosers, and understood that the chain of command prevented a subordinate from sharing in any glory that could reasonably be attributed to an idle superior. And to Corm's credit, idleness—his stubborn refusal to abandon his men as the ice crushed in around them—gave them a ship to reach. Now he realized that the insults for Palqua had been as mild and sparing as the credit. It went as a sound unheard until a similar one brought attention to its absence.

As far as the crew knew—as far as Foster told it—everyone had done alright. There were no heroes or scoundrels. As for Palqua, Foster came away mildly more impressed with the enigmatic crew member. A capable leader, nothing mind-blowing. Courageous enough to argue for it, and to go himself. None of it seemed strange, though he wondered whether men like this, dozens of voyages behind them, saw things the same as him. Did they downplay what he would see as a harrowing feat? Put more stock in something Foster half-noticed?

There was no way now to excavate what Gionn and Arthas said. Every mistold version had mixed among the crew so that he doubted that even *they* could recall the truth. It became a patchwork pieced from the versions that trickled forward, mixed with their own imaginations. Foster wondered, though, if his own tale had done something more than he intended. Like the general mood of the ship, he committed to nothing. Almost as if he didn't dare count himself for or against his crewmates for murkier reasons.

If Palqua was a jackass, someone would have said it. Himself, or for sure Gionn. This was no admiral, anymore. His own men—former men—may have been loyal, but the others would have delighted to bring down a foreign officer to their level. No one did. With great care, they avoided putting him anywhere near their captain, but Foster suspected that whatever the obscure sentiment might be, Palqua stood far higher than an arsehole above a bucket.

No one called Foster "Squain Skipper" after that. Corm headed off criticism by referring to the whole ordeal as "a lot of work to lose a barrel." In another week, the episode seeped into board and flesh, and no longer warranted mention. That delicate balance that only stood out to him in hindsight vanished under direct inspection. In its place ran a subtle tension. He must have been the last to notice, leaving Foster to wonder how much he'd already missed. But he felt it in pangs, like the pluck of a tight line. The crew got on as well as they had since Drummoc. Men shrugged off minor offenses, and Gionn, who'd briefly returned to his familiar derision of his benchmate, again littered in "Fosters" among the more colorful names. The new accord didn't bring a feeling of ease. If he had to name it, what he felt was "exactness." It was as though every simple act was weighed and measured, full of meaning that he sensed without understanding.

"Ice sky!" Fid sounded, and the call ran the length after dawn. There hadn't been a blue one in some time. No sun or stars lent their guidance. What occupied every mind in genuine cooperation was a pathological fear of anything frozen. The *Gairhle* often sailed within sight of the coast to get bearings and refill barrels from regular pit stops with names like Bathwater Break and Maimslip. But a day before, Corm had veered from a landward course and put them in danger of running out of water before the next fill when a small berg appeared alone, a mile to starboard.

The gray clouds toward Antarctica glowed bright along the bottom, whether from ice or sunrise or imagination Foster couldn't say. He'd heard the term often enough now to know that a lighter hue got the crew worked up, while a deeper one allayed their fears. Where the boundary stood, though, struck him as a debate over paint swatches.

Corm took no chances. After a brief chat beneath the mast with Eckerd, a number of sailors jumped to wrestle the sheets. This time, it was Tamarqan who hurried forward. Foster knew him only as Moipa's mate, one of the half-dozen two-share men. No one needed to tell them by now to vacate their benches when a sailor needed access. Foster and Atalkut stood off. Elsewhere, other men adjusted ropes, usually the ones who sat nearest. A handful gave way to more experienced crew, glad for an excuse to stand and stretch.

"Lend me a hand," the Amposi said—Foster assumed to Gionn. It was Gionn who answered.

"Overboard, cunt."

Hogue dealt quickly with his knot, then crossed to help Gabol. Foster scaled a barrel and fit to the nearby empty bench, according to custom. He marveled at the heavy sail thrashing overhead as lines came loose and tightened. The boom squeaked around. Wet leather gasped at the corners against the slack. A little pitch forced one step onto a ballast rock to steady himself. Foster couldn't explain what came loose for him. In the shifting momentum around the mast, he felt a pull. Another step brought him beyond his unspoken boundary. He expected to be lit into at any moment as he passed another row. Then another. He wasn't sure where he was going, or what he would do when he got there, but each wobbly stride left him feeling airy, unable to question his own motives. He tried to imitate the grace of Corm, whose practice showed when he danced the length of the boat. It felt almost criminal. He wouldn't have dared it before the ice, but now the violation itself seemed to beckon him. There was no rule he'd ever heard spoken about how far a man could wander. He might have been kidding himself. But Foster moved as though he walked a mountain creek, ice cold and glorious, beyond some invisible border.

Just as sure as it drew him out, he felt his feet catch as he passed Fergo and drew even with the empty seat of Pitras, occupied farther back. This was the last foamy sputter of the tide that washed him aft. No one said a word. Maybe they never would have. Foster preferred to think himself an initiate of the roaming crew. Six or seven rows. That's what his trials earned him. A sudden awkwardness took him, and he felt the need to excuse his presence.

"What's it mean if you see a seal swimmin' beside the boat?" He asked Fergo.

"Did you see one?"

"Maybe." He hadn't. But he felt a cold gulf between him and the man he inadvertently—absurdly—offended. Pitras advised him to apologize. Instead, he asked for advice. On a ship where everyone guarded whatever low status he held with jealous pride, it was the humblest thing a man could do.

"Means grab a fuckin' harpoon!" Fergo growled, and showed his disinterest by returning to the rope he braided.

Foster headed for his seat, stepping aside to let Tamarqan pass. Behind, he heard the sound from the sail that meant it was set and full. She pitched to port, away from the faint glow of the ice sky, that may not have been a glow at all.

Gionn cast him an unreadable look when he returned.

"Bucket!" Atalkut scurried past for Ordacles, who pointed him to Jonn on the bench before. The frozen sailor had returned to duty, but his former vigor seemed frayed.

Soon as the lines were set, the night's damp clothes ran up every free rope. Corm asked Arthas something, and after a nod, hung his watch cloak over the man's bench. On the very last row, Uldred complained to Tawatu that Bosc got a bigger portion for breakfast. Forward of the mast, Fid turned around on his bench to chat with Otsander. A song sprung from the lips of Banno or Bannan—Foster'd heard him called both. It wasn't a grating work shanty that counted off some mundane task, or a lament for a faraway lover, but a nostalgic romp about a basket. A second voice joined. They praised it as a cradle; for bearing a gift for a bride, and good mud for building; as a raft on a river, a funeral litter.

Laughter drowned them when Gewar, who sat even with the mast, rose on his bench dressed in a long tunic ornamented with beads.

"Hoy, lads! Kiss for your bowl?" He offered in a high voice while the food came around.

"Sit on me lap til I starve!" Hogue pleaded. Gewar pranced over the cargo, dodging lustful hands and propositions. It was a dress, Foster realized, and he couldn't be sure if the entire crew was rollicking in the performance, or had been honestly seduced. They howled and whistled and cheered him on. The Amposi sailors in particular seemed to lose control. Gewar fled the grasp of Imau'y, who chased him with disturbing persistence until he was tackled by Eckerd and Nolan. Gewar threw off the garment in a panic, and if he hadn't been looking at a fully-clothed sailor, Foster would have thought a woman had just exposed herself to the crew by the reaction. Everyone lost themselves in gasping fits except Gewar, who crumpled the dress into his bag in an act of survival.

"Perfect timing, Bucket," Gionn said to Atalkut—though his eyes fell to Foster—when the men finally cleared the lane for him to return. "You brought what I require. Any later, you'd have a mess on your hands." He pulled down his trousers. "Aye, you'll have the best of fair Gionn, *now*." He emphasized.

Foster understood well-enough. It was at the moment of balance that things could tip. All that day he watched as the sail whipped and the skies shifted; benches creaked, and laundry flapped in the wind; conversation roared over unusual distances, then ebbed to silence. His habit was to face forward at intervals, opposite his rowing position, to watch the seas ahead and chat with the Mattaka boys. That day, when the notion hit him, it came with anxiety and the kind of self-awareness that imagines all eyes are watching. They still spoke to him, but he answered into his shoulder until they gave up, and cringed when they had a brief exchange in Mattakatan. Days earlier, someone would have reprimanded them. No tongues on the ship. Now, it passed without comment, as if calling attention to it were more grievous than the offense.

He caught himself studying the aft benches, who always faced forward except during a rare call to oars. A couple of times, someone turned away just as he glanced over. If it were his first day, it could just as well have been ship life. Nothing in the carrying-on hinted at trouble. There was no reason he could think of why anything had changed. But the men felt it. The ship felt it. He didn't know what happened, or where it was heading, but Foster couldn't shake the sense that things were different, and full of danger.

Parks returned to him. Less and less, now, but the thought of filling in his buddy and hearing his side comforted Foster. He brushed away a fear of the worst, reminding himself that his friend was one-legged and alive until he heard otherwise. Costig and a gold coin would see to that. In his love of peace, Foster had forgotten that his mission required the opposite. The things that made his stomach tighten and sowed unease through the ship were exactly the ones he needed.

His desire for a frank conversation extended to Gionn. Foster longed to plot openly, and beg some kind of assurance that if he paid up, the bastard would follow through. He would have to settle for a cryptic utterance and a strange music through the ship to confirm for him the time had come. Time for what? Foster couldn't even imagine what would bring this ship in at Nunoc. He knew only that it wasn't Corm and a loyal crew.

"What would you do?" He asked.

Parks sat on a rock near the coast, his stump dangling. "You know how I feel about Gionn."

"Do I? You were his best bud not too long ago. He broke you outta prison. Twice."

"After he fucked us."

"Keep in mind that if I can't pull this off, could be the last you see of me. And you'll have to take care of Tunguk and Kjartke."

Parks shrugged. "Sounds like you made up your mind."

"Wouldn't be here if I had."

"You just want me to confirm what you're already thinking."

"Which is what?" Foster took in the apparition, and though it was himself, clung to it with a frustrated innocence.

"You can't do it alone. Maybe Gionn's not so bad."

"He's a goddamn menace, but he knows a lot of shit."

Those broad hands wrapped around his left thigh and placed the remainder of his calf across the other leg. "Know what, dude? I've been thinking about that. Everybody knows a lot of shit. Everybody except us."

"Yeah, which is why we need their help."

"For how long? We just keep throwing ourselves at people's feet, screaming, 'Save me! Save me!' I don't know what your future plans are, but it seems like sooner or later, you and me are gonna have to figure shit out for ourselves."

Foster nodded. "Eventually. But I don't expect to do it by tomorrow mornin'. Now I hear what you're sayin': to hell with Gionn, and you got every right to say it. Let me play devil's advocate, though. It's true, he always fucks us at first, but doesn't he always come around in the end?"

"Maybe. But now we know there's consequences for being wrong," Parks squeezed his knee. "So he comes around in the end. I guess the question is, has he fucked you, yet?"

Foster spent the evening prying at the ciphers of movement. Every sound conspired, and every remark cast doubt in his translation. He might as well try to learn a language in a day. Before long, the sea murmured with them, the weather cooled, and he found himself scratching for omens in the few birds that ranged home from their fishing grounds. Overcome with paralysis, he returned to his earlier pastime of observation without comment. He brushed aside theories and the names of sailors, refusing anything that didn't bear directly on his senses. In this, there were no more answers than in all his fussing, but he could breathe again.

The sun rolled down to an early bunk. Soon, he could stare at the silhouette of the man across the bench without fear of arousing suspicions. It felt quiet and unimposing in the dark. A man, like the rest of them.

Foster napped until the cold woke him. All but the watch slept. In the cover of dark, he eased himself from the bench and lay prone where a ballast stone butted against small cask of whale oil. He pulled his right arm free of his cloak and threw it back, then rolled up his sleeve. Bracing for the shock, he plunged his arm into the bilgewater up to the elbow. The chill ran all the way to his ear. Foster traced the seam up and down, and came away in a mild panic when nothing stopped his fingers. He composed himself, tried again, and considered abandoning it, along with his hopes.

But he found a calm eave beneath the panic, and scraped his nails over the thick board until they fell into the next seam. Foster traced slowly toward the keel while his heart throbbed on the rock. His fingers stopped. His eyes shut tight. He closed with gratitude around the top third of a metal disc wedged between the wood.

7

BAND OF DESPERATES

From a distance, the aklu looked little more than a mound of snow. Not until they were upon it did a few blocks appear, half-buried in drift. Norwet stood before the dug-out entrance with Mentewat and Polc. Behind them waited a half-circle of marines.

The first still sky in five days glowed a dissolving gray. Their boots sunk in virgin powder at the end of their trail. Not a paw, or a rust-brown speck marred the site. A single track led beyond them, then turned to the grooves of sliding knees where it disappeared inside. Mentewat pressed upon the boy with a look that, beneath its intensity, preserved a deference for the fact that Norwet might undo him.

Snow shuffled out, followed by a thick head. Costig gained his feet and sheathed his knife, brushing his trousers clean.

"No sign of the lads." He surveyed the fresh blanket across the slope. "Could lie a foot away, and we won't find 'em til Spring." Costig trudged to Mentewat. "And thank your luck you don't lie with 'em."

Norwet cringed at the choice of words. Mentewat had ridden the storm in a trail tukit at the dog camp with Polc and three men from their crew. They'd requisitioned Norwet to drive them to Drummoc as soon as it lifted, but not halfway there, the trio met Costig and a complement of marines marching to search for their men who had not returned. Mentewat's tale weighed their hearts. That boastful mustache rearranged itself during the lie. Norwet's apprehensions only swelled that Costig let Mentewat bear out his story in earnest. He insisted on haste, as if there was a hope of catching the fugitive holed up through the storm.

"And you're sure he was alone?"

"Maybe someone hid inside," Mentewat pointed at the aklu. "As for us, he needed no help."

Costig grunted. "Must have swallowed a few nails since I met him. Help or not, we know the jumpers fled before the storm let up."

Norwet swallowed past a lump. Mentewat did a fine job of pretending that he thought Costig referred to the Leopard Seal. The admiral's bright pale eyes at last pierced the boy.

"That your measure of it, lad?"

Norwet gave a weak nod. "Aye," his voice rasped the word to clear his long silence. "It is possible another man helped him escape." He perhaps dreamed the puff of amusement that brightened Costig's face.

Wendell meant to turn himself in the moment the blow ceased. His mate thought him departed more than five days ago, and the sooner he took the initiative, the lighter the sting of the lash. When he found the admiral had left with a deck of marines to bring back the search party—the one dispatched under exactly the terms Wendell had advised—he felt ashamed. For days, he groomed his excuses, first to Costig, then to himself. The grime under his fingernails from the meeting with those captains, under the "stain of lamps," as they say, had not left him with easy thoughts.

Win the Marines, that was all they asked of him. Costig wouldn't fight it, but if he did, he wouldn't have the spears that he had when he ousted Turrha. Besides, his company would be happy to have their sergeant-at-arms back, he assured himself.

But even the Navy couldn't help but notice.

"Went himself," the caskip beamed. As Costig was prone to do. Not a man on Drummoc had a quarrel with Wendell. His easy manner allowed him to pass through every jealous door on whatever task he set himself. He offended none because few noticed him. His way was to settle the knots before anyone knew they needed tying, and be gone when they realized it. When he and Costig first cleared the town in search of the Leopard Seal, the men followed him hut-to-hut not out of fear but as though they were happy to repay a favor to a mate. And that same humor that kept him free of grudges and the maneuvers of rank also ensured that no man loved him like they could a Costig, by whose passion or whose wrath—or both—all lay seduced.

To win the Navy would be no great battle. The Drummoc lads turned with the tides. All it required was most of the dozen captains—thirteen if

Polc counted. Three already stank of it. Throughout most of the Amposi service, "loyalty" meant only a lack of immediate opportunity.

Each boat was a sea kingdom unto itself, varied as the nine shores. The captains swapped the best and worst of men between them like iqina tokens. A good sailor who pressed his advantages could serve three or four crews in the single season before he deserted. There were a hundred different motives for following an order, and none of them were discipline. Among their favorites was treachery, and a mutiny was near the only secret they knew how to keep. That meant Wendell could depend, in a roundabout way, on the sailors to stand against the loud marine who rowed them to blisters and barked them up volcanoes like foot soldiers.

Marines were a different lot. There was no one higher on the island than a sergeant-at-arms—three of them besides himself, but he led no company. And Costig never reassigned his own command. He probably felt he could avoid the full disgrace of admiralship if he fancied himself still a marine. That meant fifty saw themselves answering to no one but the admiral. The other hundred pulled in cadence with their man. They were far from the sort he'd heard told of in the years when glittering steel emptied north from Hiade like the Barereto River.

The nature of their task forged them. By order, they protected the decks of Ampos, first to board an enemy, first to receive him. But some time ago, it shifted to keeping order among their own sailors, especially on land. Were he to convince their sergeants-at-arms that Costig belonged among them, not in the admiral's quarters, it may do no good. Marines followed most orders, but were keen to the kind of treachery famous from the Navy, and wouldn't suffer it from their own commanders. He would have to win them one-by-one, and one is all it would take to inform Costig.

So if it were marines he needed, he resolved to start with the finest. The storm had been their first break in the siege. The peninsula gleamed white like a holystoned deck all the way to the water's edge. It was the coal and no other that brought Ampos, and thus the warships of Donnab, to this harbor. If the sleds could run here, they would fly at Camne Drumlag, and some weeks before anyone expected it.

Wendell set a company of marines and the crews of Liam and Bruco to knock loose the dog ships *Juhketappat* and *Orin's Thief*. It would take more than that, but if Costig returned to find a lane scraped to the launch, it would please the man whose forgiveness Wendell expected to need in fair portion.

The drift rose up the hulls like a frozen wave. He tapped at ice that sealed the oar ports shut, while powder sloughed past them from the covers. A group of marines shoveled clear a path through a foot of snow so the rollers could lay on rock. Wendell knew the sailors would do such a thorough job brushing the ice from every cranny of the ships that there would be no time to join the marines in that miserable task.

"Did you think we'd run off if you didn't set Gua to bite our knees?" Liam teased the Amposi sergeant-at-arms, his shoulders as broad as he was tall.

"Aye. In fact, I did," Wendell said.

"You'll need to fetch your company as well if you hope to keep this mendicant at labor," Gua retorted.

"The only company I keep is you two lads, and me own if I have the luck," said Wendell.

"We all know Costig means to pass his lads to you. Who else? He wants you to ask." Gua jabbed with his elbow.

Wendell blushed at the thought he never considered. "Stuff your flattery. It's his. He leaves it vacant because he knows he'll soon tire of fussy officers and ministers, and riotin' squains."

"Ha!" Liam planted his shovel and rubbed his hands for warmth. "Admiral's pay comes in silver, and I've only seen a man tire of it for gold."

"Steel is Costig's metal," Wendell assured him. He started to add something, then stopped himself. It was a measured act, as from a mate who wishes he could say more, and Gua took the line.

"What's he said to you?"

"Oh, nothin' like that. No! And I'd never break a confidence." He hesitated again until they stiffened with curiosity. "It's just that when a man's ready to sail home, only a god or a woman can hold him to foreign shores."

"Squain gods!" There came a maniacal laugh that made the lot of them flinch. "Squain cunts!" Another burst cracked beside them.. A crazed sailor took Wendell by both wrists. "They don't let go." Black eyes clung to him in anticipation, while it seemed that bright creatures darted back and forth between the surface and an abyss. Liam freed Wendell with a shove.

"Hoy! Were you born arse-first?" Liam slapped him about the head. "Go chew your bench!"

"Sail with me!" The sailor offered Wendell. "There's a secret entrance to the harbor. Fuck! Shit on a whale's back!" He cried out not from Liam's violence, but as if he'd forgotten something important. "We could have rowed here in half the time." Each phrase from his cracked lips seemed to have little to do with the last. He cowered away from Liam's blows, but addressed Wendell as he faded. "There's very little to do here. You can keep your broken fingers! I know a mutiny when I see one."

Liam gave him a final kick, then returned shaking his head. "Must like you. That's the most I've heard out of him."

Wendell chuckled in agitated relief. "Go easy on me new mate. At least until he shows me the secret entrance."

"I've got somethin' to plug his secret entrance," Liam muttered.

"Pride of the Drummoc Navy. It's a wonder your admirals flee," Gua crossed his arms in satisfaction.

"Aye, that's me prize for thinkin' I could pass one on the new captain. Offered a blind trade, me worst for his worst, and I knew he took it too fast."

"Who'd you wager?" Wendell asked.

"Sowe."

"The second mate?"

"He's not a mate. Everyone thinks he's a mate, because he thinks he's the captain. All he knows of the mast is which side the shade is on. The blaggard tried to mutiny Rixtan during drills! Made us laugh so hard, they pulled with a new spirit, but he was dead serious. I should've carved the 'M,' but I thought no way Polc's got a worse cunt. Not all the way down from Ampos on a ship straight from the king or the farri or whatever Tolba dreams himself—admiral of the nine fuckin' shores."

Gua fell into uproarious enjoyment, but Wendell ceased his chipping to tug at a stray thought.

"You say he's one of Polc's?"

"Aye. Teague. Why, are you short a marine?"

Soon after the lanes began to sing of the people's emergence, the door flap bristled under a swishing hand. Kjartke gripped the spear and knew the old man's knife would be faster. But Hastate announced herself, and slipped in to fire a lamp. The poye's granddaughter startled, and Kjartke herself was surprised to see Brother sitting upright and alert. She took the rustling from the sled to be his usual agony.

It was the first time he sat without threats. His long hair hardened to his face with grease and he slumped to the right. The girl wrinkled her nose at his stench, which Kjartke no longer smelled.

He drank of the lighted tukit, bare but for these three, and a little pile of their things. "Where my dogs at?"

"Cut loose," Tunguk said. When Brother seemed betrayed, he added: "They know the way home."

Hastate lay a little sack at the end of the sled and flipped back the blanket to reveal the foot, still bound in the parchment he carried like some sacred relic. This, she examined first, peeling back the map with care. Her small hands squeezed his toes, and she watched him writhe in response. After a moment, he eased and let her do as she might. The foot was swollen and tender, but by the light Kjartke saw the dark colors fading.

"This one can stay," Hastate proclaimed. "The cold is gone. But you must use it, or it will spoil."

"I was gonna check out this Zumba class later," Brother said strange words to no one but himself. He winced in anticipation when she peeled back the pant leg on the other side, then his face flushed in the lamp light.

Hastate ran her fingertips along the stitches, and said they could come out. Then she probed the drainage hole that Kjartke and Tunguk labored each day to keep open. The flesh near the end was purple and and fat.

"You were supposed to knead. Like this." She wrapped both hands around his lower leg and squeezed with all her strength and she slid them toward the base. Brother screamed. Kjartke leapt across to cover his mouth, and scolded the girl for him. But she did not stop. All around the leg she pulled with vigor against his cries.

"We did," Kjartke objected.

"Every day."

"Every day," Tunguk confirmed.

Hastate found the claim quaint. She attacked it as if she stripped flesh from a carcass, the knot of muscle popping under her palms as she rolled across. Tunguk had to join on the other side to help restrain Brother's thrashing. It won no sympathy from Hastate. She wrung until the fight left him folded in Tunguk's arms, whimpering. Her efforts closed more and more near the bottom, where she squeezed right up to the edge, dipped her finger inside, and scooped a hateful wad of rot, bile on a black lump that appeared hard and soaked with blood. The girl held it up as if to reproach them, and Kjartke felt ashamed.

Hastate flicked it across the tukit, then kneaded again until only blood welled out of the opening, then less and less.

"*Now* we close it."

After the torment of cleaning the wound, Brother hardly flinched when the bone needle dipped through his flesh. The girl sealed it with a fine leather, unlike any Kjartke had, then cut the old stitches and withdrew them with care. She pulled a pinch of something out and started to place it in her mouth.

"No herbs," Tunguk said.

"It will help."

"No herbs," he repeated. Kjartke had told him little of her dealings with the poye, but he understood well enough. Hastate shrugged, and gathered her things.

"Wait." Kjartke caught her. "Whose tukit is this?"

Tunguk wore the face of a father who is proud to see his daughter learn something he did not expect.

"A whore," Hastate said without disdain.

"When your grandmother forced her to leave in the storm, what purpose did she give?" Tunguk asked.

"A Navy officer. We told her one with coin is very sick."

"Was she not angry?"

"Aye. And grandmother promised he would die soon." Hastate smiled sweetly. "Don't worry, the people will not look. But she has many suitors among the Navy, and the storm was long. I will be surprised if no one visits."

They called Foster to the mast during the first bearings. Gionn allowed himself a moan of disgust, scheming ears be damned. He perhaps overstated the situation when he warned his mate that the time to lay gold upon his palm had come. The laundry disaster of the previous day left him sure of the direction, but he less believed in the imminence of the event than he did the weight of an argot.

Yet with Foster tripping over barrels toward a navigational debate between Corm, Eckerd, and now Ordacles uninvited, the course was clear. Gionn was far from certain Foster understood his warning, much less what he was walking into. His hopes remained high from the previous night, though, when he heard the cunt rummaging beneath his bench with interrupted breath. Either he'd end the day with a coin, or his mate had nearly drowned in the bilge while he shook a reef out of the old sail. Valuable as the hold of the *Gairhle* might become, Gionn preferred his pay up front. Then let the benches turn as they may. He need only stay on the skyward side of the sea.

Foster hardly reached them before he tripped and sprawled on his face. The rest of the crew enjoyed it, and he added his voice: "Ha! Die from your wounds, scum!" Too harsh, he thought. *Idiot! Clench your arse before you speak!* He should have went with "cunt." That one was reliable. He'd only needed a little distance, and now he'd overdone it with "scum." They'd think he tried too hard. Gionn lashed himself over the insult while Foster stumbled again in the effort to find his feet.

They spread his precious map between them. Good that someone would get some use of it. But there could be no doubt where they were. Nothing but Hiade lay south of them, and the bearing was west, always west, until they hit the Arm, then north toward the Orin. Foster could've plotted it, himself. The only trick of the journey would be to stay off the ice, which wasn't on the map, and to round Nunoc without being seen.

Then again, these three were the thickest of mates from the original crew. Had the bubbling fears stirred them to bicker over some trifle, or was there another motive for their meeting at the mast? Every man on the ship watched and wondered the same as he.

Gionn despised a slow mutiny. Admittedly, the fast sort had their troubles. Tended to be a bit incendiary, with no time to mark who stood for who and side accordingly. A man could be roused from a nap and forced to decide in a stupor. They could go well, too: every man rises in a wave and the captain's off without a commotion, as it were with Oduy. He'd even heard of deposed skippers swapping benches with the new lad and rowing the rest of the season on a share. In the trade around the Aubatanes, he could be put back at the helm practically by the end of watch. Or it could end with all hands overboard—as it were with Oduy.

The advantage, as he saw it, was that he need not spend weeks calculating laundry like some bead cunt. So far, Gionn was unimpressed by Corm's composure. Could have headed it off a dozen ways, and he missed every one. Hanging his cloak over Arthas was a weak move. Should have had it up first, and high enough that it bothered no one. But he waited til the lines were full except the low places. A captain couldn't hang it off the mainstay. To do so aft was a sign the ship would be divided; forward, an omen of a reckless end. But Arthas was an even worse choice than wearing a damp sheet.

Gionn couldn't explain it, but he was certain the two were mortal enemies. There'd been no cross words between them, and the mood under the tarp when they shared tales was as light and enjoyable as a tavern at port after a good haul. But something about the way Bentos spoke of them upset him. Arthas and Jonn left the crew at Drummoc, and rejoined the *Gairhle* only in the second lot, after Turrha and his bunch were ousted. The reunion couldn't have been either man's first choice. Hogue would know, just a few benches away, but at this point he may as well ask Corm, "What's all this mutiny stuff about?"

For the captain to hang a garment over a man's bench meant that man was marked and owned—an act of intimidation and a warning to the rest of the crew. But to first ask his permission as Corm had meant the opposite: the captain favored him, and wanted all to know it. Not asking would have been worse—no less than to stir a grudge and make a threat against Palqua. To court Arthas, though, seemed a beggar's tactic.

If anyone, he should've let his laundry flutter in Foster's drooling face. The simple maid probably wouldn't even take the meaning. But he was as neutral as they came: a shareless imbecile whose count would make them all richer, and a member of Palqua's rescue party, at that. Aye, that would have drilled the Amposi's hull had Corm any sense. Maybe he realized it now, and made a show of bringing the map up to consult.

Gionn knew not how many men were once Corm's, or in what esteem they held him, but neither the captain nor Palqua had called for a bucket in days. Palqua seemed to have the numbers if he went by Navy alone, but didn't take them for granted, or the deed would be done. Both were keen on winning the lot from the ice, and the new lads, in particular. That left him in the unpleasant position of mattering a great deal. Men would look to him as a pennant to show which way the wind blew.

To side with Corm would serve his purposes if Corm survived. It'd get him killed, otherwise. The task as he saw it was peace. He recalled many lectures from pious cunts of the bachla, the eight natures from which man could be born. Eight streams flowing from the loins of the eight daughters of Nim at the angles of the world. Though a man could travel far and cross the waters he liked, his bachla lay always behind, sweeping him ever along the course of his birth. It was Eirgren who left no footprints, whose wake sat calm as oil upon the sea. She talked honey from bees, brokered peace between enemies, and put the scattered stones in order.

Gionn, he was told, belonged to the one who lay opposite. Nachreann sat her guests upon splinters and coals, served each from his neighbor's cup, and promised her hand to rivals. From her issued all strife, worms, and the unraveling of rope.

Foster wobbled back to his seat. The order came from Eckerd, and the sail shifted in a trivial correction. He needn't reunite the kingdom under one farri, Gionn reminded himself, only get a ship to Taclann. Still, as he watched Foster fold the map, he envied the easier task. At least it would be easier if it were him. But Foster was no son of Nachreann, nor did he slide out of chaste Eirgren. Gionn marked him as a Deana, or an Ainsome. Neither was fit for his duty.

"You get a glimpse of it?"

"What?" Foster asked.

"Taclann." Gionn nodded at his map. "It's closer than you think."

Foster paused. "You wanna see it?" He half-unfurled the map between them. His right thumb gripped Nunoc conspicuously, but only the Buckets had a naive view of it.

"The blessed isle," Gionn fawned. "Where we'll count our debts in gold instead of copper."

"I didn't think much of it when we left. Just wanted to get the hell out of Drummoc. But I gotta admit, you sold me on the idea." He smiled and placed his fingertips surreptitiously on his boot, and Gionn's heart chortled. "I just hope you ain't overpromisin'." Foster might as well have winked.

"Mate, the men of the *Gairhle* will have all they can handle, and enough to throw overboard," Gionn swore, and even he thought he meant it.

Costig couldn't decide who had the initiative to ready the dog ships, and there were fewer still who could have got the Marines to work at it with the Navy. Part of him stirred with the hope that his long efforts finally began to seep into the garrison. Were it a sign of a changing wind, they might make a siege of it.

But he doused the thought. The elimination of his next errand did little to staunch his ire that five of his men would not be found. It felt something of a betrayal, too. He'd done all he could to give the lad a head start, to be repaid in blood. Costig remembered well enough it was he who broke ranks first. But they couldn't have known his intentions had changed. An inept game of chase conducted with a wink had now gone to blows. The shouting matches with Corm, the late chats at Ingputka, keys wrapped in letters—it all seemed as distant as it was fanciful. That was not Costig's world, but whoever killed his lads had squarely entered his field.

He turned over the two glinting argots in his palm. The sooner they returned to the treasury, the sooner he could breathe the truth. Costig was not ashamed to admit an error. He longed for it. The opinions of captains stole no sleep from the marine. But with the assistant viceroy engaged in matters unknown, for purposes as murky, he couldn't afford to tip his defenses, or cost himself his command. Three argots stood on the beads with Willakuy. Three would have to go back.

Now he knew where to find it. According to the audit, the bureaucrat had taken ten Amposi coppers, two-hundred twenty-two decairs, and one gleaming piece of the farri's gold. When his marines recaptured the purse, it wouldn't seem strange to Willakuy if a few coins remained unaccounted. Few suspected they were taken out of an abundance of scruples to begin with. So the missing argot would belong to Alexicus, and Costig's debt would be paid.

He had only to get to the assistant viceroy.

The admiral sank in fresh powder, his lips heavy with a prayer that the snow held. Two days, maybe three to ready the ships. In the meantime, he had his own preparations.

He found the one he sought in the navy hall, regaling Polc's crew while he warmed himself with a hasqa.

"Aymos!" The Amposi captain called for a cup, but Costig waved it off. "Would you say that five days is sufficient time to weep in Ampos?"

"Two weeks, if there's no storm. But for a squain, it will suffice."

"Lift the mournin' at sundown. Take your crew out back of town, and stake your arses to the plain between Drummoc and the dog camp. I'll have no traffic either way."

"Sir. Through the night?" Costig stared in disbelief, "It will be quite cold."

"Is it not your crew's turn to march Urkuk?"

"Are we still doing those?"

"I don't know, is the war still on?" Aymos started to protest but Costig cut him off. "I just lost five marines to the Leopard Seal, and I find you shirkin' your exercises to guard the casks. The dog camp gets tossed tomorrow mornin', and you're not to let a soul pass in the meantime. Not a squain, not an officer of the Navy. Or I'll consider you aidin' the fugitive. If it's cold, bring a fuckin' blanket!"

Costig realized the revelry across the hall had fallen silent.

"And what of the rest of you? If I have to take the time to recall which two crews belong to Rixtan today, you'll swim the harbor instead of row! The rest of you lads, find the bottom of your cup, then clear a launch for me dog ships. Those of you who survive Donnab's ships can have a feast day when they turn for Bernica."

A reluctant murmur washed over the hall. Some of them rustled with their bowls as if to hasten their effort, while others glanced at their captains, or brooded over a drink in sullen resistance. Costig decided to let his officers do the rest, and mark who did it with a will.

"Hoy! Admiral!" It was a lad who couldn't have realized the disrespect of his hail. He huddled under his cloak, nose and cheeks burned red. "Can I be excused of it?"

His mates intercepted Costig's fury, and pulled off his boots to show his toes, dark and bulging to twice their size.

"Is it your feet I'm excusin', or your dull wit?"

"Feet, sir."

"You should see his plumb bob," a man added. Costig bubbled with laughter, and the tables joined in, eager for the relief. "Thought he'd pop around to the brothel in the middle of the blizzard."

"Glad to see the girl didn't stab you."

"Was me who did the stabbin'," he swore. "She was so cold, didn't even charge me." The young man boasted.

The sailors boiled over in taunts. "Aye, and which one was it?" A suspicious mate asked.

"Didn't catch her name." They jeered him and waved him off. "I mean it! Look her up yourself! Long black hair…"

"Was it?" Costig led the mockery at what was a description of every woman on the island.

"Aye. And tattoos on her chin."

The admiral's smile collapsed.

"Aymos!" The captain slunk over. "Never mind the watch. And see that the mournin' is extended, and all know it." He brushed the bewildered captain off, then pulled the lad aside.

"Save the tale for your mates."

He hung his head. "I couldn't find it. The brothel. She saw me lost. Brought me back to barracks."

"Saw you lost. Out in a blizzard?" The sailor shrugged. "Where?"

Kjartke did her best to keep her hood between her and the woman who emerged two doorways down. The other had her face on full display, and from what glimpses Kjartke stole, it was a lovely one. Most of the time, she studied the sky, the lanes, the leather flap of the tukit behind her with some resentment. She felt exposed, or engaged in a bluff.

After the second time some drunk sailor tried to barge into their tukit, Tunguk insisted she stand watch like a working woman. Only an angry flurry drove the man back out—it was brother's voice, "Hoy, cunt!" He said in pathetic imitation of Gionn. "No spectators!" The dark and the noise seemed enough to hide the sled and its occupant.

She warmed at the memory of his unexpected help, and the growing sense that they now cared for a living thing. His nights as a corpse were slept. His ghost moans were lowed. Some time during the howling storm, a spark had caught, and now the fevered sleep and the misery belonged to a man, flaring up here and there among wet tinder.

She stood certain this other woman was the one whose tukit they occupied. Her gaze clawed at Kjartke, as if trying to peel back the cloak. Maybe she wondered why she relinquished her tukit to an "ailing officer," only to find a young whore in her place. The bile in the air left only when another sailor spoke to the woman, and they disappeared into the tukit.

Tunguk had not said it, but she knew it, curling her toes for warmth under a single glowing cloud that wrapped the sky: this was no place to rest.

She had thought no further, and did not know if he expected her to. Between the scorn of her neighbor, and a strange exhilaration, Kjartke's visions darted all ways but the one she must go. Brother's lie to the visitor made her heart quicken, and she wished she could share a laugh with him the way she had recently laughed with Tunguk, or Armenuk. It felt a fine ruse, to stand here as if a girl of the poye for all who passed, and him, a sailor heavy with pay. In truth, she did not know who he was, or what bonds held them. He was no kin, no lover, and they shared no debt. The uncertainty of her position, here before a brothel, enjoyed a kind of appeal over the permanent lines of Drummoc, its jagged stone and mortar of snow.

"Soapstone bowl." A pair of marines stood before her. "For the both."

Kjartke blushed as it occurred to her.

"Where's Lanallike?" The second demanded when she saw her face.

"No more." She turned, hoping they would leave, but the two men consulted one another without a word. The first shrugged.

"Fine. The bowl, but we come back tomorrow, too."

Kjartke scowled at the dish, probably stolen from the mess. She did not know what women exchanged here, but the sight of these faces and the shape of their offer cured her of the excitement of her ruse.

"No."

The men appeared to delight in the rejection. "Just today, then. Both." She shook her head. "Come on, love. Is it that good?"

"Snow isn't Winter, is it? No Winter prices. Bowl," the second man chopped up his speech for her. She did not know what snow had to do with anything, but she pointed to the white path, chewed by feet. He rolled his eyes. "No Winter. Autumn." She did her best to ignore them.

"Copper," the first man blurted. "And we come back tomorrow."

"Lanallike," Kjartke deflected. "Copper for Lanallike."

"How much for you?"

Her throat tightened as she searched for anything to deter them. The memory surfaced of the shining coin she handed the poye, for all its trouble. "Silver."

The men burst into laughter. "*Silver?*" Good, she thought. She had feared they would pay it. "We're here for a toss, not a bride! Copper, and you'll be glad for it. Only because you're new."

"What's this shit on your face?" The first man grabbed her by the chin, and she wrenched away, causing them to howl with anticipation. "No copper."

"Fair enough, I got a ship in the yard worth many silvers. She's yours." They cackled at the joke.

"No silver? Fuck off," Kjartke spat.

They still smiled, but their frustration began to crack through. "Love. I'll forgive you if you hadn't heard, but there's a fuckin' siege comin'. A fleet of ships sittin' off that harbor until we starve enough that they find the bollocks to sack this filthy camp, whereupon every last man of 'em will do exactly as he pleases with you, and you won't see a scrap for it if you live. We're the only ones who might turn 'em back, and right now, you're not makin' us want to."

"You? You will not turn back boys with stones."

She felt she had gone too far, but it was already traveled. The marines glowered, then the nearest one seized her arms.

"Come on. Copper, and we'll be back." Kjartke tried to twist free, but the other caught her by the waist. They shoved her toward the doorway. Kjartke screamed curses in Mattakatan, hoping at least to prepare Tunguk's blade. Then she thought better, and bit her tongue. These were no Kapadak children. It would not be so easy for the old man, and if he took them, she feared others would come. She felt a flash of hatred for Brother, how he enjoyed such a reputation, yet could not stop these marines.

Kjartke pressed a foot against the wall and pushed, falling to the ground but failing to escape their grip. They hardly struggled to lift her. Their force was light, like a reproachful relative against a child.

"Behave, love. Or I'll tell the poye you're extortin' the garrison."
With another jerk, she pressed herself against the cold stone as if she
could stick to it. Kjartke forgot the men inside. She fought with the
stubborn futility that was her custom by now. It was a waning effort, one
that accepted defeat but refused to welcome it. To do as little as was
demanded, without pleasure, like the daughters of Ajatse who made a
home but answered no prayers.

"This is what you came for, isn't it?" She heard the voice of the
Leopard Seal in the spirit world. Not Brother—somehow the tone
belonged to that false name, though it did not differ. The marines peeled
her from the stone, and pushed her feet ahead under the flap as she
arched back into them, a mere gesture.

"Robbery!" A woman's voice shouted. "You take without pay!
Robbery!"

The marines looked up at Vatjate. The woman stomped in and
swatted them about the ears. "Robbery! Let her go!" She cried in the
farri's tongue for all to hear.

"Off, you milk dog! We agreed to pay!"

"This is how you agree?" She said of Kjartke, now crumpled in the
snow. "You go, or I bring the spears. I tell the admiral!"

"Tell him! She gets more than she's worth."

"Robbery!" She boxed them again, and one flung her back. Now
more women emerged, one of them with a sailor still dressing.

"Come on, lads, we just had a riot! Pay, or fuck off," the sailor
insisted.

Shouts from the women in Mattakatan interrupted their response,
and Vatjate flung a handful of snow in one of the men's faces. They cast
hatred upon Kjartke, but receded toward the harbor under the volleys.

She took hold of the outstretched hand and gained her feet with
Vatjate's help. They waited until the onlookers tired of the scene. Kjartke
noticed Vatjate linger on the tukit. Her eyes were pregnant with curiosity.
She knew what guest lurked within, and she had not come here by
accident. Kjartke gave her no satisfaction.

"The mourning is still on. No one can be arrested. But you must be
careful. We don't think it will last for long."

"We mean to move soon," Kjartke lied.

"Where?" Vatjate felt her hesitation. "You don't need to tell me. Nowhere on Drummoc is safe." Kjartke nodded her agreement. But Vatjate could not know that Costig aided them. She despised him for what he did to Armenuk, but he was why they had not been caught. He gave them a key, she supposed. And a bucket. Perhaps she could make them safe right where they stood, if only she let him know. Then he could once more bend his men around them, that they arrived always too late.

"Camne Drumlag," Vatjate continued. "He must throw himself on the mercy of the new official. My oldest speaks well of him, and says he has cause to hate the admiral. Ask for Haraket. And my husband, Mennetsatletaluk."

Kjartke snorted. "It is a long swim."

"That is why I've come. Will you speak with my friend?"

The ruckus died, but Parks' pulse didn't slow until he picked out the faint voices of women speaking Reverse-Eskimo outside the door. Metal dragged against a sheath and fell quiet. He'd come to know the sound in the permanent darkness by the honed senses that only cripples and superheroes develop. Eskimo Joe had drawn it when the men came. Now the knife was home again. Parks had fumbled in the dark, but his bat sonar wasn't as developed as his hearing. He nearly fell off the sled trying to lay a finger on the spear.

It creaked beneath him as he eased back. He swung a hand overheard and pressed his palm into the jagged stones. The feeling gave him a hand and an arm, an outline he suspected but wasn't always able to confirm. Now that the fear of another intruder melted, rage seeped in to the vacant crevices. It was hard to understand them with their stupid accents—all of them, Kjartke, too. But he wrangled a few words, and filled in the scene with the worst things he could imagine. He burst through the door at the last second and staked them to the wall with the spear he couldn't find, again and again, spattering the snow red.

Parks shifted, and the fantasy collapsed under the pain throbbing from the raw nub. There would be no heroics. He sank back clutching his thigh, and resented her for going outside to begin with. It was too risky, and he might need her here. And Joe: why had he refused to help, as if they could do what they pleased with her as long as they didn't come inside?

The thin line of light along the side of the door fluttered, and he willed it to flash brilliant gray for a second. Just a second. That would mean she was back, and it would give him a burst of the world he starved for. There was always a blanket, a wigwam, an igloo, a snowstorm, the black night between him and anything meaningful. Deprived of his senses, he ceased to exist. Not all at once, but he felt it descending, like a sunless winter. Between dreams, he would awake somewhere new and bleak. Simple things escaped his memory, as if they were tied to a sight or a sound he couldn't find. They ached as holes in himself—a reluctant face, a missing year, words that abandoned him. He couldn't imagine relief, because there was no present to extend. Body parts vanished until he thrashed them against something. Parks rapped the ceiling with his knuckles and hyperventilated. It happened so often that it wasn't as scary anymore, but the panic still came when he was unable to connect himself to anything solid. He had no footing in an intelligible world, and so no hope of moving anywhere better. This was what it must have felt like to decompose. For the breeze to pick off pieces of him to scatter over the ground.

Parks hummed. That was his trick: a thin thread of sound issued forth without him choosing it. Soon, it jerked taut like a fishing line under a nibble. He let it play out until it repeated. Then words.

"On a dark desert highway, cool wind in my hair. Warm smell of colitas rising up through the air."

Eskimo Joe shushed him. The brief acknowledgment slowed his breath. "Can I go outside?" His voice broke like a teen. "Just for a minute. A very short period of Eskimo time," he clarified.

"Rest," came the reply. Parks felt the word rebound off the walls and brush the hair on his neck. Again, he settled by a degree. Parks lowered his voice.

"So I called up the captain. 'Please bring me my wine.' He said, 'We haven't had that spirit here since nineteen sixty-nine.' And still those voices are callin' from faaar away." Joe's hand closed over his foot to silence him.

"Fine. Then you talk. Pretty please?" Eskimo Joe didn't respond. Parks felt the opening. "Why did you leave?" The question hung, and his gut told him Joe wasn't refusing. "Drummoc," he said. "You're from here. But we found you somewhere else. How come you left?" The pause that followed stretched until Parks was sure he would have to pester some more, before it finally broke loose.

"I was sure I would die if I did not."

"Dude. Tell me about it." He meant only to agree, but Joe took it as a plea for elaboration.

"There was a time I looked around, and I could see nothing new. The tukits sank into the snow. The same ships came by sea. The people sank, too. Into their trails, or the mines. I knew I would follow. You ask why I would leave. In Drummoc, I saw only as I had learned to see. But North, I saw as I dreamed. I am ashamed now to say what. Perhaps you, of all people, can understand. Suyu is an uncle of a people near Mabhan, the Hamarqeta. He wears the head of a serpent, the wings of a bird, and the tail of a lion."

"Of course. I, of all people, understand."

"He is a shapeshifter. Like many of the kaim, and like Urkuk. But Urkuk calls men home. The Mattaka have no name for Suyu, and it was many years before I recognized him. But I know he speaks here, or one who is kin to him. He calls the people *away*—in the shape of a woman, or a ship. A shore that is known by many, or only told of. Just as you think to reach him, he has turned again, and it is another that calls you. He is only known by remembering, because when you see him, you will not know yet. No boy of Drummoc knows this, but a man can look around with disappointment and say, 'Ah. It is Suyu who led me here.' Then he must be careful where he chooses to go next."

Parks thought of the drab town, fossilized wigwams under a fading sky. Freezing and dark. So dull that the entire place turned out to celebrate when a ship full of dogs showed up. So hopeless that men fought and conspired for a seat on the last miserable boat. Having a prison seemed redundant. He could understand why young Joe hauled ass out the second he got the chance. But from where he sat, the whole thing beckoned to him. The mill of people, the crowd pushing in the tavern for a bowl of fish. He missed being upright, and towering over people. He'd forgotten what it felt like to take a single breath where nothing hurt. All he craved was to plant firmly under an autumn sky, without hiding, without fear, as immovable as the place itself.

"What about your homies? All your friends and family. Were they—"

Eskimo Joe silenced him with a short hiss and a pause, as if he were listening for something. Parks listened to, and didn't hear it at first because it wasn't a sound. It was an absence. The women's voices had stopped. When Joe peeled back a corner of the door flap, then let it fall, Parks knew that Kjartke was gone.

Arthas was first to turn bluecoat. Corm at last left the ship—where he ate, slept, and peddled—to dress the sore that festered in his crew. The men spoke to him with respect, and only when they had to. None of them, not even Eckerd, mentioned that name or his new employment. Maybe they didn't know, as they insisted. Pitras alone had called to pay out early, and it was for other lads, not himself. No one brought it up again, but Corm had a captain's sense of the rumblings. The price for repairs was robbery, and all knew it. He hoped it would come down once the merchandise turned to silver. Now, he suffered evil dreams of the entire crew shattering the moment they got their coin. It was no good to force them to play nurse to the sale if he hadn't an oar left once she was seaworthy.

That morning, Eckerd sent Pitras to man the market in his place. If he lost the mate, he was sunk. Corm seethed, and channeled his venom at the betrayal into reorganizing the wares on display, and having the watch holystone her like a Navy docogon coming in for review. The flurry of work allowed him to consider that perhaps Eckerd had sent Pitras for something other than his own laziness and dissent. A good mate knew his first duty was to hold the crew to her captain. He could have wanted Pitras out of the tavern, if the sailor spoke too much of cutting loose the inconstant among them—or if he had gone that way, himself.

Trade collapsed to the same sailors returning each day to inquire if the prices had dropped, and penniless squains on the browse. Corm decided it was Arthas who divided his crew, and after talking down his own spear, he left Pitras in command and stomped off to treat with the blaggard as though he were a man.

They spotted each other at the same time. As Corm approached, Arthas fell in with a group of sailors. Palqua, who hadn't shown his face since they first made land, waved cordially from a distance before the whole lot streamed inside the navy hall. So it was no rumor. Only a man on the rosters could enter that building. Arthas had defected without pay.

Anger lifted him like high swell and he waited for it to set him down again. Corm decided not to return to the *Gairhle*. They would see his fury, and someone was bound to ask why he left for such a short walk. More than that, he hated the ship as he never had. She leaned like a wounded animal, full of fine refuse that no one wanted, manned by a crew who scraped their boots on the rock in anticipation of the moment they could jump. It was a fair luck that gave Corm so much recent practice in quelling his moods. By a feeling that grew familiar, he set upon the tavern. There would be no more hoping for new customers, for better terms, for Eckerd to tend his crew.

He found those who weren't on watch at the market cautiously pressing their tabs over a bowl, among those navy who shirked the hall for one reason or another, and a few squain drunks taking a head start. None of his lads could afford the brothel yet, but he laughed within at the thought of the local whores adorned like Amposi noblewomen if he was forced to part out the merchandise as pay.

"A cup for every man of the *Gairhle*!" He announced. Eckerd hailed him from the corner, and the crew begrudged a little cheer.

"And what of the brave navy who defends your port?" A man challenged.

"Let me alone a moment with your cup, and I'll fill it, too." Corm returned.

"I don't fault you, mate. I've seen your trade, and if you've not heard tale of Drummoc tabs, you'd be wise to deny a drink." The sailor finished the last of his hasqa and clapped the empty cup to the wall to signal for the pitcher.

"Aye, I've paid a few, and heard the tales. They'd have me believe that a single man skipped his debt on a whaler, and two warships chased 'em for a week. When the captain refused to hand over the lad, they rammed him and watched the whole crew drown."

"Don't believe it, Captain. They wouldn't drown a whole crew on one man's account. In fact, they pulled five of 'em from the sea to tell of what happens to tab jumpers, and let the rest drown. Ask me how I know."

"Don't surprise me that sailors are prone to embellishment," he scrutinized the man. "If you've been drinking with me lads, you've no doubt heard your share, and you'll know me name's Cormdran, and perhaps a few names for me worse than that." He extended a bent arm, and the sailor hooked it in his elbow to thud against the massive chest.

"They call me Foul Hand Waits. Not Foul, or Hand, or Foul Hand, or Foulie, and I'll have me honor back from any man who says otherwise."

Such names were common among the canoe peoples, who wouldn't stand a foreigner to steal from his tongue, but there were also halots who earned one and prided themselves on it. This lad was much fairer than any of the clans Corm had seen. His long black hair swept straight back full of grease and hung in curls over his shoulders. His mustache thinned to waves of dark smoke, and the more Corm searched for it, the more his origin flashed along some feature from one place to another.

"Your luck has found you again, Foul Hand Waits. I'm down an oar, and don't intend to be carrion for the Navy." Corm must have been the last to learn of Arthas, but now they could wonder how long he'd known, and what he knew of other things. "Swear to me bench, and if you churn up any trade, I might shake loose some blubber for you."

Foul Hand Waits touched his chest in humility. "Undeserved, Captain, given what I've heard of your command and the high esteem of your crew. You'll forgive me if I keep me place on the rosters, given you've yet to pay out the shares, and the bill to get you back in the water is," he lowered his voice, "frankly, a fuckin' ransom."

"Forgiven, and the offer stands for that seat, and any other you can fill with good barrels. Oh, and the Navy likes to set certain recruiters among the whalers to nick the weaker lads. Let it be known that if you, or any other man spots such a dog and gives him his due, what I lack in silver, I lavish in fine goods." Corm winked. "As for you men of the *Gairhle*, I'll have every hand who counts himself among the shares mustered in the mornin'. We sail for Camne Drumlag!"

Foul Hand Waits winced. "Don't think Palqua will like that."

"Is it Palqua, or Turrha who's the admiral?" The sailor avoided the remark. "As I understand, there's over two-hundred navy and marines there, and the gods only count how many squains. If no one at Drummoc cares to buy, we'll go where they will."

"And not a one of 'em has a coin, nor will he get his pay until the coal is loaded, and he's back on Drummoc in Autumn."

"That bead cunt'll come along if he wants his count. They pledge their pay, and I'll be happy to sail back and collect it. As for the squains, wouldn't surprise me if a few gave over their family's larder for a trinket— or pledged his wife."

Eckerd caught up to Corm as he stalked out with new vigor.

"I'll have 'em where you say, but the mast is out until we get a wedge. Are we to row the whole passage? Won't help our repair bill if the Navy sees how we limp."

"Aye, mate. And if I don't sell them goods, I won't have a ship to embarrass me or a crew to see it."

The sun never set on the men of the *Gairhle*, and Corm sweated the morning. He couldn't mark the line that cleaved it from the night, and with each man who trickled in, he thought the rest had left him. But by a dozen different interpretations, every member but Arthas arrived at a morning of his own reckoning.

The pile of rollers gave him equal distress. Long wood logs, cut from the forests of Ampos and smoothed by the keel of a hundred ships, they lay stacked at the end of the yard where the dry fleet reclined. If he wanted in the water, he'd have to set them one by one beneath his ship, and run the last to the front again as the crew pushed her to the launch. That's where he expected to greet a throng of Navy, and where so far, only a single captain stood in wait. Could have been that their lads were off sogering and would arrive shortly. Corm needed them now. His own men expected him to hurry over before anyone could stop them. That was the intent he meant to give off, but far from the truth.

Eckerd's warning not to show weakness by going under oars was as wise as unnecessary. Corm had no desire to wet his hull. He knew a loud boast of a passage to Camne Drumlag would ruffle the admiral to action. Had to. This time of year, she bustled with coal ships, and squains loading basket after basket on every inch of deck while their captains cursed their pace. They wanted off and out of Hiade before the ice and the gales ever raised a distant standard. A whaler full of goods, unheard of as it was, could only crack the delicate operation and leave it to founder. Palqua would remember his threat to ram the vessels if the Navy didn't give him fair terms, and with the repair bill as it stood, they could scarcely entertain the notion of letting the *Gairhle* ply her trade at the mines.

If he went, he'd get pennies, or get sunk. He didn't want trade. What Corm needed was an enemy.

A crew held together on few conditions at sea—fewer still, on land. Silver always did it, and he hadn't even the pretense of that. Instead, he recalled with pride the way his motley lads barreled up in their run-in with the angotaks. From the scuffle for the cargo to the perilous flight, they pulled as one. It was "drop bollocks and raise a cry" when they had something to fear. Everyone wet his blade, and though they could have stood for his mutiny half a dozen times, they held. With some regret, he thought of their faces when he brought them in to Drummoc before the storm, and wondered if he might have lost faith too soon.

He had no silver, but they would recall their mates who fell on the decks between here and Taclann. If he wanted to hold them, all he needed was a fight.

So after as much stalling as he dared, Corm approached with bewilderment. Captain Bruco had the honor again. No man had yet spoken to him twice, perhaps because the kind of things they were sent to say required a stout marine on guard. This Bruco had a pitiful way that didn't warrant the effort, and they must have taken it to mean Corm found him agreeable.

"No rollers today, Corm. Suspicion of rot."

"Aye, I smell somethin' like it. Stand aside and I'll have a look."

"Me orders are clear. The carpenters have to inspect the pile before anyone uses 'em."

"They'll be around any moment, will they?" Bruco could only smile. "By your own laws, it's an offense to hold a free ship in dock."

"No one's holdin' you. Launch if you care to. You just can't use the rollers."

The crew grew restless, and Corm let the murmurs work their way through. "Are we to carry a sixty-seater laden with goods and drop her in the sea?"

Bruco shrugged. "If you're not strong enough to move her, at least you got enough dresses to go 'round."

Coming from a different officer, it might have irked them, but Bruco teased out the insult with as much uncertainty as rehearsal. The men laughed with glee, and only enjoyed it more when the officer failed to conceal his pride. Whaler or sailor, here was a man who stiffened in hope that someone would believe him a captain.

"You got thrice the logs I'll need. If we find a rotted one, we'll set it aside for you." He glanced to the hall. Bruco did the same, expecting the same reinforcements as Corm. All they found was a scattering of disinterested loafers.

"Sorry, mate. Orders," was all the officer could contrive. Corm tilted his head, and his crew streamed past to wrestle logs off to the *Gairhle*. "Hoy!" Bruco protested. "If you're lookin' to be striped, all you have to do is ask. Pile 'em back!" The crew ignored the empty plea.

"Carry on, lads! The Navy won't rest until we sleep in the poorman's quarters or the prison."

"It'll be the second if you don't do as I say!" Bruco puffed up to Corm. The whaler rose well above the little officer. A menacing squint sufficed to send him off after a man lifting one end of a log. Bruco grabbed him by the elbow. "Stop, or I'll harness you to a coal sled!"

"Unhand me lad!" Corm reached for Bruco, who slipped free of his grasp and shrunk away. Corm hoped he would tussle, but Bruco just placed himself between two men and pushed on their log until they had to set it down. When Corm started after him, he retreated to the pile.

"Marines! Take this man!" He called to no one within hearing.

"Stand aside, bucket." In truth, the whalers had the run of it by then. Bruco could do nothing to get in the way. Corm collared him, and dragged him from the rollers. No other captain of a squain boat would have suffered that treatment without offering a fist. To Corm's frustration, Bruco merely straightened his coat, the faded pompous blue of the Navy.

"We'll see your courage when Costig arrives."

"I swore your terms, and by every god of the sea you can name, we've a right to sell, and a right to leave. To take a vessel by force is *piracy*." The word sent a ripple of unease over the crew. "No surprise, that half your men come from the whalers, and perhaps yourself." Bruco gasped at the insinuation. "But if you choose that trade, King Tolba will regret no evil treatment or unkind word visited upon you. You stand between these lads and their wage—their hasqa, whores, and silver! Aside, turncoat!"

Bruco's lips trembled. He stepped off three or four paces while Corm wondered what he'd have to say to find the man's spine. The speech hadn't roused the lads like he hoped. If this one wouldn't give him what he needed, someone else would have to.

When Bruco glanced back, Corm seized the hesitation. "I said, '*Aside!*'" He cocked back his fist and dropped it through Bruco's face. Only the pile of rollers caught his stumble. The men paused in confusion. The officer looked up as if he had his feelings betrayed by an old mate. Blood welled over his gums. Corm stung with humiliation on his behalf. Bruco looked a child about to bawl over his father's discipline. He gained his feet, and scurried off with haste.

"Was that necessary?" Pitras hefted his end of a roller.

"Aye, if we mean to sail," Eckerd defended Corm with little more than a sense of duty.

"The lout wasn't in me way, at all," Pitras said. "But now the Marines will be, soon enough."

"Then make a song of it before they get here!" Corm suggested. But no one picked up a work shanty. The men fell to their labor in silence. He looked off after the pathetic officer, and again at intervals when Bruco disappeared. The marines he expected never issued forth. Before long, the *Gairhle* sat on rollers with her oars turned about.

Corm ordered the first heave. She creaked a few inches over the logs, and the next effort did little more. He no more wanted that ship in the water than a blade in his belly, but the captain fell in alongside the men. There were plenty of positions. They were twenty-seven and himself when they made shore, now two short. The *Gairhle* still had sixty benches and a bulging hold.

"With a will, lads!" He encouraged even as he pushed with a faint effort. "Now she knows the way of it," he said when they cleared the first roller. The pace should have pleased him. It would be a midnight sun before they wet a timber. Corm, though, was a captain. He had them working as a single body, but it was a wraith, visiting to mumble of its own death.

The fault lay with him, he thought. He'd never suffer such a poor effort. They felt the divided spirit of their leader, and gave him the same. Corm released his oar and stalked up and down, snapping off from the bottom of his lungs. He reminded himself that whatever disadvantage he gave by showing his limping ship, the Navy lost far more if they let him make Camne Drumlag. He needn't go so far. Only to the nearest fight. They would probably make him exhaust his crew before marching out to meet them. All the better. A wasted effort would infuriate the whalers. They knew the Navy terms to be unfair. Let them think the admiral kept them from their silver entirely, and he would again have the lads who boarded an angotak vessel like they were a Fire Nose crew of the farri.

A spatter of curses drew his attention to the prow. A group of squain lads danced in mockery where they had turned the next roller so that it lay across the following pair. The men at the forward oars chased them off, and set it right. But within a few pushes, the same lads appeared round back, making off with a roller between them. Corm didn't bother to order chase. There were plenty more in the pile. By the time they replaced it, though, their heave for the launch had become a spectacle for a growing bunch of youths of the sort that caused bootstraps and wet laundry to vanish.

Another group made a run for a log and Corm intercepted them, forcing a retreat. A rock thunked against the hull. Nemas stopped pushing to go after him, but the lad ran just far enough to not be worth the effort. They waved their hands at the crew—a grave insult from a squain that hurt no halot's pride, except they knew what it meant and boiled with indecision over whether to take offense. Now there were enough of them that logs turned or sprouted legs the moment all hands committed to the heave. Corm set four crew, two ahead and behind, to dispatch them. It worked well enough, until their legs grew heavy from the portage. Sixty barrels on the oars and a little help from the Navy at the ropes would have done the deed. They had less than half that at work, and he felt the frustration mount in the men every time he had to stop to reset a roller.

"Hoy, me son!" Corm called to one of the older lads present. He backed away at first, but Corm climbed over the side of the ship and returned with a bundle of leather. "A fine dress for your mum, if you stab the next little bastard who touches wood." His mate laughed at the offer, but he extended his hand. "When it's done," Corm said.

The lad drew his stone knife and strutted in front of the ship while the other squains heaped insults at the betrayal. The hired hand swooped after a few of his kin like a lazy falcon, but they retired to the rear to harass the rollers.

Corm fell back to guard their wake, so the unflogged orphans took rollers straight from the pile and placed them in haphazard arrangements across the path ahead. The falcon considered it too far from his dress to oblige, and at the rate they moved, it would be a fortress by the time they got there.

"This is the admiral's work!" Corm warned the crew. "They're each a penny heavier this mornin'." No one took up his outrage. He ordered a rest, hoping the squains would grow bored, and knowing he had the daylight for a month or more, yet.

Corm marched himself toward the obstacle, letting the men decide who would volunteer their help. When he arrived, only Eckerd trailed behind.

"What'll it take? Extra shares for the return. That'll put a thumb in their arses."

"Too soon," Eckerd advised. "It's no trouble to fill a northbound whaler if you get the repairs. But do it now, and you'll just have two-share men quittin' for the rosters. Bad look, that."

"If *we* get the repairs." Eckerd looked perplexed. Corm clarified: "You said, 'if *you* get the repairs.'" The first mate smirked in dismissal, and bent for his end of a log.

With the obstruction clear, the push resumed amid the squains. They circled like gulls after a fisherman. Here and there, one considered his wage earned and fell off. Most delighted in the sailor's grim chore. The sound of feet slapping on wood alerted the crew to a pair who climbed up unnoticed and darted over the benches howling at one another like a boarding party. They ducked the men Corm sent after them, and swept under outstretched arms when they hopped off. The one he hired gave the air a vigorous slash that sent them skipping clear.

The *Gairhle* gained weight with every heave. To let go an oar to chase off a lad made it twice as heavy when it was taken up again. Corm's muscles sang with relief when half a Navy crew at last appeared sauntering in their direction. But only the men rejoiced when one Captain Aymos offered to help. It was their duty, after all, and apparently neither Bruco nor whoever contracted the little mercenaries thought to inform them that the ship was to be held by all efforts. With a man at every oar, she leapt over the rollers as though the wind found the sail.

Corm was never so distressed to see his ship near the sea. The Navy had everything to lose, but by brilliant anticipation or incompetence, they waved on his bluff. Night couldn't hope to save him. White foam crackled up the landing to beg him on. Nothing he could gain at Camne Drumlag would make up for the loss of revealing that his wedge couldn't even hold the mast for a day's passage. The failure would be his to bear, with no grudge to unite them against the Navy. Here on land, all they could do was jump ship. If they sailed, though, he feared whether he would even return as captain.

Bruco spared him. Corm halted the effort when he spied the officer stomping his way with renewed spirit. A dark stain welled out from the bridge of the man's nose under his eyes. Rather than broach Corm, he stopped short and called for Aymos, and snarled an order that seemed to interest the other captain very little. With a shrug, the Amposi returned to Corm.

"Bruco says you can't use the rollers until the carpenters inspect them." Corm opened his mouth to protest, but Aymos cut him off. "We will leave you to return them to their rightful place." It was as much as permission to push the last sixty yards themselves.

"How're we supposed to get back to shipyard?"

"Use the rollers," Aymos suggested.

"We can't push on another sixty yards, but we can go back over a hundred?" Uldred snarled what all the crew thought.

"Wag your black tongue at the admiral. This man's deliverin' orders," Eckerd silenced him, knowing the injustice of it meant little when they could launch as they pleased.

"You push us all the way to the launch, then ask tired arms to heave back without help?" Now the first mate looked at Corm with some confusion. Surely the captain knew better. Aymos, too, didn't know what to make of it. He'd all but waved them on about their affairs.

"Aye, we'll help you back. If you like." Aymos offered, trying to sort whether he'd accidentally caused some inconvenience.

"You'll damn well help if you want use of the launch. As we sit, no ship comes in or out."

Eckerd leaned in for a whisper. "Captain. Let 'em go and we can make it out from here."

"There's a trick to it," Corm lied. "They wouldn't make it so easy if they hadn't other plans for us." The mate, though unconvinced, wrestled with enough doubt that he returned to his place.

The captain belted the command. "You heard these Navy cunts, lads! You're not allowed to sell your goods and earn your pay! The admiral would prefer to starve us over pickin' an honest fight with a half-crew of true barrels."

Even Bruco, who simmered at Aymos' concession, failed to hide his surprise. Both the whalers and the Navy were so taken by the order that Corm had to repeat himself before they started the ship in the other direction.

The squain boys dispersed, and the older one who he hired to drive them off had the liver to speak.

"You give me a dress." The Navy, who hadn't heard the wages, laughed.

"You were supposed to see the *Gairhle* into the water. You want a dress? Bring me an admiral's hide and I'll stitch you one!" He swatted the lad away.

The turn sickened Corm. Not a man spoke, except to grunt in unison with the Navy crew each time they heaved. He saw no other way, but a gulf rippled between them, impassable as it was narrow, as if he stood on shore and watched while a yard away, a ship full of men shoved off.

By the time the men reached the dog camp, Norwet busied himself harnessing a fresh team to one of the more suspect sleds. He watched Costig and the marines pass atop the ridge, Mentewat trailing. Only Captain Polc peeled away to slog through powder for his post. The three men he left hardly took notice. They bathed in the sun, as they had since the storm lifted, seeming to care for no one and nothing.

The sight of the admiral renewed his brothers' harassment.

"At least tell us what you found," Ferrakut bargained. He sat on the sled in a row with Saunlauk, Siguvik, and Ulwet. It creaked already at the pulls of the few dogs they'd harnessed. His father Alakset would never have run such a thing, but Sawi was desperate. If it fell apart now, only Vjarku and Seleku would tumble—no firestone.

"They didn't find him. I can see by their shoulders," Saunlauk guessed. "Of course they didn't find, him," Milak joined from beside Norwet. "Tunguk is no fool. And Norwet's shoulders say more than the admiral's."

The storm had been long for the eldest boy. He spent it under interrogation. First they begged, then heaped abuse, then offered many favors in exchange for the story of what passed at the aklu. Before the weather broke, they beat him for his silence, but he fought back with enough vigor to repel them. If it was shoulders they trusted, Sawi and Onag had much to say before they disappeared into the men's tukit for the duration. His throat burned to speak it. The pride of how he caught the man who would have destroyed them battled with his secret fear of the deed. The sound of the knife thumping through leather haunted him. He did not feel shame or regret. But the faces of his uncles upon seeing his blood-painted tunic had startled him, as though the sudden sight of his reflection in still water was not as he expected.

Norwet worried less, though he still worried, of the tangled lines that speech wove. He did not know why an admiral helped the same man he sought, or a mercenary took up spear against that same master. For all the trouble it gave him, he did not want seven more mouths to keep in order. He might have spilled his secrets during the blizzard, but they soon turned to guessing, and their dreams were more interesting than anything he could say.

First, Leopard Seal was dead. Norwet stained his tunic when he cradled the body. But they knew Sawi left with gold in his eyes, and returned somber. So the marines got there first. Norwet failed to delay them, and they forced him to perform the burial. Or was it Tunguk's blood? They took the woman back to town to have their way before executing her.

His brothers saw he was not bothered enough for it to be true. The whereabouts of the marines who did not return to camp with Norwet and Mentewat, Sawi and Onag, became the focus of wild tales. Perhaps Norwet *had* led them astray, stranded in the storm to freeze. But the blood was too much. Someone must have fallen to a blade. The marines lay slain.

But by who? Tunguk was too old, Leopard Seal lame, Norwet and Kjartke too weak. He bristled at the remark, and nearly broke, until Milak frightened him by suggesting Tunguk turned the dogs on them. The three of them fled, and Norwet only just finished burying the bodies when Sawi arrived.

It was as close as they came. The question of Mentewat became the mirage that wrecked them on the rocks. The Amposi in turn fell under an evil song of Tunguk's; betrayed his own after a glimpse of Kjartke; recognized Leopard Seal from Urkuk, or as the soul of Barduk returned. Briefly, Foster and Gionn never left on the whaler. They ambushed the marines, and forced Mentewat to swear an oath in exchange for his life. But soon, they found the sea again. Mentewat acted under orders of the assistant viceroy to preserve the hero. Or Norwet tricked him—but Norwet was not clever enough for tricks.

The boys' dreams reminded Norwet he knew little more than them, and though they might come close, it was not possible for men to dream the truth.

"They were not gone long," Milak ventured. "They found the place where he camped, but no trail of him."

"If he left after the storm, there would be a trail. He fled in the blizzard." Saunlauk added.

Milak lit up. "To run to the wilderness in a blizzard, he would be dead." The others didn't immediately follow. "There is one place he could be."

"Drummoc?" Ulwet said tentatively. The others scowled, then gave it consideration.

"He will seek a ship. There is nothing leaving but dog ships, for Camne Drumlag." Milak's guess rang through Norwet. It was the only sensible way, but he heard as many sensible lies from his cousin already. "We must help him when we load the dogs," Milak continued.

The boys yipped with excitement. Norwet, wary of error, cautioned them: "Because you can't see him in the wilderness doesn't mean he hasn't outsmarted you. We must find a way to stay here when the ships leave, in case he has deceived us all."

"Then who will help him at Camne Drumlag? Sawi?" Saunlauk scoffed. Norwet didn't find the notion so absurd, if Sawi knew what was best. But as much anger as he held for his uncle, who lusted to turn a free man into gold, he felt he could not betray too much.

"We will all be expected to go. Someone must find a way to remain behind. In case."

"*Norwet!*" His uncle's voiced pierced their hushed tones. Norwet carved fresh snow all the way to the teams, where Sawi and Onag harnessed fine dogs. He felt the scalding in his chest again, as his uncle saw more of him now than he cared. But he stood fast as he had under the blows of his brothers, and wondered if anyone could harm him as easily as he once feared.

"Me and Onag go to town to check the snow. I think it will be good. And if it is, we must stay to hire drivers." Norwet nodded. "Everything here must be ready when we return. We may sail in a month, or it may be a few days."

"I will see to it, Uncle."

"Senadak will see to it. You and the boys will do as he says." Norwet puzzled over it. He nodded again, and started to go. "Norwet." Sawi caught him. "What do you know of this Mentewat?" He shrugged. "Did he speak to Costig?"

"He lied."

"And you?"

"How could I say otherwise?"

His uncle could not dispute the answer. "A sled goes as the dogs who pull it. Be careful who you harness this family to."

The unusual frankness of Sawi fanned Norwet's courage. "You must drive the dogs you have."

Sawi glared, then levied his gaze on the three mercenaries, and the tukit where Polc and Mentewat had shared quiet words over the outing.

"It's good we have these protectors here to spy on us. The admiral thinks they will tell him that we aid the Leopard Seal," Sawi said.

"Then they fall on their own spears."

"You are right," The admissions surprised Norwet. "But these men have another secret. One we don't share. They watch you. You will watch them, too. You have cost this family great riches, Norwet. Your father disavows you among our ancestors. But if I can't claim the reward for the Leopard Seal, maybe there are other things the admiral will pay handsomely to know."

Costig stopped cold in the powder when Wendell appeared on the deck of the *Juhketappat*. They saw each other at the same moment, and neither could contain the mischief of a smile. Behind the marine, a strange sailor appeared with the sharp movements of a tatter in the breeze. Wendell steered him down the ladder and back to his crew. Costig watched his old mate approach with a scolding admiration.

"Swore I saw your ship off for the huntin' camp."

Wendell tilted his head sheepishly. "Aye, it weighed on me these last days," he joined his commanding officer. "But not as much as it would have if I'd gone to gather meat when I knew I could better serve here."

The two dog ships hummed with the clink of chipping ice, and snow flew in a wide lane leading to the harbor. "I'll take your apology under consideration," Costig said of the bustle whose source he now knew. "Walk with me." The pair curled around the ships and didn't speak until they cut past the marines clearing the way to the landing.

"Fresh snow," Costig commented as they tromped the new layer near the waterline and turned west across the thin lip of coast between the ships and the Attavaik Sea. "Too muddled back there. I like to be the first prints in it."

"That's why we get on. It's the other lad's tracks that draw me."

Costig paused to watch the shallow peaks of water trade places in the wind. "If we got this much powder here, should be a silver road straight down from the mines. Might be the first thing to go our way since Tolba called up the fleets." He gnawed on the end of his mustache. "I won't pretend I'm not pissed. If a marine shrugs me off, I'll hate to see what an officer of the Navy takes for leeway. But if you're right, you won't do me good laid up from a lashin'. I'll be interested to see what you bring me, and why it's more important than feedin' the colony through a siege."

"Me nose has it that there are more vital matters than either of us understand, yet."

"If you don't understand them, then hurry, mate. I've already got an admiral as dumb as me, and most of the time, he does as I ask."

Wendell shoved his hands into the sleeves of his cloak and braced against the chill. "I won't insult you by grovelin'. Did you see the lad I spoke to on the dog ship?"

"The twitcher?"

"That's the word for him. Wouldn't even go in the hold with me on account of the dark. But get him apart from his crew, and he suddenly finds his tongue."

"Liam's?"

"Aye, once he traded barnacles with Polc."

Costig grunted. "That's twice now he'd lied to me. Good lad otherwise. Suppose I shouldn't ask too much of a mercenary."

"I can hardly fault him from where I stand," Wendell admitted. "Maybe I could ask the nature of the tale."

"The first was about Camne Drumlag. He said everything was fine."

"How do you know it wasn't?"

Costig hesitated. Foster told him, but Wendell couldn't know that, and he was less than sure the man wasn't just trying to save his mate. "Same way you would." He tapped his nose.

"And the second?"

"This mornin'. Not him, but his man. Mentewat. I can't say for certain," it was Costig's turn to lie, for he was as certain as the sun overhead. Mentewat had clearly never seen the one-legged fugitive. "But I have cause to doubt those marines fell to Leopard Seal in quite that manner."

Wendell puffed his cheeks in surprise at the news. "A suspicion of trouble and a lyin' subordinate? They could have you on the same charges!" Wendell chuckled. "That aside, I think me admiral's instincts were better than he can justify." Costig raised an eyebrow. "Teague was last man on the boat. They got him in Gharnadil to replace a dead sailor. So he had no mates, and trust me that he isn't the type to endear himself. Now that he's off for good, had a lot to say. I wish I'd asked of Camne Drumlag, but the voyage down was interestin' enough."

"Oh?"

"Polc took on almost the whole crew at Payaqura. Then straight to Ampos. Only stayed one night. The men weren't even allowed to leave the ship. Just the captain went off, to speak with his contacts of work. He came back in the mornin' with a contract and a man of Tolba's court, then they were off for Drummoc."

Costig turned the story over. "What of it?"

"That was me first thought, but like you said, I noticed an odor beyond that of me immediate company. Do you know of Payaqura?"

"Aye. It's one stop north of Ampos."

"Bit of a backwater, and close enough to pass if you can bother to make Ampos. Were I a mercenary with a ship, I'd do just that, and gather them in a port where I'd have me pick."

"Maybe he didn't have the crew to make Ampos."

"Sounds like he didn't. Teague wasn't sure, but he guessed no more than six or eight men were with the ship before Payaqura. How she made it there, or what happened to the rest, he couldn't say. Maybe they found a better crew, but were I a rower lookin' for work, I'd hold out for Ampos rather than jump in Payaqura."

"There's a thousand causes for it. Damn you, Wendell, you've got me defendin' the cunt." Costig bristled.

"As I'd prefer. If I'm wrong, you'll tell me." Wendell clapped him on the back. "She's a 48-seater. Forty men signed in Payaqura. Tough to find so many good lads, even if they didn't turn down every Atlantean. Polc refused to take a single man of Mabhan or Laconos, too."

"Wise, if you're workin' for Tolba."

"But how would he know he'd work for Tolba? He hadn't been to Ampos yet, and the declaration's still private. Tolba only sent word to his officials. He won't make it known across the seas until Spring." Costig pursed his lips in concession, and Wendell went on. "Now ask yourself how men fill boats. In me experience, two and three at a time, in that trade. Only way to rouse an entire crew of half-decent lads is if you got a lot of coin on hand, or there's promise of a big job—as we saw with our whaler. But again, how could they know in advance they'd hire to Tolba?"

"They must have. We just can't see it." Costig tried to count how much coin a man would need to lure what he measured as a rather fair crew in such a small port. They must have stripped a few from every vessel.

"Aye. I can't see what else would do it. But so they sailed to Ampos. And in the mornin', the good captain returned with a fine contract, and a representative of our new farri to help convey it. Couldn't get his name, but Teague called him 'Many Twats.'"

Costig ruffled like a bird on a rock. "That's not so strange a tale."

"No, not so strange. And I admit, that's the worst of it. Lost a man before Gharnadil—not to the seas. Polc executed him, though me informant never heard why. Then they sailed to Drummoc. Not Nunoc, or the viceroy. Not even a stop on the way."

"Gods know we needed the men and the warnin'. Nunoc can care for herself in a siege."

"I agree, but that's what I learned, and it's yours, now. Take it with a drop of spirits, too, mate. That Teague also claims he's drowned thrice, and thrice been rescued by maims. I didn't bother to repeat all the nonsense I had to sift through to get that much out of him. He also claims the lad from the whaler—Foster—stole his map, challenged him to knives, then swam the last fifteen miles to Camne Drumlag to avoid the fight. And that the Leopard Seal is either one of his uncles, or married his mother—he was unclear. And did you know he was swallowed once by a whale? This was distinct from the three drownin's, as it were."

Costig snorted. "Didn't happen to know where I could find his stepfather, did he?"

"No. But I'd say that when a man's prone to such fancies, the ordinary bits ring in the ear."

They stood a while, as if Wendell's caution applied to every lap of surf, every sift of snow and ringing pick on ice. It felt ill-advised to interrupt what might be the piece that toppled the pile. Costig spoke with some reserve.

"Be that so, Polc may be the least of the captains to worry over."

His mate made a sound of agreement as if he'd said something so obvious, he'd wasted his breath. "Anything particular, or is it the nose, again?" Wendell asked.

"You know this lot. Testin'. Gnawin'. Testin', like a dog on his lead. He does just enough to upset you, so he can see how you react and do it again," Costig puffed out the hair on his lip.

"Say his name, and I'll have his carlin and beam."

"Forget it, mate. Just check me numbers: I've got twice twelve as twenty-four."

"Aye, I'm sure of it." Wendell said without hesitation. "And so are you. What's twenty-four?"

"A number that impresses squains. Are you sure you don't need a count?"

"The smallest darraig is that—two sides of twelve. That's four sixes. I can count to twelve sixes by six as easy as to ten. Seventy-two, if you wondered."

Costig let out a low whistle. "Then I can rid meself of Willakuy! When'd you take the oath of a number cunt?"

"Keep him. I know me sixes so I'll know when the squains are out for trouble. And you know yours well enough, if not from squains then from the fact that every ship of character seats in twelves if it can muster 'em. You wanted me to know you got twenty-four of somethin' set for mischief, and I'm to wonder what. Fair enough. I intend to regain your trust in a roundabout way that you'll see when you see it. Just know I share your—let's not call it a love—your interest in Drummoc."

"Aye, you just doubt me methods."

"I doubt nothin' you set your will to."

"And where do you think I've set it?" Wendell didn't reply. "He's in town." A look sufficed to answer the marine's confusion.

"Are we still mournin'? I'll round up the lads for another search."

Costig shook his head. "I've got a better way."

Vatjate peeled back the door flap enough that the light fell on Ostuk's face. It sparked a vision in the spirit world: two ships stretched out on either side to dangle her on a line between: one rain-black through a storm, back to Nunoc; the other, dusted white, cutting the channel to the vague shadow of Camne Drumlag. Just as soon, they vanished. Her instinct begged her to flee to her tukit. This man had given too much, and she knew what she must ask if she were to stay. Better to stand watch at a brothel where every moment may bring a flurry of spears as had visited Mennetarmenuk. Would they not come soon enough to all who knew her face?

Kjartke felt the spot on her chin where the freezing sailor touched her marks that gave her womanhood. Ostuk had seen what trouble they were. Why would he come? A better brothel. That was what Tunguk promised of this place. Now she had her tukit. Many times, she walked away from Brother and told herself she would be a fool to return. She wondered why she allowed herself to care for him as a mother would. Now seeing this man, she recalled the ship. It was not for them she came—not for him and Foster. They had come for her.

Tunguk should have kept them in Nunoc, and let her work there. He told them they must find a northbound ship in Drummoc. Even with their maps, they could not spot his lie. He should have left them, but he returned always to them, and so it was for Tunguk they came.

She did not understand why, but Tunguk came for her.

This obligation, it was like a fine knife given among her people again and again to whoever needed it, until none could recall who held it first.

But these were not her people. They were strangers, all of them. Ostuk, Norwet, Armenuk—maybe Costig, too, who hurried the boy to Urkuk. This flurry of gifts tied them the way it would a band of Jargadak, so that the obligation was not to one, but all. Vatjate, the little girl. The strange bead man at Nunoc. Gionn. She thought herself alone when she went with Klimut to the Kapadak. Now she feared she belonged to a band of desperates. What was this gift they passed? She knew only that all may ask it, and what anyone gave was not their own.

"Kjartkene," Ostuk said with a timid smile. "I did not hope to see you again."

She stooped through the doorway, and Vatjate closed the flap behind them.

At dark, she had still not returned. His sunset was a dimming of the thin slit where the leather failed to touch the wall. The dark felt infinite as the void of space, except for the stale air that hinted at his narrow confines. He wasn't sure which shortened his breath more. He used to think he was the kind of dude who would never break under torture. They could throw him in solitary, waterboard him, pull out his fingernails—nothing could make him utter the name of the beautiful spy who he promised his silence.

Now he lay on his back, gasping for the breath that would make his lungs feel full just for a second. Parks wished for a torturer. He would confess to any treason and turn over his mother if they would kill him quickly. There were no villains to take mercy on him. All he had to look forward to was the return of that sliver of light, hours from now. Change, of any kind. That was what he craved. Eskimo Joe shifting, or a burst of voices from outside. He knew he wouldn't sleep.

Not with her gone. Even more than light, he wanted the rustle of her figure swishing through the door. The wait reminded him of staring at the black screen of a phone in anticipation of some text that should have come by now. He fumed at her, because she forgot about him, or left to hang out with some Reverse-Eskimo dude. She was working, he told himself. A woman's got to pay the bills. Then guilt seeped in. Something had happened. Someone kidnapped her, or she lay bleeding. Or worse. His anger turned to her attacker, and his chest tightened.

Parks sang to calm himself.

"Last thing I remember...runnin' for the door. Had to find the passage back to the place I was before. 'Relax,' said the Night Man..." He sat bolt up and gasped, ignoring the pain in his leg. Before, Joe would have had to pry him up. Now, his back ached from the sled and he felt like he was drowning if he lay down for too long. His lungs stretched in relief as cold air bottomed out. His breath evened, but everything began to tingle. His ears rang.

"Joe?" He whispered. A light snoring greeted him. It seemed to run around the curved sides of the wigwam until he wasn't sure which direction it came from. The bare sound orbited him, the only thing between his body and endless space. Voices rose up and dipped away. He knew they weren't from the street. They hissed in Reverse-Eskimo, or quoted popular movies. A sailor offered to paint a ship. They lacked the sinister undertones of the ones the heard when he was drugged. It was as if they carried on without realizing he was there.

Now the orbit of sound wobbled like a top. A few notes from the guitar solo of Hotel California. The hiss of lava hitting snow. His mom reciting a vital password like a recipe. Nausea gurgled in his stomach. Parks felt the terminal collapse grow imminent. The featureless wigwam spun faster as it faltered. He stabbed a hand upward for anything at all.

His palm braced against the ceiling. It was so low, even from sitting he could reach the place where the stones converged, the peak of the structure. The maddening spin stabilized in a dance around him, like a maypole. He felt a tremble rise through him like an approaching train. His eyes rolled back and his teeth clamped down.

Everything died off with the imperceptible ring of a fading bell. It took several seconds for the colors to bleed in so that he recognized himself on the open deck of an old-fashioned ship, mast above, empty benches on either side. A wide back and a clump of red hair drew him to the work of the only man aboard. Three coils of frayed twine lay at the feet of Gionn. He braided them around a gold wire to conceal it.

"*Hoy*! No lookin', cunt! I'll send you boatless to Manhas!"

Parks startled back and stumbled over something. He rose on one leg as easy as if it were two to find a body wrapped tightly in a sail and bound. A movement aft caught his attention. Foster struggled to pry open a barrel. With effortless strength, Parks lifted the corpse in his arms. The man seemed even bigger than he was. Suddenly, he knew who it was, like a secret he couldn't allow himself to think or else it would be spoiled. He took it by the feet, wound back, and heaved it into the water. The shroud and its contents dissolved into millions of pieces of frail paper the second it hit.

He felt himself back in the wigwam, braced between the sled and the ceiling. The walls flashed on all sides like a projector screen. The most inconsequential memories darted past, like someone shaved them off a stick with a knife. There were no formative moments, no triumphs or traumas. He spoke of a homework assignment with a 5th grade classmate. Smoothed his bunk on a specific day before leave. A stranger asked him a question about the road work outside at a 7-11 while he picked up an energy drink and a can of dip. They followed in a hometown parade, disjointed and out of tune. Parks felt grateful for the reprieve from boredom. Interspersed were things he knew never happened. He practiced with a bullwhip in his parents' backyard, then Eskimo Joe sat beside him at his favorite bar in Santa Cruz. "Can you show me where to go?" He asked. The flurry accelerated, and with each, he forgot the last. The details blended, and they nipped at him like a toenail clipper that took off a little too much. He worried over the two dogs they cut loose in the storm.

Parks saw his own glowing flesh. Pieces of ash fluttered away from the log of his body. The crackling core shimmered with orange vein. Panic gripped him. He was disintegrating. His other hand pressed overhead against the first one in a vain attempt to stabilize himself. But a cold wind reared up, and with each swirl, stripped him until he became as thin as Gionn's wire. He slipped through an infinitesimal crack, and found himself sitting on the roof of the wigwam, whole again, one leg sloping off.

The sky was full of crystal stars. The moon shone in a single wide beam like a spotlight, somewhere across town. A terrible yipping sprang up all over Drummoc, not from dogs, or men, but something close enough to both that he felt stranded on an island amid horrors. What followed, he could never say. More fevered dreams, with no sound or vision he recognized—just a sensation of everything warping in on itself.

Near the end, he saw Kjartke as she first appeared, with a babe in her arms, that one breast protruding over the slipped-down shoulder. He seized on the moment of clarity and slid down a fireman's pole.

Parks woke as he left, holding up the roof. Joe snored lightly. The sled that served as his litter creaked beneath him. He waited an anxious moment to be sure the vision had passed. He could see no part of himself, and nothing stirred. Parks was back among the still and the dark and the whispers. He took his hands off the stone, and his stomach became queasy. He tried to remember the last time he could see anything, or move on his own accord. A glimpse of Tunguk and Kjartke prying him to his feet collapsed. He caught a few words from Foster in the lamplight of the tent before the cutting started. Farther. His run down the side of the volcano—it was just a hallucination. Like everything since then. A brief blink with groggy eyes, people doing things, then sleep.

Here he was in another sensory deprivation chamber, tripping balls and pulling it together, a little more and a little less every time. The labored breath returned. It felt like there was no hope of ever leaving, of the world going on, or making a place for him. The wigwam became a coffin. He pounded at it with every sense he had: spinning blackness, choking gasps, rotten odor.

He remembered the sickening feeling that drove him from their wigwam after the dim jailbreak. He hallucinated then, too, but he rose from his pile on his own two feet and walked halfway up a goddamn mountain. Parks succumbed to the claustrophobia and cast the blanket off his lap. He started, and failed, to peel his tunic free. It was a coffin, and he was buried alive. No one could hear him. Soon, there would be nothing to say.

He thought of Kjartke, still gone. She had come after him. Found him frozen and chewed his seal for him. He wanted to cry out for her now, but the formless air suffocated him. If he wanted out now, it was up to him.

Uma Thurman, he told himself. *You're Uma Thurman. Punch through the coffin.*

Parks flailed and yanked back his hand when it cracked on stone. He prayed the door was straight ahead, as he had when he stumbled into the street to meet Wisconsin Johnson. With both palms, he pressed into the ground beside him and curled his right heel to slide his butt forward.

When he extended his leg again, it was off the sled. He lifted and pulled. The walls closed. The air drained, and he wheezed in panic, oblivious to the pain. His butt hit the hard rock, and he feared Joe would wake and stop him. Parks kicked and scraped until his foot burst through the flap. Leather washed up his thighs and over his face in a slow wave, then broke.

The sky was a starless cloud. His hands stung in blue snow. Darker mounds of wigwams rolled around him. Parks recalled the terrible yipping monsters, and had to remind himself it was a dream. He scooted around the side and pressed his back against their wall. The icy carpet brought a welcome chill to his left leg. The whole stump tingled, and in the thin light he watched it as though it belonged to someone else. Fog sprang from his lips, and he noticed his breathing had slowed and deepened. The cold air was water in a thirsty lung.

Parks dug a trench with his right heel until he felt solid rock. He placed his palms against the wall and pushed, lifting his butt until it braced on the bottom of the sloped rock. His foot slid free and he plopped down, but on the second try, he stayed up. A reposition of the heel and hands, and he scaled one rung higher. Before long, Parks draped back over the exterior of the wigwam like a blanket.

He collected himself, then turned on his side, adjusted his foot, and pressed off. With a wobble and one hop, he freed all but his left hand from the stone and rested again. His body seemed to waver around the single post on the ground. The movement became smaller until his weight found the balance point on its own. Parks stood.

He didn't dare take the hand off the wigwam. The rooftops of Drummoc stretched out before him, not a one taller than him. The lanes shone with reflective snow. Any second, he figured the old man would be out to drag him back. There was no way he hadn't heard the shuffling escape. Then again, he wasn't much stealthier the first time he broke free. Wisconsin Johnson had warned him to stay quiet. There was no Wisconsin Johnson. What was it that told him, then?

Was he afraid if someone heard him, they would kill him? For days—was it a week, or more?—Parks wished for death. He knew many worse things now. Besides, Joe would just come to drag him back by his ear. That's not why he left the wigwam in the first place. He went to meet a man he knew, because he knew he couldn't live by the grace of others.

He wanted to find a way home, even though he didn't think it possible. Or to rescue his shipmates and carve out a place for them here. What he feared was being nursed for the rest of his miserable life. Saved by women and children and geriatrics. He had to be quiet, because he wasn't strong enough to be loud.

A little cough spilled out. Parks muffled it without thinking. When he realized it, he took a breath, and let out a short string, followed by a big hock and a spit of ancient phlegm. The graveyard of Drummoc begged him to return to the wigwam. He knew he had to, but he would have preferred to be torn apart by wild animals. Parks came out here for a reason, and he couldn't remember what. A breath of fresh air, before another interment in darkness?

It started as restlessness. The feeling ran through his stomach, and he thought he would be sick. But it spread through his limbs like an insistence that he could neither deny nor place. A little moan escaped. He folded forward, and looked down at a single foot sunk in snow. The dangling tatters of the other leg filled him with anger. A beast held him in its jaws, and if it were going to devour him, he wanted to gouge its eyes before it snapped down. Sweat beaded on his face. Parks straightened, and weeks of silence reared up in a cry.

He screamed a long syllable, and as it trailed, it turned into a high howl. His lungs emptied. After a gasp, another feral shout rolled over the rooftops and echoed back from some unseen rock face. He expected to see neighbors issue out in their pajamas with flashlights. A third followed close on the tail of the others.

Only then did he noticed a slight pressure, fingers closed around his free hand. She looked up from a loose parka, reproachful scowl between a curtain of black hair, and without a word of admonishment, gave him a gentle tug toward the fold of the wigwam.

The evening sun nestled like a brilliant argot near the horizon, and Gionn wished he could force its head beneath the waves. The deal was struck. Only by night was it safe to burden his palm with the coin—even a nit like Foster would realize that. Then the rudder belonged to Gionn.

He knew the cunt thought low of him. A certain voice told him to give Foster exactly what he expected for his trust and his gold. But Gionn had not planned any particular treason beyond accepting his pay in advance. Long experience refused to allow him to count his purse while it hung empty. And if his honorable mate understood the desperate balance of the ship, he overestimated his fellow conspirator.

As Gionn saw it, the litany of things that could fuck him shrank considerably once he held Costig's coin. Costig himself vanished from that list. In truth, he rather liked the lad across the keel, or at least felt a certain favor for him at the moment. If the mutiny went a certain way, it would be no trouble to move at the right time to set her in at Nunoc.

But Gionn hesitated to count both coins and allies so soon. Had he been damned to keep peace and see her to Taclann, he'd have lost a fair amount of sleep over the two numbers. Now, Taclann and a full roster would serve him just fine. So would Nunoc, or any isle, under any captain, at any strength, so long as his own arse remained on a bench. If it turned a certain way, he'd get a perverse pleasure out of honoring his bargain. Yet he knew there were more likely destinations than the careful courses of the admiral or the captain.

His heart brimmed with generosity. If it weren't much trouble, he planned to steer Foster off the inevitable blunder. As for what that would be, the examples sprawled as numerous as the eyes of Bilata, and depended very much on whether it was Cormdran, or Palqua, or the Greater or Lesser Bucket who made the final move.

Out of the corner of his eye, Foster dropped a pair of wet boots on the barrel between. The sop never once peeled off his skins to dry, claiming it made his toesies cold. Gionn couldn't help but dream, with some consternation, that the coin lay at the bottom, and this was the Wife Seal's way—leave them to dry overnight, and let Gionn sort through them. He swore vengeance upon any man who upset them before that.

Then again, he may have just pulled them off to retrieve the coin for a less fumble-fingered exchange.

In his eagerness, Gionn lost sight of the happenings across the ship. Foster flitted over his position like a nervous tern. Gionn wanted to slap him still, but had vowed not to interact again that day. The Buckets debated in takka-tak, whereon Bentos cursed them quiet. The breeze shifted and pitched them a little too far to port, and a few hands wrangled lines to adjust the sail. He heard the tap of the lid hammered back onto the supper barrel. The commotion amidship crested slowly. Not till more backs rose to converge did Gionn's attention lurch that way.

A fist arced over the shoulders. Two men—he couldn't see who—grappled near the mast. Shouts broke, and others joined the fray. Gionn's heart iced over with dread. He glanced at Bentos, who shared the same fear: *mutiny*, started without them. No hint of who stood with who. The forward benches hesitated. Corm hefted himself over a man and tumbled into the melee.

Gionn tried to catch Foster's eye, but his mate rummaged in the rocks at his feet as if searching for something he'd lost. The squains held a stupor, and the pitch-painted lads around him snuck their hands toward their blades, waiting for a sign of where to turn them.

Every confused rower backed to the beam, so that only the sea stood behind him. The distrust among the forward rows was unanimous: Chirim and Bentos, along with Juru and Yuray, Hogue and Gabol, kept a firm watch on Gionn and only an ear toward the trouble. He preferred his sword out, but worried it would spark assumptions. Spiteful cunts! He meant to retreat to the quarter deck, but the squains already held it not out of defense, but for a better view.

Gionn considered the wet boots. *Soon as they turn*, he thought. *Grab 'em and fish the coin behind the Buckets. Let 'em tire, side with the numbers, bash heads. You know the paces*, he reminded himself.

Foster snatched them off the barrel and inserted his fist into one, then the other, oblivious as ever to the fates unfolding beneath the mast. Gionn sickened. Now he'd have to keep that one from going over with his argot, as well.

A cheer and a laugh went up—a strange thing for a mutiny. Corm's head reappeared. Just outside the melee, men hurried to put up blades. Confusion rippled to the stem in place of panic.

"*Arse down!*" The captain ordered. "*Arse down!*" One-by-one and not without circumspection, tense sailors lowered themselves until Gionn could see Gewar and Bale, each bloodied and restrained by a pair of benchmates. The rest of the ship settled like foam sputtering out on the sand. Only then did Foster notice and take his seat.

"Whose is it?" Corm demanded.

"I had it before he pried it," Bale insisted.

"I saw it first, and you blindcocked me." Gewar lashed at Bale with a foot.

"I don't give a fuck who seen it or who touched it. Who brought it aboard?" They fell silent. "Who among you?" Corm addressed the entire crew now. "I'm no thief. You'll have it as soon as you explain how a low dog sailor came about it, and why it's on me ship." Only the boards groaned in response. "Because if you can't," Foster's eyes swelled in horror, and Gionn's knuckles whitened with rage.

Corm held up a glittering coin between his fingers for all to see. "I'm richer by an argot."

8

WEDGE

Cormdran stalked bench to bench, stopped, and held the gold coin in the face of each sailor. No one moved. Not a man spoke. The captain asked nothing of them, or maybe it was asked and answered in the scrutiny—as if the portrait of the owner was stamped into the metal, and he only needed to find its match.

It started at the aft-most positions, with Uldred and Bosc. None escaped. Palqua, who Corm had taken pains not to ruffle, had to hold his gaze like the rest of them. The little argot radiated with a new power that transfixed the men and filled Corm with a confidence that begged to be tested. Foster felt the sharp corners of every eye on the ship poking at the rest of the crew all the while. Each loping stride brought the captain closer. The mounting pressure was relieved only by the fact that Gionn couldn't afford to lay that hexing stare on him.

Juru and Yuray. Bentos and Chirim. He crisscrossed the cargo all the way. Foster had rehearsed the encounter in his mind. Confused and respectful—those were his watch words. But in the last pause before the step that brought the captain to bear, a pit tightened at the memory of a previous visit: nothing but a morning walk, and Foster collapsed with anxiety before he turned away. Too little, too much—there was no way to meet the man's stare that didn't betray himself. So he didn't.

"Wrong end," Foster stated flatly before Corm could come to rest. The first words in many minutes caused every seat to shift with anticipation. Even Corm was taken. "Of the ship," Foster clarified. "Lookin' at the wrong end."

"The milk-whelp found his courage. Tell me, lad, if you know his name. Or I might start to wonder what could cause you to speak so surely."

"I don't know whose coin that is, but I know he ain't up here. You found it by the mast, didn't you? We don't go up there—except to fill a bucket. And you know squains carry gold like whalers carry honest men."

"Remind me, Wife Seal: were you not up there this very mornin' to share with us your fine map?"

The air pressure seemed to drop around them, and a chill rippled over the deck.

"Sure was. You think if I brought a gold coin aboard I'd carry it with me the one time this whole trip I been more than four rows that direction? That son of a bitch'd be stuck in some dark hole as close to my bench as I could find. And who said it came out today? I reckon it was wedged in some crack until the sea wiggled it loose to get kicked around where we could see it. Unless it slipped out of somebody's unclenched asshole while he was out for a stroll, you got maybe five, ten dudes could've brung it. Ain't none of 'em up here."

Corm savored the boldness. Foster felt the momentary surge of confidence falter with every second the captain didn't reply.

"Then you know why it's here."

"Aye, sir. Somebody's up to no good."

Corm smiled back over the crew. "You're the number cunt. Could a man not have come by it honestly? Saved his silver and swapped 'em for a lighter load?" It was clear he was being facetious, so Foster bit his tongue. "How many silvers to an argot, anyway?"

"Don't know, sir. Never counted that high."

"Never seen one? Nor I. As I understand, sometimes the Navy hires squains for odd tasks. One of you lads?" The boys shook their heads furiously. "And what would you do for it?" Corm held it closer to Foster.

It looked like one of those gold dollars that circulated for a few years when he was younger. Or a rough arcade token. Foster wondered what it amounted to in US currency. He never had the chance to really examine it. There it stood on end, a strange face, a strange word, disconnected from anything he could dream of. In his own world—as for these people in theirs—he may have lusted after the end of his troubles. Here? Nothing Foster wanted went for gold. If all it got him was an unreliable ally, he'd throw it overboard to watch Gionn swim.

"Name it." He held out his hand in jest.

"I'm sure a man could ask many things, but what's got me in irons is who on Drummoc could spare the argot for the askin'?"

It sounded rhetorical, but the pause again made him anxious, as if Corm expected a response. Foster shrugged.

"I doubt anyone short of an admiral could peel off one of those." It struck him as obvious. How could the captain not see it? It was Costig—Foster knew that, and any man aboard could guess it. He didn't even have to lie, except about the most recent owner. If he couldn't keep it himself, at least the coin still worked on his behalf. A mutiny was one thing to worry about. A spy set loose to destroy the ship, another entirely. If Foster couldn't mount a contingent against Corm, the captain's own imagination would do it.

He expected to see concern, frustration, even a backlash of anger swamp that face. No one else in the crew was positioned to notice Corm's grin. The cussing and shouting he expected never came. Nothing changed but his awareness of a patronizing stillness among the crew, and a growing sense of a mighty mistake.

Corm stepped to Gionn.

"Turn aside."

"Pardon?" Gionn said. A thick hand clasped his chin and twisted him to profile behind the coin. "You got Mil's nose."

"Can I have a look?"

"...If it birthed from his arse."

Corm's fist swallowed the argot. He spun for the mast without molesting Tunguk and Atalkut. Each bench fell in turn to pastimes and duties with the dull resolve of a chain being dragged out over wood. No one had the heart for the theatrics of the previous days. Once more, Foster felt himself at a loss to understand a new current among the crew.

He placated himself by counting seats around the mast, and taking roll of the men he'd just implicated: Gewar and Jenneker, Nolan and the two carpenters, Igonus and Aldan. Eckerd and Tawatu were close, but probably beyond suspicion—they'd been with Corm since the journey south. Bale seemed unusually familiar to all of them, but Foster knew he joined with Palqua's boys. Moipa and his friend Tamarqan were close enough to be annoyed with him—not the best set of enemies, he told himself. But if he couldn't wedge the captain from his core, he'd have no hope of driving them in at Nunoc, and returning to Parks in Spring.

Rather than going beneath his tarp like he often did in the evenings, Corm settled on his bench, two up from the last one and directly opposite Palqua. At least the former admiral was far enough back to escape the blast radius of the fumbled coin.

Foster burned with panic.

No one needed to tell Corm that Costig had it in for him, least of all the dumbest sailor on board. Why had he pressed Foster? The captain had Eckerd, Ordacles, dozens of men with unapproachable experience. He knew the Navy and the whalers. It would make as much sense for Foster to ask Corm about the politics of life on the carrier. Corm didn't need an answer. He needed someone dumb enough to say what no one else could risk: only an admiral had that kind of money, and Costig wasn't the only admiral around.

A mutiny was delicate. If someone could command more support than Corm, the rest of the crew may just shrug and give up their captain without a fight so long as they had the golden dream of Taclann. But if there was a chance that man acted not out of a selfish urge to helm the ship, but a secret intent to destroy them all for Ampos…

The rest of the crew ignored Foster out of hatred or pity. Palqua and Corm chatted amicably about something trivial. Men took in their laundry for the night. The wind cooperated mercilessly, driving them over crisp seas toward their destination. Foster squeezed his cold toes into his boots and wrapped his oilskin against the plummeting temperature. At some level, he hoped he'd wake to a cut throat courtesy of Gionn.

There was no such reprieve in store. He'd boarded with a gold coin and a single friend, and made a gift of them both. If any man on the *Gairhle* owed the smallest favor to Foster at that point, it was the one he came to overthrow.

The sail appeared running along the coast just after dawn. The *Juhketappat* and the *Orin's Thief* creaked in file over rollers through the lane the marines cleared in the snow, bound for harbor-side where they'd sprout ropes and sails and fine appointments. The visitor found Wendell among the crews of Liam and Korrel, where he hoped to hear a sign that the concerns regarding the admiral had spread to the fleet. Liam prodded his men with an easy manner. Wendell wouldn't have called it impunity, but it wasn't a pace meant to impress. It reminded him of the work a man gives on hire for the day, knowing he'll return to his own captain by supper. By that, he surmised that Liam knew. Korrel didn't. It was too soon to tell the junior officer.

The appearance of the ship sent Wendell shuffling through the powder to where Costig held court with the other two sergeants-at-arms. It was a company where he was always welcome, yet never felt a part.

"Every time I see that damn sail I piss meself thinkin' Donnab's van's arrived," Costig complained.

"Who is it?" Obrachar asked.

"Haraket." Costig didn't bother explaining. "Comin' from the Calm Harbor." The others looked to Wendell.

"Squain lad, took the supply darraig to Camne Drumlag a bit earlier than planned. Maybe he's worked up the bollocks to return the ship." Wendell clarified.

"You know as well as I he's scoutin'," Costig snorted.

"Scouting? For what?" Gua laughed at the notion.

"Shall I have Rixtan run him down?" Wendell offered.

"Bollocks, alright: he's as close as he can get, and still have time to slip off if he sees an abiama launch. No, don't waste Rixtan on a fool's chase. *Fuck!*" The outburst rattled through his usually unflappable defenses.

Gua shrugged. "Let him look upon the place he will never set foot again."

"He's seen the dog ships," Costig snapped.

"So? The dogs come every year. It's a petty official playing king of the miners, mate. Not an enemy admiral." Gua clapped his back to tease him.

"And he's got me *Juhketappat* crew," Costig ignored him. "There's not two squain sailors left to knock together this side of the channel."

"Use Navy," Obrachar tossed his head without concern.

"Got to be squains this time." Costig met with bewilderment. "You'll know why when you see it."

"Or when you tell us," Wendell said pointedly. "We're not grassbenders guardin' a cup of hasqa. If there's somethin' we can do to help—"

"Keep those Navy loiter-sacks pullin'. Beyond that, I've learned to ask of a lad what he can give, and I'll ask plenty of you in Spring."

Wendell heard the wound of betrayal in Costig's voice. "You'll forgive a dull wit if he keeps the counsel of his spear."

Parks woke to rough hands wringing his leg in punishment. Kjartke scolded Eskimo Joe in a sharp whisper of crackling Reverse-Eskimo that matched the rhythm and ferocity of her hands. She must have saved it up from the night before. They had to huddle in silence when she brought him back, in case someone went out to find the source of the howling. Now they were both taking it for their failure to keep quiet and babysit, respectively.

The grating massage felt both harsher and less effective than when the little girl did it, but the pain barely rose to half of the first time. He squeaked and sputtered. Parks focused on those guttural syllables to distract himself. It sounded like someone dropping handfuls of the flat, jagged wigwam stones into a pile, hocking up the occasional vowel. How could a language have so many K's?

He closed his eyes—redundant in the dark—and searched for the lines that marked the end of a word, even a sentence. The language was an assault on the senses. He caught "Brother" a couple of times, but it rattled on at a pray-and-spray pace. Even if he wanted to learn it, he doubted anyone could give him a verb conjugation table. Maybe if he strained his ear, he'd figure out "yes" and "no." At least pin down the cuss words so he could dish it out in Reverse-Eskimo.

Mattakatan, he admitted to himself. Foster used the word, and he knew it just as well. Probably the only one outside a few names in his vocabulary. He concentrated to sift the stream of speech.

Eskimo Joe finally got his reply, a short one. Kjartke laid into him again, and they exchanged a few more phrases. The voices paused, and she wiped clean his stitches. When she started again, her tone had changed. The words came slower now. Parks nearly leapt with excitement when he heard a sequence of sounds from her sentence repeated back by Joe—a word. Then came something familiar: *tukit*. That meant wigwam, he was sure of it. Once he separated a few from the herd, he began to pick out snatches of sounds in almost every phrase. Most of the time, they shifted as they passed between the speakers, giving up an ending or adding a syllable in the middle.

*Ostuk e*merged in one of Kjartke's lines. It broke on him like cool water. The captain of the dog ship, his homeboy Ostuk. Parks felt like a spy, sensing meaning where others suspected a drooling idiot. The shape of the conversation began to show itself. First, she eviscerated the old man for letting him into the street to bawl like a maniac. Parks found himself on Team Kjartke—it could have been a costly mistake, and he, too, blamed Eskimo Joe. Once that left her system, it turned to a discussion. She told him something at length, probably where she was, and as it went on, Joe asked more questions, which left Kjartke sounding less certain of herself. It revolved around that name, which became two names. At first, he didn't distinguish them, but soon he found a word that sounded a lot like the other in their accent: *Costig.*

Kjartke loosely bound his leg. She seemed content to play messenger, passing the burden to Joe. But he said something she didn't like, and a new argument erupted. This time, she sounded like a recalcitrant teenage daughter pleading with her dad. In disaffected tones, he spoke last. Light blinded Parks. Kjartke left the wigwam—the tukit— in bitter silence.

"Never too old to pimp." He knew Joe was waiting on an explanation. "You think it's a good idea to make her stand out there on the corner?"

"Yes."

"Sorry I got your balls blistered."

"It is good you are feeling strong. The admiral has kept his oath. Now you must keep yours."

"The worst is over, kemosabe. A month or two of chewing my own food, maybe a couple of crutches, and I'm your huckleberry."

"Two days, or three." Parks couldn't imagine what Joe was on about. It was the old man's turn to clarify. "The admiral calls for Amposi mourning. All may return to grieve, and none will answer for past crimes. This will not remain—I think only until the dog ships sail. He means for us to go. Kjartke has arranged it."

Parks puffed his cheeks and blew a long gust of resignation. An old anxiety crested again: he sat in a hut full of old ceramic vessels with Gionn, listening to the distant yelp of dogs. Another ship to make.

"Then I need to you to get me a meeting with Costig. There's something I gotta tell him, white man to white man."

"What?"

"The last time I saw Foster. I can't believe I still remember. I was drunk as piss on my death bed. He told me something about whatever-that-place-is-called. The mines."

"Camne Drumlag."

"That's the one. It's supposed to be vital intel. But it sounded kind of boring to me, so just in case, I've got a few ideas to spice it up. You know, add much paint and beads to make appealing."

"Do not speak of it yet," Joe advised.

"Got to. That was the big selling point for giving me the job. Just think of it as a gesture of good faith. He gets the teaser, then I'm off to find the real dirt."

Eskimo Joe thought long on the matter, like Parks' old man before handing over the keys to the car.

"I will bring your meeting. But I ask of you, Brother: do not add much paint and beads."

The harbor rung with the collision of competing songs. The sailors belted their cadences up with block and tackle. The Battle of Icua melted pitch on a coal fire to paint in the crevices. An unusually cheerful lament for the beautiful Debora carried provisions from the storehouses to the decks—enough to last a quick shipwreck. The full strength of Drummoc doted on the *Juhketappat* and the *Orin's Thief* like vessels under blessing to cross the Atlantic, though the channel was scarcely a day's sail. The snow, the smell of black smoke, the rhythms of the season greeted Wendell like an old mate. He could almost hear the dogs add their own woeful song, as they would soon enough when the drivers marched them down to their labors.

In the joint where the peninsula met the widening foothills, another wail peeked out in the gaps of the nearer voices. A group of Mattaka gathered, their faces smeared with coal dust. The mother of the boy wore a brilliant dress fit for a great daughter of Ampos, loaned to her for the occasion. Wendell wondered how they lifted such an exquisite good off of Cormdran—or what unspeakable deeds someone did to earn it.

The water of the harbor rippled by the two darraigs on maneuvers. They sat with grateful oars raised while Rixtan spoke over the side to a little daille sculled by two men, Costig's head bobbing between them.

"I can almost hear Aymos gasping," Bayochar said of the near darraig. "Can you believe Costig made them row the day after a march up Urkuk?"

Wendell whistled his sympathy.

"In fresh snow!" Bayochar added. "I hear they barely made it passed the dog camp before the marines had to let them turn back from exhaustion."

"I hope the other captains are in good spirits." Wendell gauged his speech even though he thought they were far enough from the next man. Bayochar caught on.

"Aye, I put nine in good spirits. The rest will come around when the time is right."

Wendell calculated. "Etan's off at the hutnin' camp. Korrel and... Bruco?" Bayochar grinned with admiration. "Believe it or not, I've come on an errand for the admiral. How many of your lads have sailed Camne Drumlag? Not stationed—sailed."

"More than a few. Why?"

"We're short nine sailors. I've heard tale of a few squains I might ask, but it'll go better with Navy on the ropes."

Bayochar gave a dismissive laugh. "The captain knows the course. You just need men who can listen."

"Surely an esteemed commander such as yourself has nine of those and nine to spare."

Bayochar waved him off. "Ask Folmon."

"Check with Bayochar," Folmon said when Wendell found him dividing the provisions between the dog ships. "Can't spare a lad just now." They stepped away from the bustle. Wendell thought it imprudent to mention to either the other's suggestion. He nodded gratefully.

Folmon lowered his voice. "You know Lanillike?"

"By her fine reputation."

"She swore to me she knows where to find the Leopard Seal. Won't say until the mournin's lifted and the reward restored."

"I know a good many men in the habit of believin' what that one tells 'em. But Costig promises he's got an iron in the forge."

"Does that mean you haven't spoke to the Marines?"

Wendell cringed at the insinuation—the bare fact—that for once, the Navy had organized itself first. "Not yet. It won't suffer a rough hand. By Hadalis, they'll want to know who stands to take his place."

A low rumble seeped out of Folmon. Wendell understood it wasn't the first occasion for the captain to worry over the matter. "We've got most of the captains' support. I'm afraid if we put a name to it, they'll turn to bickerin'. Once he steps down, we'll stand for it."

"Just the Navy?"

"Just the captains."

"Well on that," Wendell admitted, "all the ones I've spoke to seem to agree."

He had a long wait for the daille, and spent it at the shoulders of the mourners. There were enough of them that another riot almost broke out over the splashing of Rixtan's crews. They claimed that a burial at sea couldn't take place while men upset the waters. Sometimes he thought the squains contrived new customs when it suited them, but Costig offered no challenge. Instead, he waded out himself to hold his crews. Wendell could think of no other admiral who would have done the same. Nor could he think of one who would have put the lads through their paces to begin with.

The body lay wrapped in leathers. It looked a trivial thing, small enough to fit in a sailor's sack. Once that daille reached shore, they would sing themselves to a coarse grit, then march as far up Urkuk as they dared to escort his spirit.

Costig had no more enviable walk. Wendell shushed the pity for his own task—it was not a treason, he reminded himself, but a restoring of order. No one could carve the garrison into fighting shape like Costig, and without the distractions of the office, what a mighty force that would be!

There were lessons for the next admiral, whoever it was. Not just mistakes to learn from, but genuine acts of pluck and prudence—even grace—that stood like cairns for uncertain ships, if they bothered to look. Wendell just prayed for the love of his mate that he misunderstood the missing argots.

"I spoke to the captains about your crew. As you'd expect, lots of recommendations and no volunteers."

Costig stepped ashore, and helped the sailors after him. It came as a mild jolt to Wendell that the men sculling were not gruff blues, but Gerachay and Wayranapan.

"Just as well. I found 'em meself."

"With Rixtan, then? Aymos, or Rapana'ekunata?"

"Neither. I've been over what you said about Polc. Can't find a thing that worries me, except that it worries you. I may as well leave him short a few hands while we scrape his hull."

Wendell gleamed. "I'll ask after who's been with him the longest. Won't hurt if some of the lads came with him to Payaqura."

His last talk was the shortest, and the hardest. Wendell made straight for the sergeants-at-arms, that they would see him leave Costig. He greeted Gua and Obrachar, then searched for the words, as though flustered.

"I've been thinkin' on this mornin'," he said. "Costig." He wrung his hands. "Do you—" He caught himself, and regrouped. "I was just wonderin'," he trailed off, and waited until their impatience surfaced.

"Out with it!" Obrachar barked.

"Eh, you know, forget it. Probably nothin'." Their frustration mixed with concern in a speechless slurry, and he left knowing he'd found the mark.

Eckerd's manner made it plain before he reached the *Gairhle*. Corm only wondered the damage.

"Four more."

He grimaced. "Pitras?"

"Not just yet," a voice startled them. Pitras sat up from where he'd slept in the hold.

Corm stuck his hand in a sack and produced a handful of beads. He painstakingly counted them out onto the flat of an oar, one for each man of the crew—twenty-six, besides himself.

"Arthas." He separated one bead. "And three. Now four more," he dragged them apart from the main pile. If one of them managed the count before he did, he had the tact not to call it out. "Eighteen left." The names meant more than the numbers, anyway. "Anyone I'll miss?"

Eckerd shrugged. "The lad went. Jonn." The mate knew how much Corm favored that one, though he'd never admit it. No one called him "Grassbender" after how he stood to the angotaks. Corm could name no sons, but the departure struck a surprising blow. There was a betrayal to it he never thought he'd feel in the endless dance of whaler crews.

"Arthas," he growled under his breath.

"Maybe," Eckerd said with something else on his mind.

Corm straightened up. "Two shares! Sail north with me, Pitras, and you'll start with two." The man was a good enough sailor that Corm had little hope to keep him, short of handing over the boat. Eckerd would chide him later for having a two-share man jump, but Corm could no longer worry about how it looked to the crew. He had to hold someone. "I've got eight shares on offer: one for each of the jumpers," he said of the goods languishing beneath them. "One for you, and one for Eckerd. Let the other six dangle for a good man who cares to earn 'em." He knew as soon as he said it he'd have to offer one to Ordacles to avoid a well-deserved mutiny.

"As long as I've nothin' to do, might as well have somethin' to dream of." Pitras hooked arms to seal it.

Gewar caught their attention scurrying over from town as fast as he dared. None of his men had moved with such purpose since landing. It seemed that Euskus had awaited his generosity, and arranged it that some good news might find him no sooner than he dealt the spoils.

"Got a looker for you at the brothel." Gewar grinned.

Corm struggled to keep a disinterested pace. What awaited, he couldn't say, except that it wasn't a woman. When the two men arrived, they found Nemas and Muir guarding the door to one of the stone huts.

"You won't mind that we gave the woman a gob of pigment to tell us when he came 'round," Nemas greeted him. "*Hoy!*" He called within. Oterec and Fergo emerged on either side of a man with long, greased black hair.

"What was it? Foul Hand…" Corm made a smug search of the air. "Waits."

"I'll thank the lads for grantin' the men a word in private." The sailors laughed in mocking. "Aye, your captain knows it. I can't well offer me help in the tavern, can I?"

"His 'help' was to offer me a bench this mornin'," Nemas said.

"Me as well," Muir admitted.

"Blind bastard! Didn't offer me a bucket to shit in!" Fergo complained.

"Aye, I needed a fine barrel like yourself to tell the old man." Foul Hand Waits straightened with a near-convincing pride.

Oterec raised a little purse and emptied five coppers into his hand. "Its his third day in a row by the brothels. The men of the *Gairhle* have been kind."

Corm snickered. "Three days. Navy pay's what? A copper each week? Either you've saved your chum most of a year for these poor girls, or that's a fine commission and you're expectin' more."

"If you kill me, they'll know who done it. Your crew'll swear the rosters to get out of prison. I won't insult you—you know what comes of you and your ship."

"Aye, you're right. Killin' you's not an option. Lads!" He gathered his men's attention. "For your troubles, each of you just earned a full share of the cargo, and another half-share on the northbound leg."

"Fine goods," Gewar pointed out. "You promised to lavish us. I'll have an Amposi dress." The other sailors whistled and called at him like a street woman. He pranced seductively over to Oterec and tried to nick a copper.

"A dress for none but Gewar, for there's none lovelier." The laughter felt a tonic to Corm, who couldn't recall the last time he heard any favor from the men. He waved them off, and they crept away, wondering what mischief he would lavish on the recruiter.

Foul Hand Waits' courage drained. He clung to just enough honor that he could smile a little, and stop his feet from running away. Peeling whalers for warships was as common in every port as the flow in the other direction. But he would have heard tales of what happened when it was done with too little discretion.

"I'd pity meself what's comin' if I didn't feel sorrier for you."

"Allow me to free up your sympathies," Corm reached for him, but Foul Hand Waits collapsed and embraced the stout knees.

"Free me, good captain!" He wailed. "Free me! If only you could!" The recruiter writhed between his legs and scooted away as Corm clasped at his ankles. "Are there two lower souls in all of Hiade? Mercy to the lost! How will we find our way?" He moaned. Corm caught one leg and dragged him back a few paces before he kicked free, only to have the other captured. "I see how you suffer! Look in me eyes, that you may see your own!" With a heft, Corm caught Foul Hand Waits around the midsection and lifted the twisting body over his shoulder, where the little man crawled like a fleeing rat. Two thick hands found cloth and tore him free, and he spun again like the maims of legend from a fisher's net.

Foul Hand Waits found his feet, and Corm noticed the lightness of his belt when he saw the blade the man held to his own neck. He laughed and picked up his spear. Foul Hand Waits retreated pace by pace toward the brothel, ever-threatening his own life.

"I would pledge your ship if she had a hope to sail. Manhas is a foul place for one who goes by his own hand. I wouldn't dare it, but I hate the words I must tell you, me captain! I stand against me own admirals, though I gain nothin'. Poor souls! The lucks have left us both."

"I've heard every manner of self-sparin' lie, but I don't believe I've ever seen a man threaten to cut his own throat to get out of a spot." Corm lowered his spear. "Go on."

Foul Hand Waits placed the blade on the ground. "I'd make a miserable wraith. It's true, I took your commission. But it was yourself who gave over those men, and there's more to follow." Corm listened, amused at the unbidden confession. "You'll never get your repair. I'd sail for you if you did, and drill any hull I could to get us out. But you don't know what you've hauled into. You think the whalers are full of mutinous laundry-hangers? Serve half-a-season in the Navy of Ampos! There's no captains, only admirals-in-waitin'! The garrison's thinner than she looks, and there's at least two 'commanders' here—more on some days. Every last man's anglin' his way off. If you knew half the truth of it, you'd shed a tear for me, a stranded wretch, as I have for you!"

"I've no use for blubberin'." Corm collared him.

"A wedge, then." The captain stopped. "I don't speak of the part for your ship, but of another kind. It's fitted in the seam of two things, and by the smallest effort, rends them. You haven't spoken to Palqua. You think because he wants your ship, and will let it rot beneath you before you sail. It is true, but he cannot speak to you because Admiral Turrha ordered it. He believes Palqua botched the talks, or claims to. Was he too hard? Too lenient? His error was to be Palqua. Turrha would have your ship himself. There are few enough rams in Drummoc. Whoever claims your ship might prove himself master of this place. That's all I dare say, but a wisp of what I know.

"Leave me whole, Captain, and hold a seat. I want nothin' but to see Drummoc drown. We will get you a wedge, or give them one."

Weeks passed before Foster glimpsed an opening. He expected a witch hunt, and hardly slept for all the lies he practiced. Palqua tried to unload the crew's burden on the second day. He urged haste. Corm should question every man, and make a search of their belongings, in case there were more conspirators. Costig's spy—and he was always sure to mention that name—had no choice but to put them in at Nunoc if he wanted to live. There was nothing beyond that could stop them, and that island grew in their minds, especially as they passed a place called Galliput that Foster couldn't pick out from the monotonous coast. Palqua even offered himself to be interrogated in front of the crew or under the tarp, as Corm preferred.

The captain assured them that he kept watch even as he dreamed. The man would be found. He had to reveal himself to accomplish his purpose.

In fact, Corm did nothing. When accusations were cast, he staunched them, reminding the crew that Costig—and he used that name, too—wanted them to turn on one another. After a few tense days, the ship found her rhythm again. Foster still felt the weight of eyes, but it came in a different character than when mutiny rumbled. Whatever secret communications prowled the deck now vanished. Suspicion was unanimous. No man said a word that could be construed as harmful to the well-being of the *Gairhle*. They bailed with enthusiasm, tied knots with a snap. The way the captain swooped in defense soon cured them of pointing fingers, for fear the act of pointing would seem calculated to cause a rift.

Corm alone basked in the new mood. He would have paid an argot for it. Whoever may have wanted another captain set it aside out of self-preservation. The enemy was faceless among them, and the only man who couldn't be guilty was Corm. He presided over a single body, a watertight fortress of heavy wood that left Foster helpless.

Compared to the slog aboard the *Juhketappat*, they raced before the westerlies. Even during a brief storm, when they carried only a slip of sheet and spat seawater that ran down into their lips for days, the *Gairhle* closed with unwavering determination on Nunoc. It was a rope, sliding past him and soon to run out. He only had to reach down and grab it. But Foster didn't know how.

Gionn had no reason to help him, if he ever meant to. His gold hung in a purse, nailed to the mast to taunt its owner. Foster came to recognize Gionn's friendly charm as a sign of bitter enmity. All the while, the coast trailed behind him, teasing the end of the line that would soon pass without an effort on his part. He laughed that his first instinct was embarrassment at letting Costig down. Never mind that he could never return to Parks, Tunguk, Kjartke, let alone home.

The opening started as a hiss of voices at the mast. Corm and Eckerd discussed the daily course. For only the second time, the captain shouted and beckoned, "Wife Seal!" He approached, and while they consulted his map, he let his eyes drift to the little purse above their heads. The men around him glared, probably none too happy that he had implicated them in the crime.

The debate hummed around how close they were to the Antarctic Peninsula, which they called the Arm. They had to turn north-northeast. Corm wanted it now, but Eckerd thought it was too soon. It would put them too far out to sea, out of reach of their lifeline—the freshwater and seal of the coast, which they would have to call on eventually.

"We got nearly seven barrels of water, and food for a month. We'd be mad to make land," Corm argued. The suggestion surprised Eckerd. He'd never heard of a ship remaining at sea all the way around the Arm to Taclann. "How many days we been at sea?" Corm turned to Foster, to emphasize the feasibility of his point. Foster made a face like a kid called on in a class he didn't know he was attending.

"Was I supposed to be countin'?"

Corm grunted a dismissal. "Three weeks, we'll be in Mag's Harbor."

"We're not as close as that to the Arm. Four weeks, and six or more if the wind don't favor us. You know how it is at the joint—dead, or turned in your face as often as not," Eckerd countered.

"Aye, that's why we turn now." He traced the map. "Cut the angle, save a week and the doldrums. We ride all the way past Nunoc, sight ourselves at Breidoc, and run for the West Pillar of the Sun Gate." He slapped the parchment with the back of a satisfied hand.

Eckerd held his tongue but not his expression. "Adventurous."

"Tell me, what choice have we?" They made no pretense of quieting their argument from the crew, and Foster felt they addressed the men as much as each other. "Anywhere close to Nunoc, we not only risk the Navy and the angotaks, but our golden lad," he slung the last part over the benches.

Eckerd thought it over begrudgingly. "There may not be seal at Breidoc. Penguins, if a luck smiles on us. Anseloc or Bannoc would be better to rest and stock."

"I said 'sight,' not 'stop.' Shore is where he'll strike."

Foster's gut rung with the suggestion, and the fear of it. The first mate folded the map and returned it. "Right," he said after a bleak pause. "Steer for Breidoc, keep her wet til Taclann, then?" As a crew member who froze or starved or drowned with the rest of them, the concern and the easy surrender of the mate worried Foster. He hoped the argot hadn't given Corm such power that he was immune to common sense.

"Don't see as we got a choice," Corm replied. Early in the voyage, no one fretted over questioning the captain, or even insulting him. Now a stiff silence shrugged its consent. Corm didn't immediately give an order, or stomp off to his bench. He seemed to wait for something. "You lads can weather it. Weren't too pleased the last time I came in early, were you?" The challenge wavered with nerves. He searched for something— a laugh at an inside joke, maybe. Corm's chin dropped in contemplation. Some old battle rumbled beneath, sending up cracks in his certainty.

"There it is, lads." Eckerd took the lead. "Give me one wedge to port, less a shavin'." Foster knew only that he referred to some measure of the horizon by the stars.

"Arthas?" Corm's voice surprised them, Arthas most of all. "What do you say?" The sailor didn't know what to make of the question anymore than the others. "Keep to sea, cut the angle for Taclann—that's me itch. But you've had as much of the angotaks as anyone. If I'm givin' too much berth, I won't have you sops fingerin' your earholes while I sink us."

Arthas paused as long as he dared. Even Foster saw that Corm might read into any answer for dissent. It felt like nothing less than a snare, tugging at a leg in anticipation of a pull. A look to Eckerd didn't give him any guidance. After a false start, he managed to speak.

"This season, they'll be north of Nunoc. Well north, makin' back for the Sun Gate. That's where I'd expect 'em, and that, we can't avoid."

"Then you think it's too much. But we won't make Taclann on these barrels if we fondle the coast," Corm pointed out.

Arthas looked at the barrels, as if they could tell him anything. "Nor at all. I've never heard a ship go from the Arm to Taclann without reprovisionin'."

Foster and a good many others expected an outburst from Corm, but the captain nodded. "Aye. But if the weather holds…"

"The weather at *Hiade?*" Eckerd ventured. Even Corm had to chuckle.

"Better to keep to the coast. Stop if we need to—and we'll need to." Arthas eased by a fraction.

"I don't say you're wrong. But you forget there's a navy at Nunoc, and a man aboard who'd see us skinned."

"He must be a fine one if he'd do it for nothin'," Arthas nodded to the gold adorning the mast. "Why pay him to begin with?" A number of crew hooted their consent. No one seemed to have considered the possibility that a hired hand wouldn't risk his life for pay he'd already lost.

"Nunoc won't patrol beyond the shadow of the harbor after the sun levels for Autumn." This time, it was Palqua. "Between ice and desertion, they can't risk it."

"Coal ships!" Fergo shouted. "They leave Nunoc with steel this late. And they got escorts."

"Aye, escorts!" Someone echoed.

"They'll leave us be if we leave them be," Bale waved it off.

At that, the deck erupted in debate. Barrel capacity and rations, the habits of every ship to plow these waters, the dangers of the Orin and the Attavaik—everyone had their say. Foster was surprised so many supported Corm's sea route, which required perfect execution with no margin for error to avoid dying of thirst, or drowning in the massive seas of the Drake Passage—that was the Orin to them, as far as he could tell, and the Attavaik, the Antarctic coastal waters.

But he realized that the new confidence of the sailors to speak their mind may not have extended to everyone. Some shilled for their captain. Or they genuinely believed that he, an unpaid "grassbender" acting alone, could ruin their dreams of fortune. He realized his own inclination was the coast, for more reasons than his mission.

"Weiroc!" Irilo the spinnaker suggested when they debated what islands were safe to refill their barrels.

"Too easy to sail past," Eckerd scoffed. "And if we miss, there's only Hup'atele's Cairn, and not a drop on it."

"Anseloc!" Another voice cried, and Foster got the sense the less-traveled had begun to name-drop.

"Yunoc's got all we need." Tamarqan stood. "Can't miss that one. We will stuff every barrel in a week or two, and we can skip those rocks that pass for islands you halots so love."

"Aye, Yunoc's fair, but gimme back me argot and I'll see the lads at Nunoc have our barrels brimmin'!" Gionn sent the whole boat into choking laughter that rolled over the first attempts to return to debate.

"Too much traffic. Yunoc might as well be a brothel. You're bound to knock against someone." Pitras settled the hysterics.

"Not all of it." Foster spoke for the first time. "I came through there on the way down with a squain guide." He cringed at using the word, and hoped Atalkut and little Tunguk would forgive it. "He knew every nook and cranny between here and the Sun Gate," he hoped he used the term correctly. "I know a place you can't see if you pass within a hundred feet of it, but it's got all the water and food you need. The natives tell me no white man ever goes there."

Gionn must have sensed his move, but he'd already claimed to have met Foster at Nunoc, so he couldn't warn the crew away from Lenet's camp without exposing his lie.

Corm gathered himself. "We'll talk islands if we need. Right now, the question is coast, or sea?" The benches ruffled with contention. "Arses down!"

Everyone settled into place. Foster started for the bow, but Corm placed a hand on his chest. "You haven't got a share to stand, anyway, but I'll have no shirkin' your position. What'll it be?"

He scanned the entire deck to disguise a momentary look at his redheaded friend. Gionn betrayed no warning or opposition. The last time, Foster saved face despite wanting that man and his companions to die on an iceberg. But the votes were already tallied, and the way was clear. It didn't matter what he thought now, either, but this time he would have to admit it upfront, and they would remember him for it.

"Coast."

Corm smiled with contempt.

Tunguk emerged from the line of buildings to find two blankets laid upon the harbor grounds. The first was that of Gjetsene. Hers stretched white and without fault to the sea, and the glare made him squint. The snow came early, he thought, but he was no recent authority. Now the sun burned through the clouds like a face in a porthole. The heat told him the storm had made its run without support. Her work would be undone. Soon, there would be nothing to drag the sleds across, and another wait to send the dogs. They had to go soon. Once in the mountains of Camne Drumlag, they would have plenty to glide over to the mines, no matter what came of Drummoc.

The second blanket was black. It lay in front of the warehouses, and on it stood the Seleku brothers, Sawi and Onag. A grandfather spoke to them, not of work, but of dogs, and snow, and firestone. He remembered for them things they had not forgotten, and older things about the runs of his youth. Tunguk waited at a distance for him to tire.

"Have you found many good men?" He addressed the brothers.

Sawi scoffed. "Good men are at the mines. We have found most of what we need, though. Children, old men. A few criminals." He lingered on the visitor.

"And two more. We drove for Ulmar, among other occasions. Tended dogs for Ostuk. We will see them to the ship, and across the channel."

"The crossing is short. My family will see to them once they are loaded."

"It is no bother. You do not have to pay us. We work out of gratitude, for the help you gave a friend." Tunguk saw the dog man choke on what he wished to say. Sawi could only nod once in his resentment. "What is this?" Tunguk motioned to the tavern, where dozens of people pushed to get in.

"Troublemakers' meeting," Sawi answered.

By the time Tunguk arrived, the doorway swelled with rough youths and women fighting for entry. He glanced along the face of the building, and saw the familiar boy waving him over to the low window. Tunguk crawled halfway in, but could go no farther. An impatient shove lifted his feet and sent him tumbling, but the room filled so quickly that he landed on a woman's shoulders. Two more boys crawled in behind him before even the window clogged.

Lamps blazed on the bare walls and a stifling heat rose from the breath of Mattaka pressing into one another. A line of marines separated the crowd from the front of the room, where the admiral sat at a table next to an Amposi official who another old man told him was Tuilapoy, Minister of Colony. Two more Amposi officials flanked them—camp aides to the admiral.

Tuilapoy stood. "By order of Alexicus, assistant viceroy of Drummoc under the esteemed guidance the viceroy of Hiade, I convene the weekly, or nearly so, public meeting for the airing of concerns and grievances of the Mattaka people, 'to be heard and dutifully addressed in all earnest sincerity and with forthright expedience by all officers and officials in whose power it is to remedy said injustices, that all who feel wronged shall be heard, and all who are heard, restored.'"

Costig's stomach wafted sulfur into his throat at the sound of the minister's prattling. He'd no one to blame but himself. He could have canceled it again, but in his short tenure, he noticed that the squains responded to the ritual of it. The last time he pushed the meeting, a certain prisoner escaped and a rock-toss followed. He preferred to sit all day in an airless room—chosen to limit the crowd and choke them out sooner. As much as he hated the assistant viceroy, he had to credit the lad: things went peaceably when the locals got to complain, whether or not anyone did a damn thing about it.

"Alright," he roared to silence them. "What of it?"

A little girl front and center tried to get his attention, but shouts from around the room drowned her out. More seal. More blubber. Half those present barked their outrage over the food until Tuilapoy managed to single out a woman to speak for the group.

"Admiral. They steal from our larders. We have none for winter. No money until the men come. Give us meat! We will pay when our husbands return." The crowd cheered her.

"If you want the meat stolen from your larders, ask the one next to you. If they won't return it, I've opened boat traffic. Go and get it."

A round of shouting in Mattakatan surged through the tavern, and the marines braced them back. Again, the little girl tried to flag him, but older voices prevailed.

"Why you take the reward? Put back the reward!" An older man shouted.

Again, the officials struggled to quiet them enough for an answer. "The reward for the capture of the Leopard Seal will return when the mournin' is done."

"When? You never end it! You just want your men to find him first!" Another woman waved her arms at him. "Let us try!"

"It ends when I say it ends. And anyone who shirks his duties or disrupts the affairs of the colony to find the Leopard Seal will *not* be eligible!" He didn't expect them to thank him for the period of reprieve, but Costig began to see the truth to his old captain's warning that no mercy went unavenged.

While Tuilapoy fielded another round of outbursts, Costig spoke into the ear of a marine. It took a dozen calls for quiet before they settled to hear the girl who his men brought to the front of the table. His cheeks swelled at the sight of her black eyes, pleading with her courage as the din settled around her. She looked to Tuilapoy, who nodded in a fatherly manner.

"I have a grievance."

"Go on, love," Costig grinned.

"I am Adelate, cousin to Mennetarmenukne. I am grieved that you murdered my kin, who harmed no one. He lay in the tukit beside me when those people were killed for their treachery. For days, he could not move from the blows your men gave him. The knives you seek still sleep among us, and walk the lanes. You know this. It is murder, because he did no wrong. But it is more. You slaughtered my brother to quell the spirit of the people, who are selfish and wish only for blood. So it is a sacrifice. The gods forbid us to sacrifice our fellow men, even our enemies."

She pulled a silver coin from her dress and held it between them. "Here is your blood price. I will return it to you when you have done what you must. Fall on your spear. Sacrifice yourself to spare the people. If you do not, there will be retribution for your black song. Last night, many people heard terrible howls in the streets. Some say it is the evil kaim who gather to drink when the gods destroy this place. Others say it is the cry of the Leopard Seal, come to avenge the people. It does not matter. Either way, you will die. Fall on your spear, that you die alone."

Costing blinked. He glanced to Wayranapan, then Gerachay, and back to the girl who held her ground. "I'll consider it." He waved, and the marines removed her into crowd.

The litany followed. There were those he genuinely regretted, and sought to remedy: a report of sailors trying to force a prostitute for less than what she asked, and someone shitting with regularity in the poorman's quarters. Others struck him as personal affronts to his leadership, but escaped resolution. When a woman claimed a sailor entered her dwelling during the storm and, "used her in a shameful way for two days," he understood why they went so quickly to heaving rocks, but she could offer no name, and saw nothing in the dark.

"Then who would you have me lash?" He finally sent her away in desperation.

Others, he could not win. The Amposi mourning period was too long, depriving them of the reward; too short for miners and criminals to take part; too Amposi.

His lift of the boat traffic ban earned the fair criticism that the best men weren't around to hunt, and grandfathers could only harvest so much. There was not enough hasqa with the new rations, and not enough women according to one eager lad. Costig fielded issues of confinement. They wished to be allowed to join the Navy, or sail beyond the Attavaik, or hold the meeting out of doors. It felt as though when he tried to find resolution, they brought matters he hadn't the authority to resolve, and when he tried to explain what couldn't change, they found matters too absurd to treat. In turn, he felt like a quartermaster, a bead man, a poye, a scheming god with the things they asked.

The storm was blamed on the Navy, or the admiral, himself. Crews angered Urkuk by marching up and down his face, causing him to spit fire. A group of Mattaka stood accused of making offerings to an Amposi sea god known to bring flooding. His mustache was said to offend several deities, most of all Utsetaret, who sapped men of their fertility in response.

Lesser spirits also haunted the discussion. The ghost of Turrha roamed the shipyard on the moon of his death, seeking passage to the Amposi sun lands of Wat. Meanwhile, tricksters slipped down the mountainside by night to lure the people to their destinations. Local singers set evil words on their fellows. Some among the crowd took up the little girl's complaint of human sacrifice. Another young woman, budding beneath her tunic, accused the Leopard Seal of impregnating her.

Punctuated between these like beads were reports of rowdy lads who stole, spoke loudly to elders, and called to the wives of men known to their fathers. The siege, too, pupped its share of schemes. The people should be allowed to keep steel, or forges, or be given firestone for protective offerings. Each successive plaintiff built on the liberties until every male twelve or more was entitled to full Navy issue, rations, and pay as a defender of the colony.

Personal grudges were levied, with the Mennegur family accused of many secret meetings to aid Farri Donnab, and the Vetkannar family, of spreading lies about the Mennegurs.

Conspiracies gave way to prophecy. A mother shared her dream that the young sons she lost the previous winter had returned as dogs, and begged Costig to spare them the arduous work of hauling down firestone in their first season as pups. Not to be outdone, Barduk himself had returned as either the Leopard Seal, the dead boy Armenuk, or the bead man Willakuy, depending on the source. The most passionate came from a seer who dreamed for six nights that the coal ships *Queen Taral*, *Maraigh*, and *Pallaia* succumbed to a sudden flood that now surged toward Drummoc. Perhaps it was this that reminded a flurry of interested parties to complain that he had failed to send out search ships for the dog ship *Kurrhatetgiuk*, now surely lost. None of it mattered to an old woman who said that Tannawauk would return from his hunt early this year to catch the miners sifting through his hoard, and that no wrath known to the Mattaka could exceed what would follow.

Costig cared little that the clans of the Arm supposedly grew too poor for deserting young men to raid, or that the inside of the latrine smelled foul to the squains who were not allowed to use it. He woke briefly when a woman warned that Lama's rot had returned, but she refused to disclose any more for fear her kin would be destroyed.

Near the end, after some of the crowd had already trickled out, the old man pushed to the fore.

"One is known to me who would speak to you of Camne Drumlag," he said. Costig would have recognized the voice even without the lamps that played over his face. They most often spoke in the dark. "He overhears the men who rowed under the dog captain speak of the official there. He is bad for the people. You must go to Ingputka to speak with his man."

Costig had to stop himself from sitting up. "Ingputka's under three feet of snow. Only way to find it's to fall in. Can't you say? He's not like to hear across the channel."

The old man shook his head. "It is sailor talk, and I do not wish to harm myself. I am too old to mend. He will whisper it in your ear, and we will see what you choose."

Costig gestured to Wayranapan and spoke in a low tone, then addressed the frail gray rope on the other side of the marines. "My man will find you after to make arrangements." When the old man stepped away, he called over Gerachay.

"When the meeting disperses, have the captains announce that the mournin' ends at sundown."

"Aye, sir. Will it be better to wait until tomorrow, that they have a full day's warning?"

Costig curled his toes around the argot he lay before the wounded lad all those years ago, it seemed, in the hut. He'd kept only his promise to the scoundrel Gionn. This one stood a broken oath that haunted his step. He wished he could let the lad play spy, but he saw now that Drummoc tolerated no subtlety. Parks fell, a casualty of Costig's stupidity. Now the question turned to the third argot and his word to Foster to care for the two squains. He still meant it, if the old man could find the wisdom to stay clear.

"No."

Willakuy intercepted him after the meeting. Costig felt a flicker of disgust, and wondered if he preferred public complaints to private ones.

"Well-dispatched, sir!"

"Purpose," Costig pushed by him and forced the bead man to keep up.

"Eh. Very good." The official hesitated at the loss of whatever drivel he had prepared. "As you know, I finished the count of the treasury."

"As I ordered," Costig reminded him.

"Wisely so. It is good to know what rests at Camne Drumlag."

"Purpose," he repeated.

Willakuy's fingers twitched as though sifting invisible beads. "I should say, it is *almost* complete." Costig's brow sent him into a panic. "Eh, no. I mean, it is done! Only—well, there are I believe a very small number of coins belonging to the treasury I have failed to count—confirm." He corrected himself. "I understand the three silvers that you, eh, withdrew, and held for the reward, have been distributed to compensate for the deaths of three Mattaka." Costig waited for the rub. "Is that so?"

"Aye."

"Oh, very good! Then my work is half-complete."

"If I have to ask you one more time—"

"I have only to count the other three!" He rattled. "Do you—eh, are there three more for the reward, that I might count?"

Costig stopped and ushered Willakuy away from the straggling squains. "Aye, I've got three argots out for the reward, as you well know." He thought a rough glare would be enough to put off the bead man, but perhaps Willakuy saw that they both desired to be somewhere very different. Or perhaps his persistence came from elsewhere.

"Excellent, sir! A lively reward, of uncommon generosity! Eh, may I count it?"

Costig weighted his foot to feel them, the pair that never left his person. "Three. One, two, three. That right?" Willakuy's mouth twisted, then he nodded. "Anything else?"

"That is all, sir. But, oh!" He regathered the admiral. "I do not doubt your count, but it is my sacred duty that I may only string what I mark with my eyes. You understand! It is such a low number, I know you are correct—not to say you cannot count high! A man like you," he wagged his finger," I suspect has many numbers at his command. It is just...to oblige my oath to Potxl."

"If you had to insult one of us, you'd choose me over Potxl, would you?" Costig reached out and gently stilled the bead man's fidgeting fingers within his own. "Who told you to ask me?"

"It is no trouble!" Willakuy yanked free. "We can count them later, you have much to occupy your thoughts! So many complaints!" He laughed of the meeting, then worried over his wording. "Undue, all of them! Such ingratitude, it is hard to fathom. Thank you, sir! I take your leave." He scurried off.

No one ran to the dog camp, but the man coming down the bowl from Drummoc carried an admirable pace for such a journey without snowshoes. He toppled into the tukit, and soon three of the men emerged, leaving only the runner to speak with Polc and Mentewat.

Norwet's instinct was to ignore the wishes of Sawi. He cared little what mischief occupied Mentewat, so long as it steered wide of his own. His uncle's lust to turn some man into a piece of gold seemed ill-born, certainly when that man knew what he did of Norwet. Besides, it was a rough crew sailed with Polc. They cast a grim shadow over the wisdom of Sawi's snooping.

But another feeling blew gently through the hearth of his chest. Norwet couldn't shake the sense that his work was pretend, and his mischief became his work. Every turn of a strap over wood, scrape of a runner, spit of ice, dash of a sled felt as they do in the last sunlight before a feast day, when the lure of the uncommon life seeps into every routine and fills it with an impatient wonder. It seemed not to matter if the sleds got ready at all, for some god would swoop down and set them on a different fate soon enough.

He didn't think it wise to watch Polc. But he needn't pass on what he learned if it might endanger them in the clumsy hands of Sawi. Norwet knew enough to understand that danger reached the overconfident, first. The cautious driver saw farther. He took his brothers over the crevasse field of Gjeplate not because he knew the place, but because he knew the risk, and that they must go.

No reward called to him, but if he learned more of Polc, he might know where to ease his team. Who had seen more of the Leopard Seal? Who better to drive the family than he?

"It will go faster with more hands." He approached the three men with Milak. "Sawi hires in town. You stand here looking bored. Help us ready the sleds for the ships, and you will be paid when the counts are settled."

"Lookin' bored pays better. Fuck off, mate," one replied.

Norwet shrugged. Soon, he and Milak raced through the camp behind the latest pair of cobbled sleds, Saunlauk and Siguvik riding each to a deck. They drug their feet to slow the dogs as they passed near the three sailors, who shrunk at the sight of the animals. White balls of snow flew from the riders and smashed across the men's chests while Ravitak and Arnake cheered nearby.

Polc's men swore at the laughing teams and begged them to return without the sleds. They paused at a safe distance to claw up more snow, then circled back for another barrage while the drivers hurled insults. One took it worse, and raised his spear as if to cast at them, but a companion held his arm. The man stomped off in pursuit, and Norwet merely stopped his sled and grinned when the sailor realized he would go no closer to the barking monsters.

Instead, he flung himself after Ravitak and Arnake, his two mates in pursuit. The boys fled for the main pack and dove into the wall of white teeth to laugh at the man until the others collected him. Norwet and Milak drove tight arcs around them all the way back to their post.

"These two work well, cousin," Norwet said of the sleds. "Should we pay these men for helping us try them?"

Milak tossed something to the angry man, who shielded himself at first, then retrieved a leather flask from the snow. "My father will not miss it. Or he will, and I will tell him you stole it. That way, Costig will give him three more for the offense!" Finally, the men found their smiles and saluted the boys as they returned to their work.

One more sled sat ready to try by the time the man emerged from the tukit with Mentewat. The two of them set off up the bowl again, not running, but moving with intent. Polc invited the three back inside to warm themselves, leaving the boys once again to their own supervision.

Only then did Ferrakut and Ulwet slink with padded steps from the backside of the trail tukit. They gleamed at their eldest brother.

"What did you hear?" Norwet begged.

"Lots."

"Lots of fine things," Ferrakut echoed. Now Norwet saw their course, and soured. "Just tell us what you know of the Leopard Seal."

"Tell us of the blood," Ulwet added. "Is he alive? What of the marines?"

"And Tunguk and Kjartke. Was there a fight? Where did he go? If you leave anything out, you'll hear nothing of the talk."

Norwet sneered. "Because you heard nothing, yourself. Nothing of interest."

"That's it," Ferrakut admitted with a crafty look. "Nothing to worry over."

"It was *my* plan. You can't deny Milak, and the others. All of us pulled."

"It's true. We will tell Milak," Ulwet offered.

"And Saunlauk, and Siguvik. Ravitak, and Arnake. Only Norwet who is too tall to speak with his brothers," Ferrakut cackled.

Parks edged the butt of the spear forward and planted it in the snow like a staff. With his other hand, he put such pressure on Kjartke's far shoulder that he thought she would crumble every time he took a little hop.

The portion of moon over the harbor made no headway into town. Here and there, it died in the gaps between the square bodies of the main drag, swallowed by shadows as black as the bowels of a wigwam. Just behind the workshops, they inched through midnight blue slush. With each hop, he expected to catch his toe on a drift and die face down in a snow angel. But while the sides rose a foot or two up the walls, the middle was well-tamped. This street had the most traffic by day. No matter how many feet passed, though, it wouldn't have been enough to give clearance to his pathetic efforts.

They followed in the wake of Eskimo Joe. The old man shuffled somewhere ahead like a plow, clearing a lane wide enough for the one foot that needed it, as if someone had simply dragged a timber or a bundle behind him. Parks felt for the margin with the spear like a blind man, steadied himself, and hopped again.

It took too much concentration. There was no way to review his notes. Foster had told him about the miners when he was drunk and mutilated, near death. He hoped some portion of it would bubble up in time to show Costig he was still the man for the job.

He couldn't remember how wide the town was. One hundred yards? Two? Most of it still lay ahead. Already, his foot numbed and his calf cramped. Parks burned with futility. He considered quitting, not because his body insisted, but out of shame and frustration. If for a second he allowed himself to remember that he'd have to retrace every last hop, it would paralyze him.

A sound ahead broke their stride. Kjartke's grip around his waist tightened. The clatter of voices spilled out past the next corner. Whispers that sounded foreign at first, then condensed into English.

There was no time to retreat to the alley behind them. Kjartke steered him off of the path toward the building.

"Quick, pretend we're making out," he suggested. She palmed his face away and pressed him into the wall, then flattened herself beside him. The voices rounded the corner and turned toward them. Four vague heads appeared silhouetted over the top of a wigwam to blot out a few stars. Parks took a deep breath to stifle his panting. Could they see? Even if it was too dark, they would collide when they passed.

They don't know you, no one's looking, he told himself. Joe assured them there was a period of mourning. No one could be arrested. None of it settled him. In seconds they were upon him. Parks closed his eyes, as if that could help.

A boot rolled over his toe, and he bit off a scream. The voices trickled past. The sailor never felt him underfoot.

Tunguk squatted at the edge of a passing cloud to wait for the men who followed him. They appeared on the open harbor ground several buildings behind where he left them. Perhaps they retraced their steps, thinking they overtook him. Only then did he step into the dim moonlight, returning himself to their attention.

"It is the wrong way," the boy at his side said of his course over open ground for the shipyard. "Who will clear a path for the cripple?"

"The cripple. We must lead them off."

"But what if he finds your trail and follows?"

"The woman will keep him. They will wait at the edge of town."

"Ha. Are you so sure?" The boy challenged, and Tunguk had no answer. He waited until he entered another shadow to look back. Four men crouched quickly until they, too, found a shadow. "Costig betrays you. They will take you at the meeting."

"We will see. I think he needs us, yet."

"Do not hold yourself so high. No Amposi, no son of Hadalis needs an old squain."

Tunguk nestled under the hull of a docogon and searched for them in vain. "I wonder. Do they mean to watch me, or take me?"

"Take. One man can watch."

Tunguk scaled one of the braces holding the ship, found a foothold on an oar port, and with some effort, pulled himself over the side onto the deck. He moved to a part of the ship glowing with silver light and leaned on the rail for some time. The sea was too far, but he spotted the direction he intended and measured the ground. It lay open and lit. Anyone who looked hard enough would see him cross it.

He retreated to the shadows and knelt at one of the hatches. With the butt of his knife and the spine of the blade, he hammered and pried loudly until the winter batten gave. In that fashion, he loosened the others until he could lift the hatch and throw it aside with a slam.

"You may as well shout where you are," the boy complained.

But Tunguk did not descend. Instead, he crept over the dark part of the deck and dropped into the snow with the fainest swish. There he waited until he heard the sound of boots on wood. They paused at the top. When the first started down the ladder, he hurried over the open ground at his best pace.

"You were right," he said windlessly as they reached the last building on the main row. "It was 'take.'" The next street over, a movement caught his eye. Something seemed to tumble forth with the noise of a seal wounded by spears who hurries for the water. The shape retreated with some fuss, then a quick whistle sounded. He responded in kind.

"You cannot still intend to meet," the boy said when Tunguk searched the coastline. "A madman escapes his enemy to walk into his camp."

"Maybe they did not belong to Costig. We must honor the terms if we can."

A block away, Parks and Kjartke watched the figure crouched at the corner for some indication.

"Who's he talking to?" Parks frowned over the faint muttering.

"It is bad when old men who speak to no one. Worse when they listen," Kjartke said.

Tunguk once more inspected the harbor grounds. Drunken sailors shouted somewhere across town. The watch stamped in place for warmth near the dog ships. Some boys, up to no good, scurried between the buildings. The men who had followed him never reemerged from the ship.

He signaled Kjartke to hold. Tunguk stooped toward the coast at the far corner of the harbor where the people often launched for a sea burial. There, he found a rope tied to the mooring stone and coiled tall. The line bobbed slack to taut against a knot. With caution, he peered over the edge. The dark water took its time to show him the ice crystals shattered off from the moon. They sparkled around a dull blanket that took on the shape of a daille, and the broad shoulders of a single rower, close enough to shore that a man could step aboard with little trouble. Tunguk watched the motion of the boat until he was sure there could be no other lying in wait.

It was as Costig said: enough rope to free them from the ears of the shore. Tunguk backed away from the edge unseen. The boy had gone his own way. He worried a little how he would haul Brother up from the daille after he made his talk, but Costig was strong. Tunguk made the sound that signaled them to approach. He watched the shadows where he last heard them. The delay did not seem strange, at first. Brother was clumsy, and would likely have some words of complaint, or a joke for Kjartke before he could be prodded forward. When no one came, he signaled again.

After showing his patience, Tunguk started for town. His feet eased into a heavy track left by the mourners. He thought it no loss if Brother decided not to meet. Their passage to Camne Drumlag was set. Costig's blessing remained a formality. If the admiral wanted to catch them, it should have been simple enough. Still, the more ground he covered, the more grateful he felt to be far from the daille. He signaled again, believing they might not have heard.

Now someone moved from the side of the buildings. The figure of a woman stood, spear in hand. The sound she returned to him was not the one of acknowledgment, but of warning. The crunch of boots alerted him to what he overlooked in his squinting after his companions. A group of men stalked toward him from the same direction, now yards away. Kjartke raised her spear like a question. He abandoned their whistles.

"Go!" Tunguk shouted in Mattakatan as the four reached him, line abreast.

Perhaps the kaim who covered his sight slowed his hand—it could not be that he was old and weary. One of them caught his wrist before he could draw his knife. A fist came upon him, and he fell to four limbs in the snow. Tunguk hardened himself as he learned to do when a thing could not be avoided. The boots that struck him seemed to belong to giants. He remembered a boy staring seaward from this spot, wishing for a ship. His breath escaped in whimpers with each blow. There had been many worse beatings, none as bad as this. It was a quiet end, he thought, curled like a babe. He felt no peace to arrive at last, after all his longing, and he knew then that he hoped in secret that he would live.

A man collapsed beside him and cried out, grabbing his leg. He could not see farther, but heard the shouts of boys. The other boots left him. When he raised his head, two of the men chased after something toward the town, then gave up. The other helped his wounded friend to his feet.

"They fuckin' stabbed me!" He protested as the other two returned. The man cast aside help and drew his own knife to bear down on Tunguk. The others restrained him.

"Easy, mate! He said not to kill him!"

"*Hoy*!" A great boom that could only belong to the admiral came from the direction of the water.

"Come on, let's go!" One of the men hurried them.

"You like that, squain? We know where to find your family! Any word to the admiral is your last!" They sprinted off.

Costig marched his way from the harbor. It should have seemed the arrival of an ally, but though Tunguk could not say, he felt he must avoid the man if he wanted to continue. Sickness gripped him as he took his feet, wavered, and fell again. The next time he kept his balance. Every movement felt like a ship groaning apart, sucking the sea through a ram-wound. No longer was he sure if he even stumbled toward town. His head could not lift, or he refused to try.

A hand on his tunic startled him. There was no fight left. None was needed. A pair of boys slipped themselves under his arms and bore his knees up. They felt weak, as if they would tumble with any step, but soon the shadows devoured the moon and thrust him through winding channels and the familiar brush of stone.

On the first night the *Gairhle* ran to sea, Foster dreamed a game of Battleship. Parks sat across the table in the *Qarapara* with one of those floppy hats common among the whalers. He wore an eye patch, and had two legs. Every shot his friend called was a hit.

"F4!" Parks snarled. Foster couldn't make out the pieces, but he knew the number.

"Sank my squain boat."

Tunguk studied their moves from between them like a chess master. A pang of guilt struck Foster for using the *S*-word. One-by-one, his ships fell: the carrier, the destroyer, the *Qarapara*. At some point in the game, the bunk room setting shifted to the deck of a large wooden ship he didn't recognize. A crowd appeared around them, betting and cheering against him. He ran out of red pegs, so he pulled a bloody tooth from his mouth. Something told Foster that Parks had a spy at the top of the mast looking down on them, but Lenet, who seemed to have some stake in the contest, insisted he keep his eyes on the board. When only a dog ship remained, he protested that he never got a chance to shoot.

Parks offered him, "one guess for every copper in a silver, and one for every silver in a gold." Foster rattled off letters and numbers, which he heard strike the water with a hollow slap. "F1 through F10," he said with waning confidence. Kjartke laughed at his futility. Without explanation, Tunguk had transformed into Gionn. "You cunts should've stuck together," he lamented.

No letters remained. Foster tried every alphabet he knew. "Delta, Eckerd, foxtrot, nineteen-ninety-two." The last salvo transformed into a bird and fluttered away.

Parks turned his board to show Foster empty water, never a ship at his command. He awoke in distress when they put him ashore with Gionn's knife to cut his own throat.

In his daze, he ran his eyes up the mast and found it uninhabited.

A cold breeze snapped the sail. He was used to not seeing land for stretches, but it always came back. There was no more thought of that to pin his hopes on. The vote went Corm's way—it had to. Now the morning navigational powwow took an urgent tone. They traded landmarks for sun and stars, which grew shy as the Autumn gray deepened.

Maybe a third of the ship stood with him for the coast—he didn't have to count. They wouldn't sight a bluff again for weeks until they turned for the tip of the peninsula, a safe distance from Nunoc. He remembered that anything you won't die for is not a virtue, but a convenience. A costume, like Gewar prancing in his dress. Figuring a way to get a whole ship to a certain port he couldn't find on his own would have been hard. There were a lot more ways to make sure the *Gairhle* never reached Taclann now that he shared in whatever he did to the crew. Foster wondered again why he agreed to this mission, and knew it wasn't for Costig. If he never returned, there was enough gold for Tunguk and Kjartke to die at their leisure on Drummoc. He doubted he could be that noble. Or was it for Parks? To go home? None of it rang true.

By the end of the day, a small light reached him. Whatever Corm gained from his course, he gave up his ironclad consensus. No one feared a saboteur, or any number of them, out to sea. The rollicking mood of the debate unshackled the men. Everyone offered opinions on the swell, the wind direction, the flight of birds, or anything that gave them a semblance of course. The spirit of cooperation returned, and with it, the blistering insults and second-guessing that put him at ease. Gionn went back to calling him Wife Seal, among more colorful epithets.

The real count had to be closer to even, if not in favor of the coast. The old man was no fool, though. He gave them a chance to stand against him, and they faltered. It was a bold trade: his stranglehold on opinion for a course that undercut Costig—or for all Corm knew, Palqua.

Once, when Foster took his bench after a round with the loose nails, a memory came to him. He sat on a rug in his kindergarten class. The teacher spoke to them—maybe she was reading a story—but he remembered in precise detail the way he picked at the rug, which was covered in animals and confetti, blocks of letters, arithmetic, and balloons. He pulled red threads from an "R" with a yellow backdrop beside his friend Cooper. Nothing before or after stuck out. In all, he could list maybe another five isolated moments from that year of his life. When Foster reflected on the weeks that followed on the *Gairhle*, they came in the same kind of marooned recollections that seem trivial, except that he remembered at all.

The first three days left him with a general feeling of relief, and men committed to a destiny. All he remembered of it was a single event: a sheet fluttered slack on the port side. Pitras and Fergo hurried over to help Qawa and Imau'y wrangle it. The four of them laughed over gentle teasing, and though Foster chuckled, he soon forgot what anyone said.

On the fourth, the swell picked up and a gale buffeted them from the west. He was sure of the timing, because some of the sailors had argued that the fourth day after a change of course would tell the future of the voyage.

Before Corm could take his first walk, Foster awakened to a man called Boot, who told him to swap benches. He blinked from confusion to panic. Captain's orders, the man said. He searched his neighbors' faces for a pardon, but Gionn shrugged.

"Off with you."

Foster hugged his inundated belongings and tripped his way aft in search of an empty bench. He crossed the mast. Three rows beyond, he found the vacant spot behind Aldan, the carpenter. Before his ass could touch the wood, though, Corm bellowed and chased him to the bow.

"I said *Bentos*! Drain your ears, dotard!" He harangued Boot. Foster resettled while Bentos gathered his things and made the long walk to the other half.

By evening, debate swirled. A number of crew thought they had crossed from the Attavaik into the waters of the Orin. Eckerd assured them it was just weather. More disturbing to Foster than the higher seas was his new neighbor. He wondered if the man got his nickname and his reassignment because his feet constantly encroached on Foster's sleeping zone, and no amount of kicking could dislodge him.

None of the others seemed keen on his presence, except Hogue, who traded an endless volley of jokes as though a relative came to town for a visit. By now, Foster knew the OG's—the seven crew who sailed down with Corm: Eckerd, Gewar, Tawatu, Hogue, Pitras, Fergo, and Ordacles.

Through banter, he came to understand that a portion of Palqua's men were whalers who jumped ship for the Navy in Drummoc, only to return in a confusing drama that involved the previous admiral and his gang deserting for the whaler before being arrested by Palqua, who then deserted himself. There was no telling how many Navy were veterans of the *Gairhle*, but he reckoned Arthas, Jonn, and Boot at the least.

In the wake of the newcomer, a familiar tension returned. Autumn hung a curtain that never quite broke. It may have been the settling chill, or the way that nothing dried entirely. The ship once again took on a strange music. It never grew to the pitch of the days when he lived in both anticipation and dread of a mutiny. Still, he often had the sense that something meaningful fluttered back to its perch the second before he looked. Needles danced through leather and rope wound in braids. Tiny knobs of oakum filled a sack. The captain called him to the mast so he and the mate could hover over the course. On the way aft, three different men turned to face the bow in order to greet him.

The sun or a star caused a ruckus like a woman paying a visit when they deigned to appear. Old omens were subject to reinterpretation. Corm thought that the pod of killer whales—the angotaks—favored the route because they remained between the ship and the coast. "Had enough of Jonn," Corm slapped the kid on the back. He grinned sheepishly, and a few of the old crew whooped an approval. Now and then, they ran back towards the unseen continent to catch a fair wind or keep off the Orin.

Their rations of dried meat began to taste less dry and pleasantly salted. Foster noticed some men squirreling portions away for later. Pitras made a stink of offering some of his food to Bubba—named so by Foster in a tremendous private victory of social influence. (His real name was Bubua.) Tawatu began under-serving the men who were "too stuffed to eat" until Corm quashed it and demanded full rations.

Soon after, the current water barrel became salty as well.

The first clear day saw Gewar take his life into his hands by donning his dress. What followed struck Foster as surreal. He chased the captain off the mast. This time, the sailors restrained their passions and left him unmolested, but all sat rapt while he danced around the pole and sang a song that would have embarrassed even Parks. The response was polite. Then, in a woman's voice, he tore at his chest and implored the men to offer "fair portion" to the sons of Uinab. The prayer that followed must have struck only Foster as a cringeworthy contrast to the raunchy performance, because several men shed tears. Gewar proceeded bench to bench, collecting pittances like a hunk of fish, a scrap of leather, or the wringings from a hat in a small basket. He blessed each man, whether they gave or not, then flung the contents into the sea without a word, disrobed, and sat down.

The Amposi grew restless. In particular, a stretch of benches just aft of Gionn that held mostly native sailors had to be warned several times to stop chattering in their own tongue, and they only complied when Tamarqan lit in. The next day, they demanded that Gewar loan them the dress to "perform entertainments" of their own. He refused. They became anxious, then hostile. Yuray, humorless and insistent, marched halfway across the ship to repeat his demand of Gewar. He appealed to Tamarqan when the whaler told him he "hadn't the stuff to fill it," which brought Corm down. Imau'y moved to flank the older man, and suddenly Foster felt a rumble among the benches that filled him with terror.

Whatever line had been crossed, Corm and Tamarqan joined forces to regain it. They placated the man by allowing him to pray for safe passage in the common tongue. He insisted on a lump of coal, and got it, but failed to spark the wet powder for an offering. In the end, he drew marks on a few faces, then threw the remaining lump into the sea.

Luckily, the conversation turned to things Foster could understand. Speculation ran wild about the rations. Some of those closer to the barrels stretched for a peek at the contents every time Tawatu opened one for meals. Moipa bet Jenneker on how many more days it would last, and Chirim volunteered Foster to count how much was left in the barrels. The crew took it to be an absurd notion, but Foster assured them it was possible to estimate the days based on the number of crew and the portion size. Still, he never got his chance to quell the fears.

The gambling seemed to increase as the temperature fell. They woke to ice every morning, by then. Foster found a small relief to his suffering in that he always suffered, but now he could see others suffering, too. There was little work for most of them, and men now stood on the gear and shimmied for warmth, or paced their areas. A few dared a longer trip, and he heard men bet on what bench so-and-so would turn at. They bet on the weather, how many whales would be spotted, or personal histories like the number of brothers a man had, or Foster's land of origin. Men wagered shifts on watch, a bite of food, rights to marry some female relative who was always among the most beautiful women anyone had seen, a bootlace, prayers on another's behalf, claims to possessions upon death, a chunk of ice broken off the gunwale, the next cup of hasqa, a penny. He turned down every offer that flooded his way, sure that they would make a sucker of him, but it only made him more of a target.

After a blow stung them with water sheared off the surf for hours, someone tried to cheer up the crew with a shanty—the only one Foster could remember hearing in all those weeks. It got off to a grating start. A voice joined here out of boredom, there out of spite. Once Corm struck in, the entire crew followed, and even Foster figured out the words.

Each night, he spent less time sleeping and more time shivering. It came half an hour at a time, until he found himself so exhausted that an entire day and night became a single alternating cycle of nodding off, then fighting hypothermia by doing jumping jacks and pushups on the quarter deck with Atalkut and Tunguk. He taught them to count to thirty with him. As the cold increased, so did the frequency of their baffling regimen.

His sinuses never cleared. His fingers and toes wrinkled and whitened. Foster wandered the ship like a spirit trapped between the waking and the unawakened worlds. He no longer believed he would see land, or feel warm. No determined ethic roused him to action like it did on the *Juhketappat*, where he underestimated the salvation the dogs gave him. It was Groundhog Day, without the clear demarcation of new and old. Sometimes he woke, sure that they had turned to sail in the other direction. He would have sworn the waves came from bow to stern. It took minutes to realize his mistake.

The fear of death he held for breaking the rules evaporated. When he thought he couldn't take the cold anymore, he walked back past horrified faces, hoping for a spear until something inside him spun him at midship. Someone suggested they have him count the ballast rocks to clear his head. Foster ignored it. When he got back to his bench, he couldn't bear the thought of sitting. Instead, he perched on the quarter deck to survey the ship.

It was as he figured: there wasn't a virtue in him he'd die for. But the misery of an open boat in Antarctic waters gave him a roundabout gift. While he hoped to live, the *Gairhle* remained safe. He couldn't sacrifice himself. In his desperation he remembered his friends. Foster would have traded all of them for a cup of coffee and a warm, dry bed. But now he saw a glimmer of relief in his mission. If he had to hang on for them, he would let them go. Dying, however, had some appeal, and doing it in the service of a promise felt close enough to virtue that he might just count it. If he found a way to send the ship under, he'd suffer only a minute or two, and they'd have everything they needed.

He tried thinking up a plan. Each time, he dozed off before he could gain momentum. When he lay awake praying for the gray light of dawn, he tried out a bumrush on the captain; boring holes in the water barrels at night; prying apart the hull itself. Foster staged a mutiny that ended in mutual slaughter, without ever fussing over how he would get it started. In a darker moment, he resolved to throw one man overboard every night and let the terror rip them apart. Then morning broke, and he looked in the swollen faces of the Mattaka boys, or at Gionn's flushed pout, and faltered.

Meanwhile, the spinnaker took flak for shoring up the stitches of the squain boat. Corm followed the tirade with another swap: Tamarqan was forced to trade with Nolan, who sat in the very next seat forward.

Foster drank a bladder of salted water with supper, and another for breakfast. The ratio of seawater to fresh in the barrels crept toward equal parts. He mounted the quarter deck, though when he gazed over the benches, he couldn't bring himself to exercise. The Mattaka boys' jumping jacks ceased amid his hesitation. Their abortive routine garnered more eyes than usual, and for once, no shit-talk. The crew appeared as a gauntlet of enemies. It seemed everyone knew his thoughts before he did.

The first thing Foster recognized was a sadness. Two rows lined up for a burial at sea, while he searched for the corpse. By now, he knew he could sit down and come through this. He suffered more than most, but nothing would take him that didn't kill the crew as well. The sadness was for himself. There rested a North Carolina boy, succumbed to shame and the conviction that nothing he could do was good enough to overcome these fifty-two men. He wouldn't make it two benches through this gauntlet were he to run it.

And he forgot whole days from that passage, but he remembered this: as he stood, those columns bore a striking to resemblance to the huts of Tunguk's village; the icy trail at Camne Drumlag; the lanes of Drummoc; lined with every face he met. He saw also Yunoc and the channel, the hidden throng with their coal ships. The way home. These things were separate, but he couldn't separate them. The miles of the earth stretched between him and the stern.

The first step would be the end of the Foster who weighed the risks and what he could still endure, and who huddled in a leather sack from the spray. He wondered what the moments would feel like between that and the instant when the spear found his breast. He reckoned he might feel so alive that those seconds would constitute the entire span between his birth and death.

Again the view shifted. He saw the crew not as one body, but as cold and frightened men who stared up at him like their captain. His own burial lay before him, but so did that of the crew. These timbers curled around them in a shroud. They might sink together, but it wouldn't be to a different death. Those frigid waves, barely held at bay for countless thousands of attempts would ease the Gairhle beneath the surface and forget her. He felt Parks among them, and with it, a choking regret. There was too much sweat and seawater to reveal his wet eyes as he contemplated Tunguk, Kjartke, and the boys from the dog ship. His Navy friends who he tended with the dogs, the sailors and Ostuk, Barzos. If he ran it now, it was their burial, too. He wouldn't see them again. They already drifted like his loved ones from his own world.

All of these things were separate, but he couldn't separate them, so he faced them all, and stood to lose them at the same time. The ship pitched to stern, and he let the momentum roll his stride off the quarter deck. He was past Gionn before he realized what he was doing. Everyone watched with gravity. They didn't stop him, and he couldn't see a one. Only Cormdran waited like a distant mountain.

Foster held no spear, but Gionn's knife dangled at his side. The back of his throat burned with salt and snot as he rehearsed. *Costig sends his regards*, he would say. No, *The Leopard Seal says, 'What up, bitch?'* He wobbled over irregular cargo past Fergo and Pitras and Bubba. He'd probably only get one sentence out. And what did those dudes have to do with anything? Neither one of them was here, walking right now to his destiny. Nothing he did could be blamed on another, or credited. This belonged to him.

The name's Foster, he considered as a nod to their Wife Seal moniker. He recalled saying something like it to Lenet's people from the deck of a coal ship. If he had time, he could add, *And Gionn's with me*. The bastard would have to fight for it then, or go down like he ought to. With a little luck, he'd take a few out. With a lot, they could incite a riot that carried on their task after their deaths. Nothing else would do, he realized as he crossed the mast. Plunging a knife into Corm would only gain a new captain. The ship had to be turned on itself, shredded to tatters.

The captain stood and stepped to the middle from his bench, three rows from the back. Foster didn't need to fight the whole ship. He just needed to invoke the wrath that already simmered. The threat of mutiny, the rumor of a traitor—he could call on both at once. Men wouldn't even know which battle they were fighting.

Palqua sends his regards, he repeated silently. Corm started forward. Foster caught himself on a man's shoulder and forged ahead, searching for the moment to go for his blade. He glanced up at the clouds and became dizzy.

His next memory was of hanging from Corm's arms, his feet trailing behind.

"Easy, lad," the captain said. "Grab his feet." Palqua took his ankles from across the way, and they carried Foster under the tarp that covered the last benches.

He had no idea how long he was out. A few flashes remained of the time that Corm nursed him, as he had Jonn, wrapped in blankets, rank water pressed to his lips until his hypothermia left him. His interment must have lasted days.

The crew cheered mockingly when he emerged under his own power. Foster shed the blanket with some regret, and bristled in the fresh cold air. It hurt, but only superficially, as raw flesh just exposed. When he made his seat, the boys looked on in awe and terror. Gionn smiled admiringly.

"Could have just asked for a cuddle, mate." Foster blinked.

"Aye, Gionn's quite warm. Just make sure to take the back side of it,," a man said in front of him.

"I meant yourself, Bentos."

Foster realized that Boot had gone back to his seat. As he scanned for him, something caught his eye. A man scaled the mast in a climbing belt. Gionn delighted in his bewilderment.

"He'll say he's lookin' for land, if you ask him," he explained.

Bentos smirked. "Be a few days yet, I'd say."

"Welcome sight, no less." They shared a laugh that evaded Foster and the boys.

One at a time, the angle of the sail, the pitch of the deck and the direction of the waves registered, then the bright mood across the benches. During his stay under the tarp, they had changed course. The *Gairhle* shuddered in the face of the sea route and ran again for the coast.

9

MUTINY ON THE *GAIRHLE*

Pay was issued the day before the dog ships meant to sail. Adelate first regarded the unmistakable line with disappointment. She expected a poor sailor would give her more hearing than one with copper. Tears came for this little inconvenience, as they did each day since Armenuk's death, and she moaned through her nose and kicked a plume of snow. The dark sanctity of her family's tukit called a retreat, but a small kaim bid her to stay.

Work on the ships ceased during this ritual, though there was much work left. Perhaps the Navy should have waited. When they took their coin, some of the men never returned to the harbor, heading the opposite direction instead for the public tavern. The Navy had heir own casks in the hall. To make sure these lasted, they would spend their pay on the people's hasqa when they could.

She knew that these men would be broke by day's end. The shirkers would not remain in the tavern where they could be found and pressed to work. She followed a group with new-filled hasqa skins until they entered one of the storehouses looted during the riot, where laughter awaited them. Adelate did not hurry. Now she understood why the kaim held her, and felt ashamed by her outburst. If she meant to find a hire among the sailors, she could ask for no better audience than destitute drunks in hiding from their masters.

Hasqa took time to run its course, and the noise of the room intimidated her, so she loitered all morning until a portion of the men trickled away.

A single lamp burned amid a circle of crouching wretches. Against the wall, one man already snored. The others protested when she tied the flap open, then gave her a lewd greeting.

"Just in time, love!"

"It's a child," a man with long, greased black hair belched.

"Let her be the judge of that!" The first cackled.

She froze in the arch of light inside the doorway and could not bring herself to step beyond it. Adelate knew that fear, for her, was a rope around her breast that slackened with hesitation. The Mennegur men claimed they did not know fear at all, but she saw the lie when her mother Vatjate had words for them. Nuk himself once told her that if he ever felt it, he need only remind himself that his family rode to this place on the backs of angotaks. Adelate tried this when they gave her a sack of provisions to bring to the Leopard Seal. The story did nothing, but when she simply waited, the rope eased, and she moved on. It returned before she spoke to the admiral at the meeting, but came loose even sooner.

"I come to make you rich," she said flatly.

The men couldn't contain themselves. The eager one nearly fell backwards with delight.

"Leave us, girl," the black-haired man warned. When he turned toward her, she saw he had no earlobes. "But do send your sister."

She produced the silver coin and raised it for all to see.

"I would've done you the favor, but if you insist on payin' me, just as well!" The vulgar one boasted.

"What for?" The voice of the snoring man jolted her from feet away.

"Back to sleep with you, Teague! She's not come for a madman!" Said He-With-No-Lobes. The sailor closed his eyes and was snoring again within moments. "You'll be after the might and the grace of Foul Hand Waits. Hear me, love, that's not Foul Hand, or Handy, or Foulie, or any other arrangement. Name it, and I'm your lad." The others barked over one another to refute him and offer themselves in a senseless din.

"One silver!" She shouted them to silence. "To the man who brings me the jaw of Costig."

They roared with laughter.

"You're the one from the meetin', aren't you?" Another asked. "Best of 'em, by far! Lads, this is the cunt I told you about. The 'blood sacrifice' girl!"

"It'd have to be," Foul Hand Waits said. "I've no admiration for you lot who go around demandin' parts cut from the body, which is beautiful

356

and full of wisdom." They snickered at his remark, but she detected a dark sincerity among the humor. "But that aside, Costig's a barrel."

"He's not a barrel, he's a fuckin' cooper. Not a man on Drummoc could stand to him." Said a thin man with few teeth.

"Aye, there's some more barrel than he," his neighbor claimed.

"Who? You?"

"Barrel or not, you address several who Costig freed from prison after Palqua unjustly detained us. I think it would be easier to arrest you for hiring the murder of the admiral, and to confiscate your silver." Foul Hand Waits stood, and the others followed with uncertain legs.

"If you have no courage for Costig, then you should not want to try Adelate. I have only to breathe your name, Foul Hand Waits. Arrest me! Six hundred Mattaka will await the moment you take a single step into the town by light, or beyond the hall while it is dark."

She had not considered what he proposed. Now Adelate prayed he believed her words more than she did.

The man came toward her. She stood bound in her arch of light. Adelate could only wait.

"Then hire one of *them*." Foul Hand Waits brushed past her, and the other men followed. The last leered at her, and she felt a great release when they left her in the storehouse.

"Fuck it. I'll do it." She jumped, surprised once more by the sudden revival of the sleeping man—Teague, they had called him. He extended his palm for the coin. Adelate closed her fist around it.

"When I hold his jaw."

Kjartke woke to the old man's wheezing and daylight under the door flap. She wished to linger in sleep. The night's foray kept them out long, and even when they returned, she tossed restlessly in her blanket. Tunguk still sat where she left him, upright against the wall. He complained of drowning when he lay down. She said a reluctant prayer of thanks for the boys' arrival. Were it not for Ferrakut and Ulwet, Milak and Saunlauk, Tunguk would have more than sore ribs.

The gash over his eyebrow would need mending, but she decided to wait. Hastate would do better work. With heavy eyes, she pushed out and stood rumpled at her post. The other women already preened beside their tukits. Lanallike met her with a cold glare, then stomped off.

She and Brother had heard the men approach while listening for Tunguk's signal. They could do no more than move around the corner to the side of the warehouse facing the water. Kjartke was certain the oaf would cough or fall over or sing to give them away. They breathed into their tunics to muffle the sound and steam. Motionless, they listened to the shuffle of the four sailors until Tunguk showed himself. There was nothing she could have done, she reminded herself many times since. When she stood to offer her spear in support, she hardly meant it. His dismissal washed through her with relief, but not without regret.

Kjartke calmed Brother even as she surrendered to the hopelessness that he was hers alone, frantic under her stone demeanor, until the boys burst in with the old man between them. The morning brought small consolation. She swished her boot over the many interesting tracks before their door. Tunguk must wake soon. He would know what to make of it.

The lies and wishes tangled in her thoughts like many threads, tugging at her painfully when she tried to sort them. Had her father ever wrapped himself in such matters? To a girl, it seemed not. These ways belonged to the visitors. To the Kammatuk. Among the clans, Jargadak were called tricky and inconstant. It seemed a slander of the defeated. Kjartke was grateful that her part was to stand in doorways.

Lanallike returned, and this time, beamed a smile of delight at her new neighbor. It so unnerved Kjartke that she failed to notice the shuffle of boots in snow. When she blinked her sleep away, the lanes on all sides filled with sailors bearing spears. An officer appeared before her.

"I understand it'll cost me a silver to get inside."

Costig arrived breathlessly just after Folmon. It was Wendell who pointed out the captain's crew hurrying into town. A handful of marines caught up as the admiral sifted through Navy lads to the captain's side. When he saw the marked woman, he lost his words for a moment.

"Hoy! What's all this, lad?" He denied the captain his title.

"Thought you'd be pleased, Costig," Folmon returned the favor, "when I handed you the Leopard Seal."

"In a brothel?" Costig ached with apprehension. One more day. Let the dog ships run. That was all he needed, and this, the gold, the Lord of the Mines—all of it would have been sealed.

"I have it on reliable authority."

By now the poye and dozens of onlookers had gathered. Costig deployed his men to keep back the crowd, but they showed no signs of anything other than curiosity, though the old woman was quite tossed, and she knew it.

"Then tell your commander. Are you mad? Rushin' in with the bilge of Drummoc at arms! I lost five good marines to this lad, each of 'em equal to a dozen of yours."

Folmon could only shrug. "Marines had their thrust. Couldn't risk 'em slowin' us down." His men beamed. "Stand aside, woman!"

Costig knew well the look of a man who faced his fate, and he saw in her eyes this one would walk through a spear before she wavered.

"Leopard Seal!" Costig growled. "Nothin' more for it, me son! Out with you!"

"No Leopard Seal," she insisted. "This is my tukit. I work."

"No one in there, eh?" He forced a grin. She troubled over it before she responded.

"I care for grandfather."

"Let's have him." Costig said. She shouted in Mattakatan. Nothing moved, as he was sure it would not. Thin odds this would go off without blood. But as he readied his next warning, the leather ruffled. The old man supported himself on the stone, then transferred his hand to her shoulder. He doubled over with an arm across his chest. Dry blood caked his wrinkles in a few small cuts, and a wound the length of a thumb hung open above his left eye.

"Fine care you're takin'," Folmon quipped.

"Who else? Last chance," Costig warned when he got no reply. He grinned and clapped the officer on the shoulder. "Were you with us when we cleared tukits the last time, Folmon?"

"Didn't have the pleasure."

"Ah, that's right. Simple enough. Can't fit more than two, so you pick a scrappy lad to press on your arse. I like to circle to the right, but you can go left if it please you."

"What, me? What happened to the vaunted Marines?"

"This lumber-foot killed five of 'em at his snow hut. Beside that, you found him. Take your glory, me son, but don't harm him. I want him alive."

Folmon ground his teeth while a few marines moved the woman and the old man clear. "Jordy! Rald! You heard the man."

Costig consoled himself at the officer's humiliation. The two he named looked no more eager. With their spears confiscated, they leaned at the side of the doorway. "Leopard Seal! Will you walk out like a man, or be carried like a prize?" It did no good. The order came. The two sailors looked ready to jump ship, but a foul word of encouragement from the admiral drove them in. They heard a crash, like a man falling. No onlooker risked a breath. A prolonged quiet strung tight over the tukit until at last, Jordy and Rald emerged.

"Empty!" Rald proclaimed with a shameful relief. At that, the poye found her courage.

"You see? This woman is good. I hire her so she may care for her grandfather. Jealous!" She cast a scornful eye toward one of the prostitutes. "Someone is always jealous to be the new girl."

Costig gave a mighty laugh at Folmon's red cheeks. He took the marked woman by the arm and pulled her in the tukit for a word.

"Thought you were done, for certain. Can you hang on til the mornin'?"

"Will you send more men for us?"

"These aren't mine. And neither were those who tossed the old bastard. If I find the one he nicked, on me word, love, there will be a fine procession of souls down Manhas-way. Do you know who they were?"

"No."

"No matter. I trust me man has spoken to you." She wisely held her tongue. "Ostuk," he admitted.

"Aye."

"Dog ships sail tomorrow. That's the last I can give you. Sort the details yourself."

He took her outside again.

"Useless! Alright, lads! Back to the ships! And the next time one of you means to single-handedly save the Kingdom of Ampos, speak to me, first."

Folmon gathered the admiral in.

"Costig. You know well-enough he was there. These came off the ship with him."

"It'll be 'Admiral,' until I grant you the familiar. Aye, I've little doubt you're right, but these are delicate matters, me son. Did you not think I knew the Leopard Seal was in town? Now you've smashed the false confidence I worked so hard to give him. Marines arrest people. Sailors paint pitch. If this spectacle delays me dog ships, best lie low a few days until I've had a chance to calm meself."

He gave Folmon a hearty slap on the back.

Norwet heard the four of them leave the tukit during the night. He sulked at his exclusion, falling asleep and waking many times before the long absence troubled him. By then, there was nothing Siguvik, Ravitak, and Arnake could do to prevent him. He was the eldest by many years, and they were anxious, too.

Leaving only the youngest, he took Siguvik and Ravitak to ready a sled. They would say nothing of their kin, no doubt in fear of their older brothers, but all had a sense by now that things could turn very bad, and that petty grudges should not prevent them from helping their own. The timely arrival to avert disaster had become nearly an expectation by now, and he knew they longed to be the team who rounded the bend as much as he.

But in the short moments it took to secure a sled, the dogs alerted. They found Milak and Saunlauk gathering a team. The boys were happy to unburden them of the sled, and assured them in excited tones that all was well—no need to accompany them. The pack howled in jealous rage when they left.

"Lash those fuckin' beasts!" One of Polc's men stuck his head out.

"The kaim are about tonight," Norwet excused it. "Best to make protections."

He heard nothing more, so relief found him in the morning when he emerged to see all four boys milling before one of the supply tukits. At the same time, a lump of longing rose in him at the thought of all he could not be a part of.

They looked proud, almost taunting when he arrived.

"Is all well?"

They could no longer contain themselves.

"We saved Tunguk," Ulwet proclaimed.

"We saved Tunguk," Ferrakut repeated. "Some men attacked him, but me and Ulwet fought with them."

"I stabbed one!" Ulwet boasted.

Norwet looked to Milak in disbelief, but the older boy smirked his confirmation.

"We will let you know when we've had time to make a song of it," Milak said. Norwet peered over their heads at the supply tukit. When he took a step, Milak moved to block him. "You needn't worry," his cousin assured.

Norwet frowned. "I didn't tell you of the marines for your good. You didn't see what I saw, or you would fear for your kin, too. It's no longer a game with sleds."

"You didn't see what we saw. But don't worry, we will protect you," Ferrakut offered.

"Enough! How can we help Leopard Seal if we bicker? You want to know? Fine. They found him, Sawi and Onag. Found Tunguk at his aklu. I came with the marines. Uncle had no choice. We set the dogs on them. Sawi knows. Onag knows. They won't say, because they fear Tunguk. And me." Milak snickered.

"It is true," Norwet continued. "I killed a man. Where is the one you stabbed, Ulwet? Mine is buried out there with six hundred holes. But that is not why I feared to tell you. Polc's men are more dangerous than you think. And Costig is no fool. You think he wonders who was in the other cell? After what he did to that other boy, we can't take this lightly. I did not want you burdened by lies as I am."

"We don't care," Saunlauk said to Norwet's shock.

"Your story is already old. We know what must be done," Milak said. "Kjartke gave us instructions. We won't burden you with them, except to say we have agreed with what you said: someone must stay behind when the ships sail for Camne Drumlag, in case help is needed here. We think you would be best, since you are oldest. But if you are so bold, you can help by keeping Sawi from that tukit."

Norwet stung with bile. "I told you, Sawi knows."

"I don't think my father would leave you unwhipped if he did. But maybe he deceives you, and plans to betray our friend, yet," Milak said.

The boys stood in a bitter wall. "You grieve me to act so small. I've done all I can for this family. But if that is what you ask of me, then so be it. Uncle!" Norwet shouted at Sawi from a distance, then waved him over. The younger boys stood aghast at the casual disrespect of the summons, but Sawi came. Norwet squared to him.

"Do not enter this tukit, and allow no one else to enter. Tunguk asks this of you. Once the ships sail, you will be free of him for good." Sawi narrowed as if to challenge, but nodded and shrank away. Norwet stopped him.

"Uncle. I will go to town today with Onag to see to the ships. My brothers have much to tell you of Captain Polc and his men." A little light returned to the face of the dog man, and Norwet basked in the slack-mouthed surprise of Milak and the boys as he marched off for Drummoc.

No one needed to tell Corm who picked through his wares, though he had never seen the man. A great Amposi beak hovered disapprovingly over the oils, flanked by two officials, while Costig lingered at the war club as if he could afford it. The new visitor's blue coat faded under rich beadwork and begged for fresh dye—that shade being one of the few things Corm had sold out. The black braid wore as many beads as the garment, in contrast to his native trousers, seal pelt sooted with coal in an effort to elevate it above the Mattaka fare. It merely gave him the appearance of a miner who clung to mended Amposi boots, which he fancied held some prominence over new fur seal by a perversion of vanity.

The admiral didn't bother to look up.

"How much for your reed grass?" He teased his finger over the bales, torn into thin curled strips like hair until they couldn't be split one more time.

"Curious, that. Happens to be the same as a new wedge."

"Too bad. An uncommon luxury! I have truly never seen it here. But then Drummoc is a difficult post, for an admiral as much as a whaler. It is not a question of *if* we shall have to do without, but of *what*."

"Difficult to reach, aye, but she's been good to me before. There's a certain advantage you can't enjoy in the crowds of fairer ports. Here, a man can practice bein' what he thinks he ought to be elsewhere."

If the remark stung his pride, Turrha wore it.

"I see it as a place where a man must rise or fall to what he is." He draped one dress, then another over his forearm and handed them to one of his officials to hold. "Pity, no trousers, but this is good material. You are a man who understands trade. Will you really hold such a grudge that you turn down good coin?"

The sailors straightened the wares, pretending to take little interest in a rare transaction.

"Ten silvers. Each."

Turrha muttered under his breath in Amposi. "It is high for both! But if you agreed, I would see it as a favor."

"I'm not talkin' about the dresses. You want to trade with me? You owe me ten silvers a head in compensation for each of me men your underling swiped. He seems to have confused me with a mine, and these lads as coal. I believe it's twelve now, Eckerd?"

"Aye."

"Which one?" Turrha pretended to be taken aback.

"You know."

The admiral waved his hands and argued with himself in Amposi, then turned on his camp aides. They tried to explain something to him, but it only aggravated the torrent of reproach. When he faced Corm again, he had conjured a warm smile.

"Were I a scoundrel, I might have left your crew to jump until you stood alone in your daille. But I suspect you are a captain, as you have come to fancy yourself. Drummoc alone will tell. With respect for your efforts, I shall offer you two-hundred decairs for your ship."

Corm reeled inside as though he had been throw overboard into icy water. "The *Gairhle* is mine, and so she'll be until she sinks beneath me feet."

"Can you see no farther than your prow? I would not strand a man such as yourself. You will join the rosters at the rank of captain, and you may yet go down with her. I'll have the lot of goods, and each of your men who enlists will receive three decairs, six for the mate. You, I suppose, have half the shares, and so beyond the two-hundred for your ship, you shall receive the sum of the crew's shares."

"I've nowhere near half, and no man's share is worth as little as three silvers. Two-hundred is a pillage. You couldn't get a decent ram down here for twice that. For that matter, what would I do with such a fortune, anchored to Drummoc? I'd be dead of whores and hasqa long before a tactician such as yourself sent me to drown."

"Then we shall see what you will take in a month. As for you lads," he raised his voice to the sailors. "If you tire of false promises and sign to the rosters, I will award you double pay for the first year, and guarantee one trip to Nunoc for each. Palqua has no authority to offer you either."

Turrha lay the dresses back in their place. He pivoted for the navy hall with the two officials close behind. Within moments, Elward and Broom jumped down from the *Gairhle* to hustle after them.

"Go, you rank cunts! Heavier the purses of better men!" Corm barely collected himself to meet the gaze of Foul Hand Waits, who stood where they arranged, a short distance away. He tossed his head, then feigned an impatience that brought them together too close to where Costig lingered for privacy. They ignored the sergeant-at-arms' presence.

"Tell Palqua I'm prepared to hear of the matter we discussed earlier," Corm lay the tip of his wedge in that receptive ear.

The *Juhketappat* advanced over log rollers under the steady heave of the Navy. A sailor leaned into every oar, and two at those fore and aft, outside the shadow of the false desk. A pair of ropes descended from blocks high on the mast to the amu. On the far side, lines of men dug their feet to keep it off the ground, so that she rode level and only the keel glided over the wood. But the real weight bore on many smaller lines trailing from the port beam over the false deck and under the amu, where they rested on the shoulders of as many men as could stand in the length. Norwet didn't know how they decided who would push under the false deck and trust his mates to hold it aloft, though he didn't think they could be favored souls.

Behind her, the *Orin's Thief* gave chase. When the second ship cleared a roller, four men hoisted the log between a pair of straps and hurried it to the front. A work song belted from the lungs of a stout man between the ships, sweating despite the snow and his idle hands. In one part, he sang on his own while the sailors rested, and in the other, they answered him in chorus and with a shove.

Along the quay, the cargo stood ready. Barrels of water and food, and many frozen blocks of dog food. He ached for sleep when he considered how they would have to start well before first light the following morning to get the dogs to the ship in time to sail.

It must have been the new sailors who waited nearby with the last of the rigging to be fitted once the ships were in the water. He recognized none of them from the voyage south. That crew, he understood, had fallen out with the captain and fled to Camne Drumlag on an unauthorized voyage that would surely bring suffering to someone. The choice of replacements seemed optimistic. All were Mattaka. Most of them weren't much older than he—perhaps the only boys left who had so far avoided the mines. Among the other four, two were old enough to have retired from the mines. Another had lost the ends of eight fingers to the frost, and by the way he walked, Norwet suspected several toes, as well. Only the last seemed of proper age and vitality, which meant he should have been a miner, a smith, a hunter, or something other than an unemployed man of Drummoc. As to whether any of them had sailed anything larger than a hunting boat, Norwet had his doubts.

He shuddered to think of making his first crossing with anyone less than every man aboard. Those sailors, those rowers, even the strange stowaways. He thought the storm would have taken them if one woman on the boat had not been there, or if another dog had succumbed. Like these men urging her back to the water, it took every hand.

Now the short run to Camne Drumlag, the place that forged his family and fed them. It should be of no consequence compared to the voyage he already survived. He wondered if the *Juhketappat* was as apprehensive as he.

"She always looks smaller on land." Captain Ostuk announced himself. "When I'm at sea, I think her as permanent as an island. But when she rides the log waves, I know I must be mad to set foot on such a thing."

Norwet nodded politely.

"Come. I want to show you something." Ostuk pulled him from his uncle Onag and steered the boy where the knocking chant washed between them and those who might listen. He motioned at the mast, but his words did not match his gestures.

"I don't want to drag you into a current with me, but I'm afraid you are close enough to it, already. Listen with care. You must speak to Kjartke—and don't tell me what she says."

366

The mutiny on the *Gairhle* resumed where it had broken off: with Foster stumbling about the mast. A fumbled coin briefly secured Corm's authority and destroyed any hope the idiot with the funny accent held for misdirecting the whaler. Gionn knew better than to assume wisdom and forethought in a man's actions. Still, it never ceased to infuriate him when he couldn't find such a thread. Something about Foster's presence made a fool of those within his wake. Not even Gionn could bring calamity with such regularity. It was perhaps the only trait of Foster's he admired.

Corm could have had his course without hearing a peep of it from the benches. However, Foster and whatever mischievous luck cavorted around him robbed the captain of his senses. Now the loyalties of every man aboard seemed to turn as often as a sidecock shunting across the breeze.

Corm signed Foster against good judgment. That should have made him a Corm lad, through and through. But most of the ship swapped him to Palqua after their ice frolic, and Gionn agreed. In truth, he was Costig's worm, but the only course to stopping the whaler ran through the captain. The crew might have done it for him, but he returned the ship to Corm when he loosed an argot beneath the mast. Foster sealed it when he all but accused Palqua of plotting to assassinate the captain and put in at Nunoc. Gionn couldn't have ruined it any better if he tried—and he would have.

The misery of a quiet crew full of suspicion was tempered by the certainty that he would not have to draw his sword. With his argot nailed to the mast, Gionn's enrichment hung on a safe and timely arrival at Taclann. He did, of course, fancy half a hundred ways he could nick the pouch. His own luck leered at him from the gunwale, plotting a new round of sabotage. But Gionn stuck fast to his bench, and his lips to one another. He often relished his new role as peacekeeper, who needed nothing but goodwill to prevail. He woke one morning with the sense that he rode as a god: knowing the troubled hearts of all, and that their fates would come to no trouble while he sat majestic, tugging this way and that just out of sight to keep them under the auspices.

It was Corm's fatal seam that he developed a love of maps. The man had sailed Hiade before without one, but more and more often couldn't resist calling the troublemaker to the mast to have a go at the wet sheet. Gionn himself never used one—not from his lowly posts. He came to suspect there resided in them some curse that caused men to see what wasn't there. The coast, the waves, the sun—had not great kings plied their fetch by these before the priests conjured the shores onto a parchment?

Eckerd knew the way of it. In a world where all good things were possible, Gionn would cut the bowels from both Cormdran and Palqua, and let the mate steer them. But the captain still feared the obscure assassins, who were a single man, and the most inept of them. He also harbored a murky dread of the angotaks. There was a story there, Gionn was sure of it, but he hadn't the time to root it from the veterans. Foster's map worked its dark glamour, and convinced the captain that he could sail a thousand miles in the care of an image, without food or water or sight of an island.

Perhaps Corm felt unpopular. Gionn again strained for the wisdom of it. The sea route was mad. All Corm accomplished by letting the lads stand for it was to revive the mutiny.

Then there was Foster again, standing in opposition to the captain when he had no shares and should have sat. Were Foster a clever man, Gionn would have thought it a ruse to deflect his intentions. It was as maddening as playing feachle against someone who moves at a whim.

Instead, the entire ship shuddered as the enigmatic number cunt backed like a wind before a storm. Corm got the count out of a lingering fear, and so it was both the suicide route and the mutinous dance.

Gionn stood with Corm despite his objection. So did Palqua, so did Tamarqan—those too obvious to risk a display. The coastal holdouts included Arthas, but mostly fell within a bunch Gionn took to calling the Blue Quarter. The unpronounceable names held a line of about a dozen on the forward quarter, port side, centered around Qawa and Imau'y. It could have been more or less, depending on where the lads near the mast fell. The insurrection resumed before the last arses hit the seat. Sailors at every station hurried to adjust to a seaward course, but the Blue Quarter dallied.

Every order thereafter, certain men lagged when the ship pitched to sea, and the same hurried after the ropes when she pitched toward the coast. It was too foul for laundry. Other signs of strength and caution traded places. He glimpsed a mutineer's pass—an extra turn on a certain knot—spread through the ship. "Grassbender knots!" Fergo near kindled the fight when he crossed the keel to retie their efforts, as though it would move them into the captain's lot. Stoppers soon appeared on loose tails, the work of hands loyal to Corm.

The next day, the Blue Quarter let a sheet come loose to signal their readiness. Pitras and Fergo raced to help secure it. Had the others acted at that moment, Gionn worried that they could have taken it. But the former admiral gauged it otherwise. Palqua had to quash it by folding his oilskin over the thwart between himself and Corm in plain view, wounding the zeal of his companions. Worse, while Corm couldn't have failed to notice the signs, this one lay so bald and bare, no one but perhaps Foster could pretend they faced anything other than open battle.

Like many, Gionn held the belief that the fourth day after a course change would bring omens of the voyage. So it was to his displeasure when a gale rolled through. Corm decided to forego his walk past the Blue Quarter. Instead, Boot came to swap with Foster.

The move sent him into a fit of turmoil. The passes were becoming too bold. A bench swap always played as desperate. Gionn's instinct considered how he might signal a switch to Palqua. Corm had lost it, and only an overwhelming count might spare Gionn getting nicked up. A captain set his benches when they first boarded, to the extent he could. The best and worst seats were always assigned with much intention, and in a crew like this, Gionn had no doubt that loyal men heard whispers of where to settle ahead of time. But there was no way to dole out every spot without seeming like a cunt. Palqua's lads would have scrambled for good positions where they could. It was clear the forward port quarter was their stronghold.

Captains only swapped if they thought it would break a mutiny. It should have been to isolate an important adversary, or to strengthen a key holding. Boot for Foster reeked of madness. Which did he think was loyal? Gionn pegged the former for one of Corm's lads who left at Drummoc to return with Palqua, putting him under suspicion on both sides. Foster was no good at the mast if Corm counted him an ally, and if not, even moving a weak enemy to your center invited defeat.

It took longer for Gionn to realize the true source of his distress. He knew Foster, and if he didn't consider him a mate, he was at least a harmless neighbor. Boot came with no such assurance.

When the stupor wore off, he noticed Corm fixed on him like a buzzard. Having gauged his reaction, the captain promptly returned Foster and called for Bentos.

That was it, then. Corm counted Boot for himself. It was the bow he couldn't judge. If Gionn's fears showed on his face, Corm saw how he trembled at losing an ally for a stranger. Foster, Gionn, the squains—they were one, or at least Gionn thought so. The move meant to secure the bow against the Blue Quarter, and expose Bentos to harm, which meant Corm also counted the new carpenter Aldan and probably Jonn among his blades. Bale and Nolan, too. The mast was too valuable to swap a loyal spear for a Navy lad unless he felt it stacked in his favor. Gionn's head spun. So Bale and Nolan, as he thought, were also men of the *Gairhle's* original crew. Bold to count so many for their former captain against their most recent one, but if he couldn't, there was no way for Corm to hold the ship no matter where the men sat.

Now Gionn saw a flash of memory. When the fight broke out over the argot, most of the bow thought the mutiny was on. He could only wonder if Corm judged their reactions then, as well. Perhaps the man knew his ship better than Gionn allotted. He belched with relief when Foster slunk back to his spot. A bench swap could signal desperation, aye, but also great confidence, especially that a single trade would suffice.

Boot's fast affection with Hogue confirmed it. They belonged to the old crew.

Kill Chirim and hold the bow, he advised himself. *If the numbers go against you, turn your sword on Boot and Foster to show for Palqua's side. And watch the squains. Squains love stabbing things.*

The numbers troubled him. As the nights grew frigid and the seas sided as usual with the opposition, Gionn lay awake among a hundred battles. The ship rose fast or slow, in a quick slaughter, a prolonged siege. Palqua's crew looked an army to Corm's few oars. He couldn't be certain which of those men remained loyal to the giant after all, and he knew that time under a given captain could turn a man toward the nearest alternative. Still, each night the men faded to silhouettes and disappeared without a fight into the rush of water and the groan of wood. He set them on one another again and again, changing as few as one to this side, or that, while by day they tried to announce themselves to their respective allies in manners subtle and bold.

It wasn't until three men spun to greet Foster on one of his forays to the mast that Gionn sorted it. Palqua spent as much time as he did fretting the count. Of those that spoke to Foster, he had one firm for Corm, one for Palqua, and a third undecided. To about-face normally signaled mutiny, but they weren't signaling the captains. They were courting Foster.

Both captains had set the men to their deaths in the melee as many times as he, and like himself, they realized that success or failure hung on the bow. For that to be so, both must have assumed Corm had strength at the mast, as any halfwit captain would. Were that all, Palqua would have leapt to his feet so fast as to topple overboard. He held his Blue Quarter back because he awarded the bow to his rival. Gionn, Foster, and a couple of buckets. Little enough, but he knew if they and Boot climbed up to the quarter deck, joined perhaps by Hogue, it would be impregnable.

Man-for-man, a seasoned whaler would toss a flat-footed Amposi squawker. It was the honor of the former admiral to sit beside the captain, with the guarantee that Corm would kill him first. If he lost the bow, the ship was striped—alternating between the two sides, a guarantee of a bloodbath that wouldn't leave enough hands to make Taclann.

Were Foster clever-enough to see it, he could make his squain pups signal for Palqua and it might be over in a rout. That would do fine by his purposes, but hardly Gionn's. The omens were by now thrice-crossed and keel-up. The only predictable victory was a clean passage under Corm.

The captain blushed at nothing. Swapping the bench so soon was bold, and perhaps bold was all that kept the Navy at bay. Gionn worried it came off as a near-false confidence, but he watched admiringly as Corm stopped to chat Pitras and Fergo, turning his arse to the Blue Quarter.

"Well-strung," he gripped a rope beside the men for balance, and they both stood to address him, as bold as their captain. The voice of some luck pleaded with him not to meddle. That meddling always got him what he wanted, which was ruin, most of all for himself. But one softer and more insistent prodded at his breast. He stood, leaned toward the sea and gripped a rope overhead with his left hand, as if to stretch. Seaward meant support of the route, and to stand with the others may as well have been a spear launched across the deck at Palqua.

"This one's tight, too. No slippery knots out of Chirim," he at once warned the man of his first thrust and offered his loyalty. No sign came either way from the Amposi, but Corm grinned and nodded his approval. That was it. It was too much, and he was convinced he would be killed for it, but his heart could flutter itself to a cold grave now. He'd beaten Foster to the thrust.

So it was with horror that he watched when Foster said, "Good idea," and climbed the quarter deck. The entire ship froze in a stupor.

"Could use a little warm-up, myself." The madman jumped his feet out to the sides, and at once clapped his hands overhead, before slapping his thighs and hopping back to place. He repeated this obscenity in rapid sequence, counting aloud each time until he reached thirty, which all knew represented a majority of the ship and enough to win a mutiny. The offense of Gionn's open pledge melted under this act of war. Foster, as if senseless of it, dropped his chest to the deck, and began to push himself up and down with his arms, as a mongrel might in his first act of love with a woman. Gionn collapsed to his seat, with Fergo and Pitras close behind. Corm looked like a prey animal trapped where he stood. It might have gone to blades at that, but Foster doubled his taunt by prodding the squain lads to join him. They mimicked his convulsions while he counted to thirty again and again. Gionn felt ill. He knew he shouldn't have meddled, as well as he knew he would. Now, despite his every wise bone crying for him to hunker down, he searched for some way to ease the tension.

"Twenty-nine, thirty!" Foster doubled over for a quick breath.

"Hang on, cunt! Let me climb underneath," Gionn said as Foster started in on another round of deck-humping. The crew forced a chuckle out of the same desire to ease their nerves.

"That's what the Buckets are for!" Fergo said of the boys.

When Foster started over with his jumping fits, Arthas shouted from the stern. "By Hadalis, will we never learn what comes after thirty?"

It was enough. The ship bubbled with glee, and every man aboard added his own lash to the offense. Foster ignored them until he tired and took his seat.

Three things could reliably turn a crew against its captain: food, water, and shares. As the seas grew heavy and the days dim, more than one made his case that Corm had steered them into the wicked Orin. They bemoaned the salt that crept into their rations.

Gionn drained his slurry under watchful eyes without complaint. Uncertain hands marked themselves with their swooning over the rations, and Tawatu retaliated by trying to starve them when the slop bucket came round. Meanwhile, Gionn found an uneasy peace. By nature, he preferred the center of the chaos, and the greater portion, leaving others to flounder in his wake. Now, he rested on the knowledge that none of it mattered as long as the bow held. Let them fidget at their loyalties!

And fidget, they did. He learned that peace was not so restful for the unaccustomed. For starters, it had to be defended as actively as any battlement against the bothersome details that tried to upend it. He often fell victim to cold seas coming over the beam. All was well, and his to lose, he reminded himself as he wrung his cuffs.

Despite his confidence, he searched each day for reassurance as Foster mounted the quarter deck for his "exercises." What seemed an egregious effort to taunt Palqua's lads grew more bewildering by the day in more eyes than Gionn's. The crew began to question if he really might be that simple. If Foster meant it as a statement, no one spoke his tongue. Gionn suspected there was some thread to the madness. He wasn't smart, that one, but he had his wiles. Everything served a purpose, if only in his head.

The sickness spread to Gewar. Perhaps he had smitten himself with the success of his last performance—or the bench-biter never missed a chance to put on a dress. His choice of song stirred something in Gionn he couldn't name. It was neither a workman's favorite nor a bawdy cup-clanger, but a children's tune known well enough to all but never sung beyond an early age. Gionn couldn't recall hearing it at any particular time, it had been so long, but felt the words return to him a beat ahead of Gewar.

It told the tale of a lad whose mum had to go to sea to feed her son after the father was lost. Gionn hated the notion of a woman working a ship, because it was a lie, and a disgrace. Each season, she returned with one more mouth to feed, until the starving lad lamented that he and his siblings would not live to meet the next one. Why any foul nurse would teach such a thing to a child, he couldn't fathom. The song first burned his cheeks with embarrassment that he recalled it. Then came the outrage in which he longed to cut down the singer and all of his brothers and sisters, and finally, the whore of a mother. They loomed in his visions until he could not see Gewar through them.

Last there fell a sadness, though not for the child. It recalled to him the sight of a bay under clouds, lapping from a distant storm. There were no ships and no men. The seas remained low, but every fisher and seafarer sat in a damp hut somewhere with little to say until it passed. He stood on shore and felt the rough chop as their trade, as their maniacal repetition of a single task, the lonesome determination behind it, the endless generations growing thinner and farther adrift, but most of all, he felt the sea itself. His nose burned as though he inhaled a breath of salt water.

The chorus came again, an idiotic turn for whelps: "Hoy Berga, knobbedy-knee, a comb for her locks and a gannet for me."

The prayer that followed was a farce. A feast of words for undeserving Uinab. Gewar appealed to the brotherhood of all mariners, who live but by that sea god's grace, and named several drowned cities while leaving out others. Where it brought certain crew a sorrowful sense of connection, Gionn retched. True, though the death throes of that deaf king still inspired awe, the vagrant had not answered a call since his grandfather's time. Habit alone kept his name on the tongues of sailors.

It was all in poor taste. Gionn gave nothing for an offering, and quietly forfeited the blessing Gewar muttered, with a *none for me, fair or foul.*

"No takka-tak!" He warned loud enough for all to hear when it sent the Blue Quarter into a stir of Amposi. Gionn realized they saw the performance as ill magic directed at the mutineers. He couldn't say he disagreed.

Corm's lads needed to see their weak position and stop trying to incite a confrontation. They followed in the form of their leader. Never had Gionn witnessed such blatant displays that failed to lead to a general standing of the crew, if not war. He was perhaps the only one aboard whose blood never lurched when Yuray confronted Gewar and it looked to come to blades. Even Foster noticed for once. Gionn kept his seat and his nerve, and rippled with excitement when it fizzled as he knew it would. Yuray bumbled through an ineffective counter-curse and wasted a little coal, and he, Gionn, had once again decided that all should remain well.

It upset him no less how they clawed at his good intentions. Why must these cunts feel so eager to gash the ship and gnaw one another's bones while she lurched and swallowed great gulps of water? Could they not see past their wet noses? An air of superiority warmed him, flushing out a tremble from his spine. He and Foster had swapped roles, and he bested the imbecile at this, too.

Where he longed for the wart's cooperation was the numbers. Gionn could count as fine as any aboard, he suspected, but each time he ticked off the rows, passing over the uncertain seats, he found himself starting over by the last third. To keep a pair of running counts while weighing the signals made his eyes cramp. Often as not, he got a new figure on the recount. Men of rudimentary numbers probably had a better guess than he. They knew which lads among Palqua's once served Corm, and how it stood with them.

He worried that he put so much stock on the bow because it was all he could understand, just as Foster worked under the graces of ignorance. Then a revelation found him. Ordacles wagered Arthas that he'd give him a copper for every clan of the Mattaka he could name, if he would give Ordacles the same for every one he couldn't.

"Twelve in all, as I see it," Arthas confirmed.

"It'd have to be. Squains can only count to six, and they count sixes after that. They won't suffer an eleven."

"But the Kammatuk on Drummoc were the southern clans before they joined up. How many do you credit me for that one? Neither you nor I nor those buckets in the bow ever heard the names of that lot."

"Depends on how many were in the southern clans." Ordacles turned sideways to look at him, across the way and aft by a seat.

"Must have been five. I can name seven in the north."

Ordacles grinned skeptically. "Can't have been that many. I know of nine in the north, and there may well be some I've missed."

Had it not required a shout across the ship from his cold throat, Gionn would have swore them inside out. No self-respecting squain would have merged any more or less than six clans. They so loved their sacred number that they'd probably expose a seventh child if they had the misfortune of the birth. Probably chewed their food six times and stabbed as many sailors by their twelfth birthday.

Arthas rattled off a list of names that should have gotten him lashed for speaking takka-tak.

"Aye, and the Hupadak and the Onadak," Ordacles added.

"I'd want to know what sailors told you of those. I've known men to make armies and old lovers of rocks on the shore when they've been at sea too long," Arthas contested.

"It is the other way," Baghar said from his seat in front of Palqua. "I know only three clans along the Arm. The main body resides on Drummoc."

Gionn hardly restrained himself from stomping aft to correct this last idiocy with the back of his hand. There were few crimes he held such disgust for as being wrong in a loud voice.

"Five, you spoon-puller, and it may be four now. None have seen the Kapadak in some time," Gionn shouted from the bow.

The argument went on, but something struck Gionn like a cold wave. However little they knew of squain relations, they all agreed on a dozen clans. Unless they had secret insight into the traditional names of the Kammatuk, it was five in the north and one in the south. They might have gotten off with the chat had Baghar not fouled it.

No one consulted the Buckets on the matter, because it wasn't bucket-bearers they spoke of. Twelve had to be the number of Corm's men who defected to Palqua—he was sure of it, now. Ordacles merely asked a guess of one of their lot—an ally or an enemy, Gionn couldn't say. Regardless, Arthas saw it at five against the captain.

Gionn tried again to count—there were eight of the original crew, and if they had only seven more, and grant them the four in the bow, and the two carpenters—it should have been easy, but again he struggled. He got twenty-one, then twenty when he recounted, and gave up on taking that portion from the fifty-three on board, but had Palqua's side at comfortably over half. Foster would click his tongue and have the answer, but Gionn had no Foster.

Nor could he be certain he took the signals right. There were so many, shifting and often contradictory depending on the land of the sailor, where he learned his ropes, and his personal fits. If Ordacles had to ask, few could be confident in anything except that Corm's ranks dwindled.

Gionn resigned himself to the frigid rivulets that poured off his oilskin and hissed through the rocks under his boots. Every time someone leaned too hard or wrung a garment to this side or that, visions of defectors careened before his eyes. The little sack with the argot slapped the mast in the wind. Gionn wondered how he would signal his switch so that Palqua could be sure of it before he acted.

Chirim, now grim as the weather, asked Foster to count how many days rations they had left. What he wanted—other than to sow general dissent—was to give the Wife Seal a chance to declare for Palqua under the misery of the Orin. Any time a man said "count" on a ship, it gave cause for suspicion. He knew only that it slipped from Corm's hands like a greased rope.

While Foster argued with the crew about the sorcery of counting unopened barrels, Gionn grasped that the mutiny had gone on so long because the lads were simple. They were confused. He didn't need to hold the bow—rather, that wouldn't be enough. If numbers cracked their heads like a rock, he would give them numbers. If they knotted themselves up with the meaning of every word and movement, he would give them rope.

"This cunt's got you lot wrung and hung. How can he count *bowls* of meat in a barrel while the bowls are in our hands?"

"Obviously, there ain't literal bowls in the barrels. I meant the quantity. That'll tell us—"

"Nonsense, Wife," he interrupted Foster. "Last time I rowed on a sixty-seater, a barrel of meat lasted us three days on full rations, at best a week on reduced. We got four barrels left. Four weeks at sea."

"How many days in your week?" Chirim snorted in disbelief.

"Five, same as yours, and six weeks to a month."

"Aha! Ampos marks three weeks to a month."

Gionn feigned surprise. "Bein' an idiot don't make a barrel run out sooner. I put us in Taclann in three weeks if the wind's good. A month, you'd call it, but I'll be there in half the time!"

That sent the crew into a furor, where the angry voices of so many expert navigators fixed them at anywhere from a week short of the Sun Gate to eight; from bearing too far north to sight Breidoc, to having crossed into Manhas without noticing.

"You cunts better not count shares like you do months. If you think you'll take two silvers for every one of me own..." He trailed off, and let the Blue Quarter shout and clutch their chests at the suggesting of a swindle.

"Wait, yall only got five days in a week?" Foster interjected.

Gionn blinked, suspecting his luck had awakened. "Why, mate? How many do you count?"

"Seven!"

Gionn grinned. He couldn't have hoped for such a favor. "Wonder what else you've gotten wrong."

"Hell, you can call a week what you want," Foster waved him off as the rest of the crew strained the blood in their foreheads. "Numbers are numbers."

It was no use. Any man who could tick off coins knew Foster had the trick of it. Between the twofold weeks of Ampos and the ringing of so many false figures, though, each had cause to doubt himself. And if he didn't, he could doubt his mate, or his favorite captain.

Not long after, Gionn turned to the Bucket behind him for perhaps the first time.

"I wager you the first copper I earn that I spot a whale before you do." Gionn didn't even search. Bets were a common man's way of asking a mate who he'd stand with, or telling him your own disposition, or that of another. The message could be encoded into anything from the terms to the coin and who won it. Lesser Bucket, as he'd taken to thinking of the smaller one, wasn't likely to know that. As it happened, it was also common for sailors to gamble out of boredom, desperation, and the lure of taking part in one's own ruin.

Those nearby couldn't help but wonder what sinister message he had exchanged, and soon the ship seethed with wild promises. Every one was an opportunity for misinterpretation, and recourse to another count none of them could make.

Many wagers took Foster as their subject, though he wisely refused to join in. The crew flapped like a fish on the deck. Meanwhile, Gionn made a bet with himself. *You'll find a way, cunt.* On freezing nights when he wished only to fall asleep so he might never wake up, his own mutiny stirred. *A makebate like you. You'll cock it up, yet.* He long knew and could not avoid that as his confidence swelled, he would soon follow down the other side. He'd outsmarted them, because he was able and good. Now he'd try again, and make a botch of it—his sword hand would tremble, his charm stutter at the moment of destiny.

No, he'd fire the ship and flee to some shithole at the first chance. Anything to save him from the trough. The trough, where his stomach dropped out. Of all the places, he wished he could like it the best. That's where he knew himself. The dashing man of the mast toppled among the grassbenders in the bow. He lay free of conceit, of hope, of the hundred wakes that crossed behind him. But with that knowledge came the quivering surrender and the longing for the sea to raise his barrow.

Soon he would beg the gods he couldn't bear to name to restore him to the last person who showed him kindness, as he did on Drummoc after he betrayed Foster and Parks. He craved the senseless bond that tangled them through any danger—the one he felt briefly for Oduy at times, and others before him. Even the old squain got to enjoy it with his two nurselings. He would forswear gold and steel, take up the far-flung life if he must. Pay his debts. Sought by no man, and praised by as many.

Gionn would work the ropes without a word in some honest trade where he'd barely earn his meal, and love it like a home. He would run no more from the Shitstains of the world, ask no favor or mercy, if only he could be rid of the plunge into fear and ignominy. The crest of self-celebration could only lead here, because it was as false as he. To face the spear beside a mate, a true mate who he counted without a thought, an idiot mate, too dumb to love himself more than the other. Give him that, and he'd forfeit another thirty years of argots and narrow escapes to die satisfied in a week—the five-day kind!

But where was Foster, after all? A smug tinge came over him. It was he, Gionn, who pulled Parks from prison. And he, Gionn, who got Foster on the boat. What had they done for one another? He felt an angry betrayal fomenting in his gut. For all their noble posturing, what had they done if not leave one another? Parks was probably already dead. Foster wouldn't be long.

A sort of vindication salved his wound. If they couldn't do it, why should he? Gionn was who he was, because no one deserved any better. Not Foster or Parks, or Corm—not himself.

Gionn kept them in a muddle for a few more days beforee lost the heart to litter stray numbers and encourage the crossing of signals. The weather sensed their flagging. The clouds dropped and the wind backed. His trembling fingers struggled to grip the bucket when he bailed. Hard men of the southern passage hid in their oilskins while Foster danced his vile ritual.

As soon as it lifted, Fid broke into verse alone. *Half by Hadal* was a tacking song known to all because of its use to signal the start of a famous mutiny off of Daloni. The *Gairhle* had a following breeze—she was not tacking.

Gionn long suspected Fid was one of Corm's who turned bluecoat. Now he confirmed his wretchedness in a moan that dropped out at intervals due to a parched throat. These were the worst, these jumpers. These ship straddlers, pitching this way and that with every puff. He couldn't fault Palqua's lads, especially the filthy Amposi, for siding with their own. Foster did it for his mates—almost admirable, if not for his flailing. And Gionn, at least, never once seemed loyal to any man. Wasn't fair to use the word "betrayal" when the fault rested on another's presumption. It never ceased to impress him how many rotten oar-polishers, having once shared a laugh, confused him with a faithful wife.

But these cunts! Jumped a whaler, deserted a navy, and belted out for a mutiny in a single season! To spot a lower man always elevated Gionn from a funk. This time, he watched it unfold. When the gentle tug came whispering of his cleverness and begging him to toss the disloyal howler, he watched it as if from beyond himself, and realized when he sank his lowest, he saw no distinction between himself and Foster, or one of the squains. Gionn pitched between no man his equal, and no man lower.

Another voice joined the song—Gabol, from Gionn's end of the Blue Quarter. For a moment, he sat lost. Shame took him, and reproached him for seeing something he shouldn't look at. He stood outside himself, though he knew the danger, and felt the hatred of the traitor pull him aloft, and resisted. He felt the annihilation of hope and ugliness pull him into the bilge. Again, he resisted. Now he drifted, broken from the current. A finger attacked the throbbing in his wet ear. Someone else sang, he knew not who. Gionn craned his neck to the top of the mast where he thought he saw a light in his periphery, and found only a towering black sentinel. He sensed this moment apart from others, an opportunity, though for what and how to claim it, he hadn't a glimmer.

The sack containing the argot knocked against the mast. Pride tugged him toward the bow, the only man who could hold it. He'd sworn to Corm, and before that, to Costig. To Foster, and Oduy, and Guil. Gionn despaired of their faces. If only they were as wise as he, to ask no oath—he caught himself, and yanked free of the satisfaction. There must have been one who was first. Each promise made the last one impossible. There had to be one, he swore, ancient of days, buried under years of silt. If he could but find it, and honor that! Let a single act of fidelity steer him. He closed his eyes and strained after it. When he blinked open, every choice looked as wretched as always.

His jaw quivered. Words formed and died in his throat like the first stirring of some emetic. Boot and Juru and Hogue noticed, and their rapt attention drew others who stared in suspicion and anticipation.

Another voice loosed from the stern with a great crack. Corm stood on the cargo between his seat and Palqua's, and belted along with the men. He waved his arms for all to join, and with timidity at first, then raucous release, the entire ship joined in *Half by Hadal.* Foster sorted it soon enough, and the Buckets, too. Gionn's throat ached, and only late did he come in with half a heart. When it finished, the crew stretched out spent as if they'd just lay with a woman. The faces and oaths settled again into the mire. The looming mast, the boards of the *Gairhle,* and the many hopes she bore shed their luster.

Were it Corm's strategy to suppress the mutiny by battering them against the Orin until they couldn't lift a finger, he neared his mark. The following days proved that the captain's clever parry of the shanty call-to-arms only earned a delay. No one needed to count to see the tide, anymore. The only question was how many had a fight in them. The Amposi took it worst—soft Navy lads grown in the jungle swelter. Foster added strolls to his dancing and carrying on. He couldn't have realized that only his painful innocence spared him for the affront. That, and his seat in the bow. Mutineers huddled for warmth and measured the vigor of those forward three, always jumping and humping on the quarter deck, as a show of strength.

Meanwhile Gionn's choking at the song earned him a lurid attention. Both sides lobbed petitions for a clear sign of his loyalty. Every argument against this mad course unfolded one-by-one. The *Gairhle* tossed starless and wayward; the rations, salted; the wind and the wills, swerving. Gionn hadn't considered that their refusal to stop for seal and water also meant there would be no addition of ballast to the meager remains. The barrels lightened, and the swell only teased at the tumult ahead.

When Irilo was caught sewing up the squain boat by dark, few could wonder where matters stood. Be it a symbol of putting out a captain, or a mad reassurance against disaster, he might have thanked his gods he only earned the hot breath of Corm.

After that, the dull anticipation that rubbed and creaked about them took on an imminence. They awaited what was no longer a possibility, but an event. An unusual sound brought eyes—and sometimes heads—on a swivel. It might come from any quarter, and to notice late could leave one carved. He hoped there would be a general stand to give them a chance for a peaceful offing, but Gionn suspected it might be a liberty the mutineers could ill-afford. Men pissed where they sat. He imagined spears under every huddled cloak.

Bubba turned on his bench to face Pitras. Fergo turned to K'sem, and Reed to Hogue. Chirim kept watch on Gionn over his shoulder, as did others where a neighbor was like to be an enemy. Courting was over. Gionn lay a hand on the pommel of his sword.

The captain alone seemed at ease. Corm sat straight, but without tension. His own palms remained exposed, draped over his thighs as if he listened attentively to a man who thought he had something important to say. There was no melancholy or ignorance in the deep lines of that face, carved by water running from that grand hat, and perhaps other vigils of the sort. He had the measure of it, alright. It was the look a man who sees the inevitable, and with a grin born of understanding, no longer desires to flee. Corm was still the biggest barrel on the ship, more stout than the enormous Leopard Seal of undeserved legend. Whalers could run many a captain. There were trading captains and sailing ones, crew's captains and clever pilots. In a shiver, Gionn knew at once this was a boarding captain.

"Nolan!" Corm croaked in a mighty voice just beginning to suffer the elements. "Swap with Tamarqan."

One seat—like asking Foster to trade with the Bucket behind him. Any swap now resigned him to a fight. He could have moved lads until a fight broke out, but he chose a single change of neighbors. Tamarqan hesitated as though he hoped the crew would have a go of it before he must comply, but Nolan loomed over him until he gave his seat. Now Palqua's second-in-command found himself between Gewar and Nolan, where he would be killed in the first blows. Palqua could have felt no better, knowing Corm would strike at him as soon as someone stood. Neither could still hope to call off their crew.

Gionn let out a low belch and tasted bile. Two ropes drew him in opposite directions, and stretched him to tearing. It was too late to affirm his loyalty, too late to jump sides. The bow wouldn't hold. Perhaps he could take it just to make sure, then surrender without a fight. No assurance he wouldn't just be executed, though. His preservation teetered on a deeper panic: he didn't know where he stood.

He glanced at his mate across the way. Foster barely held his eyes open. His chattering teeth sounded over the taut silence. Gionn considered warning him. A small gesture of goodwill. But of what? Foster wouldn't grasp it, and Gionn didn't know what to advise himself. He again choked on a word he didn't know. In the hesitation, he felt a parting of ways—a lovely trinket he had to leave behind in a hurry with one more rueful look.

Foster swayed to his feet. The entire ship held it's breath and Gionn swore the very sail stiffened around a puff. Hands that did not know themselves tightened under cloaks. The fatigue of battle already teased at Gionn's racing heart.

The Wife Seal, the Number Cunt, the stranger of strange lands mounted the quarter deck. Both squains followed dutifully, and began to jump and clap their hands. Foster, though, stared rapt. Perhaps he *did* know. He stretched his eyes over the crew, and the confused squains ceased their jumping. There appeared nothing behind the face, and everything. Had he seized the bow already? No man would commit his own blood to guess at the idiot's purpose. He was shaky, yet insistent. There undergirded it a sorrow that struck Gionn as if his own. Beyond it all, Foster might have even looked a terror had he remembered to bring his spear.

A pitch seemed to throw him down, but he caught it in stride and the purposeful walk held all commitments at bay as he passed between the stunned oars. Chirim nearly strained himself blind trying to keep one eye on Gionn and the other on the man stomping aft. Corm stood, and a warm squirt escaped down Gionn's thigh. Foster's gait stuttered. He collapsed into the captain's arms.

Most of the bow jumped to their feet for a look, ever darting their necks for a sign of violence, as Corm and Palqua lifted Foster between them. Again, an opportunity came to act while Corm and one of the aft men were under the tarp. Palqua could not have survived it, under there alone with them, but it was more likely general confusion that held them off. The back row peered under in a vigil. Accusations of fakery already circulated against Foster by the time the warring leaders reemerged.

Palqua sat, and Corm rested a tender hand on his shoulder. "Alright, old bastard. You've convinced me." Gionn expected the Amposi would be dealt his death, but Corm went on. "You hear that?" He called to crew. "Costig's black-hand, you'll have your chance, if you've the bollocks to thrust! First mate!"

"Aye!" Eckerd replied.

"Steer for the coast. Find me a fair island to fill our barrels, and let the angotaks thank Palqua."

There should have been a whoop, but most of the men crumpled with relief. Here and there they found their wits. She bent to starboard and the promise of a mercy.

For a day and part of another, they remained on alert. Gionn didn't know what side he took, but the Blue Quarter, who had drifted into his sympathies, began to look miserable and chattering and Amposi once more, while Hogue and Boot sparked his favor—that is, until Corm returned the seats to their original owners. Bentos grinned at him as if sighting an old mate who he didn't think to meet again.

Arthas made his way to the front of the mast and called to Corm: "Care if I touch your sack for me luck?"

"Thought you'd never ask." The hollows beneath the old man's eyes filled with shadows, and his flesh hung loose as if it sank overnight from the relief of a massive burden. The giant waved him on with permissive hand that seemed barely to have the strength for the motion.

Arthas closed his fingers around the little purse that contained the argot and tugged against the nail. He felt out the shape of the thing, and lost his gaze elsewhere as he peered inside with his heart's vision.

"Jonn! Have a go at this." The lad joined him, and Arthas bid him brush against that inadvertent talisman. Jonn hardly understood, but he humored the veteran mate and warmed to the weight of the piece on his hand. That symbol of betrayal, fastened out of torment, seemed to glow without as the sun sheared a distant cloud and bathed a patch of water, still not ready to show its face. Now it hung as the miracle snatched from the palm of treachery. It was the first gold most of the crew had ever seen, and it became their trusted pilot. Gionn could well see the face inside, the last of the minted farris. There could be no better token for a whaler destined for rich hunting than this—if only the pilfered palm weren't his own.

He couldn't summon as much bitterness as he would have liked. The settling seas and the promise of land underfoot eased his pain, and now this: no surer sign that Arthas and his mate had switched camps to the captain. More subtle would have been to announce, "Hoy! We're off this Palqua cunt. Count us men of the *Gairhle*!"

Had anyone known for certain they'd once gone the other way, it would be the little Amposi at the helm. Gionn laughed to himself when Foster finally reappeared. If anything had spared them, it was the timely march of the one man who couldn't afford a peace.

The mutiny on the *Gairhle* thus ended without blood when Moipa scaled the mast—running up the pennants, they called it. Corm took his first walk in some time, a sort of victory pass that lingered in the bow. That night, he was kept up by the sound of quiet weeping, as some men do after battle. More disturbing was the spot on the mast that glinted like midday. Gionn saw it through his closed eyelids. He felt the radiant heat.

By blinding powers, it bound the ship against one snoring imbecile. He was sure now that Foster was born of Deana—of the Bachla, that daughter who goes alone, even among her own kin. Deana who sees her face in every stream, who let Hadalis serve her a meal and offered him nothing in return. A fine mother for a farri like Donnab who suckles from his kings. Her sons shone with a beacon that gathered a hundred ships in their wake. But their charm owed itself to a mystifying air. Men love what they least understand, and no comprehension could pass between one of Deana's and his subjects. They sought only themselves. Marked by early promise, those. While they handed out gold, their mates were many, but their fists always grew tight. In the moment when they must give their last to reach the whirlpool at the center of the crossing streams—where a man may make any and all turns—they closed around their gifts. Their attendants saw them through the glare, saw an incomprehensible creature afraid of all the world even as he hoped to master it. If their ascendances were inspiring, their falls were spectacular.

Though Deana denied him, Hadalis was their father by virtue of the meal he put in her belly, and they followed his tack. Yet for every Donnab, there were many hundreds like Foster: trivial, grasping, mate to none but himself.

In his satisfaction with the new peace, Gionn felt the stream of Nachreann slacken behind him. Her waters ran crosswise through those of Deana and her opposite, Bronna. His aunts, in fact. That meant enemies and allies often came from their waters, and he held influence over them as much as he received it.

It was Gionn alone who knew something of the strange visitor from America of rumor. If this pitiable wretch who couldn't strike the ship apart at its nadir decided to have another desperate go of it alone against half-a-hundred whalers, it would be the new Gionn who dealt him his blow.

The first plaintive cry pierced the harbor just before dawn. More voices joined, and soon the foothills echoed with the unseen mass of dogs driving from the interior. A squain here and there howled in response from the crowd already gathered quayside. The dogs responded in kind, and the two packs bristled with excitement as their songs converged.

The first gray glow found something like a feast day, or the arrival of a dignitary. Every Mattaka turned out. Nothing would be hammered, no two folds stitched that morning. Yawning sailors mixed in pockets with their crews. Marines marshaled with spear. When the body at last writhed into view, it looked a river flowing thick with sediment and boulders, coursing down the slope to devour those assembled.

Costig hadn't slept a wink in his warm bed, and he doubted those drivers got much more, but he wasn't yet tired, and for all parties, rest remained a distant possibility. The sleds came by twos, a half a dozen dogs fanned out before them. He recognized Sawi at the head with his brother. A black bundle of the trail huts favored in the clan's more impermanent days lay fastened to the deck of every leader. Behind them, tow straps dragged trains of additional sleds, some piled three high, or carrying provisions and other tools. Six dogs dragged as many sleds behind, straining into the harnesses in practice for the uncountable loads of coal they would soon haul down from the mines.

What seemed a mighty serpent gave up its boasting as the light grew and the tail came into view. The sled chains dwindled quickly until a few boys drove a single rickety piece laden with a sack of personal gear. There may have been enough sleds for every team, but the drivers were too few. Dogs trailed off the backs, snapped neatly along by women and girls with crops. Everyone came. Every member of that bestial dynasty brought with them everything they could think of to add pomp to the procession and beg fortune of their capricious kaim. Ribbons of scrap leather and auspiciously-shaped rocks adorned the decks. Costig knew things to get larger and more intimidating as they closed distance, but this terrific parade only rattled apart and showed its ribs until the only magic left was that of the unnatural monsters harnessed to foreign wood who gave a fright to sailors, and twice to those of Ampos.

He spotted no one-legged fugitives among them, but took note that those leather bundles had the proportions to make a fine funeral shroud. No one ever said the Leopard Seal had to come on with the dogs, either. It mattered little how the bastard made the ship. If Ostuk said he'd board, he'd board.

For a moment, Costig succumbed to the temptation to worry about the next thing before the first was in hand. Under no divine intervention could Willakuy have summoned the courage to ask him—no, *demand* of him—the return of the gold to the treasury. Costig suspected the inspiration was rather mundane. Some captain held him in suspicion. Likely a cohort of them, because a treasurer doesn't confront an admiral with a single bluecoat in support. With a competent luck on his side, it would be settled by nightfall, and he'd only await the return of a ship from Camne Drumlag.

But he brushed aside that maneuver, and returned to the one streaming to the quay.

"Hood down," Gerachay stopped the driver after Sawi. The man peeled back his parka to show a flat squain face before Gerachay waved him aboard the *Juhketappat*. Wayranapan stood across the way at the *Orin's Thief*, giving its passengers the same scrutiny. Most of this lot couldn't be trusted to do anything but drive the dogs down from the camp, and wouldn't sail with the family. Nor did Costig want to capture the Leopard Seal so easily. He merely felt obligated to feign an effort.

The crowd sang well-wishes to send to their relatives. The ships rocked against wooden buoys while the serpent forked and creaked over the gangplanks. As the tedious process of loading and securing began, Costig made no intervention but to keep the crowd clear. He meandered to a marine wrapped in a bulging watch cloak, too warm for the occasion.

"Sergeant Poznatxen." He greeted the sinewy Eribath Islander. More than a few from that chain found their way into foreign service, especially that of Ampos. Standouts among the auxiliaries of Tolba, Poznatxen distinguished himself still more among his sort. If one or two had quicker spears, he surpassed all with an even head and an undeniable spirit that won the faith of his fellows. He'd brought Costig the squain boy. Perhaps only the endless distractions and a touch of nostalgia had so far prevented Costig from promoting him to his own vacated place of sergeant-at-arms.

"How fares it?"

"Ready and whetted, sir."

"Good man."

Costig quickly distanced himself and found Wendell waiting nearby with a confused bunch of sailors.

"Hope you didn't pry them from some important duty," Costig clapped Wendell on the shoulder.

"They promised to resume savin' the kingdom as soon as you're done with 'em." Wendell replied in his cheery way.

"Which of you's the mate?"

A man stepped forward hesitantly. "Neal, if you like, Admiral."

"Fine bunch. I recall the way your lads handled that tussle over the body of the Leopard's Seal short, fat look-alike. Do you remember how to sail?"

"Think we can remind ourselves if need be. Shall I send for Captain Polc and the others?"

"No need, me son. The nine of you's enough. I had a squain run off with me darraig, and I'd like it back. You'll have your fare to Camne Drumlag on the *Orin's Thief*, with Captain Ghrane. When you land, I want you to secure me boat, and if you can, a squain called Haraket. Don't return right away. See the coal onto the ships, and see that the dog ships don't get stuck there the way me darraig did. When all's ready, you'll send the dog captains ahead and return in me ship. I know you're thinkin', 'That's a twenty-four. We haven't the oars.' Nine squains stole it. I suppose nine good lads can return it. If you need help, you've me blessin' to conscript the twenty-six Navy lads who're still stationed there."

Neal looked like a snared animal who'd given up on pulling.

"Assistant viceroy may not be keen on all that."

"I hope he's not, but I don't anticipate it'll matter."

The mate chewed over the uncertain taste of his promotion. "I'll just send for Captain Polc."

"What for?" Costig challenged.

"He'll be sore if I don't keep him abreast. And he may prefer a different roster than these," he said of the other eight gathered. "Rasden's turned his knee. Better to trade him for fresh legs."

"Then let him be sore at me. You're posted to me garrison, and I've chosen me lot. Report to Ghrane. I'll be sure your captain gets word."

Polc's men looked as if they'd been waylaid. Costig stuck around until they started off for their assignment. He hardly failed to notice that one of the men lagged behind, forcing his stride through a quick jerking motion that spared his left leg.

Norwet broke off his stare as fast as he could when the admiral looked up at him. He halted his team to let these nine sailors pass toward the *Orin's Thief*, then fixed his attention on the long rolled trail tukit before him.

"Up, up!" He urged the dogs, and they clawed for traction in the already-thinning snow. The sleds behind him snapped into tension and he maneuvered his cargo with uncommon care toward the *Juhketappat*. Two cloaks emerged from the crowd and intercepted him at a listless pace.

"Your brothers struggle. Let us help," said an old voice in Mattakatan.

"Thank you, Grandfather," he paid the formality, and recognized the marked chin that protruded from the hood of the other hire. Norwet turned over the sled train to the man, who bade the woman steer. Ferrakut and Ulwet handled their loads ably, but Norwet wandered over to "help" them, nonetheless. As he did, he risked one more glance at the admiral. A fright ran through him when he found those penetrating eyes waiting for him, and he looked away again with secret exhilaration.

It was enough for Costig to curl a cracked lip under his frosted mustache as the two new drivers approached Gerachay. He felt relief to be proven right about the bundles—that a few squains hadn't concocted a method of smuggling a man aboard that he couldn't fathom. His faithful aid turned back the hoods of the two, and surely recognized the old man whose nocturnal meeting he arranged. Gerachay stole a glance at Costig for approval, but the admiral occupied himself elsewhere. The camp aid could only shrug and motion them to the gangplank.

Once aboard, Costig struggled to follow the old man's load. Sleds jammed and thrust atop one another like ice in a bay. What few Navy ventured on deck clung to the rails while lads and aunties fought to secure dogs. The shifting quarters set the howling mass upon itself in pockets of brutal warfare to seize early claim to some yard of space. Leads tangled. Blood leaked onto light fur. The chaos reminded him of the grifter's game, in which a pebble under a cup changes places while the mark assures himself he still knows the one that hides it. For the better part of the morning, they wrangled dogs until safe patches appeared where the brave Navy could piss themselves while lashing sleds and gear. Through it all, Costig held his leather hut in sight, motionless for so long it threatened to disappear into a backdrop of his own impatience.

His reward came after midday when the old man appeared from below and recruited several of the Mattaka sailors. He argued them away from their own clumsy preparations to help him and a hooded driver who must have been the woman untie that same bundle from the sled and hoist it with great care between them. The old man seemed unable to bear any weight, but he hovered near the load and directed their every step in furious Mattakatan. When the load went through the hatch, he insisted that those on the ladder hold it high above their heads rather than tilt it down and let it slide. Though it irked them, none of these fresh hands could mount a resistance to their elder.

Costig smiled, satisfied to witness an admirable spirit. Men often gave just enough, and slipped from one task to another, that he felt kinship to a well-salted barrel who could set every part of himself, however feeble, to the one thing and hold it as long as he drew breath. He recalled a promise to Foster, and hoped he could at least spare this old man and the woman. That, he reckoned, was up to them. He could only show their task futile, and hope they saw it before they irritated the wrong marine.

Between his usual crew and nine capable lads from Polc, Ghrane had the *Orin's Thief* squared before the *Juhketappat* even looked like she might get off in the same day. None jumped to help the other ship, though she was docked until her mate was ready. Costig made it clear that the *Juhketappat* would land first at Camne Drumlag. Her crew was Mattaka to the last, and he didn't want the sight of the interlopers on the *Orin's Thief* to spook the assistant viceroy—though neither Ostuk nor Ghrane yet knew the real reason for it.

Norwet leaned over the bow to gaze at the madness aboard the *Juhketappat*. Sawi had charge there with Onag, and all the boys except he and his brothers wrestled tooth and strap to little avail.

"The Navy is stupid," little Ulwet reported behind him.

"Very stupid," Ferrakut echoed. "I'm surprised they didn't search the sleds." The boys joined their brother in watching the scramble aboard their sister ship.

"Save your rejoicing for Camne Drumlag," Norwet cautioned. "I'm not yet sure we've fooled them."

"We did. Ostuk told you—"

"Ostuk says what he is told," Norwet interrupted Ulwet. "And I don't like these Navy men on our ship. They are Polc's."

"I saw one limping," Ferrakut grinned mischievously at Ulwet, who shrunk away.

"It was a sneaky kaim who helped you get away." Norwet faced his brothers. "We cannot forget. We are small, they are big. We are few, they are many. We have been favored; it may not always be so. You two ran the rite around the Eye with me. I didn't go alone. We became men together. I think there is more danger now than we understand.

"I felt brave, and thought I would protect you with my silence, but I see now I was wrong. No one can protect you. Or me. We can't run like dogs who pull every which way. It was me who broke our stride, and now I beg you restore it. Lay the blame at my feet, and be done. Vjarku, Seleku, it doesn't matter. We live or die as family. I have told you all I know, and you know what you must do."

"Why do you say this?" Ferrakut asked.

"I must go," he nodded toward the *Juhketappat*. Their eyes grew. "Why?"

"To make sure."

"Will you return before we sail?" Ulwet pleaded as though he already knew the answer.

"He must be sure Milak stays. Someone has to stay behind," Ferrakut reminded himself as much as his brother.

"Then we will see you on the other shore," Ulwet tensed his lip proudly.

"I hope it is so." Norwet made for the gangplank.

Costig watched the eldest boy march solemn and purposeful to the *Juhketappat*. That sealed it. He was not unwary of some trick, some betrayal, or foul luck against him, but when the dog lad left his brothers to join the melee, there could be no more doubt.

The sight of him reminded the admiral of the key, slipped into a note, that the same one delivered on his behalf. That key loosed the fugitive. Something that moved unsettled beneath his worries boiled up. Costig knew, as he had all along, that the Leopard Seal was his own creation. To know it was much less than to face it.

There would have been no call to arrest him in the first place, except to conceal their conspiracy. He first estimated the lad too highly— thought him capable of tact and discretion. Had he given up his mistake and greeted the fool when he approached, he would have lost a guileless spy, and no more. Perhaps he could have put the lad on the *Gairhle* instead of the shiftless Gionn, but he could no longer stomach wondering what became of that mission.

For pride, he scrambled to salvage the big oaf. What was his name? He could hardly remember, now. *Parks*. It was no crime to be an oaf on Drummoc, and in fact, a pastime of men of some credit. Who, then, was the real fool? It was Costig who seized him, Costig who maimed him. He had another chance in the hut to right things, but the old saying rang true, about a blunder half-made being easier to finish than quit. When the squains rallied to him, he yet again might have found him had he not aided the escape, instead.

He saw it well-enough, now. It took only a jailbreak, a riot, the life of a lad and five good marines. Costig knew he bore the embarrassment at first because he thought himself so clever. Now the captains whispered against him, and even Wendell skirted orders. All that, he could bear. If the viceroy or Tolba heard his tale, he'd be fortunate to get a demotion to the regulars and keep his life. That, too, he could stomach—even a whip, or a heavy blade on his neck.

What gutted the old sergeant-at-arms was that he must soon look upon Parks—who earned no such moniker as the squains gave him—and feed the broken lad a spear. If he outlived this mistake, Costig knew it would worm him through as few things had: jumping ship from the angotaks in Pone; the raids that culminated in Ampos, before he found his wits; now the torture and murder under of an ally betrayed.

He learned much from what he might have done those other occasions. Perhaps there waited a lesson here, too, after many years left out to cure.

With sickening anticipation, he waited until the loads were all but stowed. The timing had to be impeccable for the second part to go off. When the first of Captain Liam's sailors began to disembark, he nodded to Gua.

The sergeant-at-arms wandered toward the ship, and the milling of his company became less dispersed. From the opposite quarter, Sergeant Poznatxen led a handpicked twenty-three of Costig's own between the ships so deliberately that the crowd hardly took notice.

On board the *Juhketappat,* Norwet leaned back against a strap to take all the slack. Milak helped guide it down, where they wrapped it through the gaps in the false deck and tied off the stack of sleds.

"You know this place best," Norwet was muttering. "Besides, would you rather face Sawi when he sees what we've done?"

The younger cousin seemed to forfeit his argument at the thought. He tested the knot. "I know Camne Drumlag better, too. But you are oldest." Norwet allowed the boast to go unqualified. "When do I go? Sawi will have a fit if I leave now."

"I don't know yet. Look for my sign. Hoy!" He rushed to the main deck where Saunlauk and Siguvik tugged in vain at a dog fight near the forward hold. Soon Ravitak and Arnake joined, and even Onag left his work to quell the battle.

As the barking subsided, Norwet noticed it first as a strange swell in the voices of the people gathered at the harbor. A few shouts lost themselves in the whining pack. Then a rumble, like thunder but close and too thin.

The false deck lay to port. Norwet looked down in time to see a flood of marines rush between the cargo and stream in all directions for the side.

"On your arses!" One cried. "Stop your work! On your arses!" A pair of hands seized him and flung him down. The dogs went mad, and the invaders squeezed together to avoid the rage of their leads, while Saunlauk and Siguvik escaped altogether by immersing themselves in one of the teams.

The Navy crew looked just as confused, and several of them sat before they realized what had happened. The first wave, dressed for some purpose in cloaks, captured the hatches and slid down the ladders into the hold. Behind them, more lightly-dressed marines secured the gangplank and the false deck. Sawi looked at his nephew in a panic, searching for reassurance he couldn't find. Soon there were so many marines in addition to the crew that no one could move. Every foot was man or dog, many of which had to climb upon gear.

The Navy captain tried to clear his men from the deck, but the marines refused to let anyone off. All their careful lashings were pulled loose. Tukit rolls unraveled and the framing bones spilled from the middle. They pried open barrels of dog food, turned out every sailor and driver. A sergeant ordered the Mattaka to form up on the false deck. Sawi could not rise for weeping. Norwet and Onag had to lift him. His toes dragged behind as he did his best to die in advance of what he anticipated.

While his heart fluttered, Norwet held with all his might to prevent himself from looking at any of the other boys, or worse: across the quay at Ferrakut and Ulwet, who he knew watched in horror from the *Orin's Thief*. Shouting emanated from the hold. Soon, provisions passed up on the deck.

These brave warriors followed narrow lanes to the bow or stern or false deck, anywhere free of teeth. Where the dogs couldn't reach them, many turned their anger on one another. What started as a crisp raid collapsed into a slog of uncertainty. The Mattaka were not permitted to help, or even to soothe the dogs.

Men climbed down to the hold, others came up and changed places. It took little time to undo their morning of work. Soon, leather lay strewn over every surface of the ship, lids rattled underfoot. No one yet appeared with what they sought, but Norwet knew that there were few places left to hide, and if they didn't act soon, all would be undone.

Ferrakut eyed his brother with uncertainty, and received the same in turn. Many taller bodies gathered behind them to watch the proceedings on their sister ship.

"We will never get off, now," one of the Mattaka sailors moaned.

"I'd hate to be Sawi. Or one of his kin," Captain Ghrane said. He slapped Senadak, their older cousin and master of dogs for this ship, playfully on the back.

"Suppose we're next," said Polc's first mate. "Should we make a mess of things to speed 'em along?"

"Don't be so sure." Ghrane indicated the empty quay in front of the *Orin's Thief*. "I think they know exactly what they're looking for, and where they'll find it."

Ferrakut agreed with the captain on the first count, but the mate as well: if they didn't find what they sought, they could expect quite the mess in turn.

"I hope we don't have to re-lash every fucking stick." Ulwet declared. The men burst into laughter at the smallest boy aboard griping like the saltiest old hand.

Ferrakut switched to Mattakatan, and aimed his tongue at the captain. "Everything is ready here. We should shove off, just in case."

"Are you speakin' to me, lad?" Ghrane replied in the farri's tongue, and a hush fell over the crew.

Ghrane was young, thin, with a fierce charm in those sea-colored eyes. He claimed to hail from Pone, and wore his fair hair to his shoulders. But there glowed a tint from beneath his light skin, and his yellow beard and mustache grew in a pattern familiar to any Mattaka.

Ferrakut knew him well. At least, he saw this man each of the seasons he sailed his ship to Nunoc, though he was too young to remember the first few. He and his brothers stowed dogs on the man's ship, and he wondered if he was a fool to think that this man would remember him, too.

"I am Ferrakut, son of Alakset, of the Vjarku." He switched his tongue to match.

"Forgive me! I hardly knew I addressed such infamy! Good captain, while you serve on me vessel, do us simple men a kindness and speak the common tongue, that we might understand you."

He shrank from the mockery, and sulked off to the false deck. Ulwet hurried to catch up. Ferrakut stood at the edge and squinted at the figures on the opposite ship.

"Can you see Norwet? Maybe he will signal."

"Signal what? We have to sail," Ulwet said.

"He won't."

"You hardly asked. Try again. He won't listen to me."

"Nor me," Ferrakut nearly pouted.

"Try!"

Ferrakut shook his head in apprehension. "He will just say no."

Ulwet huffed, then hurried to where the gangplank lay tied to the deck and began to unwind the rope. "Then help me!"

Ferrakut started to protest, but found himself loosening the rope on the opposite side of the gangplank. There were so many moorings left. He staggered at the futility of their effort. A few navy drifted on the quay. So far, all seemed more interested in the *Juhketappat* than what two boys were up to.

He stiffened in terror when a pair of firm hands took he and his brother by the collars from behind.

"What are you doing!" Senadak scolded. While Ferrakut searched for a lie, Ulwet answered.

"Shoving off!"

Senadak dragged them aside and bent to speak in a low tone, no less harsh. "What do they search for on the *Juhketappat*?" The boys shrugged. "Do not lie to me. I want to hear it from your mouths." They tried to sink within their shoulders, but he gave them a rattle. "Tell me! What have you done? What will they find on the *Juhketappat*?"

"Nothing," Ferrakut insisted.

"Do you not think we hear you? Running around at night, whispering to one another. How clever do you think you are? If you know what will harm this family, it is better you say it." He leaned in. "What will they find on the *Juhketappat*?"

Ferrakut raised his chin. "Nothing!" Frustration brimmed on his cousin's face, and he opened his mouth to repeat himself, but the boy spoke first. "They will find nothing...on the *Juhketappat*." He glanced down at the gangplank, and the lines that held them to Drummoc.

Senadak recoiled as the meaning sank in. He turned to look back at the deck of the *Orin's Thief*. Ferrakut felt the grip on his collar melt. Their cousin hesitated only a moment, in which many seasons of tribulations stretched out over his face. Then he shouted to a pair of Mattaka sailors and waved them over.

"Finish," he nudged them toward the gangplank. "I must speak with Ghrane."

"Wait!" Ferrakut stayed him. "It is my fault. I will tell him." He expected nothing, and was surprised when his cousin nodded and took his place at the edge of the deck. He and Ulwet lifted the ramp as the Mattaka sailors joined them, and heaved the end ashore.

Ferrakut arrived breathless from the short run. Three more sailors reclined idle beneath the mast, while Ghrane laughed with Polc's mate right beside them. The boy started for the captain, and froze when that eye glittered his way. Instead, he approached the sailors and spoke in his own tongue.

"Have you seen Ostuk's new crew? If dogs could tie ropes!" They grinned in agreement but paid him little notice. "The old crew was better. Very brave. We sailed with them from Nunoc, and they saved the ship many times. But nothing was so brave as when they stole away in the admiral's ship to Camne Drumlag! That is what the people say."

"Nothing so foolish," one said.

"Maybe. But I don't think many will remember them after today. No one will seem as brave as the crew of the *Orin's Thief*." They scowled in confusion. "It is a shame the captain doesn't speak Mattakatan," Ferrakut met Ghrane's wry smile out of the corner of his eye. "We have to shove off. Now."

"What are you on about, boy?"

"You know who they seek over there. It will look bad for the crew where he is found." They followed his eyes to where Senadak and the other two sailors fought with the mooring lines.

"Are you mad? You will get us all killed!"

"We have to wait for the *Juhketappat*," another said.

"You can say you were confused. The captain will be grateful when he learns what trouble you saved him."

"While we're waiting, you may as well get your lads and come with me below," Ghrane said to Polc's mate in their tongue. "I'll show you to your berths." The captain waved the sailor on, and let his gaze linger on his crew before he guided the halots down the ladder into the hold and out of sight. He'd done nothing to acknowledge Ferrakut's warning, except to abandon the deck to the care of the Mattaka.

Costig stomped impatiently onto the *Juhketappat* and snatched one of Gua's marines. "Bring up the woman with the marks on her chin." He didn't see where a man could hide in the mess on the deck. Everything big enough to conceal a pup had been shaken out. They were searching in the dark below, but he had not planned for his moment of triumph to take so long.

The admiral pulled Ostuk toward the pack, where their yelping and lunging hid his voice.

"Light's wastin'. Where is he?"

"I don't know. I told them what you asked of me, and it was agreed. But they didn't tell me how they would bring him on."

The woman weaved her way between a guard. Costig led her to the very stern of the ship so they could be crowded on three sides instead of four.

"We'll have him soon enough. Save us the trouble, and I might find a tender heart for you and the old man."

"I feed dogs."

"Me mercy expires at the end of this chat."

"I feed dogs," she narrowed her black eyes on Ostuk, who could not meet her.

Costig bit his tongue and waved her off. "Have the false deck stowed. I want her all but ready to sail when we bring him up." Ostuk nodded and left his company.

The admiral turned and leaned over the water beside the enormous steering oar. He watched the sea lap the ship with a patience he couldn't match. The sergeant-at-arms cleared his throat from behind.

"Costig. There is no one below."

"Check in every bundle and coin purse. Bring the crew up top."

"We already did." There was a tedious quality in Gua's voice.

"Then check again. Get lamps down there. I assure you, you've missed something."

"Aye," the marine nodded reluctantly.

When he returned his attention to the water, there was a peaceful quality that unsettled him without cause. The sea glistened with a lightness that became a sense of something forgotten, then the pain of an absence. The quay sat empty. A hundred yards to sea, the *Orin's Thief* dipped oars to bring the prow toward Camne Drumlag.

"*Hoy!*" He shouted furiously. The captain was nowhere visible. A handful of squains on deck did a fine job of not hearing. He snapped around to the quay, where Folmon and a few of his men traded yarns, perhaps exactly as oblivious as the squains.

"*Fuck!*"

He hurried onto the false deck and hollered to the nearest captain, which by an ill humor of the gods was Bruco.

"What have we got ready to launch?" The idiot went into a spin, and shouted something inaudible while pointing at one of the darraigs they used for drills under Rixtan. It had no sail, and by the time he got a crew, they'd have a swimmer's chance of catching the dog ship.

"*Fuck!*"

Costig snatched Ostuk as he passed. "Where in Uinab's bowels does he think he's goin'?" The captain had no answer. "No matter. You land first, hear me? Stow your deck, and overtake him in the channel."

Only then did marines hurry past with lamps fetched from the navy hall. Across the way, he watched the woman support the old man, who appeared drubbed and unable to pitch in. Boys argued with one another, or soothed dogs as much as they reassembled gear and secured it. He recalled the sight of the ancient squain directing a rolled hut—the one he followed so carefully aboard from the sled—down into the hold. How had they failed to search it yet? A blind man feeling around below couldn't fail to come across it. Stashed in the bilge, perhaps? The oldest of the boys had switched ships for a purpose. Costig chewed his mustache over it.

The same creeping absence that stood bare in front of him before he noticed the *Orin's Thief* had launched now returned. He had decided where a thing ought to be, and saw it there, until it vanished like a pebble under a grifter's cup.

When the sail ran up on the shrinking dog ship, Costig grew ill. They could burn a keg of whale oil searching every cranny of this ship in search of the Leopard Seal. There was no one to find. Meanwhile, every ship's length that Ghrane pulled ahead was one more Ostuk would have to recapture. His main purpose had foundered. The admiral knew a defeat well-enough when he saw one, and didn't care to cause another by fussing over it. Ostuk must land first.

Norwet's head rose as Costig thundered about the ship, threatening their efforts and ordering an immediate launch. The marines had just begun their second pass below when he stamped at the ladder to call them back.

Costig caught sight of the boys, and appeared as if he wished to say something, but glared instead, then swatted after an idle sailor.

"You must take care," Norwet said to Milak. "Costig is no longer with us."

"With us?" Milak puzzled over the statement. Norwet remembered that he never explained the whole of his dealings with the man, or the key he delivered to Kjartke. He told the boys their roles, but hadn't bothered with the details of Ostuk's warning. Now his throat burned to tell his cousin all, to bring him within the circle so that he might be prepared. Milak knew Drummoc, but not Mentewat, or the tale he forced Norwet to relay. Costig wasn't thick to the events of the morning. If he couldn't have a Leopard Seal, perhaps the execution a dog boy would satisfy him. It would be good if he could give Milak a word to use before he left. The adult men were all on the ships. There were but women for his allies, and Polc watching their camp. Now he cursed his silence, and recalled his advice to Ferrakut: "We live or die as family," he had told the boy.

"Milak." He got his younger cousin's attention. A marine jostled past between them. Costig practically shoved them down the gangplank in a column to clear room for the crew to work. Norwet saw in that moment his course. Perhaps he knew it when he left the *Orin's Thief.*

"See to my brothers," he said. The other boys searched each other for his meaning. Norwet hoisted his sack of belongings and slipped into the tall bodies of the marines hurrying off the ship.

While the Navy and the crew fought to secure the ship, Kjartke led Tunguk below to rest. His busy hands fell still. As often happened, his pain returned to invoke his hospitality in that idle time, and marveled that he had done so much when now he labored to raise his ribs for a breath. A few wheezy laughs refused to deny his joy, and he paid dearly for the indulgence. Kjartke thought it funny. For so long, nothing amused her. She wished it would be so again, as much as she enjoyed his every stumble.

"I am not so worried now, though I may die soon." He said low in Mattakatan.

"Who gives you permission?" She answered without concern.

"Tell me, was it you or Norwet who made a fool of the admiral? Brother will do well without me." Tunguk sunk in, humbled in the way he thought a father must be when his son first takes a seal that he himself missed. There was no embarrassment. He felt low, like a moon past full as the dawn swallows it, but it came as a relief. The length of a journey comes upon a man at the end, and his thirst for honors wanes. Tunguk was tired.

He hugged his chest, and the pressure eased him. While he danced on the deck, he worried. He had no say in the matter. It was Kjartke's commands that moved him, and he admitted now he did not trust her completely. He worried he might fail his bond of akmanuak. She could not understand the workings of ships and sleds and navies as she needed to. Brother would be caught, and he knew unhappy days would await them both in Urkuk.

Now, he curled up and grinned. He wondered if he could have slipped them past were it his own plan.

A pair of fingers pinched gently around his brow, and he jerked at the sharp prick of a needle.

"Hold still," she hissed as she passed the first stitch to rejoin the wide wound.

The thunder of feet overhead took a long time to fade. Finally, the sparse group of Mattaka chattered down to find a bench. Dog drivers slipped and collided oars while a man called directions down in Mattakatan, as uncertain as they were wrong. When at last they came under sail, Kjartke let out an anxious belch and took several greedy breaths.

"Rest," he advised.

"I will rest when the sea lies between us and those men."

"I doubt it. There will be plenty of trouble for us at Camne Drumlag."

"Shh! Do not invite it."

"It is already with us." He touched her ears, and she pulled away. "Listen." Nothing met them but the chatter of boys. "Many men left the ship, but not all. Four sixes of marines went below, dressed for a journey. I did not see them come up. You are a clever woman, now. It will be good if you can guess their purpose before we land—and they show us."

10

WHERE THE WORLD BENDS

The crew of the *Orin's Thief* formed a half moon around the aft hatch. The Mattaka sailors craned like expectant dogs at the opening. Polc's men bunched at the center behind Captain Ghrane, arms folded, whose smirk offered no hint of his disposition. Ferrakut, alone, blocked the way.

From the moment they shoved off, the boys raced down ahead of the curious. The tukit that concealed him had been snatched up and carried roughly below by some navy hands during loading while the boys prayed on a single breath they wouldn't realize what they held.

"Brother!" Whispered Ferrakut and Ulwet as they tapped rolls of tukits in the shadowy hold. One groaned and shifted, and they tore him free gasping as feet shook the ladder. Norwet meant them to hide him for the duration, until a triumphant reveal at Camne Drumlag.

But as soon as these men took their oars to clear the harbor, they taunted the darkness.

"Leopard Seal!"

"Show yourself!"

"Hoy! We know you're there. Come on, we don't bite!"

"*He* does! Killed five marines in a single swipe."

It was their duty at the oars that held them back, not the two dog boys. Once under sail, Ferrakut saw it was lost. He could not keep them away for long. Ghrane gave no assurances of his safety when the boys promised to bring him up top. He could not even say how his cousins Senadak and Umatbarak felt. If their Leopard Seal hoped to continue, the man must inspire the same awe as his name. Huddled in silence against the snapping voices, doubt crawled beneath the boy's skin.

Now he faced them with a wounded pride. He knew the stories, too, and though he knew them false, he believed them in a way and took part in their glory. A ragged pang accompanied the intuition that all of them would be revealed as the same fraud.

The crew perked up at the sound of feet on the ladder, but Ferrakut knew them to be too fast for Brother. Ulwet appeared, and took his place beside his brother to signal the arrival. The dogs themselves raised their ears and ceased their fighting. A low whinny here and there awaited whatever these men were so bent on.

A black head appeared. Senadak broke the surface with a rope trailing over his shoulder. He gained the deck and pulled hand-over-hand, maintaining a gentle tension on the line. Some long movement passed hidden from sight before each tug on the rope. The crew's faces twisted to guess what spectacle mounted the ladder. Ferrakut himself forgot what the man looked like, and made him a giant with golden hair.

A hood crested, and a wide hand on the rope. There was a pause, then a strange jerking as more of him rose. All but the captain stepped back at the same time they leaned in. When his waist stood at deck-level, he paused. A filthy beard protruded. The Leopard Seal placed both hands on the deck, leaned forward, and moved another rung. He looked up at those gathered.

The face was drawn thin. Weathered garments hung loose on a creature hunched in a stiff curve. He peeled back the hood to hair matted with grease, hanging in stringy locks over his cheeks. The weary eyes found the captain with indifference. As he navigated another rung, he bore all the majesty of a wounded man, stripped of dignity, trudging out in surrender after a long siege.

When his knees lay just below, he shifted to his right and sat on the deck. Umatbarak's hand pressed his bottom the last few inches from below. The Leopard Seal swung his leg up. He rolled to his knee, and the other trouser followed, dangling empty amid soft gasps from the crew.

Ferrakut and Ulwet hurried to his side, and with their cousins' help, raised their friend and stood beneath his armpits in support. One of the dogs sounded—the young male with the hateful kaim in him, who returned to camp only a day prior. The rest of the pack joined him in a song of recognition.

They helped him, this one whose name seemed more like Brother, to a seat on a stack of sleds. Umatbarak passed a stone spear to Ulwet, who placed it in Brother's hand like a scepter. He slumped forward irredeemably, his good leg splayed out to one side.

Ghrane approached with some amusement.

"Of all the dog ships in Drummoc, I praise the luck that drove you onto mine. It is an honor at last to meet what remains of the Leopard Seal."

"One! Two! Three! Four! Five!" Parched voices rang in unison. Foster dropped off to let his growing workout crew growl the numbers. He balanced on the edge of the forward quarter deck, now crowded with Chirim and Bentos in addition to the Mattaka boys. Here and there down the line of the ship, men stood on uneven gear, lowering and raising themselves in as many ways as there were attempts, none of which struck Foster as a squat.

He'd given up the jumping jacks when Fergo turned an ankle. Swollen and hideous, it didn't stop the gravel-throated sailor from participating with a hateful glare that seemed to blame Foster for the injury, the cold, and the forced labor all at once.

They brought the weather with them to the coast. Numb limbs did more to recruit new participants than any encouragement out of Foster. In truth, they hadn't found the coast, yet.

Several days prior, the *Gairhle* came upon the ice. It floated loose, in crisp shells that collapsed against the prow, like a mass of scattered refugees trudging west. Still, Corm wanted no part. They sighted a ghostly peak on clear morning that most agreed was Yunoc, then turned north to trace the open water for some warmer island.

The most brooding clouds became their lighthouse. Each time they tried to ply inward, some bright-bottomed stratus warned of pack and sent them seaward again. He often couldn't say if it rained or simply blew. The effect was similar enough. Each morning, the ship bloomed with ice, and the hacking away kept them circulating until the meal. Every day, the sun came later, and he woke more sore than the last. There wasn't much to eat, and between constant exercise, ice-breaking, shivering, and sitting, the crew seemed to wither. He had no fear of a mutiny now, however naive that might have been. Their rations were too lean. Every third day, they got a piece of blubber—otherwise, they choked on no-longer-dried fish and seal that never quite satisfied.

Foster couldn't sit on the bench. When he did, he had to shift back so his hamstrings bore the weight. His ass felt like two enormous open sores, though he didn't think it was a good idea to drop trouser and ask someone to confirm it.

"Pushups!" He called out the change. "It ain't too late, Gionn."

"Aye it is, for a good many things, cunt." The big redhead rubbed his thighs vigorously for warmth.

While Foster bounced back from his brush with freezing, his friend only grew more anxious and temperamental. His usually-funny comments took on a note of bitterness and sometimes barely rose above whining. Many more than just Foster had noticed.

Anseloc and Bannoc. The names remained vague lumps in Foster's mind, sibling islands where they meant to fill water and hunt seal before the final push to Taclann. He'd already missed Nunoc. Now Yunoc lie days behind. He couldn't imagine how he would fulfill Costig's request to bring the ship in to the viceroy, and to be honest, he dreaded success. But depending on how those shapes carved themselves out of the horizon, he might still find a way to do—something.

"Ice!" Gionn cried. He shot up and fought to free his oar. Before anyone else could move, a churning patch of sea swept past not thirty yards to port. Gionn abandoned the effort and the entire ship fell still to watch the green waters foam around a submerged iceberg the size of a small house.

"Thick cunts! Are you tryin' to have our bowels out? Have a look off the bow between your spasms, if you can fuckin' bother!"

Foster could find no excuse. He shook from the feeling of the *Qarapara* slamming to a stop, the groan of metal like banshees peeling their way into the hull. His old world bled into this one, like debris in the water from a wreck. A white barrel flashed, then he saw a light strobing beneath the surface. From the corner of his vision he thought some of the crew wore orange until he turned to spot Corm stomping towards him.

"Enough of your dancin'!" He cuffed Atalkut and slung the others back to their seats. "I want two hangin' from our lady luck while it be light, from here to Taclann!" He thrust a fat finger at the carved figure that rode under the prow—one who Foster had only noted after he joined the ship, and never saw except the barest details along the outer edges. "Gionn and Foster! First watch."

It proved frigid work, but the healthy breeze carried their words off the ship.

"I don't guess there's anything to salvage?" Foster probed. When he got no reply, he added: "Just remember that if I find myself starin' at my execution, I might want some company."

"Then all you've done is recruit me to see you off at the earliest opportunity," Gionn replied without taking his eyes off the sea splitting around the prow. He flashed a smile. "Fine. Tell me your plan. I'm in."

Foster rolled his eyes. "So you can screw me before I get my pants down? Nah. I reckon I'm on my own."

"You can't be trusted there."

Foster tried to lean out for a closer look at the statue before them, with little success. "A smart fella once told me, you can have faith, but not trust in—wait, what was it? No. I may not trust you, but you can trust me, and if I can have faith in your nature, but you have your doubts—" Foster blinked hard.

"Iceberg!" He stood and shouted aft. Gionn strained to see what he saw. "Two of 'em!" Foster added. He held out his index to the biting cold until his watch mate echoed him.

They must have been enormous, though they came as little yellow specks so many miles off. Bodies crowded in, and the more optimistic thought they had arrived unexpectedly at the islands. Eckerd gave a course that set the *Gairhle* seaward of the bergs. The Mattaka boys loitered even after the others returned to their seats, staunching a rare chance to speak with Gionn.

"Don't get lost in the distance and let one slip under us, cunt," the veteran warned.

Foster batted his eyes and braced to the wind. Over the next hour he became dutifully hypnotized by the patch of sea before them, occasionally shaking himself awake to check on the bergs, which hardly seemed any nearer.

Only later would he learn of a phenomenon well-known in the southernmost waters. Here, it was explained to him, the world bent. Currents from the farthest kingdoms gathered like loose threads. The orderly gods didn't sail here. So a man could take a step and meet what he sought or fled, though he assumed it leagues away. He might also travel miles, enough to mark the nine shores, and vanish without seeing a soul, or leaving a trace.

It was on account of the loose rules, as far as he could tell, that things gained the power to turn into something else. Men became stones on a snow plain; a bay, the mouth of a glacial river. A skerry shapeshifted into a whale. Sheer cliffs appeared as harbors until you were upon them. Islands sprouted that no one had ever reported, and ice, especially, lured visitors by all sorts of transformations. It sounded to Foster like some magical power that increased as the latitude dropped. They swore no such thing was possible in the warmer climes, where more respectable gods ruled.

As soon as he heard it, he remembered a dozen examples to support what he reckoned to be some polar effect of light to mislead the eyes. When the two icebergs they'd tracked for so long traded places and became a pair of sails, though, it felt more like that terrible magic.

"Ships! They're ships!" He nearly collapsed in relief that he called it before Gionn. His shout cast the illusion from the eyes of the entire crew. Men clamored to the quarter deck so fast and thick he thought they'd push him overboard. Corm peeled them aside to breathe down Foster's neck. A pair of nimble vessels now danced just over a mile off the bow.

"Is it Navy?" K'sem stood on his toes.

"Last I was at Nunoc, they weren't sendin' out no more ships this year." Foster said.

"Aye, they wouldn't. Not this late," Bentos confirmed.

The crew quieted, and it disconcerted Foster the way they gave up their theories and hung on their leader in absolute stillness.

"To your benches," he said in a voice so soft it wouldn't have been heard except for the silence of the crew. He pushed through them and hopped off the deck. "To your benches!" He repeated as if surprised by his initial tone. "Ready oars and spears! Eckerd, bring her around and keep off the coast."

A U-turn, Foster realized.

"Who is it?" Little Tunguk asked Foster, and Corm heard. He grinned full of mischief, threw off his cloak, and folded it with unusual care.

"Angotaks," the captain replied.

The stack of sleds shifted beneath his weight and Parks leaned to his right for balance. The knuckles of his left hand whitened around the spear. He braced the butt against the deck and squinted. After so many days wrapped in blankets, confined to a wigwam, taking little hops by night, that his vision buckled under a dull gray afternoon. He already felt queasy, whether from balancing on a rocking deck while down a leg, or breathing for hours in a stale, filthy tent.

Parks took his time, allowing the blur before him to settle into his late twenties, in the outline of a Reverse-Eskimo but too light at the face, and with the proud stance of a white man. There were others around—too many for it to be good. Navy, he figured. A shade too tall and too pale to trust. Parks looked to the little dude who seemed to be in charge of his travel itinerary, and wished he could remember his name.

The guy standing in front of him was probably waiting for him to speak. There were always lots of things offering themselves to be said, but Parks held back. Something about all this didn't feel thoroughly planned, but more than that, he felt embarrassed about what was missing from his person, and that all the world could finally see.

"Broke the prison, led Costig on a merry chase, single-handedly put down five marines. I suppose single-leggedly, too." His crew laughed. "If I'd have known a man of such reputation was travelin' with me, I'd have arranged a more comfortable berth."

Parks made contact with the part of the blur where he had grown accustomed to finding a man's eyes.

"No worries, my esteemed sea amigo. Yours is the finest vessel I've ever stowed away on, no offense to my boy Ostuk—the weather didn't do him any favors. Who do I have the honor of inconveniencing with my presence?" He thought his familiar lingo would buoy his confidence, but even Parks spotted the impostor.

"Captain Ghrane, born of Pone, and you may call her the *Orin's Thief*. It's no honor to be the finest dog ship, but I wager there are none in the Attavaik who would boast her equal."

One of the dogs bayed and scampered over to Parks, his chewed-off lead dangling beneath his neck.

"Barbados Slim!" Parks said with surprise. The lunatic young male from the sled team propped his paws on Parks' tender thigh to sniff his neck, then began to gnaw on his tunic collar. Parks shoved him off, and he bounced back as if he didn't notice. Parks pushed him again with a friendly tousle of his head. "Me and him go way back," Parks explained to Ghrane. "I was worried about you, buddy. Heard they cut you loose in a blizzard." Parks slapped him on the behind when he went for the collar once more. Barbados Slim took it as a challenge, and Parks gave him another playful slap, with a little more pop. Slim took his wrist in his teeth, circled around, and began to hump at his leg. The two Reverse-Eskimo boys converged to wrestle him free.

"I can see you're the best of mates."

"Aye, sir. I know I don't look like much, but I'm a good mate to have. So long as you promise to let my leg remain chaste." Parks extended a hand. Ghrane left it hanging, he hoped out of confusion.

"Unfortunately, it'll do me no good for the likes of you to call me mate. I'm sure I'll curse meself for shovin' off with you aboard, and for askin' this." He let out a deep breath. "What're your intentions at Camne Drumlag?"

Parks shrugged. "If you believe my reputation, then I've come to overthrow the assistant viceroy, raise an army of Reverse-Eskimos, and sail on..." He looked to the youngest boy. "What's the name of a city I definitely shouldn't sail on?"

"Ampos?" He ventured.

"Ah!" He slapped his forehead. "Should have thought of that."

Ghrane smiled. "I never gave you leave to board me ship. As far as anyone here's concerned, you were confined to the hold, where you'd stay until the admiral relieved you when we returned to Drummoc. I should hope you make no effort to slip off at Camne Drumlag, and I warn you of the consequences." Ghrane winked and stepped forward. "Now, what did you expect me to do with that hand?"

Costig pushed through the ranks of marines to join Wendell and Folmon before the brothels. He took in the sight without surprise or revulsion, and without the coldness with which certain men, accustomed to terrible visions, add a notch to memory and move on. His hands folded across his front, and his steel eyes held the woman's body—if what remained was a woman—for a long while without speaking. An ache of admiration lifted Wendell amid the unpleasantness, and reminded him of a sacredness of duty that certain men shared.

Lanallike lay bare, white as virgin powder in a slurry of stamped snow and blood. A rash of purple wounds scored her body where the knives fell—a hundred, if there was one. Her jaw turned up first, on the steps of the navy hall before dawn. Folmon couldn't bear to look on the young beauty. Wendell had often heard of this most severe Mattaka penalty, but to see that row of teeth hanging over a bloody absence mired him in despair.

"Have your lads see to her, before every thirsty kaim curdles this lane in filth.," Costig said to Folmon. The captain had only to nod the order. His lads hurried to cover the wretched girl.

"Bad enough to stab an old man and a runt," Folmon lamented. "This is beyond the pale. I'd say your example went unheeded," he recalled to the admiral his execution of the Mennegur lad. "If you'd like, I'll see to the one who done this, and I doubt the squains'll forget it so soon."

"I would *not* like that, and you'll do nothin'. Look at her." Folmon managed with great effort. "I don't have to wonder who did it. That's no gang of boys. Only women are so cruel, all the more when they feel betrayed." He looked into the crowd of Mattaka where the poye stood among her girls. "I'd have to flay every prostitute in Drummoc."

"They left her jaw on your doorstep. Do you mean to shrug and step over it as you go about your affairs?"

"Aye, it weren't for me. That's the jaw that set the Navy to search among her sisters, and it's her sisters who it speaks to, now. I could sooner keep this colony happy if I staked up Tuilapoy and Lamachar and the rest than to gut the brothels. Besides, what do you think would happen to any tradesman who sold his kin? If a smith gave over a smith, or a dog man, a dog man? By Euskus, what do you think would happen if a captain of the Navy turned on his fellow?" He lingered on Folmon.

Costig made the sign of Hadalis, that no wraith would follow him, and left them to the task.

"This has carried far enough," Folmon said as he steered Wendell away from the others. "And what was that debacle at the harbor? He makes a fool of me for turnin' out a brothel, then sets half the fuckin' garrison to sift through dog shit for nothin'! We've got the support for it. Tell me the Marines won't bother."

Wendell held his tongue, though he knew he couldn't for long. Somehow, it felt better if he made Folmon pry from him what he wished he didn't want to say.

"The squains have lost all respect for us." The captain squared to him imploringly.

"I make no guarantees. I fear if I ask Gua and Obrachar outright, it'll go badly. But if you set the lads, I'll grant them a word of courtesy before you act. It may be enough."

"They don't have the numbers to stop us," Folmon bargained with himself.

"Aye, but you're not after a fight, are you?" The captain shook his head. "Besides," Wendell explained, "Costig's own company's weaker by half." Folmon puzzled over the statement, and Wendell grinned. "Did you not think the *Juhketappat* looked a little low in draft when she sailed?"

It came as a small delight that when Costig asked after his sergeants-at-arms at the navy hall, he learned they were at the forges, seeing to the fit and finish of the steel. They may well have been avoiding him after his embarrassment at the dog ships, but at least they were on to the next thing, as any good marine after a defeat. He felt little enough of that embarrassment by now that Costig wondered if he'd slackened under his new rank.

It was less of a rout than it felt, though. Camne Drumlag was no distant shore, and no escape. The best two dozen in his company lay ready in the hold, and the moment she docked, there'd be stiff leather and good steel marching on the prince across the channel. Costig could hardly imagine who would care to stop them, but there was no one over there fit to try. They'd have the lad bound dockside, ready to pull their way home on the darraig that Polc's men were to secure.

Poznatxen was no fool. If he spotted a one-legged Leopard Seal hopping about, he'd be happy to provide the assistant viceroy with company—and how he could miss the big lob, Costig couldn't foresee. Even if he did, there was nowhere to go. They'd have him with the next ship, or the next. He knew that hitting his mark depended less on the skill of the first effort than the willingness to repeat it as many times as necessary.

A group of squains broke him from his thoughts. The dog family. Women and girls, haggard and wet to the knees from their march before dawn, trudged away from the harbor for their home. A lone male trailed listlessly behind them.

"*Hoy!*" Costig beckoned Norwet. His aunties stopped to wait while he strode back to meet the admiral. "Aren't you supposed to be with the dogs? What are you doin' here?"

Norwet shrugged. "I don't know. Maybe I will be needed." The lad stared at Costig's boots.

"I suppose you'll tell me you've no notion where the Leopard Seal is."

"He is on the *Orin's Thief*."

The frank reply jarred Costig. It hardly matched the slumped shoulders and timid gaze. He studied the lad for a sign of his angle. "Because you put him there."

Norwet nodded. "He was to go on the *Juhketappat*, but we thought it was your men who attacked Tunguk, and suspected Ostuk may have lied to us."

"It wasn't."

"I know that now. My brother stabbed one. We saw him limping the deck of the *Orin's Thief*."

Costig smiled inwardly at the memory of Neal and his lot. "Believe I saw the one."

"Why did you betray us?" Norwet blurted. There was more hurt in his voice than anger, and his eyes rose in a sort of plea. Costig could not answer right away. Even if he had the words, it would have been a meek dismissal of an accusation to which there *was* no answer, and he knew he had to stand his turn in the fire of shame.

"I've asked meself that, to no satisfaction. What I've come to believe, though it gives me no peace, is that I'm loyal to Drummoc. Always have been. Your mate promised a service to this colony. I found him unable to fulfill it, and a nuisance to boot."

"He will, if you let him."

"No matter. I've already seen to it. And now that he's rent apart your people as much as mine, I've no choice but to settle me error."

"You may turn so quick, but he is still our mate. My family is involved. We thought we served you."

"Aye," Costig granted. "That's the only way I've justified keepin' you around after you lied to me for Mentewat. We both know the Leopard Seal can't have a piss without help." He leaned in. "Who killed me marines?"

"I did." Norwet held his ground like a child admitting to his father he'd stolen the last lump of meat. Costig scoffed.

"All by yourself, then?"

"I had help."

"Who?"

"Tunguk."

"You and the old man?" The skepticism in Costig's tone remained.

"And the dogs. We loosed them on your men, and finished what their teeth did not." The amusement fled the admiral's face. "And you helped, too," Norwet added. "For sending too few against us—because we are children, and old men. I did not lie for Mentewat. He lied for me. If he had not, I would have killed him, too."

Costig's jaw tightened and his round cheeks flushed. "You speak as if there's no consequences for what you say. Have you got your fuzz in?"

Norwet hung his head and shook it. "I speak the truth, because I am afraid to lie. I concealed things from my brothers, from my uncles. Because of me, they nearly came to harm. It is the last time I will make that mistake."

Costig placed a consoling hand on his shoulder, but couldn't think of anything to go with it. He withdrew, then admitted, "I thought you'd run when I saw you. Probably should have. As we stand, I'm havin' trouble thinkin' of any way this conversation ends but in your arrest."

"For what? I am loyal to my mates. And like you, I am loyal to Drummoc. I thought to help you prepare for war, because if there is war, the dogs cannot run. What will my family do if there are ships of the farri in the harbor? What will we do if they come ashore?" He looked back at his womenfolk. "I don't know why, but I cannot trust Polc and Mentewat. I think they are bad for Drummoc. If you let me go, I will watch them. Tell you what I see. Maybe there is a reward for my family."

"I'm done with spies and rewards, me son. Whatever you meant, you and your lot have put yourselves between this place and her enemies. Do you expect me to walk away?"

Defeat seeped across the lad's face. "Then I know why I stayed. Please. You cannot harm my family. They thought they ran for you. You say you defend Drummoc? What will happen to the mines if you arrest every Seleku and Vjarku? Who will keep your dogs, or drive them at Camne Drumlag and Nunoc?" Costig had to concede that. He started to answer, but Norwet drove on. "I know now why I stayed. If you are done with your betrayals," he said flatly, with no hint of disdain, "I will ask your word. Let them go. There is no other who is guilty but me. I will take you to your marines."

Here and there, sailors and Mattaka still churned out. Costig extended his bent elbow. He knew he owed no gesture, and it was ill-advised for an admiral to offer such a thing to a squain lad—a criminal, no less. But he cared little for what others thought of his command, now. There seemed no redeeming it in their eyes. He offered the oath because the lad was right. The young dog driver had learned what an old marine should have known: that he must give himself to the worthy act, not the clever one, the safest, or the most praised. That these would guide him, one after the other, and if he followed, it would be to a worthy end, whether it came quietly to an old man, or with all haste, as it now must.

Norwet looked once more at the women, still waiting, bewildered, then turned to go with Costig.

"Leopard Seal," a sharp voice popped one of the stitches in his ribs. Another ripping sensation popped at his ankle. Parks could not see himself, but somehow he knew that his entire body was held together by uncountable sutures. Every time he moved, he felt them rupture, or tear through his flesh. "Leopard Seal!" The voice insisted, and a line snapped in sequence over his brow. He had to hold still. Every way pulled against the other. He unraveled somewhere, no matter what he did. To bend a knee, to think a certain thought, may be the act that tore the last thread on which some part of his body hung.

"*Parks!*" He woke to a swift kick from the smallest boy. One of the adults crouched over him, the other brother at his side. A whoosh of water under the false deck returned him to the ship, its cargo outlined against the struggling dawn. He hadn't bothered down the ladder again, preferring to curl up under the loose tail of a leather covering and shiver. He was used to shivering, by now. The cold and the open air felt like his anchor.

"Sup, little dude? Who's that, Norwahl?"

"Norwet is not here." The boy blinked. "We have done much for you. Do you not remember us?"

"Easy, tiger. I remember. It's just so dark. Tell you what, I see there's a new face, maybe he doesn't know everybody yet. Let's just go around the circle and introduce ourselves real quick."

"He is our cousin," the boy protested.

"My name is Parks, AKA Brother, AKA Leopard Seal. Go!" He pointed at the boy.

"Ferrakut."

"I am Senadak," the man said.

"Ulwet."

Parks muttered the names to himself several times under his breath.

"Senadak has something foul to tell you," Ferrakut interrupted.

"I don't know, I have a pretty well-developed taste for foulness. You'd have to get up—even earlier than this to surprise me."

"The captain means to betray you," Senadak leaned close and checked that there were no sailors nearby. "Neal told me. He is the first mate of Captain Polc. Ghrane means to take you back to Costig for the reward."

"*Really?*" Disappointment marked his voice. "He seemed chill."

"He wishes to surprise you as we land."

"Why wouldn't he just have done it back there? At the harbor?"

"If Costig found you on his ship, Ghrane would be blamed. And there is no reward for the Navy's arrest. But if he returns with you, Ghrane will be paid. He has asked Neal to take his men off, so they do not ruin his reward. He will pay them handsomely to depart. To his Mattaka crew, he promises much silver for their help."

Parks brooded over it. "This Neal—why would he tip you off?"

"I don't know. But he will offer no more help."

For hours more, Parks awaited the light. He tossed and turned and pried at the problem in his head, like some twisted wooden puzzle that refused to yield. When he began to feel like Foster with all his plotting, he clenched his eyelids and tried to shake clear. Their faces marched past: Foster, but also Joe, and Kjartke. The boys—*Ferrakut-Senadak-Ulwet, Ferrakut-Senadak-Ulwet*—he took the opportunity to drill. Somewhere, a Norwet. Grom and Blowhole, more names surfaced. He pushed Gionn aside when the red hair flared in his vision. He was not used to solving these things, because he despised them, and they belonged to others.

As soon as the crew could half-see, the captain had them raise the sail. They'd anchored some way off for the night, some bank, he heard. Now she nosed into a wall of cloud. He watched the dog men slipping through the packs, offering water, untangling leashes. The two boys hung close and spoke in low tones. Maybe they would have something for him, after all.

Then as if by appointment, a sail appeared from the gray wall off the port bow. It caused some excitement among the crew, and the captain leaned against the rail to study the visitor.

Parks groaned himself up to a seat, then waved the boys over. With those skinny crutches, he made his way to Ghrane, propped himself on the rail, and shooed them away.

"Still working on my sea legs," he explained as he steadied himself against the pitch. Ghrane gave him a polite smile, then refocused on the ship. "So how long you been doing this?" Parks let go with one hand to make a quick motion over the deck before bracing again. "Ships and dogs and whatnot."

"I've made five seasons."

"No small feat. I saw that trip you make firsthand." He whistled. "You're a better man than I if you can do it a second time, much less five." Ghrane again kept his mind on the ship. "Stackin' coin? You make good money?" Parks translated.

His face fluttered, as if he took the remark as a dig he couldn't deny. "Any man can eat. When I eat, I am called Captain."

Parks considered clarifying, apologizing, but something prevented him. "Dope. Well, I just wanted to say thank you for your hospitality. I have great respect for your profession," he bought time, because he had no idea what he meant to say. "Dog workers—you know, the fine people of the canine profession, which is by the way, my favorite animal—you people have always been good to me. Anybody who thinks that dogs suck, or that they're a lowdown, unclean animal like those Amposi pricks do, has no place with me."

It came to him. "I just can't figure out why those Navy dudes don't want anything to do with you."

Ghrane looked way from the approaching the ship, and it was Parks' turn to stare out over the water. "Surely you intend to explain your insult."

"There's no reward." He saw Ghrane contort inside, flailing for some sense in the words that felt too close to home to be meaningless, but so vague as to shake the captain's careful guard. "They told me." He let Ghrane reel a moment longer. "I guess whatever you promised to pay them wasn't enough to lock arms with a dog captain."

Ghrane settled in the realization, gathering himself in a few breaths. "I don't see what it changes."

"Nothing. Because either way, there's no reward. Listen, even though you want to sell me out, I still recognize what you did for me. You took a risk, and whatever you intended, you haven't done it yet. So let me return the favor.

"There never *was* a reward. You said it yourself: do you really think I could break out of prison, sled my way across Drummoc, kill a bunch of bad ass dudes, and escape on a ship with one leg and a couple of kids to help me? What I'm about to say is a state secret. Not only is there no gold waiting for you, but there'll be a treason charge if Costig finds out you blew it. The three ingots, or whatever they're called—the gold doubloons, they're an excuse. Costig needed them to pay his agents.

"You might have heard about a little war on the horizon. What you didn't realize is that *our* admiral planted two of the deadliest assassins ever to shit over the side of a boat on that whaler. I would be shocked out of my Eskimo shorts if they haven't already commandeered the vessel, or run it aground and slaughtered the crew. There's your first two pieces o' gold. Men like that don't come cheap.

"The third, you've probably guessed, belongs to yours truly. I'm here to spy on the assistant viceroy. Get the admiral the dirt he needs to arrest the man and put his head on a pike. Now it's no secret those two don't like each other. 'The enemy of my enemy is my friend.' What better way for Costig to slip me in than to chase me away shaking his spear? Do you really think the admiral is so stupid, he sent dozens of men to tear one ship inside out, then let yours drift off without a second look?"

Ghrane flinched in consideration.

"Optics, dude. That means 'how things look to those who don't look close enough.'" Parks tapped his temple.

"For all I know, he sent those Navy guys to make sure you didn't try something idiotic. Or maybe they just don't like you. But I like you. No bullshit. I was hurt when they told me. Part of me doesn't believe it, even now."

"It's a fine tale," Ghrane spoke at last. The ship drew alongside them under oars. The boys stopped to watch, and shouted with excitement when they realized the crew was all Mattaka.

"Take me in if you want. These dogs are getting off. Up to you whether they say Ghrane was the man who helped me escape, or the one who betrayed a friend of his people to the admiral."

"Lower your sail, follow us under oars," came the shout from the boat. "We will pilot you in."

"*Hoy*! Leopard Seal!" Another voice leapt up. Parks made out the form of a hand extended out from a thigh. He returned the salute.

"Who's that? I swear I remember your name, I just can't see that far."

"It is Anset, of the *Juhketappat*!"

"Of course, Anset!" He assumed it must have been one of the sailors, or maybe a rower from his time in the hold.

"If you are what you say, what will the people think when they learn you are no hero, but a spy of the admiral?" Ghrane offered his salute to the darraig.

"Don't know, kemosabe." He placed an arm around Ghrane's shoulders for all of the pilot ship to see. "Maybe I can be both. Maybe you can, too."

The wind off the starboard took Foster in the ear as the *Gairhle* did her best to avoid being driven toward the coast. He was exhausted, having yet to pull a stroke, or tie a knot, from hours at the ready.

The second they turned, the two little sails shifted almost imperceptibly, though it felt like a predator broke from the tall grass. Corm had to shout over every opinion on the ship, and in the ensuing madness, Foster learned as much about sailing as he had in his entire life.

"Cap'n, we out-sheet 'em, and sheet's our only advantage. We put the wind behind and run for the coast," Arthas shot a finger at the thick haze and the land that lay somewhere behind it, any number of miles away. "If they lag back, we slip north once they lose sight."

"You saw how that worked last time." Corm retorted. "Eckerd, keep the wind on our beam!"

"We were goin' a different way, then. They caught us when we had to turn south at the cliffs." Pitras threw in a voice with Arthas.

"If that wind backs, if we have to cross it, we're dead." Arthas said of their present angle.

"How come?" Foster said soft-enough that only his neighbors could snort at him.

"They're runnin' claws," Bentos explained. "We got more sheet with the square but they'll have our bowels out close to the wind."

"I won't give up the weather-gage and pin meself to the rock before I have to," Corm fired back, and that was that.

"I thought an angotak was a killer whale," Foster admitted.

"Aye, it is a whale," Atalkut confirmed.

"Mate, I'll bear no more from your stupidity," Gionn warned.

"Who are they? Are they allies with the Navy?"

Gionn narrowed in suspicion. The comment had been innocent, but now Foster understood his benchmate worried he might try to use this to his advantage. He wondered how he would even signal them—how they might believe him.

"Best we tell you after the fight. Keeps your spirits up." Bentos gave him a patronizing slap on the knee.

The angotaks heeled and fell behind briefly as one dug to seaward against the wind. The other matched the wake of the *Gairhle* in steady pursuit. Foster's panic—entirely the product of those around him—soon settled into a humming nausea. For hours they looked up at the sail, aft at the enemy, and back. Fergo tried without success to light a coal fire, then resorted to pulverizing a lump and blacking out the captain's face. Imau'y stalked the length of the ship shouting, "If you have moonstone, throw it over! If you have moonstone, throw it over!" But found no takers. So many men tied strips of leather, beads, little charms where they could that Foster wondered if another mutiny weren't brewing. They struck up a round of a song called "Beithel's Breath," then another, and another, each growing in urgency. One man switched his boots to the opposite feet. The more pragmatic whet their edges.

Despite it, the pursuers grew like fangs in a gaping jaw. For a while, the wind began to puff and falter, cutting their lead. Corm nearly dipped oars before it returned, and he ordered them to save their strength.

By afternoon, a low sun peeked out to watch on its way home. The breeze backed as Arthas promised. Faced with a wind just off the bow, Corm had no choice but to turn directly for the peninsula. One of the angotaks carried past him before it bent that way, and the other followed just short of their own route to bracket them. It seemed every twist, every gust, every sticky wave brought them to bear.

The captain did his best to keep the wind from creeping in front of him, and at times, it seemed he gained on them. But it was nowhere near the lead he required to disappear into the haze. As the skies dimmed, Foster recalled the slap of bare feet on rock. He saw the gray head of Tunguk chug into view. He and Parks fled, naked and confused, begging the terrain to cooperate—for a flat stretch, a little more land. The old man was slow, and they outnumbered him. Neither advantage was true here.

"Abiamas," someone said, and he knew the type that caught them on the *Juhketappat*. Thirty-six or forty to each. The crew stopped making suggestions. By that alone, Foster had no doubt that Corm was a fine skipper, and he did all in his power with the ship he had.

When the angotaks closed within half a mile, he could make out the detail of heads, dark and round.

"Is it the same ones?" Hogue called back to those with a better view.

"Can't be," Eckerd said. "We put a ram in one. No time to repair and re-crew."

"Could be the other one, if she dumped the survivors in Nunoc and found a new mate."

"No, they always hunt in pairs. If it's not the same, it's two fresh ships. Or the same crew on a fresh abiama." Eckerd insisted.

"We can only hope," Corm said. "Might dump ballast and run when they recognize Jonn!" He shook the young man's shoulder, though his excitement didn't spill over to Jonn.

"At least they'll be short a few," Hogue said hopefully. "And we're near full again."

Corm squinted into the bright cloud bank. Long strides carried him to the bow, where he leaned off the quarter deck as if he'd forgotten there were anyone else aboard. Suddenly, the wide hat whipped off his head as he waved it and hollered with joy.

"We'll see what they got for stomachs now, lads!" Foster and a few others stood and searched the horizon. A low white line wavered and began to separate as they drew near. Loose petals from a jagged flower floated delicately toward them. Wide stretches spread between the sheets, and the sea glinted like broken glass.

"Drop sail! Wet your oars, you barrels! We're goin' into the ice!"

Camne Drumlag came out of the fog like a black fortress. From the edge of the false deck, Parks could see nothing but a little slip of white land that ran up sharply between the base of unseen peaks. Wigwams protruded like boulders out of the drift. As they neared, he saw shapes darting in and out of the huts, some toward the shore, others back into the mist that swallowed everything a hundred feet up. It was no port. More of a pathetic fingerhold in a gap where the mountains lost track of the sea. It reminded him of the place they stayed with Lenet, except that the shroud hinted at something more severe.

The *Orin's Thief* entered a sidelong drift. Parks checked over his shoulder once more to be sure Ghrane wasn't coming to arrest him. His fine speech wasn't enough, and he had to offer the man a piece of silver out of his argot. It seemed to offend the captain—not the bribe, but the amount. He demanded ten. But Parks had no idea how many silvers made one gold, and suspected a trick. His hunch told him it was exactly ten, and Ghrane demanded the whole amount. He refused to budge, and under the close watch of the pilot ship, Ghrane relented.

Poles on the shore reached out for the lip of the deck at his feet to ease her in. To either side, Ferrakut and Ulwet braced him upright. *Ferrakut and Ulwet, Ferrakut and Ulwet. The little one's Ulwet,* he reminded himself.

At the last minute, he'd decided a Leopard Seal needed a grand entrance. In his right hand, he held his spear, the same that got him arrested in the first place. In his left, a pair of short leashes with Barbados Slim and Winnie Cooper—his old team. The handlers were glad to pawn them off.

He wobbled when the poles caught. The boys hugged his ribs with their tiny might. He'd tied a knot in the pant leg just under his stump, and put on his most regal expression. A ripple of Reverse-Eskimo chatter ran through the gathering miners at the sight, and he immediately felt self-conscious. Their mouths rounded in shock. They had to be saying something about his leg. His nose twitched, but he composed himself.

The ship gave a gentle lurch as it struck the log buoys. Parks handed the weapon to one boy, the leashes to the other, then wrapped his arms around their shoulders. A great many men closed in anticipation. The distance to shore was mere inches, but shore was a slurry of mud and snow. His swollen foot felt like a concrete block from bearing all his weight. He negotiated a hop, but thought twice.

Ferrakut and Ulwet sensed the dilemma. They each straddled the gap, one foot on land and the other holding the false deck. Parks leaned in, tested their support. Decent for a pair of groms. He rocked out and back twice, then pushed down and felt them give a little too much. Somehow, their posture held. He lifted his foot and swung forward as though on parallel bars, clearing the gap with miraculous grace.

His foot stuck. They pushed off the deck to keep pace with him, but Ferrakut slid out. Parks bent his knee to absorb the shift. His stomach dropped, as if falling from a height. He landed on his face in the snow, and felt Ulwet crash down on his back. The miners howled with laughter.

From the *Juhketappat*, Kjartke watched with relief as the men hurried to lift Brother. He swatted away the hateful dog, who thought it a game, and brushed powder from his coat. The men offered their hands, and Brother closed his around them, moved them up and down, while many crowded in to repeat the ritual.

They lay off in the harbor a hundred yards, where they would wait their turn to unload. As soon as Drummoc left sight, the marines took the ship. They urged Ostuk to overtake the *Orin's Thief*. He could not, until they found it at anchor. The leader demanded he sail on, and there was much cursing, but no threat could make Ostuk try a night landing with a new crew and "ten-thumb rowers," as he called the marines.

Now they hid below. Kjartke's relief could not last. Brother had made it to Camne Drumlag, but none on that ship knew what creature the *Juhketappat* bore in her womb. They warned the crew that if any shouted to land, or made a signal, they would be killed before disembarking. Tunguk said these were not men who feared to follow their words. Over the hatch, a pair of eyes regarded the deck like a hunter at a breathing hole.

Go, she begged. They could not miss him, so tall, surrounded by a throng. *Up the mountain. Into a tukit.*

He pointed at the *Juhketappat* as he spoke. Brother meant to wait for them. He could not take two steps on his own, and those boys who held him knew nothing of this place, or the dangers just behind. Tunguk had praised her—once, and in his own way—for moving him to the *Orin's Thief.* She did not want to enjoy it, but even now it brushed through her like the fingers of her father Oljarbaruk over her hair. If Brother did not move soon, her efforts had lasted but a day.

An older man spat something in Reverse-Eskimo—*Mattakatan*, the word nagged him—and a pair of teens set a basket of coal beside Parks and covered it with a blanket. He got the memo, and lowered himself with a groan that belonged to his dad locating the recliner with his ass.

The ship swarmed with people. Chains of hands passed off supplies, and the boys left him to see to the dogs. Something like an itch caused him to look into the harbor, and he spied the lines of the other dog ship, bobbing offshore.

The lazier men hovered near him, taking their turn to feel at his clothing, his hair, or to tap his knee.

"Hurt?"

"Ow, *yes.*" Barbados Slim growled at someone, and Parks reached to pinch the back of his neck like he'd seen in *The Dog Whisperer.* "*Tsst!*" Slim reeled around and gave him a warning nip, and Parks slapped his nose in annoyance. "Bastard!" Winnie Cooper curled behind his leg, wishing to recede from the frenzy.

A number of the younger ones now giggled and darted in to tap him quickly on the forehead, or the chest, or the upper back.

"Leave him alone," someone halfheartedly scolded.

"You speak English?" Parks asked the sympathizer.

"I don't know English. But we all speak Atlantean."

"I don't know Aladdin."

"You're speaking it now." He grinned. The others circled around. Parks felt the bore of their attention—curious, amused, or unimpressed. They were lightly dressed in filthy leather, their hair matted, faces and hands smudged black. The crowd struck him as a different race of

Mattaka altogether. He expected to notice little horns, or pointy ears. For all their interest, he got no impression of fear, or respect. They knew who he was. He was a different man to each of them and, he couldn't help but feel, a disappointment to all.

They began to pepper him with questions. "What news of the riot?" "How did you do it? Did you really break the prison?" "I heard the farri sails on Drummoc!" "Have you got word of a woman named Natjate? Our child was due a month ago." "What is it like where you come from?" "Where's the rest of you?" They laughed at his missing leg.

"Let him speak, fools!" A man slipped to the front.

Parks opened his mouth but couldn't get anything out. He'd prepared his bragging points on the ship. There was no way to keep living on the lam. These dudes would have to embrace him with all their hearts, or he was done. There was the problem of his actual presence, though, and the discrepancy between what he was and what he needed to be.

"You know what they call me." Someone said a word in Mattakatan that sent a laugh through the crowd. Parks looked at his thighs and let it settle. "The stories you've heard—none of them are true. You know who gave me that name? I did. I've never even seen a leopard seal, not outside the Discovery Channel. I came here because I got lost. My matey left on a whaler. I'd be dead, except some grandpa named Tunguk took pity on me, and gave me akmanu…akamanuk…"

"Akmanuak?" The man in front asked, as if he found it novel.

"That one. After I saved his life. But I didn't, really. We just walked him home. And I didn't break out of jail. I did, but Tunguk opened the door, and a bunch of little dog boys carried me, because I was out of my mind on some potent shit. Some witch lady poisoned me, and I would have died, but I got—" He couldn't say it. Parks waved at his leg. "This."

"You attacked the admiral." A voice said, almost a question, a plea. "You came for him with your spear."

"I was going to say, 'Good morning.' He misunderstood. I think he's under a lot of stress." Parks couldn't bear to face them. The miners rustled with disappointment. Or was it his own disappointment he felt? He knew the truth of everything he said, but he knew it in the background behind the boasting and the legends. He had no choice but to think himself the Leopard Seal.

425

He came here with even finer credentials: the wise Navy vet, educated and well-traveled, connoisseur of magical technologies, man of great promise and many friends. Even when the world failed to see it, he clung to it like a life preserver. He didn't belong here, or anywhere half as bad. He had more richness of character, of experience, than all of those blackened souls before him. Parks could see the entire world in a map in his head. He'd heard a thousand tongues, drank a thousand drinks, and known the women of many ports, prettier than the fairest of this backwater. He came as a king in his mind, and when they couldn't see it, he called himself by another name, and made up a resumé of things they could understand. He was a man of destiny, a hero of stature and of mystery, waiting for someone to recognize his greatness and promptly ferry him home.

"My real name is Parks. Son of Marion, Jr. and Terry. My uncles are Gary and Frank. None of that's even true, anymore." He motioned his hands over his ill-fitting clothing, his sagging posture, his cringing pain. "This...*this is it.*"

The man extended his palm like the others, and Parks took it.

"I am Sagalak. And to name your kin, that is how the northern clans greet. Which one does your mate Tunguk belong to?"

"He's this one. You guys. And my girl Kjartke, she's from the one where the women have tattoos on their faces. You know, marks?"

"Jargadak or Haumak?"

"Pretty sure the first."

Sagalak's smile managed to warm him while it patronized him. "When the people there meet, it is not their family they name. Your father is those gods who favor you of late, and your uncles are those gods who bring you troubles. Do not tell me of your mother."

"I don't know how the gods feel about me, but if that's the case, Tunguk is my father, and Costig is my uncle." A little sympathetic laughter washed over the crowd and brightened Parks.

"You are not afraid?" A different man pointed at the dogs.

"These guys? *Psh!* I was raised by dogs." They slapped at one another with horror and exhilaration. "Everyone where I'm from has one. Except cat people." They puzzled at the word. "Antisocial murderers who always have hair stuck to their shirts." The Mattaka nodded in understanding.

"You must be from very far north," Sagalak posited.

"Very far."

"What god or madness brings you to Camne Drumlag?"

Parks shrugged. "The sea. Or luck, though I can't say if it's the good kind, or the bad."

"A luck. Aye, here we call them kaim. It is hard to see the nature of yours."

"Kaim." Parks rummaged excitedly under his tunic. "I got one of those, too!" He produced his arrow and held it out for Sagalak, who regarded it but refused to touch it. He grinned at his friends with disbelief.

"Your lover, she is Jargadak."

"Lover? Ha! I mean, not saying I wouldn't, but…I had more limbs when she made me this. I don't think she's into no-account cripples."

Sagalak nodded sympathetically. "You do not have to tell a miner of women who flee when misfortune comes."

It wasn't what Parks meant, but he thought of how Kjartke left her husband on his death bed, and their child with him, to sail with a pair of strange men. He looked out at her ship again, and though he knew better, her absence filled him with dread.

"I do not know what you hoped to find here," Sagalak went on. "But any nephew of the admiral has our hospitality." He started away, not for the ships and the long work of unloading, but toward the mountain.

"Wait," Parks stopped him. "You going to see the assistant viceroy?"

Sagalak hesitated, then put on a smile and strolled back to Parks. "I will announce your arrival. And theirs," he tilted his head at the Navy men who came off the boat with Parks. "Do you know these men?"

"No," Parks admitted.

"They came before, asking an audience. Demanding, I would say."

"Hope my homeboy wasn't rude to you." He broke into an exaggerated drawl. "Fella who sounded like he just a-came right down out of them thar heels."

Sagalak startled with recognition. "Your mate who left on the whaler?"

Parks nodded. "He is a good man. He would not let the Navy kill me."

"He's aight," Parks raised a shoulder. "Any chance I could come with you?"

Sagalak pretended to consider it. "Alexicus is very occupied. Do not worry. I'm sure he's glad to have you as a guest, and will introduce himself as soon as he is able." The miner motioned to a number of men, and started off at a brisk pace with his posse.

The *Orin's Thief* shoved off. Under the oars of fresh miners, she pointed to sea. When they were far enough, her bow spun and the oars pulled hard to gain momentum. The unladen ship glided past Kjartke, where she crouched to test lashings on the false deck, hoping the next tug would reveal to her how to signal Brother. With a terrible scrape, the keel of their companion drove up the launch, where many hurried to pull her ashore.

"One of us has to do it," Milak said low in Mattakatan as he shook cargo needlessly. "Or we have done nothing."

Kjartke lifted her chin and saw Brother rise with the help of the boys, a head above any man. They helped him toward the quay.

"The one who does it meets the spear." She avoided making a suggestion, though there were many little dog drivers with big lungs.

"Maybe they will not harm a woman," Milak guessed.

"Maybe they will not harm a child." The vision of Armenuk protested her remark. In truth, she did not wish to see any of them go. Kjartke glanced again at Brother, ignorant of what approached, of so many things. Low as these boys were, they had a bit of courage. They would make capable husbands to whatever kind of girl would stoop to marry a dog man. She wondered if it were not Brother's turn to give something, Brother's turn to be brave. At the same time, she hated that there was no one eager among them—no more eager than herself.

"See to the dogs on the deck," Tunguk spoke from his seat, curled over his ribs. "I will choose who warns him. I will say when it is time."

Kjartke snorted. "An old fool fools no one: you mean to sacrifice yourself. But he dies without you."

Tunguk took in the eager beads of eyes around him. "I think he has what help he requires."

"Everyone off the false deck." Ostuk stood at the rail of the main deck, and they knew it was the sergeant who gave the command. The height of the border was several feet. From a few yards back toward the mast, none of them could hope to be seen from the shore. Not even Brother was tall enough. Reluctantly, the boys streamed over. Kjartke glared at the sergeant, and he gave her little in return. It was enough to be sure he would not care who disobeyed him. She hopped down after the others, then tossed her head.

"Arnake!" She scolded the youngest boy. He stood atop a barrel on the false deck, just feet behind Ostuk, who jerked around, surprised to see someone hovering over him.

"Down! Listen to your auntie." He sent him scurrying over to Kjartke.

The Mattaka sailors and drivers gathered around the mast, and she pulled the little one to her leg. The sergeant motioned to the marines behind him on the ladder, and they climbed up and crouched over to where Ostuk stood. At the sight of the strangers, the dogs raised their fury. Sawi and Onag worked to calm them. The marines all knelt below the rim of the false deck in preparation.

"Everyone below to row," the sergeant raised his voice to Ostuk. Kjartke squinted up at the clouds, and knew she must find a way to remain on deck. She bent and whispered harshly in Arnake's ear, and worked her way around so the mast stood between her and the marines.

"Milak," she called the eldest brother over.

Ostuk soon found them. "I am sorry." He opened his hand toward the hatch.

"Tunguk and I cannot row. We will remain to quiet the dogs." The captain knew them well. He argued for them with the sergeant, then returned.

"You two can stay. Everyone else, below."

She nodded Milak his leave.

"Hang on!" The sergeant beckoned Milak over. Before the others could make the ladder, he addressed them under the din of dog song. "This one stays with me. If I hear a word of you two," he addressed Tunguk and Kjartke, "if your hand moves a way I don't like, if you make a dog bark, shake a rope, or yawn too wide, I cut the throat of the firstborn son."

Sawi plead with them in silence as he retreated below with the others.

"I can't believe I made it here on that thing," Parks remarked from the quay as the dog ship eased in under oars. "It looks like a fucking canoe with a..." he searched for the right expression. "Sidecock."

He toed the edge, clinging to Ferrakut and Ulwet, *Ferrakut and Ulwet*. Who was that dude he just met? Sagat? Miners pressed in behind them, ready to strip her bare the second she touched.

On board, Kjartke listened to Ostuk call out the strokes to the relay at the top of the ladder. "Seventy-two yards," he said, and she knew it was the marines' demand that he say the distance. They meant to rush as soon as the *Juhketappat* struck the buoys.

"Forty-eight yards." Ostuk announced, and Kjartke looked to Tunguk, where they soothed dogs beneath the mast. He nodded almost imperceptibly.

"You have to go. Now." She said without excitement, so softly that the men who watched them like patient hunters could not hope to hear.

"Where is everyone?" Ferrakut wondered aloud as the false deck came into view.

Parks marveled as one bank of oars struck the water then lifted, sending the dog ship into a sideways spin. It was the second time he'd seen the maneuver today. He thought the *Orin's Thief* did it too late, and expected to crash into the dock at the corner, but she came around in perfect time to catch the poles and ease in flush. This one looked like it was doomed to overrotate, but he was willing to be impressed again. A deep breath slipped out of him. He felt like a kindergartner, standing proud with his lunch pail after the first day of school, watching for his parents' car. They would be back to get him—Kjartke and Eskimo Joe. That was the only thing he dared believe.

Parks felt Ferrakut's fingers dig painfully into his side. "Something has happened."

Ulwet frowned at his brother.

"Twenty-four yards," they heard the captain's voice for the first time from the quay. The throng gathered so tight behind them that Parks had to lean back to avoid getting jostled into the drink.

They drifted so close now that Kjartke could see nothing of the men who waited, only a sliver of white mountain before the clouds. She dared not look up the mast to risk drawing the eyes of the marines. If they saw him, they said nothing. Milak, too, met her gaze, and knew not to search where the two of them boosted his brother. But Arnake was even thinner than the long tree. He had disappeared behind it, where he waited in the climbing belt for her word. She heard no sound to suggest he meant to heed it. A knot bound her. Someone must look up.

"Ferrakut!" Ulwet pointed from shore. Parks could just see a loose rope, or a banner of some kind flapping at the end of Ulwet's finger, halfway up the mast.

"It is Arnake!" Ferrakut replied. "What is he doing?"

"He taunts us. Look at how he waves his hand overhead!"

Ferrakut startled. "Leopard Seal. We have to go." Ferrakut turned and tried to squeeze through, but the miners ignored them and refused to part.

"Poles out!" Ostuk warned from the deck with insistence.

Parks didn't understand, but he felt the terror of the boys as clearly as if it soaked from their skin into his own as he watched the empty false deck bear down on them.

"Can you swim?" Ferrakut asked.

"Me? Of course. I mean, I could, before my operation—"

"Grab the buoy!"

"The what? Grab the—" He never finished. The false deck rotated perfectly into the poles at five yards out. It seemed to accelerate for a split second, then an icy shock crashed into Parks as if he'd been plowed under. An old panic swallowed him. He thought he saw a flash of survival orange. He tried to open his eyes, and realized they were already open. He was underwater.

From the mast, Arnake saw the splash and the edge of the false deck snap against the buoys like a jaw. The marines vaulted from concealment and ran for the quay, where they stopped at the mass of miners. The Mattaka stepped back in surprise, then closed ranks that the men could not find a foothold on the land.

"Kjartke! He fell in!" Arnake shouted now with impunity.

The woman dashed off, and Tunguk contorted around his tender sides to raise himself. He found her crouched behind a barrel of dog food on the false deck, unable to go farther. The marines leveled their spears at the men who blocked their exit.

"Stand aside. We're here to meet with the assistant viceroy."

"He is at the mining camp," a man answered.

"Who will show us?"

"No one," the same replied.

"No matter. We'll see the trail. Now fuck off, the lot of you! By order of Admiral Costig, we have leave to kill any man who stands in our way."

"Six hundred men stand in your way," the defiant miner crossed his arms.

"Then we'd better get started." The sergeant thrust his point into the man's breast and kicked him free into the crowd. When he jumped ashore, the miners parted in fear. Marines followed, swiping their black steel to discourage the people who had no arms, not even a knife among them. They stumbled back until a lane formed. The marines hurried through, and up the mountain.

"Ice starboard!" Atalkut called from the quarter deck. Foster craned around and stabbed his oar into the edge of a brittle blue flow. Bentos joined him, and they eased the bow around before once again finding the stroke.

Tunguk manned the port, and together the Mattaka—too small to be much use as rowers—served as the eyes of the *Gairhle* while Cormdran stalked the length of the ship.

"Clear lead comin', lads. Good for half a mile, maybe more," he encouraged them. The ice was loose, and with care, they avoided collision. Those patches that formed were still thin enough to chip with the blade of an oar. When they first entered the field, they simply plowed everything aside without fear of damage to the hull. Rather than keep to the edge, Corm drove them into a thicker concentration toward the coast—still invisible, and anyone's guess how far.

This was nothing like the jagged floes that trapped them near the iceberg. This ice seemed young, drifting unalert to their presence. It reminded him of walking through a herd of grazing cattle. Foster had come to understand that "ice" meant practically nothing. It could be rime on a sail, crushing floes miles wide, rolling mines that lurked ready to detonate on a ship, towering bergs, or crisp little patches with puddles of water on the surface like these.

In a certain light, it could even transform into a pair of angotaks.

He had to grant them a certain pluck. No one thought they'd follow the *Gairhle* into the ice. But without hesitation, the sails came down, the

432

oars extended, and the two ships picked their way nimbly after them. Now in a rowers' duel, they could no longer make relentless headway. The *Gairhle* carried more manpower, and could afford to use her stature more recklessly against the lighter ice. But the angotaks had them on maneuvers. They took care to keep always seaward, one out wide and another just off her wake.

She'd turned to run parallel to the coast, but the wind came over the beam when it puffed, nudging all parties—ice included—toward the peninsula, and in all likelihood, a swelling autumn pack.

As the light failed, they secured themselves to a meatier floe. Neither side could risk moving in the dark. The crew talked optimistically about waking to find the angotaks had fled, with no stomach for ice, or a real fight. Foster hardly slept, though, and from all the shifting around him and the anxious stomping of the watch, he didn't reckon too many others did, either. They awoke to clear, gummy ice across the whole of the sea, which broke into slush at the first movement of the ship. The angotaks remained. They exchanged some code via pennants, then resumed the chase.

By keeping to sea, they ran in water looser by a hair. Whenever the *Gairhle* found an open lead, she put distance between them. When the ice jumbled, the angotaks closed. By noon, the ship behind them was close enough for the taunting to begin. Foster was impressed by the coordination. Man after man stood in turn like a rolling artillery barrage to hurl his foulest at the pursuing ship.

Some of them made no sense, and when little Tunguk tried, it came in Mattakatan, but most of his shipmates made Foster cackle with delight. Half the point seemed to be to boost morale. None, though, were as practiced as Gionn. At first, Foster couldn't make out the responses, and gauged the volley by the laughter that followed from the other ship.

Through careful negotiation, their shadow slipped closer until a single stubborn floe separated them.

"No use runnin', lads! Save your arms for the fight!" One of the angotaks shouted. Now that he could see them in detail, Foster tried to pick out what made them so terrifying, but only found variations on the men of the *Gairhle*.

"Been a mix up," Eckerd excused their flight. "We thought you wart-whales were angotaks from afar!"

"Is that your captain at the mast? He's lost his cock to his gut and his neck to his jowls!" A new angotak lobbed his voice. The ice gave it a thin, cracked quality.

"Every time I swear that's the ugliest woman I've tossed, there comes a filthier temptress," Gionn complained through cupped hands.

"If you handle your spear like that oar, you couldn't toss a seal in heat!" Someone retorted.

Foster stood for the first time. "Hey! How's your wife and my kids?" No one on his ship had so much as a snort, and he lowered himself with embarrassment.

"Better oaths! Or keep your seat," Gionn said.

"Angotaks don't marry, Wife Seal." Hogue moaned. "*Hoy!*" He belted. "I know you can't count past your fingers, but our number cunt says it's bad for you."

"I'd say you got just enough to fill our barrels with fresh meat." A man in their bow estimated.

Gionn rolled his eyes, then went out of turn. "I'm sick of you gammers tryin' to frighten innocent whalers with your man-meat rumors. It's only cannibalism if you chew!"

"I mark your seat, lad." A bald little fellow growled.

"Already surrendered to our wit, and straight to the empty threats?" Gionn said with disappointment.

"If you make it past the arrows, ask for Moipa!"

"Sit with Foster, Moipa!" Gionn complained with sincerity. "No more Amposi oaths! You lot've got as little guile as an angotak."

"Pick who meets us at the beam, and the rest of you'll outlive him by a thrust." An angotak boasted.

Gionn fell beside himself with disgust. "Can I have *one* fight where some poltroon doesn't give the old, 'Choose who goes first because the first is dead' bilge? Have we agreed to abandon the noblest portion of the battle to bark like urchins before they start pullin' hair?"

"Fuck you!"

Gionn took up his stroke like a man who'd given up on anything decent. The rest of the ship, however, fell in stride with the angotaks.

"Better to wait for the other ship if you hope to put a single man aboard the *Gairhle*!" Tamarqan skirted Gionn's ban on lame Amposi threats.

The angotak vessel whipped into a frenzy. "The *Gairhle*!" Foster heard the name repeated. "The gods are good, lads!" One of the rougher voices celebrated. "Twice in a season we drink from her veins! There'll be no shirkin', this time!"

Several of the men muttered curses to themselves. "Is it the same ones?" Hogue asked Fergo.

"Pray it is," Pitras replied. "You're lookin' light for crew," he hollered. "Is that a new ship? Ours is yet full and unblemished."

"You forgot this!" The angotak called for some object, then lobbed it underhand so that it skittered across the ice between them—a half-rotted head.

"Who's that? The man who made you face us a second time?" Corm growled.

Foster turned quickly from the sight. He instinctively stretched with his oar as though he could push the ice farther away. The barbs continued, but the jarring reassertion of the situation froze him in the memory of the shivering waters as he waited beneath the prow of a ship with Tunguk, knowing he would have to board. He heard the saw again, as it passed through Park's leg bone. Foster shut his eyes and forced his limbs to keep moving while the rest of him gasped for little breaths and blew them out with excessive force in an attempt to slow the tingling flood of adrenaline. When he opened his lids, he noticed that across the aisle, beneath the flurry of brave speech, Gionn curled between his shoulders and gave the same attention to his own oar as Foster.

The angotaks bounded and frothed, rabid for revenge. They angled their prow toward the floe and smashed into it, as though to foul the oars of the *Gairhle* with its drift. It was a move of desperate impatience, but it frightened the crew into doubling the stroke. They plowed through a thin patch rather than waste time maneuvering. Foster settled himself by giving his entire body to the rhythms of rowing. He couldn't look at the other ship—either one. He didn't bother to turn and spot the ice, placing all his faith in Tunguk and Atalkut. When he thought he might pass out from anxiety, Corm found a lead, and they opened her up with all they had, putting the nearest angotak temporarily out of earshot.

By afternoon, the way ahead looked blocked by solid pack, circling clockwise out to sea. The second angotak sensed the trap and edged in to cut off a route around it. The only open way was a densely-littered lead that ran as much eastward toward the coast as south. It looked like a cul-de-sac, with ice on all sides, but Corm calmly steered them into the lane of stubborn chunks and stray rafts.

Within a mile, an alley south showed itself, barely wide-enough for the oars to span. Everyone knew they were as likely to be iced in as caught, but good manners prevailed and they pushed on with the angotaks in tow. It soon narrowed so that the oars struck ice. The ship behind them had no room to turn, so they hopped benches and backpaddled to the mouth of the slit, where they anchored for the night.

"They'll be gone at dawn," Chirim huffed. "If they wanted us, they could have come."

"A chase is a long thing," Hogue offered gruffly.

All night the creaking hinges of the ice closed around them, and the watch kept them up smashing at it with oars, or chisels. The angotaks remained.

They looked to be frozen fast as the *Gairhle*. In the first hours, they managed to free themselves, but all around them, the ice held—thicker tables webbed with lanes of single pane glass. Their consolation was that their enemies couldn't reach them unless they abandoned ship for a hike. No one seemed too consoled, though. To become trapped so late in the season would mean wintering on the pack with a few weeks' provisions.

Once they gained purchase for the oars, they battered through slush and collided repeatedly into a budding floe, gaining inches at a time while the quarter-deck rang with the shouts of sailors who pounded at the crease. The current ran swift, though, and spun the whole mass north and east until just after midday, when the sun crossed the shrouded coast and warmed the surface just enough that it shattered on all sides.

The *Gairhle* had water again, and though exhausted from the morning's efforts, everyone leaned into his stroke. The way behind them closed, but the angotaks found a new route to pursue them by.

"Lead west! We can make the sea!" Nolan declared.

"Not before those bastards. Mark me, lads: they'll quit first," Corm insisted.

As if they heard the suggestion, one of the ships broke off to make nearly a mile to more open water before resuming parallel to the coast, while the other kept as near as she could. There was no breaking free without a fight—even Foster understood that. Despite a lot of brave talk, every move of the *Gairhle* told him that a fight was the last resort. Corm was prepared to face pack ice and starvation before a pair of ships he apparently got the better of once before. The angotaks would blink first, or all of them would freeze.

And they did, the following night. On the next day, the *Gairhle* didn't so much as pitch while the ice held fast on all sides under an overcast sky until the current asserted itself and busted them free again. Both angotaks fell off to sea another half mile and got the crew's hopes up before they resumed course.

"Got us now, cunts. They'll just sit west in the shards until we're bound up, and dust their hands of it," Gionn theorized. Foster grew delirious from lack of sleep and constant anxiety. It should have felt like victory. Just over a week ago, he staggered after Corm with a knife in a last futile effort to derail the ship. Now, one way or another, it looked like she was done. Yet no part of him could rejoice. The men around him felt like his own, and their fate a common one. The sacrifice he so often considered now loomed: himself, for the security of those he left behind. If it was ever more than a story he told himself to feel noble, he despised it now that the choice had been snatched from him and made on his behalf.

At sunset, a clear lead opened to the southwest. Corm had sworn off the sea, but fear of mutiny or a kindred desperation of his own sent them hurtling through it. The angotaks still smashed and picked, losing in minutes what distance they'd won over days. It widened as the sun quit in an oil painting of pinks and purples and blue-greens that enraptured Foster. Not even the two black silhouettes bent on their death could mar the peace that robbed him of his desire for escape, or victory, or the warmth of life. They were every bit a part of the beauty, indispensable as the sun or the ice.

While the heavy night tones seeped in, the order came to row through the dark. The way lay open, and wasn't likely to last. Each stroke where they heard the splash of the oars and the water parting around the ram felt like a theft. Foster braced for the jarring impact of ice. Instead, it came as a gradual slowing. By the time the rowing felt like dragging a straw through a fountain drink, he imagined them far behind. Finally, the oars fouled. She buried gently into an unseen chunk. With any luck, they were nearly in the open sea, and the sun and the current would free them by early afternoon.

It was the best sleep he could have had under the circumstances.

But dawn brought a bitter fog that hung on the ice so they could hardly see past the side. No sun reached them, and the wind died. They sat frozen and blind until a gale whipped up in their faces out of the west. Through the next evening and the following day, they cowered as the ice shifted all around them with hellish cracks. Grown men whispered of evil spirits, and even though he knew what he was listening to, their fear infected him with each unearthly moan as sheets slid across one another at the seam, broke up, and twisted. The ship itself turned in the pack. The wind spun again, out of the north—or was it the *Gairhle*? A snow of frozen seawater stung them broadside. Hardly a man lifted his head for three days.

"Lord, free us," Foster tried his hand at prayer. He would have to find another way to accomplish his mission. Or let them go. These men had their hearts set on a place, same as him, and who was he to take it? He'd overpromised—to the admiral, and most of all, to Parks.

As he pressed against the boys and shook, he remembered Kjartke's words. Or rather, he forgot but recalled her meaning when she talked about the threads—the *onik*. He saw her kneeling over Parks, sewing his gaping leg with short, tight stitches.

"This is the best we can do," she announced.

Then Foster knew they were on their own. He didn't even want to help anymore. It was insane for a man to want anything in a place like this. The lines on his map unraveled and withdrew, until he could no longer close his eyes and see a Drummoc, or a Taclann, or a North Carolina. Any direction may as well have been the other. He ceased even to imagine the cold expanse beyond the hull.

So he shivered with the rest of them. When the wind flagged and returned to its normal station, the steady breeze swept away the fog. One by one, they sprouted from their black piles of leather and became men again. The snow climbed up one side of the ship in a drift, The slush was gone; the glass, the blue patchwork was gone; the jagged little floes, the rolling boulders, the yawning leads were gone. To land as well as sea, a single pack stretched beyond sight.

Coming out of the low sun, a black rock broke the surface a half mile north. But by now, Foster knew that at the poles where the laws of nature bend, everything awful and ordinary gains the power to transform. He pointed without a word, and they watched as it became an angotak.

Kjartke arrived at the edge of the false deck on the heels of the marines. A miner gasped his last in the bloody arms of his brothers. Her head jerked from side to side in vain, then fell on Ferrakut.

"Where is he?" She demanded.

Ferrakut and Ulwet snatched up two of the poles used for receiving the ship and strained to press it away at her feet. The other drivers hurried to help them. Men lined the edge and she followed their gaze at the water with the horror of understanding. Tunguk joined her as the deck separated from the buoys and the sea hissed at them from the gap.

"Brother!" She cried. One of the log buoys lifted and turned as the water lapped into the rock and receded. There he dangled, arms wrapped in a shivering embrace. The men started to reel in the buoy, but Milak shouted, "Stop! He will fall!"

"We must bring a line," the older cousin of the Vjarku boys said. "Who can swim?"

Not one of the Kammatuk spoke. Her father, or any man of her clan would have joined the water without hesitation. Any hunter of the northern clans—even Klimut, with half his strength—could manage it. These southern dogs were so long separated from the womb that birthed them that they feared it, and buried themselves in the mountains out of shame. Tunguk moved, but she stopped him. He would not come up again. The crowd parted, and several halots pushed to the fore. A man of the Navy from the *Orin's Thief* peeled his boots and tunic, took the rope, and stepped off the quay. The captain, Ghrane, went after him. Together, they fixed a rope so that the miners could haul Brother up.

He made many noises of complaint as he scraped over the quay. There, he shivered and snapped his teeth while the boys pulled off his wet clothing. When he noticed her, he became shy, and said, "I'm cold."

"You are always cold." She did not want to dirty him on a miner's shirt after his bath, so she had Ferrakut and Ulwet wrap him in a blanket from the cargo.

When Ghrane and the mate stood once more dripping before him, he said, "Thank you," then muttered the same to the boys, to the men, and became troubled as he saw he had so many who acted for him. Finally, he settled on Kjartke, and a strange look came over him. His throat moved, but no sound came. What passed between them left no need for a short word of gratitude. She did not want him to speak. The more she heard men say this, the more she knew there were other things they felt no thanks for.

A discomfort took her. She wanted to remain in sight, but spun for the ship to see to the hateful dogs.

"Let him sit," Senadak told the boys. "We have to unload." They left Parks in the care of Tunguk, or whatever semblance of it an old man could provide by stooping over him. Parks hadn't seen the old coot since they bailed on the meeting, and he looked a few years closer to death. His brow was stitched, and he shrunk in on himself more than usual. Wrapped in his blanket, reeling from the water, Parks' present state sparked his memory. He thought of the man they led home after a heart attack.

The whole scene gave him the sense he'd walked into a party after something dramatic that no one bothered to explain. A miner lay dead. Instead of rushing the gear off the ship, the others gathered around the wet sailors and the rest of the Navy from the ship. Several miners argued in spirited Mattakatan—they seemed to want the others to follow them, but only a tenth of them jogged off toward the mountain. The others discussed the crew of the ship, and without knowing a word of gibberish, Parks knew it wasn't about what kind of banquet to throw them.

"These men came with me. I didn't know of the marines, and I doubt they did, either," Ghrane defended in English.

"I vouch for these dudes. What's it called? 'Stand.' I stand for them. My boy Neal just saved my life, when every Navy fucker on Drummoc is trying to kill me."

"They are here for the ship," a miner challenged. "Haraket's ship."

"We're here under orders of Captain Polc. For the second time," Neal retorted. "To deliver a message of great importance from Farri Tolba to the assistant viceroy of Drummoc. Dock your ship in your arse and slaughter the marines, for all we care. Just let me shout a word to the man across a field and I'll be off."

Ostuk stepped forward. "He speaks true. I was captain when they first came. You won't recall, because all but a few were at the mines. As for now, it hardly matters. Haul in the darraig and fill it with coal baskets. Place a watch. They number only nine. These men can't steal your ship, but there will be more crossing the channel if they are harmed."

The debate broke into dozens of side-chats between little groups that little by little resigned themselves to the work on the dog ship. Ostuk looked Parks up and down.

"Sorry I keep fucking up your nautical journeys."

Ostuk smiled. "I rather enjoyed them. Anyhow, you and I have made our last. Costig is no fool. There is no return for us."

"Maybe we can get this big rod assistant viceroy hustler to go rattle his nuts for us. Show Costig what's up."

Ostuk made sure no other Mattaka stood nearby, then lowered his voice for Parks and Tunguk. "I'm not sure there is one."

"What do you mean, one what? An assistant viceroy?" Parks blinked.

"I'm certain there *was*. But no one has seen him or spoke to him. And I don't see what few navy supposedly remain. I have been here twice this season, and many times before. Only twice have I seen Mattaka carry on as they please."

Parks searched Tunguk for an answer.

"He means to say what man was here is sent to Urkuk. You will not meet the assistant viceroy, because there are six hundred of them."

A firm hand gripped him in the lamplight of the wigwam.

"Parks, can you hear me?"

"Hm."

"Parks. I need you to listen, brother." It was Foster. The wrath of a thousand hangovers rang in Parks' head. He came back, where something gnawed at his flesh, and his innards twisted. Back to the sense that this vessel that bore him could only be abandoned. There was nothing worth salvaging, and the only thing holding his spirit to it was the grip of his friend. He prayed it would fail.

"You have to remember this. Costig wants info on Camne Drumlag. You have to tell him this. Or actually, don't tell him. Not til he guarantees you the job."

He returned to the mines. Men handed supplies off the dog ship, and he could feel the weight in his arms. The memory of Foster's warning had stuck with him, and that, he also felt, along with the throbbing of an impression from the grip. He was supposed to tell Costig, before Tunguk got jumped. Supposed to pass along *something*. There were only a few dudes at the mine. A cave-in. Couldn't see the assistant viceroy.

It felt incomplete, and now he knew why. He heard Foster once more, when he clasped his palms together and squeezed.

"If you ask me, wasn't no one to see," the message returned to him. "They were actin' strange. Ostuk said it. I wouldn't be surprised if the assistant viceroy got smoked the minute he set foot in them mountains. Costig's worryin' himself over a ghost. The miners want him to believe there's still someone there. Don't tell him that part. Keep it to yourself, until you're there."

That much, Parks managed.

By the time the ship neared completion, a platoon of miners bounded down the mountain and mixed excitedly with the others. They turned around to hurry up again, and now a good portion of the camp abandoned their work to join them.

A quick baying snapped him back. Barbados Slim panted proudly in front of him, a gnawed leash dangling from his neck. Parks snatched it before he could bolt.

"Son of a bitch. Slim! I can't take you anywhere," he gripped the dog's snout and shook it playfully. He could hardly blame the guy.

"Can I let you in on a secret?" Slim closed his mouth and perked his ears. "I'm here to spy on the assistant viceroy," Parks put his finger to his lips. "Shh! And you know what? There might just be a way."

He flagged down one of the dog drivers.

"Excuse me! Can you bring me a sled, and a few more dogs? I need to speak with Senadak."

"I am Senadak," Senadak replied.

"Or—what's his name? *Sagalak!*"

The boys helped their cousin haul over a sled and fresh rope. Parks beckoned for a knife. He sliced the ragged tail off of Barbados Slim's leash, and paused for some memory he could not quite conjure, fascinated by the clean cut in the line. Working with difficulty under the unwieldy blanket, he tied a bend to fix Slim to the longer lead, then hitched it to the sled.

By the time the dog ships were hauled ashore, Parks rattled up the mountain gripping the sides of the deck. The dogs strained through snow that clung to the runners and bumped them along at a pace that allowed Tunguk and Kjartke to easily walk alongside. Ferrakut yanked this way and that to free them every few feet until the temperature dropped, the snow hardened, and the boy's heavy breath found its stride.

The mist soon snaked between them. Black rock sprouted from the snow like an unearthly forest, and spires only hinted at their height. The trail narrowed to single-track, and Parks saw the disturbed prints of the countless feet that pounded up ahead of them. They smoothed the work for the dogs, but they would only pull now if someone went ahead of them on the switchbacks. Ferrakut tied into snow shoes that none of the others enjoyed, and let Kjartke jerk them free when the dogs jammed a runner into a rock. The air grew thick enough to chew, like a cold drag from a pipe. Tunguk had to stop to rest, and warned them to do the same—if the marines came down this way, they would have nowhere to go.

But Ferrakut refused to halt the dogs. Senadak had cautioned him that they couldn't afford to be caught on the steep trail in the dark. The mountain seemed to glare at them like trespassers who couldn't be stopped, just yet. Despite the many tracks, Parks couldn't shake the feeling he plowed into some haunted wilderness where no man had tread.

The trail branched. Every way looked traveled, but they took the one packed down by the most dense traffic. Barbados Slim and Winnie Cooper clawed with the rest of the team, and Kjartke's whip snapped over Parks' head when they had second-thoughts.

When dusk settled, Parks' head clanged like hammers on rock. He imagined glowing mines, and the groan of men under heavy load. The dogs seemed to morph into Mattaka under the same whip. All the while he felt the imperative of silence. Not a silence of the team, but of the whole. Brave whispers, the silence of hope, of the human will, in the echoing walls of a prison where a sleeping vengeance waited for the stumble that would wake it.

Dark folded around them, and he felt the thin fright that he once felt at the well of the dead, except there, it poked at him, spat venom in his ear. Here, it carried on in ignorance, as though he existed outside the rhythms of the place, and that if he ever found them, ever found his welcome, he, too, would no longer believe that anywhere else was possible.

Just as he thought the mountain interminable and wondered how he might sleep on the sled, an orange haze broke over a ridge. The mist thinned to tatters. As the ground leveled, a bonfire caused him to squint. Shapes passed to and fro in front of it as it spewed black smoke. Voices sounded in alert, and several men came to see who it was, then wandered off disinterested. The dogs pulled for the fire, and Ferrakut stopped them as they pierced the edge of its warmth.

Two men carried a basket over and dumped its contents into the flame. It lurched above even Parks' head when Kjartke helped him to stand. Outlined in the fire, speaking busily to miner after miner, a familiar face smiled at him.

"Sagalak."

"Leopard Seal!" He excused himself. "Now you have met Camne Drumlag."

Parks stood transfixed. "I miss a good fire. This is probably the best one I've seen."

"It is not often we burn our labor. There was some trouble with the men. We must see them if they sneak back."

"The marines. Where'd they go?"

"Here. I saw them coming up the trail. Ran ahead to warn the Midshipmen."

"Midshipmen?"

"It is what the assistant viceroy calls his guard. Twenty-six men of the Navy. The marines came in strength, four sixes. No Mattaka would stop them. But the Midshipmen faced them here, where you see this fire. It looked to make a battle, but there was an archer. Marines do not use them— they think them shirkers. But this man gained the high ground," he pointed into the dark. "Forced them to retreat. They sent a squad to flank him, but then the people saw they broke numbers. It was five that left the main force. Neither was in sixes, so the people got their courage. We chased them into a mine, and they cannot come out, but we cannot go in. The squad has disappeared. So we light the camp, in case they return."

"Then they didn't find the assistant viceroy."

"No, thank the gods. I must apologize. With all that has happened, I have forgotten to announce your arrival."

"And these navy I keep hearing about, but never see…"

"They hold the entrance of the mine."

Parks nodded. "Convenient. I like this setup you got going. You guys are organized. Probably don't even need someone to tell you what to do. I bet this whole mine could run just as smooth—maybe better—if the Navy just left you alone."

"I think so," Sagalak granted.

"Only problem is Costig. He sends his goons over here because he thinks your leader is giving him trouble. How many did you say it was?"

"Twenty-four."

"Twenty-four. And how many do you think he would send if the miners revolted?" Sagalak grew still and waited for him to clarify. "If there were no officials or sailors here to watch things. How many would come? The whole Navy?"

The miner considered it. "Aye, perhaps. But we are no fools."

"I think you're a hell of a lot smarter than he gives you credit for. So what's the end game? You have to go home eventually, right? Then you come back next year. No chance they let you go alone."

Sagalak stared into the darkness as if he wanted no part of dealing with the question. "Alexicus is making plans. Many of us will winter. When the firestone ships come, we will make a new arrangement," he said confidently.

"You know I can't leave, either. Let me help you."

"How?"

"Letters. I can write, and read. We send messages, signed by this 'Alexicus.' Talk to them in ways that sound like one of my people is negotiating on your behalf. I'll give 'em the old riverboat hustle. They'll never suspect a thing. And your people get to rule themselves. I don't want the title. But I'll play the white man's game for you."

"Why can't the assistant viceroy do this, himself?" Sagalak said warily.

Parks took a hop forward and caught himself on the man's shoulder. "Because he doesn't exist." Several men had gathered, and they traded unspoken deliberations with Sagalak. Parks sensed the opening. "You smoked him as soon as the Navy turned their backs. Or heck, maybe he got a nasty cold, or fell off a cliff. But you and I both know that whoever may have presided over this camp has…moved on. What we've got is a classic *Weekend at Bernie's* situation. If anyone on Drummoc finds out he's dead, they'll storm the shore with every ship they've got. But as long as they think the assistant viceroy is the one who went off the reservation, your people are free to do as they please."

Sagalak laughed. He backed slowly around the fire, pulled aside the door flap of a wigwam and spoke a few words before returning to Parks.

"See for yourself."

The opening flared, and a man stepped out behind the fire. Parks squinted into the blaze as the figure worked its way around to stand silhouetted in the wavering heat, coal fumes pouring from his hood. He peeled the fur parka and handed it off, revealing a sooted tunic with intricate bead work like Parks had seen among the officials at Nunoc. He was clean-shaven, with a face reddened by a recent scrubbing of snow, and the stiff posture of one accustomed to puffing out his chest.

They stood off with one another as if waiting for the flickering shadows to finish the work of bringing them to life.

"When I heard about the exploits of the legendary Leopard Seal, I knew he would turn out to be a fraud."

"When *I* heard there was a guy who called himself the assistant viceroy, I knew he'd turn out to be a world-class douchebag," Parks retorted.

"Then I'm glad neither of us had to live through another disappointment."

Parks and Carabiner fell into a sobbing embrace.

11

BOARDED

Joy streamed their faces as they gasped with laughter. Parks squeezed with a strength he hadn't felt for some time, and found it matched. It didn't matter that it was Carabiner. He held on as to an artifact that surfaced impossibly and might slip away the next second. A solid body, a link to everything lost. It became everything, itself. The deck of the *Qarapara* and his entire naval career unfolded from his arms. Home, a common world, a grid of stars whirred to life. Here stood a memory unraveled long ago, strewn over the surfaces by wind until he gave it up as a lie. Now it stared back at him with a sheepish grin to confirm his place on the earth.

He couldn't let go for some time. This one presence seemed to forgive his every error. He thought and blundered the way he did because he was from a certain place, and it made sense there. None of it was his fault. That place was real. All anyone had to do was ask Carabiner.

Parks pushed away and sniffed.

"Never thought I'd be happy to see you. Quick: go away before it wears off." He held both of Carabiner's shoulders for balance. Carabiner raised a foot and swished it lazily across the knotted pant leg that dangled from Parks' knee.

"I guess we've got some catching up to do."

Sagalak beamed with excitement. "You know each other!" He proclaimed to the miners, and they hooted in celebration, as if their pride gained from it. A face moved into the perimeter, catching Parks' eye. Tunguk shuffled up haggard from the trail, unsure what to make of what he saw, but sensing the gravity.

"The second I landed, a hundred guys shook my hand. I didn't even wonder where they might have learned it."

Carabiner held up a finger and ran back into the wigwam, leaving Parks' to catch himself on Sagalak. After a minute, he reemerged shaking a piece of parchment bound with leather string.

"With everything that happened, I forgot all about this. Some guy came by a few weeks ago and wrote me a letter. Friends of Barzos, he said. How did I miss that? No one says 'friends,' here. It's all 'mates,' mate."

Tunguk approached and handed Parks a strand of beads that had slipped his memory more thoroughly than Carabiner's letter. He passed them over.

"That's our reference, in case you doubt we are who we say we are."

"We." Carabiner skimmed over the letter again. "*Foster*. Where is he?" Parks didn't immediately answer. "Alive?"

"It's complicated."

"You have no idea," Carabiner admitted.

"I love gossip. Sleepover?"

Carabiner tensed like a man yanked in two directions.

"Parks, nothing would make me happier than to roast a few marshmallows and swap sea tales," he gave an officer's assurance. "But right now, my guys have a bunch of hardened killers pinned down inside a mine, and more on the loose. It's me they're after, but I tell you, those boys set the line of scrimmage today. They stepped up in a big way. If I'm half the leader they deserve, I should put in an appearance with the Midshipmen. Get the debrief, take a first pass at a harebrained plan for just what the heck we're gonna do about the situation."

"Gayest name for an elite personal guard I've ever heard."

"You know, at the time, I didn't realize anyone would think twice about it. Hopefully, the *Leopard Seal* can forgive me." He winked. "In the meantime, where are my manners? Take a load off, bro! You must be exhausted. Sagalak! See to it these people receive my full hospitality."

"Sir, it is unwise to go to the mine now. We do not know where the other marines went."

"Normally, you know how I feel about that word—'unwise.' But in this case," he waved off Sagalak's apologetic stutter, "*In this case*, you're absolutely right. That said, what kind of leader would I be if I cowered here under a blanket while I asked unarmed miners to stand between me and my assassins? Let it be unwise that I'll take first watch."

"Aye, sir!"

He turned to Parks with exaggerated distress. Carabiner wrapped his arms around him, this time, in a more formal embrace. "No words. No words for what I'm feeling."

Parks nodded, and shooed him.

"…Before it wears off."

Marines spaced over the hollow like beads on strands, flinging snow aside. Every remaining man from Costig's company volunteered. The squain lad was sure of the place—a crease where the heights of the cliffs over the Calm Harbor folded down into the plain, coastward of the dog camp—but the recent storm smoothed the features. Costig wanted to dig himself, but already the shovels were taken, and spare planks put to service. A foreboding sky mentioned in passing that they might want to hurry if they didn't care to start again on a fresh blanket in a few days.

"Got 'em!" One of the men waved his comrades over, and they churned the spot inside out. Patches of black cloth, gray skin rose and connected until five marines lay exposed, stiff as ice. The company held tongue and temper, but the looks that fell on young Norwet were quietly ravenous. He kept his chin to his chest as he had since they arrived.

There was no prison for him yet. The work of clearing the loose walls to return it to a single cell had yet to find priority. Wherever he stayed, it wouldn't be long. Costig ached for the lad, swept into these affairs like the Leopard Seal ahead of an admiral's clever notions—but he ached more for his marines.

"Take 'em to Gjoraslag. Build a cairn, higher than Turrha's. Send for me when it's done." He placed a hand on the lad's arm, and felt no resistance.

"*Heave! Ho! Heave! Ho! Heave! Ho!*"

With every other word, Foster and half the starboard benches pulled on their ropes. The ice gave no footing, and they slipped as they yanked. Steel chinked at the ice around her hull on both sides, and if Gionn and the port pulled their ropes, too, they were just as effective as Foster. The *Gairhle* remained fast.

Corm moved them in shifts between hacking at the floe and trying to rock her free. A shallow trench stretched the length of the ship without hitting water or loosening the grip of the floe.

"Grit your teeth and clench your arse, you bastards!" Corm threatened. "Or you'll swim in Spring what you can't walk in Winter!"

Foster didn't need anyone to tell him it was bleak, but the odd comments he overheard confirmed it. When he stepped out onto the ice for the first time, he had the sense of coming onto land. The act felt like an arrival. Now the captain nearly admitted it in his threats. They were breaking her free to avoid being crushed by the ice. The *Gairhle* would rest on top. There was no more chipping from within the ship, or forcing a free lane with the prow. This was to be their home.

The activity remained too frantic for anyone to experience the full repercussion of that dawning fact. No Taclann, or riches. No safe harbor. He knew they must have denied it, or there would have been a general collapse. After all these men did to get free, Foster expected some heave of desperation.

So far, they hacked and pulled. Maybe there wasn't peace-enough for it, yet—let alone for his own celebration. Barring a miracle, he had won by no heroism of his own. It gave him no pleasure. He couldn't even be happy for Parks.

"Water!" Someone on the port-side exclaimed. They attacked with renewed vigor, and the cry began to pop off all around as they separated the ship from the floe.

"*Heave!*" Starboard collapsed backward on their ropes. "*Ho! Heave!*" By the end of the round, the vessel tipped a few inches. Corm didn't bother to swap the duties. He started up another call without rest. The *Gairhle* creaked over, then sprung back the other way.

"Run her up!" The men rushed for the oars, already reversed in the locks, and pushed with all they had. But time and again, she stuck against the lip of the ice. Corm gave the order to unload, and they scurried aboard to hand down whatever they could lift. Personal belongings were strewn like bodies over the side. The spare sail passed in a dozen pairs of hands. Finally, the barrels were broken free where they'd iced to the deck and hoisted from a block over the boom while the idle bodies fought to keep her free. When the ship neared empty, they returned to the ice, and in a gasp, ran her keel on top. With nothing to support the ship, they had to clear the oars and lower her unceremoniously onto her side.

A few congratulations passed among the exhausted crew. They would at least have something to sail if they made the spring. Foster couldn't share in it. If anything, he felt guilt despite having no part in their predicament.

It was ice. Ice, as far as the eye could see. He squinted against the glare. A light breeze sifted plumes of powder by their feet. To one side, he reckoned, lay land. To the other, open water. But the only marker that broke the frozen plain lie a half-mile off.

Close enough that Foster could make out bodies milling around it. Their mast was already down. He couldn't see enough of the keel to know if they'd gotten out as well, but she didn't seem to be flopped over like the *Gairhle*.

"Guests arrivin'!" Jenneker sounded from his stance atop the gunwale. "Four," he looked dead at Foster, as if to bask in his mathematical prowess. Corm and Eckerd stopped working to take a look. Foster couldn't imagine they were coming by to borrow a cup of sugar.

"Get that mast down. Rest of you, circle the barrels around the open side. Pile what you can, and man the wall!"

The *Gairhle's* hull lay to the angotaks. Sailors hurried to form a defensive line of gear on the opposite side, with their backs to the benches.

"It is just four," Tamarqan attempted to stall the rush. "Surely they will stop short to scout."

"Could be too eager to wait for their mates. Angotaks are mad enough to try it." Gionn warned.

"Four against more than fifty?" Tamarqan said, incredulous.

"Go and greet them if you like. I'm sure they'll be relieved to hear you're an officer of the Amposi Navy," Corm spat. "The rest of you, battle line!"

Tamarqan fell into tilting barrels as fast as anyone. There weren't even enough for a waist-high wall that covered half the open side. It felt more like a stall for livestock than a fortress. They crowded in, with only Jenneker up top able to see their visitors' progress. Foster clutched his stone spear. Atalkut held a stone knife, while Tunguk had gathered broken bits of ballast rock into the tail of his coat.

"Who are they?" Foster asked.

"Amposi service, though you'll hardly find a son of Ampos among 'em," Gionn explained.

"Whalers hunt merchants. Angotaks hunt whalers," Bentos put it simply.

"Then they're some kind of navy? I guess what I'm askin' is what's the difference between them and fuckin' Chirim?"

Bentos snorted.

"We haven't time to recite you the annals, cunt, but I'd hang back from the fight if I were you. Or me," Gionn added.

"Full kit!" Jenneker warned from above. "Short spear, sword and shield."

"Bows?" Corm challenged.

The lookout paused to assess. "No."

"Captain, we have two archers among your navy recruits," Palqua suggested. "Shall I send them up?"

"They'll just dance off with our arrows. Put what shields we have in the hands of your best. Your lads hold the gap. Eckerd, whalers to the wall. The rest of you, fill as they fall." Corm waved them into position. Palqua hurried his men to seal the opening where they'd most likely be assaulted. Even in the teeth of an attack, these two were still duking it out, Foster thought.

"Number cunt!" Corm caught him. "Cower in the ship. I haven't given up on findin' a use for you. Bucket squains, Gionn: see that no one scratches me scholar." He slung Foster to the boards, where he climbed into the side-lying vessel with embarrassment. His privileged status earned him no affection from the crew. It also served to remind him that he lost all value without the spoils of Taclann to tally. Whether Corm had another purpose for him, or just didn't want to demoralize his men before a fight by admitting that dream had sailed, he couldn't say.

With that, the captain climbed up to join Jenneker.

No one so much as whispered within the little corral. Foster's torso ran with chills that snapped out through his fingers. He hoped no one would turn to see him shaking. A glance at some of Palqua's sailors reassured him that he wasn't alone.

"Just the two of us," Corm said so casually that Foster thought he spoke to Jenneker. A pang shot through his stomach when the captain added, "The rest are beneath the ice. Show us mercy and we'll make your palms heavy."

The hull muffled a response from the angotaks.

Corm dropped down into the ranks of whalers. "Comin' around aft to draw our arrows. Hold your ground, lads. Make 'em reach if they want it." He pushed to the wall just behind Eckerd, eager for a test. Palqua, Foster noticed, also stood in the first line with his men—Foster couldn't help but feel because Corm's courage forced it.

The sight of someone rounding the corner made him sick. Four filthy little men sauntered into view ten yards off the wall, each a steel spear in hand and a round wooden shield dangling lazily at the hip. They loped with space between them the length of the barricade and continued around as if to turn into the gap, but didn't.

"Still clear," Jenneker confirmed the lack of reinforcements on the field.

"Hold!" Corm repeated.

The angotaks looked no different than any other whaler. A mixed lot, all of them smaller than Foster's former 165-pound frame, though he figured he had withered to their level on this voyage. Yet they all wore the aura of reputation. He twisted their unassuming features and exaggerated the hard lines until the men who stood across from them radiated with might. He'd granted the same transformation to Moipa after their tussle. It had the effect of diminishing his own stature to swell the others'.

They circled back toward the wall. The angotaks exchanged a look, then screamed as they charged the line of barrels. Shields cracked against the staves. The whalers leaned their hips into the provisions to keep them from tumbling. Spears thudded against the wood and pressed them back. The last angotak to arrive jumped and placed his foot on a barrel. He shrugged off a thrust with his shield as he pushed back from his leg, toppling the section inward. Corm snatched the collar of Pitras, nearest the new gap.

"Hold!"

The angotaks stepped back just out of spear range and stood like neighbors who'd come over to the fence for a chat. Pitras wrestled the barrel back into place while they laughed.

"Hold is good advice," one of them said in a voice that was wasn't as deep and snarling as Foster hoped. "While you can." He lunged forward and slapped his spear across the row of protruding weapons. The others stepped in to swat at the blades and back off.

"Don't you dare attack us, you wilted cunts!" They taunted.

The shortest of them, a man of maybe 5'2, walked around to face Palqua's line. "Have a go at these! If I stand here long enough, they'll rattle themselves to death!"

"Hold!" Came the captain's chorus.

"Hold!" An angotak repeated.

"Hold!" Said another.

"Come over when your tongues tire, loud cunts!" Gionn cupped his hands.

"Hoy! The one hidin' in the back offers his hospitality!"

"That's the clever one from before, the red one. Make a lane, and leave him for me," he told his comrades.

"Shut your fuckin' mouth, idiot, idiot cunt," Foster heard Gionn mutter to himself.

One of them darted in again to draw tense thrusts of the spears along the battlement. This time, he didn't bother to raise his shield, instead leaning back just out of range.

"We'll be right back, mates," the angotaks announced. "I'd say we'll need four more." They stood off, and Foster could hardly believe that a mortal enemy could relax yards away with impunity. Apparently, he was not alone. One of the Amposi sailors raised a bow and fired. The target jerked up his shield and the arrow snapped into the wood.

Corm wheeled and threw the archer to the ice. "I said *hold*, and the next one who donates an arrow, I'll garrote with his bowstring."

The angotak admired his catch while they strolled off to their ship.

Costig stepped out into the hall and pulled the door to his quarters behind him. He braced the load in his arms that he could turn the key. The bolt set. He rearranged the armor—his cuirass and helmet, vambraces and greaves, in a pile under his left arm. By his right, he bore his spear while two fingers clutched the end of a thin sack that held the rest of his things.

The room was full by now, and lamps flickered on the tables. He did not mark the quiet until he settled his load and faced the men. Every head fixed on him. The captains stood at the fore. The appearance of an admiral in the hall was no occasion for reverence. He should have to shout for their attention. His instinct searched and settled on the notion that word of his five marines had reached them. The show of respect warmed him.

"At your ease, lads," he nodded them back to their meals.

No one took it. Wendell appeared at center, blushing. Just above the sincerity of that ever-present smile, his brow arced in the middle and ran off in slopes of sadness. He spoke with difficulty.

"I'm sorry you couldn't hear it from me." Wendell verged on tearful.

"Hear what?"

Confusion passed between the marine and the captains around him. Costig tightened his arms around his gear unthinkingly. He spotted Gua in the crowd, but soon realized there were no other marines in the hall. No bowls out for the men. His body staggered from the blow before it occurred to him.

"Movin' out?" Folmon asked.

"Aye. For a night or two."

A sigh escaped Wendell, not of relief, but of a man who's confirmed the worst of his expectations. Costig seized with the strange feeling of knowing something was terribly wrong but being unable to name it.

"Mate." Wendell stepped forward with heavy feet and clasped his hat before him. "I've been asked to speak on behalf of the lads." He paused, as if hoping Costig would guess his intention, that he might not have to say it. "I know no other name but yours—in all of Hiade, on any deck in the kingdom, none but yours I'd name to stand before me company. I'd board any vessel, man any wall you could point at. I think we all agree that whatever fleet we face, there's none better to lead the van when they rush ashore."

Costig's lip quivered, because he knew his mate spoke his truest heart, as well as he knew what must follow.

"You're a marine's marine. We won't cut it without you. As for the colony, I don't wish to speak ill of past and future commissions, but we all know there's a certain spectacle to the job unbecomin' a spear-straight man. Chores and personalities that sap the vital force. I'm sure you'd agree that listenin' to squains gripe of booze and omens is an undue burden for a man facin' the navies of Donnab with a winter garrison." Wendell waited for some sign of acknowledgment that never came. "With all the madness here—two admirals desertin', criminals on the loose—it would bring the lads a much-needed comfort if they knew you were focused on the marines, and meetin' what sails for us even now."

Costig lowered his things gently to the floor but kept his spear. His eyes burned and his skin stiffened. A tear betrayed him as he faced the room, and he resented that they drew it like the first nick in a fight.

"Is it mutiny, then?" He replied gruffly.

"Mut—*gods*, no, Costig!" Wendell looked around for support in his exasperation. "It was always a temporary arrangement. Much as I admire it, we both know that as soon as the admiralty in Ampos got wind of a marine—soon as the viceroy in Nunoc heard, even—well, you couldn't have expected much, even if you sent Donnab back drippin'."

"Of the admiralty, I expected very little." He glared at his mate.

"I've done as you've asked me, and I will again tomorrow," Wendell promised.

"Mostly. Is this why you hung back from the huntin' camp?"

"Costig, please. I'd rather be first over the boards against the stoutest vessel than have this chat with you."

"And on what grounds? Would you have me say it? Aye, I botched it! A bastard of the mangiest breed escaped me. A man who couldn't lick a squain lad, or steal a pinch from a bucket, a man of no importance has roused the colony on a false reputation because I missed him. He'll see himself off soon enough if me lads don't already have him. I've already taken his conspirators. The squains'll forget him before the sun goes down. You want me to pay for that? Pass by Gjoraslag. I've suffered me error more than most, and there's a cairn to remind me why it'll never be enough. If those lads asked me to fall on me spear, I'd have done it already.

"But you lot! You can only see what's before you. Believe me, there's more to this command than an ambitious captain can fathom. You've lost yourself in that spectacle. You see a fugitive instead of a war. You see the thrusts gone wide and not the ones that found blood. Or you see a title, and a job. Not the service of a sacred thing.

"Aye, the admiralty can remove me. Which of you here holds that rank? When a junior officer stands to his superior, I call it the only word that suits it: mutiny."

Several of the captains sneered off his remarks. Wendell took the sting, and in a voice as composed as it was meek, he asked, "Will you be returnin' the argots?"

Costig laughed to himself. "You, then. I knew Willakuy hadn't the bollocks to broach it on his own." He noticed now that none of the officials were present, either.

"What word does the admiralty use for lightenin' the treasury?" Folmon challenged.

Costig ignored him with difficulty. "Aye. I *will* be returnin' them."

"When?" Folmon pressed. "Have you got them now?" The room hung on his answer.

"No." Murmurs spread. "They're currently engaged in the betterment of our defenses. But I'll have 'em soon."

"I don't understand," Wendell said. "Are they spent, or will they be returned?"

Costig realized his error: he'd intended to pass off the assistant viceroy's purse as the missing coin and blame him for the discrepancy.

"Secrets of the farri. Had you asked me man-to-man, I'd have been happy to discuss it somewhere other than a crowded hall." Costig stalked over to Wendell. "Tell me, mate: of all the admirals you've endured without treason, am I truly the worst?"

He didn't wait for an answer. Costig marched across the assembly to his fellow sergeant-at-arms. "Gua! Will you stand for this mutiny?"

"It's no mutiny, Costig."

"I know you're insulted. It's an obscenity," Wendell raised his voice to deflect from Gua. "No man should thank us for it. I had hoped you'd see the compromise, though. You're asked to step down voluntarily. To resume the duties you love, at which you're unexcelled. You'll still be in charge of the defenses on land."

Costig made his way back toward Wendell, but stopped short at the captains beside him.

"And if I refuse?" He tightened the curtain of mustache, daring a commitment. Of the hundreds opposite him, none found his voice.

Costig lay torn between the defense of his command, and repulsion at the thought that he would have to go on serving these rot-snout blaggards. "Who among you fancies himself admiral?"

"It hasn't been decided." There was a note of exhaustion in Wendell's response.

"It has." Now Aymos spoke. "Bayochar will be Admiral of Sea, and all affairs related to sail and oar. Folmon will be Admiral of Land. He'll tend to the colony and the coal."

Wendell slackened. He appeared to plead at Costig, but his jaw moved helplessly.

"I don't recall the Marines being asked to stand," Gua protested.

"They weren't." The sailors behind Bayochar delighted in the memory. "The Marines had their opportunity. Once per mistake, I tell the lads," the captain of Ampos preened.

"Sergeant-at-arms!" Folmon addressed Costig sharply. "Turn over the key to the admiral's quarters. I'll grant you leave of your senses for the night, owin' to the shock. At dawn tomorrow—and from here out—you'll report to me. I'll be eager to work on your proposals for the siege preparations."

"This is not what we discussed!" Wendell complained timidly.

"Aye, it's one thing to discuss a course, but the doin' often requires a different tack." Folmon said with no great regret. "Of course, if he intends to remain a free marine, he'll find those argots soon enough."

Costig shook with rage. To hide it was futile, so he wasted no effort. His veins burned with the venom of battle. Beads of sweat singed his cheeks on their way into his whiskers. He gripped his spear as in a storm that howled around him, and yet another stood—a man within himself. That one watched the gale and felt it swirl, but remained unmoved. He begged the other wait. From the storm's eye, he let it lash them both because it could not whip forever. He could not even see Folmon, so narrow was his vision, but whatever Folmon saw of him detained the captain. At last, Costig turned to Wendell. The loose skin of his neck pressed into the throat as he lowered his eyes like a man who won't beg for mercy.

The clouds and the bolts rumbled into the distance. His grip loosed from the spear. Costig opened and closed the stiff fingers, then fished the key and placed it in Folmon's hand. He gathered up the armor and the sack at his feet, and thus routed, stumbled through the heavy door of the hall.

Norwet didn't know what sounds to expect. He'd never been in such a place. But though he could only find a word here or there, the strife was unmistakable. His ear was still pressed to the door of the admiral's quarter's when it flung open.

He froze in the face of the officers. They regarded the room, stripped bare, and frowned at the unlikely boy.

"Who the fuck are you?"

"I am…" He hesitated before saying his name. "Prisoner. Of the admiral. The cell is not ready, so he keeps me here."

"A fine arrangement for a thievin' squain!" The tall man said. "Whatever you did—don't do it again." The man slung him out and pressed a boot into his bottom to guide him. "Fuck off!"

Assistant Viceroy Carabiner woke, by habit, well before dawn. He met the urge to sink back into the warm sleeping bag with a vigorous scalp massage, and several rough tugs of his cheeks. As the dread of the cold settled into the pit of his stomach, he took quick shallow breaths and discharged them forcefully, "*Hee-hooooo, hee-hooooo,*" counting them down from ten in his head. With the last, he kicked himself free of the warm blankets as if he'd discovered their betrayal, snatched up the sleeping bag, and crawled with undue haste out of the tukit.

Carabiner marched in place to wake the blood in his toes while he snapped the stiff bag, turned it inside out, and hung it on a line to dry.

"Morning Ratjuk," he greeted a graying man with a lame foot who sat whetting a knife. "Morning, gentlemen!" He called to the wider line of men he could not see, but knew had waited on his perimeter all night in their blankets.

"Good morning, sir!" Someone replied. The others shifted restlessly. They knew before long he would rouse them for good.

The embers of the coal fire blinked in the breeze that slid down out of the mountains of Camne Drumlag. The hollow whip down the pass and the moan below told him the boys at the harbor were getting all they could handle. Carabiner didn't dare approach the coals. There would be no coming back from the temptation of their heat.

"I rise to all occasions. I rise to all occasions. I rise to all occasions," he affirmed under his breath for a ten count.

After another pass through his hyperventilations, he peeled the fur seal parka, followed by the supple baby seal coat he wore fur-side in, and finally his tunic. Carabiner dashed into the snow and flailed through his calisthenics. Premonitions of death faded to chattering teeth, and by the time he dropped his bare chest to the ground to begin his burpees, the cold fell around him in a failed assault, leaving him the mightiest being astride the southern continent.

The dark stood watch for him as he dropped his pants in layers. He threw himself on the ground and rolled in the snow. A quick pass of his hands brushed the powder over his bare skin, then he raced back into his garments. Carabiner scooped a pinch of snow, well away from his wallow, and gargled it before scrubbing his forefinger across every surface of his teeth.

Ratjuk handed him the blade as he returned. With throbbing fingers, he felt the stiff new whiskers along his neck and guided the edge over every rough spot until the skin was smooth and raw. A two-handed scoop of snow stung his face for the brief wash. With needles forming in his veins, he teased out his hair until it hung just atop his ear, curled just onto his neck, and shortened it by a flick of the blade.

The stars began to sink into astronomical dawn. Carabiner found the elegant strand of Amposi beads the viceroy had given him on the ship. He genuflected and gripped the first, muttered the Apostles' Creed, then moved through an Our Father and three Hail Marys. The beads never felt right for the full thing—a particular inertia never let him go farther. Instead, he slipped the necklace over his head, took the sides in either hand, and finished with the prayer to Saint Christopher that he'd composed for himself before he left for Annapolis.

"Saint Christopher the Christ-bearer, faithful giant, lift up this sailor o'er the waves, and set me gently on the golden streets the Lord hath paved. Amen."

Once his fingers thawed in his mittens, he took his breakfast among the Dawn Council—his trusted advisers—along with Ratjuk and an old man who had arrived with Parks and couldn't sleep. Though no Mattaka had ever tried it, he reminded them for the sake of the newcomer that no business was to be discussed until everyone had finished their meals. Haraket had returned by now, and it was Carabiner who had to exercise his will to feign indifference toward the recent events at the harbor. The elderly guest ate a meager portion but it took him twice as long as the others to gnaw at each piece of blubber. Carabiner forced a warm smile for the duration, then called the council to order.

"Edrasut, go for weather. How about some good news, my friend?"

Edrasut shrugged. "Autumn. There will be not so much light. More cold."

"Fantastic. Anything on the fog report? Are we just socked in? No, nothing? Fair enough, keep those eyes skyward and let me know if anything changes. Haraket, you're a go for harbor."

The infamous ship thief knew what his superior wanted, and he did not disappoint. Carabiner lavished in every detail of the pilot voyage, the arrival of the *Orin's Thief* and *Juhketappat*, and the heartbreaking murder of a man who was only just rescued from the mine cave-in after a harrowing burial. He noted with interest the crew of halots lurking harborside and the measures to prevent them from stealing back the darraig. There was even a dramatic rescue of one Leopard Seal, dunked into the sea to spare him the marines' charge. Haraket was a rare breed in any rank, and Carabiner had to restrain himself from showering the man with praises. Ego was the besmircher of talent. Where he inflated the miserable, he preferred to discourage the excellent.

"I'm sure I don't need to tell you that those keels stay high and dry unless I say otherwise. Did you bring their admiralty letters?" Haraket handed them over. "My man," Carabiner allowed. He tried again: "And do we have an inventory of the dogs and the sleds? All the provisions landed?"

"The dog men may know."

Carabiner smiled as though trying to hide his disappointment. "Do you mind following up on that for me?"

Haraket nodded with embarrassment.

"Sooner rather than later?" Carabiner qualified. The man cleared his throat and excused himself from the council.

"Provisions! Perfect segue. Nutillen-Amalset," he executed the full name to perfection.

"I did not count, sir," he reported his some hesitance after Haraket was sent away.

"Don't sweat it, *akjuru*," he settled Amalset with the Mattaka word of endearment among male friends.

"One month. Two if we don't mind so much being hungry. We must hunt before the light goes."

"Arrange a party."

"Sir, the weapons we have from the Midshipmen are few, and not for hunting."

"Can we fish?"

"I will tell the men to braid lines. But we need good spears. Perhaps we can club penguins with our tools, but we must go to the hunting grounds of Drummoc." Amalset did not seem to think highly of the proposition.

"I hear you. Go ahead and braid that line. See what that gets us. I'll get back to you on the penguins."

Satletaluk filled him in on the open mines—only a pair, and yielding poorly. An unusually low number of bushels lay ready for the dogs to haul down, due in part to the 'firestone that hears our hammers and hides deeper each season,' but largely to the bouts of inactivity surrounding Carabiner's presence, which Satletaluk tactfully failed to suggest.

The only new injury to report was the death of the miner at the hands of the marines, though Utrupanuk mentioned that the emotional status of the workers was happy and full of excitement. Sagalak had no news of Drummoc. Carabiner started to ask Attibatbarak for a rare report on guests and hospitality, but instead, turned to the new face in the circle, grooved and unmoving as the range on which they sat.

"Please accept my apology for my unforgivable rudeness. I didn't catch your name, Grandfather."

He seemed to wake from a trance. "I am called Tunguk. My father is Akawake. Perhaps also Kurrhatet and Oset. We will see. My uncles are Wakanat and Hawe, Uppinikuanatuk and Piktuk, Junnlauk and Gunnlauk. And Tannawauk," he finished as though uncertain whether he had remembered everyone.

"He is from the north," Satletaluk remarked. "What clan?"

"Tunguk," the old man repeated his name.

"Tunguk," Carabiner granted him every man's reward, the sound of his own name. "Welcome to Camne Drumlag. I trust my men have given you everything you need?"

"Yes."

It had been so long since he'd heard anything but "aye, sir," that the response charmed Carabiner. "Excellent. I owe you an immeasurable debt. My buddy Parks, he's not the kind of guy who can take care of himself in a place like this. I have a feeling you're guilty of aiding and abetting the Leopard Seal." Tunguk smiled blankly. "That's a joke. Soon as things settle down, you and me. Cup of hot water. Have you ever had hot water? In this climate, nothing will restore your humanity faster. The purest mineral snow, that burning finish—subtle notes of charcoal. *Mm!* I can't wait to show you." He leaned in to exaggerate a whisper. "That leg! My god, I'm dying to know." He shivered with excitement, and quickly redirected to Sagalak.

"Just as soon as we deal with our *other* guests. Sagalak, any developments on the hospitality front since I left last night?"

"No, sir. They remain in the mine."

"*Ah!*" Carabiner held up a finger. "Always start with the greatest threat. That's the one we need to act on first. What about the five men who escaped?"

"I don't know, sir. We will search again when the light comes higher."

"Organize the parties. Twenty-four men to each. Don't engage, just find them and fix them. I don't want some hero with a hammer getting himself killed for no reason. Gentlemen! As always, it is my pleasure to share in your wisdom. Today, I leave you with this thought to contemplate while you go about your duties: Be noble to all you meet, from the mightiest king to the most pitiful scoundrel. Because you never know who you may one day call a friend, or when he'll turn up in the unlikeliest place."

He nodded to Tunguk and adjourned the council.

When the first rays broke in the east, he opened his parka to rub clean the beads on his Amposi dress. The leather itself was long ago lost to the coal dust that filmed every surface and muddied the snow. These, at least, he could maintain with a semblance of pride, though the ones of undyed bone dimmed little by little. He drew his knife and trimmed the flags from his seams, then raised it to catch the light. The bright new steel had grayed even through its daily polish, but there wasn't a spot of rust. In his dim reflection, Carabiner twisted the blade until he was sure: a black streak on his jawline. He cursed at having missed it, dipped his hand into the clean snow of a nearby bank, and scrubbed. The miners had forfeited that battle. Their skin was so uniformly dark he often thought it was the color of their race until some visitor reminded him otherwise. No doubt Parks would smear himself soon enough. It wasn't about hygiene, though. He knew what he believed, and what he needed to keep believing.

His stomach rustled with excitement as he neared the last act of his long morning ritual. Carabiner untied the square leather pouch on his hip and lifted a smaller piece of fur from a young seal, hair-side inward. He set it on a clean blanket and carefully unfolded it. Checking his fingers for soot and moisture, he removed the parchment and stretched out its soft creases as delicately as he could, until the entire map unfurled before him. The world sprawled out beneath the crisscross of wind roses, its landmasses bulbous and warped. A pair of dragons guarded the poles, the southern one dark and winged, the northern, clear and slithering. Ships and beasts plied the waters. On the shores, colorful pictures spread rumors of the people and goods of every coast. A slender mass jutted up from the bottom, overlain with a naked woman stretching her hand the length of the peninsula. She came short of a twin, just the other side, whose figure draped across the horn of South America and stopped at the turbid waters between.

Carabiner traced the top-heavy continent to vague islands near the equator and the leg of Florida. No other part of the United States was recognizable. He swerved up the hatched coast far enough that it could have been Maryland, and planted his finger.

Then folded it carefully and returned it to its home on his hip.

Eight sailors stepped out of the navy hall at arms and paused to chat. Costig noted them without breaking stride. Amid the bile of his parting, he hadn't left with a destination but now realized he turned toward the marine barracks out of habit, though he hadn't slept there for some time. The discussion on the steps broke. Four of the men—he couldn't make out whose from this distance—ducked into town, while the other four strolled over his trail.

He'd agreed to nothing. Whether the captains thought they got away with it was anyone's guess. In the moment he stomped out, Costig was far from sure they hadn't. What could he do in the teeth of the entire garrison? The marine in him made several suggestions, but he steeled himself against a foolhardy outburst. He trembled from the thunder of a ram that appears broadside in the churn of battle, the flat crack of wood and everyone thrown from their feet. There was no doubt the captains were restless. He dressed himself down for not grasping the extent.

If they kept the Marines out of the hall, most of the lads would be at the barracks, except his company raising the cairn. Whatever Gua thought—and it wasn't clear—the spears would find their patience tried by a navy plot. Would Obrachar be there to reassure them? Had they been informed already by their sergeants-at-arms, he might get little more than a word of consolation and a "Welcome home."

Nothing upsetting about a few sailors out from the hall. They had to turn one of two ways. None of it eased his gut, though, and the prophet of doom in him whispered that those other four meant to head him off before he could reach the barracks. Why? He was demoted, they claimed. Had they wanted to arrest him, they could have done it when they outnumbered him by hundreds.

Costig hastened while a fresh flurry dotted his armload of belongings white. His feet knew his destination a moment before they reported it: Gjoraslag, and the remaining twenty-one of his own company.

"Good evening, Admiral!" Gerachay hailed him, and started over. "Looks a nasty turn, doesn't it?" He remarked on the brooding sky.

This one didn't know. Costig saluted and hurried past, to the surprise of his loyal aide. He used the opportunity to steal a look over his shoulder, and found the sailors had hastened their pace to match.

The burial grounds of Gjoraslag lie northwest of town, a sharp turn at the harbor then uphill until the cliffs offered a vantage of the sea. It was the first place a weary ship could find a sign of the imminent harbor when the fog allowed it. There, the esteemed dead kept watch in their strongholds of piled stone.

The hardened leather was light, but its bulk and dangling straps conspired with his sleeping sack to slow his progress. "Advance light, retreat lighter. Only the victor earns a burden," he was fond of advising his men.

With each alley, he searched for a flash of running feet. Whatever he did, he needed to do it before the parties linked up again. They'd come too far for innocent purposes—these sailors behind him could only mean to overtake him. Four or eight, it hardly mattered. He should drop and run.

When his gear hit the snow, a resolve swept him. His body did not recognize the order, so it fell back on a familiar sequence. Costig slung his cuirass across his chest and turned to face his pursuers. They broke into a run. He stretched his stout arms as far around his side as he could to tie in, and would have cursed one of his men for knotting it so loosely. There was no time for a remedy. The round helmet cupped his head and the straps cinched against the top of his throat. The vambraces and greaves would only slow him. He scooped up his spear and sack and abandoned the rest of his armor.

The foaming snow squeaked underfoot. If they gained when he made the turn, he commanded himself to leave the sack, as well. Costig huffed his cadence to hold his composure. Shouts leapt up behind him. Only the dread of exposure kept the sack bouncing on his shoulder.

"Bayan, warra, hula, basda," he huffed in Amposi. His boots struck on every beat, twice per word, and a pause of equal length before repeating. There was no faster cadence than an open run, but Costig knew that in the snow, with a brutal hill forthcoming, he couldn't risk it.

The harbor reached out to meet him—the same place he waited for the Leopard Seal. He bent around the buildings, and saw the sailors had gained considerably, but already faltered under the sprint. He kept his sack. The narrow line between town and the coast reared up ahead.

A man stumbled out from the huts clutching a spear. He saw Costig approaching, and slowed himself into position on weary legs. Soon, another broke the town, and a third, with the last surely soon to follow. Costig veered toward the coast as much as he could, forcing the early arrival to resume his run. He saw the last emerge, and marked the line reeling to intercept him. The lead man blocked the path and urged the others on. He raised his spear, a steel point, and just longer than Costig's. The lad wore no armor, only his coat. The other closed just yards away.

"Halt!"

Costig did as he warned his marines never to do, and launched his last spear when he was still several strides off. The unexpected missile caught the lad in the left chest and staggered him. His weapon dipped. Costig grabbed the shaft as he passed and tore it free. The others fell in pursuit behind him, but they'd outrun themselves. Costig allowed himself to slow to half the cadence. They gained within a throw. He braced for a strike on his back.

"Bayan, warra, hula, basda," he timed his footfalls. When he could no longer maintain even that, he turned to face his pursuers, and found them gathered at their dying mate far downhill.

Snow marked the level holds up the backside of the outcrop against the steep black rock. They lay so many and so near that it rose as the steps of a high building. Tunguk swiped the loosest deposit from each before he went. A younger man might have run up without fear. It was the simple tasks that worried him—he would not fall when it mattered. But there were not many falls left in him, Tunguk supposed.

"It is a difficult shot," he remarked to the archer as he summited.

"By fuckin' *Euskus*, old man, you nearly upended me." The young sailor clutched his chest in surprise. Tunguk peeked over the edge, twenty feet to the ground. This man probably did not worry as much about such things.

"Fifty yards to the narrows." A pair of sharply slanting walls pitched like the roots of a wet tree on either side of a crease. In the middle, a dark patch gaped. "Twenty more to the entrance."

"I can make a hundred if I need. That's why they put me here. Why the fuck are *you* here?"

"I go where no one stops me."

The archer sniffed at him and returned his drooping eyes to the mine. On the field between them, twelve tukits spoke of hasty assembly. An uneven line of Mattaka pressed around the gate to the narrows, twelve sixes in all, as brave with their digging tools as the twenty-six sailors in the van with their steel points. In the rear, the assistant viceroy passed orders with much assurance among the escort that guarded his journey to the mine. Several of the Dawn Council attended him. He leaned forward and placed his palm in front of him, as if resting on a table, though nothing was beneath it. The others rested their hands on top of his in the same manner. The commander gave three low grunts that Tunguk could not hear, then the entire body shouted, "*Firestone!*" And threw their hands in the air.

They broke in many directions. Sparks showered a bowl where two men struck flint. The others brought up a basket of firestone between them and dumped half of its contents on the snow. When the bowl was lit, they placed it carefully in the basket, and many hands piled the coal around it and on top. Black smoke appeared, and soon billowed. They hurried their efforts when a red glow pulsed over the top. As the last of the firestone was replaced, the basket growled with an angry fire.

The men who lifted it had to turn their faces from the flame. The Mattaka rear guard parted. Several of the navy advanced with spears at ready while the fire bearers hid behind the van. No marines showed themselves for the archer. When the sailors came close, they, too, parted. The miners ran forward and tried to hurl the fire into the opening.

It spilled over the entrance. The basket stopped short, and several coals rolled into the dark. The fire spread to the container and no coal remained unlit. A flame licked above the mine while a plume climbed the mountain like a serpent freed from the earth.

Tunguk descended the archer's perch and made his way to the assistant viceroy, who none were eager to stand near.

"I think you would smoke them out," he said. "But the wind does not blow into a hole."

"Thank you for pointing that out. My men could have used your insight when they failed to throw it *in* the hole, like I asked."

"It is difficult to lead men who follow most of an order," Tunguk acknowledged. "May I speak as one who means well, but does not know he offends a better man?"

The assistant viceroy snickered. "Permission granted."

"Your archer is tired. It is good to have fresh hands on the bow."

"Great minds think alike, Tunguk. I said the same when I got here. But sometimes, it isn't quite so simple. That archer is the only reason those marines are cowering in a mine instead of hacking at my boys. He's the only one who poses a real threat to hit something."

Tunguk nodded. "How will you hold them at night?"

"Same way as last night: a bonfire in front of the entrance. If they try to come out, we'll see them, and beat them back in."

"Then it is a fine archer you have, who can find his mark through smoke and darkness."

"You know, you're right. What was I thinking?" The assistant viceroy struggled to bite his impatience. "What do you think of this? We rest him tonight. Someone else mans the bow at the front—can't miss from that range. You got Parks this far, more or less. Maybe you can help his old buddy, too.

"Here's the intel: I got nineteen marines holed up in an abandoned mine, no connecting tunnels, I already thought of that. We got 'em outnumbered and out-armed, but the boys tell me they can fight. We can't go in, they can't come out. Now you look like you might be an original warfighter. What we call an 'operator.'" He spoke in the way that the young humor their elders.

"If you suddenly found yourself in command of this unit, how do you get them out without taking too many casualties? We could starve 'em, sure, but there's work to do and loads to haul. The coal—the firestone—that's our blood. We can't let our blood stop flowing. That what makes us who we are, and it's the only reason anyone north of Drummoc has to care about what happens to us. You got just over eight-hundred men, and you can bet they're all watching. Here, across that channel, and on the fair shores of Ampos, they're watching, because nothing you do matters, unless you screw it up."

Tunguk waited until the ring of words fell quiet. When the asssitant viceroy seemed satisfied to have impressed him, he replied.

"There is a man in there who leads men, too. They watch, and the admiral watches. The admiral showed them the way to fight. And this man watches you. I will tell you what he sees. Fire blinds your men who stare all night. The marines will sleep until it is early. Then six men will come to fight, if they are clever. No archer will find his mark from the ground, in smoke and flame and shouting. They will make a good fight for your sailors, who do not work together like marines.

"The others will run through your lines. They will go far, and meet where they have decided. At dawn they will attack your rear. Your men have no spears. Their flesh will dull the edges of the marines' spears. The Mattaka do not know this kind of fighting. They will go every direction. Very confused. I think you will be killed. The Leopard Seal will be killed. Then they will capture the ships and return to the admiral. Soon, more ships will come, and the weeping of women for their husbands and sons will be heard across the channel.

"This is what the marine leader sees. But if you look, you will see he must do this, or meet his end. What else do I see? There, above the narrows, a man can stand," he pointed to a flat section of rock twelve feet above the ground outside the entrance. "A hatch from the ship is good to hide behind when spears fly. Bring up a mast, and a climbing belt. Any man who has fired a bow can hit from here, and if there is no fire and smoke, it is easy. Send fresh archers, and withdraw the mast from where it leans until the watch ends.

"Your men are too few. I will guess five-to-one, or six-to-one. Good for a fight among skilled soldiers. Not enough for a siege. Twice their number is better. If you bring up dogs and tie them before the mine, they will tell you when the marines come, and make trouble for them. Amposi have a terror for dogs. There, they will stay for two weeks. Then their hunger will make them treat. They will surrender without fight."

The assistant viceroy did well to hide his contempt in a voice of friendship.

"You know, I've always believed that great superiors surround themselves with men who are superior to them. You keep it up, you might just found yourself a place on the Dawn Council. I only have one question: how do you think eight-hundred men are going to feel about themselves if their leader has so little faith in their courage, their intelligence, their initiative, that he orders them to halt work for two weeks and stare at a hole with nineteen cold, hungry enemy who they can't face? How will they feel the next time I ask something of them, even if they want to do it? From a tactical standpoint, I can't fault your wisdom, which you've earned over many hard years. And I hope you know that it's with sincere respect that I point out the one thing you've forgotten. There's winning, and then there's victory. You have no idea what lies ahead of these men, and neither do they. But trust me, where I'm taking them can only be reached by victories."

Tunguk followed far enough behind the column that escorted the assistant viceroy that he would not mar them with odd numbers. Here, the trail narrowed so that two might walk side-by side and no more until it opened to the flat of the camp ahead.

The camp in daylight showed its modesty. It was no city of tukits, but the meeting place of many rivers—trails to the mines, and the harbor, where others like it stood. Many places of great reputation had disappointed Tunguk when he came to them. This one, he could not blame. It was not a rumor of glory that misled him, but the repetition of the name. From six hundred tongues Camne Drumlag issued. It was his own vision that built vast mines and the clamor of work, and erected mighty tukits that now collapsed into the muttering shuffle of the place. Gone was the wonder, and the dread.

Perhaps ten twelves lived alongside the official, with the rest scattered to corners that retained their mystery. As he returned from the besieged mine, Tunguk saved for himself the sight of The Last Place, as it was called. He held it between his fingers like a sapak bead, the small hard lines that stood for the glory of a memory. There was more to it, of course, but this was enough to shape it. All things in the world had one of eighteen shapes. In his last days, he was not fool-enough to expect another.

It was Nutillen-Amalset in the lead, and the man of the council announced their arrival with a shouted joke to one in the camp who he called Nephew.

A plume of white spilled from the wall beside the column. A man appeared in their path, and drove his spear into Amalset. Snow showered the front of the line. Three more with shields and spears slid down the steep face to land among the Mattaka. Those at the head gave their death cry and fell. The others rushed forward with alarm and smashed their tools on the stout wood.

The back of the column seemed to eddy against itself, and Tunguk saw that four men rushed the assistant viceroy to the rear as the others hurried to meet the marines, yet failed to reach the battle on the narrow trail.

Tunguk hurried forward, all the while with his eyes on the slope above them. From a jagged section some yards up he spied what he expected: another burst of snow fell on the assistant viceroy as he reached the rear. The fifth marine caught a hammer on his shield and opened the belly of the miner with his spear. The others swung to menace him as they stepped backward. He rolled the next blow toward his spear hand, causing the miner to slip. There, he met his end before he could find his feet. Tunguk arrived as Edrasut and Utrupanuk swung with the might of miners against the discipline of the battle-cured. The marine repeated the same movement. Twice, he passed the blow toward his weapon and twice, he thrust. They did not fall so easily, but he crushed the face of Edrasut with a swipe of his shield. Utrupanuk saw his fate, and stood like the greenheart tree in front of his master while many thrusts pierced him. It seemed he would never fall. But the marine pushed him with the shield, and like the frame of a burned hall, he collapsed.

The assistant viceroy lifted the pick of Edrasut in retreat. A man who came alone to strike the leader would be the best among them, Tunguk knew, and he pressed to deal the blow before help could arrive.

Tunguk drew his knife and raised his arm for a wild swing. The marine lifted his shield as he had done with the others, but Tunguk gave an old trick. He drove his right shoulder into the shield instead, and spun his back over it to find himself behind the man. His hand lifted the chin and he would have cut the throat, but the marine spared his error by strength alone. He shrugged Tunguk into the snow near the edge of the trail. When he moved to thrust, Tunguk placed his foot so the marine stepped on it, and swept it out, causing him to slip to the ground. The assistant's viceroy's pick dropped in a clumsy swing, and this warrior again made use of his shield. Tunguk saw his spear-arm braced on the ground and his defense raised, and knew he could not stop the knife. However, the old man attacked much slower than he expected, and the marine hardly struggled to avoid it.

Tunguk pulled the assistant viceroy toward the rest of the column, and the men now saw the attack on their rear and hurried over. The marine feinted thrusts at the old man to make him commit, but Tunguk held at the ready. When the true strike came, Tunguk stepped aside and passed the shaft with his off-hand. He meant to slice the arm but the marine knew the maneuver and struck with the flat of his shield, toppling the old man once more.

By then, Mattaka arrived from the column with heavy blows. Shouts from the camp streamed their way in great numbers.

"Fall back!" The leader shouted to his men opposite the column, who risked being surrounded if the rest of the miners arrived. They hurried to a trail leading down the mountains, and the sergeant fled by a different route.

Parks wondered at the commotion outside of camp. When the shouting began, he sat on a sled that the boys arranged for him by the fire. With his spear, he raked the last coals closer to warm his foot. Distant fields of vision weren't really his thing. At first, he paid no attention when a few men ran off. But soon the the camp foamed with men yelling at one another in tongues. They took up hammers, picks, rocks, or nothing at all if that's what they could find. In waves, they sprinted past him for the trailhead.

Kjartke came out at the noise, listened a second, then asked him where Tunguk was. When he didn't know, she ordered him to stay put and went after the men. Suddenly, Parks felt the pull of a crowd he couldn't be a part of. He yelled for Ferrakut and Ulwet—he yelled every Mattaka name he knew. Finally, the boys appeared, and darted off again when he told them to harness a team.

By the time they returned with the dogs, people were walking again. They clustered at the trail. Little groups ran this way or that. Larger ones headed back. The warmth of the fire said it wasn't worth fitting out the sled to turn right around to a cold pile of ash. He sent the boys away again, and stirred anxiously with his spear.

Kjartke was among the first to return. Close behind came four miners carrying a fifth between them, screaming and dripping blood. She hustled them into a wigwam—*his* wigwam—without explanation. He looked up at the blurry groups still on the approach with foreboding. They came in turn with someone limping between his friends, or refusing help for his wounds. Another came gasping and singing on an empty sled carried as a litter.

Then a group arrived slowly. Some ways out, they set their patient in the snow, where he didn't move. Another was laid beside him. A small line formed. They received no treatment but looks of confusion or regret. A man rushed out to meet them and fell on one of the dead, weeping.

Then the main body started back. A section broke off and hurried down the trail Parks had taken from the harbor. The rest postured with their tools, watching the rear, watching the heights. At the center, Carabiner took shape, stained in blood.

"Yo! Carabiner! What happened?" He shouted. The group ignored him. Miners came by to check on their assistant viceroy and wipe him with their own sleeves. He reassured man after man. Parks searched in frustration for someone who could escort him into that circle.

A quick movement from the royal wigwam caught his eye. A small, dirty face appeared between the flap and the wall, staring at the men. The face of a girl. She noticed his gaze, and pulled the flap shut. He worked his boot back on over stiff toes, creeping back to life with every wriggle. Parks knelt, planted his forehead and hands in the snow, and pushed himself back until his foot was flat, then used the butt of his spear to strain himself up.

With both hands on his staff, he hopped and shifted, hopped and shifted the short distance to the wigwam where Carabiner held court. No other had a canopy over the front—a porch, with mats and hanging clothing and casks to sit on.

He ducked under the guy rope.

"Hello?" Parks tried through the door. "I'm a friend of the assistant viceroy. Coworker, some would say."

"Parks!" Carabiner waved him over. When he didn't move, a pair of miners came to help him, and nearly carried him to the front of the group. "I thought I was glad to see you *last* night."

"I rarely disappoint." He looked over the matted blood in Carabiner's furs. "I see you've been traveling with my buddy Joe."

"You'll have to forgive me if I haven't found my sense of humor yet. I just lost ten men, three of them members of the Dawn Council, and not all of the wounded are going to make it."

"Was it orcs? Sorry. Sense of humor." He cleared his throat. "What happened?"

"Marines. Ambushed us coming off the trail. I wouldn't be here if not for your friend," he announced to all present. "We took heavy casualties on both ends of the column. He and I barely managed to hold the rear, and Satletaluk stonewalled them in the front until reinforcements arrived. Which reminds me: Sagalak! Have the mast of the darraig and a climbing belt sent up to the mine, and one of the hatches from the ships. I'll explain what to do once they're here." He nodded to Joe. "Don't worry, Parks, I'm fine. This isn't my blood."

"I mean, I figured. You weren't squealing and writhing on the ground. Um. Sorry about your men, though."

"Thank you." Carabiner placed a hand on Parks' shoulder that made it feel even less sincere. Then he looked up past Parks, as if startled. Parks turned. Halfway between them and the wigwam, a little girl stood, swallowed in oversized furs. Her hair matted to her cheeks around the rim of her hood. "Sophia, everything's fine, sweetie. Go back inside."

Carabiner seemed to sense the curtness to his comment. He walked over to meet her and took her hand. "I know it looks bad, but I'm alright. I have a few things to take care of out here, but I promise I'll be in soon."

She looked past him at Parks.

"You're alive," Sophia grinned with satisfaction. "I told him you would be."

"Come on. I'll walk you back." Carabiner ushered her toward the wigwam.

Parks frowned. His brain wheezed like an old motor. The volcano returned to him, and the ascent with Wisconsin Johnson. He remembered the night he heard the man speak through his window in an American accent—which was no accent, at all. He saw Wisconsin going last over the rail to join his family, to join Carabiner, and a wet face, hair spilling in thin matted strands outside the orange hood of a survival suit.

"Hey!" He stopped them. "From the ship. You're from the ship! Joe, I know her! Hey! Come here!"

"Parks, I'll be right back." Carabiner held up a finger.

"Sophia!" The girl turned again and was reticent to move. "I know that chick," Parks explained to the miners. "We go way back, many moons."

"You have met the wife of Alexicus?" One of the miners asked with surprise, the one Carabiner had called Satletaluk.

Parks twitched. "The who?"

"Missus Sophia, wife of Alexicus. She is known to the Leopard Seal?" Satletaluk grinned through his bewilderment.

Parks snapped back around to Carabiner. He didn't understand why he began to hobble that way, but with each hop on the spear, he felt a growing heat beneath his skin. He held the severed line to the life raft of the *Qarapara* in his hand. Kjartke sat on the rock of Yunoc, and told him of Klimut's raid on her village, his sea amigo Klimut, who slaughtered her family, and threw her son into the sea. He felt the shame of approaching her, and how nothing he could say then or now would spare her.

He wanted this one to disappear, like the man who led him up a volcano. He wanted him to show his true face. He'd come so far. Every uneven step confirmed it. He would not be misled again.

The embarrassment welled in him. Grief welled him. A helpless terror welled, and where they met, they overflowed the banks in rage.

"Your *wife*?" He blurted.

"Parks, hang on, buddy," Carabiner protested. The miners looked on, uncertain of what they witnessed.

"You sick son of a bitch!" He swung himself one last step and raised his spear to strike.

Carabiner kicked at his leg and Parks landed on his back so hard the sky flashed above him. A hand snatched his weapon away, and he heard laughter from the onlookers.

"It's not what you think," hot breath stung his ear. "Easy!" Carabiner stood and cautioned the crowd. "A misunderstanding between old friends. The Leopard Seal can't help but point his weapon at commanding officers, it seems. Lucky for him, my sense of humor is already coming back to me. How can I hold it against such a pathetic creature when I've got real threats running around my mountains, endangering my people? Besides, I think he realizes that if he *ever* points anything as sharp as a hammer at me again, I'll cut off his other leg and beat him to death with it."

Parks moaned and closed his eyes.

"Ease her down, you sons of Euskus!" Corm's voice seemed to strum the ropes that ran from the beam. Foster and half the ship heaved while the other side pulled the slack out of their lines to catch the *Gairhle* as she crossed center. A number of men ran around to aid, while Foster and Gionn took up oars to press her away. Ice and urgency overtook them. She tipped and fell the last feet onto the berm of snow and ice, erected from the drift and what they could chip out, braced with what barrels remained full.

There was no time to put her level. That would take days. The *Gairhle* opened her lip toward the field between themselves and the angotaks, and fell no farther. They rushed up the snowy slope, as their visitors soon would, into the relative security of the ship. The rest of the cargo flew in like some barrage, with the heavier items raised on ropes.

Foster turned to take the lay of it. The ship seemed frozen at the low point of a pitch in a storm. It was near-impossible to stand on the starboard half from the grade. Rather than a wall and level rampart, they stood on a mountain slope and braced a foot on the curve of the bilge, the port hull, or some object to keep from spilling back out. The gunwale bowed politely to receive. The carpenters frantically fixed the tops from every barrel at intervals along the side to increase the height and provide cover from arrows.

Hogue bashed nails into a pair of leather straps on the back of a small cask lid, bent the ends, and looped his arm through the makeshift shield that didn't reach his elbow. A few others took up the idea, but the barrel lids soon disappeared.

"She's not braced to starboard. Clear the hooks or cut 'em if they try to pull us over from behind," Corm warned. "Archers, to bow and stern," he moved their two bowmen, Chapa and Mene, to the quarter decks where the hull rose sharply for additional cover.

"How the fuck did they level her so fast?" Boot complained of the angotak ship.

"Didn't. She's fast in the ice, and splinters in a week or two if they don't raise her." Eckerd theorized.

The angotaks had other priorities.

"They just sent off two men the opposite way," Eagle-eyed Jenneker announced.

"Search party. They would be mad to attack before they find their sister crew," Palqua advised.

"And they'll never live it down if their mates arrive to find they haven't killed us outright." Gionn ushered Chirim between himself and Foster.

"If they have weakened their rank before an attack, I will be most grateful." Palqua attempted to cheer the men.

The *Gairhle* shipped with only three proper shields. Corm took one up himself, and none doubted he'd put it to use. He considered the crew, then bestowed another on Jonn. The young man grinned politely but without enthusiasm. That left the bow.

"You look a brute with that fine club," he extended it to Gionn as he admired the stout little sword.

"May you live to regret your decision," Gionn snatched it. The honor fixed him to one of the gaps instead of the "support" role he would have preferred in the second line. He sat on the gunwale with his back to the field and let the weapons rest on the deck. The more seasoned men found their ease, but Foster and most of the ship could hardly stop moving.

The battle could have been an hour off or a day. It stressed Foster that the men of the *Gairhle* stood divided between panic and complete lack of urgency—in many cases, born of panic. K'sem and Reed fought one another to stow and restow the gear at their feet for some microscopic advantage. Qawa removed his coat and rubbed ice free of the cuffs, then decided it was the perfect time to holystone the entire garment.

Foster had assumed they would fight where they sat, and most did, but a good quarter of the sailors already deserted their posts to huddle near friends or hide behind someone they thought had a better chance, leaving gaps in the wall that no one bothered to fill while the Amposi pressed three-deep behind Moipa—so tight none of them could possibly raise a weapon.

"Comin'!" Jenneker called their attention to a single man marching across the ice. The angotak carried only a spear, and stopped just short of arrow range. He began to gyrate around his feet in widening revolutions. When it looked like he would fall, he broke into feverish dance, his arms flailing, spear in orbit, distant voice skittering over the ice like pebbles.

"The fuck is that, his war dance?" Foster wondered aloud.

Gionn looked over his shoulder an insufficient distance to see. "Cursin' us." To Foster's wide eyes, he replied, "No worries, mate. Got every lad born under a dark moon knockin' it down."

Foster surveyed the crew, and noticed Fergo in a possessed fit. Several Amposi gestured as if to catch something and fire it back with ceremony. Tawatu drummed on Corm's shield and pointed at the witchman alternatingly, then bashed his forehead several times on the bronze boss at the center and mimed a death rattle.

"None of this bothers you?" He pleaded at Gionn.

"Everything bothers me, cunt. Ice, battle, ships…you. Now spare your strength, and mine." Gionn pulled him close. "Don't jump until you see me do it. I've got this bit down, and I don't care to die on the pack alone."

"I save me last throw for the first foot to touch the ice," Hogue overheard as he passed to relieve Foster at the rail. Boot joined him from aft, sent by Corm to reinforce the green end of the ship.

"That's it! Here they come!" Jenneker said a moment before the little black shapes dotted Foster's focus. Corm planted himself at the mast.

"How many? Number cunt! I counted eight empty benches when she closed. A true thirty-six—not a man aboard who don't pull."

"Thirty-six minus eight is twenty-eight," he shouted back.

"And two off to scout their mates," Jenneker reminded.

"Twenty-six." He stirred it over. "And we got fifty-two. That's twice what they got!" Foster grinned optimistically.

"Aye, may slow 'em down, if they don't get aboard." It took Foster a second to realize the captain intended no sarcasm. "Grievous on a deck, those bastards. Keep 'em off if you have to plug the breach with your corpse!" He shouted to the crew.

A black line streaked the ice, and became two, then broke into uneven figures spread the length of the ship. Foster confirmed his count. Every one of them had a round leather helmet, only a little more than a cap. Many came under shield, but near as many stripped to the tunic or the waist, with just a spear or a short sword. He shivered at the sight in his coat. As with their earlier visitors, nothing about their stature impressed him. While he counted his strength, they loped like black wolves who never thought to number their prey. They came to have their fill.

"Hold your volleys til I say, and strike down the man who don't!" Corm threatened the archers. "Heave no spears away!"

The angotaks didn't raise shields when they came into range. Their contempt for the whalers' threat carried them just tens of yards from the snow berm. There, four of their own dipped their bows from their backs.

"Cover!" Echoed down the boards. Every man squeezed as best he could behind the battlements. The second line sat on their heels to get low enough. An arrow sailed over the port gunwale. Moments later, another threaded between barrel tops and found the inside of the hull. They probed at lazy intervals while the archers dialed their range. A lid near midship studded with four like a round target. Then the fire ceased.

Atalkut and Tunguk crouched forgotten against the rise of the fore deck with their single stone knife in Atalkut's hand.

"Stay there until someone falls, then grab his weapon." Foster probably didn't have to say it, but they were grateful for direction. There came a lull, and he resisted the temptation to peek out into the line of fire. Foster lay along the upward sweep of the starboard side with his feet above the bilge. He clutched his Mattaka spear, unsure of how to stand, where to stand, what to do. Gear littered the hold, and the thwarts checked any movement along the length like hurdles. Some order, a fierce shout was bound to signal the battle. He begged for it, though he feared what would follow. Death was the welcome cure for his sickening anticipation.

It came with the faint crunch of snow. Wood knocked the side just fore of the mast. Moipa and Deowa filled the gap and planted their spears into the shield, driving the man off the side and onto the berm. The second he vacated, an arrow threaded the opening between the battlements and found Deowa's lung.

Another rusher arrived unannounced nearer Foster, amid the line of Amposi navy that held the forward quarter. Asdosa knocked him off, and again an arrow arrived as if fired at the angotak's back in expectation of his fall. The deserter of Ampos fell back with a cry, clutching the shaft in his shoulder.

Closer still. Gionn spun and went shield-to-shield with the angotak, while Chirim gave a shove of assistance. In the same movement, Gionn shoved Chirim aside and swung his shield to catch the arrow he knew was coming.

"Don't linger in the breach!" He warned the rest of the ship. Foster understood their enemy had pinned them with the threat of fire to sneak through an opening, or to earn a free shot if anyone admired his work. Gionn wrenched the arrow free with difficulty.

Now the shouts pealed, an otherworldly whoop rising to a sharp stop and starting again from the low chest. Foster couldn't move. Move where? An arrow waited for a glimpse of him. He clutched his spear and prayed no one in front of him fell.

Their cries raced up the berm. The gunwale sagged waist-high above the top. Shields cracked against defenders the length of the *Gairhle*. He first wave stumbled back. Arrows sailed. A second crested the side almost before the whalers could rebound from cover. Gionn just pinned his shield in the gap between two barrel lids and held it like a door someone tried to hammer open. A spearhead found a hole between his shield and the gunwale and snaked blindly for a target. Boot reached over the top and jabbed his where he thought the angotak might be without drawing blood.

Foster saw someone aft tumble backward into the ship.

"Fire down the beam! Archers! Fire down the beam!" Corm tried to make himself heard over the clash.

Chapa loosed at the next man to stick on Gionn's shield. His arm flailed with a feather in his tricep as he retreated. The archer searched for another shot, but didn't have the angle to aim far down the line. The angotaks knew it, and leveled the next charge amidship.

Spears on both sides darted into the openings. Fid spurted from the thigh and retreated. The angotak got his foot on the gunwale before Otsander swung a hand axe that forced him to lean back so far, he slipped off again. An angotak burst onto the ship at the mast, but Eckerd and Jenneker, Gewar and Bale fell on him with vicious thrusts while Corm regained the breach.

"Asdosa! Give your spear to the Buckets!" Foster yelled at the man with the arrow wound, but he didn't hear, or ignored it.

In front of Foster, Gabol shifted, causing Yuray to lean into an opening. He folded into the bilge beside Foster with an arrow through the side of his head.

"Fuck me! Fuck!" Foster threw his trembling hands around the man's hand axe. He thought of keeping it himself, but handed it back. "Here!" He had to insist to get Tunguk to take hold.

Another pop amidship fell back, but each one caved the whalers a little more, and the shouts of panic bled into the wails of the wounded so that he couldn't pick out a word unless it came within a few yards of him.

Steel thunked behind him, and Foster thought it an arrow at first. A three-clawed grappling hook scraped up the side and found purchase.

"They're comin' over the back!" He said, expecting someone else to move. No one did. A second landed farther down. He and Bentos looked at each other, neither eager to rise into the arrows. Foster hoped a man would rush Yuray's gap soon to block him, but when he heard boots on the outer hull, he braced for the punch into his back and seized the hook, pressing his foot again the hull for leverage. It freed, and he bore the weight of a massive catch in the second before he let go and heard the angry crash of a man hitting the ice. An arrow flashed by as he dove again for cover.

"Clear it!" Pitras said, and he took the other with Bubba, but the hook was stuck fast. Tarvin reached a hand over and sliced the line with his knife.

"Bentos! Someone!" Gionn warned a moment before he sealed off a fresh collision like an offensive guard against a surging tackle. Foster noticed Chirim on the deck squirming away from Yuray's corpse and babbling to himself uninjured. Gionn swatted with his sword at the spear hand that probed over the top. Bentos caught the shaft, and Fergo rolled under thwarts to help. Between them, they ripped it free. Bentos chanced a wild toss over Gionn's shield that couldn't have done anything but return a lost weapon.

Two more hooks came over near the mast. Bodies fell over one another to reach them, while Corm shouted, "Shoot the fuckin' archers!" Chapa showed himself only long enough to fire and ducked the return. He sent volley after haphazard volley as though Corm had commanded him to get rid of his arrows.

"Someone else on the shield," Gionn panted. No one volunteered. Foster started to move. "Not you!"

Boot came up and laced his arm through the loops while Gionn sank against the hull and took a tremendous breath. Another angotak hit, and Boot sent him back with Hogue's help. Now they studded the line like fat drops of rain on a tin roof.

"Someone take up the bow!" Palqua's plea found a space in the noise. Foster looked abaft and no longer saw Mene. An angotak body burst through the line onto the ship near Corm's tarp. He couldn't see what happened, but a pocket of whalers spread outward. A head rose, and the angotak swiped himself a clearing. Dunn went to meet him then disappeared beneath the sea of heads. Foster once more saw the angotak flash like a fox among the hens.

They were boarded.

Another breach broke between Qawa and Otsander, in the heart of the Amposi quarter. The angotak jammed inside of spear range and landed a wet hack on Otsander's wrist, then peeled down his barrel-top shield and smashed his short sword into the whaler's skull so hard that he barely fended off Reed while freeing it.

"Hold the gap!" Shouted Gionn and Hogue and Boot in succession, to remind those near the hole that more would come through if everyone turned to fight this one.

Casey fell on it in time to dislodge an oncoming shield with his spear. But the fury of the boarder put the navy section on its heels. They leaned away from his blows, and with no one to engage for that split-second, he ran his point into Casey's back.

Moipa lunged with his spear and seemed to land a flick behind the shield, but in the chaos Foster was unsure and the angotak turned on him unfazed. The sailors rallied to his defense. The angotak spun like a devil, swiping at the spears with his shield and crossing his sword, backhanding it. As they pulsed away again, the blade caught Reed's spear and tore it aside, and the return blow cleaved his collarbone.

Blood arced far above the battle as the angotak found Fid, lying on the deck from his wound. Pitras chanced a thrust but an arrow sent him diving. An explosion rocked the battlements like a cannonball hitting the mass of bodies as another angotak burst the line. Fergo and Gabol spilled back. The invader ended Gabol on his way up, then struck at the men who separated him from his comrade. He bore no shield, but the sailors threw themselves over the next thwart to avoid his whizzing short spear. Only two benches separated him from where Foster lay paralyzed. By divine mercy or good tactics, he fought the other way in an effort to link up to his man.

Whalers stumbled at him with guarded thrusts while the angotak danced over the gear and the uneven deck like a figure skater. He crossed a thwart without using his hands and pierced K'sem through the sternum.

"Fuckin' shoot him!" Hogue appeared ready to cut down Chapa until an arrow zipped into the deck—a terrible miss from such short distance. Next fell Basa'u, and Bentos tripped against the makeshift battlement. An angotak arrow glanced the top of the barrel lid and rolled high over the side amid chips of wood. Only another effort from Chapa spared Bentos a fatal thrust. His shot took the man in the oblique. While he shook the next arrow on to the string, the boarder turned and hurled his spear into Chapa's chest, then liberated a new one from the dead.

Fergo and Bentos attacked in close formation, herding him abaft.

"Gap!" Hogue shouted as he and Gionn stepped over Foster to reach the action. Foster looked at Boot, holding the bow alone by shell-shocked Chirim. The Mattaka boys stared wide-eyed and immobile.

"Grab that spear!" He ordered Atalkut to relieve Chapa of the missile that set him down.

The men at the battlements shook against renewed attacks. Foster jumped to his feet by some compulsion he could not explain and clambered over the awful footing to the gap vacated by Fergo. His first peek over the edge revealed a small mass of angotaks gathered in relay at the berm. One of them had gained the top in front of him. The edge compacted and chewed under their assaults. But this one wasn't trying to get in. He reached to pluck spent arrows from the ship. Foster raised a spear and his reaction caused the snow to break out in a chunk underfoot. He rolled to the bottom, where Foster realized there were no archers. Several bows lie on the ice. Only the one who he sent back still held onto his.

"They're out of arrows!" He yelled to his crew. "Out of arrows!" A couple of voices passed it down the line, and the men of the *Gairhle* rose where they could in a bloody grin of broken teeth. It seemed impossible that there were so few. Had someone deserted?

The mast rallied, and by stolen glances Foster saw the man with the shield driven forward. Imau'y got caught between the converging angotaks and earned a spear as they joined their backs to defend themselves.

Gionn and Hogue arrived to wall off the bow with Fergo and Bentos. On the other end, a wave of sailors spilled forward from the mast, including Gewar, Nolan, and Tamarqan, to support Juru, Lozeder, and Igonus the carpenter. While the whalers awaited their comrades, the angotaks hacked pieces from the bodies at their feet and threw them at their foes to taunt them. Both were baptized red and probably wounded, breathing heavy in the welcome respite.

Another wave charged up the berm, now serrated slush under the traffic. The line pushed them back. Foster waited for the shield to appear beneath him, and slammed his spear with both hands, then shoved the man free. The stone tip broke off in the wood. He threw the useless stick at the next one who charged, catching him mid-stride and causing no damage but spoiling the run.

Now Tarvin and Bubba and Pitras made an assault on the two angotaks from the starboard. The one with the shield sunk his sword in Tarvin's arm to the bone, but Pitras used his uphill position to steer through the other's guard and gash a wound down his bare chest.

Fergo and Bentos thrust to finish him, but he tap-parried and popped the edge near Fergo's grip. The sailor collapsed holding his bloody hand. Gionn and Hogue arrived in time to spare Fergo a follow-up. The other angotak covered his companion with the shield as Gionn hammered down with his short sword once, twice, three times with such force that the man was unable to mount a counter.

A cry from the battlements drew Foster in time to see a spear withdraw from Horrio and plunge again into the man's face. Another angotak mounted the gunwale, but Bentos thrust his spear into the attacker's side then steered him back out and lost his grip on the weapon.

Atalkut and Tunguk arrived behind Foster.

"Spear!" He took the steel point from Atalkut. Another angotak broke from the huddle at the bottom, noticeably slower, and Moipa fended him off with ease. The archer tried another run on Foster, this time having armed himself with a spear. Atalkut saw it, lifted an empty cask, and Donkey Kong-ed it at the man with a satisfying crack.

"Hell yeah, brother!" Foster tousled his hair.

"They are slowing!" Moipa called.

A roar went up from the stern, and the wild slashing stopped, telling Foster the aft-most boarder met his end.

"Hold 'em!!" Corm handed off his place on the wall to Eckerd and rumbled toward the remaining boarders. "Clear those rats from me deck!"

As though they feared the arrival of their own captain, the whalers renewed their attack. Now they moved together, and Moipa risked his spot on the wall to get in a slash that opened the hip of the man with the shield. The angotaks buckled in body but not spirit. They knocked away thrusts and blinked through pain, men who knew no equal on this ship, men who held no thought of safety, of victory or defeat. They fought as men nurtured in blood, made whole by death. Foster stood awed by this rare sight of some creature, made for one thing, in the act of that thing. Glinting steel and dark spray radiated like a halo around them. He knew it was a holy terror he witnessed.

A blow from the short sword dislodged the angotak's spear. Pitras dealt the thrust that stilled him. The other could have fallen to any. Someone seized his arm from behind. It was Moipa who lunged again from the wall and ran him through. Then everyone rained their points on him in furious revenge.

"Comin' up!" Eckerd warned. Foster hit the shield with steel this time, and the boys pushed on his back so hard he nearly fell over after the man. Down the line he saw the wave of angotaks retreat. Three more followed, and one gained the side over Qawa with a deep breath, but the freed hands closed and cast him off.

Another looked prepared to rush up the berm, but his friends stopped him. Foster saw a few bent over in exhaustion from charging, leaping, being pushed back. Some of the angotaks bled with minor wounds where a lucky slash had found them at the gunwale. They saw by the activity their men aboard were gone, and turned to limp for their ship, content with the first sortie.

He ran a quick count.

"Twenty," he said quietly. Then, "*Twenty!*" To the ship. "We got six of 'em." Foster surveyed the carnage. Blood drained from the dead into the bilge and froze in the seams of the wood. His boots caked with it. Corm and a few others cheered the retreat, but most threw themselves on the deck to gasp or clutch their wounds. Several tended to Tarvin, who screamed in agony. An arrow still protruded from Asdosa's shoulder. Fergo raised a quaking hand to admire the stump where his pinky used to sit.

He didn't dare count their own casualties, but the *Gairhle* lay gutted. No less than a dozen dead, just his side of the mast. Thirty able seamen, at most, for the next attack, and the next—eventually to include the reinforcements of the other angotak vessel. He saw below that some of their enemies had dug out the ends of the berm as much as they could without ruining their entrance, the initial effort that would topple them to the ice when complete. They may not even have to board again if they returned at night to knock her over.

"We gotta go. Come on! They're tired!" He pleaded.

"What are you on about, cunt? Did you survive?" Gionn said with genuine surprise.

"We can't hold off another attack. We gotta hit 'em now, while they're trashed. Look at 'em!" He pointed at the scattered group shuffling over the ice, cold and bloodied. "We gotta counterattack!"

The whalers stared blankly.

"I mean it. We didn't just run half a mile, sprint up and down, get smashed off a boat twenty times. We're a little tired, but not like them."

"Meet 'em in the field? You're fuckin' mad, Wife. I didn't see you in the fray." Hogue countered.

"I seen him on the wall, though. He did his bit," Bentos defended.

"It ain't half as crazy as waitin' for 'em to rest and come back with another shipload. We gotta do this now, or we lose more every time. We didn't win that fight! You saw. We fuckin' lost by sittin' here, shakin' in our boots. We gotta try somethin' different, or agree to die when they come back."

"He is right. We press the numbers. He knows the count." Moipa granted.

Corm's shoulders heaved in the cold air. He worked himself out of his shield and with what seemed his last bit of energy, tossed it most of the way to Foster.

"Go, then. If you can. Any man who can, die with Foster on the field if you prefer it. I'd go meself if..." he lay back and never finished the sentence. Even through the small effort of a few easy blocks, Foster felt his own lungs burn. He wavered, then looped the shield on his left arm. The weight surprised him, and he set it down again. Instead, he walked to the quarter deck and gathered Chapa's bow, and a few remaining arrows.

Several of the men lifted themselves to their feet with hesitation and awaited his move.

"Let's go, bitches!"

"With Wife Seal!" He heard Palqua from the stern.

"Up, you sogers! After Wife Seal!" Eckerd commanded.

Foster threw down the spear and bow ahead of him, then gauged the drop before jumping down. The berm gave and he slid out in a painful tumble, but righted himself on the ice and looked back to see Atalkut preparing his leap. He gathered his weapons and started to jog as fast as he dared. One more glance, and he saw only the Mattaka boys hurrying after him. *They'll come*, he told himself. *You can't look unsure.*

He heard other voices, other feet, but didn't dare stop to count his strength. Ahead, the angotaks spotted the advance and put a pep in their step to reach the defensive walls of their ship. He could hardly believe they didn't just turn and fight, but he soon understood as their line spread thin with the wounded and the exhausted trailing behind.

A man with a leg wound dropped behind the others. Foster closed within ten yards, then stopped. He'd fired a compound bow plenty of times, but he was far from accurate even with modern sights. He undraped the wooden recurve from his shoulder and aimed the tip of the arrow at center mass. Foster felt a sting in his cold fingers at the twang. The arrow struck the man near the base of the neck, throwing him chest down. When he came up, the angotak simply looked at him impassively, as if grateful for the rest. Foster stepped on his back and yanked the arrow free. They regarded each other as he wondered whether he should finish the man or just move on.

The Mattaka relieved him of the concern when Atalkut and Tunguk fell on the angotak, punching furiously with spear and knife.

"A proper squain back-stabbin'!" Gionn appeared in a trot with shield and sword. Now Foster risked a look and saw the ice teeming loosely with whalers in a scattered line of variable enthusiasm, each trying to catch up to the one ahead of him.

He grinned, and didn't wait. The next angotak turned to face him. A lump of intestine bulged from a puncture when he let go. Foster stopped and nocked the arrow. It rotated away like a clock hand in his frigid grip as the man shuffled toward him. He corralled it, but slipped on the draw. It squirted harmlessly a few yards ahead. For some reason, he hurried after it despite half a quiver dangling from his elbow. Foster caught up as the angotak raised his spear.

Gionn bulled him over from the side with his shield, and Foster rammed the dart through his eye before he could recover.

Ahead, the angotaks shouted in disarray, alone or in twos and threes, the raiding party spread over more than a football field with dozens of yards between them. Some planted for a fight, while others urged them back to the more defensible ship. One with a shield readied himself to buy time for his crew. Foster kept his distance and started to nock, but Hogue interrupted.

"Press the attack!" Hogue, Gionn, and Boot spread around the man. Atalkut completed the encirclement.

Foster understood. He hurried wide with little Tunguk, pressing the last quarter mile to the ship.

They passed a cannonball of a man with a shield, reduced to a spirited walk by exhaustion. He regarded them, and Foster hurried by, choosing his route like he was slipping blockers on kickoff coverage. Another pair went by, and he ached with the fear and excitement of being behind enemy lines. As terrifying as these bastards were boarding a ship, he reckoned none of them had ever experienced a retreat, much less on land. Foster could have drifted a semi-truck through the spaces. Each hammered his stiff pace without a notion of where the next one was, hell-bent on reaching their vessel. On that deck, no whaler could stand with them. None would board. He saw in their determination that he ran not to reach them but to overtake them, and keep them on the field.

Foster readied an arrow as he came upon another, head down and unaware. He couldn't afford to stop, or with eight left, miss. With a burst of speed, he fired in stride from just feet away, wounding the man in the lower back and knocking him to the ice while they peeled around. An angotak still sporting the arrow he earned at the *Gairhle* fell behind them next, and shouted a warning ahead.

Rather than cut him off, the remaining leaders dug hard into the ice. One tripped. Another's face beat purple from an effort Foster had to admire, but his fresh legs carried him by all, with Tunguk tripping over his heels, until three remained ahead.

The first angotak reached the ship, and scaled one of the ropes left hanging, then helped a companion up. Foster came as close as he could and fired at the third on the rope. The shot zipped wide, but made the men aboard cover. He hurried closer while he drew the next, and dropped him from his climb with a hit on the shoulder blade. The flat fall onto the ice knocked his wits out, and Tunguk slammed a hand axe into the man's forehead. Foster yanked him out of the way just as the man above readied to throw his spear.

They pressed their backs against the hull under an outrigger bench that shielded them from above—a design he'd seen before, where six more men on each side rowed above their crewmates. Now it was their turn to pant. The approaching angotak lost them in the shadow of the ship. Foster allowed himself one more gasp, then popped out three quick shots as he closed, piercing his thigh and hip, and catching the shield as the man hobbled back toward the open to escape. An archer met him, and pulled the missile from the shield to return fire. Foster loosed first, and missed. He threw himself aside while the response split the timber by his ear.

He started to aim again, but didn't want to give the man another shot. He tracked a wild-looking angotak galloping at him and Tunguk.

"Hold your cock, Wife!" Fergo sprinted up shaking his spear and flapping his stump of a finger.

"Over the boards!" The man on the ship encouraged his mates to fight their way in. The archer took the shield off the arrow-riddled man, who could only lean on his spear at a distance awaiting a fight, and made toward them.

"Shoot his leg!" Fergo demanded.

"I can't aim like that." Foster offered the bow, then remembered the finger.

"Fuck it, let's board." Fergo ushered them to another rope at the stern, and Foster pinned it in his boots for one good push to reach the gunwale. He scrambled over uncontested, then pulled Tunguk as one of the angotaks spotted them and started their way, the other helping his man aboard.

"Come on!" Foster looked down to Fergo, who shook his bloody hand in reply, then ran into the field. He hurled his spear into the chest of an arriving angotak, who staggered into Moipa's steel.

The whalers trickled in.

Foster spotted the man he shot in the back being riddled by Ordacles, Eckerd, and Aldan. The remaining angotaks herded together in their run for the ship. Bentos hit one with a toss. Pitras and Bubba forced a stand from the cannonball, but Hogue, Boot, and Atalkut surrounded him with vengeful thrusts.

From the midship came Gewar, Bale, Nolan, even Tamarqan, while Arthas and Palqua and his man Baghar showed for the aft deck. A third angotak boarded, but the rest disappeared beneath the outrigger in a clash of spears. Foster saw whalers hurl their spears, and felt some thud into the hull, but others found their target without a sound.

"Grant me a fight before you kill us. Spear to spear," the approaching angotak said of Foster's bow.

"Sorry, brother. There's no fair fights." Foster snapped the arrow into his right chest. He tried to raise his arm to cast in return, but it wouldn't go. When he took a seat on the thwart, Foster saw that he was no young man, though he'd run like one. The angotak aged in the pristine glare of the ice, lost in the silhouette of the distant *Gairhle*. Foster felt ashamed, as when he watched a deer he wounded rest in the tall grass with no more thought of escape. For the second time, he noticed the sublime nature of the beast—their unquenchable fury on his blood-soaked deck, and now the grace with which they finished their course. He could not see—but sensed the presence of—a litany of deeds that lay beyond him at his finest.

"At least I'll arrive in me ship." He looked to Foster, as whalers scaled both sides of the ship. "Come on, lad. Don't let these shirkers at me. I'll have it from the first aboard."

Gionn climbed on across the ship, and waited behind his shield for reinforcements while the other two angotaks dug in for their stand.

Foster cautiously crossed the benches to the man he wounded, sensing a trick. A hidden blade, a final kill.

"You the captain?"

"We don't need captains." He let his weapon fall to the deck and rose to face Foster, who leveled a tentative spear.

"Turn around."

"No."

Six whalers, then ten, fell upon the other two in a frenzy, then started for his man. Foster drove his spear through the angotak's heart, uncontested. Across the boards, the whalers howled with the joy of surprise, of astounded relief as they mounted the high places to wave at the *Gairhle*.

They hugged and slapped one another, and little Tunguk fidgeted like a pup begging a rough pat on the head while its tail thumped back and forth. In that first moment of safety, Foster cast down the bloody spear and placed a hand on his shoulder behind a weak smile.

"Good stuff, brother," was all he could manage. The gesture sent the boy wandering in mild disappointment toward other celebrations.

The two ships, frozen apart and painted with the deeds of the day, filled him with a longing for something unnameable, so near he might reach it in a short walk across the sea, yet at the same time, a shell, going nowhere, having arrived at its end like so many voyagers on this field.

A conspicuous quiet brought him around to the crew, grinning eagerly at him from all sides.

"Three grassbenders I saw on the beam this mornin'," Gionn started in. "A number cunt, and a couple of forge-jumpin' squains. If you'd make 'em an honest man, stand as you do now on this angotak prize. And any man who'd deny 'em a full share, head back to the *Gairhle* and take your seat." When no one moved, he sheathed his blade and tossed his shield aside.

"*Now* you're a fuckin' whaler!" Gionn led the charge, and as the crew enveloped him, Foster glanced out over the boards. Two angotaks—returning scouts—watched the spectacle from the ice, then turned back the way they came.

12

LANDS OF THE DEAD

The *Gairhle* rose from her slump by block and brace of salvaged wood. The better portion of the angotak's outriggers wedged her on both sides until her deck leveled and their lady luck gaped over the plain. She'd no idea of the serious debate that almost abandoned her for the other vessel. It rowed thirty-six—the number of survivors to a man not counting Corm—and Mahal didn't look to be with them long. A faster ship, an easier pull at winter's end.

"Last in Winter or first in Spring, Taclann awaits!" Corm reminded them which boat held more provisions for the journey, and booty at the end. The men who served with him longest made no effort to separate him from his beloved, with a wry shake of the head that told the rest of the futility. Besides, the angotak vessel would have to be dug out of the ice, and the whalers were too busy relieving her of spoils.

It weren't much, as Foster saw it.

Those man-hunters had a spartan sense of comfort. Their barrels were down to a film of rotten meat that looked well-picked over. A worn oilskin and a sleeping sack, maybe a dull coin and a change of shirt—the dead were light on treasures, or they treasured different things. But the crew made off with every black sliver of steel and green boss.

When given first pick, Foster claimed the spear of the last man he killed, and earned ridicule for passing up a bright sword or one of the fine shields they salvaged. They took bows and hard leather caps and cut charms from the vanquished. No barrel retained its lid. Good rope and the main sail, even the mast made its way back on the final trip.

Only when the *Gairhle* squared herself for the next bout did they begin the grim work of securing their own dead. No man kept his weapon or his purse, but the whalers saw that each went off the ship with a knife, even if one had to be appropriated from the angotaks. They retained their boots and their coats, and some of the trophies—painted strands of bead, animal bones, discs of bronze and tin, rocks tied up or bored through for a thread—were fixed to the departing crew. Those survived by good friends made sure their water skins and sleeping sacks were attached. Pennies found their way into boots. The only speech was an occasional praise, earned or not:

"Only an archer could have got Yuray."

"All of you got Reed to thank that you breathe."

"Nakos made a battle of it—I saw the surprise on the invader."

In mere hours, the bodies were frozen stiff. He expected his companions to discard them like trash. Instead, they carried out the duty with as much tenderness as any of those rough hands and tongues had shown for anything. It was a solemn honor to bear them off. Men quietly jockeyed for it. Foster was lucky enough to help Chapa down. The sons of Ampos flaked tears from their cheeks. There was no way to know how many of the fallen had been Corm's defectors, returned under Palqua, but all of them were navy.

Seventeen went over to port—it had to be port. With no sign of an enemy, they chipped dark sheets of blood from the bilge, bow to stern. Fergo rejoiced when he found his severed pinky, but for the others, their friends' blood frozen under their nails, it was grim work. The very air on board seemed to throb like an open wound.

Every member of the crew joined the procession that bore the bodies away from the stern. There, the axes worked a hole in the ice until the sea bubbled through. Corm brought up a bucket of water and Tawatu stirred it to prevent freezing while the captain consulted the crew on which sea god to entrust with the man in front of him, then dipped his fingers and flicked a pattern of water on the body.

"Mearfannan, storm-drunk, by oath, he died aboard. Bear Uldred o'er your fetch to fair waters. A boat! A boat! To bear him up!"

"A boat! A boat! To bear him up!" The crew answered, and Uldred was shoved under the ice, feet-first.

So they went to Uinab, or one of his sons; to the Amposi gods Chatsikuy or Adim, or a best guess, like Jalopong, Mintalus, or Awala. After a quick prayer from Corm, sometimes Tawatu as well, the crew called for a boat and their brother slipped beneath the pack. When the last had gone, Corm announced to the hole: "Off with your luck, you lot, and sail not the *Gairhle!*"

They returned to the ship by a different path. The whalers were reluctant to board. It felt like months since they moved freely through space, and the thwarts still twanged with the memory of battle. Corm hurried their minds elsewhere.

"Let's settle up. A two-share lad fights twice as fierce. Wife Seal! Seventeen roam the sea, and one was Irilo," he mentioned the dead spinnaker, a two-share man who'd earned his portion by the indispensability of a good sailmaker. "I count it eighteen to award, but the captain squares at sixty."

He'd had to forfeit some of his half, down to fifty-nine-and-a-half to avoid a riot after the miscount.

"Then it's seventeen-and-a-half."

"And I understand some were awarded after the battle outside me presence." He made a show of snarling with contempt, then broke into a grin. "Well-earned. You and the squains sail with one each."

"Then it's fifteen-and-a-half." The difference of two seemed to confuse them, and he anticipated the gripe. "They were at half a share, so another half to each, plus mine, is two." No one seemed to understand, but they didn't raise a fuss given that they had more to go around than expected.

"No more of these half shares. Put every man to full and tell me what's left."

Foster rounded them up in his head and checked his work several times. "Twelve left."

"Twelve. And you're sure of it? Well enough. Palqua, who showed his steel aft?"

"I cannot name a man who didn't. But of those, Baghar, Arthas, and Ordacles."

"Out of Baghar and Ordacles?"

Palqua ruminated, then named the man who as Foster saw it was his personal guard. "Baghar."

"And Eckerd? Who carved a share for himself at your side? Leave me out of it!" He joked.

"If I must. Ordacles, or Arthas."

"Ordacles has his third share, then, and I name yourself as well. But that's all I'll name. It was everyone's battle, and you lads have your say. Who from the fore showed himself a barrel?"

"Foster." Arthas blurted.

"Aye, Foster's got his. Who else?"

"Give him another, then. We would have lazed about waitin' to die if he hadn't led us over the boards to rout 'em."

The captain prickled at the insinuation that even Foster couldn't miss.

"It was the captain who sent us, and who held the midship from the worst of the angotaks," Eckerd came to his defense. "The only part of the ship that went unboarded."

"Can I stand for meself?" Hogue interjected to a welcome laughter that drew the debate away from Arthas.

"Aye, and you'll have it!" Corm confirmed him.

"Outside of Tunguk and Atalkut, Gionn was the first I saw on the counterattack, and he straight beasted on the ship." Foster further deflected their attention. He received a near-unnoticeable glow of acknowledgment from his benchmate.

The rest of the shares went out in the same fashion, with a number going to what Foster thought of as the O.G. whalers—Corm's crew who never left for the Navy. Of Palqua's, only Boot and Bentos earned one for their bravery, and Tarvin for his wound. Foster noted that Tamarqan—the highest-ranking naval officer after Palqua—also received his third share, putting him one ahead of his former boss.

When the gathering broke and the men milled to congratulate the wealthy, Foster drifted inconspicuously to Arthas.

"Hey brother, 'preciate the support."

He shrugged. "I'll never see it. May as well go to someone who's earned it."

"None of us should've got one, unless we hope to take on the supply lines of both Ampos and Atlantis at half-strength," Gionn leaned in.

Foster blinked at the familiar name he'd heard before and thought nothing of. It felt like a flicker on the tip of his memory that couldn't quite spark. Gionn continued.

"I suspect the new lads we sign will want a share, too, and they won't get mine. Unless Corm intends to be generous with his half, they should've been held in reserve."

"Aye, but he wanted to cheer us after a bollock-scraper," Bentos overhead them. "Give the lads somethin' to fight for when the angotaks return."

"There'll be more shares to hold back before we're under sail. Mark that." Arthas slipped off.

"Cormdran!" Palqua raised his voice beside the ship. "Have a look at the mast."

The captain joined him where the pole lay on the ice in the lee of the ship. "Aye?" Palqua beckoned him to make a closer inspection. "I don't see nothin'," he growled.

"It's what's *not* there that I thought you should find remarkable." The men gathered in curiosity as Palqua bent to extract a nail from the wood with the spine of his knife. He handed it to Corm, whose brow arced over cavernous eyes as he closed his fist around the iron.

"Plunder o' Euskus! Which of you is heavier by an argot?"

Several dozen sleepy miners ringed the Dawn Council just outside the range of polite conversation. They'd finished breakfast in the dark. Carabiner didn't permit the customary bowl of coal fire to see them to the first rays, for fear it would mark a target for the marines. The light confirmed the outrage: they were four, now, plus Ratjuk and Tunguk. Nearly half his councilors fell in the attack. Beyond the specter of the slaughter, something deeper haunted Carabiner: their utter vulnerability. The impenetrability of the place, the seclusion, the horde of enthusiastic men—all of it lent an aura of security that a handful of marines managed to shatter without taking a casualty. These were still his men. His army had not deserted, and nothing yet could make him believe they would hand him over to save themselves. But whatever kind army he still had at his command, it was not one of soldiers.

He waited another couple of minutes out of courtesy, but when no one appeared, Carabiner convened the meeting.

"Gentlemen. The events of yesterday hang over us. There are no words. I will not say them. Now I ask that the council bow their heads in a moment of silence, so that each may honor those who are missing in their own way."

They followed his lead, and soon Ratjuk sung a mournful wail.

"Ratjuk! A moment of silence, please. Shh!" The loyal servant took his meaning, and his apologies had to be silenced, too. As Carabiner searched for the right way to address them, a commotion kicked up on the perimeter. Dogs whined with excitement. A sled pushed through the line of miners.

"Dawn, my ass. It's still fucking dark," a voice complained. "Ow! Slim, *no*! Mush! Mush!"

"I see them!" A boy's voice offered.

"Joe! Is that you?" Parks rattled up on a sled, conveyed by a small gang of Mattaka youth and six dogs, which they'd harnessed to travel the forty yards from his tukit.

"Sup homies? *Owwww*!" He moaned as the boys helped him take his seat on a cask around three taller barrels. "Were all the wigwams taken?" He shivered and pinched his parka tail between his legs.

"Amen. I guess that'll do for the moment of silence. Good of you to make it," Carabiner nodded to the new arrival.

Parks squinted, then looked to Eskimo Joe instead.

"If you young men will excuse us…" Carabiner said to the boys, and Sagalak said something to them in their language that started them off.

"Don't go far," Parks advised. He couldn't tell if Carabiner was glaring at him, but the still figure and the pause raised his hopes.

"As I was saying, the events of yesterday hang over us. But it's dawn, gentlemen, and it's this day we must face. When tragedy strikes, we confront a choice: we can fold and forfeit," his voice seemed to rotate towards Parks. "Or we can level up. Take each challenge in our jaws, and consume it like a lion does his prey, so that the next time something like this threatens us, it's a hell of a different lion they're dealing with."

He went on, but Parks zoned out and tried to catch Joe's gaze to see if anyone else was questioning why he had to sit through a motivational lecture from a pedophile when it was colder than a penguin's taint outside. He'd been relieved of his spear at the line. Maybe Joe still had his knife?

"—Which means we have vacancies," the voice broke through on the emphasis. "Many a great man got his first shot before he was ready simply because there was a job to do, and no one better to take it. But I'm confident that whether a post comes as the destiny of one who's spent long years in deserving labor, or the luck of a scoundrel, each man is chosen for a reason. Not by his leader, but by God, Himself, and that reason, however uncertain it may seem, is the one that will see him through. When his boat arrives, there's nothing to do but board it.

"Weather. Provisions. Injuries and the Emotional State of the Men. These are the names of boats our brothers sailed with skill, but now they're rudderless, and without captain. I don't expect you to fill the boots of those great souls, but I do hope you can walk in your own. Tunguk!" The old man perked up, and Parks convinced himself these were the first words his friend was hearing.

"I'm sure you could hold just about any position on the council. The things I saw you do, and at your age! I tell you, fellas, don't turn your back on this one! What do you say? Do any of these topics fall within your expertise?"

Joe gave it great thought, then answered, "No."

"Oh come on! Don't be humble. I'm sure you have great wisdom in many subjects. What about weather?"

"The weather arrives for me as it does for you."

"There, you're sadly mistaken. I'm so clueless on the elements—especially in a place like this—that I could be the lead meteorologist for the six o'clock news!" He laughed alone at his own joke. "Parks'll explain that one to you later. Tell me, will you accept the job?"

Again, Joe surveyed the faces around him. Parks recognized a certain fatalism he'd often seen over the course of their travels.

"Yes."

"Outstanding! It'll be 'aye, sir,' from here on out, but I already feel a thousand times safer—sorry, *six hundred times safer*, with you at my side." He awaited some expression of gratitude that never materialized. "And Parks. Leopard Seal! Most of you are probably wondering why this man sits before me at the council table, rather than bound for execution. Had any other man come for me with his spear, I can't say he would enjoy the same treatment. But—call me soft—I don't so easily forget my loyal mates. He served under my command on two occasions. Not with any particular valor, mind you, but he is nothing if not competent. You men know I love a good underdog story. Where the admiral saw fit to mutilate him, I spy with my little eye the spark of redemption.

"There was never a threat. Even if he was capable of harming me, I have to believe that he would have stopped at the last second. Look at this man! Where you see a giant and a rebel, I see an awkward kid from the land of Santa Cruz, California, spat out in a place he can't possibly belong. They cut off his freaking leg!" Carabiner waved. "The pain of that! I can't even begin to imagine. The trauma! And he survives, only to be chased across the water at the tip of a spear, a refugee, seeking amnesty in our humble mountains. To say he made an error under significant physical and emotional stress would be an insult. I admire him for the mere fact that he draws breath. That he pulled himself from bed after all that, and took a dog sled to join us at the council table, for no other reason than his old mate Alexicus asked it of him."

"Who the hell is Alexicus?" Parks interjected. "I know an Alexander Aramis *Ca-ra-bee-nay*," he laid on a thick French accent for the surname. Carabiner pretended not to hear.

"Leopard Seal. Parks. I'm sorry for what you've been through. If I could take it all away, you have to know that I would—at *any* price. But as I said, it's *this* day we must face. And if you're afraid, if you're confused, no one here will fault you. Not under my watch. I ask only that you bring me the matter man-to-man, brother-to-brother. And I ask, humbly, that you do me the honor of joining my esteemed council."

"Pass." Parks replied without hesitation.

Carabiner's eyelids seemed to cramp mid-blink. He cleared them with some effort, then said:

"Gentlemen, I'll meet with each of you individually. If you'll excuse us for a word…"

Parks pretended to admire the fog-bound sky. He could feel Carabiner's eyes on his cheek, working through one of his persuasion tricks. He probably thought that he could will Parks to turn his way if he imagined himself astride a white horse, red cape flowing over his gilded armor; or some cockamamie crap he got from one of his books he couldn't stop recommending for "personal development." Parks had seen a few chapters. He got the gist. Knew the playbook well-enough to frustrate it. For a solid minute—agony to both of them—he pouted over the vista. A second before he succumbed to a cathartic outburst, Carabiner spoke.

"Bro. I'm trying. Really, really trying, here."

"Don't try. Stop trying." Parks practically cut him off.

"I'm trying to—"

"Stop trying."

"Can I finish?"

"There's nothing to start."

"I've started. My mouth is moving."

"Is it? All I hear is, '*Wak wak wak, wak wak*—" He snapped the jaws of his hand at Carabiner.

"Oh really? Then how are you responding if you can't hear?"

"'*Wak wak waaaak.*'"

"Wow. You've really matured since I last saw you. I'm awestruck by your evolution."

"'*Wak wak,* um, *my* name is Rear Admiral Carabiner," Parks sniveled. "Assistant Ballsack Polisher from Annapolis, my, um, daddy says—"

"For the love of Christ, *shut* the *fuck up!*" His voice echoed down the pass and every miner whipped around to look. Parks made the slow turn to watch the noble officer compose himself. "All good!" Carabiner saluted them cheerfully. He leaned in and whispered harshly. "I didn't want it to go down like this."

"This is exactly how you wanted it to go down. You're the king of the fucking mountain on parade. No one here to call you out, or tell them who you really are. No one who can stop you from doing whatever sick shit you can dream up. You won't even have to resign your commission this time."

Carabiner's hollow jaw tightened under those high cheekbones that would have passed for regal if they weren't so thin. Parks could see him rummaging deep in his bag of tricks for something to use against the man who was always the kryptonite to his douchebaggery. Instead, he seemed to settle himself, and when he looked up, he had learned a new guise—that, or there was a sincerity to him that was almost pleading.

"I'm not a pervert, bro. I wanted to speak to you first. Things got out of hand here, but..." he dismissed some troubling thought. "You don't understand this place. It's more complicated than you want it to be. We're not just in Camne Drumlag, you know. There's a whole world out there, and you don't know the capital of your own selfish asshole. Heck, I'm only one step beyond you. But let me speak from there.

"She's my wife."

Parks' demeanor flashed like the fading embers of a fire.

"That's what I tell them," Carabiner explained. "*Had* to tell them. There was this man…" He searched for the thread to take. "Never mind the details, but he was a viceroy. A powerful man, who can do very good things for you, or very bad ones *to* you. And between you and me, he was looking a little thirsty. In the market, if you know what I mean. These people don't have statutes for consent, bro. I had to swear by it, make him believe it, for her sake.

"These miners, they're cool. I don't think they would hurt anyone under my care—not as long as I live, anyway. But like I said, it's a much bigger world than where we sit."

"Why should I believe you?"

Carabiner shrugged. "Ask her."

"You grooming her?"

"For Christ's sake, she's twelve!"

"Is that your answer?"

"No! I am not groom—you know what? I'm not going to justify myself to you. Think what you like. It doesn't matter, because there's nothing you can do about it, or need to. I wasn't bullshitting when I saw you. I know our history. But tears of joy, that's all I had. We don't have to pretend we ever liked one another. But I thought just maybe, given the circumstances, we might want to take another crack at it."

Parks crossed his arms and scanned over the waking camp to avoid him. He wanted to buy it as much as he refused to admit the possibility of an error. He located his companion, waiting with cautious interest at the sled. The dog boys watched him. The miners, Carabiner. Almost imperceptibly, he straightened out of a sense of duty and grasped something of his old…*coworker's* predicament. He settled on Kjartke.

"If you care about her, I'd advise you to make the same claim."

Parks blushed, realizing Carabiner had spotted his object of focus.

"This is no world for a lady." The assistant viceroy left him to await his sled.

The navy response was encouragingly slow.

"Keep pilin', lads! The dead'll have their stones back soon enough."

Costig added another to the rising breastwork as the crews began their slog up the hill to Gjoraslag. Had they come the evening before, it would have been a tidy rout. The twenty-one marines and their commander had time for little else but to modify the unfinished cairn for their fallen brothers into a waist-high pen too cramped for movement. There, they huddled through the freezing night with scarcely a windbreak.

By morning, Costig found his resolve. They stripped a number of nearby cairns to expand their fortification. "Not Turrha's!" He warned. "He's got cause-enough to be pissed at me." When the reinforcements arrived, Costig squeezed sideways through the narrow entrance and poked his neck over a rough wall punctured with gaps big enough to fit an arm through. His men hurriedly patted snow into the more suspect creases, hoping the temperature would make a mortar of it. The wall was no stead of Tamar-Atxl. She'd lay down fast as a Mattaka prostitute for the first worthy effort. But while he wouldn't hire himself to rebuild the prison anytime soon, Costig couldn't help but feel a pride for the place.

Two crews, near a hundred lads, encircled them under captains Aymos and Folmon. The latter positioned himself in line with the narrow gate behind a wary shield.

"No need to cast your men out of favor, Costig. You're the one who plundered the treasury and murdered a sailor. And yet I could find the weakness to show you mercy if you make it easy on me."

"I already explained your mutiny to me company, and ordered any man who saw it otherwise to return to his post. Care to guess how many did?" Costig leaned out, watchful for archers.

"You've built a fine cairn for yourself."

"And how do you hope to fill it? With navy? Gua and Obrachar told you to fuck off, or I'd be lookin' at the Marines."

"Have you got much food in there? I've enough men to refresh the siege thrice a day."

"I don't suppose you'll be stickin' around to lead 'em."

"The former admiral left me too many messes to clean up." Folmon motioned up an archer to cover the only egress, and formed a spear line three-deep. The rest of the sailors made themselves cozy on all sides of the little hold.

Gionn ravaged the sack of a dead sailor. Out spilled a baleful sortilege of bead and leather, and the range of Amposi superstition: the feathers and wood chips and rotting rations where their luck lived. He turned up his nose and seized upon the clothing, which he wrung out between his fists before tossing it overboard into a growing assortment. His own possessions lay somewhere among them, cast by some other violater. Had the second vessel of angotaks chosen this moment to attack, they would have been repelled by the volleys of filthy gear.

"Up, cunt!" He kicked at Asdosa, pale and half-frozen with an arrow still protruding from his shoulder. Gionn yanked off the coat laid over him like a blanket, squeezed it for a wayward argot, and thought about tossing it over with the rest. He checked to make sure Foster wasn't watching, then returned the article to its owner.

"That's all of it!" Tamarqan announced, and others confirmed from their stations. Corm wouldn't let them rest, though, until they ran their fingers through every crack and crease where it might be stashed.

"Right, then. If it's not among your things, then one of you has it. Give your mate a pat!" Corm demanded.

They eyed each other warily.

"That ain't gonna do no good," Foster volunteered. "Not unless you're tellin' us to strip butt-ass naked and trade cavity searches. You know," he answered the confusion. "Check...*holes*."

"You first," Gionn countered.

"Corm next," added Bubba.

The captain's ire retreated at the prospect of unanimous mutiny. If the missing coin lie on someone's person, there it would remain.

"Hold it for now, you bottom-sucker. That piece is a prize of the *Gairhle*, owed to each accordin' to his shares. You'll find soon enough a thief has no mates. And if it be yours by trade—if Costig's lad has it back— then get on with it! Do alone what the angotaks couldn't. The *Gairhle* is fated for Taclann. I feel even it now, more than ever. Omera's bite will come up empty, and among these barrels row sea kings, ascendin'!"

Arthas scoffed. "Your admirer is as like to be dead now as among us."

"You're as wrong as ever, Arthas. Who among those we buried would Costig have sent after a man like meself? Not one could have coaxed a penny from him."

It didn't go over well with Palqua's bunch, but Gionn knew it was true. They hadn't even managed to outlive Foster—the surprise of the battle as far as he was concerned. Besides, it wasn't Foster's argot.

"When did you see it last?" Foster insisted on inserting himself into ill-advised affairs.

"It was on the mast when I ordered it stowed under the keel."

"And who stowed it?"

The reluctant answers trickled in: Eckerd, Irilo, Gewar, Bale, Ordacles, Lozeder, Baghar, and Palqua. Only Palqua and Ordacles would swear that they saw it.

"There was a mess of hands goin' about before we boarded, though," Bale deflected for the others.

"Aye, and don't forget the angotaks were down there. One of them could have taken it." Ordacles added.

"Angotaks don't stop to open little purses in a fight," Corm replied, growing unsure of himself. "But we'll search 'em all. They haven't got far."

Gionn was among that portion of the crew sent to tramp after the bodies of the slain angotaks for a feel-up. They traveled under shield and spear, anxious that the other crew would happen upon them in the open. A cursory search left them trotting home to the safety of the deck empty-handed.

They found the rest of their mates repeating the scrape-down of the ship with waning enthusiasm.

"Hoy, Wife Seal! Help me with this stone." When Foster joined him away from the others, he risked a whisper. "Mate, give it if you got it. You've bought me loyalty. Don't look at me like that! Only great cunts change—it's a foul sort who think the same thing, over and over. Besides, we're dead if we stay with these buckets. We've got to abandon ship."

"What's that?" Corm boomed from much nearer than Gionn remembered.

"I said, 'We've got to abandon ship!'" He shouted for all to hear. Some of the men laughed, suspecting that anything out of Gionn's mouth was a farce, but he wondered how much Corm had heard.

"Have a look around. We're besieged by ghosts! Not real ones, you idiots," he allayed the fears of a few. "Our enemy is nowhere in sight, yet we sit on our last barrels of food wagerin' whether we'll starve or be cut down. There's no winterin' on a few weeks' meat. We got to head for the coast and hunt."

"Then they circle behind us and take our ship. Or meet us in the open," Eckerd said. "That rout's left you with a false confidence."

"Foster's charge only worked because we were as confused as we were. In the open or on the ship, doesn't matter. You saw what they did to us." Gionn planted his feet.

"The deck was low and off-kilter. She's level, now," Eckerd countered.

"A level deck won't suddenly teach the Navy how to fight."

The better part of the crew ruffled while Eckerd couldn't wipe his amusement away long enough to respond.

"I didn't see Corm's lads rushin' to help when they boarded," Bentos retorted.

"Of course not!" Tamarqan exclaimed. "It was our men in the fray, while the others huddled at the mast or the bow."

"That's because the mast and the bow didn't let 'em aboard." Hogue snarled.

"Aye, and we surely cleaned up the Navy's mess!" Pitras set off a barrage from the navy contingent that the whalers answered voice-over-voice. The men charged one another with shirking, tiring, or fumbling their flaccid spears. The spacing and the order at the wall were to blame; the hold too full; someone put his foot in the wrong place to defend an attack. Gionn backed away, wary of a sudden mutiny breaking out. Yet he couldn't resist heaving a remark about the terrible archers. Moipa and Gewar swung at one another, and it was hard to tell if the men nearby were intervening or adding their blows.

"Chill, bitches!" Foster wedged himself between Bentos and Hogue. "We all did what we could from where we were at." The poor imbecile couldn't incite a mutiny if his survival depended on it—which it did, Gionn thought. The blessing of the man of the battle eased the tempers across the ship until Corm wrested the deck back from its latest brink.

"I'll hear no ill of the dead, and the livin' have earned their keep!" He took up Foster's effort. "And we've all paid too much to abandon our ship to angotak firewood."

Gionn knew he had sufficiently dodged his own comment, but now he was quite convinced he was right about something, and it offended him that others should go on being idiots when his arguments were so clear to himself. That he had meant only to cover for a stray remark when he made the suggestion to Foster hardly weighed on him.

"Our jumpin' will be only temporary. Once we fill our barrels with meat, we'll return to sail in the spring. The angotaks won't bother us in their state. Those of you who boarded their ship," he shielded off any potential reply from Corm, "you saw their larder. They were half-starved and full-mange, and their sister ship would have been no better off. They need food worse than us. Their scouts saw we won, and they slunk off with their tails tucked. We'll have no more trouble from them."

"We both have to hunt. The only question is when?" Palqua steered in his assured manner that never overcommitted itself.

"And where." Tamarqan said of the endless pack.

The bitter bile over who carried the fight found a quieter outlet in a sailor's favorite debate: that of his location. The *Gairhle* drifted half the course of the Attavaik Sea in the quarrels that followed. She lay at once just off Bannoc, or two hundred miles from the Arm. Each speculation had to meet the requirement of being more improbable than the last, until finally someone suggested they were so near Taclann that they might walk. Every swell and sky was paraded out to justify a claim. Finally the ripples broke on the far shores and found their center, crossing somewhere north of Yunoc, south of Geiroc, and optimistically close to the long limb of land that stretched for her sister across the Orin.

"There's whale seal on Geiroc," Fergo swore. "Many a man has said it."

"But Yun is the mother of seals," the taller Bucket spoke up. "From Spring to Autumn, her belly swells with them."

"Won't do us no good if we're closer to Geiroc." Fergo insisted.

"No choice but to head for the coast until we find ourselves, then we turn to the nearer of them." Eckerd's good sense showed that he had seen Gionn's side of it. Corm's hand was forced, but he would have to cut off his piece before surrendering to the crew.

"The only way we can be sure they won't harm the *Gairhle* is if she's the only good ship on the ice. We can made sleds of the one we took, but we have to find the other and scuttle her. That way, no one sails without the *Gairhle*."

"Unless the angotaks decide to make scrap of her, and die with us out of spite." Arthas' remark went ignored because it came from Arthas, and because it was too sensible to admit.

In the glow of another victory, Gionn found the angotak vessel, a black stain across the ice. He stood once more on the edge of that temple of Omera and turned to his own ship, just a ways off and so nearly missed in his desperate scamper. Now they proposed to journey an unknown number of miles to an undetermined island, and back again across the twisting pack, over its breaks and unordered drift. How long would it take them? Just a few weeks would be enough for this place to travel far out to sea, or wind north in a maze of hummocks. He couldn't have been the only one who knew it, but more than that, Gionn always feared a coincidence. Mere weeks had passed since he shunted off that goddess to drag himself aboard. Their reacquaintance was as improbable as it was accursed. Perhaps it was no fair toss that brought him to dance once more upon the white fangs of Omera.

Many men came to the camp of the assistant viceroy from the harbor, from the mines. They arrived with their tools, full of eager apprehension, as if sent for. Kjartke had never seen so many Mattaka men in one place. Not in the camp of her father, even when the bands of the clan gathered for ceremonies. In Drummoc, she saw many people, but they were women, the young, and the old. She had seen sailors formed up in ranks, and sailors on the ship that chased them from Nunoc.

So many men were unaccustomed to seeing a woman, too. Their eyes darted to her as they spoke to one another. Perhaps they only meant to work. This was a mine, she reminded herself. But they were raiders, too. They came in force to steal firestone from Tannawauk. As the water gathers up in a wave, so she felt amid groups of men, and she expected it to break with the same care. When so many men came together, it meant war.

"Carabiner says you have to pretend to be my girlfriend." Brother told her when she fitted the mended boot onto his foot that changed shape so often. "It's for your safety."

"Girlfriend. What is it?" Kjartke had her suspicions, but if he insisted on using strange words, she would make him explain them.

"Like a female partner-in-crime, who possibly lives in the same wigwam."

"We share a tukit," she pointed out.

"Right, We do. Sometimes girlfriends have their own place, sometimes not. I'm not saying you have to actually be my girlfriend, or that I would want that. Just that we have to make these jokers think you are."

"It is a wife?"

"Definitely not. But a girlfriend can turn into a wife."

"Then it is a woman you visit in her tukit at night—the cousin, or sister, of your wife?"

"No." Brother blinked. "No, that's called a mistress, and your men are some dogs if they're getting after your relatives like that. It's like, a woman, and there's mutual affection, but she's not your wife yet."

"I see. The one you are promised."

"That's a fiancee. A girlfriend is less severe. *Maybe* it'll work out like that, if you do all the right things. But it's more like a ladyfriend who may or may not live with you, but there's some physical stuff— and I'm not saying you have to do that part. Pretend. We just look at each other like we might. It's definitely more physical than a wife, maybe on par with a mistress—but things could fall apart at any time without consequences. There would be a lot of anger and broken hearts, but both parties know it's kind of a trial period. You know…taste the seal meat before you trade many beads for it. So there's a constant mistrust. On the other hand, unless someone is just afraid to be alone or using the other person to abuse them in ways they subconsciously have to have in their life, there's also this hope. We—or real boyfriends and girlfriends—are always hoping that this might turn into a fiancee situation, and then maybe down the road if nothing better materializes, a wife."

"It hurt?" He looked at her with his mouth open until she tapped the bottom of the boot.

"Oh. No." Brother stamped it on the ground, then grew quiet as he did when he wanted her to talk. Eventually he asked, "So what's the Mattaka word for 'girlfriend?'"

"Mattaka have no word for this."

"Right on. Should we make one? I don't really know how your culture does things, but it's a really useful concept. Prevents you from getting stuck in a marriage with someone you don't like. Although, the divorce rate is still like, fifty percent. But without girlfriends, it'd probably be ninety-eight percent."

"*Atatapalatet.*"

"What?"

"I make you a word."

"Thank you. Atala…"

"Atatapalatet."

"Atapalapa—atatapal—atatapalapat—"

"Atatapalatet."

"Atatapalatet," Brother said. "Atatapalatet. Atatapalatet."

"Pretend," Kjartke said.

"Right. For your safety. You know this word, 'pretend?'"

"I think so," she answered.

At that time, the assistant viceroy came with a man she had seen meeting with Tunguk and Brother. Several young men stood behind them.

"Leopard Seal! We need your spear, my friend. There's an acute shortage of weapons in the camp, and unfortunately, a lot of things that need to be stuck."

"I mean, sure, I'll do what I can. What are we talking?"

"My apologies," he touched his chest. "Not you, just the spear." The men amused themselves at the confusion. "Satletaluk will return it as soon as we're done."

Brother hesitated, and started to hand it over when she squeezed his foot.

"Ow!" Brother jerked back. He looked to her for guidance, and the men saw.

"If you are hunting and you make a kill, and your enemy tries to take it from you, how will you stop him?" Kjartke asked him, her eyes downcast from the others.

"Ma'am, I appreciate your logic, but Parks isn't exactly in hunting shape right now, nor does he need to be. You're our guests. Our food is yours, and I promise he'll share in the glory of any kills we make with his weapon."

She did not say anything to this man, but looked strongly at Brother.

"Sorry, fellas. What does a man have left if he gives up his piece?"

"What's left is a very valid question," the assistant viceroy cast his gaze on her.

"You know how it is." Brother made the sound of a whip cracking, and though she did not know why, it seemed to satisfy his clansman.

Satletaluk awaited permission to take it, but the assistant viceroy said, "Very well, gentlemen. If it's hammers we have, it's hammers we'll sharpen." He waved them off, then knelt beside Brother. "Do me a favor, bro. I want us to talk—all of *us*. You, me, Sophia. But wait til I get back. I wouldn't let any of my men speak with her alone, and it'll look bad on me if you try. Just as I would never speak to your...what should I call you, ma'am?"

"Atatapalatet," Parks answered.

The assistant viceroy smiled. "Just like I would never approach this lovely companion of yours without your blessing. Tunguk!" He called the old man to join his party, and they left Brother where he lay.

"What I say—it is too much for a girlfriend?"

"Embarrassing me in front of the guys by forbidding me to do something? No, that's pretty standard. In fact, I'd say you were amazing."

Kjartke started to go, but Brother caught the leg of her trousers.

"Can I get a favor from my girlfriend?"

She waited until the men admired themselves marching off behind their leader to slip into the tukit. A strange odor met her. It was unlike leather and the fragrance of bodies that she expected. Only the scent of the poye's home, with its many herbs, came close, but did not prepare her for the strength of it. Kjartke staggered and a strange world raced before her. She wondered if she had not violated some curse by her entry.

"Hello?" A timid voice called to the dark. "You're not supposed to be in here. I'm armed," the girl added when no answer came.

"Forgive me. I will leave." She had nearly recovered from the smell when the girl stopped her.

"Don't!" Kjartke heard the sound of blankets cast aside. "You're the woman. The one who came with Parks."

"Aye."

"Are you his girlfriend?"

She thought it over. "He say to say I am. It is for my safety. I do not think any man fear Brother, though."

She laughed, then cut it off sharply. "Is he OK? I literally cried when I saw him."

"He is important to you?"

"Definitely. I mean, he's one of the only people left from my…ship. My land."

"You are family?"

"No," she said with humility. "We were just on the boat together. It's hard to explain."

Kjartke smiled to herself. "I understand." It was not why he sent her, but now she sensed a thread that ran out of sight to some tucked away coil. She did not often wonder after him. But meeting two on this far shore who could speak of Brother drew her like a girl to rumors of a visiting stranger. Foster, the assistant viceroy, now this young bride: it must have been a strange voyage that gathered such a crew.

"He is alive. But he is not careful. I am not surprised he sink his boat."

"It wasn't his fault. Or his boat. He's like, the last-in-command. Even Foster outranks him."

Kjartke took a satisfaction in hearing it, as well as a sting to learn she had attached herself to one of such low status.

"A rower."

"Not even," she giggled. "He's like, a deckhand, but mostly he just took us out in the little boat and cooked for us. But he was my favorite. He always cracked me up, making fun of my parents, Alexicus, everyone. And his food was ridiculous. He made the *best* ravioli. It was frozen, but he made the sauce from random things he found in the galley, and I swear it was way better than anything you could find back in my land. Wait, so how do *you* know him?"

"We were on a boat together."

"I really want to talk to Parks, but Alexicus doesn't like me going outside without him."

"It is bad to sit inside. Winter is soon. You must get light, or you will be sick. Sit outside the tukit with me."

"You sound like my mom," she laughed with pleasure. "I'll ask him if that would be alright. It's been a while sine I talked with a woman."

Kjartke sensed her withdraw into herself. "He send me. I am to ask if your husband treat you well."

"Can you keep a secret?" Kjartke did not answer fast enough, and she went on. "He's not my husband. I just have to tell people that so they'll leave me alone. But he's really nice to me. And people listen to him."

"It is well. Brother send me with his word: if you want him to kill Carabiner, you must sing the team song of *Frozen* in his hearing."

"*Theme* song?" The girl asked.

"Perhaps."

"Thank you. I don't need that. But please tell him that's very sweet of him to offer."

"It is good you do not ask too much of him."

"I know he's not your boyfriend," she said suddenly. "And I said he was the lowest-ranking guy on the ship. But he gave us the life boat when the ship was sinking. He saved us."

"This, I know he will do. If he can."

They found the second angotak vessel at sundown, and crept as close as they dared, advancing a little more as they lost each degree of light. It was Foster's hunch that the two scouts who returned to find them sacking their ship would lead them to it. There was even a trail of prints to guide them, at first. Step by step, Gionn became convinced, then insistent, that it was his idea. When they lost the track, he suggested they hold the course as though that were some revelation, until their northeasterly hike brought them to the black carcass.

Foster didn't bother arguing. It was the man's consolation for his presence. The crew had quickly decided that a direct assault was madness. They loaded the remainder of their offering coal along with fresh kindling from the conquered ship into a couple of sacks, and elected the "blacksmith's jumpers" to set a fire beneath the hull. Foster was chosen to go with them because he was believed to be favored by a luck since the battle—to these folks, the word didn't mean good chances, but an invisible spirit hovering nearby like a ghost and manipulating human affairs to its liking.

When Gionn heard who their success was entrusted to, he was beside himself.

"*Those* cunts? They'll wander out of sight, count to thirty, and say they done it. Even if they find the ship—and I'll scarf me face with Corm's trousers if they do—they're as like to start a fire as me chafin' thighs. Only an idiot who's never fired a ship thinks anyone can fire a ship. If we mean to do it, we'll send a couple of barrels like Arthas and Ordacles. Otherwise, there's easier ways to free up a few shares."

It was a convincing argument, most of it. Initially, Foster thought he did it on purpose to get a chance to speak in private. But they never got any privacy, and Gionn's rage over his own selection lasted too long for theatrics.

Once they found the ship, they had to freeze on their bellies until it was dark enough to approach. Gionn led the way when the light failed, and what should have been a ten minute hike meandered for over two hours as they doubled back and looped frantically in search of their vanished target. Foster literally stumbled upon it when he tripped over a length of wood laying on the ice. They crouched in perfect stillness until voices guided them to the cold touch of the hull.

She'd been cut free of the ice, but fell most of the way over from where a hasty assortment of ice blocks and oars had tried to prop her. These they tripped over, as well, and only a ghoulish helper could have saved them from being heard. Yet the voices carried on while Gionn filled the sawn-off cask top with coal dust and feathers of wood. Foster heard just two angotaks—as many as they'd seen milling around from a distance—though he knew many more could be resting in her belly.

He found the ship. He carried the flint. Maybe the Mattaka boys would be the only ones who'd believe it, but he was bound and determined to start that fire.

The first *clack* sent a dribble of sparks to die in the nest of kindling. The sound was so loud it paralyzed them where they crouched in the cavern under the keel. When he heard the voices continue undisturbed, he hacked off another one, a little better. It seemed deafening. He waited a long time, expecting an attack any moment, before he made a third attempt.

"Have you got tits for hands?" Gionn chastised in a whisper. He snatched the flint and battered the stones in a furious succession. A shower of sparks fell in and around the bowl. Gionn tried to blow them to life, but they smoldered out again. Before he could repeat the effort, Foster grabbed his wrists.

"Too loud!"

"They'll think it's the ice."

The stones clacked in another machine gun burst. This time, Gionn suppressed a scream and doubled over. "Me finger!" He moaned as his cold digit throbbed.

Atalkut took the flint and drenched the bowl in embers with a few effortless flicks.

They piled on wood and coal in graduating sizes. The flame bathed the underside of the ship in a warm glow, and the four of them gaped in disbelief. A cavernous hole stretched nearly the length of the ship. The outrigger hung gutted. Scraps littered the ice. And a pair of feet dangled through the opening from above.

"Hoy! Whalers! Good of you to warm us."

Foster dumped the rest of a sack on the fire in a panic. They seized their weapons and backed away, guards up.

A second voice laughed gleefully. "Good whaler!" The thick accent echoed. Two obscure heads leaned over the side to get a look at them.

"You got a hole in your ship." Foster hoped to alleviate his terror through small talk.

"A what? *Pinipa!* You let someone gash us!" The first man complained, and now Foster noticed a subtler accent, different from any he'd yet heard, but colored by the prevailing speech.

"Got you surrounded, you wankers, but we came for your ship. Behave yourselves, and we'll return to the only seaworthy vessel without spillin' your cups," Gionn warned.

"What, the four of you? We saw you creepin' a mile away, you fat bastard."

"Hoy! I'm solid as a bullock, you squainsguard gammers!"

"Aye, it's plain which end of the bullock."

"Come on," Foster reached his arm between Gionn and the angotaks. "We're done here."

"Saw you on the *Alabax*, didn't I?" The angotak directed himself to Foster.

He weighed whether to respond, or just hustle into the darkness. With all their turning, though, he wasn't sure which side of the ship they came from.

"You're the scouts."

"We're angotaks, like the rest of 'em, mate! And before you congratulate yourself, you'll know we haven't had a full belly in weeks."

"Left you behind for jumpin' ship under attack, did they?" Gionn prodded.

"Left us, aye, to unname the ship with honor, and see to our dead." The angotak's tone took on a strain of defense that soon eased. "We were headed to the *Gairhle* tomorrow, to ask truce for burial, or take your battle, as you prefer."

"We'll stay out of your way."

"Who do you swear by?" The angotak demanded.

"By my mother's good name."

"Will your mother avenge us? Swear by one of Uinab's sons."

"I swear by 'em all," Foster said with a new confidence.

Gionn muttered some kind of disapproval. Then: "Most of yours died off the ship. Short work for you, mates."

"We have a way to call 'em back aboard before we send 'em off. No angotak goes boatless in death—so long as you haven't defiled their corpses."

"I knew we forgot somethin'."

"Where'd they go?" Foster realized his question came from left field, and it was the living that concerned him. "The rest of the ship."

"A day's sled ahead of you, and well off to Yunoc."

The name of the island rang him like a copper cymbal. "Are we close?"

"Thought that's where you were runnin'," the angotak said.

"We were just runnin' from you," Foster admitted, and he felt the man to gleam through the darkness.

The fire now glowed from deep within the heavy timbers at the bottom of the ship and crept at a glacial pace outward. The first hunk broke in a swirling cloud of embers and hissed on the ice. He wanted badly to stand beside it, just for a moment, to warm himself on the smoldering corpse of their pursuer. These men felt bewilderingly human, nothing like the wild beasts that breached his ship. Only that name made him tremble—*angotaks*.

"Take care of the *Gairhle* for us, mates," the angotak straightened up and moved closer to where the flame now licked through the hull. It played on a face, streaked with grime and a longing that he probably didn't recognize himself. The labors that caked him couldn't hide his youth, a man in his early twenties who had sounded so much older. "We'll sort out who gets to sail her in the spring."

Atalkut and Tunguk tugged at them, nerve-wracked by the whole exchange and eager to curl up in the relative warmth of the hold. Foster felt the cold again, and knew this man warmed himself at the price of all his crew and ships. He took two steps, then called back:

"See yall at Yunoc."

Winnie Cooper pressed her brow pathetically into Parks' thigh as he scratched her neck. A constellation of little rocks lay before him in the snow, connected with zagging strips of rope. He steadied himself on the dog, and extended his toe to tap a central rock, then turned his head right and left to take in the camp. Lines branched from it in four directions, and from those in many more, connecting with other rocks, or stretching to hint at a distance that dwarfed their scraps.

"And is the elevation to scale? The ones farther up the slope are higher?" He asked of the grade on which the map of the mines lay.

"Some are up, some are down, or many ups and downs," Milak answered.

"This mine," Senadak pointed to one at the far end of a long piece of cord, "you could see if there was no fog. But it is high, and a long journey. Your people ask, 'How many miles?' For us, it's not close or far, but hard or easy to reach."

Parks contorted his neck to make sense of the representation. It annoyed him that the farthest rock might only be a half a mile away up a hill, while a closer one may lie eight miles over parallel terrain. But he had to grant it a certain logic, especially for a man who traveled on one leg.

"We know they bailed out down here," he traced the main and only trail leading downhill from their camp, the hub. "But then they could have gone here," he indicated a pair of very close rocks to one side, "or anywhere back up here." Another trail ran unbroken to the south for a great distance—or height—then shattered into many smaller trails and mines.

"If one among them knows Camne Drumlag, it is here," Senadak touched the long trail. "This is where the active mines live. When the sky is clear, you can look down on the whole trail, and on this camp itself, to see where your enemy moves. Or steal food from the camps up there."

"But these are closer?" Another trail branched only a hand's-length from the main artery in the opposite way, where it ran into a tight pair.

"Those are among the oldest mines. My grandfather was too young to haul firestone from them. There is nowhere to go but back, nothing to see, no camps to raid. A bad place to hide."

"Then no one thought to search them." Parks shook his head at the elementary mistake.

"The men searched there, and all the mines. The fresh snow steals their track."

"Then where else could they be?"

"Inside a mine," Milak said confidently. "No one will go in after what they saw. The search stops at the mouth."

Soon the sled careened down the hill along the highway to the harbor. Milak drove, and Ferrakut and Ulwet went in front to restrain the dogs from a suicidal pace. Every bump felt like a hammer blow on his leg, yet the movement thrilled his lurching heart. When was the last time he traveled faster than a walk? If it was on the ship, he had no sense of it. Not since he got...*here*. Wherever this was. Each time the runners drifted sideways toward the edge he imagined a motor rumbling beneath his feet, tires squealing, and some piece of him anticipated the long fall over the edge with glee. It disappointed him to arrive so soon.

In a matter of minutes, they fought the sled up a short rise onto the first branch. The legacy mines gaped like the eye sockets of a picked-over corpse. Plenty of recent tracks ran both ways from the miners' search, but they met no one.

The holes lay at the back of a couple of gouges in the shape of a crescent moon. Parks understood the rock probably lay flush at one point. It was a surface band of coal that drew them here, and an unbelievable amount had been hacked out to a height that he couldn't explain. Over a hundred feet up, he saw the band continue to rise in the mountain, at last safe from their picks. And there, they carved on at ground level, boring into the rock through inhumanly small openings that the shortest of Mattaka would stoop to enter.

The place felt alive with a lore he mostly invented. Parks imagined boys breaking off a strange chunk of rock and marveling when a spark ignited the dust. There were hordes with tools on massive scaffolding. Fires lit every corner; men danced with fire in wild celebration. He imagined a conflagration in offering to the Great Spirit, or whoever their coal god was—maybe a seasonal orgy. The mountain stripped and their thirst unquenched, the ancestors of these dog boys pressed far into the range in every direction.

They filled their kayaks, sunk their hunting boats with their new wealth. Everyone lit fires. There was fire to cook and fire to warm, fire to celebrate birthdays and holidays, or to light the way to pee at night. Dogs pulled a burning sled. Smoke signals filled the air, men were burnt alive. Someone learned to juggle. Growing bored with fire, they awed their distant cousins with their magic, and one day, someone decided to impress a visiting crew from Ampos.

Milak stopped the sled hesitantly far.

"Accuse me of thinking like a lazy bastard, but if I just slaughtered a bunch of people, I'd probably run to the closest place I knew. Especially if I didn't get what I came for, and knew I'd have to go back and try again."

"We should tell Sagalak," Milak suggested.

"Or Satletaluk! He is minister of mines," Ferrakut countered.

"They'll never listen to us," Parks said pridefully.

"They will listen to you. You are the Leopard Seal! You are on the Dawn Council!" Ferrakut lit up.

"Maybe." Parks wondered if either of those things were true. "I once ran a boat with the assistant viceroy—he calls himself Alexicus, but his name's Carabiner, like a little clip you buy at REI. We had to take this annoying couple out in the little boat all day, to whatever cold, stupid piece of coast they wanted to survey. They had a really long expedition planned on Christmas Eve, which is like, the night the Great Santa delivers all his gifts to the people of the world in our culture. Neither of us wanted to spend all day on the goddamn ice, so I suggested to Carabiner that we convince the lady to bring out the daughter as a special treat for the holiday—she hadn't been on the zodiac at all. I knew the kid would complain after a few hours and we could all go home.

"Carabiner said my idea was negligent and dangerous, and that I was barely qualified to operate a zodiac at all, much less with children's lives at stake. He gave me this big speech about how it's doing the hard things that we don't want to do that are the best gifts we can give to others, and how if I go on this stupid little run, I'll have more confidence when I go home because everything seems so much easier in comparison.

He said to think of the people who paid all this money to rent our boat, and how this means the world to them, and if an old guy and a lady can do it, we shouldn't bitch out.

"Next day comes, and the lady tells me the girl is going on the boat with us to see the ice up close. I can tell the man is all pissed about it, but that argument's already in the books. So I figured, whatever. Maybe she was tired of it, too, or just wanted to actually spend some of her family trip with her daughter. Then after I take a picture of the whole family standing on some little hunk of ice in front of the mountains, she turns to Carabiner and says, 'Thank you so much! She really appreciates us including her.' And he proceeds to tell her how he arrived at the insight that the coastline will still be there to survey in a couple of days, but special moments with your family last forever."

The boys seemed to understand as well as the dogs.

"So fuck it," Parks clarified. "He thinks we're worthless? Just a bunch of dog drivers? We'll keep our ideas to ourselves, and see how he feels when we bring him the men who carved his ass like a butter board."

With halting steps, they steered the sled toward the mines at his urging. When the four of them stood before the open wound in the mountain, Milak dared the obvious:

"What will you do?"

Parks had not considered that. Or rather, he remained a believer that the next step in life would present itself to him as his foot fell.

"Do we go in?" Ulwet demanded, and earned a look of reproach from his cousin.

Parks wondered that, himself. There was no way he could expect to capture the men. Maybe if he could confirm their presence, he could come back with reinforcements. He looked around for he-didn't-know-what: empty tin cans strewn on the ground, a smoldering fire, a blood trail. The mouth offered no hints. The blind emptiness contemplated him, a corpse of a mine that seemed to have died mid-sentence. It had been ages since it last led a Mattaka to the underworld. These boys would follow if he asked them. But some force like a magnet within the mountain itself met him, north to north, and he knew that none of them were ready.

The harbor made a nice consolation for them all. The trip couldn't have been in vain, and when he saw ships again and smelled the cold of the water, he remembered that he always withered in their absence, no matter how they abused him.

A surprising bustle greeted them, and familiar faces: Ostuk and Ghrane, the rest of the dog boys and the navy men under Neal. He'd assumed they were tucked away in the camp somewhere, or scattered through the mountains, but most had never left. Not a bushel of coal had been hauled down, but a swarm of Mattaka under Haraket busied themselves over two of the ships.

Only the littlest boy, Arnake, gave him a hero's welcome by throwing himself on top of Parks with painful abandon. Arnake's old man and uncle left when they saw the sled approach. One other Mattaka who he didn't recognize called out, "Leopard Seal!" And waved frantically. Parks returned the salute, and the man pointed down to show off his own amputated leg, with a wood prosthesis strapped to the nub.

"Same," Parks acknowledged patronizingly. "Right on." He quickly flagged down Ostuk to avoid having to approach for a conversation.

"Going somewhere without me?"

"I will be glad to finally sail without you on my roster," Ostuk joked. "Don't worry. We will return in a month or so."

"There are no winter provisions at Camne Drumlag. Ostuk and I take our ships to the hunting camp on the far side of Drummoc." Haraket took a break from directing the loads. "You will have to tell me of the Dawn Council."

"Am I still on it?" Parks made a face. "Maybe we can switch jobs. I'll drive the hunting boat."

"I would be glad to, mate. But if we can't take enough food for nearly a thousand men, all of us starve."

"Where have I heard that before?" Parks said sarcastically, then realized no one present knew of their troubles at Yunoc.

"Hey, can you bring a message for me?"

"To the hunting camp?" Haraket asked, puzzled.

"Yeah. What's left of them." Others gathered, drawn by the remark. "If I tell you a super top secret, can I trust you dudes not to run and blab to the admiral?" They nodded with concern. "Tell them their families are safe with my boy Lenet, and that they'll be reunited sooner than they think."

"Lenet?" Haraket didn't recognize the name.

"Drummer on the *Queen Taral*," one of the miners confirmed. "They are on the Nunoc passage."

"With two other ships. Sadly, they ran aground and all hands were lost." He delighted in the reactions during his pause. "At least, that's what me and Foster told the viceroy at Nunoc." Parks grinned. "They found a nice winter harbor at an undisclosed island, where we gave them whale meat, and made sure no one would come looking. If there really is a bunch of warships heading down to besiege us in Spring, let's just say they may have to get in line." He winked. "'Signed, the Leopard Seal.' Don't forget that part."

A stir of Mattakatan whirled through the miners. Parks squinted fondly at the sea, his old amigo, at the end of the southernmost route, where all waters came to break against the black rock of Camne Drumlag, and ripple back.

They placed their hands in the center on top the assistant viceroy's, and seeing no other way, Tunguk added his to the stack.

"'Hammer' on three. One, two, three..."

"*Hammer!*" The circle yelled without him. He felt the air crack as they lifted their hands, and came away somewhat impressed at the ritual.

Tunguk stood with the rest of the Dawn Council in a place of privilege, behind the line of the Midshipmen and under the heavy guard of Mattaka. Half the men at Camne Drumlag mustered. Near the entrance, he saw that a mast leaned against the rock wall, near where he suggested, and an archer sat behind a ship's hatch.

The marines retreated out of sight into the mine. For all the men present, only twelve came to the fore, half of them Midshipmen. They carried two shields, and the young Mattaka among them borrowed the steel weapons of other Midshipmen who waited in the second line. No more could fit where the high walls narrowed to the mouth. The shields took up in front of the entrance, with the others stacked behind.

Two men carried a bushel of firestone around them and set it at the edge of the hole. They took up shovels, and in turn flung a powdery mix of small fragments into the mine. Tunguk thought he saw the trick, and smiled to himself. When the bushel was empty, they retreated. Two more miners came with lump firestone, and poured it at their feet. They brought it to smoldering, then the first shovel threw smoking red shards deep into the mine.

"More dust," He advised the assistant viceroy.

"Plenty more where that came from, Tunguk. Let's just see what happens."

The miners paused only to let the flame spread in the pile before tossing in many shovels full.

"He does not listen." Tunguk regarded the boy with surprise. "You are an old fool—that is what he thinks."

"He moved the archer," Tunguk answered.

"I sure did, grandfather. Thank you for the excellent suggestion," the assistant viceroy repositioned himself so that Satletaluk and Sagalak stood between him and Tunguk.

"That is all. Just enough to blame you if it fails." The young visitor scowled.

Tunguk pushed through the guard and was pleased to see the boy follow him where others would not interrupt. He advanced as far as the second line, and squatted near a wall away from the others, careful to keep his distance so he did not add to the numbers, though by his count the shovel men already fouled the two sixes of fighting men. Here, he could see much better.

"I did not expect to see you away from Drummoc," he told the boy.

"If you can take me nowhere better, I must at least go somewhere different."

"Perhaps there is nowhere better for you than here. Many things are happening."

The boy snorted. "I see miners shoveling firestone."

The chink and scrape of their rhythm captured Tunguk. He watched many embers fly, until there came a different sound. A shovel tossed its load, and a roll of cracks returned from the mine like hail striking the deck of a ship. The miners noticed it, too. The next flung his load, and the cracks came again. They tensed and waited. Now the first tried another toss, and the firestone broke across a shield as it raced from the mine. The men with the shovels threw them down and fled just beyond the point of a spear.

The Midshipmen with the shields met the marines who sallied forth. Six came, as wide as the line would allow. An arrow fell from somewhere above Tunguk and took one of the marines between the shoulder and neck, forcing him to fall back to the mine. Mattaka lunged with spears. The shafts clashed, until more arrows forced the enemy to raise their shields overhead and return to the mine after a battle of only moments.

The assistant viceroy came forward. Tunguk worried over what name to call him by. He had heard Alexicus and Carabiner, but could not recall which came first. He decided on the first, because he suspected the other was a vile word concocted by Brother.

Alexicus cheered the men, and ordered a "shift change," which was explained to them ahead of time. He claimed it was a tactic he learned when he served in "youth hockey," where every man was changed often for a fresh team, as one changes dogs. None of the young Mattaka were wounded, and they refused to quit the field. It took many threats to remove them and place their weapons with a new team of Midshipmen and miners.

The marines were few, Alexicus said, and they would tire quickly as they faced new warriors. Tunguk thought this clever, but now they could not get the marines to come back for another fight. Much firestone went in. They tried a weapon unfamiliar to the Mattaka—the sling. The assistant viceroy had shown it to the people. Tunguk knew it well. He saw it first among the Naopawi people, who used them to raid each other for wives. They were not as true as arrows, yet a fated toss could kill. The youth took them up with zeal. A terrible whirling sound cast stones into the mouth of the mine. For much of the light, they tried their slings, their taunts, and spared no burning firestone, but none of it could draw another battle.

The boy remained with Tunguk, making scornful comments. This was no battle, and held no glory to him. At dark, Alexicus pulled his forces back, complaining that the archer was so close as to frighten the enemy off the field and spoil the attack.

"It was a thin firestone," Tunguk said to Satletaluk as they prepared a tukit. "The first bushel. Did it take long to crush?"

"Hardly. It is from a mine at the beak of Tannawauk's bird. The firestone there crumbles so easily, it cannot be used in the forges, though the mine is still rich."

"I think it is you who suggested to put dust in the mine," he guessed, and Satletaluk grinned.

"Any miner could tell you the dangers of it. And any wandering old man," he gleamed, "that more dust is needed."

"The moon finally looks through the fog," Tunguk admired the pale glow. "I think I will walk back to camp. See if the dog drivers are restless. I know something they can haul."

"By yourself? There are marines out."

"If I do not return, tell Alexicus the weather will grow cold and clear." He started up the trail, and heard the crunch of the boy's steps behind him.

As the trade died, Cormdran spent much of his time counting. He rejoiced each morning he made it to sixteen—that not one more had jumped. Most of them reported for duty only to be tapped on the chest. Having confirmed their enlistment, they wandered off to spend the weekly pay he now issued to prevent a total collapse of morale. The men each received a palmful of beads or a bowl, or some charm or token to trade with the squains for hasqa and other favors.

He salved himself with the rumors that reached him via Oterec, who communed over a cup each morning with Foul Hand Waits. Palqua had fallen sharply out of favor with the admiral. While most of the sailors did less each day than Corm's loafers, Palqua's lads man-hauled sleds up Urkuk to stuff water barrels with snow, or scoured the rough spots off of skeleton ships that would never sail again. The sight of Arthas cursing this way and that may have done as much to hold Corm's numbers steady as anything.

While those who jumped the *Gairhle* were confined to Palqua's roster, others wormed their way onto any crew who would take them. At least a dozen men abandoned the captain under Turrha's harassment. The other captains dared not speak to Palqua in public, for fear of association. He could hardly cross the harbor grounds without that marine, Costig, making no effort to conceal his pursuit.

Palqua broke on the morning that a darraig under some lieutenant of Captain Bayochar returned from the hunting camp with scant provisions. He probably thought he would be sent to sort out the squains. For the first time in many weeks, the Amposi approached the *Gairhle* with Costig and a squad far enough back that they couldn't help him if he pissed off Corm.

"It is clear you will not sell enough to pay for your repairs." He hurried on before Corm could retort. "I do not wish to strand your men. Hiade is too narrow to court enemies. If you will trade one out of four of what remains, you will have your wood and carpenters, your nails, all that you require. Another one of four, and you will be provisioned when you decide to sail. That is half of a cargo you will never need, unless you trade your oilskins and trousers for the costume of a noble woman of Ampos."

Corm knew his answer, but had learned to consult his men. They stood unanimously, and without debate.

The next morning, the navy carpenters arrived to fashion a wedge and repair the wood the mast had blown out when it fell. It bothered him to see Arthas and Jonn, Fid, Otsander, Casey, and the rest of his lads among those who came to carry off the same goods they won so hard. Corm denied them the finer pieces—the statue, the war club, anything of unusual taste. He felt a lightness as it left, and suspected the men felt it, too. The only joy greater than a good haul was the same cargo discharged.

So it brought a special bitterness when Costig returned later with a full company to recall the carpenters. They carried off every board and nail while Corm spat on their necks—orders of the admiral.

Though as an unenlisted merchant he was barred entrance, the little congregation of sailors on the step of the navy hall saw it wise to let him pass. An Amposi sergeant-at-arms tried to stop him for a word, but he bouldered past and knew, having never been inside, exactly which door to beat on.

"Out, you honorless lick-boot! You corrupt bastard! Unwed thief!"

There were enough men in the hall to remove him by force, but they only gathered at a distance and pleaded in consoling tones for him to wait outside. Corm had none of it. He pounded the door again, and settled for a considerable wait before it finally cracked. A squain girl squeezed out as though afraid to open the door more than necessary, and scurried out of the hall.

Turrha took his leisure to arrange himself, then condemned his idle men with a look. He didn't protest Corm's presence in the hall, or ask why he'd come.

"Speak with Palqua."

"What?"

"I never agreed to such a price. A few armfuls of cloth for so much wood?"

"Cloth, aye, and jewelry and housewares you'll not find for thousands of miles!"

"What use do I have for it?" He waved his hand dismissively.

"Then I'll have every last bead of it back at me ship before I return, or I'll breathe your name on every shore as the foulest port-swindle this side of the Atlantic, a shame to your king and your kind!"

"I do not have it. Speak with Palqua." He smiled and closed the door courteously.

The little siege at Gjoraslag became the latest spectacle for the Mattaka. In its second full day, the people arrived with the light in greater numbers than the besiegers. They lay blankets on the snow, and the children played games behind the navy circle. Clever women came with warm mittens and skins to trade the sailors. It was not a hardy crew. Many parted with all they had for a small comfort. They brought bladders of hasqa, and took home copper for a single cup. Some offered prayers or charms, and others, to curse the sailors' enemies for a small fee.

Norwet resisted as long as he could. There was plenty to do to ready the camp for Winter, and besides the women, he had only the elderly father of his aunt's first husband to help him. As soon as the sled materials were stowed, he left his cousins to tend to the larder and made the long walk by himself, envious of the boys at Camne Drumlag.

The stone ring was poor. It would have toppled to the first ram. The marines lazed about inside, covered only up to their waists. No archers waited. No side tested the other. He tried to spot Costig, but many lay against the low wall out of the wind. A passing bird rested atop the entrance, then left for more promising grounds. Norwet did not even approach as far as the rest of the Mattaka. It seemed a wasted effort. He prepared to return to his chores when a girl came to him from the people.

"Did your family arrive safely with your cargo?" She asked politely, then twisted her lip to show what she sought. His hesitance seemed to offend her. "It was me who brought the sack of food to your camp—when the blacksmiths beat you up."

Norwet hadn't recognized her, and knew only that Milak said her family was large and difficult. "The blacksmiths did not beat me. As for our cargo," Norwet shrugged. "It was not seized at the harbor. That is all I know."

The girl tried to follow what he stared at through the siege, but in truth, he only meant to look past her.

"A fine battle," she said.

He snickered. "We are spoiled by excitement. But I admit, I am bored to watch the Navy seek a fight with an admiral who was caught stealing and run out of his post."

"I can't stand it. But I won't miss seeing him killed. He murdered my cousin. As for these others," she said of the Mattaka, "they don't have the guts to commit to a side. I saw a man walk right past the navy line and try to sell to the marines over the wall. No one stopped him! They simply had nothing to pay him."

"I can't blame them. They have already had new officials, riots, and news of war—and an infamous prisoner who cannot be contained. Everything moves. What is there to commit to?"

She considered his argument without being impressed. "Of all people to say such a thing. You have now escaped twice from what I hear. Who is the prisoner who cannot be contained?" She smiled over her shoulder as she returned to her bloody vigil.

They found the *Gairhle* by the low signal fire, and when Gionn called out, a cheer went up before they could give the news. The blaze from the angotak ship had arrived well ahead. Already men tripped through the dark, gathering tools and putting the ship in order. No more praise came their way. The crew reamed them for taking so long, for resting beside a fire or stopping for a cuddle. They were called shirkers for not giving a proper battle. Pitras wondered why it took four of them to light a bit of wood.

Yet they stretched their ears for Gionn's tale of mayhem—the panic that ripped through the sleeping angotak vessel, dozens of men flinging themselves to safety on the ice, the shrieks of those overcome by the flames. He produced a ring he apparently cut from the finger of a man who fled his way in the confusion.

Foster and the boys remained quiet. No one hassled them for huddling in the ship for a few winks while the rest of the crew hurried across the ice to finish stripping the nearer of the enemy vessels of all the wood and leather they required. By the time they woke, the pleasant hack and scrape of wood played from all quarters. The carpenters took advantage of their opportunity to fling men this way and that for a certain adze or a nail. Everywhere, men split and shaved beams for the skilled hands who made them flat and true.

Bone by bone, four long sleds came together. They were as simple as two runners joined by planks spaced a foot apart, no handles to complicate things. Foster thought they looked like pallets, but he had a suspicion that the thin runners, so fussed over by Aber and Igonus, had a method to them he couldn't quite guess.

All who weren't occupied by the wood work dressed the ship for Winter. Everything that wasn't coming with them went aboard. Foster helped five other men lower Mahal off the ship. The Amposi couldn't even sit up on his own from his wounds, rudely sewn with leather stitches that looked too fat and too few. He joined Tarvin and Asdosa, none of them in a condition to work.

In his uncertainty about what to do, Foster gravitated once more toward Gionn. Along with a number of Corm's men, they worked a stolen mainsail over the ship like a funeral shroud—no easy task when the leather was frozen solid. It had to be beat with a vengeance to bend or to straighten. It was too short to cover the whole ship, so their own spare sail had to round it out. His hands stiffened on the cold sail and peeled raw as he snapped edge after edge into place, sneaking warmth from a sleeve when he could.

When he saw her in that state, forlorn and huddled against the wind, he could hardly believe that crusty little lump had been his home for so many weeks. As much as he despised it, wanted to smash it on the rocks, Foster felt a painful severance. He couldn't imagine ever seeing her again. Not if anything went as he hoped.

For the others, the effort was meticulous. One seaworthy ship remained. No matter how far they sledded or what happened, it meant nothing if they couldn't find her again before the ice broke up.

"To arms!" Tamarqan hollered from the ice, and the call echoed through the men. Foster snatched up his spear and met the others to find them pointing at a distant pair of figures standing a few hundred yards off the angotak ship. Those whalers gorging themselves on her wood fled towards the *Gairhle*.

"Just two of them. We must attack before they are joined," Moipa insisted.

"They ain't here to fight. They came to see about their dead."

"Then let us reacquaint them with their mates." Palqua backed his man, but Foster shook his head.

"I swore 'em a burial truce on the sons of Uinab."

The whalers groaned a disappointment that concealed their relief at not having to face the angotaks again.

"Good that you had a moment between burnin' their ship and cuttin' down the stragglers to negotiate a burial," Bentos sneered at Gionn.

"With the *angotaks*!" Hogue panted. "Do you know what courtesy they'll show *your* corpse?"

"Hell, they can do whatever they want. If I'm dead, what's it matter?"

He thought it was a smooth parry, but a horror of quiet disbelief danced over the whaler's faces. They turned to Gionn as one does the parent of a misbehaving child. His exaggerations of their victory were already forgotten for some crime that Foster couldn't grasp.

"Matters very much where you go next, mate, and in what standin' you arrive," Gionn clarified.

"Where I go next, huh?" He said with a derisive confidence that impressed no one.

"Aye. Do you expect to find you're trapsin' the only world of worlds, and that you'll get to vanish without consequence like a drop of water in the midday sun?"

The crew was coarse and treacherous, illiterate and violent, so Foster often forgot how delicate they could be about matters of superstition. They thought him an idiot, or reckless, and he wanted to show them he knew what they meant, he just didn't care.

"You mean the underworld. Where the dead go."

"Under, aye, among other places." Gionn answered with a measure of sympathy for his ignorance.

"Nor only the dead," Fergo added, and Foster noticed the man's severed pinky now hung gray from a cord around his neck like a charm. "The gods visit in disguise, as do men: Glaumus, Iop, Tercatitl, Avernase, Jorn's wife—lots of cunts."

"Aye, and there's more places that the dead can't go at all. What about Tlintaat?" Jenneker leapt into the mix.

"Gods, heroes, wayward bastards," Gionn cast a judging eye, "and even the unburied."

"And here you are, fittin' out your enemy to meet you!" Hogue threw his hands over the field of angotaks, as equally sure that a mistake had been committed as he was resigned to honor Foster's truce, apparently.

Foster stung with the rebuke of having assumed he knew something. A few glorious accidents thrust him into favor, only for him to forget that he was still the stranger here, the fool. He resolved, as he had the other times, never to speak confidently again. His pride, however, begged to be eased down. He grasped for a question, a gesture of humility.

"Do they ever come back?"

"Many claim it, but when have you ever met a man just returned from another world?" Gionn asked rhetorically.

"All those I named, but Jorn himself!" Fergo contested.

"I don't mean the old tales. A real salt and blubber cunt roamin' the fleets."

"Many times!" The wiry stoop deepened and Fergo seemed to curve like a wisp of smoke when he immersed himself in his oddities. "I've met men back from the Pillars, and Obdu Caran, and a lad who was stolen by the Uhkru off to Wisk before I was born. He escaped after many years and when I met him, looked a youth though me own hair had its gray. Even rowed next to a lonesome sort who was born and brung up in Manhas, and lost on our shores. He saw I knew more than most, and often asked me how he might return. I gave him me advice, but don't know what came of him."

Gionn coughed with laughter. "If you claimed you were a dwarf giant cast out of mad Hafalras, I'd sooner believe it, you wank-wit. No one passes 'tween worlds like a brothel door."

Palqua smiled at Fergo with incredulous charm. "In Ampos, it is only a great hero who can make the journey, and he must trick a man into trading skins to return."

"In Ampos, aye! Better men know the way. There's half-a-hundred: sailor-priests who'll show you at great expense, or certain initiations where the goin' and the comin' is part of the rite! You can find it by certain maps, stumble on it through awful trial, or if you're set on it, and don't care to dally, you sail from the port of Noina at neap tide under the dark moon, with two bulls on your barc and no metal, nor can you break the water with an oar, but you go only by sheet. With stone or wood, you slaughter the first bull, and spill his blood only in the sea; the second, only in the ship. Then you beg a sign of the serpent Tamash, and drink when he spits fire, and light a bowl when he tries to drown you. If you survive it, memorize the words he gives you, and forget not the sounds. You'll need them after you sail four currents, two up and two down, under four skies. And you must never steer for a siren, or fail to help a stranded man. When your ship at last sinks, utter them quick, before you drink your drink!"

Foster was relieved to see that the rest of the whalers were as bewildered as he was.

"Is that all?" Gionn asked.

"Aye, and there's a good many temples that have it as a secret teachin'—to go between the worlds, that is. Three or four in Atlantis alone, and on most of the nine shores."

The crew fell into loud debate. Foster was forgotten as they levied challenges at Fergo. They gave evidence of other worlds and legendary passages, or dismissed a far-fetched example. Lies and dreams were traded, and where they agreed on the place, the route differed, or the kind of people a man would find there. Shouts crossed until they hardly seemed to respond to one another as much as take turns expounding their own topics.

But a single word hung. He had heard it once before, an afterthought in a song when they first sailed. *Atlantis*. It meant nothing to him, except that it was familiar. Maybe it shouldn't have struck him at all. There were plenty of recognizable things. Parks, for starters. And though Antarctica had a different name and a marginally warmer climate, it seemed familiar enough. This was no alien planet. He knew ships and spears and they spoke his tongue. Often, it slipped his mind that he was anywhere else at all. It had arrived suddenly like the ice on the sea, a bizarre layer, come for a season.

It shouldn't have bothered him, but now it sparked like the little beacon on the *Gairhle* the night before, that lined him up between the burning wreck behind and his passage home.

A name, among many names. What was it to him? A drowned city, he figured. Some fantasy at the edge of his memory. Fergo had mentioned it so casually, like it was Pittsburgh, or Spain. Though he couldn't recollect it from his own world, it was as though for the first time, he spotted a feature of the shoreline that looked something like his map.

Tunguk once told him that to avoid being lost, he needed two places: one to stand, and one to orient by. In the thick of the whaler, with its mutinies and battles, he thought he came to bring down a ship for an admiral, to save his friends. On some level, he always knew the real reason: a promise to Parks of a way home. But the impossibility of that promise required him to bury it. He would have broken if he had nothing but that to hold him.

Now it swelled in him again as a turbulent sadness. These men, this ice seemed once more a layer on the surface. Beneath it pitched a wave that upset his hard-won belonging. Tears froze on his lashes. He brushed aside the thin crust. If he could just get his nail under the edge, he might peel this whole world away. His sadness was for the things it covered: beautiful cities, friends, lovers, and kin. A humanity this place couldn't afford. He'd deceived himself with the worries of the world around him. It mattered to him where a ridiculous little boat ended up. He wanted to win, and to be liked.

He glanced over the whalers who minutes earlier, he sought to impress. Even the ones he cared about—Atalkut, Tunguk, and hell, maybe Gionn—weren't more than appearances. They'd shown up uninvited. Now he wished they would recede before the sun.

The crew carried their debate to their work with fraying commitment. Most of them cut ice blocks to build a stand for the mast. The carpenters scraped at the sleds while every bit of gear was lashed into place. Atalkut claimed to have worked a season helping brings the dogs to the harbor, and he showed the men the Mattaka way to ice the runners by spitting water onto his mitten and wiping the thinnest layer of water that froze immediately, again and again until they would glide like skates.

Foster watched the angotaks venture into their ship. He walked out a little ways and gave a slow wave to confirm his oath. Gionn drifted his way, clear of the work and the wild stories.

"I'm keen to see how they get 'em back in the boat," he offered. "You wouldn't know, of course, but if you die in the water, thus you'll arrive in

Manhas. Men go to great lengths to stay on board, or make land. That's why you should only jump ship if you got somethin' better to jump to."

"Mm." Foster made a distracted sound. They stared at the distant enemy as Gionn tried to suss out some magic from the process. Foster's words stuck in his throat, like he was trying to say aloud something that shouldn't even be whispered. Finally, he managed it.

"Is there really such a place as Atlantis?"

He was so prepared for the scorn he would receive that it almost disappointed him when Gionn took it in stride. He draped a brotherly arm over Foster's shoulders.

"Fuck Fergo. You're the one seems like he comes from another world."

The remark brought Foster back to the ice, and he stared in detail at the miraculous patterns of tiny frozen swell that swept past their feet. Under the weight of that arm, watching the angotaks tend their dead, everything became solid again.

"I do. Where I'm from, we control the land, the sea, and the sky. We got great wonders you can't even dream of. Everybody else just tries to be like us—to dress like us, talk like us, move next door to us. But at the end of the day, I would rather be a regular guy in America than the king of every damn place yall just named—especially this one."

"Aye, that's Atlantis, cunt. You just got a strange name for it." Gionn left him for the crew.

Foster looked back and saw the whalers press hand-over-hand to raise the mast in its icy brace beside the ship. Atop, a vertical line of three red pennants fluttered. That alone marked the place they would have to find on a shifting pack if they hoped to die aboard the *Gairhle*.

13

MATTAKALAND

Norwet ached under the weight of the sack and the long walk from the dog camp. The meat, still frozen, burned his arms through the leather and made him rattle with cold. As the incline leveled, he grew alert. Soon he would encounter the navy line, but the dark would not tell him where.

He listened, stepped, listened, stepped. The first angry mutters reached him. Men shifted in their frigid sacks, unable to sleep. Norwet bent around, unsure what he hoped to find. Quiet didn't mean an opening, but it felt safer to him. If his last visit could be trusted, the men lay not in a close-woven circle, but irregular clumps of companions. When he had traveled half of the circle against the sun, the invisible line could be felt to thin, not by any sense, but by a dog driver's intuition. Certain places felt open for a sled to pass. Here, the pitch night beckoned him through—he hoped not simply because he was tired.

With a hoist, he repositioned his arms under the sack, closed his useless eyes, and started forward. When he was sure he must have passed the sailors, he put his attention to the backs of his wrists, the first things that would feel the stone fort of Gjoraslag.

Norwet did not notice the hand that seizes his ankle until he toppled forward. The strong grip dragged him back, and he heard feet shuffle in the snow.

"Where you off to, lad?" A rich voice asked with cheer. Two men snatched him upright.

"Who's there?" A tense voice demanded nearby.

"Nemas and Muir. Got ourselves a visitor, Captain," the first sailor replied—apparently Nemas.

Many hands felt over his head and his face, his arms, his burden.

"Squain," Muir confirmed. "What's in the sack?"

Norwet saw no cause to lie. "Meat. For the admiral."

"Oh, come on! Grace us with a tale, at least!" Nemas said. "Haven't you got your dead grandmother's remains that you got to bury before the sun's up so she can marry an Amposi prince in Urkuk?" They laughed at him.

"He'll need a better one for Admiral Folmon. Search the bag," the captain's voice approached.

Norwet expected to feel it yanked from his grip any moment, but its weight remained through a long silence.

"What's to search? Meat. For the admiral." Muir said.

"Could be weapons, as well," their captain said.

"Could be all sorts of useful things, but they're not for you, are they? He said they're for the admiral." Nemas' voice carried through the hand on Norwet's shoulder and shook his bones with its calm insistence.

"I'll alert Folmon," the captain sounded to stutter with frustration.

"Captain." Nemas' tone was one of loving concern. "This one'll pass."

"Are you mad? He would feed the marines!"

"Do you think we're fine men?" When the captain couldn't find his words, Nemas said it again. "Me and Muir. Are you glad to have us on your crew?"

"Well…*aye*, but—"

"Don't you recall we signed to the *Gairhle* with the once-admiral Turrha? Whereon the new admiral Palqua arrested the lot of us and threw us in prison. Costig could have executed us for jumpin', but he reinstated every man without penalty. Now me fourth admiral has us freezin' half to death every other night 'cause he's too soft to knock a wall and have it out. Seems to me you've Costig to thank for men like us. Don't begrudge us repayin' a debt."

The captain spoke many half-words and made noises of a gurgling animal. Then Muir spoke.

"Why don't you make a round to check the rest of the line, sir? We never saw you here. Oh, but Bruco, if you breathe a word to Folmon, more than a few of your lads'll visit you where you sleep."

A frantic stomp fading away told Norwet he was alone with the two sailors.

"I can't foresee what he'd do with the news, but we'd thank you to tell Costig that Nemas and Muir have another shift night after tomorrow on the east line." Nemas clapped him with a blow that nearly toppled him, then the night grew still, and Norwet hurried to feel out the cold stones.

The sled caravan wound into the forward camp on the third day of the battle. Carabiner and his lieutenants watched the procession in annoyance. Most of the drivers urged their teams on to the front lines, where they unloaded their covered bushels. Senadak broke off from the main group, and two more sleds followed. Atop the cargo rode Eskimo Joe.

The old man hopped off and helped guide the next sled broadside to Carabiner. The second it stopped, Parks threw his stump into the snow with a cry of agonizing relief.

"*Owwww*, fuck me!" He beckoned at the two boys who drove him. "Service dogs," he demanded, his eyes cringed shut. He groped until they unharnessed Barbados Slim and Winnie Cooper, who worked their heads under his fingers.

When the burning vibration of the ride eased enough for him to look around, Parks squinted over the idle camp. "Is this it? I don't see anybody fighting."

"Tunguk!" Carabiner glared disapprovingly at the panting invalid. "What's all this?"

"Dust," he answered.

"I don't recall ordering 'dust.' I suppose this is your way of trying to anticipate my needs?" Joe smiled his response. "In that case, thank you very much. I think we all saw how well the dust idea worked, but I can appreciate initiative, even in its clumsier forms. Though I will admit, I was disappointed to miss your weather report the past two mornings."

"Clear and cold," Joe looked up at his breath against the unusually blue sky.

"Right. Satletaluk told me. We'll speak later about the procedure for being granted leave of the front, but for now, maybe you can tell me what *he's* doing here."

"I was summoned," Parks bellowed.

"Oh? By who?"

"By me," Satletaluk tipped his head apologetically. "Haraket tells me you have word of my son," he addressed Parks.

"Uh…" Parks rotated his stump so that a different part lay on the snow. "Of course. I have many friends. I'm sure your son is one of them. But don't be jealous, Carabiner. I'm really excited to see you, too. I came to apologize."

Carabiner's eyebrows raised guardedly, as though considering whether he should allow him to go on with what was bound to be a sarcastic rear assault.

"I'm not normally one to make excuses," Parks ignored the snort in response, "but I just haven't been myself, lately. No one tells you how bad it sucks to have your leg cut off. I know, that was weeks ago. Every now and again, I think I'm turning the corner, and I try to stand up and hop around a little, take a sleigh ride—and every time I do, I end up laid out under some blanket like a corpse for the next day and a half. If I were stateside, I'm pretty sure I'd still be in a Navy hospital out of my mind on ketamine.

"As it is, I just start the day trying to talk myself out of a suicide attempt by reminding myself that there aren't any guns or places to hang myself anyway, and the cliffs are too far of a walk. Then I spend the next thirty minutes trying to get my gooch to unclench. Can anybody explain to me why my gooch hurts? I didn't know that was connected to my shinbone, but goddamn! I might could deal with the leg if it didn't feel like someone was stomping my junk from the inside."

He lifted his stump out of the snow, placed it on a folded blanket, and gently squeezed his calf for warmth. "Anyway, I asked around. This is the first place I've ever been where every single person I meet speaks highly of you behind your back. They say you're noble, or kind, or generous, or they tell me how you take care of your wife," he let the word hang to show he could say it without animosity, "as if she were your favorite sister. I didn't speak to her, either, but she speaks, and what she says of you…well, it isn't what I remember. Nothing is.

"So maybe I owe you an apology. I showed up in a bad mood, and you're just so easy to take it out on. *So* easy. Like you ask for it, with your little face, and the way you—" Parks stopped himself. "You're a different man. And maybe I'm not. Not as much as I'd like to think. You tried to include me, and I insulted you in front of your friends." He scanned over the Mattaka councilors and the miners gathered at Carabiner's side. "It was a dick move on my part. Like I said, my junk hurts. But no excuses. I don't even know what we're trying to do here, but it'll be hard enough if we work together.

"I'd almost rather hack off my other leg than say it, but here it is: I messed up, bro. I was an ungrateful little bitch. I've come to ask—no, I've come to *beg* that you reinstate me to the Dawn Council. I'm willing to start at the bottom. Work my way up. I can be head of janitorial operations, I don't care. Latrines, personal grooming standards, whatever. You have my pledge of loyalty. The Leopard Seal is your bro again."

Carabiner approached slowly for drama, but his lips curled tightly in satisfaction. He extended a hand, and Parks took it.

"Welcome to the team, bro. I would never put you in charge of personal grooming. But as it turns out, there's a vacancy in injuries and the emotional state of the men. Something tells me you would be a fine ambassador there."

Parks patted him lovingly on the knee cap, then squeezed at both joints enviously.

"How many in my platoon?"

"*Munikjuta!*" Carabiner held out his hand, and one of the men filled it with an ornate club that looked like a man's hip. The stone head fit seamlessly in its wooden socket, while the length was painted with bands of patterns and figures. Two strands of beads hung behind the business end, and a shiny leather glistened at the grip. "These men don't follow orders. They follow leaders. Whoever does what you ask—that's how many are in your platoon. *Kanetlakhuratwe!*" He said to the men. They snatched up their tools, and formed around Carabiner.

"You speak Mattakatan?"

"I won't pretend I'm conversational, but I can say what I need. It's hard to be around these fine people twenty-four-seven and *not* learn something."

Parks receded with embarrassment.

"When you get back to Eagle Camp—that's my translation for where you're staying—do you mind checking on the construction of the forge? As soon as it's done, I've asked that one in twelve of each metal tool is melted down and made into spearheads and arrows. Counting isn't their favorite pastime."

"I got you, homey."

Carabiner started to correct him, and Parks knew it was because he failed to say "sir," but the assistant viceroy thought better, and pointed at him as if he'd made a clever joke. The troop of men followed him toward the front, leaving only Joe and Satletaluk.

The trusted adviser on the state of the mines waited for all the men to pass. He stood a head taller than most of them, which still made him short in Parks' book. But his presence extended well-beyond his stature. Satletaluk had almost no gray hair despite being in his early fifties. His face showed signs of an occasional shave. His body bore the toll of his work: an impossible bony protrusion on his right elbow; hooked fingers, flattened and bent; most of all, a tempered hardness. Here stood a man who rung from thousands of hammer blows, having long ago shed every part of himself that couldn't bear it. He was the miner who other miners looked to. Under the grime, there was an almost noble quality about him. But while the other Mattaka often came across warmly, Satletaluk wore a serious calm that didn't need to speak to make a threat.

"Stab in the dark. Is your boy a rower on a coal ship?"

"Aye. Two sons, in fact. Mennetungiliamuk on the *Queen Taral*— you may know him as Muk. And his brother Mennethiadetartet—Hiad, only sixteen, on the *Pallaia*." Satletaluk seemed to hold back further detail, as if testing Parks.

"I've got to admit, I suck at names."

"Hiad is quiet, but if you knew Muk, you would not forget him. He is first to speak, and last, and you will soon decide how you feel about him."

"Sorry. The one I talked to most was Lenet. He seemed to be the man in charge."

"If Lenet speaks for the people, it is a bad sign for Muk. Tell me, what word do you have of the ships?"

The miner's reticence dawned on Parks. "Your plan worked." Satletaluk only stared in response. "They're safely harbored for winter, and I personally delivered their admiralty letters to Nunoc. As far as the Navy's concerned, they're all dead."

"Muk does not ask his father for plans, or take advice. But I thank you for your help. You say they will return in Spring?"

"Maybe. Lenet's boys want to come out swinging, but there's a lot of guys who don't."

Satletaluk glanced at Joe, who confirmed Parks' account through lack of protest. "If it is even possible, then we must make preparations. There are many things Lenet does not know, and if they fail…" He drifted somewhere far away. "I must speak of this to Alexicus."

Joe watched him go, then sat on a coal bushel next to Parks and swiped Barbados Slim aside with a leg.

"Your friend, he has sailed many days with you, yet he does not hear your empty words."

Parks shrugged. "It's hard for some people to doubt a compliment. He'll figure it out, eventually."

"Then it is good that your bond can stand so many betrayals." Joe signaled to the boys and said something in their language. They harnessed Parks' team for the drive back while the old man wandered toward the mine.

The runners jammed again, and the growls from the harnesses were instantaneous. Foster and Palqua hurried to pry the sled free with their planks, as they had every few yards. With no handles to grip, they could only stick the end of the wood as far under as possible and lift violently until the sled lurched over the sticky young ice.

Mahal shuddered, and hardly noticed. The wounded man lay white on the load. Theirs was by far the lightest—spare wood, weapons, rope, and an empty barrel—yet two sleds shrank in front of them, and only the behemoth that carried the majority of their food and water lagged behind.

Palqua caught Foster staring at the rider with concern.

"If you want to know where the dead go, he will show you soon enough."

"I'm sorry to hear it, brother," Foster lamented out of duty. "I know you lost a lot."

"I offered to leave him on the ship. He would hear none of it."

"*Hoy!*" An outburst from the front drew them. "Hop on the sled if you fancy a ride, cunt. Every time I look, your line's bent! The squain pups are makin' a better show of it," Gionn lit into Jonn.

"If you pulled like you talked, we'd be there. Shut it or I'll bash you," Jonn shot back.

"If you could reach me for a bash, we wouldn't have a problem."

Foster hated to admit that he was right. Four lines fanned from the sled, and Jonn's tightened and sagged in alternation. Tunguk and Atalkut leaned harder at the threat, even though it wasn't aimed at them.

"Baghar!" Palqua called to the last member of their crew, walking near the front to clear stalls with his plank. "Swap with Gionn." The operation halted while the two men traded the harness. Foster knew it wouldn't be long before his turn came up again. He'd taken only two shifts, and both times he felt that if land and salvation were a hundred yards away, they were doomed.

The ice despised their passage. A field of mud would have allowed smoother progress. The runners seemed too thick, though he knew as much about building sleds as submarines. The whole thing was too long to maneuver. Four men could pull it, but eight would have been better. Within minutes, he would fill his lungs with freezing gasps until his ribs splintered from the inside, and his empty stomach threatened to heave. On the first shift, he attacked it so hard that he could barely get tension into the rope afterwards. His quads seized up and his boots constantly lost traction. Foster tried turning the harness around to pull backwards, found it worse, and suffered Gionn's ridicule for the experiment. "One more on the long list of things you do arse-first."

It took half a day to lose sight of the *Gairhle*. As miserable as every step remained, they were flying compared to their early efforts. Nothing but ice and uniform gray to guide them. He hoped whoever was in front knew the way.

While they took their sweet time with the change, Foster leaned in to make sure steam still rose from Mahal's mouth.

"Hang in there, brother. I can see the coast ahead," he lied pathetically. When the sled started up, he could only dress his awkwardness with a thoughtless joke. "Don't forget to search him for that coin before we go diggin' holes in the ice," he warned Palqua.

"I had nearly forgotten it," the navy man said without conviction. "But I wouldn't worry. Gold makes its own voyages, and it's too bright to travel long in secret."

Foster thought he would leave it at that, but it seemed to spark hidden thoughts. Palqua gave the impression of organizing his every word before he spoke the first.

"It is the less interesting question don't you think—who has the coin? Any man desperate could find the courage to take it. I have wondered more often how it came to our ship at all."

The stomach cramps returned, and this time, Foster couldn't blame the sled. "Corm sure has his theories."

"Aye. But he is not the man to uncover the rascal."

"No?"

They stopped as Gionn leveraged the front of the sled over a lip in the ice. Foster and Palqua popped at the back until it slid clear.

"He has too many choices, I fear. You will hardly blame him if he has cause to suspect me. But I have the advantage that I *am* me, and a man knows himself, more so the less he can share it. I tell you, Foster, Corm and I have not always been mates, but I have not come to upset this voyage.

"I wondered of course if one of my lads would have done so. Among them, I found only fools, shirkers, bootlicks, and more than anything, good, honest men. Nor do I think Costig has such affection for them that he would try to hire their loyalty. There is but one name who might do it, and *could*: Arthas.

"We must also consider Corm's lads, though. You arrived late, but their fortunes looked quite dire for a while, and perhaps…just perhaps. The coin was found near the mast, and of his loyal crew, Eckerd and Ordacles are beyond question; Tawatu hasn't the craft; Hogue and Fergo sat too far away. That leaves Gewar, or more likely, Pitras, who came only infrequently to midship.

"Then there are the new lads on the roster. Do not be offended now—I accuse you of nothing. Since you asked of the coin, though, and I have suffered under the intrigue so quietly, I thank you for allowing a fool to think with his mouth.

"Two carpenters, two squains—none of them worth an argot. Yourself, and Gionn. Of all the men I've named but Arthas, none would be so likely as Gionn. He'd do it for a copper, I suspect, or a wild wind in his hair. The problem is that no man could possibly believe he wouldn't just slip it into his purse and go on his way. Could Costig have been such a fool? I might have thought it when he was sergeant-at-arms, but once I saw him in the admiral's seat, I was freed of the notion.

"Corm has many names, but I am left with four. Arthas, Gewar, Pitras…and perhaps, yourself. I did notice you visited the mast not long before it was found. Would have been a clumsy thing to lose it in so brief a visit. And I do not know if you're the sort who is capable, as I said before, or who another man would *think* capable, which is more important. I mention it only to be thorough."

"Flattered to make your list, brother. Whoever it was, though, they ain't got much left to do but get their pay."

"On the contrary. If we survive at all, we will find ourselves once more on the *Gairhle*. To prevent us from finding food, or returning—that would be easy if he didn't mind the sacrifice. But such a zealous man would have required no coin. The fact that he was paid tells me he'd prefer to live to spend it. So the task remains. You seem a clever sort, at least in some faculties. Will you help me keep an eye on those names I mentioned? I think two wits like ours will be difficult to escape."

Foster sensed the rope his mama would feed him when she'd caught him in a lie, and wanted to see how far he'd run with it. He nodded earnestly.

"I'd be honored."

The sled stuck, and when Foster tilted his plank under the edge, Palqua rested a hand on his forearm to stop him.

"Come. Let us not shirk our duties."

They took the harnesses from Atalkut and Tunguk. The team strained into the leather until the runners scraped to life.

"Knock, knock," Carabiner poked his head through the door.

"Alexicus!" Sophia threw off her blanket with glee. "Wait…*who's there?*"

"It's me," he answered a little bewildered.

"Oh, I thought it was a knock-knock joke."

"Knock knock," he repeated.

"Who's there?"

"Nadia."

"Nadia who?"

"Nadia regret asking me to make up a knock-knock joke on the spot?"

She laughed. "Definitely. Are you *back*, back?"

He sighed theatrically. "Wouldn't you know they refuse to come out and fight me? I left Satletaluk in charge so I can head down to the harbor to see off the hunting expedition. Now I was thinking, the trail from Eagle Camp to the harbor is the only safe one in all of Camne Drumlag right now…"

"Oh my god, yes. I have to get out of here before I go blind."

"Have you ever ridden on a dog sled?"

The Mattaka were always eager to lend a favor, but when the two of them went anywhere, they practically lined the path offering their bodies to walk on. Lady Sophia, as he'd taught them to call her, held a sacred presence in the camp. They couldn't so much as take an afternoon walk without a throng shuffling after them. When they first arrived, both of them were foreign novelties. They garnered curiosity, and no more, until Carabiner established himself as the master of Drummoc and of Camne Drumlag. He never issued any decrees, but soon after, he noticed that the men did all in their power to avoid walking in front of her. When they traveled in snow, the Mattaka jostled for the right to walk exactly in her footprints.

Carabiner was initially horrified at the Mattaka practice of giving gifts to other men's wives. He thought the only girl this place had ever seen had incited the miners into a brazen courtship. With difficulty, it was explained that a man shows his utter respect for his friend's wife by gifting her the thing which he can least do without. So she piled up mining tools and a stack of blankets higher than a tukit before he forbade the practice, which disturbed Sophia to the point that she refused to go out for fear of receiving another gift.

After that, they stalked her waiting for her to drop some object so they could hand it back. When her scarf blew over a vertical cliff face and fluttered hundreds of feet into the abyss, Carabiner thought it hopelessly lost. Three days later, a young man returned the article to him.

He embarrassed himself a few times by rushing to her defense, misinterpreting some cultural gesture like the gift of a knot of hair—

customary for a father of a girl near the same age to offer in symbolic kinship with his daughter.

Eventually, Carabiner recognized their infatuation as the kind a man might have for a visit by a rare bird, or a spring thaw. He probably made it worse by refusing to let her out of the tukit without him—men adore what's kept from them—but despite his trust, she was in no state to serve as a paparazzi princess. As much as Sophia adored the miners, she preferred to do it from a distance. Their kindness weighed on her like a debt she wasn't allowed to repay. Their attention, even when modest, even when she glowed from the warmth, later unsettled her. There were too many things for her to miss, too few for her to do.

Above all, Carabiner was a man of foresight. He could not imagine they would be long for this camp, and however good these men were, he'd already seen enough of the others beyond Drummoc that he meant to set his boundaries now, while they were still easy.

The men fell over one another to harness her sled, and they went like a homecoming parade to the forge. Carabiner expected to find Parks, but was perfectly happy when he never materialized. The forge itself was nearly done, days before he expected—half a dozen ovens, semi-circled in a natural hollow. He repeated his instructions, not quite trusting Parks to get them right, but insisted they check their counts with him once work began.

They stomped down the trail with four dozen guards, minus two, in keeping with the local superstitions that called for even groups of six. Carabiner walked astride the sled down the trail to the harbor in a practiced silence. He knew nothing of how these people expected a man in his position to treat his "wife," and with no examples to go by, he defaulted to a distant benevolence he'd seen in movies. That probably played a role in his keeping her shut in the tukit. Not a word or a gesture in front of these people came without a war of second-guessing in his mind. Carabiner dwelt in constant fear that the next thing out his mouth would be the one that toppled his fragile empire, which was the only thing keeping them alive. With her, there was the added distress of alienating his charge and his ally. It was just easier not to serve two masters, so he kept one of them on the sidelines.

Sophia didn't seem to mind. She bumped along on the sled with a blanket wrapped so that only her nose and eyes showed through. Tunguk had promised cold with the clear weather, and it came with a bitterness that irked Carabiner. The weatherman had understated the forecast by a few degrees. The girl was always cold, even when Carabiner baked in his tunic. The musty dark of the tukit must have become pretty intolerable for her to tag along without a word of complaint.

She knew, he told himself. He'd explained as much to her—how they had to act to maintain their position. And every time they were alone, he took great pains to cast aside the assistant viceroy, to make jokes, embarrass himself for her benefit. It only made him feel more guilty when he had to return to the show.

The *Juhketappat* and the darraig *Cleanthe* already bobbed under their provisions, an hour from sailing. He'd cut it closer than he intended. The ships had their orders, and could have left without him, but Carabiner preferred to associate himself with memorable events. To give them his blessing as they left, and to change some slight detail of those orders at the last second—that would only reinforce him in their eyes.

He accomplished this by having Haraket move two barrels of food from the *Cleanthe* to the *Juhketappat* in order to make her lighter, then reversed his earlier position: instead of the darraig going wide around Drummoc to avoid being spotted, she was to break from the convoy and sail close enough for another reconnaissance.

"Sir, I fear they will not be so surprised to see me again. What if they send warships, and discover our purpose?"

"An excellent point, Haraket. We occupy Camne Drumlag with more than twice their number, we have all the coal their colony depends on, as well as three good ships and men who can sail them—men who aren't afraid of testing their navy in their home waters. I'd like it very much if they understood our purpose, which is Mattaka sovereignty, and no less. Then they might understand that the only way to deal with us is at the negotiating table, with a healthy dose of humility."

Haraket nodded politely. "Then it will be as you say."

Sophia breathed into the wet patch of leather and let the steam warm her chin. She wanted badly to leave the sled. Her legs ached for it. But the sight of the snow made her feet numb. She was aware of the wide circle of attention that kept a careful distance. Even the dogs seemed curious about their passenger. Her driver held them in check with his back to her.

Instead, she stood on the creaking planks that crossed the runners and marched in place, huddled in her blanket. Alexicus teased her constantly about the cold, until one night she snapped at him. Now, she wished he would start again. She would grin and whine, and that would be her apology.

There were far worse things, she had learned, than the cold. Most of the time, she hid in her tukit like her bedroom back home, and the frigid weather was a friend of her parents'. She came down on occasion to be polite, and because the light and movement settled her. Still, she couldn't accommodate herself, and clung to Alexicus like she had to her mother on the ship. This was not where she lived, and as polite as everyone was, she cried most nights for home.

Sophia had seen the group of boys arguing and shoving one another secretly. She kept her eyes on Alexicus, even when she felt the presence of someone very close.

"For you."

A small boy, no more than eight and probably malnourished, stood beside the sled. His knife-trimmed hair matted to his temples, and his dark eyes smiled unaware of his sorry state. He extended a worn boot. Another just like it split around his right foot, while his left wiggled bare in the snow.

"Oh my god, no, no, no! You put that on. I—I'm not allowed to accept gifts anymore."

He tried to press it to her blanket, but found no hands to take it.

"Please. Put it on," she shoved back with the wrapped lumps of her arms. "I'll get in trouble with the assistant viceroy." He seemed to understand that last part, and hopped himself back into his boot without wiping the crust of snow from his foot.

Sophia shot a look at the group of boys, and they turned in four different directions.

"Did those boys make you?"

He seemed surprise when she pointed them out.

"Hm? No. I don't know those boys."

"They're not your brothers?"

He look a closer look. "Some. Not all."

She laughed, though he didn't seem to be joking. "What's your name?"

"I am Arnake, of the Seleku."

"Nice to meet you, Arnake of the Seleku. I'm Sophia."

They both waited for something to say. The boy looked back at his family. "I come to ask the queen, can you let my mate Leopard Seal to stay among you, and protect him from the Navy?"

Sophia smiled. "I'm not a queen. And he's my 'mate,' too."

"Not as much as me," Arnake swore. "I broke him from the prison, and climbed the mast to warn him of the marines, and me and my family, we drive him to the harbor and the ships, and, well mostly Norwet or Milak drive him, or last time, Ferrakut, but we all help, and one time, there was a fight with the blacksmiths, and also, we hid Gionn in the snow—do you know Gionn?"

"No, but it all sounds very brave," she said with the sweetness of a mother.

"*Arnake!*" A voice unleashed across the harbor grounds in Mattakatan, and the boy bolted to the safety of the group while a man who must have been his father chased after him.

Carabiner watched someone herd a kid away from Sophia. He'd squared things with the ships, and only waited for them to shove off, when his guards flowed around him like a shallow stream past a stone to block the path of a sudden arrival. He stretched to find a navy man, alone and unarmed amid the Mattaka.

"Sir, a word."

"A word with who?" He lobbed his voice over his men.

"Neal, who sails under the standard of Farri Tolba with an urgent message for he who commands Drummoc."

"Any word you have for me, you can say in front of my men."

"I thank you, but it isn't true. I have plenty I won't say but to yourself."

Carabiner had the men pat the sailor down, taking a knife from his sheath before they stepped only far enough to speak in low voices while the Mattaka waited fiercely nearby for a move they could misinterpret.

When he'd finished, Carabiner wondered at the privacy. He'd said nothing that wasn't known to everyone at this point.

"I got your message already, and rest assured your men will be paid what they're owed for the mission once I can meet with the treasurer, a sharp Amposi fellow by the name of Willakuy. You've done Ampos a great service. The viceroy will hear of it, and don't be surprised if a few extra coins slip into your hands as a token of gratitude," he winked.

"Fair enough, sir," Neal answered with underwhelming excitement. "Me captain, Polc, would have liked to tell you himself, but the recent admiral's got the island in a fit. Third one in a matter of weeks, you know."

"I used to be a navy man myself. Organized, effective command is not something you should strain your eyes looking for, sailor."

Neal shook his head in agreement. "Though I do know it when I see it," he looked back at the ships in their berths. "Polc, as well. He'll deny it if you repeat it, but the right men know who reigns in Drummoc." He considered a parting gesture of friendship, but thought better of touching Carabiner under the miners' watch.

Carabiner rejoined Sophia, and they offered a royal wave to the ships as they shoved off for the hunting grounds that would determine whether more than eight hundred men would emerge on the other side of Winter.

"Ask Turrha."

"Turrha said to ask you!" Corm floated after Palqua as the captain kicked a log roller with his foot, and noted where it stuck. He knelt and pulled it toward himself with one hand, and applied the blade to a little knob. The rest of his men stumbled around them in the same manner, trying to swear the logs true. Their captain seemed little bothered by the task, unfit for a man of the blue.

"Where is it?" Corm bellowed downward.

"Your wood is in the woodpile, of course. And I suspect the carpenters are checking the level of the tables in the hall under a cup of hasqa."

"You know what I mean, you clever cunt. Me wares! I'll have 'em back before I run out of breath, and turn to speakin' with me hands."

Palqua's crew drifted in, grateful for an excuse to spare them the admiral's hazing. Corm had left half the men to guard the rest of their goods under Eckerd, who would be most likely to talk him down. Seven others stood behind him—brutal good lads, but not enough to bother the sailors who he reckoned had them at four-to-one.

They came as a painful reminder. As many faces in their rank once served on the *Gairhle* as there now stood whalers opposed. Bosc and Hiren put themselves between the two captains.

"Is it your wares you want, then?" Palqua kept his eyes on his work. "Thought you meant to make repairs."

"Aye, those were your terms when you took half me goods. But if your words carry no honor, I'll have 'em back."

Palqua stood suddenly, showing the first sign of annoyance, though Corm couldn't tell what was or wasn't sincere with this one.

"By my honor, I sent the wood. It was Turrha who snatched it from you. If you mean to sail out of here, it's Turrha who you'll speak to. Of course, I can return your goods, if you care to sit upon a pile of dresses while your crew turns bluecoat. But you will get no better offer, if you get one at all.

"I find it untimely, how the admiral's favor turned against me. There's no act or ill-word I can recall that should have earned it," he squinted at Corm. "But nevertheless, I have done you a service. Even a man of such loose character as Turrha dreads being called a swindler. While the Navy has your wares, it weighs on him. He must honor the price, or he will not recover from his reputation. I am happy to return them, but then there is nothing you have that will buy your repairs. Turrha will pry your fingers from your ship, and you will need a great luck to earn a commission, or to draw pay in the Navy at all. Perhaps you can return north before the mast on a coal ship in the spring."

Corm leaned into his former crew, and it took both of them to hold him off.

"Pray that no such circumstance arises. I tell you now, you have not met me, but you will."

When he returned to the *Gairhle*, Foul Hand Waits awaited.

"You will forgive me, but I must be seen to act in my duties while we prepare our voyage."

Some hovering spirit held Corm from knocking him before he could hear the rest.

"I have spoken to your men on Palqua's behalf," he threw up his hands to protect his face. "Please! It is necessary. But in secret, I have sent to Turrha, and he blesses me undertakin'. Two of your men have signed away, I'm afraid. Nemas and Muir."

The names struck like spears in his breast. He would have given any number of shares to keep them, and never did he expect to have to. Few of the others would have surprised him, but short of losing Eckerd, no betrayal could have sunk its ram to deep. He may have dealt the final blow to his conspirator if he could have commanded his limbs at that moment.

"It isn't as you fear," Foul Hand Waits recognized his grief. "I have signed them to *Turrha*, as spies. They will draw pay to report on Palqua and yourself, but they remain with the *Gairhle*. We have spoken at length. They assure me they intend to sail with you if you sail at all. Nothing will be said that you don't desire. This way, they get a little coin, and if a bad luck has its way, they are secure."

He despised it, but Corm couldn't bear any more misfortune, so he said nothing. Nemas and Muir didn't mention it, either. They went out of their way to make a joke or a mate's remark, and Corm nodded behind a curt smile for two days.

When neither carpenters nor wares showed up, they were the first two to volunteer to accompany him to the tavern. Corm and seven of his men barged in while Palqua's crew burnt off an overnight watch, relegated to the public house while the feud with Turrha lingered.

"I doubt you've even spoken to him," Corm challenged amid the crowded room, jostled by old women and young squains and former whalers, alike.

"You are right. He will not see me. But I have sent my man." He motioned across the tavern. "Arthas!" The jumper came coolly and avoided Corm's twisted glare. "Has Turrha reconsidered?"

Arthas made as to rummage for the memory, then gave Corm a half-shrug.

"No."

A hand rested on his arm, which he realized was clenched tight.

"Corm! Look who it is!" A drunken Casey shouted to a mate. "Have a drink with us!" The jumper pleaded as if they were old sort. Nothing between them but an eager grin. It salted the recent wound from Nemas and Muir. They stood right behind him, as if they were still his lads, meanwhile scraping pay from the very man who denied him his repairs. And before him, Arthas, who seemed to flaunt against Corm's dignity by drawing breath. The crowd shifted in bands. A young squain planted his foot squarely on Corm's as if it were the floor, and didn't move. With his head and shoulders above the revelers, he felt himself afloat in a mire that pulled this way and that, intent to drag him under.

When he was a lad of five, his father cast him in the river to teach him to swim, and had to dive after him when he didn't get the trick. Those omnipotent hands yanked him coughing from the brown water and dragged him like a catch onto the mud while his older brothers feasted on their laughter. Within a week he learned, and in a few months, could cross one side to the other without getting swept downstream. He couldn't say why, but it was this and nothing else that flared before him as he gritted his teeth at Arthas' smirking face.

A right hand crumpled the traitor, then backhanded the squain off his foot. He didn't see who wrapped him and forced the left to miss Palqua. The arms vanished as soon as they appeared. He started to swing at another, then stopped, recognizing it as one of his own—but swung anyway when he recalled that Hiren counted among the jumpers.

From there, the tavern heaved around him like a storm-tossed warship. Hasqa glimmered in red arcs, and women cried out as they knocked about and spilled their bowls. Nemas cracked an Amposi sailor, and he saw his man Timor buried by three of Palqua's. Corm and Manuclas tried to pound him free, but had to turn to face new arrivals. Manuclas let out a cry unlike any punch could elicit, and sunk beneath the shoulders of the crowd.

They swung for weight and weather, and for every man who fell to the angotaks. Corm thought they might lay down the whole tavern. But Palqua's men found themselves. Cups flew, and many a local crawled for safety. A squain boy ran past and stabbed one of Palqua's in the leg—kept stabbing at anyone he could reach in a mad whirl.

The door snapped, and a voice now familiar rumbled over the melee. Marines poured in, and seeing he was committed to a course, Corm hammered the first two before they flooded in thick, bashing sailor and whaler and squain. Blood warmed his lip when he raised a defiant head to Costig and nearly reached his feet.

"As promised, mate!" Was the last thing he remembered saying.

Palqua's crew staggered into camp as the light seeped out. The two lead sleds had long disappeared. Corm and the provisions had fallen out of sight to their rear. What made it a "camp" was their inability to go farther. They stood on Eckerd's clear tracks—the only mark on the ice that melted into horizon on all sides.

They carried no sail for a shelter, and nothing to eat beyond the first two days' rations. The wind raked the exposed ice, and they took turns pointing out the white bloom of frost on each other's cheeks and noses that required a warm hand to revive the flesh. When Palqua estimated they'd traveled six or seven miles, it felt like a cruel lie. Foster could have sworn it was double that, minimum. The plan was for all sleds to camp at twelve miles, and at their pace, they'd be lucky to make it by the end of the next day.

Spending the night on the ice without shelter seemed unthinkable. They argued whether Eckerd and Tamarqan could have stopped just a mile ahead to wait for the others, knowing they had nothing to rig a tent. But Corm *did* have a sail, and Gionn was confident they expected the two laggards to camp together.

No one could conceive of dragging the sled another yard without knowing whether they had to travel one mile or seven. So they sent Gionn on foot to scout Eckerd's position, and hunkered down to wait for Corm.

Another hour blackened the ice. They lit a small signal fire to guide Gionn and Corm, but in a couple of hours, were forced to abandon it to conserve fuel. Spare wood kept them off the ice as they leaned against the sled in their bags. Jonn fidgeted and at times seemed to shift in a panic, cuddling into Foster in a much more intimate way than he expected from the strong whaler. While Palqua and Baghar traded low tones in Amposi, Foster sensed that the man's previous journey onto the ice weighed on him.

"Weirdest thing about bein' on a boat," Foster did his best to distract his companion, "is you can sail together, fight together, and never say a word to each other unless the guy sits right next to you. Don't think I've spoken to you since we were on the ice last, and you weren't too chatty then. You even remember that?"

"Not much," Jonn said politely, and soon the cold broke Foster's noble intentions. It was too miserable to sleep, though they were dog tired. The men raised a flimsy windbreak of their cargo, and within a half hour, the wind shifted to blast them from a different quarter. Their discomfort sank to concern. Eventually, they rose for fear of their lives, lashed the gear, and harnessed the sled. Only movement spared them.

The runners had frozen in place, and then they broke them, the bottoms remained caked with ice as stiff and sticky as tar. There was nothing to do but pull into the dark. Few nights on the *Gairhle* could compare. Foster soaked with sweat and slid helplessly off his feet when it gusted. Only the nauseating exhaustion forced their blood through their veins like syrup. He hoped any second to trip over Gionn's corpse. Palqua, working behind the sled to keep it free, split the night with a torrent of abuse. He'd discovered Jonn sitting on the sled—no telling how long.

Foster tried to do math. How many days like this would it take to reach Yunoc? He buckled at the thought and returned in a daze to the trail. When it came his turn to walk behind with the plank, he dozed mid-stride and nearly lost them, jogging after the sound of the scraping ice. Foster lay the tip of the plank on the back of the load and hustled to keep contact, knowing that to lose them now would be fatal. Atalkut relieved him, and he insisted that the boy do the same.

Now he relished his shift. It warmed him more than trotting behind, and tied to the sled, he was secure to the only island of humanity. Like a ship, it bore him. This alone separated him from the uncaring world that wouldn't even realize it swallowed him if his tether snapped. He must have been a dog, he thought, no notion of why he pulled or what he could hope to reach. He moved because those beside him did.

When he hoped for nothing, not even the dawn, voices barked. Startled men swiped for their weapons. Foster threw off his harness and felt the sled for a spear. Palqua had the wherewithal to announce himself just before Eckerd's crew stabbed at the darkness for invading angotaks.

They found Gionn warm under the sail tent and collapsed into their bags again. In the wavering moments before sleep, he remembered that Mahal, all this time, lay wounded on the sled.

"Did somebody get Mahal?" He asked.

They muttered a deliberation, and when no one could seem to agree, he recognized that the man remained outside. It didn't seem like he could have made it this far, anyway, and again his noble intentions flared then wrapped themselves in the stark limits of their powers and settled down to sleep, without guilt. By morning, he'd forgotten.

Foster was nearly the last to emerge after dawn. No one argued or levied any charges when they lifted the stiffened body from the deck. No part of him doubted the others had given all they could, too. They set their brother down, and Palqua searched his pockets while the Amposi Navy hacked as far as they could into the ice before the effort was abandoned.

The harness jerked Ulwet awake. By the light of the firestone blaze behind him, he saw one of the dogs snapping with curiosity at the end of his lead. The other five curled in the snow at his feet, as content as the rest of the watch to guard the fire. With the assistant viceroy away at the mine, the men never patrolled beyond the warm glow, and now, as often, they dozed under blankets.

Ulwet grabbed the tight lead and yanked several times to discourage the dog, who sniffed at the team and took a long look before circling into his spot again. He was supposed to make rounds according to the Leopard Seal, but he could not see, and it tried his cold hands to hang on to the team. One was enough, his friend had told him, but Ulwet knew as did the other Mattaka that dogs work best as six. He prevented them from pulling free of his sleepy grip by harnessing himself, and tying each rope to his breast.

Though the dog settled, the night seemed pregnant with kaim. They bulged at the edges of the orange light, pushing in and pulling back with fear. The animals returned to sleep, but he could not. Camne Drumlag was beautifully haunted. The sky people whispered on ridges dotted with stars. The rock people came up from the mines to squint at the brilliant night and lay their carvings. Urkuk, many miles away, seemed to trace a circle in the air with his burning beacon that only the dead could see, but even Ulwet could feel. Alakset, his father, would make his journey—perhaps he already had. Ulwet wondered if he would know his sons had come so far, so close. Would he visit them before he entered those lands?

Was he here now, just beyond the ring of flame?

The snow crunched with the footsteps of someone out to relieve himself, or maybe one of the watch in a moment of duty. He listened, and heard no more.

His father was much like his uncle. Were he here with them, he would sleep in his trail tukit, eager to load his sled with firestone. Ulwet would never be permitted to tie dogs to himself for the Leopard Seal. He would rest beside his father. Sawi remained at the harbor because he could not suffer the man, or stop him. Only two sons of Alakset traded shifts. Even Senadak and Umatbarak, boldly helpful without Sawi nearby, preferred to haul dust for Tunguk.

That, Ulwet did not resent. If he drove a sled for a man of ill reputation, or hauled a one-legged outlaw, at least it sung to him. It was the firestone run he dreaded, though he'd never done it. Now that he had tasted a different trail, it called him in the softest voice. The thought of hauling bushels down the mountain or riding endlessly on the *Juhketappat* felt as though it was he who was harnessed to the sled, driven on at the whip.

It was this that made him rise in the night full of the unknown, full of things he feared. He did not so much want to patrol with dogs. It was cold, and they did not understand what he asked of them. He wanted to do anything that was something else.

"Up, up," he asked quietly so as not to excite them. The dogs perked, and when the first yanked at their leads, the others followed without knowing why. One of them sounded, and a man yelled at him to silence the beasts. Ulwet stepped toward the edge of the light and dug in his feet when they tried to pull him like a laden sled. He wrestled the leads, too small to hold them if they wanted to go, but his insistence was enough to slow them.

Ulwet went out among the dead and the kaim, where he saw nothing of his team but their silver breath in the moonlight. They tried to steer him for the trail to the harbor, but he sat down until they gave up. Some yards back, the fire glowed. Ulwet paused to listen to the ringing of the voices that cannot be heard. He listened for Alakset.

Only the squeak of a patrol near the tukits competed for his ear. The same dog howled again, and he shushed it out of fear of a beating from the watch. When he held the muzzle, the snow-steps ceased. Ulwet again felt the presence of the kaim, very near—as near as the fur that brushed his legs.

It came again, and a shadow flashed between him and the fire.

"Who goes there?" He trembled. The steps quickened, and the dogs howled in fury. The other teams, tied off to the south, joined in the call.

The leads tore into his hand. Ulwet flew from his feet and dragged head-first on his back after the running team. The watch near the fire shouted, he thought at him. Raising his feet, he slammed them down to slow the run, but popped up nearly to standing. After a stumble, he again righted himself into a full dash. He saw men lunging in a flurry at the edge of the fire. Two of them dropped bundles and jabbed with their spears. Their outline could not have been Mattaka.

A miner fell to a blow, and the spear nearly took his last breath, but the dogs arrived. The second man aimed his point at the team, and Ulwet threw himself on the ground sideways to stop them from rushing to their slaughter. It was enough. Their jaws gnashed short of the blade, and the two men fled into the night.

"We believe they hide in Bekiatven," Satletaluk's voice called Parks back with a yawn. More than a day had passed between the raid and Carabiner's return. Though the sun rose later, Parks noticed that "dawn" remained fixed at the ungodly hour of Carabiner's choosing. Only now, after half the council had presented, did the stars begin to fade.

"Bird's Mortar," Carabiner translated after thinking it over.

"Aye. Or one of the old mines nearby. The men there went with Haraket, or moved to work at Vinniakten. No more food to steal. So they came here by the fire to look for you, and something to eat."

"Good thing we had the dogs out," Parks noted without pointing out what everyone knew: that it was him who assigned the patrol.

"It is good," Satletaluk acknowledged. "No one was killed, and they left hungry."

Carabiner seemed not to hear, then raised two fingers to silence Satletaluk when he meant to continue.

"And those dog patrols, they're only at Eagle Camp, correct?"

"Aye," Satletaluk confirmed.

Carabiner smiled like he appreciated the effort that failed to live up to an obvious standard. "Let's get a few teams everywhere we have men. And I want one permanently stationed outside Lady Sophia's tukit with Ratjuk. Let's hear from Injuries and the Emotional Sate of Men," he said without looking up.

"No injuries," Parks cleared his throat. "As for the men, I'd say chillin'. But restless."

Carabiner passed his fingers through his hair in amusement. "No injuries? I heard two men were wounded in the latest raid, and I know for a fact that we still have a number down from the initial attack, to say nothing of mining accidents."

Parks shrugged defensively. "Then it sounds like your men have disrespected your orders. No one reported anything to your esteemed councilor, and I can't exactly go door to door in my condition."

"We seem to be suffering communication breakdowns in my absence. I stopped by the forge yesterday evening, and the blacksmiths were under the impression that you ordered one of every *two* mining implements melted down for weapons. I recall asking for one in *twelve*."

"Yeah, these people aren't very good with fractions, so I decided to find a 'more common denominator,' if you will. One-twelfth—what percent even is that? Anyway, if we're gonna dab some fools up as often as it looks like, we're gonna need a lot more hardware."

He knew when Carabiner inserted himself tenderly under his armpit and helped him to the privacy of his own wigwam that he wouldn't like the outcome. Sophia was called to wait outside with Ratjuk, and they exchanged a look of embarrassment.

"I have to admit, my first reaction was to assume that you were full of shit," Carabiner left room for Parks to fall into the trap of making a comment. "All that business about being part of the team. Starting from the bottom. You didn't even make it one meeting before you undercut every word out of your mouth.

"I thought, 'There he is. That's the Parks I know. He said he wanted to change, not that he would.' The Navy, the *Qarapara*, here…it doesn't seem to matter. You always did the bare minimum. It hurts you to think that everywhere you go, I'm your superior officer, and like a mischievous child, you have to test. Test just how much you can get away with to show everyone how cool you are, without actually working up the courage for a mutiny. *Ah!* Let me finish," He cut off an opening syllable.

"So there I was, wondering just how much I could put up with before I was forced to do something a lot worse than threaten you in public, which may save me a little face, but let's be honest, has no affect whatsoever on you. I was asking myself what I'd be *willing* to do to you, given that whatever differences we may have, you are if nothing else, a treasured relic of my time. You belong to a place the same as I do, and any harm that comes to you feels like it's visited on me, as well.

"I wondered how you could lie so freely and feel nothing, and how much of me would be worn down on your behalf before I finally, realistically, had to pull that girl aside and explain to her in terms she couldn't possibly understand why I couldn't do anything more to save a drowning man. How I had to cut the anchor before it dragged everyone else down with it.

"But then I remembered the rest of what you said—if you meant it at all. It doesn't matter, really, because it's true: I'm not the same man. The orange guy you sent over into the life raft didn't make it. And if you could do no better, I could. I decided to apply to you a lesson I learned long ago. That is, there are no liars by nature. We make them when he lose faith in people.

"Of course, that's a lie in itself, you can see it with a moment's reflection. At least until you look to the heart of it. I can't know what goes on behind that big forehead, but when you tell it to me in your own words, you cannot help but speak the truth. You may say 'dog' when I see 'cat,' or swear your hand is empty when it holds a knife. I'd be an idiot to believe you, but the worse mistake would be to doubt it. When you deny a man's truth, you cleave the world in two. There's a cat world and a dog world, and little hope of coming to terms again.

"Have you ever listened to the *Alvin Fennimore Podcast*? He's a former DEVGRU operator who wrote a book about a system of situational awareness he developed called *Apparence*. He teaches it to military, corporations—you get the idea. And what he talks about a lot on his podcast is how there is always truth in appearance. That means not just how you look, but how you present yourself, even when it contradicts the deeper layer. Not just what you know, but what you say, whether it's God's honest truth, crazy talk, or pure manipulation. Every place, every person, every thing, we're all *screaming* the truth at any given moment. *Begging* to be understood. The problem is, most people can't see beyond the *flares*—the thin film of literalness.

"We take each other for liars, or lunatics, and in doing so, we refuse to see a deeper truth. I don't mean ulterior motives. Everyone is telling you all you need to know at every moment, and when you put your faith in them—not your trust, your *faith*—you inhabit the same world. Whether they love you or want to kill you, you come to walk in the same place, and you begin to see things that were invisible to you when you went around dismissing everything that didn't add up to your preconceived expectations.

"You cannot lie to me." Carabiner hacked a shower of sparks. On the second try, a little nub of fiber glowed, and he gave it the gentlest breath, then touched it to the spout of an oil lap. The flame cast a pale orange that stopped short of the walls. Parks grew queasy at the reminder of the place they held him down and cleaved him apart.

"Or rather, you can try, but everything you come up with is true in some way. And the rest of you tells me other things. You say you want to work as a team. Start at the bottom and pay your dues. I think that's true in every sense. If I reject it, you and I will never come to terms, because I've refused to stand beside you in your truth. I'll never see, for example, that to you, a team is a group of people who takes care of Parks, while he does just enough to avoid burning bridges. Your 'team' accepts no leadership, and anyone who tells you to do something you don't like isn't a part of it. Although you certainly don't mind when other people do what you say. Heck, who doesn't like that?

"But you'll take any stray, as long as they can put up with your jokes and have a sense of loyalty. And you'll deny anyone of great skill who bores you, or wavers in his commitment, or who threatens to raise that team to a standard you yourself don't believe you can attain.

"Your team is a flexible unit. People come and go. You take them in with hardly a thought, and exile them just the same. *My* team is a unit that transcends the individual, but if I get stuck on that, I won't see that to you, the word means something else. To you, nothing outweighs a man and his needs. Someone nearby is more a part of the team than someone far away.

"You weren't lying, or misunderstanding anything. A man doesn't sacrifice for the greater good of the team and its goal, which transcends any one person. For you, the *team* sacrifices any goal to care for its members.

"And beyond your words, I see what you think of yourself in your appearance, your posture, your daily routine. I see you walk, leaning on a spear, or a friend, or pulled on a sled, and in that, you tell me what you need from your team, and what you can provide. The old me would have dismissed you as a selfish idler. Now I believe you at every level. So here you are.

"If I take care of you and don't force you to do things, we'll be teammates. You won't do a damn thing to help me reach my goals if they require any sacrifice, but you'll always take care of me in return, the way you do for those dog boys, Kjartke, Tunguk. I hate to admit it, but maybe you're the nobler man. You would never allow a friend to come to harm for the sake of some glorious vision, some grand plan, no matter what it promises.

"Here's the rub: I believe you, but I don't have to agree. I *do* have some pretty big plans—plans that I want you to be a part of. If everything works out the way I'm hoping, everyone you see here, and everyone we know will benefit beyond imagination. It'll require a lot of little sacrifices, and some of us may have to give everything. So be it. I'll eagerly take my turn if it comes up. But it won't work if we waver for a second.

"I'm on your team, in the way that you understand it. Now I need you to stand by me."

Parks blinked away a delirium that could have been a hasqa buzz if he'd had anything but melted snow to drink. He watched Carabiner's lips until he was sure they'd stopped their moving. The apprehension of confinement pressed around him. Nothing good ever happened to him inside a wigwam. He had to transfer the flickering séance face before him to the dork in the survival suit before he could speak.

"You lost me so hard, I literally stopped listening. Sorry, what is it you need me to do?"

Carabiner sighed at the shadows.

"Satletaluk told me something you should have mentioned the moment you got here."

"You mean my boy Lenet? I figured it's all good, I can vouch for you. Even if they do show up—which, you've probably noticed how good these people are at keeping schedules—they're only pissed at the Navy."

"How many?"

"It's like, fifty...a hundred dudes, max."

"Did he tell you what they planned to do when he gets here?"

Parks shrugged. "Probably liberate their homies."

Carabiner smiled the way he always did when he meant to educate Parks in the most patronizing way possible, but shook it loose before he spoke with a note of concern.

"There are over four-hundred sailors on Drummoc, and another hundred-fifty marines."

"He's gonna get curb-stomped," Parks admitted. He snapped his fingers and wriggled to a tall seated position with great pain. "*You* have even more men than they do."

"I have over eight-hundred miners. None of them have steel weapons or shields, and except for a handful who ran off to the whalers in their youth, no combat experience, either. We got slaughtered in that ambush. I love my guys from the bottom of my heart. They would swim to Greenland if I asked nicely enough. But they can't follow complex orders without someone breathing down their necks to re-explain it a hundred times. What do you think is going to happen if we try to launch an amphibious invasion of Drummoc?"

"I can tell you what's gonna happen to Lenet if we don't." The reality of their situation had eluded him at Yunoc. He thought the ones who wanted to bail on their neighbors and make a run for it were selfish. Now that he had a clear picture of what awaited their return, he wondered if Lenet's men were insane. Yet more than ever, he saw why they meant to sail.

"Satletaluk told me that when his old man was a kid, a bunch of rowers took over a coal ship to protest their working conditions. They politely tied up the crew and sailed right back to Drummoc, made their demands, then docked the ship and returned the captives and the cargo without so much as scratching anyone.

"Every man on the ship was executed, even those who didn't know of the plot in advance. They identified the leaders, confiscated what little property their families owned, executed their sons, and his words: 'Did much harm to the women.' What kind of reprisals do you think we're going to see when they try to storm the beaches in open revolt, having murdered three crews and stolen tons of coal?

"I understand their grievances," Carabiner went on. "But I don't want to see half the colony slaughtered. History shows it time and again: violent insurrections don't work."

"Uh…have you heard of a little place called America?"

"I have, Parks, and I could rattle off more success stories than you're aware of. Those are the exceptions, and for each one of them, there are ten quiet disasters. We beat the Brits because we had immense resources, and the help of the French Navy. The Mattaka are alone. We have coal, but not much iron. Unless Ampos continues to ship it to us, that means we can't make steel weapons. No wood for ships. Even if we got our miracle and took Drummoc, then sailed on Nunoc and captured it before they knew what hit them, we'd fall in a few years at most when they came with reinforcements in fresh war ships.

"I don't want to insult your intelligence, but I've done a fair amount of investigation into the historical and geopolitical considerations. How much do you know about Atlantis?"

Parks blinked as if someone had unexpectedly changed the topic. "You mean the drowned city with all kinds of ancient alien technology?"

"I mean the empire that commands the nine shores of the known world—the one you're in right now." He read Parks' bewilderment. "Did you not even know what this place is called?"

"I know the names I need to know, and this place is Camne Drumlag."

"Right, which is part of Hiade—or Ajatse, to use the Mattaka word. A colony of Ampos, which is a major supplicant kingdom to the farri— the ruler of the Kingdom of Atlantis, and the Wind of the Wide Fetch. No? Not ringing any bells?"

"I prefer to live in the moment. It's hard enough, here."

Carabiner clapped him on the shoulder and smiled, probably relieved that he knew more than Parks about one more thing. "I hear you, bro. But the moment lives in a world of other moments smashing into one another. Nothing happens in isolation. Which is why, if you care about these people as much as I do, you'll understand that we can't fight Ampos.

"Fortunately, we have the one thing that all successful revolutions require: a member of the intellectual class who sides with the people and has the know-how to navigate the murky waters of politics. Did you know, for example, that Hiade used to belong to Atlantis before Ampos took it in a war? Or that a Mattaka warrior once raised a navy of six-hundred ships and attacked Atlantis? He had them in a sweat for a minute, until he lost every single man and brought unspeakable retribution on his people that still lingers to this day."

"Barduk." Parks guessed the only name that came to him by reputation. Carabiner beamed.

"Impressive. So you see that the Mattaka will never reach their potential by switching one cruel master for another. And they will never be free of the kingdom, entirely. We have massive resources in these mountains—not just coal. I've heard stories of beings that swim in the rock with great powers. When I asked to see one, they showed me a mineral band. I'm no geologist, but I think we've only begun to tap our riches.

"But without Atlantis and its kingdoms to buy them, the Mattaka are just a bunch of stone age hunter-gatherers with a few fire tricks. Any attempt at violence will be met with violence. We want the same thing, you and I, but I'm looking at the long game.

"Ampos has no coal mines without us, and everyone knows the Mattaka make the best steel. It's practically rust-proof—not insignificant when you consider all trade and warfare has to be conducted over a salty sea. So they take as much as they want, and pay as little as they can.

"Ampos isn't the only game in town, though. Other kingdoms, Atlantis included, want our steel and have plenty to trade for it. Now that the king of Ampos has declared himself farri, we have a unique opportunity if we play our cards right. Atlantis would love it if we suddenly cut off a huge chunk of their enemy's weapon supply while keeping them occupied on their southern fetch. When they eventually crush the revolt—and they always do—we'll be in a position to negotiate. I'm not talking about going back to being a colony of Atlantis with a better deal. I'm talking *Mattakaland*—an autonomous nation, suppliant to the farri, under its own sea king, with its own laws, like the all of the other kingdoms."

"Dude. That's gonna take forever."

"You got somewhere to be?"

"Foster's working on a way home."

"For us? Or for him?"

Parks let the remark go, but had to steel himself with resentment for the accusation to avoid considering it.

"If you think I'll ever give up on that possibility, you don't know me. But right now, this is our situation, and it's telling us all we need to know, from the bottom of its heart. Foster doesn't have the personality for this place. I really, truly hope we see him again, but given what I've encountered, I'd say we need to plan for a long stay. Maybe a permanent one."

They were Parks' own sentiments, volleyed at Foster so many times, yet he couldn't bear the sound of them from Carabiner's lips.

"And have you given any thought to who will be the king of Mattakaland?" The question brimmed with undisguised contempt.

"That's for the Mattaka to decide, once we get them into a position to decide it. Right now, above all else, we have to intercept your 'boy' Lenet. Things are contentious, but there's a war coming. All we need to do is distract the Navy from mounting a meaningful defense until it gets here."

"Meanwhile, these people go on getting fucked. And what if your war doesn't come as fast as you think, or never comes? Or Atlantis shows up and get their asses kicked? You said it yourself: they're distracted. We're an afterthought. No one knows about Lenet, or what you're up to. If we move now, imagine the reaction when our future allies find a welcome mat instead of a siege? Eskimo Joe knows Drummoc. If we ask him to help us come up with something—"

"I hear you, and it makes sense logically. It has a lot of genuine compassion behind it, and again, I applaud you for the way you treat people when they're one of yours. But if we fail, we're all dead. If we succeed, half of us are dead in the fight. Let Farri Donnab spill his blood when it's time. We can't afford to poke the bear."

"I know the bear. His name's Costig, and you already poked him."

"Costig is a caveman. I wouldn't want to get into a fist fight with him, but he can't stand up to abstract thinking and subtle ingenuity. He's fucking illiterate."

"You're underestimating him. He's not illiterate, he just can't spell very good."

"Nor can he catch a one-legged fugitive who doesn't speak the language, though he's got all the resources of the colony at his disposal." Carabiner let it sting. Parks wanted to tell him about their agreement. He wasn't the only one naive to certain complexities. But while he owed nothing to the admiral anymore, his familiar acquaintance hadn't earned the secret.

"Are we in this together?" Carabiner squared his jaw as if he didn't care what the answer might be.

"We are," Parks said at last. "At the end of the day, who else do I have?"

Carabiner lifted Parks' hand in his fingers and gave it a gentle squeeze. "Welcome to the team, bro."

Another day passed in idle. It took the collapse of the tent to stir Foster and most of his party. They cussed and kicked their way out to confront the saboteur, to find that the wind had finished its own work.

It was a slipshod rig to begin with. Freezing air drafted under an edge until someone tucked it beneath their hip, then it shot through somewhere else. Every thirty minutes through the night, the same pole collapsed until no one bothered to reset it.

Yet by sheer mass of bodies, it was the warmest night he'd spent since he set foot on the *Gairhle*. Foster hardly thought he had the energy to escape the sail. The prospect of a new day in the harness tempted him to suffocate.

He emerged to a mess of gear speckled over the ice. Eckerd and Tamarqan spoke in no subtle tones off to one side while one of the sleds was restowed. Corm's party never made it. Now the first mate wanted to lighten a sled and go looking for them. He thought it fair to bring half of his team and half of Tamarqan's, which would have taken Pitras, Fergo, and Hogue from the Amposi, along with Boot and Ordacles of Eckerd's.

"Everyone thinks he's a captain when the captain's off," Arthas remarked to Foster. "This one's just back from a life as a sled dog, judgin' by his many views on the matter," he said of Tamarqan.

"Then he's a fine naval officer," Foster said. "Knows just enough about things that are none of his business to fall in love with his own authority." The half-a-smirk he earned from Arthas felt like a victory.

"Aye, but don't think we're done with clever cunts because we're off the ship," Arthas warned. "Tamarqan suspects with that roster, it's a ruse. Eckerd means to link up with Corm and the food, so they can strand the rest of us."

Palqua stalked over to mediate as Foster stood on his sled, ostensibly to look back for the missing whalers, but in truth to put a layer between his soles and the ice.

"They wouldn't leave…" He trailed off as he considered those remaining.

"Who? You and Gionn? Brave Chirim?" Arthas tugged his coat so that he stepped back to the ice. "Better to keep your head warm," he tapped his temple.

Chirim scraped at the ice with a pale finger and came away with a tuft of fur from a garment. He tore a few additional fibers loose, and dropped the plunder in his sleeping bag. Though he seemed alert, something in the battle had changed him. It wasn't the first time Foster noticed him hoarding flecks of wood or rock, strips of discarded leather, a hunk of ice chipped in the attempt to bury Mahal.

He relished the rest, but none of the sleds carried more than two days of food. Foster had saved the last few ounces of meat the night before, just in case. This was that case.

The sled finally took off with emergency supplies only, led by Eckerd and crewed by Tamarqan, Boot, Bale, Lozeder, and Banno.

Palqua refused to let them loaf. Every sled was unloaded. They tightened lashings, added nails, and Igonus planed the top-side of the runners to thin them down. It was impossible to clean them enough to resurface the bottom, but they ground the nastier chunks of ice free to restore a semblance of glide.

Near midday, Tunguk thought he saw a seal bathing on the ice from afar. Four men were sent with spears to investigate. They stowed and restowed the sleds painstakingly, pulling them around camp to test their ingenuity and to stay warm. Palqua issued a challenge for a better tent design. Intense bickering gave them a sail strung between the height of two sled loads, a few feet off the ground at center, and weighted at the edges. Every man piled in to try it, and though it drafted between the sleds and didn't even leave enough room to sit up, Igonus was declared the winner.

What would have been a tailwind swooped in to sting the whalers, but none of them could bear the dark of the tent while it was daylight. As they grasped for tasks to busy themselves and came up short, the men drifted into their cliques and made threats against the slow "dogs" who brought the rations.

The Mattaka boys clung to Foster, and he joined Gionn, who flirted with Bosc in the fashion of a dumb, helpless rascal that Foster recognized from their first meeting. The rest shaped up according to crews: Corm's with Corm's, Palqua's with Palqua, while Arthas and Jonn kept Igonus company adjusting the tent. The hunting party returned without having seen a thing.

A number of important decisions would take place if no food came. Foster suspected Gionn had found the most neutral associate he could to avoid having to choose a losing team too early. It turned out Bosc, who he had never spoken to due to his seat in the very farthest stern, had come to Drummoc with Corm, but deserted to Palqua's navy on shore. He likely gravitated to Gionn for the same reason.

"How's a fish-thievin' pond-slapper like yourself get a proper Atlantan name?" Gionn probed their new friend. The word set Foster to stare across the ice at the frozen corpse of Mahal, as if a blink would cost him a glimpse of something important.

He'd assumed Bosc was Amposi, but with each word, the differences sprouted from his sharp face until Foster blushed. He came from the interior, as far north as any proper man had been, but driven toward the coast with his Ksit'hangi people by men more northern than himself. He was a chief, in fact, who traveled to Atlantis to pledge his warriors to the farri in exchange for help in fighting several of their neighbors. But he found no such land, and after being chased by "flesh-eaters" and blown adrift in a storm, he found refuge on an island with priests of a sun king—Foster couldn't tell whether that was a man or a god—who promised to help him if he stole ice and brought it back as a tribute. It was they who added Bosc to his name, Asahem Bosc, and his first captain who robbed him of the former, so that he roamed under a name that Gionn said meant only "Inlander."

In good conduct, Gionn never questioned a word of his claims, and didn't push beyond where Bosc gave freely.

"Your luck is with you, cunt. These bucket squains can show you where to find your ice." None of the three got the joke, but it baffled them long enough for Gionn to drag Foster off to their sled. He made like he was adjusting the lashings, and loosened the lashing that held the spears with all but a wink.

"That's five. We'll need a sixth to make a run for Yunoc. Don't look stupid if it goes to shit tonight, but better to wait for that argot, if we can. Job's done, and I'm beginnin' to think me best ship south is a coal sidecock."

"You wanna desert. Jump," he corrected himself to the whaler's term for cowardice.

"Always got one foot on the side, mate. We might try to pitch the squain lads over for a tougher cut if we can, but then again, might play to our favor to show up with a few of that sort. Easy does it," he replied to Foster's stiffened shoulders. "We can't go anywhere until you find that coin, which you probably lost on purpose, you lousy wart. But if me luck says otherwise, be ready to haul. We can always come back later to search the corpses."

The wind described their prospects in low tones. The remaining whalers split as the evening wore, checking each other with nervous looks.

Foster thought of Arthas' warning, and felt the movement of other plans, slow and deliberate as the pack they rested on. The temperature plummeted. They huddled with their private thoughts of where the fracture may break. Many of the speculations probably wondered where he, himself, would land. By now, he knew that hunger compelled men more than loyalties, and this wasn't the first time they would go hungry.

Group by group, they trickled under the tent for the night until Foster only remained because Gionn did. Palqua also sat vigil, and Ordacles paced for warmth beside Hogue. They sparked a small signal fire without asking the officer of the watch. Something irresistible drew Foster to it—he couldn't shield it for warmth. It flickered like a prayer.

Foster gave up, and found a spot along the edge in the black tent. He heard Palqua come in, and later, Hogue and Ordacles. No sooner than they settled did Gionn crawl loudly past the sled, bringing in a gust of wind. Men cursed as Foster heard him flail over them looking for an opening.

"Sorry, cunt! Hoy, what's that? A foot? Sorry."

The sound came closer, and two beefy hands felt over his back, then grabbed at his ankles unnecessarily before he finally settled on the far side.

He awoke half an hour later to a scrape, and it took a minute to realize it wasn't coming from the tent. All around, he felt the men notice and raise their heads quietly. A low voice. Footsteps. The sound surrounded the tent, and the men, with their arms outside, held their breath as if they could disappear on the ice.

"Hoy, dead men! We angotaks dine tonight!" A distorted voice sent chills through the tent.

"Fuck off, Gewar!" Ordacles responded, and the camp burst into jubilation at the arrival of Corm's sled.

He first considered asking Eskimo Joe. But Parks succumbed to embarrassment, and the lure of mischief: he bit his tongue at the surprise he imagined on the old man's face when he showed what he could do, with no help from anyone—at least, not Joe. Something told him akmanuak didn't extend so far, though.

"Akmanuak. Akmanuak," he drilled.

A sharp laugh from just behind him made him jump.

"Tunguk sleep. Perhaps I will save you." Kjartke shook loose the back of the sled and began to pull him toward the wigwam.

"Whoa, whoa, whoa! Not yet. I have to watch for smoke signals from Foster," he nodded at the horizon of slopes that obscured the sea. "And someone may need to report an injury."

She managed to roll her eyes without moving them. "Soon. Too much danger at dark. These men who watch, they are nothing."

The miners squatted around a pile of coal that would become the fire at sunset. To his other side, Ferrakut bounded through the snow on all fours like a dog while Ulwet slapped at him with a piece of leather.

He looked up at Kjartke again and felt his throat seize.

"Do not drool if you mean to speak."

He swallowed a lump and turned away politely, and she left him where he sat.

The men carried on about something exciting in words that sounded like rocks spilled from a basket to clack over one another as they raced for the ground. His conversation with Carabiner was hardly more intelligible. Every exchange with that fool left him with a cringing resentment. If that woman petty officer who reported him made it all up it because she had to listen to him talk for half an hour, Parks couldn't blame her.

Carabiner had left again as quickly as he arrived. There *was* a fight or something, but it was convenient that his absence meant Parks still had not been able to speak with Sophia. She probably didn't have anything vital to say, anyway. He just longed to be able to follow along when someone spoke, and to be followed. To bitch and joke—that was all he wanted. His injury, the cold, his once and current supervisor—there was no shortage of material. When Foster left, he had other things to worry about, and while he suspected he would come around to that loss at some point, he failed to grasp just how much he ached to make a crack about those boys playing doggie and have someone laugh.

"Yo!" He waved at them. "Oldest one. Ferrakut."

The boy approached with guarded excitement. Parks looked him up and down, dusted with snow.

"Hello."

"Hello, Leopard Seal," he replied.

"Hi. Now let's try in your language." Ferrakut remained blank. "How do you say hello in Mattakatan?"

"Mattaka don't say 'hello.'"

"Well that's rude. You don't greet an old buddy, like you just did me?"

"If we say in Atlantan, we greet. But what does it mean, 'Hello?' Mattaka don't need it. I see you. Do you mean to call for my attention?"

"Not necessarily. What do you say when you see someone?"

"We say what we need to say."

Parks would have been annoyed if Ferrakut wasn't so clearly confounded.

"Give me an example."

Ferrakut mulled it over. "*Yutpannikvautenri.*"

"Easy there, tiger. Yoot-panny-aven…"

"Yutpannikvautenri."

"That's fucking 'Hi?'"

"No. It means, 'Fish have returned to the shallow bank that breaks ships.' If that is what you want to say."

Parks took a slow blink. "Let's back up. Do Mattaka say 'yes?' Or 'aye?'"

"Aye."

He waved his hands for the boy to proceed.

"*Â.*"

"*Ah!* OK, I got this."

"*Anka.*"

"What's that?"

"No."

"Anka," Parks imitated. Ferrakut grinned doubtfully. "Believe it, buddy. I'm gonna make Carabiner's Mattakatan sound like Foster's people trying to speak English."

"*Akjuru.* 'Believe it, akjuru.'"

"Muchos gracias, akjuru. You got yourself a student. I'm holding you personally responsible for my language skills. And this is just between us—don't tell my atatapalatet."

Ferrakut drew back his chin in something between skepticism and horror.

"Kjartke," Park explained. The boy split with laughter. Parks shoved him into the snow with a shake of his head. Ferrakut hardly noticed. He choked with glee as he scampered back to his brother on all fours.

Corm's crew had lost a full day when a runner cracked, and Aldan had to fashion a new one. Every one of them pulled himself half to death, fearing the consequences of a divided party until Eckerd found them.

The captain didn't wait for morning to dress them down for not posting a watch, and Palqua caught special hell. He offered no excuse, though Foster figured that Gionn had promised to take the shift before turning in.

Another half day fell to an overhaul of the loads. At least it came on a full stomach. Food was spread more liberally, and despite the twelve men on Corm's sled, to six or seven on the others, some of their cargo was redistributed to Eckerd and Tamarqan. Two of those men were wounded and couldn't pull at all, and the sled was overbuilt—the runner had cracked not from being too thin, but too thick and inflexible.

When they finally returned to the trail in the afternoon, the angotaks had gained an additional two-and-a-half days on them. The ice was no better. It gummed the runners and the soles of their boots. They clawed for every yard. By order, the lead sled stayed within sight of the rear now. They reckoned six miles on the next full day, and the most optimistic of them only guessed ten on the second.

Each morning, he didn't think he could go another hundred feet, and by the end of the day, there were miles, but precious few, behind Foster. Rumors started of a death march. Yunoc lay a few hundred miles to the southeast, according to Tamarqan, who sailed the route to Nunoc more than any.

Eckerd swore it was another fifty. Every time they drew near the lead sleds, Foster came across the two arguing.

On the third, they reached the hummocks. Here, the sheets of new ice that locked them in brushed across the border of an early-season pack, denser and less mobile. The ice heaved up like jagged breastworks. Even the smallest crossing left them quivering from the effort to leverage the nose up and pull with all their might until the sled snapped clear with a terrible sound. It felt like jumping little fences between a network of cow pastures.

They pulled laterally as much as forward to avoid the worst lines. Turning south proved a reliable way to shrink the barrier, but it also wore on morale. Usually, they found a section ankle-high or a little worse. As they grew closer and more mangled, though, the sleds jammed against a wall as high as a man's head, and they had no choice but to trace it for more than two miles before finding a section, just wider than their runners, that seemed to have collapsed on itself. The first two teams had to harness to a single sled, guided by Palqua's group behind, to get her moving. It took them an hour to get across, and longer on the second sled.

By the time it was Corm's turn, the whalers simply unloaded every item and carried it over. The empty sled skipped onto a new kind of ice, covered in a thin, crisp snow. The runners seemed to squeal with delight. Bosc harnessed himself to the lead sled while the men reloaded Corm's, and whistled for attention. He took off jogging while the whole rig slid behind him alone, slow but smooth, where it previously took a whole team to budge.

While the men rested, Eckerd walked the captain ahead of their parties to look at the trail. Palqua soon joined them, then remained alone after a quick discussion. His solemn look drew Foster out from the teams. He made an excuse for his curiosity.

"Ready when you are, sir. At least we should have good ice for a stretch."

"Aye, and well-paved," Palqua said. Foster followed his gaze to the three curving pairs of sled tracks that ran under their feet, out beyond where any of the whalers had gone—the frozen wake of the angotaks. Suddenly the relatively smooth section of hummock made sense.

Palqua traced the marks to the gray distance.

"We shall be certain now where we are going."

14

END OF SIEGE

Wendell stood before the navy hall at the head of a bewildered column of a dozen loafers, expelled at the time of the occupation. The marines on duty had succumbed to wisdom and removed themselves to unknown quarters. A knot cinched in him as the first of the search parties trickled out from the town to puzzle over this assembly. He offered no more than a polite nod until Admiral of Land Folmon marched up in the mood of a man pulled from his breakfast.

"Gone!" He sputtered at Wendell. "Spirited off like Meabla under the watchful eye of *Bruco*, it would seem," he aimed the last bit at the hang-faced captain.

"Not quite, sir." Wendell nudged the point of his spear towards the door of the hall. Folmon needed a breath to gather the meaning.

"Is he in there?" Wendell gave a single nod. "Who got him? Not Bayochar…" Folmon said as if he would rather have Costig run free than to be apprehended by his fellow admiral.

"No one's got him, sir. He tossed out the lads and barred the door," Wendell thumbed toward the stragglers under his temporary command—half of them Bayochar's men who shirked their night watch. Folmon tensed and Wendell could hear the command to storm the hall as loud as if it were said. He quickly intercepted it.

"Tuilapoy is with him. And Willakuy. Gerachay and Wayranapan."

"Hostages?"

"No, sir. He asked to see them in order to conduct the affairs of the colony. Says he's returned to duty."

Folmon scowled in disbelief, perhaps suspecting a treachery on the part of the officials. Wendell could attest they had gone with a mix of nerves, of duty, and resignation to the perennial madness that was the mother spirit of the service of Drummoc.

"Where's me lads? And Bayochar?" Folmon looked about.

It was a morning befitting Drummoc.

Wendell had already heard the half of it from the men sent to gather reinforcements. Sometime in the night, Costig and his marines stole out of Gjoraslag undetected through the east lines, Bruco's portion. The escape wasn't noticed until just before dawn, when an old squain snuck past in the other direction to attempt to trade with the besieged men. He found the stronghold deserted, and immediately informed the third captain of that watch, Ithir, who was in the habit of giving him a single iron nail for his report on the state of the marines.

Ithir sounded the alarm. The captain of the watch should have been Bayochar, but he, his first mate, and several of his men had not bothered to attend their shift. The rest of his lads conferred with Bruco and Ithir. They searched the empty stronghold, and followed the marines' tracks as far as behind the town before returning to the site to debate whether they should pursue or call for reinforcements. Their consideration lasted inexplicably until sunrise, when they finally sent a man to bring up Folmon. They found him breaking his fast with his crew and those of Rapana'ekunta and Seander, all of whom were late to relieve the watch.

This messenger did not give the reason, nor ask for Folmon's men, so the admiral took his time fitting out for the snow and came alone.

Wendell's gaze wandered the sleepy harbor grounds, lamenting the still waters, where so recently Rixtan held court with different crews every day.

"Gone," he replied. "Someone," he didn't bother to name himself as the diligent observer "spotted the stolen darraig scouting the harbor again this morning, and reported it to Bayochar. Since his men were occupied at Gjoraslag, he borrowed yours—"

"*Borrowed?*" Folmon choked as if it were his wife.

"Aye, sir. He and Rapana hurried out the darraigs we used recently for drilling," he hoped Folmon didn't notice the note of disapproval that slipped through in the word "recently," "and gave chase." They looked over the water together, unable to spot the masts under oars. "Right before Ithir and the lads arrived to call all hands to arms for the search."

He didn't need to tell Folmon that not a single marine responded, nor did he feel it wise to weigh the scales of bad news with the fact that he had seen Costig slip into the hall as soon as it cleared, as though he were waiting for the moment. It seemed too much trouble at the time to race up the hill when Folmon would learn eventually.

Wendell also withheld the word he received from one of the expelled marines, that three of their mates had decided to stand with Costig's bunch. It seemed blunders were an ornament of the admiralty, bequeathed to the new officers even as the old sergeant-at-arms regained his effectiveness of command in the course of his demotion.

The great door swung open and the whole of the Navy snapped to, ready for a charge. It was the ministers who emerged, though, followed soon by the admiral's two camp aides.

"What are his demands?" Folmon challenged Tuilapoy.

"Willakuy is to asses the treasury, to determine for how long we can pay the lads under a siege given the denominations we have.

"As for myself, I have much to do. In the main, he asks for a report on the weapons we are forging, and on the construction at the Calm Harbor. But eh…Costig," he struggled not to guess at the rank Folmon wanted to hear, "also would like the prison wall rebuilt for what he refers to as urgent accommodations. Wayranapan and Gerachay spoke in private, but I suspect they have their lists, as well."

Folmon laughed silently, and looked around to see if anyone found it as absurd as he.

"Does he think he's admiral?"

"It would appear, sir. Oh, and Wendell, he asks that you see to bringing as much meat as possible from the hunting camp, and setting a plan to supply the colony during a siege."

"Etan's after it."

"Costig says Etan's a cunt. He asks you."

"And what tasks has our madman assigned meself?" Folmon sneered sarcastically.

Tuilapoy reluctantly produced a folded parchment.

"He would you like you to convey a message. To the Leopard Seal."

A hunting trip—it was a fine way to get out of a bit of stowage. The little bucket had already had the lads out twice after "seals" that only his young osprey eyes could see, and as many times they came back with cold toes to show for it. Now only Foster was dumb enough to believe it. That, or he was happy to risk being left behind to miss a little work. Corm promised as much if they weren't back by the time the sleds shoved off. It was more like to be a shapeshifter, or some ice daimon, but with the barrels growing shallow, they could ill afford to ignore a black glimmer.

Gionn was glad to be rid of Foster. Always lurking around him like a shifty luck. Now there were matters to discuss that would trouble his virgin ears.

"Looks like you could use another pair of hands, noble sled captain."

He manned the other side of a small cask, brimming with freshwater ice. He and Palqua turned it along its bottom on the way from Tamarqan's rig to their own.

"That Bosc seems like a square cunt," he said of the sunbaked inlander in Eckerd's party. "For the sort that sailed with Corm, anyway."

"Held his place in the fight well enough that I hardly noticed him. And not so well I noticed him, either," Palqua replied.

"That's the brilliant thing about port." He cleared his throat over the bleak terrain. "As it were. You get to meet all sort of aft vermin. Nothin' against me bow mates, Foster and the lads. Wouldn't mind stabbin' their guts out, though. They follow me around like a bunch of whelps to their bitch mum. Probably walk right off the ice if I did first. It's nice to get a different sort."

Palqua nodded congenially.

"Did you know he was a chief of his people?"

"It is a good tale." Palqua said with decorum.

"Ksit'hangi, that one. His name means 'inlander' if you don't speak the proper tongue, which bein' Amposi, I assume you wouldn't. I rather like that—you know right where he comes from. Not at all like some of these blaggards," he gave a dismissive toss of his head. "Take meself: I'll tell you sure enough I was born on Hautatlo and entered the honorable service by force when Paladris stole off with me father and uncles, and I first saw me dear mum cry from hunger.

"Course, it's a load of shit. None of your damn affairs, cunt, and I'll slap you half-a-turn round the mast if you ask again. The only one less believable is Foster. Have you heard *his* tale? I won't ruin it for you. Ships as big as cities, he says! Sorry, that's all. Do yourself a favor and beg the rest, before anything should happen to him.

"Bosc, though. Square cunt. Eckerd's fortunate to have him. Wouldn't say he's a barrel, but those are too set in their course. Now meself, I'm a proper whaler. Don't choose me wind before I sail. I pull to sea and wait for the strong one."

He and Palqua each put a hand on the bottom and hoisted the cask onto the sled.

"I agree, it is a fine thing to meet the men of the bow. They are good in a harness, and as we saw with the angotaks, fleet of foot. Of course, I am not inclined to believe a sea tale, much less the things I hear out on the pack. But if you are right, perhaps when we reach Taclann I will raise a cup with Bosc to his faithful people."

Gionn excused himself to search for a length of rope. He shivered once he got clear of the Amposi. That one was too clever for his liking. Though he didn't have to worry so much whether he got across, it did trouble him that Palqua may have taken more than Gionn intended to give. His stomach bubbled like a broth pot with the old fear. It had been some years since it came often, and only recently had it sputtered up with an unlikely acquaintance on Drummoc. Now he sensed again that danger. Through the mutinies and the ice, the gnawing hunger and the sled tracks they followed like a forsaken pilgrimage, it returned to hang its shadow. And Palqua was just the sort who could undo him over a loose word.

He drifted back to help with Corm's load, grateful for the distance.

"Hoy! Captain! Use another set of hands?" Gionn brushed Bentos aside to gather the long end of the lumber that Corm bore. They hugged it to keep the middle boards from sliding out. He debated which name to use this time, but in the end looked out to Eckerd's sled.

"That Bosc seems like a square cunt." It came out too abrupt for his liking. "For the sort that jumped to Palqua, anyway."

Corm snorted a plume of breath.

"That's the brilliant thing about port," He plodded on. "As it were. You get to meet all sort of aft vermin. Nothin' against me bow mates…"

Foster untied the leather strip that he wore like a bandit mask and squinted at first, taking his time to let his eyes adjust. A lot of the whalers dismissed them, but the Mattaka boys said their people always wore them for winter travel over snow. Little Tunguk especially had good eyes, and he showed Foster how to cut a pair of narrow slits so that the daughters of Ajatse wouldn't burn his sight for staring at them. A few of the more seasoned whalers like Ordacles and Arthas had already adopted the masks.

He, at least, still believed the boy. They'd backtracked until the sleds disappeared, and once again, no sign of the seal.

"You still see it?"

"Maybe he is gone to his hole," Tunguk suggested.

They stood on a dizzy highway of sled tracks. Seven pairs of runners grooved the crust of snow that would lead him back to his crew. There was no debating who the other three belonged to. The ice gave ample room for whispers that the confinement of the ship wouldn't allow. There was a growing body of sailors who pulled with anxiety that they would catch up to their frontrunners. Corm brushed aside the fears—the angotaks were starving, he said. While Tamarqan and others insisted that the easiest way to get a meal was to ambush the men of the *Gairhle*, their captain didn't think they had the strength for it, and the difference would only increase every day.

Until their rations began to dwindle, too, that is. Tawatu kept tight lids on the state of the barrels, leaving them to guess by shaking every time they stowed. True or not, the men believed the rations were shrinking by the slice each day, and some, including Foster, had begun to eat less than their full issue in order to build a reserve.

He reached into his trousers and untied the water bladder where it dangled at his crotch. His poor frozen crotch. There was no shortage of fresh water, on the other hand. The barrels were full of snow, and he learned that the older the ice, the less salt it contained. The men knew where to cut. The problem was drinking it.

Each day, they loosened the stitches of the seams and sewed up a chunk to melt in their armpits or between their legs. A vigorous shake spared just enough liquid to wet his tongue. Only when he got truly thirsty did he melt it in his mouth, and paid for it with violent chills.

"Cuffs and crotches, arseholes and armpits!" Gionn's advice echoed in his head. He'd tried to recruit Foster to help feel up men through any convenient touch for a brush of an argot.

"It won't be in their kit, but any crevice he can sew a coin is worth a grope. A man who don't take off his boots is not to be trusted."

It was a dig at Foster. Between the fear of an urgent retreat and Gionn's fingers, he hardly shed a layer. But the others peeled off all they could stand in the tent, which to his utter shock grew warm-enough that the rime on the ceiling melted onto them all night, the ice beneath turned to puddles, and they started their day soaked.

At least the ice was good. In contrast to the first days, they had made more than ten miles on each of the last three, and by his reckoning, more than fifteen the day before. The sudden progress filled them with guarded enthusiasm. No one knew how much farther it was, though what awaited felt inevitable. The men quarreled in the harnesses like the dogs on the deck of the *Juhketappat*. The whole column had the look of ice, waiting to break along the deep cracks visible beneath its frozen exterior.

He caught himself watching Arthas, then Gewar, before he remembered that it was *him* who brought the argot aboard. The sleds had reorganized often. Extra rations crept aboard, as well as most things they needed in case they were separated. The sail was divided in two. They slept in hardening factions, and by now, Foster understood that anyone who split off without a tent wouldn't last more than a night or two. A few men like himself and Gionn made it a point to alternate, though Corm's and Palqua's men were mixed between both tents.

So with a gnawing hunger, he took off with Tunguk after seal. Foster didn't go because he thought they would find one any more than they did the other times. The convoy, like the ship, may have been a narrow island in a sea of certain death. The absence of scraping runners calmed him, though. Gionn's talk of ditching the crew worried him as much as the fear it would split.

The dawn, when he was not in a harness, spread its gold over the pack. Tiny knobs turned translucent and every facet flashed red and pink and orange and blue. If he didn't need to eat, or drink, or warm himself, he would stay here. Something about it felt like an invitation.

The grandeur wasn't lost on Tunguk. That, or the boy kept quiet due to his dwindling reputation as a lookout. He must have been praying a fat seal up from the depths. Foster didn't doubt him, but he knew they would come home empty-handed. It was the walk, and the break he needed, and the lure of a growing hunch. The first time, Tunguk saw the animal off their tracks, north and east. Then after they crossed onto older pack and a fresh trail, the seal had appeared behind them.

He unwrapped his sleeveless summer tunic and placed a small cache of meat that barely filled his palms square between the tracks. Tunguk watched with some surprise, then looked over the ice again with new urgency. Foster touched his shoulder. Without a word, they turned and followed the lines of the runners like a tether to an unseen ship.

Another armload of mining tools fell beside Parks' sled.

"Ten. Two more."

Milak tossed a hammer and a tool with a short handle and a thin, flat blade, squared at the end. Parks would have used it to spackle an intense hole in the dry wall if he had to guess its purpose. He sized up the implements.

"OK, take…*that one*," He pointed to a pick with a long head on one side. Ravitak tossed it aside into the forge pile. The boys started to gather up the remainder, but Parks waved them off. "Hang on, that's only eleven, now. We need one more." Dumb looks followed. They were used to his puzzling corrections at that point in the process, though, and another hammer went down.

"Yep, that's the one. Forge." Ravitak tossed it. They paused for permission, then chucked the other eleven tools in the "keep" pile.

"Is that it?" Another seven tools plunked down in the snow.

"That's the last," Milak assured him.

"Huh. Well, I don't know. It's way short of twelve. I say just toss 'em all. Forge." The tools joined a considerable heap destined to make the sled journey back up to the idiotically named Eagle Camp. The most casual eye could see that of the two piles of tools present at the harbor, the forge pile accounted for a very liberal interpretation of "one-twelfth." Anyone who knew their fractions, anyway, which meant that Parks' morning of rounding and shuffling and guesstimation went unquestioned.

"Do you think there will be enough spears for each man?" Ulwet asked hopefully.

"Carabiner doesn't think so. But then, who's counting?" He winked. "Powwow!"

He waited for all the boys to meander back. Ferrakut came last from his job, reporting that he could find no one injured, and that the men were very concerned for the welfare of the two hunting ships, devoting most of their songs to a good haul, but otherwise were in good spirits.

The harbor presence seemed to have dwindled since his last visit. Many had gone with Ostuk and Haraket, but Carabiner had pulled most of the men guarding the landing to spread throughout the high mines, where he suspected the marine raiders were hiding. Only fifty men plus Captain Ghrane and his crew remained to protect the *Orin's Thief*—or to hold it hostage. He couldn't tell.

Parks shot impatient glances to Senadak, who stood a ways off talking with Sawi and Umatbarak.

"I don't think he will come," Milak said. "Sawi disapproves."

"Then he'll miss our greatest conquest yet," he watched them wriggle. "Gentlemen." He stopped himself, realizing that he sounded like Carabiner addressing the troops. Parks cleared his throat. "Carabiner has his Midshipmen polishing every knob on his vessel while he hosts bonfires at a weak-ass siege. Meanwhile, the Leopard Seal and his Dog Boys, we get shit done. You all know that the real danger is the five men who ambushed Carabiner and fled to parts unknown. Who raid our food, unsuccessfully, thanks to Ulwet." He clapped the blushing boy on the back. "They killed, what now, twelve of our men?" Ferrakut nodded in confirmation. "And wounded ten."

"Nine," Ferrakut corrected. "No. It is ten, but Vetravet says it is not so bad."

"Now they hide in our mines, confident that no one can find them, and if they did, that no one would have the brass balls to do anything about it. That's because they don't know us. What we lack in weapons and numbers," they looked at one another timidly, "we make up for…" Parks tapped his temple. "Here.

"My people have long told a story of a wise trickster. He's a dog-looking dude who walks on his hind legs, and he is called Wile E. Coyote by his friends and enemies, alike. Of all things in this world, the one he hates most is Roadrunner, who I can only describe as a really fast, flightless bird. But roadrunner is too fast for him. Wile E. runs slow, like your old buddy Leopard Seal. Luckily, where Roadrunner is simpleminded, Wile E. is clever.

"He knows Roadrunner likes to escape down tunnels. So one day, he takes a bunch of black paint—you know, like pitch—and he paints what looks like a mine entrance on the mountainside."

"So he will stick to it!"

"No, Arnake. Listen up, little homey. He does it, because he knows Roadrunner will try to escape. The next time he sees the bird, he chases him right toward the hole at full speed."

"He smacks his face!" Ulwet guessed.

"No. Somehow the paint magically turns into an actual hole, and he runs right through it. And when Wile E. Coyote tries to follow, *he* smacks his face." The boys frowned at one another. "But in theory, it was brilliant. We just need ideas like that, but better. So! Let's brainstorm."

"Brainstorm?" Ferrakut asked.

"You know storm, right? A brain is the gray squishy thing in your head, like when you cleave someone's skull open." They leaned back in awe at the realization.

"We will brainstorm them?" Milak ventured uncertainly.

"Just say what plans you have. Nothing is too outlandish. Look around, what materials do we have? We've got mining tools, wigwams, coal baskets, sleds, a ship...maybe that ship has ropes, nets, use your environment to figure out how we're going to get those dudes out of the hole and into captivity or death. Go!"

"Ooh!" Ulwet practically leapt up. Parks called on him. "We can send our best warrior to sneak into the mine at night with a spear. He can go alone, so he knows if there is anyone there, he will stab them without fear that they are his brothers. And he stabs until the men are full of holes and the mine is a sea of blood."

Parks frowned. "'K. Who's our best warrior?" They all looked around without commitment.

"We need men. Big men, to help us." Milak meant grown-ups.

"You're thinking inside the box. We have loads of options. We can make a fall pit with spikes, a trip line out of rope, or a snare."

"Wait til they come out and dump firestone on their heads!" Arnake added.

"Or that. How about this? We bury a net—I'm assuming the ship has a net we can use—bury that in the snow, attached to a rope and a pulley overhead, and when they step on it, it triggers the net to close around them and raise up. Huh?" He lifted his eyebrows a few times. "Not bad, right?"

"What is overhead? It cannot hang from the sky," Saunlauk pointed out.

"And how does the net know to raise?" Siguvik piled on.

"Like I said, there are no bad ideas. We're just getting warmed up. OK, Arnake: go!"

Arnake moved his mouth but nothing came out. The boys began to shout over one another at him. "He is dumb! And too small!"

"We make them come to us," Milak offered.

"Now you're talking!" Parks clapped. "How?"

"Like fish. We put bait." He thought hard. "Food. They are hungry."

"They are not stupid. Who leaves food outside a mine?" Ravitak fired back. "I know! We use Leopard Seal as bait!"

Now it was Parks turn to lose his speech.

"We can't afford to lose Leopard Seal, you drooler. We use *Kjartke*!" Siguvik suggested.

"It doesn't matter what we use, we are young. We need men to help us," Milak reiterated.

"You know what? You're right. Milak, go find us a few more men. Yeah, right now. Go on." He shooed the pragmatic older boy away. "And no to the Kjartke thing. Kjartke is terrible bait, for so many reasons. Ferrakut: what you got?"

"We must ask Tunguk. He will know. And he will be angry if we act without him."

"Siguvik?" Parks ignored the Eskimo Joe comment.

"We offer bribes," Siguvik said. "Wood! A pile of good scrap wood. Or a steel blade from the forge."

"We give them Kjartke!" Arnake shouted.

"What if they do not find her beautiful?" Ulwet worried.

"She is atatapalatet to him," Ferrakut defended, doubling the boys over with mockery.

Parks played it as cool as he could while they got it out of their system. As they finished, Milak returned with two men. One was the amputee with the wooden leg he had seen on his previous visit, clearly enamored to be a part of the gathering. The other had a head that looked like it was elongated in childbirth and never popped back to shape.

"Alright, alright. You got jokes. We need ideas." He turned around. "What about you?"

Kjartke blinked. It seemed to sum up her opinion of the proceedings.

"Will you ask the young girl, too?" She answered rhetorically.

"Lady Sophia!" Ravitak said. "Arnake will ask her. He cannot speak of anything else. She is atatapalatet." Arnake tried to fold in on himself to escape the raging laughter.

The sled started to move, and Parks realized that Kjartke had had enough. She gave a sharp command in Mattakatan, and Ulwet and Ferrakut hurried to fetch the dogs.

"Whoa, whoa, whoa!" He put the brakes on the movement. "I'm in a meeting. We still need to work out how this is going to go down."

The tattoos on her chin curled menacingly under Kjartke's glare, as though they had welled up from within her as a mark of her nature that he couldn't place but knew to fear.

"All will be killed. Let them stay in hole."

Kjartke marched off, daring them to arrive at any other conclusion. After a vacuum in which each of them must have braced as hard as he did to muster up a little denial, Parks spoke.

"Alright, little homies. There are a few details left to iron out, but I feel confident saying that we just curb-stomped the Dawn Council in terms of progress.

"Milak, thank you for these…two fine recruits. Fellas, 'preciate your interest. Hang tight for orders. But in the meantime, we're going to need a few more big strong bodies to help us out. I'd do it myself, but I don't have a sick wooden leg like this character." He pointed a finger gun and winked at the man.

The amputee bubbled over with delight at the show of favor from the Leopard Seal. He hobbled over as fast as he could and threw his butt down in the snow. In a flurry of straps, he freed the prosthesis and placed it on Parks' lap.

"Please! Take!"

"Nuh-nuh-no! Sorry, I was joking." But the man had already risen so fast onto his single leg that Parks thought some stage hand must have yanked him on a hidden wire. "Too much! Seriously, this is yours. Here," he extended it as the man stumbled back to his friend. "Too much, buddy. Seriously. I doubt it's even sized for me." Now Parks tried to stand, but even off the elevation of the sled, could find no way to work himself up with his hands full. He held it out again.

The amputee's friend hurried over to Parks—he thought to take the leg—but pushed it back into Parks' chest.

"You must. Please."

"I can't make this dude hobble around. How much did this cost, like a billion Mattaka bucks? He'll never work that off."

"Please. Do not give it back. It is a grave insult," the man with the elongated head said. Parks looked over at the unsteady amputee. The corners of his smile curled down, caught between the exultation of making such a gift to the Leopard Seal, and the despair of having it thrown back at him. "You must take." The friend said with a quiet assurance that showed him far less simple than he looked.

Parks' jaw hung open as they hitched the sled. His heart cracked in desperate guilt. He watched the crippled miner throw his arm around his friend and beam as if, after a life of hardship, he had arrived finally at his victory.

The door to the navy hall quickly closed behind Polc and the board fell into place. He'd hardly been gone when he rejoined the two admirals, several of the captains and officials of colony, and one low sergeant-at-arms. The corner of Polc's mouth shrugged at the rusted ram that the carpenters had salvaged off a wreck, fixed to a beam taken from the ramp they had been building for the Calm Harbor. He was meant to give them time to finish the implement.

"He asked me to carry his message over to the Leopard Seal. I can't say he was convinced that you'd burn the hall if he didn't surrender."

"Is that all he wanted you for?" Folmon asked with disdain.

"Aye. And to send up Bayochar, next." The officers showed their amusement, and perhaps a touch of admiration for the gall. "I told him that weren't likely. So he asked for Lamachar, in order to arrange the retrieval of the coal."

Wendell grinned to himself. Costig didn't trust a one of those men farther than the reach of his boot. It had the desired effect on Folmon, though.

"I can arrange that with Lamachar," Bayochar replied. "It has to be done, but we've no need for Costig."

"The dog ships are after it," Folmon said.

"It's been too long. If his suspicions of the assistant viceroy are to be believed, it may require a few warships to see that they return, and I'll remind you that that is a matter for the Admiral of Sea."

"If you care to bob off the coast, it is. Once you set foot at Camne Drumlag, it's land again."

"We can leave nothing of value there through the winter. And we know little of the officer there, or the proceedings."

"You want to treat the viceroy's man with hostility because Costig don't like him? Costig isn't the fuckin' admiral!" Folmon reminded his counterpart.

"At the very least, I mean to take a sounding of the place."

"Then do it from the sea!"

Bayochar snorted and babbled angrily in Amposi, which Wendell pretended not to understand.

"Shall I speak with Costig, sir?" Lamachar interjected, eager to loose the tensions. Folmon checked the progress on the ram.

By the rap on the door, Costig knew it wasn't Lamachar. Too assured. Yet it lacked insistence, or pride. He suspected Gerachay or Wayranapan, but was not surprised to see Wendell slip through the narrow crack permitted by their barricade. The marines declared the stair clear and barred it behind him.

Wendell made his way to the table somewhat timidly, and graciously took his seat when Costig poured him a cup of hasqa.

"A Drummoc man. That's what you are. Took me a few cold nights at Gjoraslag to sort it. I admit, I was angry enough that it was good you kept your distance. You, Gua, Obrachar—Drummoc, all of you. Loyal mates, as long as your mate's for Drummoc. It was me fault to think you should have seen it in me, too, when I did everything to avoid showin' it to you."

"Call it Drummoc, then," Wendell allowed. "What presides as the officers and the servants sail here and there. She's never introduced herself to me personally, but that's as fine a name as any."

"Did he send me message?"

"Not just yet."

"Aye, I didn't think you were here to discuss matters of coal. Terms of surrender, perhaps. Or me penmanship. Did you read it?"

"Aloud, as did Tuilapoy, Willakuy, Wayranapan, as if he couldn't trust a word until he heard it four times."

Costig's mustache stiffened with satisfaction.

"And you're right: I'm to show interest in talk of coal, while I sniff out what you could have possibly meant by all that Leopard Seal madness—expectin' the man who took your office to ferry a message to an enemy of the colony on your behalf. Brilliant!" Wendell's laugh was musical and sincere. "He may cleave you yet, but he won't outsmart you."

"Half a company of marines took his hall without a fight. What do you think Fair Donn'll do?"

"If you had any fears that the Admiral of Sea was any better, that darraig-thief came back for a look, *recklessly* close. Had the lads been in the water at their drills, they'd have nabbed him. By the time Bayochar launched the boats, though, he led 'em on a merry run east. As they were unprovisioned, they had to turn back."

"Haraket. What a burden off me, all these names. Why, by the gods, am I tryin' to take 'em back?" Wendell's own name sounded in Costig's ear. Wendell, who had sent Etan to the hunting camp in his stead, and stood by Folmon in mutiny. In bitter Gjoraslag, Costig had dreamed their ruin. If it were Wendell's lady of Drummoc that Costig served, she was faint of voice and easily drowned by those outside the hall.

"Why, by the gods?" Wendell repeated. "If I limit meself to the past few days, I could recount enough folly to make you seek the first whaler north. Leave her carcass to the carrion birds. But I keep hopin' in me madness that somehow, you go into Spring a sergeant-at-arms. Let the blue bastards feud over those names, while we handle the real colony, how we always done."

The rank sung with a beautiful longing, like youth, or an old port he would never return to.

"There's no marchin' backwards."

"Aye, not for any of us, I'm afraid. Wish you would of told me your arrangement. Not many believe it, of course—they're sure it's a tale to cover the theft of a few argots—but me nose smells somethin' to it." He tapped his nostril.

"And this is you, lookin' after the message for your admiral?"

"It is, and for me own sake. Perhaps I'm a bit simple, but I like to believe all that bumblin' after the Leopard Seal is best explained in terms of a clever man who didn't want him caught. If you meant to lend credibility to a spy, you couldn't have done a finer job—but as you said in the message, his great reputation came at the cost of your own. A mention to meself, to Gua, Gerachay, Wayranapan, any of it could have prevented this. That's all that leaves me to wonder if it weren't a song composed after the singin'.

"Course, you had no cause to mention the lads on the whaler—Gionn and Foster—except that it was clearly a message for Folmon. And if he hates your name, he's no choice but to take on pursuit of your spy as a fugitive, and all the unrest that'll come with it. Just so, he'll have to treat the assistant viceroy as an ally, spirit him away from an agent who's advised to 'arrange death if Alexicus compromises the colony.' Which is to say, he'll have to bow to a senior official. We both know how well admirals cast aside their pride. And if you're right, he does so to the ruin of Drummoc.

"Or he calls it rubbish, and lets Alexicus usurp him when you turn out right. The third way, as you knew when you wrote it—to deliver your message as you order and support your campaign—is too humiliating. That you called for Bayochar to deliver it—Euskus! I hardly contained meself when I read it. No wonder he's pissin' buckets! He gashes himself no matter what he does."

Costig strained to contain his satisfaction.

"There's nothin' I could say to convince you."

"Not just yet," Wendell granted.

Costig leaned back and leveraged his foot up, then pried off his boot. He shook it upside down until two gold coins clattered to the table.

"If you ever find it in you, I've a favor that I ought to have already asked you." He pushed one coin across under his forefinger. "That's Foster's. If he stops the *Gairhle*. Whatever happens to me, see to it that it's spent in maintenance of the old man, Tunguk, and the woman with the marks on her face. And if he doesn't stop that ship, see to it that he and his mate are outlawed and hunted in Amposi waters."

Costig slid the other coin over.

"That's for Parks. I think it'll wind up back in the treasury. But if by a miracle, he undermines our assistant viceroy, give him his due."

Wendell waited as if expecting to be stopped from seizing the argots. He gathered them uncertainly.

"And the third?"

"On the whaler. We'll never see it again."

Wendell nodded. "Of course, the others'll say you've kept one in a different boot to make your escape."

"Of course. But it's not them I need to convince. You know by now I sent a unit to Camne Drumlag under Poznatxen. Had they succeeded, they would have returned in that darraig days ago, with the assistant viceroy in irons. Nothin' short of treason could have spared him. If it's Drummoc you love, rally the Marines. I don't know what we'll need to do to get through this, but neither Folmon nor Bayochar can do it. As it stands, we may not even make it to Donnab."

Wendell took off his boot and dropped in the argots, then removed his coat and folded it on the table.

"It's Drummoc, aye. And if I do that, we'll slaughter half the sailors and a few marines, besides. None of which serves the lady. And it's in that spirit that I'll inform you me suspicion: Folmon intends to smash his way in when I open the door to leave. I think he wants to make me out to be your enemy."

Costig rose from the bench.

"You didn't need his help," he declared, and left his hostage to get comfortable.

The sleds waited uneasily just off a mess of ruts that showed the angotaks had paused here. A strange symbol blocked their path, ten feet long and drawn in blood.

"Seal," Eckered returned with a few men from a side trail of drag marks. "Speared it a quarter-mile off. Not a soup bone or a whisker left."

Tamarqan paced nervously. "We should never have followed so direct. Now we have seen their hateful sign."

"Don't matter if we see it or not, it serves the same," Fergo countered. "Just a ward. As long as we don't drive over it."

"It is more than a ward," Asdosa said with as much force as he could, his arm still lame from the arrow. "A man of Ampos can see that."

Foster closed his eyes and hunched against the wind while another debate raged over the relative strengths of their magics and whose could be trusted.

It was decided that since several of the Amposi who tried to counter the angotaks' magic had died in the battle, and Fergo had only lost a finger, he would be responsible—but the captain yielded to their insistence that something be done.

Fergo commanded that the sled party circle wide to the left, and remain together until they had regained the tracks. When volunteers were asked to stay behind to help with the defenses, few spoke up. Foster was glad for another opportunity to avoid the harness. Tunguk now only reported his seal sightings quietly to Foster, and they had remained consistent. It had been two days since he left the meat in their wake. Now he'd ssaved enough to justify another attempt if he could break free of prying eyes.

Gewar and Tunguk were requested by name. While they waited for the sleds to disappear so they could begin, Foster sent the boy to ask Gewar "any questions he'll answer." That left Fergo alone.

He waited for the odd little man to relieve himself in the open. Fergo was gaunt when they left. Now, he looked like a lie holding up a fur seal parka. His limbs bent and twisted, and his movements jerked and warped as though his body despised straight lines. When he stood by crouch-walking forward until he gradually reached his customary stoop, Foster approached.

"I can't bring myself to believe any of the things out of your mouth. Unfortunately, brother, you're the only one sayin' what I wanna hear."

Fergo studied him over a graying strap of beard that now waved downward several frozen inches, while his upper lip received the frequent attention of a knife blade that kept the stubble short enough to give him the look of a derelict Lincoln.

"Lost, then?" He nodded in confirmation of some hidden suspicion. "Aye, you're a queer sort, and your number magic, dread. But it usually happens to more remarkable lads."

"I've already forgot what you said. And I can't say I found it likely. But I'll try anything. Anything. If you can just get me to Noina."

Fergo scoffed. "Anyone can. If you're sure that's the one you want. Have you forgot there's half-a-hundred ways?"

"You said that's the fastest."

"Never said it was fast. But aye, I can show you."

"For?"

Fergo flicked absently at his gray pinky, dangling from its necklace. "Argot." His eyes singed Foster from their bead-thin abyss. "Have you got it back, yet?"

Foster collected himself. "Never had it to begin with," he said with manufactured amusement.

"A vile rumor, then." Fergo seemed relieved.

"From who?" Foster decided to go on the offensive.

"A bastard and a wretch. But one man, at least I can say that. Not like you, Gionn."

"I'm Fos—"

"Aye! Foster! Gionn! I've seen both your forms, and I'm not fooled, lad." He dipped his head and snaked it to Foster's other cheek. "Me dreams, they tell me things. Gold's the price! No liar would give an argot for his tale, nor a wayward man spare a thousand to return home."

He held his gaze as he looped around, then backed toward the symbol and shouted for the others to join.

The briefing was simple enough. Fergo scraped a circle around the blood sign in a single counterclockwise pass. He then handed the spear to Gewar, and had him put on his famous dress.

"Upon Gyresha, the ground is bare," Fergo wailed. Gewar bent like a hag and walked backwards over the sign, scraping a straight cut razor thin until he reached the other end of the circle.

"Let the point not slip or skip or lodge, but smooth, your mark!" Their conductor had warned, and Gewar held his course well.

Fergo then put himself perpendicular to the first slice with the spear in front of him like a push broom. "Upon Lailogan, the seas are foul." He walked a careful path forward to make an intersecting mark.

"And now a virgin takes the dress."

"Don't look at me," Foster frowned.

"Swear it, lad," Fergo said to Tunguk. "That you have never lain beside a woman." The boy gulped and nodded before he put on the gown, which brushed against the ice on his barely five-foot frame.

"Upon Balgeira, your thrust did err."

Tunguk, too, walked backwards with mandatory grace, slicing through the center to divide the pie in half again.

"Hands of Dannan, split your prow!"

The last act fell to Foster. He imitated Fergo, no dress, walking forward with the spear in front to complete what looked to him like an asterisk. Keeping the dulling point in the ice was harder than it looked, and required the gentlest of constant pressure. But as soon as he passed the middle, it snagged and skittered off. Fergo hurled a vicious rebuke, jumping along the edges like an enraged baboon while Foster recentered it and finished his work. A bony hand snatched the spear from him when he reached the edge of the circle.

"An argot, lads." He reminded Foster, and the plural didn't seem like an accident. "And I'll believe it was another who came to foul us."

The sled jolted over a lump in the worn trail and Parks had to brace a hand on the snow to keep from toppling off.

"Ow! Fuck! Easy, li'l akjuru. We got time," he held back his frustration, mounting with the pain. Ulwet steered, if he steered at all, by launching his entire body, undersized for his eight or nine years, into every adjustment.

"He will stop us," Ulwet defended his urgent pace by repeating Parks' fear.

"He's all the way up at the siege with Carabiner." It came out in a whining tone, from a heart that wanted to be stopped.

When Kjartke saw them take off, she slashed at them with every threat in her vocabulary before trying to get Senadak to stop the sled. When he refused, she turned her venom on him until he agreed to bring Eskimo Joe. Parks would not have been unhappy at their company, even if they hauled him back to Eagle Camp by the ear. The pit of a goodbye ached in his stomach.

He'd waited for his favorite moment: the one forced on him when everything came to bear and he had still done nothing with all his plans, had no choice but to scramble in that purposeful panic which alternated through his life with his preferred state of rest.

It wasn't one of his better days. He woke in the night to the wild sounds of the miners. Kjartke had gone out to investigate, and when she returned, she told him to sleep.

His leg had awakened, though. Each time he thought the worst was over, it returned to him like a ghost. The missing toes cramped, absent flesh froze solid. He writhed in and out of shallow sleep all night, kicking at the empty space to silence the wailing limb.

In the morning, a sense of something urgent drove him outside. He saw the horrors and connected the voices of the night. Three men had escaped from the mine. They didn't make it far. Parks only glimpsed them for a second before he had to look away. As the boys recounted it, he felt his own skin torn under the torture. The weight of men on his chest, sickness, the teeth of a saw. Kjartke chased the boys from his trembling body.

The Mattaka took it all in with indifference. He knew Ulwet was a fucking savage, but even sweet Ferrakut shrugged, and Kjartke tended him like he was a child, upset to learn that the chicken in the yard had ended up on his plate.

He fled without a plan, and in flight, he settled on it.

Ferrakut led the dogs over the rise to the old mines, gouged like unhealing wounds from the mountain. Something of the risk nagged at him. His leg whined like a dog strangling itself at the end of its leash. Parks thought that he should feel brave, or at least clever, to do what he intended. But Carabiner had scored first in the eyes of the miners. When Parks looked inward, he felt only "late," as if a ship made ready to leave without him, and this place wasn't one where he could bear to stay.

He made them drive right up to the first mouth, the older and smaller of the two. Even the dogs raised their ears, wondering what he meant to do next.

"Run down to the harbor. See if Milak found any more men to help us."

"Help with what?" Ferrakut asked.

"I'll explain when they get here."

Ulwet nodded, but his older brother must have picked up on it.

"I will wait with you."

Parks started to argue. He squinted into the black mouth, and understood that he hadn't been driven here by a desire to one-up Carabiner. Blind fear and futility pressed him. He couldn't even think of the mine. He meant to send them away for their own protection. But if he did, he had resigned himself to something other than what he told himself he came to do.

Parks quietly nodded in assent.

"Then help me up."

Ulwet scampered back toward the main trail to the harbor. Ferrakut wrestled him to stand tentatively with his arm around the boy. The touch surprised Parks, who imagined himself thicker than the bones that rested on the slight support.

"We should wait for them." Ferrakut didn't bother to ask what they meant to do. He had gleaned the desperation of the act.

"Don't worry. I got my—" He hefted his spear. "My whatcha call it?"

"It depends. What will you stab?"

"Does it matter?"

Ferrakut nodded. "It changes. If you are a hunter after seal, or a warrior after a man…"

"If everything goes well, nothing."

"*Tiuktan*," he said.

"My spear," Parks leaned on it for balance. "My tiuktan."

Ferrakut grinned. "In your tongue, it is '*pierce-nothing*.'"

The little joke settled Parks, until he felt himself between the stability of the weapon and the tutor. The pain in his stump granted him a stay, and turned into a dull throb as his heart beat a pool of blood to the swollen end.

"Yo! Ahoy, in there!" He raised his voice to the mine. "This is the Leopard Seal, and I've come to take you prisoner." Parks waited, as if for a laugh, but the hole remained dumb.

"I don't know what kind of news reports or periodicals you have access to in there, but your situation is grim. Your boys are trapped in a mine by a few hundred armed Mattaka. Last night, they feinted a battle to give three of them a chance to break through the blockade. The good news is, it worked. The bad news is that they don't know this place as well as the miners, especially not in the dark. They caught up to 'em on the main trail.

"I always thought these folks were some of the warmest, kindest people I'd ever met in my life. But apparently, they have quite a reputation for their treatment of prisoners. The assistant viceroy ordered the men to be taken alive, and technically, when he arrived at camp this morning, they were. I'll spare you the details, but let's just say that starving to death in a hole ain't looking so bad right now.

"I know you're in there, too. Everyone else thinks your men were headed to some pre-arranged point in the high mines to link up with their sergeant, give him the dirt, maybe come up with a way out. But if you're like me, you don't know this place very well, and you don't like to walk far. You'd pick the most obvious place—so obvious they hardly bothered to look—because you didn't really expect to fuck up so hard, did you?

"Now you might be thinking, 'Fine. This is the only dude who knows. Let's snag him, fight our way onto a ship, and fuck off. That would be sick, if it were possible. Two of the three ships, including the one you were supposed to commandeer, are gone hunting. You might could get to Ghrane's ship, but those lazy, no-good mercenaries have already cuddled up to the assistant viceroy—so my little spies tell me.

"But here's the exciting part: you have before you an opportunity to avoid starvation, dismemberment, and maybe, if everything goes *just* right, a chance to complete your mission. Costig probably didn't mention this, and I'll have to ask you to keep it to yourselves—state secret. You too, Ferrakut." He sighed as though it pained him to admit. "I work for Costig.

"That's right: an agent, double-agent, conspirator, hitman, call-it-what-you-will. Did you really think the admiral is so dumb that he searched the *wrong ship* while he let me sail away?"

Ferrakut looked up with concern, unsure what to make of it.

"I'm here for the same reason as you: to keep that rascally assistant viceroy in check. That's right, laddies, we're on the same team. You're the hard-nosed, law-abiding door-kickers who always get their man; I'm the clever rogue, master of a thousand disguises, who always gets the girl. You don't have to believe me, but you're so completely fucked right now that if you even find it plausible, you owe it to yourself to hear me out.

"Here's the terms: You surrender to me. I can get you full hospitality, VIP-treatment. Or if not, at least no torture. You tell the assistant viceroy lots of nice things about how I outwitted you and forced you to throw down your weapons under fear of death. You'll probably have to winter here with us, but I've already recruited a dope-ass boat captain to bring us back in the spring. Who knows? If we play it right, maybe you can even help me haul in that nasty assistant viceroy when the time comes."

Ferrakut's doe-eyes plead with him for it to be a ruse. He winked to let the boy doubt himself, and because he hadn't anticipated the discomfort of his apparent betrayal.

"It is empty," Ferrakut said. "Come, we will go find Ulwet and Milak and the men. Try another mine."

Parks could hear the denial in his tone. He was eager for something else to be true, and if they walked away, the whole story might collapse into illusion. For his part, he didn't know if he still worked for Costig, either. Had he concocted it to trick the marines? To turn them in to Carabiner? He'd felt terrible after Carabiner's speech about—he wasn't entirely sure. Mostly, because he knew a man who he gave so little credit had seen through him. But even though he thought it was bullshit, the idea that Carabiner believed him, that all he said and did was somehow true, weakened his defenses.

He wasn't quite eager to please Carabiner. If he could do good, though—especially if he could spot it first, and do it of his own power—there might be a way for them to cooperate in parallel, without too much...cooperation.

They both froze as a man ducked out of the low opening. He squinted in the low light. More than a week of crouching in the dark with little to eat took its toll on his cheeks and his gray flesh, but the way he carried his shield and spear left no doubt in Parks that what remained was plenty fierce. Another came to his elbow, then two more, helping the fifth between them. Leather strips wrapped two pieces of wood, cut from his own spear shaft, to the man's lower leg. He bore no weight.

Parks instinctively drew Ferrakut in and shifted his load on the stone weapon, pitiful to their steel. A wobbly cripple and a Mattaka boy made even less of an impression on them. They seemed to reevaluate whatever they had decided in that cave.

"How can we be sure you're Costig's man?" The leader spoke.

"I can tell you what his mustache smells like." The joke drew a smile out of the little company. "But I swear to you, I'm not his man. I'm the goddamn Leopard Seal. My people are those who help me," he looked down at his tutor. "My enemies are those who don't."

The leader checked his marines, who said nothing and gave no sign. He stepped forward so that their frosty breath mingled. The shield fell to the snow between them. He lay his spear at Parks' foot.

BONG.

The blows resounded through the hall. The eight bronze shields of the founders reverberated from their places overlooking the room. Marines rested at their posts, deaf to it. Wendell had taken up at the far end, where it was clear he offered no help or hindrance.

Costig resisted the urge to shake the battlements once more. Heavy tables turned on their sides created a funnel from the double doors to a narrow gap, large enough for a single man. Four of his lads stood in that murderous anteroom. He'd begun there, and had no trouble getting volunteers to join him, but they insisted that their sergeant-at-arms command from the far side of their defenses, with the main force. By some craven sense of duty, he obeyed.

BONG.

A little ice slid down the walls from frozen seams at the roof. He marked a tender sore on his foot where it had often bit against a gold coin and refused to complain until now, left to heal. He marked the time, the spirit of the blows. Costig thought of Camne Drumlag and of the *Gairhle*, and wondered if either of those long casts had yet a hope to land.

BONG.

At last, the board that barred the door cracked and bowed, but held. More ice, and now fresh snow showered the marines who hurried to swap it for their only spare before the sailors could get off another strike. They tore it free and dropped in the reserve. It was brittler than the first, and would not hold as long. A hurried thrust hit the door with little force. The men on the ram thought it only needed a tap to go, and found it stiff again.

One of the marines hammered at the iron arms that supported the bar. The inner pair had bent considerably with the crack. They returned obstinately. One of the bolts stripped, leaving the support to rattle loose against the bar.

He brushed his gaze up the wall, through the high rafters, down the far side of the great hall that stood for the might of Ampos. No one had come for him in the burial cairn of Gjoraslag, but here at the heart, he was intolerable. The clean lines of masterful stonework shimmered. Was he the servant of Ampos, beset by raiders, or had they caught up to him—that youth who jumped from the angotaks within scarcely a year, and set upon the shores of graceful Ampos herself with the scourge of Paladris, before jumping sides in the wake of the flood?

Ama must have known that his oath could not have been more sincere. She steered him where he was needed. He did as he was required. But here in this hall, in this seizing heart so far from the sacred shores of Ampos, he wondered if it could be her blood that issued forth to fill this place. He had not thought much of any lady of Drummoc, and if he had, he would have taken her to belong to the line of Ama. But if Wendell meant it as more than a platitude, then he was no longer certain they served the same thing. Perhaps neither of them knew.

Whoever presided, Costig could only be sure it was another who knocked.

BONG.

The sea lapped at the edge of the lead. It may have been thirty feet, or a nautical mile for all he could see. Fog hung over the water ahead, and separated Foster from his companions ranging the ice to either side.

"Hoy, beside!" He shouted the arranged phrase. To his left, he heard a thin voice repeat it, farther away than he expected. Foster looked right and waited, but Gionn never sounded off.

There wasn't much to fear as far as getting lost. Camp lay a few hundred yards behind, and two days of scouting had revealed no way through. The angotaks had for sure made it beyond. Something about ice and fog, though.

Four days ago the breeze backed a half turn until it gusted in their faces off the distant peninsula. Snow blinded them, filled their tracks. Their legs wilted in the headwind. Corm ordered the tents up, and for two days they hardly slept for hanging on to the canvas against the freight train roar. The ice groaned around them as if massive beasts prowled the pack, snapping trees as they went.

Then it stopped altogether. Fog buried them, and when they formed up to trudge through it, they immediately hit water. No one dared to mention what might have become of the *Gairhle* if the ice gave so much closer to land. They went out in parties north and south, probing for a way through, and each time came back with a solemn shake of the head.

His stomach twisted with the lightness of hunger. The expression "scraping the bottom of the barrel" took on new meaning as Tawatu issued a handful of icy meat shavings that wouldn't have fed a small dog. He kept his eye on Gionn for a break. He watched Bosc, and Corm, and Palqua. Every time they went out, he expected some group to take off—maybe his own.

The crew held, probably for no other reason than none of them could swim to Yunoc, and a morsel of food at camp was more than they could expect anywhere else. His generosity wore out. Without enough calories, even the calm air seeped into his bones until he shivered what he knew would become his death rattle.

Foster came as close as he dared to the edge, pleading for the other side. A breeze off the sea was all they needed, so of course it held out stubbornly. He threw down his spear and fumbled with his trousers, peeked out as little as he could, then released a sputter of dark liquid that dribbled and froze on the surface.

A movement from the water flashed out to him. He scanned the lead for some time, ready to chastise his imagination when it came again, unmistakable. A dark, smooth back arced just above the surface so briefly that the water came together with hardly a ripple.

Like a fisherman with a nibble, he picked up his spear without a sound. Foster wanted to holler for help, but he stuffed it down and prayed for the water to break again. Within a minute, a spray of air hissed from a snout that ducked again, followed soon by a sleek head that regarded him out of one sidelong eye before slipping under and flashing a patch of back.

A seal.

"Hoy, beside!" Tunguk called to his left, and he ached to silence the boy. Foster readied his spear to throw, and at the same time realized the stupidity of it, even if he could hit. There didn't seem to be any way to get the animal onto land where he could make a kill. He'd been spotted, and it was likely gone. Yet he persisted in his attention with his stomach singing in hope.

The head surfaced and stared at him, feet from the edge of the lead. It was long and massive—he thought maybe a fantasy of hunger—and it wore a playful grin. It dove again, then resurfaced for another look as if to tease him. They both knew there was nothing he could do.

A dark shape smeared the fog, and Foster waved frantically to Tunguk to join him, pressing his finger to his lips. The boy hurried over, and seeing his posture, drew his hand axe and pored over the water.

"Seal," Foster practically mouthed.

"What kind?" Tunguk asked as quietly. It probably mattered quite a bit for their chances. But Foster was no marine biologist, or Mattaka hunter.

There was no need to explain. The head appeared again at the edge of the ice to sniff at them. It was as angular as a polar bear, and maybe even larger. The animal smiled to reveal a jaw of canines jutting like Antarctic peaks over the smooth inner mouth. Tunguk grabbed Foster's arm. He looked at the boy for permission. It seemed so close, he had only to step forward and thrust.

"Run," Tunguk said calmly.

"*What?*"

With a burst, the seal hauled out in front of them, breaking a shelf of ice under its weight and sending them tripping back to avoid falling in. The agile body twisted onto the ice without effort like a finned serpent until its entire fifteen feet gained support. The dark gray monster reared up to reveal a light belly, spotted black. Foster froze before the immensity. He'd seen bulls smaller than this, and when it smiled again, the charm had left its fanged mouth.

"Run!" Tunguk pulled on him.

Foster jabbed at the head while backpedaling. The seal caught the shaft and whipped the weapon from his hands with a vicious shake of its jaws.

"*Uitkalpate!*" Tunguk screamed, apparently to Atalkut who roamed somewhere nearby.

"Gionn!" Foster turned and bolted. "Help, bitch! Help!"

They glanced back at the monster humping over the ice behind them. Foster thought he could outrun a seal, but his legs burned from panic and starvation. He had to shuffle to avoid a deadly trip, and it moved so much faster than its size should have allowed.

"Uitkalpate! Uitkalpate!" Tunguk repeated. "Lion!"

A blow from the snout to his heel toppled Foster. He wheeled around and had to dodge a swing of the axe from Tunguk at the same time as the jaws nipped for his outstretched foot. The seal plunged between them, parting them to either side, and wheeled after Tunguk. Foster gained his feet and froze, torn between fleeing and some futile gesture of assistance.

The boy squirmed out of the path of the bite and circled around as the animal turned like a figure skater after him, without urgency, as though the chase were a game it couldn't help but win.

"Help! Spear, spear!" Was all Foster could do.

Tunguk darted back toward the lead to escape, and the seal turned on Foster. He tried to start backwards and crossed his feet. His body hit the ice with stunning force. The head struck like a snake. He just got a foot on its neck to redirect it as he rolled. The seal bounced closer, so close he thought it would simply crush him under its weight. Again, it rose up to show him the spotted underbelly. The smile gaped, and in that moment, a spear crashed into its breast.

The seal thrashed and let out an awful sound from its depths. The shaft scraped over the ice as it turned to find the threat, deciding that it was Foster who had offended it. It lumbered forward as he slipped for his feet.

One of the men broke the fog from the left and thrust his spear into the creature. It whipped again, trying to find him with its jaws, but he held on, avoiding the deadly grip while he slid and bucked like a bull rider at the end of its rage. Another man practically leapt over Foster to yank the first spear from the seal while it fought his companion. He jabbed and twisted it free of the back three times with incredible speed. When the tremendous head spun for him, the other man pulled his spear and struck its side. The seal smashed him away with its head, but he sprung up and danced with it to regain the weapon while the other took his turn to stab the other side.

Blood pooled at the fur. They worked in rhythm to attack and withdraw as it lunged this way and that, always a moment behind and fading. The seal's terrifying threats faded to a moan. The larger of the men found its spine, and its body flattened. They attacked with ease now, stepping free of the jaws each time they gave a desperate bite until it settled for good with a grin and a glassy eye fixed on Foster.

Tunguk reappeared with Foster's spear and helped him up. They caught their breath as the two men tore into the flesh with their knives. Foster couldn't tell which of the whalers had come to their aid in the chaos, and now when he approached, he didn't recognize them at all.

At first.

His relief left him, and he braced his weapon. The fairer of the angotak scouts noticed and grinned like the animal. He raised an enormous chunk of blubber.

"More'n you usually leave us," he said. "Pinipa! Hurry, mate!"

The other withdrew from the seal covered in blood to the shoulders and holding the warm heart. They raised themselves, and only then did Foster detect their fatigue as they trotted off into the fog.

Foster collapsed, panting, and Tunguk sat beside him.

"Uitkalpate." He said. "You ask me what kind. Your people call it lion seal."

Foster shook his head.

"I've never seen one before. But I'm pretty sure my people call it leopard seal."

Daylight flashed in the crease as the board splintered. On the next blow, the rusted head of the ram parted the doors of the hall. A pair of marines pressed their backs to each side, but the deluge of sailors plowed through and jammed in the funnel of tables. Flashing spears drove back those who tried to go over, and in moments, the bodies pressed so tight they couldn't raise a weapon. The invaders urged their companions back onto the landing. The opening at the end of the funnel tempted no one. They drove their shoulders into the tables, but found them reinforced.

In the ebb of bodies, the four marines behind the doors flung them back so that they nearly closed the hall again. They fell on the surprised crews. Several men cried out as they toppled. Costig could only just see over the barricade—a spearhead, an arc of blood, the tug of bodies as the sailors replied.

"I'll find you in Manhas, lads!" He shouted, as much as a final blessing to his vanguard as a threat to those dying sailors. The mass roiled and quieted. Then like a bubble racing to the surface, a bloodied body squeezed through the opening, then another, aided by brotherly hands. Two of his men had somehow fallen back into the hall to lick their wounds.

With no one to harass their efforts, the sailors in the doorway slammed their shoulders into the tables in an attempt to part them. Marines on both sides pushed back.

"Steady, lads!" They knew the signal, and shifted to the ends of the barricades nearest the door. "Hold the gap!"

Dasseder, a sergeant of Gua's who only just took up with the company when they occupied the hall, cut the rope that held the tables' edges together—the opposite of Costig's command and exactly what he intended. The sailors tumbled forward as the gap tripled, and their mates stepped over them to get through.

"After me!" Costig shoved the table aside at the wall and entered the pen behind the enemy as they cleared into the room. The marines on the opposite side did the same. He struck down a surprised straggler who thought himself clever coming up slow. In a flurry, he and the remaining twenty-one marines cut themselves an opening and formed up in a rough shape, backs together. The sailors who had gone through now turned to tease at them with their spears, but on all sides, the navy hesitated to throw themselves into the fight.

Costig pushed outside onto the landing. He recognized Folmon's crew coming up the steps in support. He broke ranks and met one before he could reach the top. His spear found soft flesh uncontested. Then a quick parry, and he tore the next from breastbone to belly button. While the sailors thought about their thrust, he made it, and in moments the marines drove them onto the steps.

His foot struck the ram. Costig wrestled the head up to his chest, nearly lifting the entire apparatus, then sent it tumbling down the steps, crashing through the legs of the sailors. Behind them and to both sides, hundreds waited in reserve. He expected it, but resolute as he was, it staggered him.

"Strike the center, lads!" He pointed at the middle of the force, where the two admirals stood. "If you kill no one else, kill Folmon!"

It had the effect he intended. The admiral shouted furiously, waving men from the flanks to rally on his position. Polc abandoned the left flank, and Barrow Jak the right.

An arrow zipped several feet over Costig's shoulder, though he presented a square target. Before he could thank his luck, he spotted the toothy grin of one of Corm's whalers, Nemas, on the string. He fired again, hitting a charging sailor in the arse.

"Out of the way, cunt!" Nemas chastised. His mate Muir sent a shaft skipping harmlessly off the steps.

Costig found his senses. "Left!" He jumped from the landing into the snow six feet below. Marines knocked up powder behind him.

Only the crew of Korrel remained. Most of them were those who fled to the *Gairhle* with Turrha; who were imprisoned by Palqua; who Costig spared back into service. He noticed in particular the lobe-less scoundrel Foul Hand Waits, jabbing impotently at the air among his brethren in a farcical display of resistance. Korrel, himself, came up with good intentions, but those few who would have made it a fight recognized their fate and shuffled out of the way as the marines fled into the alleys.

The opening was brief. Already, Costig heard the order, and the unmistakable clamor of pursuit. This much had gone to plan. The marines had no intention of holding the hall. They already wore their watch cloaks and carried a pouch of meat. There was but one place for them, one long hope of retaking Drummoc.

They broke into squads as they found themselves, branched down as many paths. The voices made it clear the sailors had entered the town behind. He would expect more to encircle it if they took long enough. Though the marines had rarely seen a tukit beyond the brothels, the navy would be completely lost.

In the madness, none of it was familiar to Costig, except the outrageous nature of it. He knew the direction, and let the streets flow where they willed. He glimpsed faces over the shoulders of a hut, but they had no way through to him, and he veered deeper into town. The scuffling of boots left his knuckles drained of blood on his spear, for any moment he expected to come face-to-face with a fight.

He nearly killed the point man of a marine squad as they collided into one another and struggled to cross their separate ways.

"Back inside! Back inside!" He yelled at curious squains.

"Got 'em!" Someone said behind, and he was aware of additional boots in their wake. Costig meant to keep running, but the marine in the rear turned to meet them. It became a two-man brawl, as neither line could squeeze past into the fight in the narrow lane. The marine struck a grave wound that toppled the sailor, but the next man cast his spear into the marine's chest.

"Go!" Costig couldn't become mired. The third man, one of the wounded from the hall, grabbed his mate as they ran, supporting the shaft that wobbled from the lad's ribcage. The overcast sky gave no sign of Urkuk, and all the twists made it difficult to judge the glow of north, but he put it on his left as often as he could. The maze let him believe the claim that the squains cursed their own lanes to drive intruders mad.

A party of lost sailors broke their path without noticing. He heard another fight nearby, and had no notion how to reach them if he had wanted to. A brief scuffle and a jog—it should not have taken his breath so easily. He'd spent too much time sitting in admirals' quarters of late.

Another bunch spotted him over the tops, but this one cut them off.

"Two here!" The man shouted, and only then did Costig realize he had lost the other half of his squad. The one in the lead raised to cast, and Costig warned, "Aside!"

His man took his advice, and the sailor broke the vital rule that he not throw away his last weapon. Costig showed him why. The next came up with a more fierce attack. He was beaten to the thrust and could only steer it away. It was the marine behind that slipped his spear past Costig's arms to pierce the sailor. Costig added a pop from the middle of his shaft, then engaged the next man. His squadmate put a foot on the side of a hut and vaulted past to gather the fourth, and they had but a brief chat about how marines are bred to fight in the tight, uneven quarters of a tossing deck.

Now he leaned his palms on the huts as he pulled himself through. The town seemed endless. He couldn't even say which quarter they were in. He made several turns, then came upon a boy looting the corpses of several sailors—the ones he had recently killed. Costig grabbed his collar.

"Which way out?" The boy stammered before realizing he was not being arrested. He pointed back down the lane Costig had come from. "Show me."

He hardly trusted the lad, but Costig pushed him on until he smelled the wind off the mountain. They emerged behind the town to find the wounded man from his squad, without his mate.

"What are you waitin' for?" Costig knew the answer. "Off with you!"

They regrouped as confused cries rolled up the mountain from the town, stopped, and swept back. A large party of sailors trudged along the side, heading to cut off the rear. Only their half-hearted effort spared the marines so far. Ahead, two squads ran into the wilds. Costig found his pace and stomped through calf-high powder for their rally point.

When the assistant viceroy appeared, many of the men ran out to meet the procession. The boy was eager to see, but Tunguk restrained him with a gentle touch. So few stayed before the mine that Tunguk thought the marines inside should try for a run, or at least a breath of fresh air.

Word had already reached of the captives. Well before the group drew near, he saw by the walk of the crowd that they were dead. It came as relief. Brother should have been safe with so many men at camp, and Kjartke to watch over him. But Tunguk feared he would go off on his own, or do something foolish.

He had heard the taunts of the boy for days: that he shirked his duty. He stayed, Tunguk often replied, to see to the firestone.

"Do the miners need an old man to watch them throw dust?" The boy had said.

Tunguk argued that it was these men who threatened them most. That he must not let the miners allow them to escape. But even a boy could see the assistant viceroy would hear nothing of his advice. He stood accused of chasing adventure, and constantly had to deny the boy the stories of his youth, of other fights whose glory lay in their carelessness.

When the men broke free, he dreaded that an old wind had lured him astray. Brother was as tiresome as the shores of Drummoc. Had Tunguk lost another place in his wake? Was he so important here that he could not finish his obligation?

Many shovelfuls had been pitched into the mine. He made sure it was Satletaluk who told the assistant viceroy it was ready, just before he left to inspect the prisoners. In their return, he felt the sigh of a man who nearly falls overboard, and is held up by some watchful spirit.

The sled toured the camp. When it finally passed them, three mangled bodies lay stacked with a clean spear wound through their hearts.

"It is not our people's way to let them go so quickly," Tunguk said. "I think he did not like the sight, and showed a mercy."

The assistant viceroy had the sled brought near the opening, in front of the fire.

"We have been here too long," Alexicus raised his voice, and soon the men quieted their celebration. "I've heard some say it's for lack of brave men, willing to face the enemy. Others say there are many brave men here, but no good weapons. I've even heard that we should just pitch camp and wait for our problems to go away.

"Wait, like these men in the mine. Starving. Freezing. Choking on the same air as you. And if we stay put long enough, we, too, will have an opportunity to gain better things. Just like them," he put his boot on the edge of the sled. "How much longer do you think they'll hold out in there?" The men smiled boastfully. "Backed into a hole and besieged? Do you think they're getting stronger? If they suffer another day without the light of the sun, are their spirits more poised to break free and find it?

"These men are invaders. They don't belong here. They've come to your home, and forced their way in. Do you want your mine back?"

The men whooped and shook their tools.

"Why?" The assistant viceroy challenged them. "What will you do with it? Break your back for a few more bushels that will barely earn you enough food and hasqa for another year? Raise your voice if you can afford to buy wood." He listened to silence. "If you can afford a scrap of iron." The assistant viceroy's words hardened their faces. "You work for *them*," he pointed behind him. "Their shields are wood. Their blades are steel—Mattaka steel. Do you think those men are besieged?

"If they're the ones besieged, then go! Sail to Drummoc tomorrow, or Nunoc. Sail as far north as you can dream. Some of you have tried, and here you are still. Held to the waters of the Attavaik. Held to these mountains as surely as those sons of bitches are stuck in that mine.

"*You* are the besieged. The whole of the Mattaka people do not belong to themselves. They call this the last place in the world, and that is where these men have surrounded you. You're huddled in the dark, coughing yourselves to death, praying you get a chance to run for it."

He looked at the three corpses with an eye that shared their pain. On the edge of the crowd, Tunguk noticed someone signaling his attention: Senadak, one of the dog drivers. He showed that he saw, and that he must wait.

"I tell you, when we try to fight inward, to the mine, we fight the wrong way. I say 'we,' because my fate has brought me to you, by a course I cannot explain. But I know, I *know* it was for a reason. There is nowhere more south than this, the last place. Which means the world lies in every direction," he swept his hand over the horizons. "*That* is the way we turn our spears."

Many of the young men bristled like dogs at a lead, and many more made stone of their faces, unsure of what this man said.

"Not with the reckless warships of Barduk, or the meaningless raids of Vitjukvattajuk." The name whispered to Tunguk, and for the first time in the long wind from the mouth of this man, he stood among the people rather than apart.

"We will sail our firestone ships to the nine shores, along with our steel ships, our gold and minerals. And your leaders will anchor at the right hand of the farri. He will call you sea kings." The men looked to one another without knowing what to say, but if his words gave them fear, it also stirred a deeper spirit.

Satletaluk handed the assistant viceroy a torch. He touched it to the blaze, and took his share of it.

"I hereby restore this mine to the Mattaka kingdom. And by this act, I declare the end of a siege, that a great people may finally embark upon their destiny."

The miners pushed eagerly to see. Near the mouth, the Midshipmen and those Mattaka who held the front needed no order to retreat to a safe distance. Tunguk approached as timidly as he could. He offered a palm to the assistant viceroy.

"It is best done by one of no importance."

The assistant viceroy did not hand the torch, but took his palm as a friend who is too kind to point out an error directly.

"Thank you for your concern, Tunguk. This is the way it has to be."

Tunguk nodded and moved somewhat farther than the others.

The assistant viceroy walked to the mouth alone, turned, and held the torch overhead. The men gave a great cheer. He readied himself, then shouted, "Fire in the hole!" as he flung the torch into the opening. In the same act, he threw himself against the side of the mountain and turned away.

No more came of it. The men waited, but soon grew restless. The assistant viceroy remained shielded even while his frustration turned to doubt, and at last, surrender. He marched toward Satletaluk looking very angry. Before he came halfway, the mountain gave a great roar.

A serpent of fire stormed from his hole and flung the assistant viceroy to the ground, then struck at the head of the crowd.

15

Sun Dogs

The miners dove into the snow, and the fire serpent vanished as quickly as it had attacked.

Tunguk hurried to the side of the assistant viceroy, who rolled as a dog at play then jumped to his feet. The hair on the back of his head was very short, as was that of his fur seal cloak, and he smelled of burnt hair. He accepted no help, but brushed himself and looked back at the wafting black cloud with astonishment.

The miners were no worse than he for the quick puff. They danced their victory.

It was Tunguk who first noticed the burning man. He charged from the mine, his shield and garments aflame. Tunguk drew his knife to meet him, then saw that this man could no more attack than say his name. He stumbled blindly, dropped the shield, and crossed his feet in a fall that could not quite find the ground.

No hair remained. He bled from a crack on his forehead at the top of a pink rim where he must have raised his shield as the fire raced around, for the front of him was not so burned as the rear. He twisted in agony from the blistered flesh and the fire that still licked at him from his cloak. Tunguk caught his shoulder to cut the miserable creature's throat, and snatched his hand back from the scalding leather. He raised his blade to swipe instead, but the assistant viceroy called to him.

"Wait!"

It did not please Tunguk. He had no more taste for the hospitality the Mattaka showed prisoners, but he relented.

The assistant viceroy shoved past and flung the man to the ground. The miners rushed forward like dogs for a fight. Instead, their commander threw snow on the flames and patted at the singed flesh.

"Alive!" He demanded. Now all of them saw a second man crawl from the mouth and bury his face in the snow. "Take them alive!" The assistant viceroy repeated.

Tunguk had a head start on the others. He went to the second man, who was also bald, and burned more badly than the first. There was nothing for him but to step over into the cave. Thick smoke singed his lungs. The stench was terrible and familiar. Worse were the shrieks that echoed off the walls. The blast had been strong, but it did not seem to have killed anyone. Tunguk tripped on the edge of a shield, then felt a man with his foot, kicking in the dust but unable to utter a word. A hand touched his back, and the miners surged around him in the dark. Tunguk ushered them by, hunkered in the middle over this marine.

"Get them out! Don't let them die!" The men screamed, and he knew it was not out of mercy. Someone cried without ceasing as he passed, his tender skin unable to bear the touch of the hands that lifted him. Not so eager to repeat his mistake, Tunguk tapped at the one in front of him to find a spot that was cool enough. His clothing felt to have come from boiling water. In his twisting, his hand caught Tunguk's, and this, at least, was only very warm. The man squeezed his plea. To either side, Mattaka added their whoops to the din. Another marine kicked as they drug him by, and it struck a glancing blow on Tunguk's hip—enough to remind his ribs of the pain that had still not gone on its way.

Tunguk curled like a protective shroud over the wounded marine. He squeezed back with a firm grip and felt a shade of calm come over the youth, who settled at the touch. The old man eased his blade in until the fingers slackened.

"It is braced!" Norwet scrambled out from the storage mound. He'd turned three broken sleds on their sides to support the leather roof, covered in snow, little more than two feet tall at center. He could not gain his feet before Ianate shoved Banugsep, her youngest of four years, into his arms.

"Crawl to the back, sister," he used the term of affection for his cousin. "The other girls will join you."

She looked back at her mother for rescue, but she urged the girl on sharply. Norwet guided Banugsep's sister Hattrakatsep, a few years older, in after her. Already there was little room. Metkate, the daughter of Onag and Iniasep, was a year older than Hattrakatsep, and she followed with a sense of duty for the others.

Norwet looked it over, and decided that another could fit. The sister of Metkate, Saunlauk, and Siguvik was the oldest remaining child of Onag, perhaps the same age as Milak. Norwet beckoned to her, and she shook her head defiantly.

"You must keep them still, Ariatjate. They will be frightened."

The girl was too close in age to listen to some Vjarku boy who arrived with so much trouble. Iniasep did not insist, or slap her daughter about the shoulders as Norwet thought she would.

"It is your choice. I hope your sister will not be frightened." The three girls under the mound called out her name imploringly, while Norwet watched the rim above the camp with apprehension. She darted past, and wedged herself into the opening.

Norwet swept armfuls of snow to cover the entrance, and all three of his aunties helped. This was his doing. He did not need to guess how they felt, but all of them, even Sawi's wife Ebrakallite saw that this was family work now, and they pulled with him as a team. She had no more daughters, and her sons were across the channel, but Norwet thought that in the absence of her children on the overdue dog ship *Kurrhatetgiuk*, she carried herself as the mother of them all. The other women looked to her, perhaps more than the men looked to Sawi. She was not so inconstant. Though the mothers of Sawi and Senadak were much older—and the father of Ianate's first husband had remained behind— the camp belonged to Ebra.

It was plain the mound had been packed, but there was much work around the camp and no one would linger here.

"Where are you going?" The old man Baldrakut stopped him.

"To get a spear." There were but two men left, and Norwet remembered the futility he felt in the fight with the blacksmiths.

"You should go from here. Quickly!" Baldrakut ushered his hands as though pushing water.

Norwet looked up the side of the bowl that led to Urkuk, now sliced with fresh sled tracks.

"With Costig?"

"No! Away. What will you do with that spear, one boy?" Norwet felt his hair stand on end. He had run the Eye with his team, and was no boy. Beside that, he had killed a marine with his knife, and broke the prison twice. There was much he might do, as he saw it.

"It is you who gave them sleds and dogs. We cannot blame you if you stand among us." Baldrakut grinned knowingly.

Norwet regarded Uniatsate, the only other one of the children—though he reminded himself that he was a man now, and she was a year older than he. He had spoken little to her since he arrived, even less than the younger girls, though it was her he often wished to acknowledge him with a word. Though they were cousins, and not far removed by the judgment of the Vjarku and Seleku families, he was content to earn a glance from time to time, even if it came with a certain scorn.

"Go, Norwet," Ebra said.

He chased the tracks of Costig's sleds up the hill and felt them call to him, but where they went, he would not be able to help his family. He would not be at the harbor to greet the triumphant return of his friend the Leopard Seal.

With a cast of snow, he took off in the direction of the Calm Harbor, and hoped he would make the rise before the first of the sailors came down the far side into his home.

When she had sat a long while waiting for Senadak to return with Tunguk, and when they did not come, nor did Brother and his pack of animals, Kjartke began to pace the snow. Her mother called it "bring hand to mouth," the kind of person who gave so little effort to those who helped him, it was as if they must move his arms for him, or turn his jaw over his food. She had felt this of Brother for some time, even before his leg was cut. Now she also felt it of Tunguk. Must she walk herself to carry the old man to his charge?

It was the women who made it bearable. In such times, they would help one another. Mostly, they would talk about these helpless husbands, or sons, and share a laugh. Their talk was often enough to melt the toes of a man who was frozen in sloth.

The Kapadak women were cruel to her, but she often listened to them when they had complaints, for any ears would do. It seemed a mercy to be rid of them, until she was. Though they would hear no ill of Klimut, when she heard their words she felt these were as good as her own. Their arrows did much to relieve her, as if she had loosed them herself.

Here, she was alone among men. And when she thought of their journey, though she often spoke to a woman for this occasion or that, it was no circle of wives. They saw the setu on her chin. She spoke only of what matters she attended to, and they listened with stone ears.

When those same marks would have earned her an audience—with the Jargadak women who wanted to share their whale—Tunguk silenced her at the tip of a spear. Once she recalled it, black and jagged in Foster's hands, she could not shake it. It lunged at her from the spirit world, prodding at her. She thought it dared her to speak, but when she faced it in defiance, she saw it again in her own hands, when she guarded the boat while the men swam ashore to retrieve Tunguk. It was then she realized it had not come to torment her, but to seek her grip. Kjartke sat idle, waiting for idle men to act. Her resentment came as much for herself.

When she reemerged from the tukit with the spear in hand, the camp was astir. The rush of men confused her, so that she could not be sure if she had meant to go up the trail for Tunguk, or toward the harbor for Brother. Miners ran to each other, passing their words with excitement, none of them bothering to share with her. As it jumped like a flame from one to the next, they hurried from their posts—their watch, or the forge. It took little for these men to excuse themselves from a duty, but this seemed to be more.

The tukits where the wounded were tended flew open, and their caretakers joined circles of dance and celebration. Their song was one of a successful hunt, or battle. They sang the bounty in to camp.

A man hobbled out to join them, his foot a mangle of crushed bone. It was Ratjuk, who attended to the assistant viceroy's tukit. Kjartke tightened her grip on her weapon, and narrowed her eyes at the tightly-drawn door.

The procession paused before the last few switchbacks. Parks wrinkled his nose at the motley gang. Milak had only found three grown-ups: the amputee who donated his peg leg, his bullet-headed friend, and Umatbarak. The two men supported the cripple between them on the steep climb.

Seven dog boys flanked the prisoners. Parks had awarded the oldest four—Milak, Saunlauk, Siguvik, and Ferrakut—the steel spears and shields of the captive marines, while he took the fifth set. It felt like some early stage of a video game, when he finally upgraded his gear from the crappy stone-tipped stick that was only good for poking level-one enemies.

"I feel like people are gonna have a hard time believing we captured these dudes in a fight," he announced. "OK, change of story. Forget the one we rehearsed. We'll just go with the truth: we cleverly found their hiding place, then Ferrakut and I explained how fucked they were, and convinced them to surrender." He winked at the boy, hoping the credit would keep him from repeating what he heard about Costig and betrayals. "Got it, Poz? No battle." He said to the marine sergeant.

"Poznatxen," the man corrected.

"I like to give people cool nicknames. With all the new folks I meet, it makes it easier to remember."

The unyielding look of the the prisoner made Parks fear momentarily, though they were bound and unarmed.

"In the Eribath Islands, *pozt* means 'nose,' or more often, 'flat nose,' which is among the lowest things you can call a man. I'm Poznatxen, 'osprey beak.' I've surrendered me arms, not me honor."

Parks affirmed nervously. He reorganized the troop so that Milak and Ferrakut led with their shields, followed by his dogs and sled, then the prisoners. The brothers Saunlauk and Siguvik came after, with the three men limping at the rear. It was as regal as he could get under the circumstances. He hoped that the prize outweighed the presentation.

The songs reached them before they topped out, and he wondered if somehow the news had leaked.

Not a soul noticed them drive into Eagle Camp. The body of miners formed into a half-circle. To the far side, an army poured down from the trail. They were greeted with song and embraces. The crowd was so thick, they couldn't get through.

Parks diverted around the edge, riding a sinking disappointment. A roar went up, and he knew Carabiner had beat him back. The dog team lurched in a panic at the hundreds of miners who foamed the snow. The boys had to use their shields to block them from pulling in every direction. Barbados Slim turned around and climbed onto Parks' lap, stepping on his junk for a better view and a sense of protection, and it took another pair of boys to dislodge him.

As they neared the front, a man here and there spotted their little marching band, sweeping in off a dirty side street after the main parade. The prisoners were dressed inconspicuous-enough to be some of Neal's men, up from the harbor. Bodies pushed forward then flowed around, continually blocking Parks' bunch from breaking through. He realized they were moving around some shifting nucleus. The entire mass changed direction, and the boys could barely hear his orders to redirect the team.

Milak resorted to banging men aside with his shield. He shouted in Mattakatan, a blur of meaningless sound that only reinforced Parks' desperation over his first few days of language classes. The bang of wood and glint of steel began to collect the miners' attention. Painstakingly, they forged a channel as men slapped each other to point out the prisoners. The terrified dogs refused to move. While Milak and Ferrakut fought with them, the rest of the line squeezed around him and continued on despite his warnings to hold.

When they finally drove a wide-enough wedge to get moving again, Parks was the last to arrive. He found Saunlauk and Siguvik standing guard over the men in front of Carabiner. The cripple and his helpers blocked Parks' view until the boys lifted him from the sled and elbowed their way to the front. Parks struggled to hop with the unusual weight of the shield, and had to drop it. He leaned on the spear with both hands, throbbing and utterly exhausted.

Eskimo Joe lingered with Senadak over a sled that held a man stripped to the waist and blistered red. Parks gagged, recalling the morning's horrors, and wondered if his old buddy had taken part in whatever they did to this poor bastard. Nearby, Carabiner supported another marine who seemed in immense pain, despite looking a hell of a lot better than this partner.

Carabiner beckoned for Satletaluk to take the man. He walked to Poznatxen, and the two stared unblinking at one another.

"Where'd you find them?"

Parks answered, but the voices of the miners drowned him and Carabiner had to signal for quiet, which took some time. He was ready to repeat himself, when Ferrakut interjected.

"In a mine!"

Carabiner nodded as if it confirmed exactly what he already knew.

"Looks like they surrendered without a fight," he said of Parks' companions. Parks could only nod.

"Well I wish we had called on your talents to talk them out. You might say ours took a little more doing. This is what's left. I don't think the others are going to make it."

The marine who could stand gazed at Poznatxen. His face contorted in a kind of agony beyond his considerable physical injuries. The sergeant held firm, but for a slight downward flick of his gaze that might have been an apology, or forgiveness.

A sense of responsibility awoke in Parks, and he said in a voice too loud and threatening, "I promised these men full mercy—food and housing, and that no harm would come to them."

"I think it's the measure of a man that he is as merciful to the vanquished as he is vicious to his enemies." Carabiner motioned for his Midshipmen, those deserters, to take charge of the prisoners. "Good work, fellas," He gave a casual salute in the general direction of Parks' group, then marched off, the army spilling around them in rivulets that stranded them where they stood.

When they had nothing left but their own company, the cripple frowned in worry.

"You no use. You like?"

It took Parks a second to realize he was pointing where the peg leg should have been.

"Aw!" Parks feigned a sudden memory. "Forgot. At my house."

"You like?"

"Um, yeah. It's very good. But my leg, it's still too tender. Hey, do you wanna borrow it in the meantime? Could be a while before I'm ready."

"No, no! It is for you!" The man insisted.

"Right, I just can't bear weight yet. I thought you might be able to use it in the meantime."

"Try. It is good! Try!"

Parks sighed in defeat and bowed his head gratefully. "Thank you. Will do. Thank you for all your help today." He dismissed the three men.

He looked at the sled forlornly, and though it was a short distance back to his wigwam, he gathered his shield and took a seat.

"These are good weapons." Parks looked up to find Satletaluk. "You have done well to capture them. And the men of the forge tell me you are generous with your tools."

Parks made half an effort to smile. "Any time."

"I think you have earned your choice of the spoils," Satletaluk indicated the spear and shield that Parks held. "The men are glad for what remains."

He realized the boys wouldn't be allowed to keep the other four sets of weapons. Their faces sagged from the heights of temporary pride when Parks nodded for them to surrender the arms at Satletaluk's feet. He lifted his own in offering to Eskimo Joe, who waited quietly with Senadak. The old man shook his head.

"Too heavy for me."

The butt of the spear snagged on the ground when the sled started up and Parks lazily shifted it clear. He had never seen so many miners in the camp. Now that everyone had returned from the siege, he could hardly move a few yards before someone wandered across the path of the dogs and the dispirited boys who drove them.

The constant obstructions jolted him from his triumph. They reminded him pointedly that he had to scrape along staring down six dog-asses because he couldn't simply get up and go around.

Carabiner's comment loomed. A team to Parks was a bunch of people who helped him, and who he might help in return, if it wasn't too much trouble. The lone remaining shield weighed on his leg, while the boys urged the dogs on empty-handed. A few kids and a cripple. An old man. Somewhere, nowhere to see his glorious march with the captives she swore he couldn't take, a woman. He buckled before the thought that he might one day do something in return.

Near enough that he could recognize the shape, Carabiner burst from his wigwam. He yelled something at the man who guarded it, then spun frantically, flinging men aside.

"Sophia!" He cupped his hands. "*Sophia!*" Carabiner barked orders at terrified miners, and again, the camp lit up, this time with a rising panic.

In an instant, Parks knew she was gone.

At first, they looked like ice adrift off the bow. Ostuk handed over the steering oar and had the sailors take in a reef, as much for the practice as to slow them so that Haraket's darraig could come along for a word. He'd been forced to retain the cobbled bunch of Mattaka that Costig had helped arrange, while Haraket jealously guarded Arwoset and his former crew for the "warship." It was well that he did. By accounts, they'd barely outrun the navy pursuit when Haraket sailed arrogantly close to the harbor for a peek, and without skill on the ropes, may not have been able to rejoin the *Juhketappat*.

He mostly offered encouragement on the walk to the bow. Hardly an order was carried out to standard, but if he corrected every mistake, they would soon doubt their own hands. While a small error didn't cost them, it was best to let them struggle through.

"Fine work!" He called up the mast. "You are becoming fast!"

In better times, he would leave the veteran crew to guide the dry ears. Now, there were none. Most commands had to be followed by the steps required, and the many dangers that could occur. So it was with apprehension that he leaned over the bow, unsure of how close these men could come to loose ice. They certainly would not be able to go through it if it amounted to more than a morning slush.

But the floes changed form, and became whales arcing across their path before that, too, proved another trick of Ajatse, who bent the eye six hundred ways. Ostuk shouted back to lower the sail and call the rowers up. Haraket's crew followed his lead and finished sooner. A following breeze propelled them under bare poles through a crossing fleet of Mattaka hunting boats and giuks, filled with tukits and all the possessions of the people.

Their hurried paddling calmed when they saw brotherly faces on the decks of these wood giants. Women and children sat atop the loads. Nothing was packed tight, folded, lashed, or spread by weight. It seemed they had piled as many things as they could with great haste. Many of the boats slipped past them fore and aft, but some returned their greetings. Ostuk closed near Haraket and invited the people to paddle between, where he threw a line.

A man came aboard with his wife, leaving their children to hold the boat. He seemed fearful at first, explaining that they were from the hunting camp on Drummoc as he cast looks at Haraket's darraig, studying the crew of both ships to assure himself it was not halots who sailed them, or perhaps certain Mattaka he did not care to see. His wife, however, suffered no timidity, and soon grew tired of his evasion.

"Ask them who they are," she would say, and he would repeat it. She did not understand what an assistant viceroy was, but the sight of a navy darraig crewed only by armed Mattaka gave them confidence.

"Tell them of the navy ship that raided us," and he would tell. It went as such, that she explained the fate of the camp turn by turn, while her husband relayed it and added a detail, or cautioned temperance to her explanation, so that Ostuk and Haraket traded laughter that is only seen gleaming in the eye.

Although the couple amused them, their tale was full of sorrow, and soon weighed on Ostuk's breast. There had come a navy ship—the second in recent days that urged them to provide more meat for the colony. This was their task on the western shores of Drummoc: taking the seal and penguin that visited, and ranging south to the ice, or west to good hunting grounds, that the miners and the people of the island had only to take an animal here or there to supplement their food.

They were relieved to hear that Ostuk and Haraket knew of the families that fled on the firestone ships, and cared nothing for it. Because of this, the hunters struggled to take enough meat for the many sailors and families of Drummoc, and while the last man who came had been kind and patient, this new captain used harsh words.

He demanded what they had. They gave him something, but it was far too little, and they refused to spare any more. When they claimed the rest of the people had gone for whale, the captain demanded to know where. He sailed to the whaling grounds, and finding no one, returned to their shores. They greeted his arrival, but this time, the sailors had not come as allies. They rushed ashore with their weapons drawn, and slaughtered the men who went to meet them.

The people of the camp fell about in fear. The women hurried their families to safety while the men took up spears or bows. But the raiders came too fast. They struck at anyone who resisted. The wife had seen women cut down for fleeing near a sailor. Others were taken into the tukit while their children cried outside. These sailors called them thieves and said they would suffer for trying to starve the colony. Their captain, a man named Etan, declared them in league with the farri.

The people retreated from the camp to another almost a mile away, where they rallied while the sailors looted meat and satisfied themselves on the goods of the hunters. Here, they took what they could carry and launched these boats, hoping to reach Neferwet's Foot before they starved, or faced another attack at sea from the ship.

It was no use to ask them for the meat they sought.

"I will counsel with my fellow captain," Haraket told the woman.

Ostuk knew his meaning. When big decisions faced the people, they would gather to hear two men offer a path—perhaps more. Then they would stand much like the ships of the halots, going with this or that, or splitting the parties if they could not agree.

Haraket wanted to speak first to Ostuk, to persuade him before he had a chance to make his case to the crews. There could be no doubt what the young man wanted to do. He was patient, clever, slow to anger. The assistant viceroy had sent him to Drummoc because he knew this man could withstand the torments of the admiral, and at the same time, would not be fooled into taking less than he sought.

Yet before he was called Haraket, he had sailed far. Before the people named him Haraket, he was Mennetvattalatjatuk, son of Satletaluk, of Mennegur veins, and that was not a blood that could remain settled for long.

It would be wise to rest at Neferwet's Foot and take seal, with these hunters to guide the less-experienced miners. If they did well, perhaps they could harvest enough to support Camne Drumlag over winter. Haraket knew this.

When the young man took him aside, Ostuk was surprised to feel disgrace. This man saw a dog captain of half-blood who clung to the respect of the admirals. What's more, he was right. Ostuk had awaited his downfall as timidly as this husband who needed a firm wife to serve as his tongue. He had bent to Costig, and only a secret word had spared the Leopard Seal. No action on his part. In fact, it was those dog boys and Kjartke who did what he could not dare.

He had long imagined the glimmering current of Ralte darting swiftly beneath him. He feared it and cursed it even as he trembled with an excitement he could hardly admit. But in this old place, he had once again drifted into Yurutpa, the wide and cloudy waters of the many. To have tasted the cold waters briefly before slinking back—that was not the same as to sail them all his days. However few those may be, his retreat had shown him that he could not live here anymore if for a day, he might tremble in that bold course.

"If you wish to take these people to hunt seal, then I will counsel with you, and we can see what the crews say," Ostuk replied to the stunned captain. "But if you ever had another name before you ducked back into the mines, my brother Haraket, we will find the meat we require packed neatly for us in the hold of Captain Etan."

Haraket grinned.

His fingers counted boots, running lightly over the humps of toes in the dark until he came to the one he remembered. Gionn traced the line up from the inner ankle until he felt the stiff top, buried deep beneath a trouser cuff. He drew his knife along the pant and parted the two flaps, then hooked the boot with his forefinger. He meant to open it with a clean slice, but considered that the point may jump through to the leg. Instead, he worked it vertically between the skin and the leather and wiggled it until it just pierced. The leg shifted, and his heart stopped that he was done in. It soon settled, though, and he probed the blade inside once more.

It was just like he told Foster. Couldn't trust a cunt who sleeps with his boots on. Ready for midnight trouble, that one, or got something worth more than leather in there.

The tip found its mark, and he sawed at it with the smallest motions he could make. He pinched his prize and squeezed, eager for the moment the opening would allow it to slide free.

In his concentration, he hadn't noticed that his icy knuckle rested against the calf, for the most part because the warmth it gave him felt so pleasant. The leg jerked. The blade nicked flesh, and a scream shattered the farting, snoring silence of the tent. The foot kicked him in the face, sending the blade from his hand. There was no other way.

He latched on to the boot with both hands and stood, forcing the tent free of the snow as the sail bulged in the shape of a broad hunch. Gionn ripped and ran, and while the boot came with him, so did its owner. The cold hit him while the sailors inside cursed at the draft and punched at the roof that collapsed upon them.

One hand swung for his hip, and reminded him that his sword lie within. The knife gone, and with no time to strangle the lad, Gionn fell upon his third course: he twisted and tore to free the boot, careful not to make a sound that could identify him. The sailor scraped over the ice howling nonsense. He'd no notion of who he caught, only that it was no frail thing.

The heel loosed, and only the long leather backing held it when another kick broke his cold hands from their prey. The man got his feet— Gionn heard as much. He felt about in the black, and heard a whooshing that he soon learned was that of wild fists in the air. The one hit him so hard he could only marvel that his feet were still beneath him. Two more shots brought him to another kind of blackness, very different from the first. He reached for anything, caught the shoulders, and as he fell backwards, just managed to turn so he landed on top.

Gionn hammered him once before a strong buck threw them both, and they grappled furiously to no advantage. Other voices neared. Baghar shouted in Amposi while he caught Gionn's cloak. He heard Foster press in behind.

"Help! Over here!"

Their roll knocked the two men over. Gionn feared he'd be thought an angotak and receive a stab for his troubles.

"I got him, Corm! I got your man!"

The whalers held the both of them at spearpoint until first light, Jonn without the boot, which Corm removed and demanded that no man touch until all could see.

The captain finished the cut, and stood squinting at a large coin while it turned gray, then copper, almost to gold, almost.

"Fuckin' penny, Gionn!" Corm roared.

"Hoy! Lemme see that!" Gionn snatched it. "Size of an argot! That's one of King Haola's. Got to be over a hundred years old." He shook it, as if his point were proven. "Even then, these were melted down into two of Farri Mil's pieces fast as they could round 'em up. How was I to know a cunt who sleeps with bootfuls of argot-sized coppers is merely an arse and not a thief?"

"You remember, Corm. I got that on the way down, and been in me boot since. Never spend your last one, or you'll never get another." Jonn picked frozen blood from a cut on his lip.

"And you." Corm's nostrils flared at Gionn. "Decided to cut it out yourself at night so you could hand it over to me in the morning?"

"Tuck your smirk between your bald legs, mate," Gionn said to Foster. "What of the seal's heart, and all that missin' blubber? I never seen you offer a fingernail to Hadalis, and you happen to throw the best cuts to some impotent squain god in the moment before we find you? What of *him*, Corm? Lot of stab-holes in that monster for a squain and a brave archer. In league with the angotaks, I'd say. Let's kill him just to be sure."

Foster was spared the blade, and Jonn was spared the insult of pulling beside Gionn. It was Arthas in the swap, and if that was all he got from the whole affair, he was better off, nonetheless.

Gionn strained into the harness on an empty stomach, Corm's only discipline. His face throbbed at the pressure of the strap on his chest.

Palqua, sensing his discomfort, teased from the rear: "If you tire, you can walk with Tarvin."

Gionn looked back at the last sled, hoping to take comfort in the sight of the man falling behind. He despised wounds, and the wounded. Didn't matter the bastard, they sickened him, and hung like the taint of poison in a cup. Foster's seal had spared all but one of them. After the initial feast, Corm declared the man looked strong and booted him from the sled to walk alongside, which is to say, keep up or don't. It was only an arm gash, but those who looked at such things said it would do. He'd barely arrived last night, hours late.

"Hard cunt," Gionn said to entertain his traitorous company. "Wasn't that one of his own?"

"Aye, he was, til he wasn't. Jumped in Drummoc. Corm's quite forgivin' of the dead." Arthas spoke from experience.

"And the livin'," Foster quipped.

"Go toss the bucket, mate. No one faults a whaler for grubbin' a coin. What use would I be if I didn't?"

"It'd be useful to pull next to a man without wonderin' if he'll strip me bare and leave me for dead at the first opportunity."

Gionn wasn't sure how to take this sudden forswearing. Foster was ordinarily more discreet with his hatred. It struck him as carrying some secret intent to which he should probably bend his ear, but it also struck his pride.

"You must be referrin' to these *upstandin'* blues—yanked most of his crew and filled his benches with jumpers. Aye, if they live, so shall I."

"I never jumped, mate. I saw her to shore, and forfeited me shares. And I'd have a task to convince meself you've never left a doomed ship for a bright sail. I think Foster means to say that a whaler may swap benches and pinch coin, but he don't rob his own mate." Arthas became uncommonly animated, then coiled it in to regain his disaffection.

"No, you lot just leave 'em to die." Gionn felt Foster and Arthas share some look of condescension behind his shoulders. "You think because this poltroon led one charge on the angotaks and found a dead seal he's some kind of barrel? He abandoned his best mate and his woman to Drummoc, as you did your whalers, and Palqua, his king's navy."

"Drummoc is not so bad. A few seasons will bring the man out of the wood." Palqua heaved over the sled.

"That why you fled as soon as you heard Bloody Donn was comin'?"

"We left as you did, for more lustrous waters." Arthas countered.

"I was halfway gone before I ever landed at Drummoc, and I don't give the blunt end of a shit for a soul there. You fled because you knew their fate, and wouldn't share it."

"Their fate is to sit on the larders for a year at most, fishin' and birdin' and whorin' and gamblin' until Donn's captains get hungry and cold and turn for home."

"When Donn's done tossin' Drummoc, we'll hardly recognize your mates from what's left at the bottom of the larders. And how do you think the woman'll fare?" He turned to Foster.

"They already sent reinforcements to warn 'em. If they can hold out, I reckon Tolba's fleet won't be far behind," Foster supposed.

"Tolba won't send a fleet to Drummoc," Arthas corrected. "And neither will Donnab. At best, he'll peel off two or three of his least-favorite captains to splash about in the harbor while me mates from the *Gairhle* who swore to Turrha collect war pay for holystonin' Costig's pride."

"Aye, you've got that right: whoever fears a fleet at Drummoc is mad. No need to go there at all, if you just blockade Nunoc. But Nunoc's useless without Drummoc, and he means to have back what Ampos stole.

All it'll take is a few shiploads of wood to Pone. A few adhus and a borrowed docogon will hold Nunoc, and it's easier to hunt and fish and find a bit of land to rest the lads there than at Drummoc. A few more'll go on to Drummoc, but as you said, it's much harder to blockade, and that won't do. They'll land, and have a proper toss."

"A few adhus?" Arthas scoffed. "Foster can tell you how many men that makes, but I happen to know it's a paltry sum compared to the garrison."

"A garrison of whalers and the bottom-suckers of Ampos. The wise ones'll jump to Donnab soon as a sail appears. The rest couldn't hold a latrine against one throbbin' arsehole."

"I might be more worried by your wild scenarios if anything you said ever turned out to be true. Or if you ever had someone you were afraid to leave behind." Foster's dismissal felt like the punch of a blade, and Gionn searched for the words that would spare him from having to draw his sword.

"You're right. I've as many mates left as the Leopard Seal. But unlike him, I never needed one. Whatever happens now, he's fucked broadside. If not by Donnab, then by Costig." It did little to ease his rancor. Gionn found himself wishing Foster whatever blessings it would take for him to live to hear of the sack, and the awful fate of Parks, and to know the truth of it as Foster, too, breathed his last.

Arthas seemed cheered by their feud. "One like you on every ship, eh? Master of the Seas and Oracle of Battle, despite he's never been a second mate on a fishin' skiff. Drummoc's got one rough harbor, and another place where a single ship can land if the tide's right. They could bring a thousand men, and for a dozen defenders at each, they'll never get a one on land."

Gionn huffed steam and leaned into his harness with a vigor born of spite.

"They already have," he muttered.

It was a full day before the prison door opened. When they removed the body of Manuclas, dead of his wounds, Corm's first reaction was anger at the lad, as if he had jumped with the rest. He had to remind himself it was a loyal man carried out having given his last. The betrayals had left his gut as tender as the brawl had done his bones. A touch could brace him. He envisioned his ship sacked, his men killed or turned bluecoat.

That same afternoon, Costig came back for Timor, whose wounds needed tending. He enlisted Nemas and Muir by name to carry the man out—perhaps a perk of spying for Turrha. No reassurance from Foul Hand Waits could ease the feeling that he had lost four more.

No one offered to empty the single bucket left for the men's relief. They stayed another night in the putrid cell, and in the morning, Costig announced:

"All but the captain, out with you!"

Ordacles, Pitras, Gewar, and Oterec limped off, and he received a bucket of water and a small bowl of seal. The rations did not bode well for his release.

"Hasn't Palqua got enough of a head start yet?" He shouted at the closing door. Corm sank into the sharp stone of the dividing wall and sighed a lung of rank air. It seemed unlikely the Mattaka even used buckets in here. Alone, he felt a twinge of release. His shoulders abandoned the posture of command, and new pains hailed him, some from much farther than the recent toss. He felt the collision with the angotak ship, the blows that followed. Corm saw others borne off like Manuclas. Not a moment to hesitate over the waters in consideration. Perhaps the rest would do him good.

"Don't fret, Turrha won't hold you long. Just until you sell your ship."

Corm looked up the wall for the voice that came from behind.

"Palqua."

"Aye, and Arthas in the next cell."

"That smell comin' from yours, Corm?" Arthas' faint voice leaked over the walls from two doors over.

"We are men of principle, you and I. Turrha does not say, of course, but he wishes me to return your wares. I think that it is a foul trade, and one that keeps Drummoc alive—though perhaps not your strange cargo. The Navy cannot afford to break its deals." The heavy creak of a hinge came from outside.

"Palqua." Costig called beyond the wall.

"Stay the course, mate!" Palqua clearly stood as he spoke, his voice fading towards the door. A second creak told him Arthas, too, had gained his freedom.

It would be another week for the captain. Only after he lost hope that the rare light spilling through the door would beckon him did he hear that name, on familiar lips. It was not Costig, but Nemas and Muir who held the key.

"In your own time," Corm growled as he stepped into the open sky and nearly spun to the ground for the unaccustomed movement. He scoured the shipyard from afar. His relief upon spotting the *Gairhle* was perhaps premature—it wasn't as if she'd be dismantled. Doubt soon crept in. From that distance, he could make out no bodies on watch.

When Corm started for her, he realized that Nemas and Muir, rather than join him, aimed for the navy hall next door. He held, stunned and humiliated. Muir gave an apologetic shrug and went on.

Corm came about and bent for his ship with the walk of one who meant to hide a grievous wound.

"Round to starboard," a soft voice hissed before he could reach her. His head snapped to and fro. In his singular intent, he had failed to notice a bright new ship, two masts still on duty. She felt too much for a merchant, and had nothing of a warship. Corm couldn't see over, but he was certain she had a deck and a hold, though with that keel she was cut for weather, not wares. Not a man moved. It was as though the ship herself had spoken.

He stalked around to starboard.

"Turrha waits for you at the *Gairhle*, but we must speak." Foul Hand Waits stuck his head over the side.

"What's this? Come on down and talk to me face instead of me hat."

"Can't. Palqua is free, and he has men asking after me. I fear he knows of our arrangement."

"What's Turrha want?"

"Your ship, of course. The captains did not like that he imprisoned one of their own. I fear we have been too successful in parting them. I see no way but bloodshed. Both men need you to strengthen their position. It is truer now with this new official," he gestured over the barc beneath him. "Be cheered, old mate: though we seem weak, it is now our choice. Your choice."

"Where are me men?"

"Oh, about. You will be pleased to hear I recruited another spy: Timor." When Corm's face showed no such pleasure, Foul Hand Waits hurried to explain "He required treatment for his wounds that only the

Navy can afford. Now he watches Turrha for us, with Nemas and Muir. But what of Palqua, you ask? Do not forsake Foul Hand Waits. I have sent four more spies to his ranks: Uldred and Bale, Boot and Nolan."

Corm realized that the bastard wasn't only slithering that deck to hide from Palqua.

"*Spies*? You fuckin' sop! *Jumpers*! For your commission!"

Foul Hand Waits signaled to keep his voice down. "Do you not see the course? They set at each other like dogs. Do not sell yet, but promise your ship and crew to the man who grants repairs, and a winter of service. We will be free to sail in Spring, once the victor shows himself."

"I don't mean to sell at all, nor will I hail either of those cunts for a single day! As for yourself, you'll be wise to cower where I can't reach you."

Corm found Turrha leaning against his hull, with Captain Bruco and a pair of officials nearby, as well as a complement of marines. He didn't greet the man, but jealously pored over his goods, trying to decide what had been stolen with his crew away. The bitter sight of the half-empty hold only compounded when he wondered if indeed, he were the last man of the *Gairhle*.

He approached the admiral with enough intensity that the marines gathered round before he could utter a word.

"If I didn't sell me way out of prison, I won't now."

Turrha took offense. "Mate! I would not have kept you so long as a means to conduct dishonest trade! Whalers are treated well here—better than they deserve. But they must understand, you cannot strike at an officer of the Navy of Ampos."

"I struck at no such thing, but a liar and a thief."

The admiral smiled understandingly, and hesitated to show he agreed. "His provocation was noted, and disciplined. I have ordered him to return your wares, but so far, he refuses. Please do not take a slight from Palqua and hold it against me as if we were one man." Turrha waved off the marines for privacy. "It does not matter if he returns them, though. I am prepared to compensate you for the entire cargo. And the ship as well."

"Oh? And what'll it be, this time? Three coppers and a slap on the arse?"

Once more he mimed the shock of offense. "Mate, I have not come to sour the deal. It remains as before: two-hundred decairs, the rank of captain, and all the rest I promised.

"You have but eight men left. Perhaps you have not yet heard of this new official from Nunoc. I fear if you do not sell, he will simply take your ship. They do not have the manners of a naval officer, these viceroys, and do not care if they trouble the colony's reputation."

"You troubled it yourself when you left us at sea to freeze for days, and robbed a dyin' crew for three of every five of the sales."

Turrha looked away. His shoulders shook, and as the sun gathers the breeze on its rise, he lifted his smiling head. Laughter permeated his body until he cackled at the whaler.

"Three of five?" He managed. Turrha shook his head. "I should not have locked you up, but rewarded you for your restraint. Forgive me, captain. It is beneath the dignity of an admiral to haggle with whalers like some fish merchant belting over the water. Until recently, that duty and all its terms belonged entirely to Palqua."

The cramps of prison and the long fight left Corm, replaced by hot blood. He hauled himself up the side of the *Gairhle*, gripped a spear, and dropped back down. The marines came forward again, but Turrha showed only amusement. He eased the men with a swish of his hand. Corm lay bare in his gaze, the weapon, the quivering giant awaiting a decision. When the admiral said nothing, he spun for the town with quick, heavy steps.

They made camp in the afternoon with a billowing gloom in the east. Having lost the angotaks' trail after the storm, the sky's rumbling threats lifted their spirits. Several of the men who read signs in the weather said it meant land—the Arm, and somewhere at watch before it, Yunoc.

Corm lingered in a squat and scraped his arse with a fistful of snow. He could get no peace, not even here, for Arthas waited halfway between himself and camp to intercept his return. Between the angotaks and the lion seals, he carried his spear at all times, and the jumper appeared unarmed, so he did not expect this to be the call for mutiny, though this one always seemed a move away.

"What brings you circlin' 'round me shit like carrrion?" He spat on the approach.

"Good, make it look like we're arguin'." Arthas replied. The man's very presence was an offense hanging in the air, so Corm was surprised when Arthas took a crude posture, yet added: "I must be mad from some ice daimon, but I've come to your aid. Keep your eye on Gionn."

"The thief? I've never taken it off him from the moment he swore his bench."

"Then keep both on him. He thinks a split's comin'."

"And you're here to promise me everything's fine?" Corm sneered with suspicion.

"It's not, no. He offered to lend Palqua a 'hand,' and suggested he could bring along Bosc, too."

Corm laughed. "He offered me the same. Why doesn't Palqua tell me himself?"

Arthas rolled his head in a frustration that he expected Corm to grasp. The answer should have been obvious as far as the jumper was concerned.

"No matter," Corm said. "He admitted he goes which way it blows. So do you, and all but a man or two on a whaler. I don't fault him for sayin' so."

"No? Because you've always faulted me for the same, though I'm hardly a pennant in the wind."

"You're a fuckin' ram in me side. Don't ruin me shits with your intrigues again." Corm started past.

"I know who it is."

The captain halted at the cryptic proclamation.

"The argot?" He asked.

"I don't know who got it, but I know who brought it on."

Corm paced a curving path back to Arthas, trying not to appear very interested. He grunted permission to proceed.

"Jonn told me a tale recently. Somethin' he recalled from the ice—when we were stranded with Gionn and Bentos. He was out of his wits then, so I paid it little justice. Didn't think it likely.

"What troubled me from the start was that I knew Palqua would never take your ship to stop you from reachin' Taclann. He don't work for

Costig, nor does he care to be admiral of Drummoc—not when there's fatter prizes to be had. But I also knew the lads who stuck it out with you. None of them are the sort, either. Palqua told me to watch Foster, but I wouldn't trust he could reef a sail for an argot, much less run us aground.

"When they were with Jonn, though, and they thought him a corpse, they said some things that bothered him later. Gionn told Foster he shouldn't have come back, it would be, 'two closer to your scheme.' And when Foster tried to silence him, he taunted him. Asked Jonn if he had any notion what Foster had planned for him, to prove Jonn was a lump.

"Then they argued over pay for some work, and whether they could show themselves in Hiade again if it went keel-up."

Corm turned it over. "And if it were you, you'd say as much to deceive me."

"Aye, it didn't ring for me, either, until I heard Gionn and Foster goin' at it over some mates they left on Drummoc. Costig didn't want us to sail, because he knows Ampos'll send supplies in Spring. They can't spare the warships, but the merchants, they can give Nunoc and Drummoc a chance. That's why we're here, isn't it? Everyone knows what's comin'. Here's a man with mates, with a woman he never mentioned, ripe for the blade of Donnab if Drummoc falls. If only he could stop it, make an argot, and show his face again, a hero."

Arthas saw that Corm had no quick reply. "I doubt he could do it alone. He'd need one like Gionn, who knows the whalers and swings his weight. Forget you heard it from me, Corm. Think of it: they showed up in Drummoc late in the season on a dog ship. No one knows from where, or what sort. We would have never taken 'em if you weren't worried about navy infiltrators from Costig. What if he made that his advantage?"

"Why are you helpin' me?" Corm snapped defensively. The notion that Costig had outwitted him and let him sail off wormed with traitors had never sat well, and less so from Arthas' lips.

"I was never against you, mate! You made it out that way, because I didn't care for your deal with Palqua. No one did. I was just the only one with the bollocks to say so. The two of you tossed every man on that ship because you're both too proud for your own good."

"Too proud to let me crew die in the harbor, after all we did to get there? Aye! You could do with some pride, yourself. Pride in your ship, your mates, the blood you spilled for that cargo."

"You think men should be loyal, but you act without askin' 'em. The only one who benefited from comin' in early was *you*. You feared a mutiny. You see blaggards in every crease and corner, and you wouldn't know what to do with yourself if you didn't have 'em nippin' at your hems. You dreamt of 'em so much, you conjured your very fears, and now," Arthas regarded the spear in Corm's frigid grip, "you're fuckin' right."

The men would not come near them. Kjartke waited with Sophia in front of the tukit, while a runner went to the harbor to get the husband, where he had gone to search.

It was Tunguk who found them. She had not meant to hide. When he showed them out, the miners gave ugly faces. She could not tell if it was her they feared, or the anger of their leader. Few had spoken to her since her arrival, but now they danced as close as they dared, then pulsed away, like water on a shore of snow. The girl held their curiosity, yet it was no match for their caution.

Brother would have come, but Tunguk stopped him. He sat near-enough that Kjartke could hear him, talking of nonsense with one of the dog boys.

"How was I supposed to know that names mean things in their language? 'Bird nose,'" he sniffed. "It's not like I have an app to look that shit up."

"It is the same with Mattaka," Ferrakut said.

"Wait, yours mean something, too?"

"Don't yours?"

"No. I mean, not really. Maybe if you look it up online, but not that we know of."

"You have names of no meaning!" The boy could not hide his excitement at the prospect.

"Why, what's yours?"

Ferrakut bit his lip. "It is hard to put in your tongue. But I would say, 'one who is himself forged well,' or perhaps, 'steel makes him'."

Brother nodded in the way he often did when he was sure he understood something that yet escaped him. "Man of steel. In our tongue, it's 'Superman,' the strongest of heroes, but also one of the most boring."

"Superman," the boy tested the sound.

"Huh." Brother stared into the spirit world. "Now that I think of it, I guess our names do say something. Like Carabiner. It means, 'a stupid little clip for attaching a water bottle to your backpack.' And Parks. That's my family name. It is…'multiple areas of greenery, managed by the government.' Or, 'to stop and abandon a car or sled in the present, with the intent of driving it again later.'"

Ferrakut lit up at the secret knowledge.

When the one who attached water to packs came, he tried to curse her with his eyes, but she held it off as her mother had taught her. He did not speak to her, but said harsh words instead to Brother. It was difficult for her to understand, but he warned that Brother should, "control your woman, or someone else will have to." The girl went to him when he beckoned, and he placed her under guard in his tukit.

Tunguk spoke to Brother in a voice too soft to hear, and he nodded along with acceptance.

Kjartke was not surprised when he later joined her inside, scooting through the flap on his bottom. He grunted into his blankets on his own, and though it was not much trouble, it was only recently that she would have had to drag him herself. Brother did not scold her immediately. He held his breath at times, as one who prepares what he should say but has not gathered the courage.

"So how's she doing?"

"She say many things, in a great rush. Some mean little to me, but I know she wait to speak them, so I let her. Others, I think she still cannot speak. She ask of Foster. And of you, in ways I cannot answer."

"Like what?"

"Why you are called as you are. If you mean to go home. If you will be 'OK.'"

Again Brother stopped his breath. "Well, if you ever manage to steal her again—"

"I steal no one!" Kjartke snapped back. "This man, he bind his wife. She is a prisoner in his tukit. My people do not allow this. To keep a woman from other women, it is not allowed."

"Hey, whoa, easy tiger! I'm with you. Team Kjartke. I wanna answer those questions for her, and I have things I wanna ask her, too. It's not that simple, though."

She had heard this excuse, and thought it the shield of one who can neither act nor explain himself.

"Your people: What do they do? If somebody does that." Brother wondered.

"The women, they tell their husbands. Then the men tell him he cannot do this. If he does not listen, they take his wife from him. Give her to a man who live alone. Or if there is no such man, a strong hunter will take her for a wife, though he already has one."

"Huh," Brother said. "I feel like he'd be pissed."

"Aye. Do you think it good, what he do with her?"

"Of course not!"

"But you do nothing."

"Like I said, it's not that simple. There's a lot of shit going on here. A lot of moving parts you don't see."

"I see you do your will, only if there is no danger."

"You think I'm a coward? Is that it? Look at me!" He pleaded, though it was dark. "I do everything I can. It's not fuckin' easy. Even when people—when *you* tell me I can't pull it off. Did you hear I captured those marines? The ones you said would kill us?"

"Tunguk say they gave surrender with no fight."

"Because they were afraid of what would happen if they didn't."

"Aye. As you fear Carabiner." Brother had no words for her, and she spoke again before he could find them. "I cannot answer what she ask of me, but here is what I think: You are called by a name that is empty. You will leave for your home if it does you no trouble. I do not know what it mean to be 'OK,' but if she fear you cannot do this, then so do I."

The home of Mennetsatletaluk swelled with family when Vatjate pulled back the flap. She sat Norwet among the boys, next to a pair of older men at the far end. A single lamp burned in the center, and one of the grandfathers grumbled about the waste—it was customary to eat with the doors open to let in light.

"We have a guest, grandfather," Vatjate said. "And there are matters to discuss."

Norwet recognized the boy who had brought him food the past two nights where he stayed in a tukit left empty by a miner, a friend of the family. When he sought refuge, she had promised to check on his family. Norwet thought it would be quick. He did not dare ask over food, but at least this meant they had not forgotten him.

The elders asked him questions about Nunoc and the voyage down. Women asked of his family back home—they did not know his mother had passed, and offered too many condolences for something he had set aside. He answered politely, and tried to catch the gaze he felt often upon him, that of the girl he had met at Gjoraslag. She brought food to the Leopard Seal from this family, a grave offense. He knew from their meeting that she was not so mannered. This one burned to know of prisons and murders, criminals and revenge. There was nothing she could say here, and he longed for every word of it.

He new in his short time here that this family was looked upon with caution, sometimes despised. That was why he came to the Mennegurs to be hidden. They received him kindly, but said little of the matter. Norwet hoped to speak from that voice of his he used with the Leopard Seal, with his brothers, and once, with the girl across the tukit. He was the uncontained killer of marines, and each day it pained him to speak as a dog boy, even among the rest of his family.

But these miners supped like any other Mattaka. They talked of relatives through mouthfuls of meat, and told jokes he'd heard as far away as Nunoc. He suffered it until the slowest eaters gnawed the last of their portions. Only then did he catch her looking, and though he'd meant to turn away, he could not release his eyes until his stomach caught fire that someone would notice.

Norwet did not dare be so direct, but the moment it was not rude to address his host, he blurted at Vatjate: "Have you any news of the fight? I heard the marines gave the new admirals good steel." To question her of what he wanted—word from his family to return home—would have insulted her by the suggestion that she had not checked on them as she promised. This way seemed bold, and he felt the girl lift with guarded excitement, but it was the rounded path to what he sought.

Vatjate retained her composure. "You should not have helped him. Costig is not popular among the people." The subtle rebuke struck his breast. She would not have said it if he hadn't pushed, and she wanted him to know this. Now the flicker of the oil lamp seemed to stutter and avoid the girl's face. Costig had killed her cousin, and until that remark, she had thought Norwet his enemy. His honor in her sight staggered from the wound.

She scowled at her mother as if to ask why she had brought this animal into their home. Vatjate answered by addressing Norwet.

"Perhaps you thought he would forgive your crimes—that he would soon be admiral again." Norwet had not considered it, nor did he know why he outfitted the fleeing marines with sleds and tukits and a little food. He could no longer track the consequences of anything. Since his father sent him to run the Eye with his brothers, to become a dog driver, he had chosen sides many times by nothing more than what felt true. When pressed, he could not explain the good or bad of it. Only his certainty.

"He will," Norwet said with a courage exaggerated to recover face. "These admirals are weak."

"Maybe. But they are still dangerous."

In a flutter, the door flap swung and the girl was gone.

"I do not mean to speak of this in front of the family," Vatjate said. "I am sorry."

"—But we must," she added as if cut off. "If you are as I suspect." The boys around him grew tense with some expectation.

"I have spoken to your family."

He knotted within, distrustful of her tone.

"Folmon came with many hands soon after you left. They searched the camp, and Costig's tracks were plain. He did not believe your grandfather that the sleds were taken by force."

"Baldrakut is not my grandfather. He is my cousin's—Uniatsate."

She nodded. "Baldrakut is dead. The Navy does not know of you, and your family held their tongues. As the man of the camp, he was to blame, and Folmon slew him."

Norwet's spirit twisted in agony, as if felled by an arrow. He searched for some way to disbelieve it.

"The admiral ordered a captain, Barrow Jak, to take his crew and pursue as far as he could. The others returned to town. But this captain was lazy, and did not wish to trek in the snow. He thought to wait at the camp, then tell Folmon he lost the trail in the dark."

She paused too long. "It is good that you hid the girls. They were not found. But this crew is of a low sort. They treated the women...roughly."

"Uniatsate." The name fell from his mouth.

"They are alive," Vatjate attempted to soothe what could not be repaired. "I have asked friends to visit often, help them with their chores. These boys, they watch during daylight, in order to warn them if men return from the town." Norwet only half-turned to look at the ones beside him, friends of Armenuk, no doubt.

"I should not have run," his voice came out foreign to him.

"You would lie in a shroud beside Baldrakut."

Norwet tried to jump to his feet, but the boys snatched his arms and legs. The old men helped to pull him back, cradling him deep into the tukit. He flailed. No one shouted at him. Rather, they held him firm the way he would calm a tormented dog. When he realized Vatjate had anticipated this, seating him among her family, his muscles slackened.

"I must go to them," he begged. "Someone must protect them."

"A boy will protect no one. Until the miners return, there is little we can do."

"You cannot stop me!"

"You will stay here tonight. In the morning, you are right. We cannot hold you all your days. But if you are killed, what good are you? I tell you what I tell my daughter: there will come a moment. Many of us sleep with this dream. Six hundred days may pass, and six hundred things between. But if you do not forget it, or rush to your death, your moment will come."

Norwet squirmed in fury without a real effort to free himself. They consoled him as they held him down, but he could not distinguish their words. Tears carved the slopes of his face, wet his neck, seeped under his collar. His voice rose and broke, rose and broke until it left him and he was glad to be rid of it. He became as a babe, cradled to the chest of his mother. It would be many hours before he slept.

The Leopard Seal came to him restraining the crazy dog he kept at his side. He felt a crowd of evil kaim in the hold of a ship, heavily drafted, swell spilling over the deck. A man he could not make out appeared leering at him, shifting many times, composed of parts from every face he'd ever seen. Then the face of beautiful Uniatsate. He forgot the daughter of

Vatjate, stood at the prow, and stared feverishly at a distant coast knowing that one more night like this would swamp him.

Three white pennants ran up the mast of the *Juhketappat* as she neared the barc. The darraig under Haraket imitated the signal—an ally hailing to speak. The personal vessel of the viceroy of Nunoc lay moored at a low shelf of rock where the spoils of the hunting camp were hoisted aboard. The handful of men on deck stopped working to consider these two unexpected visitors.

The dog ship shunted at an angle to the barc at half a mile, lowered sail, and proceeded under oar. The darraig hung back and out to sea, though she was the faster one. Ostuk stood at the edge of the false deck and called commands to a pair of men at either hatch, who relayed them to the rowers. The hands on the barc shouted to shore, and several more men climbed aboard to line up at the starboard rail.

Ostuk motioned for them to throw their hooks, but the man at center declined. The dog ship was forced to bob some yards out.

"Hail, there! I have come to speak with Captain Etan." The men regarded one another with suspicion. "It is Ostuk, of the *Juhketappat*."

"I've seen you about," the captain confirmed. "What do you want?"

"Admiral Costig has sent me to help."

"We don't need no dogs."

"I didn't bring any. The need for food has worsened. Once the barc is full, we are to fill my ship in turn, and if we need, the darraig as well."

Etan tried to pick out the vague heads that backpaddled out in the darraig.

"Who's that?"

"It is Captain Korrel, with some of Captain Bayochar's men."

Etan scoffed in disgust, as if he suddenly realized why he was approached by a dog captain instead of the navy escort.

"Well you've come a long way to fuck off. We won't even fill the barc. Lazy squains are tryin' to starve us."

"Sorry, what was that?" Ostuk cupped his ear.

"I said, 'We won't even fill the barc.'" Etan raised his voice, then in frustration knocked the man beside him. A pair of grappling hooks clattered over the false deck, and Ostuk set them. Soon the oars came out to brace his ship from colliding.

"Nothin' against you, me son," Etan said. "Your people are full of excuses. A fair share of 'em are missin' entirely—not where their mates claimed they'd be. When we came back to confront 'em about it, they raised blood and attacked us."

Ostuk made a quick survey of the barc. Twelve men on deck. It would not be a welcome sight for his people. He did not know the strength of the crew on land, but if Etan sailed with the usual number, it may have been anywhere from thirty to fifty, all counted.

"May I serve you a hasqa on my ship?"

"Why's that blossom-bottom out there?" Etan demanded. "No, but you may serve it on mine when he drifts in. Then you can sail your beast ferry back to Drummoc and warn Costig we may have squains treatin' Gjoraslag as their larder by winter's end."

Ostuk nodded. "It is a sad fate to starve. I pray you will depart more quickly." A blush of offense swept Etan's face, but Ostuk spoke first. "But until then, could you spare a man or two to help steer me in? My crew does not know the trick of this water."

"No. Anchor off. I'll speak to Korrel, then you'd best sail. There's no other place to moor here, and we aren't movin'."

"Very well. Perhaps you can call up a carpenter to join you on deck."

"What for?"

"You number twelve. My people will be timid to see it. If one more comes, or one less, it will be better."

"Are you mad, dog captain? Fuckin' twelve! If your bastards don't like it, fuck off."

Ostuk regarded the line of sailors, their tunics browned with blood. The rail of the barc stood just higher than his head. The amu bobbed underfoot. It recalled for him the sight of Amachar and his wounded abiama, and the mercy he showed. He long thought Drummoc his home, but his stay had felt like an exile, avoiding his family for what he said was their safety, and what he knew was the sense that their safety was all that held him to these shores. The edge of the *Juhketappat*—this was his place, and he stood grateful to have returned to the spot where the choice was his.

"My mother's family is Mattaka, but I admit, I have never shared their fascination with that number." Ostuk knelt beside a pile of sleds.

"*Kettiaku!*" He shouted in Mattakatan. When the wave of crouching men poured onto the false deck and the sailors eyes grew, he rose with the spear he had stashed. Ostuk snapped the throw into Etan's chest. The men beside him clutched his arms as the captain staggered back and fell.

There were nine left on the gunwale when the Mattaka made their throws in stride. Miners with hammers and sticks vaulted onto the rail. Most of the crew fled down the gangplank, and those who didn't could not reach their weapons in time. Rather than pursue, the miners threw down the gangplank and cut the mooring lines. Etan's crew shouted one another to arms from land.

Instead, the miners shoved off, and a rope spilled onto the false deck. Ostuk gave the command, and his oars pulled away while the crew secured the tow and, yard by yard, it snaked through the water until the line went taut with a shudder.

A makeshift flag of trousers whipped intermittently from a piece of wood. *Sleds*, Foster thought. The odd shapes Corm sent them to investigate thawed from the backdrop into a pair of of low decks laden with loose scraps and a couple of barrels.

"They'll be comin' back if they marked 'em. In the spring, or by sundown," Gionn warned.

"Maybe we find goods to take," Atalkut suggested.

"Aye, angotaks are known to carry great troves of ambergris and gold with them on their dire sled journeys. You'll be wise not to touch it, though. Their fingers are black with sorcery, and anything of use will be properly warded."

The four of them fanned out and made a cautious approach. Foster wrapped around the left flank. The flapping britches seemed to notice their approach and sink with disappointment as the breeze died. A barrel blocked the view from the back. Around its edges, he saw an untidy roll of leather. Bits of odd wood littered the ice beside it.

Foster lifted his head every few seconds to see that Tunguk and Atalkut weren't signaling to him. He lost sight of Gionn on the far side as he came broadside, and stiffened at his spear.

"Don't move!" He shouted loud enough for the others to hear. The boys split and hurried around to either side, weapons at the ready. A lone man sat on the deck, his arms wrapped around his knees. The roll of leather became his leg. His tunic seemed dusted with snow, but a few careful steps revealed that he was shirtless.

The angotak sentry sat with his spear sideways in the crease of his waist. His outer clothing was folded neatly in a pile on the front of the deck. Foster lowered his point and approached. Thin wisps of beard and mustache hung with heavy frost. His milky eyes did not blink. He froze vigilant, staring longingly at the nearby clouds that must have marked the peninsula.

"Volunteer," Gionn explained when he saw the state of him. "If they dropped two of their three sleds, they're out of seal and too weak to pull. Made a run for land, and this cunt knew he couldn't keep up." There was a note of admiration in his voice. "Doubt you'd find a man of the *Gairhle* to take a last watch for the rest of us."

"Or anyone to appreciate it if he did." Foster didn't need to mention the dogged way that Tarvin and Asdosa had been forced to keep pace despite their wounds. When only a day before, Tarvin never made it into camp, no one spoke of it. If the others were no better than Foster, they probably had another name or two they hoped would drop off the list of hands reaching out for a ration of leopard seal meat.

"There!" Tunguk pointed into the distance. Soon, the others saw it, too. A rock shifted, then another. Someone moved across the ice. Foster looked back the way they came, and could still see the dim studs of black that he knew were the whalers.

Tunguk muttered numbers under his breath. "I see four. No, eight, nine, ten."

"Over there," Atalkut shifted their view just to the right. "Four more."

"Now I see twelve." Tunguk added.

The shapes appeared for Foster and slid over dark patches in the background.

"Twenty," Tunguk's count climbed.

"I have twelve," Atalkut said of his own area.

"Two more there," Gionn frowned.

"Too many. There weren't much more than thirty on that ship."

"Now there are six hundred," Atalkut corrected himself. "I have lost the count." He grinned.

"Seal," Gionn announced as they hustled into camp. "And rock too steep for snow."

"Bite it, lads," Corm bellowed to the crew. "Not a one of you utters the name, or she may vanish."

No one had to say it. They wore it on their faces. Somewhere just beyond, the pack ice lapped at the steep shore of Yunoc.

Foster frowned in surprise to find new faces in the harnesses of his sled.

"Off with you, buckets. Corm's switched the teams so we run tighter," said Ordacles. He'd come from Eckerd's squad in place of Arthas. The Mattaka boys were sent up to Tamarqan for Hogue and Pitras. While the recent arrivals stowed their sea sacks, Foster surveyed the sleds and noticed that a few others had changed as well, though he couldn't pin down the exact trades.

It didn't look like it would help, though. The biggest changes were to the teams of Tamarqan and Palqua, and adding three strong pullers to his squad would at best swap out number two and number three. Corm's molasses team had hardly changed—Bosc and Jonn might have been the only trades, but the overall numbers remained the same.

He should have been thrilled for the help. He'd grown fond of the boys, though—maybe even felt responsible. As he watched them settle into their new digs, the flaring excitement of land began its descent back to earth. Two days at most, he told himself, securing his spear with his belongings. Out of instinct, he waited until no one was looking to meet Gionn's eyes, where he found the same mixture of hope, perplexity, and exhaustion that he had brought back from the scouting trek.

By the time the caravan reached the angotak sleds, they were just as spread out as ever. Foster assumed they'd be just behind Eckerd having swapped boys for men, but Tamarqan and the Mattaka still held a fair lead. Whether he and Gionn weren't pulling as hard because they expected help, or the three members of Corm's original crew had the same idea, the result was a lackluster pace. For once, the lead sleds stopped to wait for everyone to catch up when they reached the frozen man of the watch. It was a stark reminder that better men had come this far, and no farther. Where the rest of that crew lurked, he didn't know, but at least if they came on them suddenly, Foster could rest assured that he had some of the best fighting men on the ship. He hadn't seen Ordacles in the fight, but by all accounts his defense might have been the fiercest of all—and Hogue and Pitras had impressed him in the bow.

"Another mile and wait," Corm ordered Eckerd as the last team slogged up. "We'll come to land together. Palqua, keep the same lads in the harness. Don't get so far in front of the fuckin' barge," he growled at his own men.

There didn't seem to be anywhere that an ambush could hide. The ice stretched barren all the way to the subtle dark flecks that marked some distant shore. But Foster had learned well that even on a clear day, things had a way of popping up or disappearing unexpectedly. The pack twisted all forms like a house of mirrors. The strip of leather with narrow slits that he wore to stave off snowblindness made it worse, but a number of those who waved it off had complained of headaches and stabbing pains. Igonus, the carpenter in Eckerd's team, had stopped pulling for two days, walking with his coat over his face, until he finally cut up a sleeve to make his own mask. Moipa refused, and had been uncharacteristically morose as he tried to hide the pain.

Palqua insisted on adding another harness, bringing the pullers to five. Foster's competitive fear of being the weakest link in the new team faded. The lines beside him bent often with half-hearted effort. Foster tried to slow himself, but any less on his part and the sled would have just stopped moving. He didn't have the confidence to bitch at the whalers, and hoped Gionn would do it for him. For some reason, though, his reliably cantankerous friend took it in stride.

Corm's plan to govern their speed by exhaustion worked. The "barge" often got close enough that Foster could hear their voices.

"Fuckin' cunt, there's three of 'em," Gionn whined cryptically. "Me eyes sit on needles. Mate, let me use your sieve," he beckoned for the mask. Foster peeled it free and had to squint to adjust to the glare of the ice. The sky cleared to the west, where a pair of sun dogs flanked their source—an illusion he'd heard of but not yet seen. Two incomplete orbs hung on either side as if the world split down the center, while the two halves spread farther apart in a brilliant halo.

He turned his head away from it as he reached his hand toward Gionn. They fumbled the exchange, and the mask dropped at their feet. Without hesitation, Foster bent to scoop it up, and looked back around his arm to make sure the sled wouldn't run him over. Baghar hovered over the front of the sled and in that second, finished stuffing Ordacles' sea sack back under a rope. Foster stood and passed the mask to Gionn.

"Useless!" Gionn tore it off after only a moment and flung it away. "If me mum had a son whose eyes were so close together, she'd have left me out at low tide to be raised by flounder."

Foster's accent came on so strong that Gionn hardly understood any of the violence directed at his ears. In truth, it had fit fine, and his eyes were beginning to prickle. As he saw it, though, there was much to look at—more than he could track on his own.

It was Foster's worried glance that started him. Often, Gionn could anticipate the arrival of his luck. He met it most near the bottom. Where the seas rose, or the threads unraveled, he could count in those waning moments on that crackling presence. Dragged through the coals but never left to burn—that was his fate. Each time he thought himself abandoned. It had finally tired of his fool-arse stumbling. Yet lost on the ice, stranded with Oduy, or shuddering from a ram, his ankles wet off of Taclann, it came. Never did it seem a mercy. More so a humiliation and a debt of pain. He got the least thing that would do, though perhaps for a man who had nothing, the least was a fine start.

On occasion, it surprised him. He didn't think himself in need when it stirred him from a hasqa slumber on a breezy mat in Guaracan, or from the soft arms of Julea. Those were the hardest to recognize, when it seemed no better grace could find him.

Now with the shore in sight, the promise of seal and a firm step off of the infernal ice, it mounted through his denial. He felt no fear when Corm stood over him with his life in the balance after he failed to nick Jonn's coin. Now he stole the gaze of Foster, and something in his own appearance was sufficient to silence the tirade.

All afternoon, Gionn had watched for the crack that would rend beneath them. The fog to obscure their path, or the storm to gash them. He fretted over the angotaks, and when he couldn't locate them, a mutiny.

Corm had switched them up. To move three of his best fighters to Palqua's sled struck him as so blatant that it neared arrogant. He may as well have held a knife to the man's throat and dared him to flinch. Gionn pitied the others—not in the sense that he felt sorry for them, but that he found them pitiful in their ignorance of whatever doom awaited those other than himself. He only wished he could spot it before it seized him.

The triple sun nestled like a crown over the three men on the right side of the fan. Here was another of those omens that every sailor took differently, to the point its message was shattered like a sheet of ice into a thousand facets. He had always heard it meant illusion, and things that were other than the way they seemed. Perhaps the disagreements it sparked were testament to that.

The face of the father of Hadalis, it shone the brightest argot over the sea. He wondered who had his piece. He felt very little like toiling for his pay on the deck of an Amposi barc, rich as it might be. Perhaps the light marked the whalers to tell him that none would ever see the *Gairhle* again. Foster had somehow done it, and he'd best make other preparations. The omen might have meant that one of these three took the coin, and now Gionn's luck delivered them to his side that he might reclaim it.

But it wasn't the way of his luck to fill his purse. As Gionn scraped every surface in search of the disaster, the two sleds in the front stopped to wait. He heard Corm bellow encouragement and promise rest from behind. They had only to reach their mates.

Foster leaned into the harness, practically pulling the sled himself on shaking legs while the better men slacked beside. Gionn turned to them to flay their bollocks. When he did, the three setting suns flashed on their shoulders, alternating the image of the men's heads with a stabbing pain. He clenched his eyes, turned ahead, and when he opened them, the afterimage of that light sank over the waiting teams. They fanned out ahead, free from their harnesses. The distance and the ghosts of the sun burned his vision. He could look nowhere else but at Foster, dark and near.

By some spirit he could not place, he felt overcome with the desire to fall upon the man with his blade. To stab until the wretch troubled him no more. Just as quickly, he grew ashamed. The slashing fury turned on himself, and all he wanted for Foster was to protect him from whatever brought his luck for a visit. That, too, turned to vapor, and at last, he saw it.

Gionn stopped as though at the edge of a precipice.

"Me bleedin' eyes!" He tore at the knots of the harness as though it burned him. "Baghar, you soger! At least do as the others and pretend to pull!" He flung the lines down and snatched the board they used to jolt the sled free of bumps from Baghar's hands.

"Back at your station. Corm's orders. You'll be relieved when we reach Eckerd." Palqua sanctioned him.

The sled ground to a halt.

"I don't care who, but somebody needs to get their ass in that harness before I take another step," Foster complained.

"Gionn. It is but a few hundred yards." The Amposi retreated from orders to humiliation.

"Then it won't spoil your pet. Tie in, cunt!" Gionn swatted Baghar on the bottom with the board. He came about with fist cocked, and Gionn raised the weapon ready to meet him.

"*Baghar!*" Palqua intervened. A nod toward the harness was all it took. Baghar went with the sneer of a man who had just granted someone a privileged place in his long hall of memory.

The sled growled to motion. Gionn closed his eyes entirely to savor the darkness while he kept his balance by resting the end of the board on the sled. The water froze to his lashes when he opened them, and he picked it free.

Corm's bunch had closed on them. The captain seemed to whip them on with the promise of a respite. Foster, too, pitched forward at half the angle of the others. He'd spend himself in the final effort, even as his mates dawdled. There was no way around it. They closed within a hundred yards of the meeting place. He began to make out faces among the two sleds who awaited them.

Gionn set the board atop the load and fiddled with a lashing.

"What are you after?" The old officer's bite crept back into his tone, and it was the one of a blue who wished to berate a man but couldn't because his superior had said otherwise.

Gionn yanked aside Foster's sea sack, fished his own free, and threw his sword belt around his waist.

"Angotaks are near, me captain. I'd have somethin' sharper than a board."

"It is clear for miles."

Gionn ignored him, and drew the lashing less-than-tight. The whalers on the right side of the fanning team took their turns to peer at him. He kept his eyes as near-shut as he could and made a miserable face.

To the west, the clouds once again consumed the sun. Sweat cooled on his skin and his whole surface tingled like a hand in a sacred spring. His legs drained the fire of the recent toil and began to harden with blood. Tamarqan hailed them from the center, though the two teams remained curled in a loose line. Perhaps it was too late.

As they neared the reception, Gionn snatched his gear and Foster's, hugging the sacks with his left arm. His free hand slid loose Foster's spear. The five men pulling didn't notice, but Palqua stopped, letting the sled move ahead as he shouted, "Gionn! What is the meaning of this?"

Out of spite, he hurled a desperate word: "Run, Palqua. They've undone us!"

Gionn elbowed Baghar on the back of the head and with a swipe of the spear, cut the taut line of Foster's harness. The momentum sent him into a forward tumble. Gionn caught him in full sprint, and pressed the sack and spear to his chest.

"Right, cunt!" He pointed at the flank where the two buckets idled. Foster obeyed out of panic without a notion of why he did so. Shouts chased them from their own sled. Ordacles and the others fought to free themselves of their harnesses, no easy task with frozen fingers.

The waiting parties saw them break free. Men took up weapons they had left discreetly beside the sleds and ran to cut them off. His legs didn't seem to do nearly what he asked of them. Foster kept gleeful pace without a sled on his back.

Tamarqan's team held the right flank. Gionn drew his sword. The squains looked on from the edge in confusion. Chirim the Mad and Moipa the Blind didn't move. The others made a dash for them. The buckets could have had them easy if they had been let in on the betrayal. Instead, Juru collided with the taller one. Tamarqan came within a thrust, but a raised arm from Gionn made him stutter and look over his shoulder for reinforcements.

They broke past unscathed. Most of the others fell into pursuit. He pushed Foster onward, laughing like a maniac while his lungs threatened to collapse. The whalers stomped to a halt in turn, shaking their weapons and shouting as though they'd only meant to drive them off.

The hand on Foster's back slid around his side and restrained them to a walk. Foster's arm fell over his shoulder from exhaustion. The two breathed spouts of icy steam into one another's faces, locked in an unintended embrace, unable to speak.

Gionn thanked his luck, and bent toward the black streak of Yunoc, goldless and exiled, freed as always with the least that would do to keep him going. For the first time in his fate-tossed travels, though, it did not seem so little.

16

FIRE KING GROWS WEARY

Foul Hand Waits darted into town when he spotted Corm stalking toward the harbor with his spear. Not a man could miss him. Congregations of sailors hushed. Squains scurried out of his path. The jumper Boot hailed him from afar, but dared not repeat himself. It was plain to all that the biggest man on Drummoc marched to war, and there'd be little doubt as to his adversary.

"Palqua!" He demanded of a pair of shrinking bench-fillers.

"Point me to the corpse of Palqua!" Another group shrugged timidly.

He spotted Arthas and Jonn among others that must have been the man's crew. They would know, but the sight of that mutinous borer enraged him so, that he wouldn't have spared a word for the man without giving him the spear.

"Palqua!" He shouted at anyone who would listen. A nervous walk drew him like a predator. Bruco. The boot-scrape of a captain swung his arms for the navy hall, and Corm moved to intercept him. His quarry broke into a run, but the whaler collared him and flung him to his back at the end of his point.

"Where is he?"

"Wh—who?"

"Palqua! Or I'll settle for yourself."

"I don't know." Bruco saw the spear's hunger for blood and revised his position. "Somewhere near! He is giving a tour to the assistant viceroy, just came from Nunoc."

"What the fuck is an assistant viceroy?"

"I don't know. *There*!" Bruco jabbed his finger with great relief at a party emerging from the poorman's quarters. A preening bird of an official gestured grandly to Palqua while a young woman and a retinue of snivelers—Amposi and Mattaka alike—trailed.

651

Corm made it most of the way before they became alarmed. Palqua's first mate and guard stepped in front of him. He signaled to Arthas' bunch for reinforcements but they pretended not to notice. Even the two loyal crew members, Tamarqan and Baghar, appeared to consider their alternatives. While Corm decided whether to speak before he killed them, the assistant viceroy stepped in front and held out his hand. It was enough of a surprise that Corm stopped.

"Good day, sir! Alexicus, assistant viceroy of Hiade and commander of the colony, second only to Viceroy Hurut-Atxlchar, himself. My extended hand is a gesture of honor and respect among my people, and to accept it, you only have to take it firmly but not-too-firmly in your own and hold it for a moment or two while looking into my eyes."

"Among me own people, we show respect by not killin' those who fuck off rather than aid our enemies."

"To whom do I have the pleasure of speaking?"

"Stand aside, mate."

"It is Cormdran, a rough-mannered whaler who blames others for his misfortunes," Palqua answered.

"I'm willing to believe you'd kill me. But I will not stand aside, because I'm responsible for this colony and if someone has been wronged, I want to hear about it. Now, if you want satisfaction, let's try this again." He stuck out his hand.

"Me only satisfaction will be that bastard's blood."

"I've often felt that way about someone. And you know what? Every single time, when I took a moment to check-in with myself and what it was I really wanted—I mean *really* wanted—there was always something better waiting for me to notice. Let's say you kill us. Me, Palqua, my innocent wife. What then? How long will you be satisfied? What'll you do when every man in Drummoc comes for you?"

"Let 'em come! I'll kill 'em, too!"

"And what is it that makes you want to kill Captain Palqua?" Alexicus stubbornly held his hand before him.

"He's no captain. He's a liar and a thief, and I'll see that every whaler from here to Atlantis knows that Drummoc is no port for trade. You won't see so much as a bucket for wares!"

"Whaler. A fine trade."

Corm glared at what he expected was sarcasm, but the man went on in such a way that he soon wondered.

"Where would we be without blubber? Oil? Meat? This place would be nothing! Hard, dangerous work. I can't imagine doing it myself. I'm a bead pusher. I read and write and count, I wave someone this way or that, but I wouldn't last a day on a whaling ship. Yet I need all those things, and so does every man, woman, and child of Drummoc. Tell me, Cormdran, how have we wronged you?"

"You tried to kill us! Left us out at sea after we come all this way. One of me lads died of his wounds. The crew was near mutiny, and we only got in by givin' up three of every five coin to the bead man. *Three of five*! I'd not believe such a tale if it were another man's."

Alexicus let out a low whistle. "That's a hefty fee."

"Aye, and it's *his* doin'! He peeled me crew, one by one, made me look a fool, then he took half me wares in promise that he'd repair me ship. I haven't got a single nail for it, nor has me cargo been returned."

"You know well I honored our bargain, Corm. I have told you it is Turrha who blocks your repairs. Did we not share a prison? I fare no better than you." Palqua answered between the shoulders of his men.

"Well now, that hardly sounds fair to me," Alexicus looked back.

"I have sacrificed much for him," Palqua defended himself. "Were I to return his goods, he would have no hope of his repairs. He would lose his ship to Turrha. I would prefer to see him sail tomorrow, but my aid has gone unseen, though I've suffered in reputation among the captains for it."

"You worm-tongued shirker! You and Turrha fight over me ship like a woman you'd rip from me arms."

"Then it's your ship," Alexicus said.

"What?"

"It's your ship that matters, not this man's death."

"Me ship is scrap without a crew and repairs. I got no cargo to sell, no pay for me lads, no lads, either.

"Then it's not just your ship, but the ability to sail it, when and where you like, with good loyal men."

"*Aye!*" Corm snarled at Palqua. Exhaustion rolled through him like a wave under a creaking hull. He gathered a breath. "Aye."

The assistant viceroy finally lowered his hand, and Corm slackened with the realization that this man no longer demanded of him those dignities that men of his ilk paraded around in place of forthrightness.

"So where's the other half?" Alexicus asked. "You said this man has half of your cargo. Where's the rest?"

Corm blinked. "In me ship."

"We have a lot of hungry men who sleep in these poorman's quarters," Alexicus thumbed behind him. "Maybe they'd like a little blubber, or even steak."

"Aye, but they can't eat a bronze lion," Palqua retorted.

Corm caught the girl sneaking a look at him. She hurried her gaze elsewhere.

"Dresses," he said without thinking. "And pigments, fit for a princess. Soft grass for beddin'. Beads and jewels. Virgin soil, to make fertile a marriage." He raised a sly smile at Alexicus, "And a fine Amposi war club that I wouldn't sell to any man less than Atxl himself, or perhaps a noble son of Ampos."

Their lungs burned with cold air and each leaned into the other to stay on his feet.

"How?" Foster begged of no one in particular. The whalers sank behind them into the dim evening, though not far enough. His legs stiffened in anticipation of a night's rest he couldn't give them. Yunoc— if it was Yunoc, at all—gave one last bearing and closed the folds of dusk around its waist.

"Dunno, but you saw it. Every one of 'em but the buckets. They must have sent us to scout so they could line up the ambush. Probably the first time since we sailed that Palqua and Corm came to terms on somethin'."

"You don't think it had somethin' to do with you robbin' Jonn?" Foster had not been as upset with Gionn as he pretended after the incident, but he couldn't stand the thought of the blame that hung over them settling on his shoulders, rightfully or not.

"I think it had to do with you bein' the only cunt idiot-enough to have dropped the coin. Jonn sews his Haola pennies tight while you let argots rattle around underfoot."

It was all the argument they could manage. Foster and Gionn fell into a somber rhythm, their toes fading from sight, their arms clinging to the other's ribs for warmth, and to stay together in the frigid dark when they were too exhausted to speak.

He thought Gionn would peel him free, but they went for hours in the last direction they saw. When Foster let go to adjust his grip on his sea sack, those stout fingers sunk in like claws. Neither man needed to voice his desperation.

A tailwind urged them on. The plunging chill whispered that to sleep here, exposed on the ice, would spare them one death by another. They shook until there remained no animosity between them. They lost histories, and their hopes froze into a single block. Foster dropped his gear, nearly tripped, then realized he couldn't bend to pick it up. Gionn wedged it into an armpit for him.

By midnight, the clouds swept inland. Stars rolled overhead against an impossible black, glittering in a haze near the ice on three horizons. Where they blotted out, the two men leaned. A clear sky brought the bitterest nights.

Foster's spear, swishing like a blind man's cane, finally made contact. They picked their way through broken ice with miserable deliberation until they reached what had to be a hummock. The smooth shards couldn't suggest a way through. They traced its edge for as long as they could stand. At the base, the vigorous sea breeze leapt up and swirled, then vaulted over the top with an acrobatic spin. Miraculously, they felt no wind at the bottom, even though it came directly toward them.

The sea sacks turned over their contents. Within minutes, they gave up on sleeping apart. Both men wedged together into Foster's sack, pulled Gionn's over their heads, and dozed as long as they could in their cocoon before waking to rub the frost from their extremities, so they might doze again.

At dawn, they broke the crisp shell that had formed on the outside of the sacks. The light came later and more reluctant, and by it, they saw they'd wandered into a maze of vaulted ice. It took half their daily ration of sun to pick their way out again and see that they had missed a wide-open passage. No sooner were they through than the island showed its speckled face. Brows of snow furrowed over alternating bands of black rock. Though the way around to the channel between Yunoc and the peninsula was north, they worked south, hoping to find the seals they'd spotted from the angotak sleds.

They climbed atop a footing of ice that may have been land or sea. Gionn treated it as the former. He knelt on all fours and muttered some prayer followed by what sounded like a threat. When he rose, he joined Foster's vantage and grew solemn.

Four streaks marred the ice. Foster could already see the space between the men as they fanned out from the sleds like the tentacles of some creature, come up from the frozen waves to hunt.

"How the fuck did they move so fast? Did they pull through the night?"

"They didn't spend all their time gettin' lost and found again. I'd say we got til dark before they're upon us." Gionn pointed south over a yawning crescent to a beach, studded with gray rock.

Foster and Gionn hustled down the far side to a peak that rose right out of the water except for a long gouge of land, as if taken by a divine thumbnail, leaving more than a mile of steep shore that terminated at a few hundred yards of rolling bluffs covered in rockfall a year old or ten thousand. The mountain beyond offered no way through and the clouds didn't admit to its height.

The seal lay out sunning by the dozens. It looked to Foster like a well-stocked fish pond. With a box of shells, he could have shot enough meat to last until the thaw within a matter of minutes. Instead, he tested the weight of a spear that was clearly more seasoned than he was.

It would have to be quick. Kill, fill, and retreat. His urgent elation soon shuddered as Gionn hurled cuss words like rocks at a corrugated tin wall.

"Fuckin' whale seal! Every one of 'em!" He complained.

The animals had seemed near. Now the ground beneath them stretched unexpectedly while they swelled in size. He'd grown accustomed to adorable sea dogs. These lazy giants didn't bother to flee. Their grumbles spread as the men came into sight.

"Elephant seals. That's what we call 'em. What, you can't eat 'em?"

"Aye, go over there and stab one. Just explain to him you mean to feast on his flesh so he don't snap your spear and crush you beneath his girth."

One of them raised his chest and greeted the visitors with an agitated bellow. He towered over Foster though most of his body remained on the ground. The bull stretched more than twenty feet, and made the leopard seal Foster had encountered look like a worm. Foster wouldn't have felt safe running him down in a truck. There were smaller ones, but he saw Gionn's point. The entire crew of whalers would struggle to occupy the territorial males while they took down something more manageable. If they waded into the colony, weak and stiff, they might not come out.

They walked the length of the beach, probing for a thin spot, or an isolated calf. Anything vulnerable nestled within the group, warned by the others' calls, while the indifferent hulks didn't even flatter them with a glance of concern.

The beach curved, the bluffs closed, and their hunger grew desperate. They lost sight of the whalers behind the point. Nothing smaller than a tractor separated itself from the herd. With the far protrusion that marked the shoreline closing in, Gionn sighted a motionless body.

That it was already dead became obvious before they arrived. The corpse lay frozen, its spine to the water. Dark spots ran up and down the length where dozens of spears had pierced it. The belly lay open from throat to tail fin. A pile of frozen viscera spilled on the beach. Wide sections of blubber had been stripped away, and choice cuts of meat removed. Most of it remained perfectly chilled, left like a gift for two starving fugitives.

"Angotaks?"

"Aye, but why leave it? They should have sent for their sleds, butchered the whole of it, and drove off with a thousand pounds."

"Maybe we were too close behind."

Gionn bent inside the carcass. He pulled his knife and began working loose sections of fat. Foster had no idea what to take or how to clean it, but he started to saw off stubborn blocks. The knife pried in futility against much of the frozen meat. A chainsaw would have been a more appropriate butcher's tool. Gionn frowned, and dug both arms in to reach near the back of the cavity. He came out with a broken arrow shaft.

"Squain."

"You think Lenet's men came around the island to hunt?"

"Stone arrowheads don't go through that hide, sweet prince. This was fired after it was open." He touched the point to the incision in the belly. "This is steel, done this. But look here." He touched another jagged section. "Someone cut off their supper with a stone blade."

He stood and looked at the end of the beach, some three hundred yards south.

"Angotaks got her, but the squains came on 'em before they could fill their sleds. They made off with what they could, and the carrion thieves got their ration, but they didn't stick around. Must be hundreds of pounds of good flesh here."

"Food's great, brother, but if your job is to stay hidden and you see someone you don't know snoopin' around, might be bigger things demandin' your attention."

Only Foster's appetite allowed him to gnaw bits of blubber while they peeled off stubborn strips. It tasted like gamey beef that had been steeped in rancid fish, and the cold fat coated the roof of his mouth. He'd lived off of seal and seafood, most of it of questionable condition. The next time he had cod or fur seal, he would be more grateful.

The sun still arced low over the sky like an old man out for his walk when they were startled by a shout. Gionn stuck his head over the carcass, then ducked back down and hurried to close his sack, though they'd barely slivered off a dozen pounds apiece.

"'Won't catch up til dark,' huh?" Foster couldn't help himself.

"It'll be dark enough when I stab your eyes out. Come on, filthy cunt. Up on the bluffs before they get here. They'll be after an easy one like us."

They had barely started their ascent when a ruckus kicked up among the whalers. Foster looked back to see the lead sled arrive at their seal, cutting off the way south. They unharnessed and strung the bows.

The gentle rock of the foothills offered scant protection. The snow piled deep here where it slid down off the mountainside. No outcroppings or boulders to shield them. They had no choice but to slog back north, exposed on the slope while the other sleds came up in support. Foster noticed a handful of bodies hang back, giving appearances of guarding the carcass, but most of the men joined the chase.

Eckerd's team, along with Tamarqan and Juru, led the pursuit. They followed parallel along the beach until the colony of elephant seals blocked them. With no way off the bluffs now, Foster and Gionn could only outpace them.

Out on the shore ice, Corm had turned his sled. The tired men drove back the way they came on the far side of the seals while the closer party made their way up the slopes.

"Don't panic, cunt. I been in me share of chases, somethin' opens up if you keep your head."

"Who's panickin'? I been in chases, too."

"Not as many as I. Don't be an arrogant cock when I'm tryin' to help you."

"You're the one arguin' about who's the expert on bein' chased."

"Stop talkin' so much, you'll lose your breath. *Arrow!*"

Foster couldn't react. He watched the shot bury itself in the snow ahead. A fold in the land sunk and soon he realized that a deep groove carved by spring meltwater broke their path, separating the bluff they were on from the next one over. When he turned, he saw Tamarqan nock another arrow. He felt the dread he ascribed to the angotaks that day he harried them over the ice, their wild counterattack picking off man after man short of the boat. Maybe they didn't dread him like he thought. They seemed to embrace their end when they saw it, not with joy and relief, but a shrug of indifference.

The Amposi stopped to take aim. Out of exhaustion and cussedness, Foster remembered that he couldn't understand why those men didn't just turn and face him. They were so sure the boat was their fortress, that they committed to their doom.

He planted his feet and raised his spear to heave. Gionn grabbed his collar and flung him down the slope into the depression as an arrow zipped by his scalp. They slid in deep powder and settled into a little hollow where the land eddied back. The slope up the far side looked ludicrously steep.

"I'm not panickin'," he petitioned Gionn. Every way but one ran uphill. They looked down at the path of the channel where it led into the colony of elephant seals, blissfully unaware of the struggle behind them.

Foster looked back up, expecting Tamarqan to appear at the top of the embankment any moment. Before they could move, the ground beneath their feet twisted and erupted in a shower of snow.

The forge sang an old song. Mattaka hammers had long folded steel for other men. Not since the days of Barduk had the people held their famous blades, which blackened but never rusted though they bathed in the sea. Many said the steel was never the same. None that Tunguk had seen was better, but men of all shores boasted of the old smiths. What blades remained from the days when the fires glowed in the people's hearts were jealously guarded by those who never struck at an enemy.

The smiths had forgotten how to sing the metal. Tunguk stood captive to the glare. He knew the fire would teach them new songs, if they persisted. The fire was not so removed from its ancestor. But the smiths had also forgotten the retribution that broke those songs, and the lips that carried them.

The boy accompanied him more often now. They had learned to speak of certain things without scorn. He, too, admired the forge, though his eyes were full of dreams where Tunguk's held memories.

"It is trouble when the people arm," he cautioned.

"And what is it when the people bend their backs? At least it is the trouble we choose."

Tunguk did not think the boy knew what he chose, and wondered for the first time if men made so many choices as they thought. Yet he could not rob him of that spark. To do a thing and to believe in the blessings that must follow—it had sated him many days when the truth would have starved him. Tunguk thought that no less than a hero could lift himself to do the simplest task if he knew the course of all his days the way an old man did.

Still, he felt the open promise that the fire once held for him. He could not dream as he did in his youth, but he was tempted.

Tunguk came to the side of the forge alone. The miners had built a house of stone around it to trap the heat, open only to the front. Against the outer wall, he found Brother and Ferrakut sitting on the sled, stealing warmth. A young pile of spearheads grew beside Brother, which perhaps he counted. At that time, however, they were in the making of words.

"Petty-uck."

"*Petiuk.*"

"Peti-*ook.*" Brother noticed Tunguk watching. "Peti-*ook.*" He aimed his thumb at the wall behind him as if introducing a friend. "Forge."

A look was enough to send Ferrakut on his way. Tunguk moaned to a seat on the sled. It took several breaths for his ribs to ease again, while the sudden change made his head thump.

"You are learning," he said with some relief. "*Akmanittak.*"

"And a happy akmanuak to you too, amigo. Or should I say, akjuru."

"Listen. Akmanittak. This is different. It is your name in Mattakatan, Brother."

"Akmanittak," he practiced. "There is no word for hello, so I will say," Brother placed his fingers on his own chest, "Akmanittak, Tunguk, we share akmanuak by the petiuk. Sorry, I was hoping to keep it secret from you until I could speak like a gangster, then just drop, like, a whole Gettysburg Address on you all at once and give you another heart attack."

"It is good," Tunguk placed his hand consolingly on Brother's thigh. "To learn Mattakatan for your people, not so easy."

"No, but I have a private tutor, a personal bodyguard-slash-assassin, and.,.Kjartke," he pointed in the direction of the tukits, then touched his chest, "atatapalatet."

Tunguk burst into laughter until he gasped against the pain.

"Damn, no need to be so harsh, dude. It's just for show. Keep these other dogs away from her."

"You must be careful who you learn from."

"Did I say it wrong? 'Girlfriend.' I swear that's what she told me."

"It is hard to put in your tongue, but perhaps you would say, 'tastes many times before buying some seal flesh suspected of being rancid which belongs to a woman.'"

Brother looked both to his lap, and off a great distance. He smiled and nodded. "How'd you get all that from one word?"

"Mattaka do not chop words like meat. It can be as long as a rope, and hold many things."

Frustration came to Brother's face. "Fuck me, how is Carabiner already crushing it? I'm never gonna learn this shit, am I?" He let his head fall back against the wall. "How long did it take you to learn English? My language?"

"Atlantean? It is spoken often in Drummoc. I heard it as a boy. This is the best way. You do not need to point at things. Just listen. You will learn much with your lips closed."

Brother frowned. "You fools talk too fast. And you hardly talk at all." Tunguk let him twist against the knots of his ire. Then Brother asked: "So how many languages do you know?"

"I know only Mattakatan. But I have heard many tongues in the streets, on the ships."

"Like Kjartke? Her English sucked when we first met, but she's gotten a lot better."

"She is quiet. She learns from you, now."

What he left unsaid found its place within Brother. "You taught her?"

"It is not spoken much among the Kapadak, or the Jargadak. Some men come to trade, but a little is enough. When I came to this clan, they thought it good that I had captured many stories."

"Captured stories?"

"Mattaka guard their sacred songs from vulgar ears. What you hear are not the songs of power. We believe that these must only be sung among the people. If they are captured and shared around foreign fires, they grow weak. But your people are careless. A man who listens will capture many tales. These, I told often. The people were glad to bore holes in the stories of the Atlanteans. It is better to capture a story than an enemy."

"Yeah, well, after I saw what you people did to those marines, you can have all my stories if you let me go."

"Mattaka are known across the seas for their hospitality to prisoners," Tunguk grinned. "Even the women and children take delight in it. The women, they say, are worse than the men." He turned across the camp to where Kjartke stood alone, shaking the dirt from their blankets. Brother saw her, too. "And though you should fear each clan, they are not the same. Kapadak are terrible. Worse than these Kammatuk miners. But if you face capture by the Jargadak, better to throw yourself into the sea."

The snow beneath Foster bubbled and twisted. Their feet tore out, and he clutched for Gionn. Together they flailed for something solid. He couldn't tell if they were falling or sliding down the hillside, to be buried by tons of snow. A second later his back landed in loose powder. A corner of ground kicked up in a plume. A shout seemed to issue from the earth itself.

Leather bent, and a pair of feet pedaled at the air. A white monster sprang from the groove of the channel and towered over them with a spear. Beside it, snow bounced across a moving lump that attempted to break free. The first one clutched at the edge of a sail and whipped it like a bed sheet to free the other. As the layers fell away, Foster grasped the outline of ordinary men. They had landed on a covered sail, and the campers underneath scrambled to figure out what threat had crashed their tent.

Gionn drew his sword. Foster swished around for his spear. The snow-dusted man let go his friend and prepared to thrust before they could get to their feet.

"Pinipa! Hold, mate!" His partner dusted himself and took in the rabid panic of his visitors. "It's him, again."

"Seal man!" The muscular yeti cried.

"Come to try the last of the *Abalax*?" He leveled his weapon.

"Passin' through, cunt. Try the blaggards behind us." Gionn half-lifted Foster to his feet and half-shoved him down the steep channel. They slid as much as stepped thirty feet to the beach. Unseen voices from the bluff caught the attention of the angotaks. They fled their ditch as the whalers arrived at the top.

The presence of an extra pair in flight confused Tamarqan long-enough that his shot escaped him. Rather than tumble after them, he waved the next group back to rejoin pursuit with the sled parties, then picked his way down with a handful of men.

Foster skidded to a stop. A bloated neck lifted from its nap, cocked sideways, then sounded a guttural alarm. He sidestepped it and found himself hip-deep in a winter colony of elephant seals. At the shoreline, Corm and his men worked out of their harnesses. Off the beach was into the fight, but with the southern route leading back to the rest of the whalers, rushing to join the pursuit, the only way was toward the northern point where they first arrived—through a thousand tons of blubber.

A flash of movement was all Foster needed to know the others followed in his tracks. He hugged the edge by the bluffs, hoping to avoid most of the seals. A smaller one barked its annoyance at him when he passed. A mother and a juvenile scurried away. The bulk of the animals never stirred. He checked the men pacing them parallel on the far side of the colony. The snow drift nearest the bluffs lay thick. Thighs burned to lift from the deep prints. Corm's party seemed to gain distance on thinner ground, eager to cut off their escape at the opposite end.

"Archer comin' up!" Gionn warned.

Tamarqan closed on them unobstructed from the rear with three others.

"Cover!" The angotak called up.

Cover *where*? Foster thought. The two angotaks broke from the file and darted onto the beach. Foster and Gionn bounded after for lack of options. The snow here was packed harder from the dense bellies that wormed across it. Their feet found purchase, but immediately they had to dance around shifting seals. A young bull reared, and they broke to either side. Tamarqan stopped to level an arrow. With nothing to shield them, the more talkative angotak pulled Foster down against the rough side of an elephant seal. The arrow skimmed over them and lodged in another seal, who cried from the insult. Their "shield" felt their touch and whipped its neck around to strike at them.

Foster found himself in a dash too fast to gauge distance. The beach began to alert at them. He nearly ran into a seal, turned, and had to roll out of the way of another fleeing from Gionn on the other side. Some cleared a path, others went right for them.

"Cover!" They ducked again and heard an arrow split the air from the foot of the bluff.

He peeked up to find Juru, Boot, and Bale close on the heels of the Amposi sled leader, and Boot, too, carried a bow.

Having passed them, Corm's men now started to weave into the colony to head them off. The captain could have been one of the massive males, himself, the way he stood above the rest. The two groups of whalers moved in a pincer, with Tamarqan's threatening the shot from the right while the spears closed on their left.

A nervous pile-up ahead forced Foster seaward, where somehow he crossed with Gionn and ended up just as separated.

"Stop lookin' back, mate!" The angotak urged.

Several whalers penetrated into the seal. The first to reach him was Bosc, who teased himself a path that seemed to have nothing to do with catching Foster. He grinned as he crossed in front with an elephant seal between them, dodged a lunging bite, and took a harmless angle that moved him away again.

Gewar arrived with more intent. He filled the gap. Foster couldn't stop his run. He planted a foot on the back of a seal and vaulted to the other side. An arrow struck the animal in the neck when it protested.

"Hold your string, Tamarqan!" Gewar snapped, now that the whalers mingled among the targets. Instead, the Amposi nocked another.

"In league with the angotaks!" He heard Corm bray nearby. "An extra share to the man who deals their blow!"

A line of whalers slipped through ahead. Foster was forced to stop and retrace his steps, while Corm thundered in from behind. The angotak drove Hiren to retreat with a shake of his spear. Though he couldn't see him through the chaos, Gionn ran through his full vocabulary somewhere toward the foothills.

"Whose boots did you nick?" The angotak rejoined him.

The dull hides undulated around them. A path cleared, but when they hurried in, they saw why. A bulbous trunk flared with angry breath. The bull lurched toward them and arced a dozen feet high. He slammed his neck into the spot they vacated with a slap of rippling skin. Foster backed into another screaming animal and pinballed. Four whalers converged, and he backed away, then wheeled to find Corm at a spear's-length.

The first pop sent Foster's weapon flying from his grip. He dove after it. The angotak stepped in to intercept Corm's follow-up. They clashed and parried wood, searching for an angle. A rumble from the side saw both men scatter as the bull flung itself at them. The angotak used the split to gather Foster.

"If you're gonna carry Nagal's stick, you'll have to do better than that."

He looked down at his looted steel, dumbfounded.

Corm hardly backed from the bull, dodging to this side and that. He glared past at Foster, untroubled by the seal's rage.

Foster tried to use the distraction to squirt free, but Bentos and Jenneker cut him off. Jonn and Bubba slammed the door on his left flank.

"*Finally!*" The angotak tipped his head back in praise. "I remember you!" He squared to Jonn. "Pinipa!" He hollered into the colony. "Let's knock, mate."

Jonn hesitated at the enthusiasm. He scanned this way and that for errant seal.

The angotak plunged ahead. Jonn stepped back, and his attacker's careful thrusts kept Jonn off-balance. He fell, and it would have been his end if Bubba hadn't slashed between them. Jenneker hurled his spear. The angotak saw it all the way and tapped it aside. He looked to Foster for reinforcements, and Foster realized he'd been watching mouth agape.

An elephant seal crashed past. Foster went for Jenneker, unarmed and separated from his weapon. Bentos broke off from the angotak to help, and it was Foster's turn to retreat. He knew nothing of spear-fighting, and had no intention of learning the hard way. Besides, he'd taken a shine to Bentos, and the sailor didn't pursue him. Instead, the three armed men concentrated their efforts on the angotak.

He thrust with a fury familiar from the attack on the *Gairhle*. By threatening the flanks in turn, he prevented the whalers from surrounding him. When a maneuver bought him a second, he whipped around to press Jonn. The others were mere nuisances.

Foster again forgot himself. This wasn't his friend. He hustled on his original course, but found himself faced with Gewar. The whaler's eyes rose over Foster and widened. Foster hurled himself out of the way a moment before the big bull thundered down. He jumped up to find Corm close behind. The bull lifted and swatted at the three of them. An arrow hit it in the chest with all the effect of a flimsy needle.

"Hold your string!" Corm called to Tamarqan. The other four whalers tripped over in retreat from the lone angotak. The seal swung its head and struck Jonn across the back. He accelerated face-first into the snow and didn't move. Jenneker grabbed his wrists and dragged him away as the seal followed up the attack and split the whalers into pairs. Foster parried a thrust from Corm the way he'd seen the angotak do. Another arrow went just wide of the captain and struck Gewar in the side.

"I'll kill you meself!" Corm shouted at Tamarqan, and Boot pulled down the Amposi's bow. Foster used the misdirection to throw himself toward a cluster of seals who were unsure if they fled the angry bull or the men.

The nose only brushed Gewar's shielding arm, yet sent him tumbling several feet. Corm ran his spear into the animal's throat. It hardly penetrated. The bull crashed down, snapping the weapon. The captain snatched Gewar's spear to fend at it.

When Foster looked again Hiren and Aldan had joined the fight with the angotak. With more men lunging at him between fleeing seals, he backed toward the bull. A flash of red caught Foster's eye: Gionn had a fifty yard lead on them, running free and alone, while Bosc wandered in the midground.

Foster staked himself on the right side of the angotak and wriggled his spearpoint in the direction of the whalers to a look of horror from his ally.

"Are you stirrin' a soup? Stab someone!"

He swung it like a golf club at Hiren's legs to avoid getting close. Hiren blocked it with ease, but the angotak hit the opening. A quick thrust between the ribs and a rip out sent Hiren to his knees.

"Watch out!" Foster grabbed the angotak's cloak and yanked him away from the bull. It froze the whalers with a puff of its trunk. All but one of them shrank away. Several tons collapsed onto Hiren, lifted, and smashed, its reddening chest rising again and again. The angotak thought about going after Jonn, who Jenneker dragged toward the shore, but Foster held his cloak.

Instead, they faced Corm.

"Up with you, lads!" He ordered the whalers to reinforce him from the other side, but those who weren't in retreat hesitated on the far side of the bull.

The angotak spread his arms. "Take your throw!"

It seemed impossible to miss from so close, but both Foster and Corm knew better. The angotak cocked his own arm. Corm centered his spear, ready to parry or dodge. The angotak feinted twice, then let it go. The captain tried a desperate swipe, but the spear was meant for Gewar. It thumped dead center in his sternum. Before Corm could counter, the angotak snatched Foster's spear, prepared to meet him.

The rest of the whalers saw Gewar fall, and broke from the melee. They were all Palqua's men, none eager to be crushed for a shot at Foster. With that, the bull returned its insatiable attention to those who remained. Foster guided the angotak away from its charge while the man engaged Corm's spear.

They met with a wrath worthy of two unrivaled warriors. A counter that seemed too fast for the big captain slashed through the top of the angotak's nose. He answered with a steady pressure of taps and feints and thrusts that kept Corm from timing another blow.

Soon he found his window. A flick opened Corm's forearm and blood dripped in spurts from the sleeve.

"Move!" Foster slung the angotak aside as the bull came lurching between them. It bounded after the two of them. The angotak tried to pick his way back to Corm without success. Foster once more considered running, unarmed, but held out of disgust for Gionn, who faded toward the point.

A pair of jaws nearly closed around his calf. He'd backed too close to a female, who knocked him down and growled at him. His companion pulled him up.

Corm drew the spear from Gewar's breast. He aimed for a throw, and now the angotak danced with the bull between them as a shield.

A high-pitched cry chilled Foster's bones. The second angotak rushed into the battle between his friend and the seal. He poked at it, drawing blood and stepping aside before the slower animal could retaliate time and again. It freed Foster and the other to move around towards Corm. The captain saw the field had turned against him. He aimed at Foster and ripped a throw. The angotak just got his spear shaft between. The missile wobbled into the tail-end of the bull.

Unarmed, Corm headed for the sled with reluctance.

The native-looking angotak smiled like a kid at play. He seemed to speak to the bull through his howls and taunts and gestures. Its attacks gave him no concern—they were much too slow. This man was more muscled than Foster's new partner, and if it was possible, faster.

While he gathered its attention, Foster's partner placed a foot on the bull's back and tore the spear free.

"Still got a bit of Nagal in it—for now." He handed it to Foster, then signaled to the other. The three men resumed their run while the whalers struggled to regroup on the shoreline.

The Dawn Council swelled. The new arrivals didn't have much to say, but Parks had worked with Carabiner long enough to know that any decision he made involved some amount of malice. Eskimo Joe showed no reaction when the leader of the dog family, Sawi, was introduced to replace Nutillen-Amalset, the Provisions officer killed in the ambush. It made sense that the guy who owned the sleds would be in charge of moving supplies. Parks worried that the father disapproved of his boys hanging around with him, though.

More troublesome was that Captain Ghrane and First Mate Neal were asked to advise on foreign affairs while Haraket was away. He wondered how seriously Ghrane had taken his story of working for Costig, and how he might use it.

"Two more prisoners have died of their burns," reported Attibatbarak on guests and matters of hospitality. "Though we treated them as you asked," he added.

"The two who came back with us, they're still alive?"

"It seems they will live," he answered with regret.

"Thank you, Attibatbarak. My friend the Leopard Seal promised our hospitality, and to the extent we keep our word, we'll be trusted when we bargain with Drummoc. I know it isn't your people's way, but you've treated our guests as a man of your office. If it was easy, I wouldn't need a councilor to do it. Many of us here—myself included—are guests of this place, and testament to your excellent service."

Attibatbarak nodded, and settled on Parks even before Carabiner called on him. Parks made a mental note to ask Ferrakut the meaning of the man's name, and the others as well.

When Carabiner dialed him up, he bent an ear to Ferrakut, who he'd weaseled into the meetings as his translator and aide. He hoped the honor would keep the boy from revealing his pact with Costig. It seemed like half the people present knew it by now.

"First off, I'd like to say that even though my motion to vote on ratifying the new members was vetoed, I fully intended to vote them in. Just wanted to do it by the book."

He gave the injury report down to the hangnail, hocking and rolling each syllable of the name in imitation of Ferrakut's whisper.

"And Kjartke is stricken with grief," he rounded it out. "She's afraid she offended you by inviting your wife over to our wigwam. It's a common custom among her people, and she hopes you forgive her."

There was irritation in Carabiner's smile, but the consummate politician had no choice. "Had I known, I'd have eased her suffering myself. Please pass along my reassurance that I'd forgotten the mistake until you mentioned it."

"As for the forge, it's lit before dawn and burns until after sunset. I'm personally inspecting the quality of every blade that comes off the line, and we're five percent of the way to our goal in only a few days. We're running out of good long sticks for mounting spearheads, though.

If you can requisition us some timber, we'd be much obliged not to have to put them onto old hammers."

Parks endured a long discussion about when they could expect Ostuk and Haraket, and what to do if they were delayed. When Carabiner adjourned, he mushed Ferrakut to catch up.

"Speaking of guests. What are you doing for dinner tonight? Any plans?"

Carabiner motioned for Ferrakut to give him the harness and run along. Carabiner strapped in, and walked with Parks in tow. Somehow, what should have been a show of generosity struck Parks as humiliating.

"You know, I'm a servant of my routines. I think I'll have the cold seal in my tukit, as usual."

"'Cause I was just gonna ask if you were free for a double date."

Carabiner pulled several steps before responding. "Was that your idea, or Kjartke's?"

"Come on, dude. Kjartke has one outfit that she's worn through two arranged marriages. You think she's heard of a double date?"

"I wasn't talking about the date."

Parks folded forward at great pains and caught the line at the place it hitched to the sled. He yanked it, and Carabiner stopped to face him.

"She was wrong to take her. We know that, now. There just aren't that many chicks here, if you haven't noticed. We wanna hang out. Supervised visitation."

"You know there were marines running around trying to kill people. You make it sound like I was holding her prisoner."

"You're a cautious dude. You were protecting her. Like back on the ship, when you would clean the insides of your boots with disinfectant wipes at the end of every day. It's not wrong, but you may have noticed the threat is gone. You smoked those fools. Now your fake wife needs healthy human contact, or she's going to go nuts—and so will my fake girlfriend."

"There's what we want, Parks, then there's where we are." Carabiner tucked his chin to gaze down on the sled. "Sophia is supposed to be the wife of a nobleman. She can't just run around camp gossiping like some native girl. Not if we want her to be treated the way she needs."

It was so subtle a dig at Kjartke that Parks wasn't sure if Carabiner knew he made it. Maybe the arrogance just flowed effortlessly from the officer, but he was also snide enough to mean it.

"If you're worried about her saying something you don't want her to—"

"Not that shit again," Carabiner rolled his eyes.

"No. No. I didn't mean *that*," Parks held up his hand. "Yo. It was hard getting here. I don't know what you've been through, but I notice you're a few short of the number we put in that raft. Maybe stuff happened. Hell, maybe you had to eat somebody. I've been there. I won't pretend I didn't look sideways at Foster a few times."

"It *was* hard. On all of us. You think I'm trying to hide something? There are just certain things she's best not having to relive. And if you and your girlfriend can't even respect the very minimal boundaries I've set in this camp, how can I risk turning you loose on the only one of us who isn't already completely lost?"

Carabiner saluted Ratjuk.

"Looking good, old soldier." He accepted the two bowls of meat and the snow-filled pouches the man had been warming against his stomach. Ratjuk had never apologized for his error of letting Sophia be taken out of the tukit. In fact, he had never thanked Carabiner for giving him the esteemed post. Being lame, it was a pitiful sight to watch him try to keep up with the others. Carabiner thought the responsibility would both instill him with pride, and show the miners he was a man of compassion, who made the most of even the least among them. Ratjuk carried on as with any other duty. He did most things well, but the pride Carabiner hoped to elicit was well-hidden if it ever came. Though he wanted to admire that, some part of him remained irked.

There was no use scolding him. He reminded himself that none of these men were sailors of the United States Navy. They felt pride and shame, courage and fear, to be sure, but not for the reasons he expected.

It drove him nuts when he first arrived. If anything, the able-bodied were worse. How often did they refuse to work because of some omen? He had a man mourn for twelve days when he dreamed that a family member had died back on Drummoc. Another insisted he had to stay within sight of water until the moon returned.

Carabiner broke like a frayed strap and let them fall where they may. There was no way to understand them by his own truths. He had to inhabit theirs. Mattaka or Navy, he let them shift around him, reassigned them, or closed a mine because some spirit grew restless.

Little by little, they came together in their own order. Men worked with zeal. Volunteered. In his career, he would have called them lazy and superstitious. He said worse to Parks and Foster. But once he accepted it, he began to see them—see many things that had flaunted in front of his scaly eyes.

Yet there were times he slipped. His anger begged him to dress someone down. Parks' arrival came as a blessing. He anticipated the relief of speaking frankly and treating someone according to custom. But Parks had changed, too. Or maybe he had been a kindred spirit to these people all along.

Fennimore's Apparence system had always struck him as interesting, but he never put it to use in the "old world"—he hated that term, but couldn't think of another. The constant calibration that it required left him disoriented. He feared sometimes he would forget his way back to himself. As much as Parks remained ineffably himself, there was a subtle shift that discomfited Carabiner. Besides the map that he consulted every morning, there was only one thing that tethered him to the place where his soul still resided.

"You're not gonna believe our luck: the mess hall had our favorite dish again today." He joked as he entered the tukit. "Sorry my meeting took so long. I had to get the new councilors up to speed, then of course they held me up chatting afterwards. The good news is, I think we're finally back to a place where we can buckle down and work, instead of scrambling between crises. Don't get me wrong, it's still a slog with these characters, but a slog in the right direction."

He listened to the quiet.

"Oh, and I checked on the prisoners. They're being treated very humanely, which is less than we owe them, but only right." Again he waited for a response from the dark. "Maybe after we eat, we can get back to planning our igloo. There should be enough snow at the harbor now, and it'll be a lot warmer to winter down there. I'm still thinking skylight in the living room so we can get some stars, and maybe even see the jaguar statue on a full moon, but I seem to remember you said you had the argument to end all arguments for the vaulted ceiling layout. I admit, I'm intrigued, but I have to warn you—eight years of debate team doesn't roll over that easily."

The tukit dimpled from a breeze, then returned to shape. Nothing answered but faint chatter of men outside.

"Sophia?" He jumped up and swept his arms around. "*Sophia*!" Carabiner shouted in a panic.

"I'm *here*," she scoffed with exasperation.

"Don't scare me like that. I've got your breakfast."

"Just set it."

"Set it where? You don't want it?"

All signs of another occupant withdrew into the pitch. Carabiner placed her bowl along the edge, and gnawed anxiously on a bite of seal. He hadn't been around enough lately to say that this was recent, but whether it was Kjartke or the fear of lurking enemies, something had cracked her awkward cheer.

"You know, as hard as it was for me to have those unsavory elements running around out there, threatening everything and everyone, I can't imagine having to face that cooped up in the dark." She said nothing, but he felt the quiet shift. "What do you say we take advantage of our daylight?"

Parks wrinkled his nose. The Mattaka bounded at a distance like drunk puppies. Sagalak and a few armed men followed well-back. Kjartke's knapping tapped in his ear as he watched Carabiner and Sophia stroll the camp like the royal family on a tour. They admired the forge, gazed off the precipice toward the sea, steered a wide berth from the prisoners' quarters, and passed by all the Mattaka wigwams so the miners could fawn over her appearance like a rare bird fluttering over the bleak land.

Carabiner's lips moved, but Sophia kept her eyes occupied elsewhere, hunched in her parka with a beaded dress hanging out the bottom, multiple pairs of pants beneath it.

Finally, they meandered back toward their wigwam, but to his surprise, detoured. Sophia looked equally confused when Carabiner stopped in front of Parks. His eyes climbed the legs of the assistant viceroy, and he bit down a flurry of remarks. Kjartke didn't bother to turn from her work.

Carabiner looked at Sophia. "Aren't you going to say hi?"

She struggled to gather herself from the surprise.

"Hi, Mr. Parks."

"Please. Parks."

"Leopard Seal," she grinned. "And Kjartke."

She raised her chin and forced a smile.

"Are you making arrowheads?" Sophia stated the obvious over the obsidian pile that gathered by Kjartke's lap.

"Aye."

"For Parks?"

Kjartke shrugged with a gentle scorn. "For he who can use them."

Corm's hand swelled a ghostly purple. His forearm shook as he carefully wrapped the strip of leather around it so that it closed the seam of the gash.

"Let me do that," Eckerd reached, but Corm snatched it away.

"Fuck off. Now you lot come to help," he jeered at the rest of the sleds, just arriving after Foster and Gionn's escape. His men who tasted the melee sprawled around him tending their aches. Jonn had awoken from the crack the bull gave him. The lad blinked and contorted his face, then gave his stiff back a wrench.

Palqua came close on Eckerd's heels, and after all, Tamarqan.

"I ought to stake you to the fuckin' beach! I told you to hold your string, you jungle-tramp bastard. Gewar's dead of your stupidity, and I don't care that the angotak dealt the blow. You'll fetch his corpse for burial or don't bother comin' back!"

"I couldn't hear over those beasts," Tamarqan objected. "Besides, you should have waited for more men to come up,"

Corm thrust himself to his feet and grabbed his spear. Palqua, Eckerd and several others wedged between them. He tried to sling them aside, but the battle had taken more of Corm than he cared to admit.

"They can't be far. Let us press," Ordacles suggested.

"We will meet them together, when the gods cast it. But that is not why you wish to go, is it?" Palqua asked.

"I wish to fight, not to dally with the likes of you."

"Captain! I am sorry to bring you this in your mourning. But the good of it is that you shall have your argot back." The men rustled at the statement. "Baghar, tell him what you told me."

Palqua's handmaiden stepped forward.

"Captain. It is most unfortunate. When the new men came to our team, I saw the glint as they stowed, and recalled that he was among those who stowed the mast when the coin went missing. I speak, of course, of *Ordacles!*"

A wave of rancor lifted the sleds. Now those who separated Corm from Tamarqan pivoted to keep Ordacles from dealing Baghar his blow. Corm shouted over them, but even his voice was lost. Nearly every man who could stand hurried into the shoving fray. Their hunger for a fight had not been sated, and now they threatened to turn on one another.

With a renewed bellow, and the help of Palqua and Eckerd, Corm broke the parties and took the ground between them, his strap still trailing untied from his forearm.

"Ordacles has nothin' to do with those blaggards, and I'll have no more of you men duelin' over bright pennies."

"It is no penny, captain. Perhaps he is no mate of Gionn and Foster, but it was he who stole the coin that rightfully belonged to yourself, which was sent to destroy the brave men of the *Gairhle*."

"If you mean to split us, Baghar, you ought to have picked a gentler name!" Ordacles challenged.

"It is no rumor. I saw you! You do not believe my word? Then believe your eyes. Turn over his sea sack, and you shall have it!"

Ordacles blasted through Eckerd and Aldan and shoved at the chests of Tamarqan and Lozeder, who held him from Baghar. Corm wrapped his waist with his good arm and drew him back.

"At ease, lad! No one's gonna turn you out over this cunt's mad visions."

The wind left the sails of the fight, and the men paced the ice. He thought it settled, but Palqua spoke.

"Is it not worth a look?" He said it with such innocence that no man was moved to rage.

"I said from the start I won't tear me crew inside out gropin' after a coin. We rid ourselves of the bastards who brung it, and that's the heart of the matter."

"It has been a difficult journey, these last days especially. I agree, it would cause too much distress for the crew to set at one another's belongings. I merely meant to suggest that perhaps Ordacles would grant us peace by showing us, himself."

"You want to see me kit? And when you're satisfied, I'll trade blows with Baghar until one of us falls."

"I accept your terms." Baghar said.

Ordacles marched to the sled and removed his sea sack. He gripped the neck and held it high as he returned, then reached in and fished out his purse. In plain sight, he loosed the string and spilled the contents onto the ice. The only thing that struck was the smooth ballast bit—the stone some men kept to avoid the ill-fortune of "a purse once-emptied, always barren."

"You'd be a fool to keep it there." Baghar folded his arms, unimpressed.

Ordacles grabbed the sack from the bottom and shook its contents free. His spare clothing tumbled out. A piece of wood carved from the luck statue on the prow of the angotak vessel. Two whetstones. Strips of leather, a flint. Several bone needles. A coil of thin cooper's iron, rolled up tight. A squain bead in the shape called *getjar* that he purchased on Drummoc. A tattered wreath of kelp from Darfordlann. And among its benefic leaves, the face of Farri Mil pressed into a disc of gold.

No one dared move. Corm at last approached, and brushed aside the kelp with his boot. He knelt and pinched it free of the ice. His fist closed around it.

"Restored."

Ordacles trembled with shock while the captain limped off toward his sled.

"Is that all?" Palqua demanded from behind. "This man stole from you. How can you be sure he did not mean to aid those conspirators?"

Corm barely regarded him over his shoulder. "I've sailed with Ordacles long enough. There's none his equal. He stood beside me when the men of the *Gairhle* fled like rats. He fought harder than any of you when the angotaks came. Would you have me toss a barrel overboard because it gave you a splinter?"

"Stowed!" Ordacles finally gathered himself. "You stowed it on me!" He pointed a stout finger at Baghar. "You were at the mast, too. You stole the coin and put it in me kit!"

"Enough!" Corm staunched the tide.

"Baghar has served me for many years, and I have never known him to be dishonest," Palqua said. "I only wonder how you would have treated an Amposi if he had taken the coin. Perhaps it comes as no surprise to you that Ordacles has it."

"If you wish to accuse me of somethin', say it with your tongue, and prepare to stand behind it with your spear."

Palqua let it pass out in a long breath. No man ventured to speak, none to act. A brittle air hung over the sleds that seemed ready to shatter at the touch.

"Tamarqan!" Corm felt the power that came with the argot. "Fetch Gewar and Hiren from the beach, and with due care."

The man looked to Palqua, who nodded.

Corm collapsed to a seat on his sled as slowly, the men returned to what duties would placate them. He did not let go his grip on the piece, but with three fingers, wrapped the strap around his wound a few more times until the edges folded together, and with a bite and a snap, tied it off.

They found Gionn waiting at the snowy foot of Yunoc. The relief Foster felt at seeing him was no more than habit, at this point. Gionn had probably saved him from the ambush for the same reason he now held up: no one survived this place alone. For his part, Foster held him in the same regard.

The whalers remained within sight, at most a mile back, but they'd stopped for the time, and not one of the four had the lungs to carry on.

"A fine pair, eh Pinipa? These lads slaughtered our crew, and now they've caused us to abandon our meat, our sacks, and our tent to the whalers. Good that they hung on to theirs," the angotak tilted his head at the sleeping bags full of belongings that lay between Foster and Gionn.

"Loo'tros," Pinipa said the man's name in a thick accent as if to echo the sentiment.

"Don't kill us, cunts. We're too tired to fight back, and there's squains about. You may need us, yet." Gionn puffed.

"Aye, though I can hardly see what for." Luxtros leaned on his spear.

"I'm the one gave yall food," Foster plead. Gionn shot him a sidelong glare of irritation.

"And we didn't kill you when we took your seal, nor did we leave you to your mates, who seem to hold you in high favor."

"They found out we're not whalers," Gionn threw a desperate line. It found its mark well-enough that the angotaks didn't immediately waylay them. "Agents of Ampos. Hired by the admiral of Drummoc himself to see that the *Gairhle* never reaches Taclann, where she'd prey on the supply ships that *Farri Tolba*," he emphasized the name, "sends to batten the garrisons of Hiade in the comin' war. From the looks on your stupid heads, I suppose good Tolba failed to forewarn his esteemed mercenaries."

A slow smile crept over Luxtros' face. "I expected a lie, but that's grand." It was impossible for Foster to tell how Pinipa took it. He beamed with the warmest joy now, as in every moment since they'd met. He may have sympathized and supported them, or failed to understand a word.

"It's true. Admiral Costig gave us an argot apiece," Foster added. Gionn rolled his eyes in despair.

"It's Admiral Turrha, last I heard. This Costig sounds a generous soul. I'd like an argot for killin' whalers, wouldn't you, Pinipa?"

"Loo'tros!"

"Can I see the argots?" Luxtros batted his frozen lashes.

Foster and Gionn slumped like schoolboys.

"Mine's on Drummoc. Left it with a friend."

"Foster dropped mine on the fuckin' ship. You can see it when you kill those whalers back there, and I'll be happy to scrape your share off when we get somewhere that can make change."

"Of course. No finer men than you two. If I had a couple argots I despised, you'd be me picks, as well."

Foster sensed their credibility evaporating. Beneath the cheerful demeanor, he now understood something of the nature of an angotak, and he'd have taken a ship of outraged whalers as enemies over these two, any day.

"I didn't drop it."

Gionn lifted his head.

"It wasn't in my boot. I fussed over it to make you think it was, and I even sliced a little hole in one of 'em. But when Corm called me up to the mast, it was in my hand. I pretended to trip. Then I set it in the ballast, where I knew someone would find it."

A flush as bright as his red hair melted over Gionn.

"I knew if you had the coin, you'd betray my ass. Hell, even just back there, you didn't stick around a moment longer than you had to. So I gave your argot to Corm. I figured either the crew would tear themselves apart over it, or you'd have earn your pay: you'd have to kill the man you came to kill."

His nose turned and his lip quivered, then his shoulder slumped with a sigh and Gionn hung his head between his knees. Foster gathered in the amused reaction of the angotaks, and didn't see the big bastard launch himself. They tumbled in the snow. Heavy fists pummeled him. He clung on for dear life, and kicked off when they rolled. Gionn scrambled back up and hit him with a flying tackle at the feet of Luxtros while the angotaks screamed with laughter.

Foster shoved and swung in defense. He expected the hard thump of a knife blade any second. Gionn wrapped his hands around Foster's throat and turned his face from the desperate punches of his victim. Foster's windpipe strained and he sputtered. As he thought he would pass out, he slipped a knee between them and lurched with all his might. The grip broke, and he crawled. A hand seized his ankle, and dragged him back. Foster kicked Gionn in the groin with the other leg, to the delight of the angotaks. They rolled around impotently, Foster gasping, Gionn moaning. Then in a renewed rage, Gionn went for him again. But Luxtros bumped him aside with a hip.

Gionn tried to go around, but in his exhaustion, it was futile. He collapsed, and shouted through Luxtros' legs at Foster.

"It pleases me to know that for all your high-booted efforts, you've succeeded only in blackenin' your name. The *Gairhle* will cache seal, winter, and sail for Taclann as soon as the ice melts. You won't live it to see it, but die assured, cunt, your mates in Drummoc will not survive you long."

"Save it," Luxtros gathered up the two sea sacks and handed one to Pinipa, keeping the other for himself. Foster sat on the numbing snow and looked up at the angotaks. Instead of a spear, a hand extended. "You may yet earn your pay."

For three days, they went for their walk—three days that blinked for Parks like an eye narrowing for sleep. When the pile had grown big enough, he gathered the ends around it and drove after Carabiner and Sophia, catching them just before they went in for the night.

"Hold up!" He shooed Ferrakut and Ulwet, braced himself on his spear, and hopped the last few paces. They stopped. She didn't hurry away, and he didn't shield her. They'd exchanged pleasantries each evening, and each time, Parks had let them go without imposing. He could have spoken to her now, if he liked. Instead, he fixed on Carabiner.

"I have a gift for you."

"Me?"

Parks nodded. Carabiner recovered from his surprise, and excused the girl with a smile. From his shirttail, Parks produced a dingy sheet bulging at the sides and let it fall open on a barrel top.

"Arrowheads." Carabiner sounded less than impressed.

"Half-a-gift, anyway. You'll have to requisition the wood to make the shafts."

"Your girlfriend won't be mad that you're re-gifting her handiwork to my men?"

"They're not for your men," Parks explained. "They're for you. To give to *her*," he indicated the wigwam where Sophia had disappeared. "Besides, can you imagine me firing a bow without dropping like a tree the second I let go of the string?"

"Thank you," Carabiner said politely. "I'll see what I can do."

"Don't see, just give them to her. She'll appreciate that you trust her."

"I have no doubt they'll come in handy. I just don't know if a twelve-year-old girl is the best recipient."

"Why not? She's an archer. She didn't tell you?" Parks played surprised at Carabiner's ignorance. "We talked about it back on the ship. She even used to compete, until a couple years ago. That's when her dad got her into biathlons. You know—ski and shoot. I figured we don't have any rifles, but maybe she would appreciate plinking a few targets. If you wanted to go crazy, you could even whittle her some skis."

Carabiner frowned at the image. "That's very interesting. I'm not sure skiing with sharp objects is the best idea, considering our medical facilities, but believe me, your offer speaks volumes."

"Do you ever ask her stuff?" Parks pressed.

"We talk about all kinds of things. I know you think I'm some starched officer with a stick up his ass, but believe it or not, I have a pretty good rapport with most of my people. I could tell you some things that might surprise you."

"Because you haven't asked me anything. I'm the kind of dude who, when he meets an old friend who just happened to wash up on the same distant shore in an alternate universe, has a lot of questions. 'How did you get here? Did you see anything cool? What's the best thing you've eaten so far?' I wanna put jumper cables on your nipples until you tell me every single story you can think of. It kind of worries me that you don't feel the same."

Carabiner absently turned over an arrowhead in his fingers. "If you'll recall, your arrival coincided with a bit of a distraction I had to handle."

"I would've skipped meals and stayed up for days. You make me count people's boo-boos for you every morning, and how many picks got melted down, but you haven't asked me," he waved at his leg and realized he couldn't quite say it, "anything."

Carabiner sighed. "Look. If you're feeling upset that I haven't prioritized you, that I haven't taken the time to hear you—"

"You told me that everything anyone says is true,"

"Not exactly what I said," Carabiner smiled in frustration.

"Well I'm hearing you loud and clear. You don't want to go home. You *like it* here. You're in charge of everyone, and they hang on your every word. And you know what else? I think you like being the one who can protect her. The *only* one. You don't wanna hear from me, because I remind you of the old Carabiner, picking lint off of people's lapels with his clipboard. I remind you that you're not the only one who can survive. Me and Foster made it, on our own, even though you cut loose. You cut the fucking rope, you left us to die, but we didn't. And maybe, just maybe, you feel a little bad about it."

Now Carabiner shuffled unconsciously through the pile of arrowheads to avoid looking at Parks.

"You also told me," Parks hopped closer, "she's the only one who 'isn't lost.' Like she's some map you're responsible for."

Cold recognition brought a pallor to Carabiner. He picked through a few arrowheads, then lifted the corner of the leather wrapping and shook them off as gently as he could.

"Parks, *no*." He bemoaned the state of the map. The parchment had darkened several shades. Little tears let light in between mysterious stains. A ragged serration marked much of the border, and a chunk was missing entirely. "*No*. Are you serious?"

"I know, right? They used it to bind my foot when I had frostbite. My stupid dog tried to eat it. At first I was pissed, because I thought if I hung on to that thing, and brought it to the place where we sank with the other two maps, it might open up a portal that would bring us back. But then I remembered: maps don't do that.

"I see you fawning over yours every morning. According to your Principle of Truthiness or whatever, actions speak louder than words, right?"

"No. That wasn't it, either."

"Well they do where I come from. All your parading around with your ten-year-projections for the Mattaka World Order told me you plan to be here a while. So why are you worried about a map? Because beneath your persuasion bro mind games and your Annapolis manners, you're actually a decent dude." Carabiner recoiled from the unexpected compliment. "You want to stay, or you think you have to. But you feel guilty. You know Sophia doesn't belong here. She doesn't wanna be a fucking Mattaka princess. She wants to go home. You're torn between your little empire of coal, and her. You got one foot in each world, and don't know which way to step. Trust me, akjuru, that's not a good place to be." Parks' knotted pant leg bobbed gently on command.

"You know who knows where he's going? Foster. He's hellbent. I tried to tell him it was a waste of time, but secretly," he leaned in to whisper, "*I hoped he would prove me wrong.*

"Look around you, dude. I live here, now. You want to be on the same team? Stick around. But if Sophia's going to stay, she needs to be on our team, too. Otherwise, you'd better drop this assistant viceroy crap and get her home, ASAP."

He gave Carabiner's shoulder a loving squeeze, then hopped out from beneath the awning.

"Parks!" His putrid map waved him down.

"Keep it. You take better care of shit than I do."

"You sure?"

"For all the good it's done me? Yeah."

"It's the only thing you've got left from our world." Carabiner stretched out his arm, but Parks beckoned for his sled.

"No. It's not."

The campsite was freshly-deserted. Many huts still stood. Drift crumbled at the edges of round depressions in the snow where others had been plucked, amid unfilled prints. Sewing lay in piles as though the corpse within had vanished. All trails led to the sea, where two hide boats in ill-repair looked out over the waters.

The drying racks, though, stood empty when the company limped in. Costig's marines had been days in travel, no sign of pursuit, but unwilling to tarry. Their wounded made a march of it, and now with the rations from the dog camp exhausted, they picked over larders that they found laid open in hopes of a forgotten morsel.

"Hoy!" Costig shouted to the rippling huts. "The admiral of Drummoc requests your hospitality." He expected no answer, and got none.

Their fighting retreat had cost them six lads, and several more nicked up. Those who had the strength left didn't need the order to begin searching the dwellings. Wherever the hunters had gone off to, they'd gone with unusual haste. In his crawl through the first hut, he found toys of carved bone, and a pair of boots a hunter would hardly abandon. Two more held other simple treasures, yet not a lump of fat.

When he threw back the door of the next, he staggered in fright. A pair of sooted faces gouged with deep ravines of age stared back. The old women sat around an illegal forge. Iron tongs protruded from the cold hearth. They seemed to have gathered in waiting, however, for these were no smiths. Their expressions, solemn and unwavering, hardened with a recognition that was not of a particular man, but an event that could not fail to arrive.

"Where is everybody?" He demanded, and received no answer.

Costig closed the flap in disgust. The marines returned with no more spoils than he.

After a brief rest, the urged the sleds on. There were more camps—he didn't know how many. Costig, like most, had never set foot on this side of Drummoc in all his service. But somewhere up the coast was a harbor fit for a ship, and there would be hundreds of squains ranging between here and the many grounds used to supply Drummoc with seal and whale.

What luck had led them thus far did not leave them yet. Within a few miles, they sighted the tops of dwellings—a more populous camp. He couldn't be sure it was the harbor. A pitiful one, if it was. Their arrival sparked a rustle of bodies in the distance, though. He was near upon them before he realized some of the residents had arranged themselves in a defensive line. No squain would entertain such a thing.

They left the sleds and approached two-abreast. Before he could make out the party, they broke ranks and gave a sailor's wave. The men had recognized them as marines.

"Admiral!" The words practically spilled from the first mate's lips with relief. The title rippled through Costig and filled his breast. It was his, yet he had already given up on it.

"How did you know?" The mate asked.

"Know what? Where's Etan?"

The crew gathered around the marines like pale flakes blown against a rock.

"First to fall," the mate's head bent to the sea after some troubling vision. "To the squain revolt."

Luxtros slid down off the rocky vantage with his friend close behind..

"What do you think, Pinipa?" He asked in front of Foster and Gionn. "Should we stand for these blaggards?"

"Loo'tros," Pinipa confirmed with a grin. "Good man."

"You're a soft touch, mate. Spies or not, they had no mercy for the men of the *Abalax*. This one killed Nagal," he pointed his spear at Foster.

"Nagal." Pinipa's mouth curled down and his brows arched in mourning. Then he placed his hands across his belly, smiled nostalgically, and approached Foster. His palms clamped on either shoulder and his face flooded with gratitude. "Good man."

Luxtros snorted with a resigned humor. He slung a sea sack over his shoulder. "Fine. You lads had better wait here. It may surprise you that most angotaks are not as hospitable as Pinipa. In fact, you may fare better beggin' your captain's forgiveness."

Foster and Gionn climbed up the boulder to watch the two men tramp across the coastal ice with their gear. A ways off, the faint lines of a sled sat parked near a rocky fold just inside the Yunoc channel. Foster tempted himself that he remembered this spot, which they must have sailed past with Tunguk. There was nothing familiar about it, though. He recalled the way the chop fell off abruptly, as if someone drew a line with a piece of chalk, when the looming island intercepted the wind. He also heard Parks' warning, "Wigwam!" None of them ever saw what spurred his imagination.

That same sea rolled before them like white glass. Maybe it was memory, but now, as much as then, he felt *presence*—less of people than of the place itself, like an animal raising a curious head to consider someone who wandered in on its slumber.

Gionn stood and crossed to Foster. Foster scooted quickly away and leveled his spear in warning.

"Easy, mate. I've come for a cuddle, not a stabbin'."

"Oh yeah? You've already forgot that you tried to kill me back there?"

"Aye, the cold makes strange allies. And if I wanted you dead, I'd have drawn me blade. Brilliant, that: tellin' the angotaks you turned on me. I doubt they'd have believed us, otherwise."

"It was the truth."

"I know it. Won't say I didn't enjoy our pummel. But much as I'd like to skin you for a bag, I'll admit your betrayal was the first thing you've done that I admire."

Foster frowned.

"You go about so upright, all thumb-in-arse. Yet in all me travels, I've never seen a man throw his mate's argot to their enemies and force 'em both overboard out of spite. I've stabbed meself in the foot more often than a bead man can count, but even *I'm* envious of that one. They say you become like the men you row with. It's about time you got a little of the old Gionn in you."

He dropped down hard on the snow and leaned into Foster for warmth. Foster peeled away and stood.

"What I did was out of principle. You don't get paid for goin' back on your word."

"Call it that, then. Until you get used to it."

Across the ice, Luxtros stopped well-before the sleds and waved back at their position. Gionn studied the scene before heading down with Foster. He cupped his nose in his mitten to melt the frost. His reluctant stride told of how much the prospect of joining the angotaks appealed to him. A blanket and a single ally would have been enough to desert with. By the way he watched for a sign of betrayal, Foster knew he still might choose to freeze on his own.

The angotaks didn't wait, only stopping when they reached the sleds. The roughly-packed vehicle stood broadside to the island. When Foster got nearer, he saw why. Arrows protruded from the loads like spines. Some of the cargo, roughly strewn on the ice, took form as rigid defenders, frozen where they fell. One man, out ahead of the barricade, must have given a good fight. He wore thirty arrows if he had a one.

Luxtros and Pinipa pored over the nearby rocks, or strained across the channel, trying to recreate the battle. The others must have fled— Foster couldn't imagine a surrender. The ice was too hard here, too little snow to reveal which way, and what prints remained were a muddle.

"Tokens from a brave warrior." Luxtros knelt reverently beside the riddled defender. His eyes and ears were cut from his head, and his fingers, bloody stumps. "I never seen such a huntin' party as could drive off nearly thirty angotaks. Wonder what made the squains so bold?"

Gionn's hand tensed around his pommel, then released and slumped at his side.

"Ask 'em yourself."

The scant rocks and shadows of the nearby island pulsed with parka-clad hunters. They flowed down in silence and without haste, bows and spears at the ready. There was no place to escape, and no more cover than these dead men had enjoyed. Luxtros and Pinipa slung down the sea sacks and readied their spears, untroubled. At first, Foster tried to count, but the number slipped him as the streams of men mingled into a broad line of many dozens.

They didn't fire. Instead, the mass widened and curled around the flanks, anticipating a run.

"See that you die well, and quick," Luxtros advised the others.

The hunters came within a few yards, then bent to surround them. A man stepped forward from the rest.

"It will not be so easy now to steal a ship." Vekret peeled back his hood.

"Nunoc sends their apologies. There won't be a rescue party for the shipwrecked Mattaka rowers," Foster delivered with sarcastic remorse.

The hunter who had opposed Lenet's plan to sail on Drummoc let a grin creep across his face. He held his palm low and out to his side, and Foster returned the gesture.

The furniture of the Dawn Council had already been reappropriated to Carabiner's porch. Four shorter casks sat around a large barrel. Ferrakut and Ulwet helped Parks from the sled onto the nearest seat. When he turned to offer a gentleman's hand to Kjartke, she brushed past it and positioned herself cross-legged on top of the cask beside him, which tipped precariously forward without bothering her.

She scowled at the other seats.

"This is to surprise me? I do not want to be with Dawn Council."

Parks waved the boys off. "The surprise is what my people call a double date. I told you if you got me arrows, I would get to her, didn't I?"

"You give them to your enemy."

"*Frenemy*," he corrected. "It's Carabiner one-oh-one: you want him to unpucker about something, you have to give him something else to be in charge of. All it cost me was a shitty old map, and twenty flint points to leverage the missus."

Kjartke shrugged. "If you cannot shoot them…"

The wigwam flew open. Sophia dipped under Carabiner's arm and grinned ear-to-ear. She set a pair of bundles—one flat and square, the other folded in at the corners and tied like a bandanna—on the barrel in front of them.

"These are for you." She pushed the flat one to Kjartke, who took it with a gracious nod. "You can open it."

Kjartke slipped her fingers through the knots and uncovered a long cloth that fell out as she raised it—a dress of leather, adorned with bright beads across the bosom and the sleeves, continuing down the midline in an ornate pillar that fanned along the hem.

"It's an Amposi dress. This one's a little weird for me, but I thought it would look good with your tattoos."

"Thank you. It is very beautiful." Kjartke wadded it up on her lap.

"Sorry, Parks. The whaler didn't have anything really cool that made me think of you, except the jaguar statue, but I don't think we can part with that."

"I'm flattered that my lithe and powerful figure reminds you of a jaguar." Parks untied the string and turned over a set of small ceramic jars, the lids waxed shut.

"They're pigments. I think it's supposed to be make-up, but maybe you can give them to someone as a gift," Sophia beamed coyly.

"Hell, no! This is the nicest thing anyone's ever got me." He thought twice. "Except for my arrow-thingy," he raised the ceremonial shaft from his belt and wiggled it so Kjartke could see.

"My arrowheads are being fitted right now. We had to order wood to be cut and shaped, but the men are even making me a bow. Alexicus says I can teach you how to shoot. If you want."

"Oh, I want," Parks bobbed his head.

Carabiner joined them with four bowls of fresh fish, and a larger bowl of pre-melted water—a Camne Drumlag feast.

"Kjartke, Parks," Carabiner tuned up his noble host voice, "Please accept my apologies for not doing this sooner. I can't tell you how grateful we are to finally have mature, reliable friends with whom to break bread—or boil cod, as it were."

"Amen," Parks echoed.

"I'm sure this will be the first of many occasions, and I look forward to getting to know you, Ms. Kjartke, as much as I look forward to meeting, for the first time, the real Mister Parks, stripped of those trappings of civilization that we're all guilty of holding before us on sturdy ships and in glamorous ports.

"But first, I'm sure Parks can tell you," he fixed on Kjartke, "that I'm the kind of guy who likes to air his worries and be done with them. If there's anything unpleasant between two people, I say tell them. Lay it on the table. If you don't, it'll only fester like a wound, and months later, when it finally becomes unavoidable, well, by then it's too late. What seems painful in the moment is never as destructive as the thing it will become."

Parks did everything in his power not to roll his eyes. Whatever Carabiner had planned was his retribution for the knowledge, somewhere deep down, that he had lost a precious thing to a man who would eternally be his report.

"I don't know if your people are familiar with cancer," Carabiner didn't quite ask Kjartke. "In our culture, it's a terrible illness you can't see, because it lives within the body. It starts out very small and harmless, but left alone, it grows and grows until it consumes the man who carries it from within."

Kjartke nodded. "I hear of these spirits. Mattaka do not fear them. They cannot enter without invitation. But Tunguk tell of a man lost in this way. He would hear no songs, take no remedies. Many days passed. Then he must be killed, for the spirit is captain, and it must be done with care, that it do not harm those who pull it from his body."

Parks chuckled inwardly while Carabiner collected himself.

"I think ours is different. But the point remains." He drew a folded parchment from his hip and slapped it on the barrel. "If you ever have a grievance with me, I want to hear about it. Find me in a quiet moment, when I'm alone, or with my close friends, like we are now. Let's quash this thing, before it crawls into our tukits to winter."

The cask creaked as Parks folded his arms and leaned back as far as he dared.

"You writing me up?"

"Read it."

The letter unfolded to an uncertain scrawl, etched most of the way through the single sheet.

"After all, it's addressed to you. A ship came by from Drummoc. My men didn't let them land, but they threw a parcel ashore with a few rocks to weight it and two letters," he shook the second, "closed with the wax seal of the admiralty.

"This one," he said of the one he held, "explains how Admiral Costig has been deposed for 'raking the treasury, wet-knuckling with criminals, and inciting the *s-words* to riot.' The new admirals, of which there are two, wanted to make it very clear to me that they desire good relations with the viceroy and his officers. They invite us to return to Drummoc immediately with the coal, in order to protect our lives and wealth from the farri's navy.

"As a gesture of their sincerity, they turned over that letter, intercepted from the former admiral. He writes to a certain spy called 'Leopard Seal,' who he orders to assassinate me."

An innocent horror overtook Sophia's face, while Kjartke seemed almost amused by the prospect.

"*Finally*! There's no use trying to escape, Carabiner. The Leopard Seal always gets his man." Parks smirked. "What do you want? A confession? Take it: I agreed to spy on the assistant viceroy for Costig, before my surgery, before he tried to stab me in the back. Before I knew it was *you*." Parks flicked the letter back to Carabiner. "I'd be surprised if Ghrane hadn't already warned you. He didn't just land on the Dawn Council with a winning smile and a firm handshake. But if it makes you feel better, take my seat. Post a guard on my wigwam. In the meantime, I don't recommend trusting those new admirals. Everyone over there is a jerk."

Carabiner's stern demeanor melted. "They're on their fifth admiral in the past few months. I think I'll take the advice of my councilor. You see? That could have gone metastatic on us, but if you just put everything out there—relentless authenticity—your problems have a way of collapsing in on themselves."

"Roger that, homey."

Sophia's shoulders caved in a deep exhale of relief. The four of them grinned on the verge of a laughter that none felt quite brave enough to initiate. Parks gave her a winning wink. It made him feel something of the old name again, the legend that he pronounced on ships and faraway islands, before it was laid bare for all of Camne Drumlag. The memory of having been a spy, an assassin, hired for golden wages and passed like a whisper between conspirators raised him, even though he knew it was flattery.

The weight of the task slipped away. He no longer had to hide or worry over the betrayal of—if not a friend, a familiar. Parks even felt a rush of satisfaction at having gotten one over on Costig. If anything, it was cooler to be a double agent.

Yet the reversal swept him away like a sudden current. While the conversation turned to food and camp gossip and preparations for winter, he kicked for ground beneath him. Parks felt lightheaded. He made Sophia laugh time and again, though barely present in himself. More than a mission had been stripped from him. A tatter of his own character frayed in the wind. He was not Carabiner's confidant anymore than Costig's agent. He was not a famous rogue. He was not headed home.

Maybe in time he would learn to move in this place. His tongue still tripped over rock and bird and sea. For now, it seemed every mound he raised for himself flooded and shot him farther downstream. Most of all, he no longer felt like Parks. There was no Foster to get his jokes, or roll his eyes at Carabiner's antics. All of his careful disguises had fallen, and he only awaited this last to crumble, that he could slip beneath the waters in a fan of wild hair.

Parks watched Sophia from the periphery with a secret smile. She was staying. It brought him immeasurable comfort. There was no other way to see it: Carabiner had listened. He saw he couldn't live here and bring her back at once, and with a handful of arrowheads, he made her choice. She warmed Parks because she held for him a piece of his own world.

It was one he couldn't expect her to carry for long. Parks, more than any of them, knew what it meant to fully arrive in this place, even if he hadn't done it yet. He was close. It hung like a terror in the freezing air, inevitable as winter. And it bathed him in guilt. She huddled on her cask, awkward in those ill-fitting clothes. None of the Mattaka were immune to her charm—a charm of mere presence—because she was so foreign to this place. If he had an ounce of courage and an extra leg, he would cut his way through an army to throw her through some shrinking portal with his last blood-choked breath.

Parks sat complacent. He knew that like Carabiner, he didn't want her to go. It pealed in him like a tragic bell. He knew she couldn't remain, either. Not the girl who sat across the barrel, anyway. No more than he, or the former naval officer.

A light snow blew off the western peaks and settled on their furs. The early dusk closed around them. Somewhere, against the weight of the coming season, too thick for thoughts of Spring, he felt a small lamp that he didn't know still burned shudder and go out.

Winter at Camne Drumlag came earlier for some. For these, it began in the invisible places where gods move, as a brush of air that hurries behind. In dreams. Frost grew like grizzle on the wrinkles of a tukit. A certain star winked over the horizon. Those who had dwelt longest in it knew it by their ears, their nose, their lips, while other men relished in their Autumn.

The flesh and bones of the bowl withered while there was yet food, for wise bowls prefer to be sparse rather than empty. The hand slowed. The foot slowed. The heart slowed, and beat firm in the late dawn. Tunguk watched sleds of firestone course the winding paths to pool at the harbor. It did not seem so much as in his youth, though it filled the grounds and backed up the trail. In days past, the miners would soon board ships for Drummoc. He wondered what Tannawauk would do when he returned from his hunt to find the thieves encamped with their pillage.

The Kammatuk counted the year as the northerners: many of the same day, lined up like bushels of firestone. Tunguk could no longer see it. He watched *denankikumak*, fire-king-grows-weary. The tide queen's courage swelled. She stole more and more of his fetch—*kjapadenalak*. When her succession was complete, Tunguk would mark his eightieth day. Since a boy, he had counted them like a northerner, on ships and shores under strange stars, even when the light fled the other way. Now like the fire king, he returned to the place he began, in darkness.

Ajatse and her women went about their handiwork. Theirs were the deep tides that did not concern themselves with the quarrels of gods and men. They carried on their works begun long ago—cut and stitched and knapped and stretched—works always ready, never complete. Many kings had failed to come home to them. The women hummed songs as they worked.

Kjartke, too, turned to her mending. She settled the things that required good light, so that much could be done when it left her. In her rough hands, she took Brother's stump. He cried when she wrung it. He could not escape her, for the boys were busy with the sleds. Nor did they come when the firestone runs ceased. Soon he learned that word of his alliance with Costig had moved through the camp. A name that rises on shallow words soon breaks with a whisper.

Tunguk did not stray so far in his wanderings. The forge glowed into the twilight. Many blades were fitted while rivers of green and red ran across the sky. To his mother's people, they were the eager souls who drew near, looking for a babe through which to return. But the Kapadak and others said these were the threads of Ajatse's sister Gabke, which she laid out to mend her many works. As he admired them, he saw the face of Foster also looking up, lit with color. Tunguk felt the distant tug of the bond that held them, and knew he yet lived. These same streams were the ones that showed Aku, the dog of Hawe, the way to the land of the Mattaka, as they still did for many a traveler.

The ice arrived before Ostuk and Haraket. It came broken at first, drifting past. Many worried. It was a sign that Tannawauk neared, and though they had chosen this way, the miners were anxious. Now the ships could not return. Their winter meat would be stranded. When it was fast, the Seleku family and others drove out in six directions.

Others cut the first blocks for their aklus. Most were raised at the harbor, where it would be warmer. Because Brother had upset so many, Tunguk thought it best to build theirs at Eagle Camp. No one offered help. His first aklu collapsed before he finished. The next came out ill-shapen, and he gave it to several young miners who knew the art even less than he. While he built, the trails to the high camps trickled like freezing springs until no more remained at the mines. Everyone crowded at the harbor, except for the prisoners, the dog family, and men of low status who would not fit. The camp curled in on itself and listened to its gnawing belly.

Finally, the aklu understood his clumsy intention. It arrived with a round room, almost tall enough for Brother to stand, and another small one for relieving. Tunguk lit a lamp, that the heat would settle the blocks and seal out the wind, and in that modest glow, he felt a pride that was simple and contained.

Sleds returned. The two ships had been iced in trying to round the back of Drummoc to avoid being seen. There would be stories all winter of the men who drove out to get the hunters. Many loads of meat returned, and no man was lost. Now and then, the edge of one of these stories reached Tunguk. Most did not want to speak to him, because of Brother. The Dawn Council retired for the winter, and the assistant viceroy moved to a fine aklu at the harbor. The pulse of Camne Drumlag slowed until it left him listening with uncertainty.

The breathless light withdrew with the rest of the world. The tide queen had her way. Unniakattuk—the night sailors who thundered down toward the sea—stampeded while Tunguk slept and woke, slept and woke. Faces disappeared, leaving only a company of shadows. Brother felt the agony of one who is spring-born, far from darkness. He said the walls were too close. Tunguk and Kjartke feared for him. They took turns speaking, often in Mattakatan. Like a child, the sound eased him.

For his part, Tunguk had been away very long. Even the islands of the Arm were not the same as this place. Drummoc returned to him. It reminded him of old terrors. This was the time when ghosts without ships hurried over the ice toward Urkuk, who flickered red and spit fire above the channel. Things that feared the light, great and small, thrust their heads from their hateful dens. Many tricksters roamed. They made impossible noises. Objects and trails vanished, reappeared.

The boy visited more often. In a loud voice, he proclaimed that he would not spend another winter at Drummoc. He would find a ship, or a fight he could not win. Tunguk questioned him, and when he refused to answer, it came as a relief. Urkuk had not yet sent for him. But he took the beads of his sapak in his fingers, one-by-one, and went many places.

Often, when no other light flickered, Brother sang. He must have known six hundred songs. Some, he made as he went—a practice that surprised Tunguk. With a tiny voice and a dry throat, he sang like a thin mooring line that went taut in the ebb of the sea, just holding on. There had been a time when Tunguk, too, could make a song. Now all he had left were old ones. No new voices offered themselves. They passed him over for those who could carry the song for many days. So Tunguk put in to the old ones like a deep, slow river.

Near the turning the point, when the sky was blackest and Tunguk marked his birth, an arrow of fire shot from the stars over Drummoc and struck the mountainside above the Eagle Camp. It was said to be fired by Tannawauk. Soon after, a man who guarded the prisoners tried to kill them in a sudden rage, but they overcame him. A youth from the harbor came by asking after Kjartke. He wanted her to accompany him on a journey shown to him in a dream. Tunguk told him to leave, and he headed toward the high mines. Later, it was discovered that he had killed his friend in their aklu. This youth did not return. Many of a lesser constitution suffered visions during these days. A great serpent moved through the mines, causing the earth to rumble. An avalanche at the harbor buried many bushels of coal, and several aklus whose residents barely escaped.

It was under this vengeful shroud that Brother emerged. He harnessed his two dogs on his own, and called to Tunguk and Kjartke. They drove him to the aklu of the dog boys, where he sang many songs until the Seleku and Vjarku alike came out to hear. Then he made his "caroling" for the prisoners. Three times, he visited every aklu at Eagle Camp, shouting, "Ho, ho ho." As usual, his songs had little power, but they made others glad. On the third, many from the harbor arrived to listen, having heard of this ritual. A tired throat forced him to stop just before *kjatsensak*—when the tide queen began to flee the fire king's return. But several people noticed there was no more trouble from Tannawauk. Most, but not all, attributed it to kjatsensak.

The stars dimmed a shade at a time. Guards were posted at the rations, and their bowls shrank. The boy grew restless. He spoke to Tunguk of distant glories he would soon attain. Tunguk listened, trying not to discourage the young man anymore. He knew what miseries such promise could endure. It was not settling into the commonplace that made the old. Most are common their entire lives. It was the way that dreams narrowed to match the remaining days, until they could offer little more than what stood before him. When the sun first broke the horizon, Tunguk picked the cold tears from his cheek. No crown could fill a man with such awe as that tiny rim of gold above the sea.

The Dawn Council formed again in that sliver. Their bellies had much to say. The assistant viceroy spoke of a new deal on firestone, and a return to Drummoc for the lonesome miners. He warned of the Navy marching over the ice for an attack. Anything to distract them from their starvation. The fire king had begun his return, but the seal would be in no hurry. Mattaka were forbidden from taking penguin before certain signs in the heavens. Only a few fish pulled through the ice sustained them. In times such as these, an old man would offer to go "hunt" to ease the burden on the others. But there was one who still needed Tunguk.

The boy said that he should take Brother with him. That they both came through the winter was a miracle too strange to be the work of any god. Many times, Tunguk thought there was only a little more left to do. His obligation would be satisfied.

But Brother moved well about the camp now. His longing for death had given way to a quiet. Nor could he care for himself. Akmanuak remained in place. Brother busied himself with visits to the prisoners, who found him amusing. The dog boys could not stay away, either. In the early sun, Kjartke finished the last of her mending. They had good coats and boots, again.

Tunguk had often made it known in a word or a gesture what trouble Brother and Foster were. Yet here he stood, on the edge of a season beyond his allotment. This day was not his own. Every breeze and glistening view felt stolen. Perhaps he pretended to be bothered because he could not admit he wished for more—the time they gave him, forced by akmanuak, which he could not have justified to himself without them. Or perhaps a man feels good when he believes his way has been hard.

At last, he could feel grateful. They had carried him this far, as much as he had carried them. Yet in the admission came a new worry. It no longer seemed that Brother's death would be the thing to relieve him. The illness that comes of a long period of fasting set upon Tunguk. It usually left one stronger when the feasts arrived. Perhaps it would again.

The songs of the great heroes were sung of a single man. There was no mention of Kjartke's needle, or Ferrakut's sled. Many, like a young boy who stood at the Drummoc harbor and stared out to sea, listened to those songs and thought a man could be alone. He passed from ship to ship, shore to shore, on a proud merit.

If Tunguk were young, he would sing of the many hands. The steady oar and fishmonger. The lazy man, the first to fall, and the man who knows the way. He would sing of the fire king and the tide queen, and their passage on the back of the sea. He would call a man by six hundred names. He would praise the storm for his skin, and a lie for his wisdom; an ill-luck for his fortune, and winter's despair for his courage.

If Tunguk were young, he would make his song *mattaka*—the people. He would not forget the wave people, the fish people, the wind people. He would sing unnamed in the quiet of the shroud, until any name one could speak would be his own.

In that way, he had erred. Amid the promise of Spring, he was still Tunguk, and his hands grew stiff. And if Brother were to go much farther, he would have to sing this song for himself.

17

MEN OF THE *GAIRHLE*

"At the rails, lads! We have guests!" Turrha shouted to the men of the *Gairhle*. They brushed themselves into a rough line before the ship.

"Up, you bastards!" Corm reiterated when he saw near the whole of the Navy and Marines on a march toward the harbor. It ruffled him that Turrha had given the order. He'd a habit of that, and it wouldn't draw water on Corm's ship, but now was not the time to broach it.

Most of them had been Turrha's, after all. Corm stole an admiring glance at the beauty who glimmered in every eye on Drummoc. She stood in a place of pride as near the launch as they dared. Every splinter mended, black as pitch without, and holystoned white aboard. Never had he seen a ship in such graces. More than just seaworthy, she seemed destined for the sea, for all things upon it, like a great love foretold by glittering auspices. All it took was a war.

The carpenters had barely begun work when the messenger ship arrived from Ampos. The rumor sparked on every tongue. Soon, men he had never seen arrived to beg a seat on the untouchable ship. When Corm in his bitterness hesitated, they bid each other lower, until the most desperate offered to serve without a share. Old faces, gone to Palqua, reappeared with a smile, and were told where they might find a place for their restless arses.

When the assistant viceroy's barc returned without him—an extended tour of Camne Drumlag—Turrha arrived the next morning with a sea chest. Not a sack. A *chest*, and as many loyal men as there were vacancies. Nemas and Muir resurfaced, as did Elward and Broom. No man cared to be at Drummoc when the farri's siege arrived, and all saw the visions of gold in the only whaler that might sail before the ice to pick off the rich supply runs that a war requires—and that no other ship in the fleets suspected.

697

Turrha's oath of humility lasted as long as the breath that uttered it. Yet something about a former admiral under his command appealed to Corm. They were handpicked lads, fine as any, and not so enamored with their officer that they would be bothered if Corm had to send him for a swim.

Alexicus had bought every scrap of their cargo—just enough to settle their bill and put a few coins into loyal purses. Only a turn of weather and Tawatu's pinning kept her in port now. That his imminent departure had unraveled the very navy that so abused him filled the old captain with a following breeze. The way every hindrance had collapsed at some divine nudge felt almost regrettably easy. It was only fitting that Palqua had one more thrust for him.

"Captain Cormdran!" The new admiral greeted him. "I do not begrudge you the right to seek crew or sail. But you have among you an officer who not only jumps his post during war, but does so having provided himself with ballast from the treasury."

Turrha broke loose like a yardarm in a storm. A wrathful sputter of Amposi rained upon Palqua, patient as a mollusk on his rock.

"I don't believe it. Not a man such as himself," Corm said without conviction.

"Then allow us to peer inside his trunk."

It was more a dare than a proposition. Every man there knew what they'd find, and that no captain would allow it. But Turrha had insisted on three shares—*three!*—and thus Corm succumbed to the temptation to let the two of them gut one another in his wake. When he nodded, a fight nearly surged between the former admiral and the sergeant-at-arms who came for his kit. Whalers and marines squared, but Costig wrenched it free and no one volunteered to take a spear for his officer, being greatly outnumbered.

The bead man did not have to count. Turrha swore the purse he upended was his own wage, duly saved, but it glittered too much of gold. Costig seized the coins, and his marines dragged the wailing prisoner away.

Not a day upon wave or ice passed that Corm didn't regret it. Soon, the men returned in force. "Admiral" Palqua claimed that Turrha confessed to desertion with his mates. Everyone of them had been bribed from the treasury, and according to Palqua, to formulate a mutiny against Corm as soon they went to sea.

He would not have it. Good men like Nemas and Muir denied it, and by then, Corm would drink of the filthiest bucket before he accepted a word of truth from Palqua's lips.

"Come away with them in irons, or in shrouds," Palqua told Costig before he vacated the field. The marine wisely hesitated.

"This is the way the benches fall in every port worth the name," Corm reminded him. "You think you can arrest me lads without blood? Let the first be your own."

"Aye, it will be, and yours, as well." Costig nodded and several of his men moved to stand across from Corm. The marines alone had him at three-to-one. But the assistant viceroy, in a turn of fancy, had sent back nearly every sailor stationed with the miners at Camne Drumlag. The navy present reduced them to fodder were it to come to spears, and every man of the *Gairhle* knew it.

"You will have your crew. Tomorrow." It was Tamarqan, Palqua's first mate, who spoke. "The admiral has declared that no man will be considered a jumper, up to the number of empty seats upon the *Gairhle*, provided he withdraws his name from the rosters, returns all property of Ampos, and settles his debts before departing."

Corm didn't like it, but there it was, for all to hear. He knew he should have stood the bluff. They would win if they had the nerve, but even Costig couldn't be so mad. Instead, he tried to bargain. "I've four veterans in that crew. They can hardly be deserters of Ampos. Would they remain?"

"If I allow it, will you grant me the arrest of Turrha's lads without opposition?" Costig replied.

Corm pained over it. "Aye."

At that, the original men of the *Gairhle* poured over to the captain to remove themselves from the fray. Stranded by their captain, the others were too dispirited to mount a defense. Once a company of marines had separated them, Costig came around.

"In fairness, I've considered it, and I think I'll have those four lads who deserted with Turrha."

Corm tried to respond with a spear, but Eckerd and Pitras held him. Marines swarmed the meager crew and made off with Nemas and Muir, Elward and Broom. Corm cut them all down in his visions—Palqua, Turrha, Costig, Tamarqan, every sailor and marine, like some fishing village in a raid. When the final man stood against him, he saw the source of his fury: looming and hunched under a wide leather hat, was himself. He had wavered, and there was no coming back.

That night, Corm fled through the dreamworld with a skeleton crew, undermanned, oversheeted, taking water, and assailed. He scrambled through the fight, his men falling beside him, ones he knew well and others he never recognized. At last, the *Gairhle* stood still in a squall. Her sail was full. Her enemies closed. But she did not move. He could see Taclann on the horizon, almost near enough to swim. He noticed a single rower in the bow, hidden in a rain-drenched cloak.

"You, there! Pull!" He commanded in a cracking voice. The man let his oar crash into the lock. He stood, and mounted the quarter deck. With deliberate movements, he tied three pennants to the mainstay, then turned into a bird and flew off. A second look revealed they were not pennants at all, but ragged feathers. Corm collapsed to a seat beneath the mast and blood washed to and fro around his ankles. The boat rent with each pulse of the sea upon the sharp back of a boulder of ice.

Eckerd woke him in the hold of the ship the next morning. When he climbed out, a crew of blurry faces awaited, ready to try the seats he despaired he would never fill. His relief soon fell in the shadow of a familiar figure.

"I think you will find I have assembled a far worthier crew than the appointed officer," Palqua smiled. "Perhaps you recognize some of them. Do not worry. Whoever is fool enough to call himself 'admiral' next will not have the courage to stop us, nor the law, for we sail by our own provision. Besides, I doubt you will stand so idly by should they attempt it—not if you hope to fill your benches a third time.

"I, myself, only ask two shares to Turrha's three, and would not dream of contradicting your order, or dragging a boot in the execution of it. You will find that those traits you most despise in me are equally fortunate when they work on your behalf. Don't worry, Captain. It is the voyage that makes the mates. Where we are going, I am confident we will work something out."

Corm checked his rage. Rather, it never came. Perhaps it flew with the bird of dream, or *was* the bird. But here he stood, his ship whole, his benches full, having crossed the foul winds of Drummoc.

"Aye," he growled quietly. "I think we shall."

Arthas came round and clapped him on the arm. If there was any torment intended, he let it ride beneath him and on its way. There was much sea yet to sail. No trouble for the master of the *Gairhle*.

Piled into a hand-scraped ditch, it was Rolodarn who broke the blanket of snow. He did it to spite them. Rolodarn, who wore half a dozen squain arrows, and twice the years of the younger men, got his feet first. He scorned the others to stand. All rose, but two.

They made their camp on the lee side of a foot, so that those who never woke would not die at sea. When they lay down, none had thought to see the bald head emerge, patched with frozen skin, the white beard streaked red. His voice wheezed like a saw without teeth when he mocked them. His lung had collapsed. His fingers swelled so stiff he couldn't hold a spear. With his palms, he swatted snow off the backs of his companions.

"To your feet! Once more, if you're angotaks!"

There was a little meat left, but no man asked for breakfast. A pair of scouts ranged either way. No sign of the squains to the east. But the western party returned with a grin.

"Whalers, just 'round the point."

"Did they see you?" Rolodarn asked.

"I made sure of it," Hestens replied.

The crew circled, and each stood as straight as he could. No man showed his wounds. There was no captain on an angotak ship. Any could say his course, and if he had the will, it would be done. That morning, as often, it was the course that chose them.

Chaleda had sensed the quiet urgency. Sled after sled, man after man, they dwindled. Poor hunts. Harried by squains. He had never felt such hunger, and the little taste of whale seal only made it worse. They had not fled the field lightly under the last attack, and many felt it was a mistake. But angotaks did not war with the clans, anymore than they stumbled back and forth, adrift to an inglorious death.

He had worried that they had warded off the whalers so well they would never find them again. The sighting put new color in their faces. It rushed through their ranks like a breath after surfacing. It was settled. This was the day that called them into the ice.

"You speak some Mattakatan," Rolodarn suddenly fixed upon him.

"Aye," Chaleda answered, unsettled by the strange declaration.

"Never seen so many squains."

"A war party," another man claimed. "No other call for such hostility."

"No less. Won't make the winter. Not with that," Rolodarn forced out each sentence in a wheeze. It was plain enough without seeming an excuse. "You'll treat with 'em."

Chaleda couldn't understand, from weariness or nonsense. Rolodarn saw as much.

"Capture one of 'em. Tell him. We leave him. He leaves us."

Chaleda could only shake his head in protest, the way a man dismisses a thing that cannot be, without having entertained the notion.

"Aye!" Rolodarn sent himself into a coughing fit that nearly brought his end. "Aye. Six men. Sacred number. Doran. Etxe. Pattawa. Rat. Marcans."

Of the twenty or so among them, these along with Chaleda were young and hardly nicked.

"You will need our spears. The whalers have numbers. We will go after the fight." Chaleda countered.

"Go now. Take the food. We'll eat the whalers." Rolodarn grinned.

It landed as hard as a blow upon Chaleda, for he knew the meaning. None of them would have left his brothers, either, but that this man, who was not their captain, who had awoke one more day out of spite to gasp these words, had the will to say his course.

"*Abalax*!" Rolodarn nearly whispered the name of their fallen sister ship.

Chaleda looked to his party and nodded.

"*Abalax*."

As they rounded the steep foot, six men hurried away along the northern shore of the island toward the channel. The sleds had run in tight formation since spotting the scouts. Corm beckoned them to halt.

"Tryin' to draw us into somethin', or out of it," Eckerd cautioned.

"Igonus! Aldan! See that they don't sneak back upon us." Corm had not known himself until he said it, but putting the two carpenters on watch meant he intended to fight—he couldn't spare the hammers, nor count on their spears.

He sickened with old visions. The boarding fight on the run south, the battle on the ice. He'd heard many a tale and spread his share. Now marching to his third toss with the angotaks, Corm could honestly say they were more terrible than he dreamed, and at the same time, human. When they came around the foot to find the crew drawn up for battle in the open, he half-expected to see Foster's face among the enemy.

There was no place to hide on the narrow shore. Fourteen, and not a one retained his shield over the icy haul. He ordered the stop. Their handful of shields went to his own picks. The whalers didn't approach. The harnesses had fagged them. They'd happily await the angotak charge while they gathered their breath.

But the line didn't move. The whalers tensed for battle, then lowered their spears, then sat on the loads. Some whet their blades. Others took a quick feed on their ration. Corm weighed their faces. He worried if he rested them too long, they'd lose their nerve. Palqua's bunch chatting among themselves didn't sit well. He ordered the Amposi to compose the right flank.

The scuffle over Ordacles and the argot left Corm raw. In all of the right side, heavy with Palqua's men, he allotted a single shield. The two squain lads had shown some oak, so he gave them the bows he relieved from Tamarqan and Lozeder, and placed them safely back with the carpenters and the idiot Chirim. Asdosa, lame in one arm, was expected to fight.

He felt a proper general, marching his lads slow over the ice. What he lacked in land tactics, he covered in good common sense. Each of the six shields wore a man on either shoulder. At half the strength of the whalers, the angotaks couldn't match the spread. When he saw it was all spears, he halted the line at twenty yards and ordered up the squains.

"Fuck your archer lads. Let's have a man's fight," a bald angotak jeered.

Corm motioned the squains to string up, and sent word down the line that when the angotaks charged, the whalers were to flank left. Palqua's lads tried to shade over, but Corm swatted them back. The maneuver would put their right flank in the heart of the enemy, where they'd have to make a showing.

The men must have felt it. He trembled, himself, but not so much it broke the surface. Corm pressed against Ordacles—his gashed forearm prevented him holding both a spear and a shield. The angotaks saw it would be arrows, after all. Their hand was forced. From across the way there issued a cry.

"*Abalax!*"

"For the *Gairhle*, me sons!" Corm replied, and the first arrow struck true. Even a smith's apprentice had the mark from that distance. The charge seemed to stutter and grind. There was no pace to it. Another pair of stiff legs collapsed under an arrow. Stragglers limped behind. The lads got off one more each before the whalers crashed left. Palqua's sops veered behind the center rather than meet the van. Only Moipa held behind his shield, with Banno and Lozeder.

The jumper Bosc hurled, and found his mark. The moment Ordacles caught the first blow on his shield, Corm ran his point through the man's breast. A collision spread down the line like hail on a deck. Death cries pierced the thin air. He couldn't see who fell, but to either side, the line held. Over the shield, Corm saw his left flank round the corner, and knew by the panicked Amposi voices that the angotaks had done the same to his right.

Another fell before Eckerd, and three spears darted furiously. A wild throw from one of the trailing angotaks split the shields. Nolan took two steps back, the shaft dangling from his shoulder, but did not fall. Beyond the enemy, the shields of Hogue and Pitras with their mates swept through the left flank and in moments, there was nothing more of it. Two wounded angotaks backed toward their mates. Corm and the line turned hard to meet the angotak van, which flowed away as water in the sand rushes back to the waves. The whalers' line bracketed the enemy on two sides for an instant, but Palqua's flank retreated behind Corm under pressure. The angotaks fell off to regroup, and by some god's grace, there were but half of them left.

The wounded arrived. Corm dealt the blow to the jeering man, who could scarcely raise his arm to threaten. Blood spurted out his mouth to dye his beard. He could hardly believe it. Six…now four left. The whalers encircled them for a slaughter.

But these were not so crippled. They pressed their backs and thrust with a fury that soon dilated the circle.

"Arrows!" Corm shouted.

It was a blunder to announce himself the captain. They came directly for him. Eckerd and Ordacles held the first blows. Bale, at his shoulder, countered and had his spear stripped like a stick from a child. His blood spilled onto Corm as the man tried to collect his viscera. The line broke between Corm and Eckerd, and the angotaks smashed free of the circle. Two of them hammered at the shield of Hogue, and perhaps the same who struck down Bale repeated the move to slash Tawatu. When his knee hit, they gored him with such rapid strokes that he could not topple, for one spear always held him as the other came down.

Corm's reserves scattered, and the other pair of angotaks cut down Chirim. One of the Buckets seemed poised to meet his end, but he turned as they raced upon him and delivered an arrow into the mouth and out the back of the nearest.

"Throw!" Corm ordered. He cast his spear, and others joined to fill the second angotak with spines. The two survivors saw that so many had disarmed, and ran foaming at them. Corm tried to pull his spear. A thrust forced him to abandon it. He fell down to avoid the blade, and rolled in time to see it raise again. An arrow struck the man's chest, and Ordacles blasted him over with his shield, where spears hastened his end.

The last angotak saw the tides, and a mad spirit filled him. He laughed with such abandon that his face streamed with tears. The spectacle gave pause to the whalers. It was nothing so simple as grief for his comrades, and though there was joy to his carrying on it mingled with some current that they could not guess. The fight left him. He stood unwavering, as a man granted a singular honor. Perhaps it was hasty to say that relief filled him. Theirs was a strange cult, and by their own virtues he seemed to have arrived at some culmination, launched of a distant harbor and long-sought. A babble of foreign tongue flooded out. He spoke rites over his mates that frightened the Amposi, sensitive to such things. It was enough for Corm.

"Cast!"

A host of spears sent him to his kind on what shore they sailed—pray it wasn't Manhas, Corm thought.

"Tend the wounded," he gasped, and leaned on his knees. Eckerd and Ordacles threw down their shields to aid Nolan, slumped on the ground. Lozeder and Banno appeared in a bad state, and Palqua's lads gathered over them. Moipa wandered to the edge of the field, hiding his eyes in his collar. He alone had held the right flank, but it was not the angotaks who got him. Rather, the infernal glare of the snow.

The rest of the men leaned on one another with words of congratulations. Corm caught one of the buckets staring firmly at him, and knew it was the archer who spared his life. He gave no thanks, but the slightest nod was enough for the lad.

The body of the last angotak drew him. He felt of it like a mighty fish, who after a crippling fight lays on the deck with eyes of glass looking for all the world like an impostor—no such thing, so ordinary, could have tried him like that. A few men reclaimed their spears. Nearby, Arthas looked on full of worry. To his surprise, Corm was glad to see the man had survived. The hatred that welled at the sight of him had pulled free of its knot, and it now stretched back to the day he boarded the *Gairhle*. Their victory had made him a whaler, once more.

"'Finest on the sea,' they say. Three times they tried us, and thrice broken. There's no ship who can boast that. What'll they have to say of *us*, mate?" Corm righted himself as he addressed the veteran whaler. But Arthas hardly seemed to share his pride. He appeared frozen to the spot, so that Corm actually checked his feet to see that they weren't fixed in the snow. Arthas approached the corpse belabored, spear in hand.

"I hope they say that we were men of the *Gairhle*."

Corm couldn't get a bearing on his haggard look. The crew was scattered about in their bunches. He had been on land so long that the sense a captain has for the slightest shift in his benches had gone dull. It had left him in Drummoc, too. The ship had near-collapsed under his command, with no small help from Palqua, for he was a seaman. He hadn't the balance for unshifting ground.

Now, too late, he saw that it was not only the angotak at his feet who had arrived at the horizon beneath his star.

"Arm yourself," Arthas growled. He cocked his weapon, too close to miss. Then spun about and let fly at Palqua. The Amposi swindler was caught on his heels, but Baghar shoved him aside and took the cast through his ribs.

Palqua snatched up Baghar's spear and sunk his throw into Arthas, who staggered into his captain's arms.

"*Mutiny!*" Corm shouted in an unaccustomed panic. Eckerd and Ordacles looked up from where they knelt over Nolan. It was all they could do before the lurking Tamarqan sank his spear into one, then the other.

Corm lowered Arthas and ripped one of the shafts from the dead angotak. A struggle broke behind him. Bubba and Boot locked in a tumble. Bosc fled. The carpenters tackled the squains to the deck to signal neutrality. Jenneker made a run at the flank, though it was unclear for which side.

Palqua, Tamarqan, and Juru advanced on him. Corm turned in search of allies and enemies. Certain of the men raised weapons but didn't seem to know where they stood. The three fell upon him at once. He knocked aside Juru's point, but before he could reset his spear he felt a sharp thud beneath his ribs. Palqua drove him to his back and Corm gripped the shaft with both hands as the blaggard tried to force it deeper. When Juru's thrust reared above him, he could only brace in anticipation of his end.

But Arthas, forgotten beneath them, kicked out the feet of Juru before it fell. Hogue, Fergo, and Pitras roared to his side, and Fergo split Juru's face before he could recover. Palqua wrenched his weapon free and retreated with Tamarqan. Jenneker lost his nerve and retreated, but Fergo wouldn't have it. He gave chase.

"Lads!"

Hogue and Pitras regarded his wound with horror when he raised his arms for them to lift him. An incredible warmth spread beneath his tunic and Corm could not straighten himself. He collected his spear, and staggered ahead after the Amposi worm.

"Easy, Corm! Let us have it," Hogue begged. The captain pulled free.

"Away!" He pointed them to Tamarqan. A tormented cry joined the field. Jonn crashed in from the blind side and drove Palqua's mate to the snow. He sat astride the thin chest and dropped his fists as hammers on an anvil.

Now Palqua stood alone.

Corm swatted off his men. His steps stuck as in mud as he stalked his rival, and he dared not look down at his gash. All around, the debacle foamed out. The wet blows to one side sounded from what remained of Tamarqan's skull with no sign of slowing. Hogue and Pitras finished off

Lozeder and Banno, wounded from the earlier fight and having never raised a hand. No one dared move, for fear of seeming a part of the mutiny. It had rested on Arthas, and had Arthas done his deed, it would have carried the day. Instead, Corm basked in the futility. Palqua planted and leveled his spear. He didn't seem so content with his fate as the angotak had been.

"I hope you do not begrudge me. What kind of man would I be if I did not try?" Palqua smiled with resignation.

"You were right. I knew we'd work somethin' out."

Corm slapped aside the Amposi's thrust and cracked him on the temple with the shaft of his spear. With a shout that reddened his face, he plunged his weapon into Palqua until his cloak reddened and his arms tired. Then letting it fall, Corm shuffled over and collapsed to a seat beside Arthas.

"Told you," Arthas looked up at his captain. "I'm no jumper." The whaler flashed a bloody smile, then settled into the snow.

Hunger drove Wendell out before the dawn most days. He didn't expect that it would bring relief. The widening arc of light fed him in other ways. It promised many things for the patient: the breaking ice, the splash of a hull, warmth. Long before those would come, though, other things returned to him. The wide swing of the daylight through the year brought him his boyhood, on a shore far-enough north that the cold fog brought him comfort. He had spent many seasons in places where day and night did not trade places. Always, he felt a pull or a push. To the north, or to the south, away from the busy lanes. The bark of longshoremen. The visitors of many shores and many tongues, gauging their influence. The same colors and rich trade that drew the far-flung nudged him aside to dream of those lands the sailors swore off in their tales. The busy ports that drew other youth unsettled him. They were too ordered—as if they could go on forever under their own momentum, without any man's help.

It was not safe to be out alone, he told his men. Not with the Mattaka in such a state over the food. They hadn't much understanding when they were told that they should seek their rations from the thieves who raided the stores in the riots. There had been funerals. He'd seen them on the ice. With the growing day, so mounted the unrest. The Navy hardly fared any better, but no squain would believe they didn't sleep on barrels of salt fish and seal in that hall. Yet he took his rounds, and offered his blessing that the ice fishermen may find their luck.

There should be hunts soon, he reassured himself. Etan had not returned, and there was some worry among the admiralty about the meaning of it. And though it was impossible with the frozen sea, the specter of the siege rose a little higher each day. Fears and ice aside, there would have to be movement soon, or there would not be enough shrouds in Drummoc for the starved.

A pair of lads fled up the launch from the sea—the same ones he had just seen heading onto the ice to chip at their fishing hole.

"Hoy!" Wendell snatched an arm, and saw terror in that drawn face.

"Ghosts!" He ripped free and ran toward town.

Wendell knew well that Urkuk was the last port for the Mattaka soul, and it was over the ice most of them came, for they had few boats that could make such a journey. It was not his way to scoff at another man's gods as certain sailors did. If it was so, then so it was. That concession didn't spare him the fright he got when out of the blue dawn an army of silhouettes appeared.

His knees half-failed him. As they formed into a wide line, he actually felt relief that it was not the dead, but the armies of Donnab come to slaughter them. Instead, the howl of dogs cut the vision and sleds appeared among them. In rough leathers matted with snow, the miners converged on the harbor by the hundreds.

He'd timed the night march immaculately. Most of his men had mustered ashore before the first crews ran out to meet them in disarray. The men followed their orders, waiting calmly for their rear to come up. No one raised a spear or a voice. The miners laughed at the bewildered marines. Carabiner knew they could want nothing more than to run to their wives and children. Instead, they held on the harbor grounds.

When the officers finally arrived, Carabiner stepped from the ranks to meet them.

"Apologies, Assistant Viceroy," one of the men said. "Had you sent word of your return, we would have been in a better state to welcome you."

"I'm sure of it. You must be the new admiral."

"Folmon."

"Bayochar," another man said.

"That's right, there's two of you. I got your message, and I owe you big time for outing the spy. Anything you need of me within reason—ask, and ye shall receive. In the meantime, it's no easy walk from Camne Drumlag. My men could use a meal and a few casks of hasqa to warm them."

"If we find such a thing, we'll be glad to share it. Me lads haven't seen a full bowl in two months," Folmon said, and the gaunt faces before Carabiner made him think that *that*, at least, was the truth.

"No worries, mates. I've sent a large contingent to the hunting grounds. When they get back, you'll be welcome to anything we have, once the miners and their families have been provided for."

"I shall remind you that all provisions are property of the Navy to distribute," Bayochar said.

Carabiner stared in response, until Folmon intervened.

"And provisions are a matter for the Admiral of Land, Bayochar. We welcome you, Assistant Viceroy Alexicus, but our resources are thin. I don't know that the colony can accommodate your lot."

"Accommodate? We live here. These men have homes and families. We'll feed ourselves if you want."

The officers exchanged frustrated looks.

"I notice that many of your squains carry steel. That's forbidden on Drummoc. Nor do I see any coal among your sleds."

"The coal's at the harbor, waiting for the ice to melt."

"Perhaps your men should remain there until it's loaded in the spring."

"That won't be practical. We're currently in the process of renegotiating the coal contract between the Mattaka people and the viceroy of Hiade. Nothing moves until these men are satisfied with the deal, and that contract includes provisions for private ownership of forges and steel, hunting rights, and a few other things that I won't bore you with, since you're administrators of a navy who carries out the will of Nunoc, and not policymakers, yourselves. I'm the representative of both the viceroy and the farri in Drummoc, and I can assure you I've signed off on these temporary amendments, and I'll personally hold the people accountable to the peaceable terms the agreement."

Shouts of excitement sprung from the town. Bunches of Mattaka streamed out along the edges at a cautious distance, eager for their reunion. If the admirals had planned a more staunch position, the flow of bodies from the town at their rear caused their confidence to flag.

"Look, I'm a Navy veteran, myself. I know there's nothing worse than some piss-ant official coming in from some place you've never heard of and telling you how to run things when you've been doing just fine without him. And when you've been running the show for a long time—though I know you just started—it's easy to get it in your head that the way it's always been is the way it'll always be. I'm sure you have your reservations about my policies. Hell, as fast as you're flying up the ranks, you might be the guy to change them one day. But right now, given the challenges that we face with food and a war that neither of us asked for, I think it's best if we leave the annoying details of economics and colonial administration to the piss-ants with the fancy titles. Let the real sailors worry about the battles."

The pep talk seemed to impress Bayochar more than Folmon, but it was just confusing enough to both that they couldn't mount an effective response.

"Aye, you're the official," Folmon shrugged. "But I can tell you that a load of armed squains got no place in Drummoc."

"On the contrary, we're going to need every spear we can get if you don't want your head mounted on Donnab's prow. Now I don't like guessing at where I stand. I want you to answer me in simple terms: who's in charge here? Me? Or you?"

There weren't nearly enough weapons for everyone, but Carabiner had placed all of them in the front ranks, and no one could see otherwise. The Mattaka spread in a wide half-moon around either side of the admirals' forces. Half of their strength still lazed in the barracks, and now women and children and the old, tradesmen and vagabonds from the town gathered behind the sailors and marines.

Folmon swallowed his resentment. "Aye, it's your command." Bayochar only nodded in agreement.

"Very good, admiral. I want every provision you have—every morsel of food and drop of hasqa, every piece of timber and nail, gathered right here on these grounds by midday. We're going to take a look at what we've got, and make sure that it's fairly distributed."

Carabiner knew by the nod that there was no hope of it being carried out, and learning that was his true aim. If he couldn't gain their compliance on an inconvenient order, he could expect much worse when it mattered.

"And what of the coal? Will you just leave it at Camne Drumlag to be pilfered by the farri's raiders?"

"Anyone who gets the idea to take a single lump without my permission is in for a rude awakening. That coal is protected by the blackest of Mattaka magic, by the god Tannawauk who we have propitiated with offerings, and if that's not enough, I left a select cadre of my finest men whose sole mission is to cut down any soul who tries to set foot at Camne Drumlag."

Parks leaned heavy on his spear. Beyond the quay, the ice ducked into a fog that visited every morning since Carabiner left. Night dawned to evening over the channel. His breath froze in the wisps of his beard. The quiet of the harbor at Camne Drumlag had the feel of something forgotten. It seemed like he had emerged from Winter's attic to find his parents gone, every room of the house still in the cracks of light through drawn blinds. The promise of an empty house when the outer layer of law falls away.

No, it was more. Like he'd awoken to find the world away for his own funeral. Through the winter, he'd dreamed of finding secret rooms in his igloo—rooms full of light, or clutter from a past owner, but places that he felt ashamed to have never noticed. No one told him to stay at Eagle Camp. He just couldn't think of an alternative. Winter to him was confinement. The cold walls held an air that hardly stirred. The stars sealed out the light. The good people enjoyed each other's company at the harbor, where the admiral's spy couldn't bear to go. Sometimes a rumor made it up the trail. A lamp flicked on in the igloo, and off again once its purpose was done, not to reappear for weeks.

No sleds came for him. His leg confined him to quarters, a scoot to relieve himself, maybe a few hops beyond the door. Passing in and out of sleep, the stiff blankets confused him. He tried to thrash free, positive he'd been buried alive. They spoke in tongues to soothe him. In the darkest of the season, he prayed for any change—Spring or death, so long as it came soon. He ran his hands over walls, as he'd learned to do while hiding in Drummoc. Or he sang. Anything that could touch something else.

The sound gave him shapes. He learned every seam of the igloo, every vibrating corner of his corpse. Parks didn't survive Winter. He watched himself rise from the dead, dismissed by all and left behind. He learned the shape of that, too. And once he did, it seemed just another place whose secret walls would shift to the right word.

From then, he felt more alive in the way that a thermometer reads colder or warmer. It was never good, stoked, terrible, depressed, or any of the finer shades.. Each thing made him feel more dead, or more alive.

He explained all this to Foster in the dreams. Winter, too, was full of dreams. He'd never seen a parade so vivid, so disturbing. Whatever was important about the world traded places into his dreams. He saw everything, heard prophecies, ran many miles, and then awoke to bleak confinement. Spring came to him as dreaming less, and forgetting what he had dreamed.

There at the channel, he listened for his old friend, who he struggled more and more to picture. Foster had admitted he wasn't coming back. Maybe Carabiner wasn't, either. But now he knew with certainty he was on the other side. And each day the sun felt out new corners of the mountain, and the fog drew back.

The wooden leg swung beneath him, clearing the ground by a foot. His cripple friend wouldn't take it back. It helped when he sat, though, allowing him to brace with a bent knee. It taught his wound to press against something, however light, with a little more weight each day.

Parks shooed away Ferrakut's help when he sat. Months of humility, sad glances from afar, and a fair amount of caroling had drawn the dog boys to his side again. Their worshipful tones were gone. All except Ferrakut and Ulwet left with Carabiner. Of the more than eight hundred souls, only forty remained. He looked over his inaugural council, seated on their casks. Beside the two boys, Eskimo Joe glazed over in thought. Kjartke held scowling court. Captain Ghrane had to remain with his ship. Attibatbarak retained his office of seeing to guests. Before he left, Carabiner had warned Parks that the man was impetuous. He despised their kindness toward the prisoners, and spent the winter arguing for a raid on Drummoc with anyone who would listen.

Everyone who remained was a cripple, a malcontent, a captive, or an idiot.

Or royalty.

"If I am not mistaken, it is Lady Sophia who the assistant viceroy left in command at Camne Drumlag. You were removed from the Dawn Council for your spying—a generous punishment. Yet it is you who appoint this pack of women and children and old men," Ghrane addressed Parks.

Her last-minute ascendance seemed like a desperate stroke to corral the rude personalities—himself, especially—but it was a win for Parks. Carabiner ignored his pleas right up until the morning he left, when he sent word to Eagle Camp. Satletaluk and the others had finally convinced him of what he knew all along: it wasn't safe for her to travel for a week exposed on the ice to an uncertain reception.

"Who said anything about the Dawn Council? We're a panel of equals. A flock who flies in a big clump. If you don't like it, swoop on back to your ship, Captain." When Ghrane didn't budge, Parks continued. "I propose a new name. Something way cooler than 'Dawn Council,' maybe something that reflects our more reasonable meeting time. Everyone here either works with dogs, or likes dogs. Or knows what they are," he conceded to Kjartke. "What about the Dog Pound? Alternatively: Dog Team One?" He met with blanks looks.

"We are not dogs," Attibatbarak complained.

"I get that, but it's like our spirit animal. Well, mine is also a leopard seal, but I didn't want to make it about me, and dogs are pack animals."

"Those who run far!" Ulwet said excitedly.

"Is that supposed to be a name?"

"To the Mattaka, a dog is no good," Joe explained.

"Every single one of you bases their livelihood on dogs," Parks rebutted. The two boys hung their heads in shame.

"I liked what you said before," Sophia spoke for the first time. "Council of Equals."

"'Panel.' But either way, that's severely lame. No one's gonna want to be in that group, or to do what it says."

"What does it mean, 'equals?'" Attibatbarak asked.

"It's when everyone is just as good as the rest," she explained. Even Kjartke wrinkled her nose in skepticism.

"There are ships that sail in this way. There is no captain. Any man may speak what is good." Joe pointed out.

"The only such fools are angotaks and Erdeshwe fishermen," Ghrane replied.

"Those are the ones familiar to a man if he has not sailed far," Joe acknowledged, to Ghrane's displeasure.

"How are things decided?" Attibatbarak demanded in frustration.

"You stand for them, as on a free ship," Ghrane explained. "But what is there to decide? I have my orders. Perhaps you have yours. We will see when the ice breaks."

"There's *oodles* of things. How to distribute the fish we catch. Forge production. Holiday festivities. Dog training. Employee training. Singing competitions. Who inventories the coal? Do we care? What's our plan for prisoner remediation? What happens if there's a natural disaster, or a manmade one? Communications with Drummoc. How do we know there wasn't trouble when Carabiner arrived? Do we send reinforcements? How do we make sure Camne Drumlag doesn't win the Shittiest Place on Earth Pageant for the seventy-fifth year in a row? I can keep you here all day if you want." Parks folded his arms.

"Those are all really important things," Sophia said. Parks ruffled at the likelihood that Carabiner had coached her to validate every fool so he feels heard before you smack him down. "But Captain Ghrane makes a good point. Did Assistant Viceroy Alexicus leave any orders for you?"

He blinked. "Don't let Attibatbarak torture the prisoners." He probed his memory. "Don't cause any trouble," he muttered quickly. "And make sure nothing happens to Sophia. You?"

She grinned sheepishly. "Don't let Parks cause any trouble, and don't let Attibatbarak torture the prisoners." Parks held out a fist for the man, and when he wasn't sure what to do, showed him how to bump it. "But most of all," Sophia said, "we have to turn back any ships, by any means necessary, except for someone named Lenet. When he comes, we have to keep him here, also by any means necessary. I think for now, we should stick with the orders we have, and Parks, we can talk about those other things as they come up, as long as they don't conflict with our orders."

Parks nodded in admiration. "Gold star. Look at you. First you're Annie Oakley with a bow, and now you go Queen Amidala on us. I'm impressed. Carabiner better watch out if he doesn't want to lose is coal mine manager job." Sophia flushed at the praise. "Only problem I see is that Lenet isn't coming here. He's going to Drummoc—show up and blow up-style."

She shook her head in delighted rebuttal. "Actually, he isn't. Alexicus arranged with Neal that his captain, Polc, will sail out to intercept him and explain the situation, then escort him here without the admirals ever knowing he was there."

Eskimo Joe and Kjartke found him later at the forge. It didn't bustle as it had with a full camp, but the metallurgically-inclined found a reason to light it each day, even if it was to shape some trinket. It was a new freedom for them, and from what he'd heard, something that burned deep in their nature. Maybe they feared if they let it go cold, it would be taken from them again. There were never less than a dozen men of the forty remaining members of the population idling nearby. More likely, even a Reverse-Eskimo didn't mind feeling warm.

"We did not think to see you at Eagle Camp without Ferrakut and Ulwet," Joe greeted him.

"My dogs know the way," he postured confidently. They did, though getting Barbados Slim and Winnie Cooper to pull in the same direction—or at all—while sitting on the deck was an ordeal he didn't care to mention. The snaking trail that seemed so long and forbidding at first now took a familiar bend. He'd made it most of the way by shouts and yanks of the leads before they nearly slung him over the edge to an eight-hundred foot slide. The sled lodged on a rock, and he was only able to clear it with the help of a trio of miners on their way up, who ruined his first solo expedition by driving the dogs the rest of the way.

"Kjartke wishes to speak a name."

She looked to see that the miners were far enough away.

"Daldus."

Parks waited for something to click, and when it didn't, he simply nodded supportively. "Dope."

Eskimo Joe saw that it meant nothing to him. "When a man carries more than one name, it is not to be trusted. This man is also known to Gionn as Shitstain." Parks snorted. "And to others as Polc."

"He ask that I do not say this name, except if harm come. I do not know the meaning, but Gionn say it is known. He has great fear of this man. Now I fear too, that this man make talk with assistant viceroy, and with Lenet."

"I know this name," Joe said. "Its meaning is one who belongs to the line of Dal."

"Who's Dal?" Parks probed.

"Mil was of the line of Dal."

"Who's Mil?"

Joe smiled in admiration of Parks' naivety. "Mil Daldus was the great farri who took his people across the sea to high lands after the waters came. His ancestor was Dal, and all before him were called Daldus in honor of the farri who reunited the kingdom. But after this, the sons of Mil took the name Miladus. This was so, until the brother of Aer thought to become the farri. Donn is called Little Donn by those who taunt him. He is the younger brother, but he made claims under the older line of Dal, and many sailed for him.

"If Gionn speaks the truth, this man Polc is not loyal to Tolba as he says, but to Donn. But I do not think this is what he spoke to Kjartke. It is one thing to be loyal to a farri, and another to be called Daldus."

"Polc *is* the farri!" Parks steadied himself on the old man's shoulder.

Joe laughed. "The farri is gray with wisdom, and rich in sons."

Kjartke seemed no more clear on the matter than he was. Her mouth twisted in contempt of something she had been forced to keep, that to her at least, had no bearing on her small, frigid world.

"The question is are we dumb enough to trust Gionn?"

They had no answer for him. But as he stared into the forge, a shape leapt out with the weight of a memory he couldn't place. He felt certain of something he didn't yet know.

Parks called to the man at the hammer.

"Yo! I need you to make something for me."

Corm placed a hand on Arthas' chest, at first a tender touch, then leaned into it and pressed himself up with tremendous pain. Blood froze on his hands and stirred in powder among the snow at his feet. Nearby, Boot and Hogue knelt on Bubba, subdued at the end of a knife. The struggle settled, and all eyes anticipated him. It took some moments for the field to take shape from the chaos. The mangle of limbs marred his composure—angotak, whaler, mutineer. Corm stumbled to a conspicuous heap. Ordacles choked on blood, dying atop Nolan, who fogged the air and no more. Beside them, Eckerd lay face down, done-in before he knew the fight was on.

No finer men than these two, on any ship he served. A ship with Eckerd upon it needed no captain. He took a bearing from the faintest swell or star, and rode a storm like an albatross. The crew would have left him in Drummoc, or turned on him at sea were it not for the mate. He would trade the argot and the richest cargo for the breath to return to that faithful barrel. Nothing could be plundered to equal such a man.

The spear shook of its own accord. A bellow escaped him, and Corm stomped over to Boot and Hogue.

"Move!" He hardly waited. They dove aside as he sunk his weight into every thrust until Bubba's cries fell off. Corm ripped it free and stalked over to Palqua's corpse.

"You black-fuckin'-bile-worm!" He planted the spear and held on to it as he stomped the man underfoot. "Are you mad? Are you fuckin' mad? I'll scatter your limbs to the nine shores! No daimon will stitch two bits of you back, and may the gulls that take you die of hunger! I curse you if I've sailed a day! A fate too foul to name—I speak it to the moon every night that I live!"

He wrenched the blade free and whipped around like a man in a melee searching for the next taker. Asdosa backed. He had done no more than keep up since his wound on the Gairhle, yet it made no difference. They all came aboard with Palqua, and reeked of his filth. Corm cut him down through his pleas.

Moipa crouched on the edge, shielding his eyes, unaware of what bore down on him. At last, though, the crew intervened. Pitras, Hogue, and Boot pulled him back.

"It's done, mate. You got 'em," Hogue affirmed.

"Aye, but one," Fergo led Jenneker back before his spear.

"I stood for you, Corm!" The lad swore. "Came in like Arthas and Jonn, but this mad bastard made a run at me."

"Do you think me a fool?" Corm spat.

"It don't matter," Pitras stepped between. "We need enough hands to make Taclann in Spring."

He surveyed the field. The heads that remained jutted out here and there like timbers from a wreck.

It had always been so. A good ship shed her limbs like a tree that climbed for the sun. She'd be full again, too. Since the day he took her over, she'd waxed and waned, but always found her wind. He recalled the riddle of Nurtas, his first captain: a ship changes one board in every port. When does she change her name?

Even miles away, Corm felt her. They stood upon her deck, within her lines. It was not Pitras who spoke. It was the *Gairhle*. He felt the concern in her voice, and followed her touch to his wound.

"Is it bad?" Pitras asked. A light wave overcame Corm, and he swatted the hand away.

"What do you think a ship is?" Corm challenged—he was unsure if he meant it for Palqua's lads or the whole lot of them . "Not one of you knows! A place to stow your arse? Wood and sail and rope? You're passengers, every one of you! Goin' here and there on different boards, standin' for every petty advantage. Is there a man among you who knows what it means to belong to a vessel? I grooved me bones on that ship. Every day of me life! I took her winds and her waves as me own. You think a ship is somethin' you take? Not from me! You're drifters, every one. Nothin' to carry you between the shores but a cast of fate. You have never known a ship, because you're not prepared to be devoured. I am always upon her. I am master of the *Gairhle*! You cannot take her from me, you vagrant cunts! I am the master of the *Gairhle*!"

His spear point slammed his point into the snow. With a deflating sigh, he fell to his arse before the weapon. When his back pressed into it, it became the mast. He arched his shoulder into it to admire the rigging where it passed in front of the sun, bobbing at the dock in Hustars Haven. Of his crews, many believed he had plundered her, or stolen her from a slip. He had mutinied his way to the helm. Gambled, or cheated, or built it with his own hands. If pressed, he claimed that it was so poor a thing, he did the man a kindness to take it.

In truth, Corm paid silver. Where most men got their pay with one hand and passed it off with the other, his advantage lie in the belief held since he first went to sea that he was a captain, there was a ship, and no other fate could come but that they should meet. It took most of a life, but on the back of two improbable seasons, he jumped ship from a position of first mate, with an aging captain and no other man with half the liver to deny his claim, that he would not have to wait another day.

She had her name, and he let her keep it.

Built in Batadu in the years when a raid by Paladris was a constant threat, the sea king Absha sailed to his nearby ally Netsetone when he heard they were under attack, but instead offered his services to Paladris for sparing Batadu. But soon she split from the fleet and sailed up its wake, re-raiding the gutted lands that had already paid tribute—so said the man who drowned him in detail while they waited for the coin to be counted. That fellow had won her off a captain who came on as a pilot after the previous one had been stranded in a mutiny, having taken the ship as restitution when he caught Absha with his woman and nearly put him to the sword.

The talker, who called himself Good Korrel, rowed her in after dismasting and couldn't afford the repairs. Corm could have wrung him out for a better fee, but he feared someone else would outbid him, though he knew there was no such man in Hustars Haven.

It was always the *Gairhle* he fought for—long before they met, or even leagues from the sea. She would bear his soul through Manhas. Sixty oars and a fearsome luck. Corm ringed the Atlantic while he drifted in and out of Good Korrel's blather. He squinted as the sun forged a golden sword on the waters of Hustars Haven. A bird landed on the bow, calling his thoughts back from their strange course. The same bird appeared in the distance across the ice. It took him a moment to place it, for it was no ordinary creature, but the bird from his dream back in Drummoc.

Corm never saw any omens in dreams. His own merely agitated him, and carried as much consequence as yesterday's wind. Now he forced himself upright at the massive bird in the cloak—the very one who left its bench to fly from the deck. Once he placed it, he felt a fool, for it was no bird at all. A man approached over the ice.

Nor was it a man. He rose, and the others gathered to him, alerted by his movement. The line bent to reveal another and another. A stream without end poured over a rise at a stroll.

"Mattaka," one of the buckets said behind him. Their sleds were some ways off, and there seemed little choice. The remainder of the *Gairhle* drew into a line more curious than concerned.

"There must be a hundred of 'em," Bentos remarked.

It was common for whalers to trade with the squains of the Arm, and at times to take on crew. But he had never heard of such a large band, all men by the look of it. They came up in a loose bunch and stopped at a hospitable distance.

"Raise me!" He called. Pitras and Hogue each snatched an arm, but as soon as they tried to lift Corm tore free and wrapped his arms across his midsection in agony, cursing their incompetence. They tried again under gentler leverage, and again he cried out for them to stop. The wound had set. Whatever fury had carried him this far sputtered in his throat and dribbled down onto his chest. He turned gingerly to do it himself, this way, then that. His arm slid out, and he watched it trembling of its own will, the bandage soaked through.

"Easy, old man," Hogue said with too much sympathy for the captain's taste.

He grabbed his spear for support and it fell over. A whimper escaped.

"By Euskus!" He swore, and hurried to find the way to his feet, as if it were some narrow course known to a pilot. The squain crowd closed at a walk. He felt them, and meant to meet them tall. But try after try, his innards flung him back before he could get past his elbow. Snot burst from his nose in a heave of frustration. He gripped the spear, Arthas' boot, handfuls of snow, anything that might raise him. Each returned him to his side in worse shape than the last.

He met the glass eyes of his companion, who for all his clever trade would never rise again. Arthas seemed to stare expectantly. His corpse bobbed and blurred at the edges. Corm wept. He wept that he could not just reach out and pull this poor whaler from the frozen shore back into the ship from which that scoundrel Palqua had torn him—twisted him from his companions, turned him about himself, and staked him without dignity to the ice.

The shuffle of boots near his own gave him pause. The captain rolled to his back and squinted up through tears to find the awful bird towering over him. When the hood fell back, the creature took the face of Foster, and it wore a quiet pity.

Gionn appeared beside, and the two angotaks he had battled. Hogue and Pitras and Fergo leaned over to regard him.

"What have you done to me?" Corm choked.

"Sorry, brother." Foster looked up at the tatters that remained of the crew. "Now before yall go shittin' your only pair of pants, just know that I don't blame you. Hell, me and Gionn deserve worse than we got. We came to put yall off course or underwater, but to be honest, I kinda like some of you bastards. So I been givin' it some thought. Yall seem like practical men. That means you can understand that what we done wasn't personal. My friends are on Drummoc, and if you go rampagin' through the Amposi supply chain, they don't stand a chance. That said, I reckon you're more like Gionn here: you don't care who pays you, so long as they pay.

"Here's my terms. This ain't an offer. It's a mutiny. I'm the captain of the *Gairhle*. Come Spring, we sail to Nunoc to deliver a message from Admiral Costig. Then we head north. These men beside me, they're angotaks, in the service of Ampos. We intend to honor our word by interceptin' any ship that Farri Donnab sends south to support his war effort. Whatever we take from 'em, that's yours to split. Same job, we're just tradin' one target for another. Any man who can abide by my command is welcome to sail with me. Anyone can who can't...welcome to your new home," he passed his hand over the bleak towers of Yunoc.

The Mattaka fanned out. Stone and steel emerged along the length of the force. The exhausted ranks of the whalers seemed to slump without moving. Bosc broke forward. He refused to look at Corm as he passed. A pause, a nod from Foster, and he placed himself among the Mattaka.

Tunguk and Atalkut exchanged a glance, and followed. The carpenters passed their captain on the opposite side. Corm could only watch the heads go by. Bentos and Jenneker rounded him like a shallow rock, cutting their number in half.

"How do we know you won't just cut our throats?" Fergo's rasp sounded from behind.

"If I wanted yall dead, we wouldn't be talkin'. Anybody who thinks I don't know what I'm doin' is right. I leave the sailin' to my able crew. And if you still can't stomach it, you're free to get off at Nunoc. We shouldn't have any trouble replacin' you."

"Who would you name first mate?" Pitras asked.

"Luxtros knows these waters. He'll set the course and the sails."

The answer didn't matter. The remaining men were only seeking permission from their consciences.

"Long as it isn't Gionn." Pitras crossed the ice.

Boot began his march. Corm's eyes pleaded with the men, who moved like rivulets over his surface and away. Fergo alone stopped to regard his captain.

"What else would you ask of us?" He waited for an impossible answer, then pulled free with Hogue.

Moipa knelt and placed his hand on Corm's elbow, and it surprised him to realize there was someone left.

"I did not wish to go, because I think you will say I have always meant to do so. It is true, I came like Foster with bad thoughts. My captain sat beside you. We meant to put him at the helm. I have pain that I could not fight with Palqua. But it is well. I see now you are captain."

With that, Moipa hung his head and staggered over to the others. Spittle burst from Corm's lips. He sobbed almost without noise. His fingers released the fists that he hadn't realized he held.

Gionn approached sympathetically. He felt along Corm's waist under his cloak, and came out with a little purse. With a bite, he drew it open and pulled out the shimmering argot, then turned to Foster.

"Let it not be said that Gionn don't honor his bargain."

Cormdran stilled himself. The sword dropped in a stroke.

Sophia sat beside him on the sled without a word. Parks didn't look directly at her. Instead, they watched as Ferrakut and Ulwet secured loads to several more sleds nearby under the direction of Eskimo Joe, while dog teams yanked at their stakes in anticipation.

He'd prepared his defense, but as the minutes passed, it withered in the stillness of the gap between them. The ritual denials, the sarcasm, all of it was standard fare for the proving of some officer who knew better, yet couldn't catch him on a technicality. She seemed sad, more than anything, and any less than the truth would have been a cruelty.

"Sorry," he sighed.

"For what?"

"Disobeying orders?" He shrugged.

"Like, 'Take care of Sophia?'" Parks had no answer. "Why does that have to be an order?" Sophia picked at the braided leather rope holding down the portable wigwam.

"You know, when I heard Carabiner was leaving, I was stoked. I mean, he's a great guy and all, does a lot of nice things, works really hard to improve conditions for the Mattaka…but *fuck* Carabiner." That got a snicker out of her. "I thought we would hang out more. Like on the ship. Just cutting up when the boring people aren't looking. But to be honest, I kinda feel like this place just…*tolerates* me. Like I'm some nuisance that everyone just has to deal with, who goes around messing things up. And you're the most popular kid in school. Even now, I feel like I'm breaking some rule being in your presence."

She frowned at the absurdity.

"It's true," Parks said. "I was all ready to tell you that I got some new intelligence. That dude Polc is an infiltrator for the farri. Lenet's in danger, Carabiner's in danger, the whole colony. I have to warn them. Maybe that's true, but that's not it. I don't even know where I'm going, or what's gonna happen. I just can't stay here anymore in my little wigwam of shame. I'm restless. I need to do something, even if it's wrong."

"I hate this place, too. Everybody just keeps leaving me here." She stared at her heels, alternately knocking against the sled. "Were you even going to say goodbye?"

"*Psh*! No! I don't say goodbye to people I'm gonna see again."

Sophia leaned against his arm. Others around the harbor paused at the sight, but Parks hardly cared what they thought about the pair, or who they might be in these people's eyes. Her mother. Her father. Carabiner. It hadn't occurred to him that this was not some ally of his rival, but a little girl, as stuck as him. She was more right than she realized. He *had* left her, even as he sat. Parks had convinced Carabiner. They deliberately decided that she was staying here—not at Camne Drumlag, but *here*, here. Whatever hope she had of home, they had abandoned it for her, and she still didn't know.

Sophia flung herself off the sled and hurried across the camp before he could stop her. But within the hour, she returned with Attibatbarak and a sack of belongings, which she threw at the foot of the sled.

"The rest of the Council of Equals has voted unanimously to warn Assistant Viceroy Alexicus about Captain Polc. Ghrane and his crew will stay behind to protect Camne Drumlag. We thought you could use some company."

"You? We have to cross the ice."

"Everyone thinks I'm so fragile. I made it here, didn't I?"

"Ulwet! Secure m'lady's bag to the sled." Ulwet avoided eye contact as he took the gear.

Attibatbarak stepped forward. "If we stop this man, who will stop the attack of Lenet?"

Parks shrugged dismissively. "Why is the farri attacking Drummoc to begin with? He's pissed at Ampos, not us. We're just caught in the crossfire. What if when they get here, Ampos isn't in charge? I'd say that would put us in a pretty good bargaining position, if they didn't just wave thanks and turn around."

"The assistant viceroy wish for peace. He say it is trouble to hurt Ampos. We make a deal."

"He did say that, didn't he? Hm. Well, maybe he won't be too mad when we hand him his five-year plan five-years ahead of time."

Attibatbarak grinned.

The man from the forge arrived with a leather blanket wrapped around a long object.

"What is it?" Ferrakut came over excitedly. "A spear?"

"What, a pointy stick? For a Son of Neptune? Behold, my young akjuru: the might of the *trident*!" He ripped back the cover and raised the weapon.

Parks twisted in confusion. Three steel prongs, about six inches each, flared in a V-shape with a middle finger from the end of a simple wood shaft.

"It is a big fishing spear?" Ferrakut wondered.

"No, no, no," he said to the smith. "This is…not quite. I'm going for fear and awe. This says 'oyster fork.'" He handed it back. "Is there time to fix it? I'm looking for more of a U-shape. You know, your basic parabola, with the center point taller than the other two by just a smidge. And I asked for triangles on top of each. Like little arrowheads. We need to dress it up so it doesn't just look like a pitchfork. I'm thinking double the length for the points, and if you have any shinier metal like brass or bronze, a little pop of color. A little razzle-dazzle. You're the man, you know what I mean. This is a great first effort. Let's see if we can't nail it on round two."

The public tavern brimmed with bodies. Children cried. Women shouted over one another in casual conversation. Miners stripped to the waist in the heat that sent condensation dripping from the beams onto Carabiner. He crammed just inside the doorway, and could go no farther. An even greater mass gathered in front, surrounding him and his associates. From within, harsh voices lobbed across the room. A pair of his own men argued in Mattakatan, and others came to their aid, drowning out his call for order. He had no inkling of their complaint, but everyone here had one.

The weekly airing of grievances had been mostly neglected in his absence. Now he presided over every problem for the past six months, amid the new tensions of an army of workers returning home late to hear of riots and starving families. Men wept of relatives who had been set upon the ice in their shrouds over Winter. For an hour, he'd heard nothing but these tales. There was nothing to be done. He weathered their grief with vague assurances. Ostuk and Haraket were coming with meat—too late, for those who left for Urkuk. No one said as much, but the subtext was that had Carabiner brought the men home at the end of Fall as usual, they could have forced the Navy to increase rations. He doubted they had much to give, but no sailors starved.

"*Gentlemen! Gentlemen!*" He cupped his hands. "Tell me who has wronged you, and what I can do. And if there's nothing to be done, save your strength."

They gave him what he asked for: There had been no coal issued to honor the dead. The Navy harried the homecoming festivities. Certain women demanded to know what had come of their men who weren't among the sled caravan. A seer had dreamed that the Navy violated a sacred nesting ground for penguins with a hunt, and it was taken as fact by all who heard. He was asked to placate everyone from a little girl whose cousin had been murdered by the Navy, to upset ghosts from the cemetery at Gjoraslag, to the volcano Urkuk, itself.

"What of the sailors who beat us?" A miner demanded.

"I spoke with the captain, Liam. They say the Mattaka started the fight." He had to ride the wave of a clamor. "I know! I know! I was a Navy man myself, and never has a sailor been innocent in a fight. But I'll remind you that tensions are high. Everyone is hungry. Often, it's hard to know where a thing got started, even for the people involved. Please, I urge you for the sake of your people, rest on your patience. It's coldest before the Spring. Our bellies growl. But nothing can stop it from arriving, if we can only keep our heads.

"The Mattaka are in position for a great victory, but it won't be a victory of arms. It will be won without blood, and no ground will be given. These same men who torment you will sail from your shores, helpless against the will of a united Drummoc. No ship will harbor here except on your terms, to your benefit, and the sailors will answer to your leaders. All of this is on its way. It will come as sure as Spring, unless we give them what they want: a reason to fight, a reason to crush us on the eve of our ascendance. Please. Everything that has been done to you will be repaid. I beg of you, stay proud, stay calm. If a man slaps you on the face, turn the other cheek and offer it to him. You are the nobler people. The rest of the world will have no choice but to see it."

A man pushed forward with the help of the crowd. Carabiner couldn't understand him through his tears.

"Easy, Sawi. Take a moment. Tell me what pains you."

Sawi choked down a lump and spoke in a strain. "You say offer my face to slap? These men, they—they—" He struggled for the words. "My family. Barrow Jak. He has taken all from me. The women, they have suffered by his hand. The father-in-law of my sister is slain. My wife…my sister…my niece…you say to offer them? It is mad!"

"Hang on, now. I was speaking in metaphor. Of course, what you tell me is terrible. Your family will be protected. No more harm will come to them. Satletaluk! See that we post men with this gentleman's family. They are safe," he took the man's hands, "and I swear to you, if there is a drop of blood left in my veins, this man—"

"Barrow Jak."

"Barrow Jak. This man will be brought to justice. As soon as the Mattaka people have a new deal in place, the moment we are masters of our shores, your enemy, and the enemies of everyone here, will wish they had sailed when had the chance. All I ask is that you trust me. Can you do that? When the time is right, by all that is holy to me, you will have justice, sir."

Sawi pulled away. "What is the wait? You are assistant viceroy! Strike him down!"

The crowd joined his chorus. Carabiner had to remind himself not to raise his palms over his shoulders to settle them—a call for war, to any Mattaka. But before he could regain order, a greater commotion swirled through the ranks outside. Men ran from the rear whooping. Half of his audience hurried after, and Carabiner found himself jogging in confusion until he saw the source of their distress.

A group of Navy pummeled and pulled at a boy. Mattaka joined the fight, driving them back enough for the young man to scurry free while reinforcements flooded both sides. Carabiner ran into the middle, pulling at both sides.

"Get your men back!" He shouted at a sailor.

"That squain bastard stabbed me mate!" The man answered.

"Norwet!" Satletaluk shouted a dire string of Mattakatan that sent the boy into reluctant retreat, but his presence no longer mattered. Miners darted in to throw punches at the outnumbered sailors, who slashed at them with knives and spears as they dove out of the way.

"Whose crew is this?" Carabiner collared a sailor.

"Fuck you!"

A fist cracked the jaw of the offender, but it didn't belong to a Mattaka.

"Get these lads out of here, you mannerless bucket!" The man threw his sailors into the other crew to drag them away while the miners lunged at them, waving their hands and splitting Carabiner's ears with sharp yelps. He spotted Neal and several others from Camne Drumlag among them—this must have been Captain Polc.

Only a handful of his own men helped him to break the fracas. He saw marines rushing from the navy hall in response. Satletaluk yanked him aside to a third man who had just joined.

"It is as you thought: Sagalak has not returned."

"Did he deliver the message?"

"I saw him enter the barracks," the other man said. "I waited some time, and I go to his tukit. No one has seen him."

"As soon as the meeting's over, call the Dawn Council. We've got to be careful about how we respond," Carabiner said.

"I don't think it wise to return to the meeting," Satletaluk said. "We must get you into the town, where they cannot follow."

Carabiner weighed the rushing marines, and though it wouldn't play well, he knew his general was right. It would be the perfect pretext for another disappearance. The two men guided him through the chaos into the twisting safety of the Drummoc streets.

On the fifth day, a spout of fire arced over the interminable ice. The glowing plume betrayed the cloud bank to their left as the island huddled at the foot of Urkuk. Eskimo Joe adjusted in his seat, and mashed his lower back against Parks' nuts for the fortieth time. The other amputee, Hopalong, sat between the old man's legs in turn, dangling his foot off the side of the sled. Every few swings, he swiped his boot over the ice as if he propelled them like a skateboard.

His friend Bullethead, their frontrunner, shouted the landmark to the next sled over, where Kjartke stomped out before the dogs to guide them while little Ulwet steered.

"Land ho!" Parks announced to the bundle of leather atop the portable wigwam. "Rounding Drummoc." A few moments later, a pale face wriggled out of the folds to have a look, then retreated into the warmth. Sophia traveled like a stowaway, shuddering between wigwam and sled, mummified in blankets. She spoke to no one but Kjartke. Probably, she blamed Parks for the temperature and the rattling ride. But she had come. Even in her bitterness, her presence lent the party a spark that their hunger had barely dimmed.

Six sleds and two dozen souls, drawn by forty dogs: he knew it wasn't for him. There was no more Leopard Seal. Most of them had no idea of their mission. Parks wasn't sure of it, himself. Like him, they had come simply to move. And like the dogs, they would run into the bleakest expanse of nothing if only the right person went first.

Her father told of it often. The Kammatuk thought it the rain of a red forge. The Kapadak, like most of the northern clans, believed it to be the hearth where souls warmed themselves when they arrived in Urkuk. But the Jargadak knew the fire as the blood of the life that dwells in all things. The master of this place, Oljarbaruk said, stripped the people of their flesh when they arrived so they would not be recognized, nor recognize themselves. It was for this reason that the women marked themselves with setu. That way, the Jargadak would know each other when they met in the journey lands.

The mountain still shed its fire into the evening as she approached the town alone. Kjartke had not seen it during her stay on Drummoc, but several times she saw the glow from Camne Drumlag, and now she beheld it with a quiet terror. It meant the arrival of the new dead.

Thin wisps of black smoke rose from the tukits to mingle with the distant fires. These could only be mourning bowls, lit by the miners with smuggled stone for those who had left before they returned.

It grew late. There had been no one at the Calm Harbor when the sleds left her, promising to return. No one on the trail. She did not know who of the Navy might recognize her, but her coming had so far been charmed. Now she resisted the urge to slip into the back of the town. No sailor would see her there, and it was the safest route to the assistant viceroy, where Sophia asked her to take the message she had shared with Brother.

But Brother had complicated things. In whispers, he begged her to ignore the girl. The assistant viceroy would not care who this Polc was, he claimed. The captain with the fearsome name must not be allowed to stop Lenet. Were she to go through town now, crowded with the six hundred miners who knew her from Camne Drumlag, the assistant viceroy would be warned.

She waited in the cold until the light dimmed. Kjartke walked along the flank of the tukits before joining the streets. Though she could see no one, the town felt thick. Many voices beat against the walls of the crowded tukits. Some spoke with joy, others with pain. Most spoke of worries.

Brother had not told her what to do, what to say. Only that she must find someone outside of the assistant viceroy's reach who would believe her, but not someone who would arrest her. If she chose a man loyal to Polc, she would be killed. Kjartke did not know a man who was not loyal to Alexicus, the admiral, or Polc, unless it was a man of no reputation. Tunguk had no advice. They said she was the only one among them who could say such things without coming to harm, if she chose wisely. Of this, she was not certain. It seemed they asked of a woman what men feared to do.

Her feet took her without a thought to the tukit of Ostuk, where she once lived. She did not dream to find it empty, but the quiet drew her. The window was sealed for winter. Extra blankets hung on the door. With care, Kjartke pulled back the edge. The tukit stunk of sweat and leather, and many bodies shifted without talk. She hurried away.

The tukit of Vatjate was too far and unfamiliar to find by dark. Besides, she was the wife of Satletaluk, trusted man of the assistant viceroy. She could not spend the night out of doors, though. The wind remained bitter. Kjartke drifted toward the brothels, once more unsure of what she hoped to find. The tukit where she slept with Brother and Tunguk sounded of activity, as did most of the brothels. The miners had returned with no pay, but it did not seem to slow anyone. She lingered, and let pass before her a dream of herself inside at this moment, for that is why she came to Drummoc. Someone moving on a side street startled her, and she hurried away.

Three fires burned along the row of buildings that faced the harbor grounds. She did not dare visit the tavern. It would have been easy to find a mat in the poorman's quarters, but that was no place for a woman. She would have to remain silent, and leave before dawn to avoid trouble. The last set of lamps lit the navy hall, and a pair of sentries out front.

She recalled hiding with Gionn while the guard made his rounds. No guard needed to patrol the prison now. Kjartke found the lamps there dark. The marines before the hall were so close. She had to remind herself they could not see beyond the edge of the lamp. Her finger pressed along the hole where she had fitted the key. It did not seem possible. Yet the handle gave when she tried it. The small clank of iron froze her, but the men didn't move. With great care, she eased the door open and slipped in. The floor remained littered with stone. Kjartke probed with her toe for someone who had already found this place. She climbed through the walls into each room. The other two doors were locked. None took refuge here.

Kjartke lowered herself into the corner of the middle cell. A faint air hissed through the openings near the roof. The stone was too cold to touch. The walls did no more than block the wind. Here, she shivered and fell asleep knowing that at worst, Oljarbaruk waited for her nearby, and could not mistake his daughter.

She jolted awake before dawn. The heavy door wailed and struck the inner wall. Kjartke wedged into her corner where the torn wall met the stout outer stones. Rocks skipped across the floor at a kick. She gripped her knife. A hand closed on the portion of the wall still standing near her face. It shook until several stones fell loose. They clacked again, tossed in a pile. The hand came back for more.

"You rush. Are you afraid?" A girl said in Mattakatan.

"Why go slow?" Replied a youth whose voice was new to manhood.

The winter had sharpened her ear. The sounds told Kjartke the shape of them as the boy piled rocks in the shirttail of the girl. When she heard the door close again, she realized she had scarcely breathed.

She lay a palm on the handle and the other against the door. It seemed a stubborn thing. Heavy. Not like the tukits of her clan, which yielded many ways to a person or a breeze. The buildings of the halots felt of foul magic, in that one could not be sure whether they might enter or leave. She understood a prison, but did not see how the many firm buildings of Drummoc were any different.

A group of men passed. Kjartke eased out as they faded—fishermen, going to break open their hole. There was no other food for the people, and the dark teemed with men heading for the ice. Hood drawn, she followed, and watched the reluctant sunrise. It had come a great distance, like herself, and worried to show its face. Kjartke feared she had run out of places. Would she always slink and sleep in crevices? The ice stretched far. Lenet said he would return. If it were so, there was still much in the way.

As the light gave her the shoreline, she saw another who watched the sea. His dress made him a marine, but he stood alone. When he caught her looking, he made a gentle smile. The sight cast her into the spirit world, where she passed through another great door, the first in her days, to find herself in the navy hall. Costig sat at a table, ready to hear the reports of those who would betray the Leopard Seal. As the man led her in, it was this face who passed her to take his leave with a friendly word to Costig.

Kjartke stepped to the side until she drew near.

"Always comes back, don't it?" He nodded to the sun.

"Please. Do not arrest me," she said flatly.

"And why would I do that, love?"

"I have slept in the prison."

He laughed. "A terrible crime, aye. I told 'em we got to forge a new key. Me word don't carry like it used to."

"I do not like a door. But it is a good place for your captain."

"Oh? Which one?" The man amused himself.

"Daldus," she said, and the cheer left his lips.

Three masts ran up over the ice, adorned with flags and strips of leather, anything that would flap in the breeze. Dogs bayed from the shadows of the covered decks, and the wigwams around the ships emptied to greet them. Parks had seen better motels, but no sight as welcome as this gypsy camp on a frozen wasteland.

"I would never dream that my deck should be rid of you," Ostuk beamed from the *Juhketappat*.

Parks looked anxiously back at the outline of Drummoc, not three miles north. The sled party scaled the ships with such glee they left the dogs at the harnesses. He groaned like an old man getting out of a recliner and fought for his feet. The points of his harpoon bit the ice and raised him. He plucked it free and wrinkled his nose. They had made the "V" into a "U," at least. The thin spikes didn't seem any longer, though, and it still looked like a pitchfork with a shrunken head—less diabolical and more of a Depression-era farm vibe. It would probably stick a man if it came to that. But the weapon inspired all the awe of a day laborer trotting behind a baler.

It annoyed him that no one offered to help him onto the false deck, and again when he got most of the way up and two men hurried over full of pity to rob him of the last act of his accomplishment. The frustration of the road ended soon enough when Ferrakut brought him a bowl of meat—actual seal meat. His stomach had subsisted on nibbles of old fish and gurgles of air for so long that it made him sick, yet he downed every morsel and relished the discomfort of a different sort.

"We will have more soon," Ostuk assured them. "The sleds took all they could carry, and hid the rest. A day, maybe two, and we will send word to Alexicus to feed the people."

"Hid from who?" Eskimo Joe posed it as an afterthought.

"Costig. He gives our hunters trouble. But Haraket is reinforced now."

"Maybe Leopard Seal can talk to him." One of the miners set the deck loose in mocking laughter. Parks blushed and joined in with a sarcasm that nevertheless accepted the barb.

"We do what we must, until we can do otherwise," Ostuk squeezed his knee in consolation.

"Tell this to Alexicus," said one of Ostuk's party, and again the men laughed but with more reserve.

Attibatbarak said something in Mattakatan. Parks only caught some form of the words "speak," and "wife." Some of the men looked at Sophia, hunched alone over a bowl of seal within earshot.

The chatter faded until the only noise that remained was the light buzz of Eskimo Joe snoring in his seat with seal meat on his belly, and the north wind that brought the low howl of dogs from Drummoc.

Soon after the black of Winter first blinked, they emerged. In the first hour of twilight, furs drawn, they leaned into their creaking loads. Foster paused at the opening of the cove to look back at the barest outlines of men. Voices rolled after them over the ice. The camp at Yunoc, obscure in the near distance, sung them off in gentle tones—the same thing, over, and over, and over.

The song ran after them like a rope, fed by hand until it was cast off altogether. He'd heard so many awful things about Winter. Already, he had a hard time remembering anything specific. It came like a welcome night after a brutal workday. In the first weeks he paced and scrounged for pastimes and conversations. The momentum of the previous months spun through him. He ducked between the tukits, determined to keep everyone's spirits up. There were a thousand things to prepare. If anything, Winter was too short.

Then one day, like a ship suddenly run aground, he slammed to halt. Foster slept. When he woke, he visited Luxtros, and before stopping off at Vekret's, he slept again. How long, he couldn't say. Days were hard to separate, but it was days before he made it to Vekret. Each task got drawn out until there were fewer and fewer in between rest, and at times, the breaks seemed to butt up against one another.

Foster's will collapsed. He forgot about crews and ships, curled under a blanket, and ceased to exist. He slept so much he hardly wanted food. If he dreamed, he didn't remember. The months of open boats and bloody fights, icy trails and a distant pressure he couldn't name, disasters cresting like waves one after the other—all of them broke against the cliff of the season, and he slept.

As soon as he was up, he felt it pulling him down again—that dog-tiredness that lived deep in the bones. He'd spent his waking time like pay on shore leave. Those days of long sun seemed a gift for him squander, but in the dark folds of Yunoc, it came due. More than once, he wondered if he might die from sleep, then shrugged, and let it come, anyway.

Foster saw less of Gionn. He was a snoring lump, or absent. Their clocks hardly chimed together, and when they did, it was a delirious exchange between two men who stood outside the lives that led them here and invested nothing in any particular future; two commentators making passing remarks with no connection to the events they muttered about.

Foster half-expected to rise one day to find it was Spring and everyone else had left months ago. But well before the cold eased, Vekret roused him.

"Do you still plan to sail?" He managed a grunt of affirmation. "Then you must go."

It was a long way to the *Gairhle*, and they had to find her before the ice budged, or they never would.

The others had been making preparations, waiting for the captain to say the word. Now they snaked into the channel with their sleds. He found himself wishing someone would go ahead of him. It was too soon, though. He shouldn't need a guide yet.

Foster wanted nothing more than to look back, to be sure someone still followed, but he didn't dare. Forty men watched him for a sign he was anything less than a captain—none of them more doubtful than himself.

The company was quite more than Wendell expected. Head after head ducked into the lamplit brothel until five sat between himself and the exit.

"I'll have the fair one in the middle, and the rest of you can earn your wage elsewhere," he joked impotently. Not a soul took his leave. "Did she not tell you I said 'alone?'"

"She did, but she also mentioned you wanted to speak with one 'Daldus,' and not havin' anyone by that name in me crew, I decided to bring a selection," Polc repositioned one of the lamps so that it better cast its glow beneath Wendell's face.

"Keep your advantage," Wendell shrugged. "And you're wise to deny it, at least until you've heard me out. I've been over your moves from Payaqura to Camne Drumlag, and though they pricked me nose, none have been any less wise, given your task. A tall order, me son. You must be the youngest lad. But he's got no shortage of confidence in you, and from what I've seen, well-earned. I've read your papers, had your beads verified, checked off your rosters, and spoken to the looser elements of your crew. Still, I'd never have cracked your hull if a squain woman hadn't accused you by name."

"A squain woman? Well that settles it!" Polc and his men had a chuckle.

"Aye, a Jargadak, part of that troublesome lot that came ashore with the dog ship." Wendell savored the guarded ebb of their amusement. "The kind who don't know Dal from Mil, or Donn from Folmon." He was certain that Polc was clever enough to see the relation between a mutinous admiral and the present farri. "Yet she knew your name, and asked nothin' for it."

"Did you give that whore a copper to bring me word and lend us her hut? She asked nothin' of me for hearin' it, either."

"Aye, I considered she may have been paid, but by who? She's been with the assistant viceroy all Winter, and it wouldn't be him, would it? You two are fast mates. I followed Neal here as deep as I dared into town last night—farther than he could have gone without a purpose and a guarantee of his safety. Alexicus may well know, but if he does, he don't care. Fortunately for you, neither do I.

"I've given me life to this service, and much of it to Drummoc. You've been here long enough to see what it's got me: forced against me mate by Folmon and Bayochar on false terms; me own Marines too timid to step in when it turned into a proper mutiny; a colony unravelin'; squains at riot; an official usin' 'em for his own plunder; division in the navy hall; indifference in the barracks. We both know what happens when the warships arrive with spies already ashore.

"You probably think this place is a punishment. You'd rather be sent to Ampos, or at least Jarrahil, or Eribath. You and every man ever stationed here. Lads only brag of Drummoc for havin' survived the passage—no worse in all the seas, of that I'm sure. But I tell you, this little island, young

Daldus, this place is an anvil. It made Barduk, and Vitjuk. Think of the names never uttered until after they visited these shores: Crannan and Fain. Atxlchar the Far-Skipped. Ito and Nuanta and every king of Pone. If you can weather the hammer, Drummoc will make steel of you.

"I'm too old for that, of course, but me blade will still serve. This was once a land of Atlantis, before Ampos seized upon a moment of weakness, and so it shall be again. All I ask is your generosity. I'd make a fine official somewhere warm like Nunoc. Or if you were sufficiently impressed, perhaps Ampos."

Wendell waited for the response he knew could not come, not yet.

"You're too clever to commit so soon. Allow me to explain. Somehow, you ended up in Payaqura with a fine ship and no more than eight men. These will be four of 'em, and they're no ordinary sailors. Your personal retainers, handpicked. Some of the finest, most trustworthy barrels in all the kingdom. Mentewat is another. You plucked him by design at Ampos—I'd be curious to know what grudge turned him against his king, but that'll do over hasqa another season. The rest of your men you hired at great expense in Payaqura. There's no way to recruit so many decent lads so quickly without a royal purse. They don't know who you are, and they'd turn on you if they found out now, to avoid bein' lumped in as traitors.

"If you meant to warn Hiade of Tolba's revolt, you'd have gone straight to Nunoc. You came here because Nunoc's too stout, and because it's the coal traffic and the fine Mattaka steel you mean to stop, and that's best done at Drummoc—let Nunoc rot! It's good you kept it to your most trusted lads. The others blabbed enough as it is. The only problem is that you haven't got any numbers to support you just yet. You're stuck doin' what little you can to encourage any sort of turmoil that may scuttle the Navy. If your talks with this assistant viceroy work out, that may just do the trick, but it'll probably cost you a fine title in return, and do you really care to give the squains the kind of leeway that he does?

"'Course, you can have her by bloody battle if you like. But give me a few cold months with the men, and you'll see just how few are willing to die for Tolba's pride."

The four sailors hung motionless on their commander like slack lines waiting for him to bend one way or the other. Polc's mouth peeled in a broad grin of little teeth, no two of which touched at the sides.

"Wendell, is it?"

"Aye."

"We could have used you over Winter. With tales like that, it wouldn't have been half so dull."

"Then you deny it?"

"Unimportant men like to imagine their little affairs have become the concern of kings. They hear whispers in every breeze and uncover secret plots in the latrine. My only concern is that other fools might fall as mad as *they* are."

"You're askin' who I've told, and it's no one. Can't speak for the squain woman, but I don't think there are many eager to listen to her. She probably got it from the Leopard Seal or one of his mates who recognized you. Two of those are gone now, and our fugitive prisoner is exiled to the mines. Me madness is safely contained, for now. So what'll it be? I'd name a price, but I'm afraid I'd underbid."

"If you're done, mate, me conspirators and I have a watch to report for." Polc and his men began to rustle.

"If I leave this hut without an oath, it's straight to Folmon. He won't pay as handsome as the farri, but copper outweighs an empty hand."

It was enough. Polc sat again and found the first mate with a knowing gaze before fixing it upon Wendell.

"Don't worry. You won't leave this hut."

Neal drew his knife, but before he could move across the floor, Wendell put two fingers between his lips and let out a piercing whistle. A fainter version of the same answered from outside. Neal looked to Polc, who lay a hand over his wrist.

"Wise of you lad. I'll see they don't treat you so rough." Wendell dipped his head politely as the sound of boots on packed snow whirled around the brothel walls.

18

BATTLE OF DRUMMOC

Aymos and Amachar flanked their Admiral of Sea some yards out from their crews, drawn up for battle. Their scouts had nipped at one another for days. They shouted their worst, and shook spears when it was too far to shout. Bayochar nearly caught them camped in a hollow, and only the alarm of a dutiful sentry spared Costig's force from slaughter in a night raid. As yet, no one had managed to draw blood. Costig did not believe that irritation would last.

He met them unarmed, against advice. His marines and Etan's lads held a rise behind him. The Amposi captains had dug in their heels— even they weren't fool enough to attack the high ground. But they couldn't hunt, and every day they avoided a fight was one more they went hungry, while Costig had yet days of food.

He stopped as close as he dared, and let the breeze from the eastern slopes of Urkuk swirl between them. They stood not far from the farthest point of the island, nearly opposite the colony and days from reinforcements. Fed though he was, the winter had thinned his cheeks and cast them purple, dusted by an ashy skin that had frozen and thawed too many times to heal. The season had not passed without some difficulty. By the look of the men across from him, though, he knew there was no hardship that would not seem a blessing to some poor soul.

"Let it not be said that Admiral Costig offered no terms," he shouted in a winter's rasp. They'd not ventured far from their men, and they would regret it. Costig would be sure the lads heard every word.

"I demand only the mutineers, Bayochar and Aymos. I've no quarrel with the rest of you, and you'll retain your rank and pay. But make no mistake: should you hand them over, they will be killed. Any man who cares to join me company may do so now, or during the fight.

"Differences aside, whoever survives must get word to Drummoc. The squains are in revolt. They've killed Etan, stolen a ship, and skirmished with us on the huntin' grounds. Drummoc must weather the siege, but before she can do so, we must tear out their leaders by the roots and set a terrible example—be they squain or favored sons of Nunoc."

Bayochar snorted in amusement. "Very well. Our terms are not so different."

Costig raised a hand overhead and paused, then let it fall. Behind him, the distant line of men quick-stepped downhill in formation, barely more than half the strength of those gathered opposite.

"What are you doing?"

"Bringin' me lads closer so they can hear," he said wryly.

"Amachar, kill him," Bayochar flicked his wrist in Costig's direction. The captain hesitated.

"He's unarmed."

"All the better."

Amachar turned for his crew. "You kill him."

"Aymos!" Bayochar snapped. The captain readied his spear, but something about the smile on Costig's lips held him. A brush at Aymos's shoulder startled him. Two stout men swept past to stand behind Costig, and these were not empty-handed. Over the Amposi's shoulders, a sailor from Amachar's bunch broke ranks and deserted the field. Another man, then another followed after him as the charging force lumbered downhill. Aymos backed away toward the safety of their lines. Bayochar found himself alone across from Costig. He tested the spear in his hand—an easy throw from that distance. But something in the old marine or a twitch from the two jumpers beside him gave Bayochar doubts. He showed his back and hurried to join the others in the battle line.

The sight of the admiral jogging, though, was all it took. Amachar's crew peeled toward Drummoc. The rest of the men broke like a floe in the spring sun.

"What do I call you lads?"

"Nemas."

"Muir." They answered him.

The latter offered up his weapon. Costig took it in his thick palm, and they trotted off after the sailors as on a merry hunt.

Among the sleds returning from the hunting grounds laden with meat, few rejoicers noticed the one that arrived from Drummoc. Brother waited alone, leaning on the fishing spear that brought many jokes to the people. Attibatbarak drove the dogs, and when he stopped, Brother threw his arms around Kjartke in a manner that was not customary to greet a woman, even a wife. She bore it with her arms at her side, and when his strength left him, he spoke.

"*Pannaketsittiukpan!*"

Kjartke laughed. "Who told you to say this?"

Tunguk turned quickly so Brother would not see his smile.

"Whose funky seal meat did I promise to taste this time?"

"No seal. But if it is true there is a man-fish nearby who is not equal to your spear, I fear for him."

Attibatbarak and Kjartke laughed from their bellies. Brother's eyes did a turn through his head. "It's good that the locals still find him funny," Brother said very loud. "Consolation in his final days."

The word she brought was good. The man called Polc had been arrested. Many of his men claimed no part, and the admirals knew it was true, but they could not decide who to trust, so every man of the crew was taken in. The Mattaka had been forced to rebuild a wall of the prison. They found that many stones were missing, and the second wall could not be repaired. It caused anger among the people when the food and coin the workers were promised was not issued. A fight came over it, and a man was killed.

But this news fell in the shadows to the Mattaka. They sent a sled party to Camne Drumlag to share the bounty, and someone took word to Drummoc. The people migrated over the ice like a colony of seal to beg food. Haraket and Ostuk gave with a generous hand. Nothing was withheld.

Tunguk watched the people stream to and from the three ships. The sun rose fast, and reports came of cracks and pools of water. Some said the shores near the hunting grounds would be loose any day. But here, the ice remained fast. A man on foot would be able to find their way for many weeks yet.

The more people that came, the deeper the trails that called the next. Before the ships lay the tukits, dogs, people at their crafts. Meanwhile in

Drummoc, the Navy sat with empty bellies, fearful of what might come. Marines roamed the hunting grounds. Spies pulled tight their cloaks. The dreams of the people went to tall masts, sunburnt sails on the horizon. It was no good to fear so distantly, Tunguk thought. Nor to take relief. Too many currents whirled together, and the best sailor could not say where he would emerge. But the best did not try. They looked to their ships.

Tunguk laughed again at Brother and his silly weapon. Then he went to find Ostuk.

Aber hesitated when the climb reached the unfinished sections where the sky opened up through the scaffolding. Aermon turned his head in disgust and pressed the lad's bottom upward.

"Hoy, cunt! Get your arse outta me face!" Aermon fanned his nose. "Did you shit your pants again?" At ten, he had a year on his cousin, though by size it seemed more, and he didn't often miss a chance to torment the babe of the family.

"I never shit me pants!"

"Then why's your name Shitstain?"

"It isn't!"

"That's what it says in the registers. I had 'em change it."

"What? You didn't!"

"Aye, 'Shitstain Miladus,' it says. 'Shits his pants like a squid when he's frightened.'"

"Eat your lies. You pulled me pants up until it dredged me!"

"Your fault for not wipin' your arse properly." He swatted his cousin on.

They picked their way up the crossbraces and shimmied a beam the width of the tower until they reached their favorite vantage—mercifully unimproved by the builders all year. Whatever barbs flew on the way up, a quiet truce always took them as they scooted out on the scaffold and smelled the first of the breeze whipping up over the water. The old lighthouse gleamed in celebration at the far end of the harbor. This, the new one, sat farther inland and on the lee side. When it was done, it would be thrice the height of the one erected by Mil, and taller than any that still stood above the waves.

From their perch, they could just see the crisp edge of Hadalsbank where it dropped off toward the city, though the better part of the palace and the temple lay obscured by the southern wall of the lighthouse, already finished as was the builders' custom with the wall opposite the sea.

North and west the harbor glittered, broken by a hundred shadows.

"Me father's fleet," Aber said excitedly, tracking Aermon's eye.

"And mine. And every fish boat that can bail fast enough to stay afloat. You're lucky we let 'em in. Mum wanted 'em to harbor at Calda, and she nearly got it."

"She's an idiot."

"Take it back, or I'll throw you off," he snatched the lad's collar, and laughed as Aber near pissed himself.

"I take it back!"

"Look at 'em. Paradin' like they just drove the Nuitatls aground."

"They did! Well, even better. They conquered the Fomraigh!"

Aermon snorted.

"Mil couldn't do it. And neither could *Aer*."

"Ha! Me father says they took Aftinoc, hardly big enough to dig a latrine, much less a tin mine. The Fomraigh got no navy worth the name, so what of it?"

"And set a port on the mainland. On Fomorlann, itself."

"By a fingernail! It's walled on three sides, and they have to fight back the tribes every time the moon turns. Two years gone, and a couple timber ports to show for it. But if that's what your old man calls 'conquerin',' let him burn blubber to Hadalis."

"The Fomraigh are giants, and you know it. If it was so easy, why didn't Aer go himself?"

"The farri don't kick down anthills. But now that your brothers have made men of themselves, perhaps he'll send 'em to do somethin' more important—like besiege the flightless birds of Drummoc!" Aermon laughed so hard the scaffold shook and he was forced to gather himself.

Aber pouted while the two lads surveyed the city. The people indeed looked like kicked ants. A torch flared at every corner and the censers ran in thin streams that joined a gray cloud crawling low over the market on its way to the steps of Hadalsbank, where Donn and the procession had passed that morning. The lads were supposed to receive them after their lessons, but Aermon had talked his cousin into skipping out on Harald, their tutor, knowing that he could make Aber do anything once he agreed to the first indiscretion.

Bragamil looked a proper city now, in less than a hundred years. The sanctuaries on Hadalsbank loomed with an ancient power that disputed their bright new stone, as if the old rites had been borne over the Atlantic in the fire horns that fled the waves. The apartments of the high city sparkled half-empty during the sailing season. Meanwhile a thousand tongues eddied through the streets where the men of the nine shores converged in search of fortune, favor, and the grand sight of the city: the leg of Hadalis, salvaged from the original statue and standing yet higher than most buildings though it broke at the thigh. Hadalis, a glimpse of whose leg alone cured a man of the ability to forget.

Some still called it Atlantis. Aermon's grandfather preferred Bragamil. He said that they were no Eribath Islanders, renaming every convenient place. What was gone was best let go, and what was to come would arise of itself. Besides, the old bastard never failed to point out, the whole of the kingdom bore the name now, and stood so tall upon every shore that it could never drown.

The warships were easy to spot. Any trollop could tell their sharp, slender lines from the barcs and fishing boats, and Aermon had practiced since he was a lad to make the rarest distinctions of anything under sail at a distance. Though most of them rafted together in threes and fours, he knew which belonged to his mother's brothers, and the farri's alabaster fleet. Much of the navy was strewn over the seas, but the best moored in reserve at Bragamil—a mere twenty ships. It seemed a shameful number, but there were plenty abroad, and it was Mil who decried the "boasting of tinderbox navies," wherein sea kings put as many things afloat as they could muster, whether or not they sailed or had good crews to man them.

Donn added another twenty-five—it seemed he hadn't lost one—ten of them docogons, a pair of which floated like foaming dogs at the entrance to the harbor. The others crowded to the sides, lashed to Aer's and teeming with sailors eager to be set loose on a proper city.

The common boats of every build and rigging filled out the modest harbor so that they could hardly maneuver. Now and then a puff of breeze brought them a few shouts from the water. Aermon studied Aber's hateful little face, and a sadness came over him. He'd been the big lad, had his way of things. But he also enjoyed an admiration from his younger cousin that few afforded him. Now the lad's cunt brothers were back. Perhaps they'd fancy themselves too grown to harass Aermon. He suspected that Aber would hardly bound at his heels for much longer, though.

When he glanced back at the harbor, there came a swelling of bodies like the bubbles at the end of a wave. It spread along the quay and over the decks, bending here and there. Some rush of glee had overtaken the men. Aber saw it, too, but it seemed too queer to remark on.

Moments later a faint blast from a shell wafted up to them, and it must have had something to do with the sudden jubilation. A second came, and a third in cadence, followed by a roar of voices that broke off with a lull in the wind. Bragamil gleamed in the short shadows of the midday sun, making him squint. Aermon grew restless, and started down the frame of the lighthouse.

The streets had the feel of a festival, empty in the wrong places and cracking with excitement in others. Most of the doors stood open in a gesture of hospitality, save a few that had too much to offer. The reds were out—reds of victory. Even the poorest managed a fingerful of dye for his wall, or a flapping rag. The indulgent wore it in their hair if they didn't have the natural crimson of Aermon.

There seemed a strange charm on the lanes that though they heard the citizens and saw a flash around a corner here and there, they hardly crossed another's path on the way to Hadalsbank. The lads curled wide of the main stairs, where they'd surely be harassed for their absence. Aermon had a certain luck about him that kept him out of the worst of things, and it seemed to steer his shoulders now. Their fathers would have a thrash at them for missing the glorious march to the Pied Temple of the Never-Setting Sun. It was all Aber's idea, he reminded himself with a grin.

A lad flew around a corner and nearly rammed them, hurrying past with his fair blue ceremonial tunic bunched in his fists.

"I'll have you killed, idiot cunt!" Aermon screamed after him.

Another bunch of women tore by in the same haste. The cousins frowned at one another, and detoured through an alleyway to get as close to the servers' gate as they could. When Aermon poked his head around into the street, a dog ran loose, drunk with freedom. One of the hunting hounds, to be sure. He hated dogs and they knew it. Aermon froze until the beast passed. No one came after it.

"Where are they goin'?" Aber asked. Several red-faced sailors stumbled down one street over, clinging to their mate.

Aermon didn't have a chance to answer before a flood of people inundated the streets. As if some lock burst, a mass of souls spilled in every direction. They pressed themselves against a wall to avoid being trampled. By the dress he could tell that most had come from Hadalsbank, and to the last, they clawed over one another in a panic.

"What of it, you cunts?" Aermon demanded, but no one even looked at them. He felt the tight and tiny grip of Aber on his cloth. "*Hoy!* I'm addressin' you!" He snatched at a girl and caught her wrist. Her eyes flared, and he thought he'd seen her before. A plump woman just behind ripped her free and shoved her on.

"Fire?" He said in a half-thought, and the suggestion registered with him. "Fire!" He grabbed Aber. They skirted upstream, though he couldn't say why. Curiosity, perhaps, for there was hardly a person or thing upon that awful rise that he wouldn't have watched burn.

He was sure of it, more with every step, and at the same time a doubt built in him. The tall apartments near the foot of the high bank blocked much of the sky. Aermon peered between their tops for some haze to confirm it.

"Over there!" A shout cut through the rest. Three sailors-at-arms, none of whom he recognized, pointed at them and pushed through the crowd. Aermon pried people out of his way, but made no head. He hardly knew what the men wanted, but they could go ram themselves. He flung Aber through one of the open doors.

They found themselves in a room surrounded by a little family of four generations, the able men off somewhere at their trades. Aermon broke the awkward standoff by barging deeper into the home room-after-room until he found a window big enough. They rolled out into an alley, jumped in another window, and skipped through an empty apartment until they emerged on a street. The first bunch of people passed like a wave, and in its trough they hurried to a low wall and vaulted up on their bellies.

There, they at last caught sight of the servers' gate on the northeast corner of the bank. The doors hung open, and it wasn't long before another group poured out. Aermon lifted the gentle slope of his nose and sniffed. No smoke yet. They could perhaps go up the stair for a look, though if there were more coming, it was no use.

He dropped back down and looked along the wall in frustration. Some distance off, a stiff man of gray hair and an impractical robe hailed him.

"Aermon! Lads!"

"Fuck, it's Harald!" He said to Aber. "Back that way," he urged his cousin the direction of their arrival.

"Wait!" They heard the tutor bleat to no avail. "There they are!" He called to someone as the lads ducked into a home. This one was occupied, and not by the owner by the sound of it. Fierce tongues and the upsetting of furniture issued from several rooms off. Aermon and Aber moved in the opposite direction until they found the storeroom, and from it, a servants' chamber and the postern door.

The ruckus of whoever moved through the place neared them, and they hurtled into the street, slamming into a pair of stout forearms.

"Harald! Onaster!" Pitshin collared them with his steel-benders, cracked and red as bark. He was Aermon's own Master of War, a slave taken during the campaign against the Aleoatni where he earned his office at the expense of many Atlantean warriors. Aer treasured him like a brother. His lessons were tougher than Harald's, but full of humor and a life that radiated well-beyond his short stature, for there was no hint of regret in him about his fate. He rather poured himself into his task with a sense of honor that made Aermon all the more bitter when he found ways to shirk his drills in spear and sword and wrestling.

Harald loped up, slender and meek of spirit when other men were present. The eldest brother of his mum, Onaster threw his shoulders back against his age and made a fair sight with short sword and shield. Aermon reeled at the thought of what brought these three into the same company.

"Blaggard!" Harald's lip quivered at Aber and his eyes shimmered with fury. He drew a knife. "For Aer!" He wailed as he lunged clumsily at the boy. Aermon stepped in his way and wrenched his arm aside. Only then did Pitshin and Onaster intervene in an afterthought.

"The lad wouldn't have known," Onaster growled as Harald straightened himself and made a show of his wrist hurting, grave insult on his face. "And he may yet be of use."

The men shoved them on like barrels before a stevedore.

"Where are we goin'? Are we to guess why you've gone mad?"

His uncle laid a palm across the back of Aermon's head. "Aer should have listened to your mum. Sent the bastards to Calda. It'll be Farri Donn kickin' your head through the streets if we don't make the harbor."

The two lads hardly grasped the lay of it, though they understood well-enough. They took each others' hands like little ones and ran before the men. The doors of Bragamil slammed shut now. What simple folk managed to escape Hadalsbank filtered off until for a moment the side lanes were clear again. Aermon tossed his head for an answer. His father and uncles were to host Donn and his men for the rites after battle, then off to a feast that would last eight days, though the poor character of the victory hardly warranted it. Donn wouldn't dare spill blood upon Hadalsbank—no sooner had he thought it than he knew the lie. Aermon should have been there, as well. Every subject of any name at all. How could they let it happen?

"Uncle! Where are the others? Mum, and her brothers, Admiral Neidis, the Bronze Tongues…"

"No use waitin' up for anyone who attended the rites. I was more than happy to excuse meself from that fuckin' pantomime when you two didn't show."

He wanted to press for more, but a clamor ahead sent Pitshin to the front with his boarding spear. Soon, the streets flooded with souls staggering away from the harbor, which yet lay at some distance. Dozens and then hundreds poured uphill like streams joining together. Unarmed sailors ran with open gashes, throwing aside women to speed their escape.

"Paladris is havin' his way at the ships," Onaster declared. "I'll fall today if only I deal his blow first!"

"Do we mean to sail?" Aermon asked incredulously.

"You are too fat to swim," Pitshin retorted.

"You couldn't bring about a daille in that fuckin' mess! We saw it from the lighthouse."

"Let us hope our crews are farin' better than we did at the temple," Onaster said loud enough for the lucks to hear.

"Aermon, we'll be seen!" Aber protested. He looked down the wide streets and saw the flash of wood and metal begin to arc over the heads of the stampeding crowd.

"Pitshin," Aermon agreed. "We got a better way."

There was no better pastime for a bored lad of Bragamil than to sneak down to the harbor to watch the strange ships come and go with the wild men of the nine shores. Aermon dodged many an obligation there. Twice that year, he even stowed away on some promising boat, and the second time, made it out of the mouth of the harbor before the panicked crew discovered him and turned around.

Through the Mariner's Quarter where everyone remained a stranger, a brief pass through the shipyard and back again just before the sea god's temple, where any man could call upon the name he chose. Then the fish stalls, and instead of going direct, a run inland to the back of the shipyard again. It was as empty as it could be that day—half-full of wrecks and with less cover than he was accustomed to.

Now the water came into view. The launch was a jam of dailles and fishing boats trying to land at once. They'd wedged into a single raft of tangled rigging and broken oars. No one could get through, and in their haste to clear the bloody waters, men and their sons climbed from ship to ship, abandoning their boats to flee the fight.

"We'll never launch anything!" Onaster swatted a man aside with his shield when he paused to gawk at Aermon. "And the warships are tied to Paladris' fleet."

They worked their way to the edge of the pile-up, where men leapt ashore. Among the retreating commoners, a handful of sailors slashed at anyone they could reach. Stripped to the waist, barefoot and helmed, they wore their beards long from a two-year cruise. The first ashore almost didn't notice Aermon's fellows, so drunk was he with the raid. He waited for a companion to catch up, falling over one ship into the next, until their feet slapped mud and they made for the party.

Their wind was spent, though. Pitshin tore the spear aside and drove his own through the first, while Onaster laid the second down with a blow from his shield, then hacked at him for more strokes than he needed. Another sailor made land behind, but this one had a fresher look, and Onaster recognized him as one of their own men.

"Hoy! Where are you goin', mate? Turn and fight!" The man, though not wounded, gave an apologetic look and swerved around them. Another fell into the shallows and splashed their way, drenched in blood. This one, Onaster didn't let by.

"What of the fight, lad?"

The man shook his head. "No fight. They waited until we drank our fill, then they cut us down on our own decks before we could even arm ourselves."

Some terrible vision flashed within Onaster and he did well to hold himself. "Is there no ship that held?"

The man drifted, then snapped-to like a loose sheet. "No. Dunno. Maybe the *Delba*. I was in the water, but it looked pitched up there: she and the *Bronze of Eusk* were tied in by three of Paladris' ships, but those are your brothers' own lads." He trailed off.

"Then that's our ship or our pyre. Join us! For Aer!"

The sailor regarded Aermon and hung his head. "Too late." He limped past.

A cry rang from nearby, and another of Donn's sailors hung from Pitshin's spear. He withdrew it and planted the tip in the mud, then peeled the buckle that held his excellent short sword—prize of prizes— and slung it around Aermon.

"We will see what you take of your lessons." He slapped the lad on the round belly, a hateful habit that flushed Aermon as red as his hair.

The five of them climbed onto the lowest ship in the heaving pile. She was nearly capsized from pressure behind, and they went over the far gunwale like a wall. No one had feet like Pitshin on a lurching deck, and they followed him deeper into the smash-up, wetting their toes, stepping aside the falling corpse of an enemy as the Master of War cut a path—to where, they could not yet see.

Ships twisted and punctured. The bow of a harbor pilot ran up vertical atop a little shellfish diver. Shorter vessels pressed under and filled with sea. All around, the fearful revelers climbed from one to the next, and where a man fell in he had no hope of avoiding the crush of ships slamming in from the back.

Most of them took no note of Aermon and his bunch going the wrong way. There were a number of smaller crashes in the open water, and hardly space to maneuver. The wiser skippers stayed put, shoving everyone clear with oars.

"That's the *Delba*," Onaster pointed to a raft of five ships adrift not far from the launch. The *Delba* was a docogon herself, with a swift fifty-oar raiding ship to her starboard: the *Bronze of Eusk*, one of the vessels by which the Bronze Tongues accompanied the farri. Then came two of Donn's darraigs, and on the far end, one of his docogons made a firm bracket for the smaller ships. Aermon couldn't see much over the sides, but it looked like a proper toss underway on the *Bronze*.

Decking cracked beneath their feet. Aermon's leg fell through, but a yank from Onaster freed him. They had to leap a gap of water to reach the next ship. Aber just made it. Chubby Aermon shut his eyes and flailed. The gunwale caught him in the gut, knocking the wind from his lungs as Harald and Pitshin scraped him over the side. He gasped on all-fours while they dragged him on. At last, they reached the back of the woodpile. A number of ships angled for a way to dock without getting smashed. Pitshin waved down a slender barc that looked a local build— Calda, or perhaps Ottarbaghan—yet ran two masts and the tapers popular along the Black Shore of the eastern Atlantic, and atop the prow, a Macuna standard. Her deck brimmed with knotted stacks of antlers that could not possibly make Macuna. Probably arrived from the Black Shore during the festivities and hadn't the chance to unload her cargo. Aermon felt ill when the ship showed her side and it became clear he would have to board the fetid tramp.

He felt a small consolation when the crew received them and he saw a good half wore the ebony flesh he anticipated, confirming his suspicion. The captain was one of them, certainly no man of Macuna. He probably carried a pile of standards and raised the one that best suited him at any moment. Aermon and Aber crouched beside a hillock of horns from a dozen breeds of deer while the men had low words with the captain.

Soon the oars pushed free and spun her bow for the *Delba*. They scarcely avoided several collisions in the mad traffic, and finally ran over a little daille rowed by a pair of lads Aermon's age. The locus of activity centered on the *Bronze of Eusk*, and when they approached, a contingent of men gathered at the bow ready to gut the first boarder. But Onaster greeted them, and when they saw who it was, they caught a line and hauled the five of them over the stern. Aermon noticed that the antler ship, the *Vau-Patl*, separated but hung close.

"Keep low, they still got a few arrows," the sailor on deck warned. From a crouch, Aermon could see a darraig protruding from the bow of the middle ship in the raft, where it sunk its ram. The crew aboard flung grappling hooks, while Aer's navy tossed them back. The enemy couldn't board without being slaughtered, nor could they be shook loose.

The decks at their feet washed with blood. They could not step without stubbing a toe on the slain. Aber bleached like a sail in the sun.

All around the harbor, the clusters of warships teemed with the crews of Donn and his admiral Paladris. Theirs floated like an island surrounded by thirsty raiders. Only the trouble of separating ships and the madness of the harbor prevented the whole lot of them from crashing over their deck.

The sailor who took them on explained that Bannett, the first mate of the *Delba*, didn't like the way that Donn's lads were going about. He stayed sober, and when he heard the first horn blast, cut the mooring lines as the enemy rushed on from the shore. He fell in the first clash, but it freed them from the shore where most of the sailors had gathered, and the crews aboard had a bloody fight with Paladris' brother-in-law. But the *Delba* lads were the handpicked men of Ablas, the most formidable of Onaster's younger brothers, and of course those Bronze Tongues who had not gone ashore made a hearty match for the enemy. The survivors were but twenty-two when they cleared the ships, and right away they found themselves fending off boarders.

"We got to free one these ships," Onaster thumbed towards Aermon and needed no further explanation.

"Well, we're a fair hundred short to crew that docogon," Harald said with a forlorn spite.

"Do you think me an idiot?" Onaster snarled back. "Fire the docogon. We'll take the next in the pack—Paladris' fifty-oar. Fire all these ships. Give me smoke, lads! We run for the sea!"

"There's two docogons blockin' the mouth," Aermon added his woes to his tutor's. "It's bound to be Paladris himself in one of 'em."

"I pray it is," his uncle said, then shouted the little crew into action.

Another of Donn's darraigs split loose from a raft nearby and pointed their way, picking through the confused waters.

"Aermon," Pitshin almost whispered. "Have you no words for your enemy?" His Master of War had long taught him that the fight begins before the first steel splits flesh, and the reminder made him ashamed of the fear that held him immobile. A vision of Hadalsbank, rising in the distance, flashed across the city. He couldn't see it clear, but his father, his mother, all who were not present stood just as frozen outside the temple, unable to do anymore than he. It felt the battle was in the hands of Pitshin and of Onaster, these few men. He didn't dare draw the sword at his waist. He couldn't even see them dead, couldn't imagine a drop of blood staining the garments of his family, his servants, his slaves. He felt only the absence, and the meaning of it that could not yet be spoken aloud.

"*Hoy*! You ripe cunts! Everyone's waitin' on you! You're the only shits not done fightin', if fightin' is the same as thumbin' your arseholes, waitin' for some other cunts show up to face your enemy for you!"

Pitshin threw him down as the arrow zipped through the place he stood.

"Patience, little Aermon!" A man answered from the other ship. "We're gonna make you last a *long* time."

His heart burbled with fear. Why had Pitshin made him do that? Now cries of his name resounded through that ship and across the harbor to their companions, trying to free themselves from a fishing boat.

Smoke billowed from the hold of the docogon as the men shoved her free. Pitshin almost carried him to the next darraig, where his uncle wrapped a cloak around him and sat him in full view of the approaching ship. Little flames licked at the *Delba* now, and then the *Bronze*. They set their blazes on the middle ship, where the enemy had sunk their ram, and as soon as the crew retreated to the last unburnt vessel, Donn's navy climbed aboard. A few arrows sent Onaster's crew to the deck, but they made no attempt to board. Onaster separated their ship from the raft, falling back to escape the spreading fire. The rowers nudged her nose around the docogon and slipped into a veil of smoke with the antler ship closing fast on her aft quarter on the starboard side.

By the time the enemy darraig split the haze in her wake, the *Vau-Patl* was peeling free on her own course out of the mayhem. Onaster leaned over the bow, shouting at the little boats to clear a lane. They could hardly comply. He ran around where he could, and swiped hard against a hull, only to bounce off another from the opposite direction. There could be no deliberation, however. The few oars at his disposal churned mightily, and the sails were prepared for the moment she cleared the mouth of the harbor. Through it all, a somber lad sat amidship with his cloak drawn, Pitshin hovering like a fickle luck.

She broke clear of the worst traffic and dug deep for the last obstacle, the pair of docogons that guarded the narrow way to the sea. At a hundred-twenty oars apiece, and more arms on deck, there could be no fight. The smaller darraig had to hope she could slip past and outsail them. Donn's men soon found clearer waters as well, though, and with a full complement of rowers, began to overtake Onaster.

The docogons saw the little runner, and nudged their rams like wet noses toward their prey. Onaster was born at sea, though. He aimed for the gap between them, that if they missed, they would collide with one another. The standard-ship countered by offering her broadside to his ram in order to block the lane. Slow as they were, their full benches matched Onaster stroke-for-stroke. The wind blew in from the sea, giving the docogons the weather-gage. A little dark figure stood motionless at the rail of the standard-ship while the crew sprinted about behind him, and Aermon didn't have to wonder who it was.

Onaster steered to port as though to slip behind Paladris. The sister ship went broad as well, staggered just behind the clever admiral, to seal the passage while the enemy darraig closed within a ship's-length behind the last captain of the line of Vin.

Pitshin left his charge to wait at the bow. The rowers pulled a final stroke and let their oars fall as they armed on deck. A crack skipped over the water. Paladris' hooks were already flying when the ram struck his side. The hefty ship had little to fear from a darraig rowing into the wind.

The first man onto the ship fell, then the second, and the third. It must have taken a dozen before they could get purchase on deck with Pitshin fighting at the van. Yet Aermon knew there were plenty to come. The enemy darraig scraped alongside from the back and soon had her hooks in. The battle still raged on a swarming deck when the *Vau-Patl* slipped around the docogons, and Aermon lost sight of his uncle, his Master of War, and his young cousin in his former place, wrapped prominently in a cloak.

Harald put a hand on his knee where he sat at the foot of a pile of antlers. It was cold and weak and seemed to drain his spirit rather than console him.

"We're not free yet, me son," the tutor said. "They'll be after us again before sundown. And if you think they'll give up in a few days, a few months…"

Aermon let the lecture dissolve around him with the smoke and the cries and the crack of wood until they reached a distance where only the soul of Bragamil stood like a jewel, its lighthouses at watch, the roofs upon Hadalsbank wavering in the heat under the clearest sky that couldn't name a single complaint.

The midday sun of Hiade stalled somewhat lower. Inattention led Gionn to outpace the sled during his rest, and he found himself at the front of the column beside Foster. Their noble "captain" wore a wrinkled look of worry as he scrutinized every shadow for a sign of their old track and often stole a peek back at Yunoc while she could give a bearing.

He'd found himself in some strange company over the years. No motley bunch should have surprised him. There was never an opportunity to be picky, yet he couldn't help marvel at the crude assemblage. A squain or two was one thing. More than half the crew seemed a cruel prank of the gods. Each successive boat struck him as a test of his capacity to tolerate absurdity. They couldn't have been handpicked any better by Donn's sorcerers, gathered round a spread of his old garments and toenails.

He'd meant what he told Aber back in Drummoc: he wanted no satisfaction. From the day he sailed out of Bragamil—the very moment he left the harbor—he ceded all claims in his heart. There were no titles that could flatter him. No honor to be restored. Gionn never once sought a return to the gleaming shores of Bragamil, frozen with all he knew in a vision that stood eternal, unmarred and unmoving.

Never had he given a thought to raising a crew. He didn't make a beggar of himself at the foot of some rival sea king. Harald could never let it go. He hovered in a poor lad's ear with stinging encouragement. Gionn, on the other hand, could not rid himself of it fast enough. On the few occasions his tutor caught him weeping, he let the old fool think it was for his family and his city. In truth, he wanted nothing more than to melt into the world like a chunk of ice into the spring sea. If all those ships and all those men had only known the sincerity of his resignation.

It was the sea that wouldn't have him. He tumbled and took on shapes as ice does, but could not melt. A careless word or a familiar face always found him. Only a few times did he hear that old name, but even when he passed like a wandering oar from deck to deck, he was fouled by an old manner he couldn't shake. Call it the influence of Nachreann, or his cross-grained nature. He always felt a man apart, and in the end, those he met concurred.

There was no wife for him, no red son, no steady route to sail during the season while he dreamed of Winter's hearth. He had no stomach for proper adventure. Every passage felt like little more than a stay of execution. Gionn stumbled through each humiliation with minor annoyance as he awaited the arrival of his terrible death.

He could not say he enjoyed it. There wasn't even a shimmer of mischievous glee that he had lasted more than two decades. He felt nothing, nor a possibility of it. His luck carried him, he knew not why, biting and kicking to seven—now *eight* of the nine shores. Having made no effort to redeem himself, Gionn found himself among whalers of Ampos and angotaks, an idiot from America, and a flood of squains. They marched for a ship whose stated occupation was to sail against the Navy of Atlantis, shorthanded and unsupported.

Upon the heights of the bank above his city, he saw the leg of Hadalis planted firm in the soil of Bragamil. Gionn laughed. Having gone through considerable trouble to see it otherwise, here he stood. It was true, then: to set eyes upon that weathered limb cured a man of the ability to forget. And if he did, the sea would remember for him. Across the still ice he saw the waters of the old harbor as he left them, with the calm of the city carved into the sky.

In a hot burst, the facets of the waves caught the reflection of Hadalis upon this throne. They sparkled around the shadows of ships at anchor, and the air stirred over the rooftops. The city stirred. He felt the pulse of it, like waves running beneath the pack ice. The people found their tongues. Barrels rolled over stone and rung out on decks. The market broke like the cries of birds. He smelled incense in the streets, mingling with the odors of life. Amid the bustle along the Sun Road and the coming and going of barcs, an absence lingered. It moved like the rest of the city. Down the steps of Hadalsbank it flowed, foaming on the stone, coursing the Sun Road, spilling into the side lanes, it lifted the ships in the shipyard before emptying into the harbor.

Bragamil gasped with relief. The eternal city, borne across the waves by Mil, came to life and though it had a sense of the old capital, he did not recognize it. Gionn felt the edge of a cold breeze chill him from the farthest fetch.

Foster caught him weeping, and stared without a word. Gionn brushed ice from his cheek and let him believe what he might.

Aymos' heels carved a pair of channels in the snow that ended without ceremony where the two marines dumped him at Costig's feet. It weren't much of a battle. A handful of dead lay over a mile or so of ground, where they were overtaken each in turn. Amachar and most of his crew gave up the run and defected to Costig. And while most of the other crews escaped, he did send a few quick lads ahead to pluck the choicest feathers.

"Where's Bayochar?"

The marines could only shrug, too fagged to speak.

"All the same. We'll meet him round the other side."

Aymos squealed a plea that choked off with a thrust of the admiral's spear.

"You shouldn't be in the street." Satletaluk arrived with a long lock of black hair, half-an-inch thick and knotted around itself at the top. "It is enough that you stay so close to the harbor. And with a window. If the Marines come through now, we may as well guide them to you."

"You make it sound like I'm hiding. Besides, Ostuk would be insulted if I refused his hospitality." Carabiner puffed his chest against the cold.

"We still don't know what has become of Sagalak. If he is in the prison, he enjoys the company of Captain Polc."

"Do the men believe the charges?"

Satletaluk gauged the question, as if considering all the reasons it might have been asked.

"Ours do not care. Theirs? Many do. Some think only that it is a bad time to be your mate."

"Ours would be wise to take an interest, then. It matters more than they can know."

Flecks of ice on the grizzled face of the Mattaka councilor set off the shadowed lines that seemed to deepen each time they met. Again, he took his time formulating a response—a habit that Carabiner was never fond of.

"There are many other things to occupy them. The Navy knows of Ostuk and the food. It won't be long before they demand their portion. They grow bolder by the day, and their bellies scratch at them."

"Which means we can't have too many men running out there at once. They could use the opportunity for a raid if they don't think the prison is full enough."

"It is not arrests we must fear. Since we spoke last, three of our men are dead. Two were caught stealing from the blacksmith—this is what the Navy says. We know only that they left the ships with their arms full of meat. Their families saw nothing of it."

Satletaluk extended the lock of hair to Carabiner.

"What's this?"

"Another man—a lad, some would say, in his first season at the mines—he went to see about his pay for his work on the wall inside the prison. The men gave him harsh words, and said he should be grateful he was given work, and that his pay would come with the rest of the builders when the ships arrive from Nunoc. He left without arguing. Then the captain came—I don't know which one. He said the men were too soft on the lad, and if they weren't careful, the builders would think highly of themselves and start a riot.

"Some of the sailors caught up with the lad, and made threats if he bothered them again. He just listened. Probably afraid. But other miners saw them yelling, and surrounded them. You know the kind of man the Navy gets. Sometimes, they come because they have spoiled their welcome everywhere else. They can't make it on good ships. They're slow, or timid, and just want to impress the old hands. Now that the miners are back, we have the numbers, and they starve by the day.

"They said he was under arrest, probably to make the people leave. The people refused. So the captain shouted at the sailors to let the lad go before a fight started, and more sailors ran toward them. I don't know how he came to be stabbed, but now his family mourns."

Satletaluk placed the knotted hair in Carabiner's hand.

"His mother sends this for you."

Carabiner took it with a solemn touch.

"Thank you."

"This is our way: if you accept, you promise to avenge the death, or you must pay with goods worth his life." Satletaluk kept his fingers on the end of the lock. "I know you look far. The people will not regain themselves by blood. I stand with you here. We must be patient. But he is not the first, and I doubt the last. My own nephew walks Urkuk. You must know that not everyone is as wise as you, Alexicus. There is a balance to keep, and I fear we can't be too still."

"It won't be long, now." Carabiner pulled the hair free. "Tell her she was my word: Ampos will have no choice but to make a new deal with us, and when they do, every man who has wronged the people will know justice." He tore a dangling strip from his coat and tied the strand so that it hung from his chest for all to see.

By the time the sled appeared on the horizon driving hard over the pack, the ships were locked up tighter than the deacon's daughter. The gypsy camp of wigwams with their arts and crafts fair that had prevailed around the three icebound vessels had been swept aside under Eskimo Joe's suggestion. That morning, when the daily line of Mattaka beggars failed to appear, the old man's spidey-senses lit up. He roused Parks, then shuffled through the camp whispering his warnings in what voice the winter left him.

Within an hour, the battlement of whale ribs and wigwam leather that lined the false deck doubled. Those women and children who had moved in to be with their men stowed themselves in the hull of the *Juhketappat* or Carabiner's barc.

Only the dogs remained on the ice. Their tethers ran on board where the men could loose them with a flick. Behind them, Parks estimated that more than a hundred men lined the sides of the ships. A combination of stone points and re-forged tools awaited. They were miners, crews who sailed with Haraket and Ostuk, even some refugees of the hunting camp that lived on the far-side of Drummoc. In the middle of the line upon the false deck of the center ship, Parks leaned on the butt of his uninspiring harpoon, standing as comfortably as some merman warrior washed ashore.

He imagined a great trail of dust kicked up, like a posse thundering across a desert of the West. There was nothing so dramatic, and the sled took ages to pick its way behind a single team. Long before anyone could make out the driver, Ferrakut shouted with glee. He knew his brother's style.

Norwet had not shown his face despite knowing that the Leopard Seal was near. Parks had heard about the boy's family, and wondered if he were grieving, or just betrayed. That morning, the visibility stretched clear to the coast, three miles away. The reason for the visit appeared almost a mile behind the sled before the message could be delivered. Several disorganized tails of men marched like black smoke streaming over the surface.

He was the last to see them, but it didn't stop him from shouting in his best John Wayne. "Look alive, boys. We got company—*takal*, twelve o'clock." He risked the word he understood to mean "enemy," and no one laughed, so he was reasonably sure it wasn't another trick these jerks planted in his vocabulary.

The dogs, long-alerted to something unusual, opened a barrage of angry howls when they caught sight of the team. Norwet turned to drive parallel to the ships, shouting his warning in his best Reverse-Eskimo Paul Revere. Milak ran behind, collapsing on arrival. Saunlauk and Siguvik hopped off the sled, all four of them armed with stone spears.

A dog fight broke out when the boys tried to tie up their team with the others. No one helped them, and by the time they had secured the dogs and scrambled onto the ship, the visitors were forming up in a line of battle. The dogs greeted them with rage. Soon there were two more fights among the frustrated pack and no one to pull them apart.

"A company of marines," Norwet breathed heavily to Ostuk and Tunguk. "And three crews. Folmon. Liam." A flash like sun on polished ice glinted in his eye. "And Barrow Jak."

"Do not kill Barrow Jak," Milak pleaded. "Leave him for the Seleku."

"For the Vjarku," Norwet corrected. "It is *my* knot."

Parks had no idea who this Barrow Jak was, but two days prior, a smaller group showed up with the Mattaka to request food for the local military. Haraket sent them away with one female seal.

A man Parks had never seen stepped forward, though not too close to the dogs. Norwet told the others that this was the new admiral. Parks felt a pang of sadness for Costig. Whatever had come between them, he liked the dude, and couldn't help but think they were on the same team—not the Navy, or the secret saboteurs, but some other loose affiliation of men who knew each other by a gleam in the eye wherever they met in the world.

"Leopard Seal! The Navy has always fed the Mattaka. We've come for our portion, and we won't leave without it."

The miners seemed amused that Admiral Folmon thought Parks was in charge. Ostuk patted him on the shoulder to make room for the captain at the battlement.

"It is the people who feed the Navy. Or it was, until your sailors came like raiders and drove them to find refuge with their brothers."

"Blame Costig for whatever Etan did. If but one of those beasts bites me lads, your families on Drummoc will not be grateful."

Joe spoke softly so that only those near Ostuk could hear him: "A hungry man is a desperate fighter. You must not let them leave with nothing."

Ostuk motioned to his crew, and within a few minutes, a single frozen seal carcass arced just clear of the dogs and spun over the ice. Folmon scowled a bitter reception. He split his forces and sent them around either side of the ships. On the starboard, no dogs blocked their way, but there was also no false deck—only a high side and no easy way up. The Mattaka casually swapped to meet them. The marine in charge walked up and down, looking for a clean way in, and gave Folmon a gruff shake of his head. They couldn't besiege them, and even with greater numbers, an attempt to scale the sides would be a slaughter.

They returned to the port, where Folmon waved for someone to grab the seal. A pair of men rushed forward, and their enthusiasm infected the others. More came to help, and someone made a slice in the blubber with his knife for a sample. That set the men into a frenzy that reminded Parks of the dogs at feeding. Sailors and marines shoved and grappled for position to cut a piece while their officers shouted in vain. Folmon had to back out to avoid being crushed by the forward push. The dogs almost calmed at the sight of a greater ferocity, pacing and whimpering as the men tore away pieces of the animal. Elbows fought for position. A punch flew. The miners watched in silence while the crews stripped the carcass to the bone. Someone snatched a piece of skin off the ice and scraped it with his bottom teeth. Even the captains gave up and forced their way to the meat for a choice cut. In half an hour, there were only bones and entrails. The former were gathered to haul back for soup.

The crews backed away from a wide pink stain on the pack. Their faces looked smeared with shame and no less ravished.

"The ice won't last more than a month or so. We'll have plenty of game, then. But we won't forget you, Ostuk. Your dogs won't be of any use when we come back with rams."

"And what will you eat for a month?" Ostuk asked. "I have pity on you. Don't come back again. We will send a seal each day with the people."

"Last chance to open your larders. Or this—" He indicated the remains of the animal, "is what you'll find of your kin."

The new admiral and his men turned for Drummoc.

The miners grew agitated. A hundred discussions broke out in a Mattakatan that the winter had hadn't left Parks any closer to understanding. Joe alone remained unconcerned. When he dismissed a plea from the boys with a word, Norwet turned to Parks.

"Barrow Jak marches on our families!"

"The sleds. We can catch up."

"He wants you to catch up," Joe said. "They draw us onto the ice for a battle. Folmon cannot harm the people on Drummoc. There are many miners with Alexicus."

"Who refuses to fight. He wants to meet with lawyers and negotiate trade deals."

"Leopard Seal speaks well. Alexicus is rich in words and has little steel," Attibatbarak interjected.

"It is a fool who would give up his advantage to meet a stronger enemy," Joe said.

"Then it sounds like the decision's been made for me." Parks slammed the butt of his trident on the deck. "Can somebody help me down?"

The younger of the sisters gave a piercing cry and clung to the other, a girl just in her womanhood. The pair fixed like stones upon the snowy depression of the dog camp. It was the older who wept. The little one's eyes peeked out in grim defiance at the company of men who had arrived like spirits at her home with their steel. The dogs sounded off, as surprised as the girls.

Three men came running with stone points. Their feet stuttered when they saw the intruders, but they held course. Sawi shooed the girls off toward the huts. Two lads watched keenly from the entrance of a hut.

When the sisters were gone, Sawi's tone sopped as wet as a beggar's.

"You have taken much from my family. Please. No more."

"What I've come to take, you haven't got." Costig nodded his men aside to reveal three sleds and their animals, worked but as workable as they'd left. "But I did bring back your dogs."

Eskimo Joe sat in usual post between Park's thighs, slamming into him at every jolt as Ferrakut shouted the team across the pack ice. While the sleds had seemed like a good idea, they took ages to harness. It was debatable from where he sat whether they went any faster than a man on foot, but it didn't matter, because most of the thirty men who sallied out from the ships chose to go on foot. Attibatbarak stormed ahead with eleven others while the boys were still wrestling with Barbados Slim. Now they stopped short at the lip of land that marked the Calm Harbor, and the reason was plain: Folmon's crews had set up a wall of men two-deep to greet them at the edge.

"Fuck me," Parks muttered.

"What?" Ferrakut blasted in his ear drum.

"I said, '*Fuck me*!'" He repeated at top volume. A prong of the trident tapped the ice and nearly wrenched itself free of his lap.

"Are there no more warriors among us?" Norwet challenged them when they pulled up to his posse, disgust on his cracked lips. The confidence flickered from Attibatbarak's face like a pond after the crash of a stone.

"Only miners, who know the firestone does not strike back," Joe answered.

The little force searched itself until their attention fell uncertainly on Parks.

"Hm. I mean, we did just say we wanted to prevent them from harming the women and children. I don't know about you guys, but I kind of imagined us jumping them from behind while their pants were down. In light of that, I'd say there's no shame in going back—"

While the miners wavered, the company of marines began lowering one another down the short hummock where the pack heaved upward against the land.

"*Shit.*"

"Run if you must. I will die if I do not kill Barrow Jak," Norwet said.

"I will kill him first, brother," Ulwet, all of eight years, boasted.

Eskimo Joe stood and drew his long knife. "The little ones speak the truth. They will catch us if we turn. We have made our run," he settled on Parks with a hint of something in his expression that could have meant whatever Parks chose. "Now, we must finish it."

It was as the two dog lads said.

When they saw Costig meant no ill, they bounded out from hiding and pronounced that Folmon had gone over the ice. Their fathers knew nothing of it, and fearing they meant to send a runner to town to warn of his coming, Costig left a few wounded but able men to see that no one left camp while he marched on the Calm Harbor.

He could not have asked to find them better off: backs turned, pressed to the edge of the shore. They got within two darraigs'-lengths before he tried the ploy that routed Bayochar. The surprise on Folmon's face when that low voice bellowed at his men to disarm and join the true admiral warmed Costig like no spring sun could.

Barrow Jak and Liam were not so feckless. The latter held the near flank, and Costig crashed like a ram into a soft quarter. Frozen and footsore, his men rallied to the spirit of their officer. Not a man on either side carried a shield—it was a proper boarding fight crowded within the narrow ground between the cliffs and the sea. His reputation and the way he cut down the first man cleared a crescent around Costig that left him searching for a target. Reinforcements appeared climbing up from the ice at Folmon's behest. In the brief opening, Costig strained over the edge and saw they were Gua's company, and that his was not the only bunch eager to get at Folmon..

A band of Mattaka lunged and darted back like excited dogs— indeed, dogs of the true sort ran among them snapping madly at marine, Mattaka, and one another alike, while Gua's lot below deliberated between defending themselves and coming up in support of their admiral. A giant appeared moving strangely in the melee, holding the lead of a particularly mad animal and swiping ineffectively with an odd-shaped spear. When he tumbled to the ground and an old man rallied to lift him, Costig grinned with recognition.

An opportune thrust pulled him back to the battle at hand. He deflected once, twice, then found a slash that sent the man to a knee, followed by a thunderbolt strike to finish it. "Get among 'em!" He could hear the old angotak chiding him even now, though it was but one season on that ship decades past. Costig ignored it, at least until he could find Folmon.

The uncertain battle pulsed towards the shore, and Parks hopped to keep up. He silently praised whatever blurry force had chosen that moment to assault Folmon—he could tell it wasn't Mattaka, and no more. His allies stabbed at the marines retreating up the hummock, then squirted out of the way when they came slashing back. The fight felt awkward, halfhearted, full of posture. The only ones to inflict a casualty so far were the dogs.

One of them yelped his last at the end of a spear in a bold charge. It brought up angry reinforcements, of four legs and two. The dog boys pushed ahead of men, filled with the invincibility of youth. As the last marines lifted themselves onto the shore, Norwet hurled his weapon into the haunch of a man climbing the shallow bank of ice. He slid back down, and Barbados Slim jolted free of Parks' grip. The man disappeared into a pile of fur.

A few feet above them, the crews under Folmon compacted and forced a sudden retreat. The marines loitered at the edge to prevent the Mattaka from joining, strangely unwilling to engage.

"You see this? It is wise," Eskimo Joe explained to Parks like a student on a field trip. "Costig did not rout them as he hoped, so he rests even as he fights," the old man said of the tight defensive cluster holding its ground against a renewed push from Folmon's side. "He means it to be a long battle."

While the lines tested each other at a distance, slapping aside spears without following through, Folmon led his crew in a dash through the narrow lane to open ground. *Costig*, Parks nodded. Who else? The attackers tried to cut him off, but the third of Folmon's crews rolled around and met them. There was a moment of heated combat—less than a minute—before Folmon broke free and began a fast march toward town. The other crews retreated, and it looked like Costig would have to fight through the marines. Instead, he lowered his weapons and let them pass to cover the rear of the fleeing sailors.

"Barrow Jak escapes!" Ulwet scrambled up the hummock despite the cries of warning and found himself alone at the top, facing the former admiral's troop.

"Costig!" Parks hopped toward the shore. He didn't need to say any more to get his meaning across. The bush of a mustache rustled back:

"One enemy at a time!"

By then, the lock on the prison door had become quite cooperative from use. Wendell held it wide and politely gestured the sailor back to his crew before slamming it behind. He'd got no farther with this one than any of the others he'd interrogated. The captains suggested a more hands-on approach, but it was not his way. In fact, he believed most of them were honest mercenaries, unaware of their employer. Either way, the innocent lads worried themselves sick that they'd get the same as Captain "Polc," and fear of being named party to the plot would soon coax loose whatever they might know. For that matter, if he could get the right ones, it would spare Wendell the poor taste of executing the whole lot. He hadn't the stomach for haphazard bloodshed.

On that, a curious feeling gave him pause. He lifted his nostrils to a dry breeze, and sighted a man at a trot. Like a surfacing pod, the heads appeared one after another, making haste towards town from the Calm Harbor. It was no reach to say they were Folmon's. What confounded Wendell was the nature of their scattered run. Men hurried toward or away from things, and he knew of nothing worthy in Drummoc.

Squains? He wondered as the first of the lads drew near with still more sprouting from the snow. The hollow of his stomach tugged with a deeper fear.

"Hoy! What of it?" He shouted as the first ran past, then had to repeat himself. "Hoy, there!"

"To arms!" A sailor responded without slowing.

"To arms!" A second urged him.

Wendell's spear was in the hall. At the thought of retrieving it, his feet rooted. It was impossible. There was still ice for several miles to the north; the south—the direction of the three trapped ships—was fully sealed. There was no way the farri's men could have gotten around. It would have taken an ice march of several days. He'd guessed another two months at least before they could have arrived, but given who was in that cell, he dreaded that he might have been caught, "watching for bird omens with the flood at his feet," as they said.

Perhaps Hiade was more important than they supposed. "Over here!" He waved at the men squirting past. "Defend the prison!" He needed help if they were to make a proper hostage of Daldus. But the sailors ignored his cries as they shuffled past. "Folmon!" He saw the Admiral of Land among them. Folmon merely scowled at him. Barrow Jak's crew came on their heels, everyone running for the navy hall. At last, he spied a few marines among them.

"Lad! Over here!" A reluctant young man peeled towards Wendell. "Is it Donn?"

The marine frowned. "Worse."

Wendell craned around him as the pursuers came into view, marching with composure in three rough lines. At the head, with the fearsome halo of a giant despite his stature, stomped Costig.

"Marines'll be fine. But I'd hide if I were you," the young man advised before scurrying off.

Wendell smarted at the ridiculous insult. What did Costig have to be sore at? He knew the answer, were it a lesser man, but personal error aside, he and his mate served the same spirit. He had plenty of time to flee in disgrace, but Wendell had always done what he knew was best for Drummoc, even if those who rotated through the admiral's quarters made it difficult.

The column stopped to gauge the forces mustering outside the navy hall now that Folmon had barred himself within. Those sea-bright eyes lay upon him. Costig barked something to his company, and save for a few, they formed up a battle line between the prison and the hall. Meanwhile a squad approached at Costig's elbows. He glared up and down at Wendell, firm before the cell door.

"Who's in there?"

"Polc." His throat tightened, and he could say no more.

"Let him out. If he's pissed at Folmon, I can use him."

"Sorry, mate." Wendell swallowed hard and found his voice. "Can't. It's a long tale, and if you knew the half of it, you wouldn't ask."

"I haven't got time for long tales. Let him out."

Wendell, in no way prepared to battle Costig and perhaps feeling his mate justified and harboring a secret wish for his success, nevertheless felt the opposition between them and knew he had to give battle here, upon the one thing he believed in.

"I will not, and nor will you if you serve who you say. He's a traitor to Drummoc."

Costig snorted. "You're one to talk."

"You remember how I said me nose tells me when there's somethin' off? Well, it's never steered me afoul, and sure as we stand, I finally got me scent—"

"Save it." He swiped a finger and a pair of marines took Wendell by the arms while a third fished the key from him.

"Costig. Mate, I know it's gotten complicated between us. You have to trust me."

One of the marines pressed a knife blade into his rib, and he saw in that grimed face a glint that had no pity for the one who had forced them into a bitter exile. Wendell held his tongue. The door creaked open, and he felt faint as the men poured into Costig's company. His feet dangled in the air, then a stone wall cracked into his shoulder and he slid into a darkness broken by a single rectangle of gray. A stout form shadowed the doorway.

"It's for your own good, mate," Costig said in a low tone. "It'll be confusin' out there—no way to tell who stands with who. We'll sort you out later."

Wendell slumped into a trembling pile and prayed that his Lady of Drummoc would find her way through.

They followed, in the way a dog gives chase when the object of its fascination flees, without understanding why or wishing it. The boys grumbled in frustration at the time it took to haul a sled up onto land and capture a team. A few men ran for the ship—to get reinforcements, or to desert, Parks couldn't be sure. The rest bounded at Costig's heels.

Maybe he went to warn Carabiner; to earn a pardon by helping the dethroned admiral; for some glimmer of opportunity he couldn't yet put into words. Parks told himself a half-dozen stories while the sled jostled toward the low skyline of Drummoc, and none of them did more than justify the rushing sentiment that swept them on. Even Eskimo Joe felt resigned to it, the breeze whipping his hair in Parks face while the old man gazed into a distance that seemed to span not only the yards ahead but years past to some youthful venture he didn't bother to share.

"This is what you wanted," Joe said in a way that felt it couldn't possibly have been intended for Parks, though no one else could have heard.

When the team trotted up, it had begun without them. Mattaka ran around like spooked birds on the perimeter. Costig's side slashed at the sailors gathered in front of the navy hall. Parts of the line whipped with fury while others pulled back, shouted support. This was a real fight, Parks told himself, and it looked nothing like the movies in his head. The action flared in a flash of spears, then rolled down the line and back. Some men chatted like spectators only yards from a bloody clash. Everything from orders to taunts cracked on both sides like rifles. A company of marines watched from the safety of the shipyard. Brave Mattaka boys darted in to loot the dead as they fell, driven back by furious comrades.

Costig wore the fight around him like a cloak. Every move he made twisted the lines on both sides. He fought at the front of his men, buckling the opposition. Parks could tell the marines by their leather armor, and they moved with coordination around their leader, with the allied Navy units matching as best they could. The crew opposite them fell into disarray, and suddenly broke into a run. Two more came up to meet them, and reinforcements blocked the retreat of the first group, turning them back toward the fight.

"It is Barrow Jak!" Norwet spotted his man in the fray. A handful of arrows arced over the sailors into Costig's men, forcing them to hunker. The dog boys tried to charge forward, but a group of Mattaka burst from the town and intercepted them. Satletaluk backhanded the oldest brother and dragged him by the collar back to Parks and Joe.

"Harness your beasts," he threw the boy into Attibatbarak's arms. "Alexicus will not have the people killed over one admiral or another."

"I hear Carabiner's afraid to leave his wigwam. This is our chance to make a powerful ally in Costig." The band of Mattaka whooped their approval of Parks' retort.

"We left you in Camne Drumlag because you make only enemies." More men came from the town to back Satletaluk. The blacksmiths joined him with their hammers, and even with the steel weapons they lifted from the first clash, the little party could do no more than watch over their rivals while the fight raged.

Costig pressed another attack to shield them from the arrows. In the mix, even he could not tell at a glance which sailors were his. The man fighting Bayochar's reserves at his elbow had almost certainly come over from Barrow Jak's crew moments before. Liam had been routed. Barrow Jak himself vanished from the field. Now Rapana'ekunata and Bayochar bore the fight, with a few of Aymos' strays. Polc's lads hurried to arm themselves from the fallen. Costig saw Korrel and Bruco come up to support the enemy's rear, hesitate, and scatter—some men joined their fellows while most found quieter places from which to leer. To feel the tide of a battle was a craft he had not practiced in some time, but he felt a seam—perhaps a lie and his death—though a seam that may well split the whole field.

"On me!" He shouted to whoever may come, and felt the brush of strong arms behind him. Costig did not wait. He made his run into the heart, knocking aside one man and another for those behind him to clear. With a hard plunge he pinned the next man to the snow with his spear, could not pull it free, and so drew his knife.

In a breath, he found himself at the heart of the enemy facing an astonished Bayochar. The Admiral of Sea raised a spear in defense and may as well have handed it over. Costig jammed him, slung him around, and cut most of the way through his neck with a swipe. Nemas arrived on his right and fended off a counterattack. With a few more strokes, Costig raised the mutineer's head for all his men to behold, then flung it into the enemy's midst.

With that, the waters parted. Those on the side of the shipyard threw down their weapons and ran. Ithir, arriving late, bolstered the other half until at last, Gua and Obrachar made their choice and marched in with their marines behind Costig.

"Welcome back, Admiral!" Gua saluted smartly. The sight of a hundred fresh bodies broke the spine of the remaining men. Cries of "Up, Costig!" wormed through the rotting line, with the character of the Drummoc Navy at last on display. Those unwanted sons of Ampos and scoundrels unfit for proper seas once more shifted with the winds of personal favor, and he was glad to confirm it before it was Donnab at his shore.

"Any squain on the harbor grounds will be treated as a foe," he announced, and his men echoed the warning, chasing the people this way and that from the corpses. Costig noticed the Leopard Seal hobble off on his odd staff, and decided to bother with that one later.

The doors of the navy hall held to the first ram. By the time they bent against a cracking board, the men inside shouted their surrender. They pried the bar free, and as the two great doors spread, Folmon's limp body spilled upon the top step, half-a-hundred wounds bleeding from the loyal blades of his own crew.

Costig stood once more chief of the cold rock. This time, it had been his choice. No great thing came for nothing. He got what he earned at first, and soon it left him. Now, upon this blood and the torments endured, he was an admiral.

He wondered what old Janten, the cruel angotak, would think of him—probably very little. That lot didn't sail for Ampos, and they suffered no officers. It was fear that pulled them, sure as it drove other men away. Only the most fearsome seas and the most hopeless fights held anything for an angotak, and they thirsted for it. They were not brave, as others claimed. Costig knew that what passed for courage was the terrible, sublime moment when, upon the full embrace of his fate, beneath the screaming glare of his goddess Thachta the man went ahead and felt the thing wash over him like a frigid wave, to emerge something else entirely.

Costig couldn't endure it. He was a jumper, though no man would call him that. Besides the odd pang, he never regretted it. Those lads sailed only for themselves, and from the moment he became a marine in the flooded streets of Ampos, he understood the delicate threads by which the beauty of the sea-places held together, and he wanted no more than to be one of those stitches. To preserve what other men couldn't even see. The scorn of Janten weighed on him, never satisfied, but he reminded himself of his passage. It was he who fought Paladris when the rogue suffered his first and final defeat at Ampos, and now it was he who stood between Aer's murderer and the Frozen Shore.

The men would be pardoned—he'd already decided it when he descended the steps of the navy hall, though he would let them sweat a while longer. Gerachay and Wayranapan greeted him with an embrace unbecoming a pair of aides to the admiral. There was much to do, and Drummoc was worse off than when he first took the impossible task. Costig ordered the field cleared and every man buried with naval honors, except for Folmon and Bayochar. He took a long look at the prison and felt the stab of betrayal, then forced it aside.

Every man who made the mistake of staggering too near him got a task: see to the wounded, bring in the food they cached at the dog camp, assess the work at the Calm Harbor, scrape the winter from the ships, run off the squains, wash the hall of blood, check on his old order at the blacksmith, reassemble the cairns at Gjoraslag. The hall door needed repairs. The prison wall, too.

The frustrated growl of former days had gone from his voice. He spoke almost meekly, without resentment. Much of it still bothered him, but not enough to dampen what was perhaps sheer exhaustion, and which passed for a magnanimous command.

When he ran out of nagging worries to assign, his attention turned squainward over the low roofs of huts. Before they could make ready for a siege, which may come as soon as the ice broke, there was one more fight lurking in the narrow streets. He didn't know how deep it ran, but Costig had a hunch who might be in the middle of it.

"He's gonna try to get back onto the ice," Costig remarked of the Leopard Seal. During the aftermath a second bunch of squains had come up from that direction—reinforcements—and turned right back when they saw the lay of it. "Post Gua's company at the Calm Harbor and have them stop any traffic either way."

In the fading daylight, he glimpsed a head protruding from the door of the latrine two hundred yards off. It shrank back within.

"Shirkers." He curled his fingers at Gerachay. "Check every hold and hole. I want a count of every man with a beating heart."

"Where are you going?"

"To have a shit!" Costig called back.

When he got halfway, eight sailors hurried from the door and steered a wide berth back to town as if they hadn't noticed him. The roof sagged from the winter load. Drift piled most of the way up the north wall, melting into filthy talons. He barged through the door and in the long beam of the opening, saw a pair of legs protruding from a shadow. An erratic snore issued through the hollow, and Costig regarded the roof with suspicion as he stepped over the crevasse.

"*Hoy*!" A swift kick to the boot jolted the sailor. "Safe to come out now, me love."

"It's the fuckin' tow line there, I told her she'd drag me under," the lad mumbled some vestige of a dream. "I never seen—I never seen— what is that? You've bollixed up the lady and now she's got to send a daille to find it."

"Up and out, cunt," Costig growled. "I'll have me shit in peace."

A faraway streak of movement caught Costig's attention through the door. He walked closer, careful to remain in the dark of the latrine until he saw it: one of Sawi's lads, hurrying toward the Calm Harbor. A message from the Leopard Seal, perhaps. Or a scout, ahead of the party to follow.

"Who the fuck are you?" The sailor screamed in a delayed rage.

"I'm Admiral-fuckin'-Costig, mate. Who the fuck are you?"

"Costig. Costig. Costig." The man repeated the name as if trying to place it. He fell very quiet, then answered with a clarity missing from his previous ejaculations. "Teague."

Costig turned his back in disgust, recalling Polc's mad tramp. While the man gained his feet, Costig pressed against the cool stone of the doorway and watched the dog lad, then fixed his gaze like an eagle on the corner of town from which he'd emerged, knowing who must soon follow.

Nights on the pack now came with thunderous reports like nearby armies shelling across no man's land. Two days before, the outbound sled trail disappeared into a jagged hummock, glistening with fresh sea water. It took into nightfall to get the sleds across, and they had to finish the job, for fear that if they left it til morning the two sheets may separate entirely. Beyond the fissure, the rest of their pristine tracks had drifted away.

Just that morning, one of the Mattaka took a sighting of the point of sunrise and declared that they were "rafting," cut off from Yunoc somewhere behind.

No one waited for Foster's orders anymore, or held them in any higher esteem, though they still listened the same as with everyone. He would not be a captain until they had wood under their feet. Gionn grew quiet. Whatever feud existed between him and Jonn dissolved without a word as the two hung abnormally close together, as if it were their separation at the iceberg that nearly stranded them and the proximity to exactly that one other person that brought them back again.

Whalers and Mattaka and angotaks and American citizens—it was a farflung mess of men yet the distrust he felt every minute on the *Gairhle*, and more so on the ice rescue, never appeared. Most of the Mattaka were younger, and none were veterans of the pack with the secret indigenous knowledge that he had assumed. Their nerves showed, too. Only Pinipa seemed to be in an uncompromising good cheer that the men found to be either infuriating or some magical charm that they clung to like a life preserver.

It was Foster's suggestion to run the sleds in a horizontal line—line abreast, the whalers called it—instead of the usual single file, and to his surprise, the idea was unanimously adopted. As Jonn hung near Gionn and the Mattaka near Pinipa, certain men also jockeyed to pull in Foster's team. The more distressed the men became, the more they cast their superstitions on some person who they thought couldn't possibly fail to arrive, and for the whalers who witnessed his improbable survival, that was Foster. He had to run a few off to keep the teams even.

When Hiad came veering over from his group with no particular haste, he prepared to do it again. The boy of sixteen was as quiet as he was often surprised by the most ordinary things. He had wonder where the others were enthusiastic, and while he never seemed to be anyone's favorite, he delighted in their taunts, which were gentler than usual. While most of the rowers came out of boredom or opportunity, Hiad had told Foster in all sincerity that he heard the captain had family on Drummoc, and since he, too, had relatives there, he thought they would be "fast mates." Every rower had kin, but only one was so impressed by the coincidence. And he had been right: Foster took a shine.

"Full-up, brother," he shouted and waved the boy off. But the team lit into the young man and sent him back: he had spotted a black flag.

"One of ours," Luxtros boasted. "You rotmouths only marked your trail. That's no way to find anything. Me and Pinipa put one to either side at half a mile, and even that would've been a mad gamble if we didn't have so few poles.

"Notch out of the top, rather than the bottom, means the center pennant's that way," he pointed north.

"Aye, and the next one up may be three miles south the way the ice is spinnin' on itself," Pitras rejoined.

"All we can do is work the signs we got, "Foster interjected. On his word, they fanned out east over half a mile, bearing north. He chased men away from their good luck charms to even the teams, and within half an hour, the sleds converged on another pennant, this time, one of Corm's. Mile by mile, their hopes grew despite the dark-bottomed clouds to the west that Foster had learned reflected the open water beneath. The markers held. They greeted the men like frozen sentries who stuck it out til their bitter watch was relieved.

Each one quickened his step until the pace was unsustainable. They no longer met at markers, content to wave. The sun paused a little longer each day to monitor their progress, and against exhaustion, Foster considered calling for a halt. Then Hiad returned.

A ship, on the far flank. The sleds raced, the men in the same harnesses appeared to race one another, none of them daring to look up prematurely. The other sleds came into view, stopped in a mass, no one moving, their attention fixed well-ahead.

They drew up at the edge of the water. The young waves appeared especially black, newborn from the ice. More than a mile away, a thin line of ice glinting yellow in the evening marked another floe, and on it, a low smear of black sprouted like a root from the soil. The hull of a ship. There was no way to reach it. The crew observed a drawn-out moment of silence until their denial began to crack through the mourning.

"*Abalax*," Pinipa proclaimed brightly.

"It's the angotak ship!" Fergo agreed, and the optimism of the charmed man spread through the ranks. They couldn't be sure of anything, though, except this was the end of the footing. *A day or two earlier*, he thought. *We might have made it.*

The solution was easy. They had to deny it with all their hearts. Foster made a third suggestion, and for the third consecutive time, they fell in rather than raise the mounting concern. Half of the party went one way with Luxtros. Foster kept Gionn and Jonn together in his own group, with those men who thought he couldn't fail, not by skill, but by the intercession of gods or demons. Fergo pinched the pinky finger dangling from his neck and whispered devout words. Atalkut and Tunguk produced chips of wood they had taken from the ship and held them up like compasses.

Gionn retired from his harness and came up alongside Foster as they followed the line of sea lifting shards from the edge of the floe.

"Feels odd, don't it? First time in ages we don't have to swindle our way onto a ship—just gotta find the damned thing. No tales, or thefts, or little murders. Can you ever recall such a thing?"

"Yeah, I can, actually," Foster said indignantly, then hesitated and smiled out of the corner of his eye. "But it *has* been a minute."

"Now that you're a captain, I won't have to put up with you much longer, lifespans bein' what they are. Makes me like you a lot more. Everything you do still takes the piss outta me, but I think, 'Ah, let him go, Gionn, you stupid rude cunt. The next one may be worse.'"

"OK." Foster marched on, unsure of how to take the compliment.

"What, with all the good spirits goin' around, I thought I could have a bit of a confession, and you might swear on the torment of your entire lineage to keep it until your mutiny day." He waited. "Go on, swear it."

"I swear."

"Torment of your lineage."

"On the torment of my lineage."

"I'm not who I seem, mate. The handsome rogue of a whaler, beholden to no man. Swift of sword and sharp of tongue. Anchorless as a spray of salt." Gionn looked back to make sure Jonn trailed by far enough, a mistake he didn't care to repeat. "Truth is, I was a humble fisher of the Atl-Ceru. Never raised a fist or a foul word to any man. Had a young wife fair as a spark of fire, and a son in her arms. On the day of me nineteenth year, we came from the nets to find me village a-smolder." He struggled with the word. "*Paladris.*" When Foster made no answer, he bristled. "Surely you're not so far-fetched you've never heard of him."

"Can't say as I have."

"Ah, fuck you then, awful bastard! Ask someone else. Well, even an idiot can understand it: they sacked me shore, bashed me son against a wall, and tossed me wife before they cut her throat. I would have fallen on their spears had I the chance, but they were gone to richer lands like a serpent rolls beneath the waves. What else could I do? Me first ship was a fisher, but you know how the waters have shifted. When the holds were empty, we had to fill 'em with somethin'. I tried many times to right meself, find another love. But no woman waits on a whaler, and an honest man starves. I took whatever ship I could come by. Didn't matter a black hair where it was goin', or whose wake it crossed. I told meself I didn't care. I was a whaler, and such a man has no memory. He's a shape, risin' and vanishin' from the surface.

"I thought it was coin and only that I needed. But now as I hold this argot, well-earned, I could cast it into the sea without a thought." He stared off into the slush of the blooming waves.

"I'm sorry." Foster offered.

"For what?"

"About your wife and son."

"Oh, right. Them. Eh, where was I?" He regained his dramatic air. "It wasn't until you said that name that I felt me old corpse brush against the hull: *Donn*. Whatever happened between 'em, Paladris was his man. In those days he sailed on the farri's word. A whaler don't care who he boards—better if it's easy. I should have preferred to go after Ampos, as Corm meant to. But that *name*. It stirred me. I don't know why I'm tellin' you this, or what I thought you'd do. Only that you've breathed life into me drowned lungs. This marks a new Gionn. You shall not recognize me, cunt."

Shouts pierced their confidence. Atalkut and Tunguk slipped their harnesses and sprang past. A few more men followed toward a lump that stood dull against the sea and the red glistening snow of sunset. The men needed no command. They abandoned the sleds and rushed with rope and hooks, wheezing all the way.

She lay on a floe only twice her length and width, wedged against the main pack where she had drifted in after a brief spin in the open water. The half-party threw hooks in stride, as if they expected her to flee. Foster stepped over the seam and splayed himself without dignity on the snow-laden tarps that covered her. Every brace stood. Only a single corner of leather had come loose. They tore into her like a Christmas gift, and fixed anchors to the main ice.

"Go tell the others and bring up the sleds!" Foster shouted.

"Aye, we could do that. But think of it," Gionn suggested. "Both the angos and most of the squains are with the other lot. Might be a fair time to sail on."

Laughter from the crew saved Foster the trouble of having to shoot it down. A party of men left with reluctance. The rest draped themselves over their home. Ice hung from the lady of the prow like the frost in their beards. The mast seemed frozen to the floe itself in the lee of the ship. It would take days to chip her loose, but they resigned themselves to the coming hardships with joyous denial. For these men, they were home.

Foster regarded Gionn, and every detail took on a strange hue. He wasn't fool-enough to believe everything he heard on a whaler, but he'd had enough of the man's lies to sense something of a truth that cast him in an evening glow, pink-skinned and hair afire. This man had to come from somewhere, he realized, and anywhere had its hopes and miseries. It led men to their unlikely meeting places, with whatever they could carry, brought them through in their own manner. In the extravagant sunset, he granted each of the howling crew that mystery of circumstances that made them more than his own encounters and assumptions. They had all come for some reason as inexplicable as Foster's story, which like the others, he held back because he couldn't imagine that anyone would understand.

"I suppose Omera's had her fill." Gionn watched the other party bounding up over the ice. He knocked on wood, remembering Foster's superstition. When they poured up to the ship, Gionn leaned over the side.

"Avast, you cunts! Have we forgot our manners?" The crew stopped cold in confusion. With a glimmer of mischief in his eye, he asked, "Permission to come aboard...Captain Foster?"

"What do you think this is?" Foster challenged, putting the men on their heels. "A coal ship?" He glared at the Mattaka. "A fishin' boat?" He swiveled to Gionn. "A whaler?" Foster found Corm's veterans. "This here is a free man o' war, and we fight for our people back home, wherever it is we come from. We ain't here to loot merchants. You're more liable to catch steel than gold where we're goin'. Make no mistake: the men of the *Gairhle* sail against the farri, himself, and the fiercest navy on the seas. If you don't like it, Yunoc's that way. But if it suits you—welcome aboard."

A howl like the wail of the dead raised from the throats of the men and they piled on in a gleeful frenzy. Gionn clapped Foster on the back, then sank to recline against the side, staring far out over the waves if anywhere at all.

When the men could not find Costig, the assistant viceroy came out of hiding. He gathered captains and officials and the proudest of the Mattaka, and called them his "task force." It was the first time Norwet got a look at the man or heard his slippery words. Ferrakut said he came from the same place as the Leopard Seal—that they were old friends. Now that he had known three from this place, Norwet began to hear the land, to see it in their walk, and it only grew stranger. He also saw what belonged to the men alone. These two had their differences, and both were still more removed from Foster.

This one came out of his tukit like a seal splashing from its winter den. He enjoyed the parade. Many followed him and ran from his side with messages. He held meetings, and listened with a serious face. The men he had feared were gone, and many rumors ran about Costig. Some thought he had fled a reprisal, or tired of the office. Others said the reprisal had already come. While the assistant viceroy made a fine show, sending searchers to every fold in the flesh of Drummoc, he found no sign.

They pulled Sagalak from the prison, near death from neglect, and uncovered the body of a marine stowed in an empty tukit. His Seleku family thought Alexicus had the admiral killed in the confusion, for he was very afraid of the man and had only returned when he heard Costig was ousted.

Leopard Seal was not so confident. He remained at the icebound ships for two days, and had only just come to town with great care to talk in private with Alexicus. Norwet's brothers spoke of Leopard Seal in forgiving tones. He had done well in the battle, but they still hurt from his betrayal. Norwet had known of his dealings with Costig all along. He never thought as much of their friend, or as little.

On the third morning of the search, Adelate found him loitering at the shipyard with the boys while the people crowded outside the tavern to say their complaints to Alexicus. His personal guard of sailors, who he called Midshipmen, stood nearby. Captains Amachar and Liam attended, making jokes with Alexicus.

She saw his stare, and said to him, "You look like you have a grievance to raise."

"He has heard me, and will do nothing about Barrow Jak. He says the Navy is pardoned, and we must learn to get along."

"Sawi cropped us for fighting in the battle. We think Alexicus made threats," Ulwet replied with scorn.

"Or your father," Norwet added.

Adelate laughed. "He should not have struck you. I heard it was no battle. Just a bunch of boys and dogs running behind the fight."

"It was a battle, and not my first. We attacked before Costig, and I killed a marine." Norwet boasted.

"You wounded him, the dogs finished it," Milak corrected.

"Who else among you got blood on his spear?"

"I did."

They blinked at Adelate's response. The girl unfolded her cloak, where from a strand of leather she wore a jawbone around her neck, grayed flesh on the chin, and a strap of brown hair that ran up either side and terminated in a ragged mess where the joint was cut.

"Who is it?" Ulwet beamed with excitement.

"Must you ask?" Adelate looked over at the assistant viceroy. "If he really means to find my cousin's murderer, he should send a party to Urkuk."

Norwet staggered at the sight and fell back in disbelief. "What corpse did you rob? A little girl could not have defeated one like Costig."

"And a dog boy will never defeat Barrow Jak. But if he is as clever as a little girl, he will pay a sailor to do it." She tilted her head in mocking and left them gaping at her back.

The night before Raratuk arrived in Drummoc to free his brother, the great hero Vitjukvattajuk, many people saw a lamp aglow on the deck of a firestone ship anchored out in the harbor. There had been no ship by the light, and it was not the season for them. When the sun rose, there remained no trace of it.

Tunguk was thinking of this when he nodded off on the sled. When he woke again, Brother no longer sat behind him. The others that were sent to search for Costig at the icebound ships were gone, and those ships no longer marked the horizon.

Only the dogs remained. They pulled Tunguk with vigor, and though the sun was out and the land visible, he could not get a bearing at first. The dogs ran on their own, and the ice felt smooth. This went on for some time. The surface gleamed a single shade of white, though when he looked close, he saw six hundred colors that leaned upon one another with such grace they seemed one hue. The sun glowed in the sky as a lamp on a ship. He saw only one person. It was the boy—his constant companion—walking in another direction far off and without noticing.

Tunguk put a foot over the sled and stood. The dogs ran on.

He could not say where he was, but he felt he should check on Brother and turned for the island, despite knowing that Brother was heading for the ships. It was a good walk. He found the ice not too sticky or slick. The cold invigorated him, and he traveled with the ease of rowing in a current. When he had taken six steps, he encountered a man going in the same direction.

The man was Mattaka, dressed like a miner in sooted leather. He stood shorter than Tunguk and everything about him was humble, as if he had never told another what to do. On his face he wore the determined smile of one accustomed to hardship.

"Tunguk! It has been so long since I have seen you!" The man greeted him.

"I have never seen you," Tunguk replied.

Now he noticed a rope around the man's waist, and just behind, he hauled the largest firestone ship Tunguk had ever seen. It glided after him with the sound of a glazed runner on new snow.

"Where are you going with so much firestone?" Tunguk asked.

"Urkuk. Many guests! Many guests are expected. They will want to warm themselves by a fire."

Tunguk tried to spot the mountain, but a fog had settled, and he could see only some yards ahead.

"I hope I can find it in time," the man continued. "It was easier in days past to find a guide. I hope they know where they are going," he indicated the tracks of three boots that he followed into the fog. Tunguk felt a tug, and saw a rope around his own waist that disappeared after the tracks.

"It is heavy, and far yet. Will you help me?" The man said.

The old man smiled. "Soon."

He looked to a part of the ice that was without fog, and saw the boy again. Tunguk leaned against the rope, and pulled out slack, leaving the man to his load.

"I have been looking for you," the boy said.

Tunguk felt a lurch, and his head snapped back against something hard.

"*Ow!* Fuck me!" Brother cried. He looked around and was once more on the sled driven by Attibatbarak, the *Juhketappat* looming ahead. Brother reached a bloody finger around to show him. "You almost knocked my tooth out. Next time, I'm riding shotgun on *your* nuts, and *I* get to be the dentist..." He went on with more words that Tunguk hardly followed.

The boy walked along by the front of the sled. "You dream more and more."

"Perhaps. Or the clouds over the mountain are thinning." Tunguk squinted back at the island. "It has a strange feel. The people talk of the firestone run and the mines, who will be admiral, as though the trouble will pass and they will return to their lives. It reminds me of the days after the prison burned, until Vitjuk's escape—everything unsettled, like a pile of stones ready to fall in the wind."

"For once, we agree. There will be a ship for us, I am sure of it."

"For us?"

"Do not play the simple old man. You said it yourself. There will be nothing left for you here. I do not know how it will come or where it will go, but I will leave this place. You! You did not return in glory. Do you not wish for one more try?"

"What will I try?"

"What you please!"

"I do not know what I please."

"That is why you need me. I am young, and full of spirit. I will be your breath over the old coals. And you will be my guide. You know the ways along the sea. We will not last without you." The boy turned most of the way toward Brother. "When the time comes, you must go with us."

Tunguk was surprised that the words gave him a fright. He felt the aches that grew in his bones like the roots of a tree. It was flattery— *another try!* Yet it ran through him like red veins of light in a rustle of ash, to hear another name the thing he could not bring himself to name.

He raised his head to reply, but the boy had gone.

The sounds outside the prison wall lent to a tortuous speculation. The battle pitched nearly before him, and Wendell was left to imagine the tides in every clash and cry. For some time he thought he heard it rumbling through the streets, only to realize it had likely ended long ago. He had no notion of who'd won, though by now it had to have been Costig, for he wasn't freed, and the only visit he had was an invasion of squains who pulled out his cell mate, a man in awful shape who Wendell had consoled but could not help.

They had given him a drink, at least, though not a bite, and now he wondered what had become of his fair island that miners could come and go in the cells. Crowds gathered. He heard a man speaking on occasion, and loud calls that didn't belong to any sailor. But he also heard the crews about, and thought he recognized certain voices.

Dozens of conversations with Costig kept him occupied. They'd gone quite well at first, but taken a piteous tone of late, and now of the third day, he began to wonder if the man hadn't fallen in battle. He'd been sore, but it wasn't like Costig to let a mate rot in his own filth.

When the door at last groaned, Wendell nearly lifted himself with excitement, but found his limbs quite weakened. The wide shape in the doorway raised his hopes until it split, and a pair of men entered against the night by the glow of a lamp. One of them held it beside Wendell's face, and he recoiled.

"Dingy, isn't it? I didn't think it'd be so hard to sit in a dark room day after day, but the dark—that was the worst of it. Worse than Winter, even. Winter, you can step out, have a look at the stars, or the Belads goin' across the sky. Not here. Worse than a ship, too. I never thought after that passage down to Drummoc in an open darraig that a cell would bother me.

"But after a few days where you can't see your hand, you're set adrift. You start to think all sorts of mad thoughts. I often paced wall to wall just to remind meself the size of the room. Did you flutter when the door opened just then? I know I did, every time you came to take out one of me lads or bring him back. Just that slip of light and a few details of the floor felt like a breath after bein' held under."

"Will you be joinin' me, then, young Daldus?" Wendell asked through a stranger's voice, his bright lilt faltering like a keel scraping a sandy bottom. "Aber, I'd guess by your age. Drummoc has quite an attraction for last-born sons."

"I will not, and I'll grant you that much. 'Aber.' Feels good to hear it again. Don't suppose you'll tell me who breathed it?"

"Then I won't be leavin', eh?"

Aber smiled consolingly. "It was Leopard Seal, wasn't it?"

Wendell hung his head, and looked at his fingers clasped in the tender light. They appeared to him rough and unusual, belonging to another man. He felt no fear. In fact, the opposite. The island in the darkness came as a blessing, and he began to feel a subtle warmth. He paused in silent gratitude to the Lady of Drummoc—he knew not how to call her—that he had been here, and done what he could. Then it was her holding the lamp. She was the lamp, and he basked in the small mercy of sight. He felt no sadness, either, except that there was nothing else he could do to keep that lamp from guttering out. Almost nothing.

"Aye," he said.

The second man seized Wendell and wrapped a cord around his throat. Wendell grasped at it out of instinct, but his fingers could not get a hold. His legs shifted, kelp in a wave, and the light filled the cell, wiped it of its edges, then left him.

For more than a month after the battle Parks endured a frozen exile on the *Juhketappat*. Sophia—his one outlet of sanity—had long since moved onto the island. The hunters now brought their food to town, snatching the hub of activity away from the ships. A skeleton crew passed back and forth with a little news. Sagalak recovered. Seal returned to some grounds. Norwet got engaged—to his cousin Uniatsate. Parks only saw the boys on occasion, and when they visited the ships, there was always a purpose to it and a fast turnaround.

Meanwhile Kjartke wrung out his stump every day, and warmed his frostbitten toes against her stomach. He wanted to read into it, or at least be turned on, but what passed between them felt as distant as it was intimate, two people tossing glances across a narrow channel. She told him stories for children in Mattakatan, and he hardly picked up a word. Eskimo Joe supervised as if he were afraid she would reveal something too precious. On occasion, he would translate.

The burden of his constant receiving—food and clothing and rides and divine intervention—ultimately wore on Parks. In an anxious quest to find something he could do, something to unload in return, he stumbled on the Mattaka's love of rap. Out of boredom one afternoon, he freestyled a few verses about Ostuk's obsession with deicing the ship every morning. When he noticed that everyone in earshot had gathered in fascination, he extended the rhyme with a verse about Bullethead and Hopalong, Barbados Slim and Winnie Cooper, Agwik, Haraket, even the treasurer Willakuy, who was visiting to give Parks what he called an "adjusted fee for espionage services performed," reduced from the promised piece of gold to three nickels and three pennies.

After that, he performed almost daily to decks packed with dozens of fawning spectators. He wasn't so dense that he didn't realize they considered him a clown. A clown was something, though.

During a rendition of Joe's translation of a story about a man who sees his seal breach the ice three times and does not strike with his spear because he wants to line up a cleaner stroke, Norwet appeared with Ferrakut and a team. This time, they made a beeline for Parks.

"You are summoned."

"By who? Or is it 'whom?'"

"Fleet Admiral Alexicus."

There had been furious debate since Costig's disappearance over who would take command. Most of the Mattaka wanted Carabiner, but the captains and officials wanted one of their own. He managed to secure temporary emergency powers and create a task force to search for the missing admiral, and apparently no one other than Parks saw through it. Though he didn't know how it all played out, nothing surprised him less than to hear that Carabiner had weaseled his way into a permanent command over people who he couldn't understand.

Joe worried he would be arrested. But by then, Parks relished any chance to stick his head up and keep it there. The sailors they passed gawked with curiosity. Some of the Mattaka gave a quiet cheer, and several looked to his leg and said, "*Gadra,*" which meant something between "good luck" and "*gesundheit,*" but could also signify the vengeful wrath of a god against someone who had wronged him.

He was not arrested. Carabiner's men met him at the edge of town, and instead of taking him to the navy hall, helped him between the wigwams to a familiar dome with a window.

"Full pardon," Carabiner reiterated. "One-hundred-percent free and clear of all charges, past and present, but for my sake, hopefully not future."

"And you're sure that the dudes with the spears know that?"

"I told them myself, and they were glad to be done with you. Oh, and did you get your paycbeck?"

"Yeah, about that."

"Best I could do, bro, considering you were spying on *me*, for a man who's nowhere to be found."

"How many of these silver guys in an argot?" He held up an irregular coin.

"My understanding is a thousand."

Parks let out a whistle. "Nice. I was pissed when I thought it was a hundred."

"The closest thing I've gotten to a salary so far is two different proposals to swindle the treasury and leave before the siege with accomplices I won't bother to name."

"They say it's a service profession." Parks fingered a tassel of hair on Carabiner's coat. "What's this? Got yourself a little belle?"

"It's a dead man's hair."

Parks jerked back in disgust.

"We don't even know who killed the poor guy, but his family wants him hauled up and executed, *yesterday*. Can you imagine, one of my first acts as fleet commander is killing one of my own men? No one wants this job. No one can hold it. Yet they blocked me as long as they could. I thought we were going to war again a week ago. The Mattaka are worried I'm with Ampos. The Navy is worried I've gone over to the 'squains.' The Marines think I'm some kind of…spoiled Annapolis kid." He paused in expectation of a remark. "And most of the island assumes I murdered Costig."

"I don't think you murdered Costig." Parks recalled Norwet's grim story to himself.

"Thank you, bro. But if anyone from the Navy, the Marines, or the Dawn Council were here, I'd be explaining how my best friend nearly derailed the future of this colony by spreading a vile rumor that Captain Polc is an agent of the farri."

"A son. I have it on authority of my friend Gionn, and he's never lied."

"I didn't bring you here to chew you out. Next time you have vital intelligence, just run it by me before you get fifty innocent men thrown in jail. Before you risk Sophia's safety by dragging her across the ice. We both know things. And we'll both continue to miss the big picture if we silo information."

"You don't have to believe me. Just be careful."

"I will. And you should, too. The hunters have spotted a ship skirting the ice."

Parks perked up. "Lenet?"

"Hard to say. But I'm hoping he'll come in peacefully when he hears such kind words from an old friend about the assistant viceroy and fleet admiral. And just to be certain, I'm sending one of my captains with you to make it clear what'll happen if he disregards your message."

"Who?"

"The only one who has any reason to be grateful to me: Polc."

Parks nodded. "You want me to go out on the ice with the dude I called the po-lice on."

"I'm confident you have nothing to fear. But I've limited him to a party of six, in keeping with Mattaka numerology. And you, no more than twelve."

Parks felt a sly concession in the number.

"Bring anyone you like, heavy guns if you're worried about it. Just not Attibatbarak, or Haraket, or Ostuk."

There wasn't any mystery in his deprival of the three men who Carabiner couldn't quite tease away from their ships, which had become the sanctuary of the malcontents. What Parks couldn't be sure of was the lingering look he got, which seemed to beg him to understand something grave that couldn't be put to words.

"We got Captain Polc arrested so he couldn't stop Lenet. Now you want us to help him?" Ferrakut complained. Getting the dog boys to agree to something sketchy wasn't as easy as it used to be. They were hard to find, disinterested, or begrudging of the chore. Parks had humbled himself to ease the sting of betrayal, and it had cost him his authority.

"My brother speaks well. Carabiner protects outlaws in his crew," Norwet said. "Why should we go?"

Norwet had begun to use the name that only Parks used for the assistant viceroy, probably sensing the casual disrespect it carried.

"I would love it if I could answer that. I don't even know why *I'm* going, except that I like Lenet, and as much as it cramps my gooch to say it, I like Carabiner. He's my friend. And sometimes, you just do what a friend asks you, even if you don't think it's the best."

They were unmoved. A debate erupted, mostly between the boys, mostly in a tongue that still eluded Parks. Finally Eskimo Joe spoke a short phrase. Norwet, Ferrakut, and Ulwet agreed to drive the sleds.

Polc and his five men were waiting for them when they rattled down the launch onto the pack. The sight of an old man, a cripple, and three boys amused them.

"A pleasure to make your infamous acquaintance," Polc bowed his head. "I understand you once served under Alexicus' command in a great navy. The mate of me mate is me mate, as they say."

"*Yarrr.*" Parks droned.

"We should be off, then. No tellin' if we'll find him by sundown or next week."

"Not so fast, matey. The rest of my homies are catching up."

The captain's amusement subsided when he saw seven more men coming from the launch. The ice was soup, according to Joe, and couldn't be trusted. He found an old hunter who knew it well, and also convinced Senadak—Norwet's future father-in-law—to guide them.

If there was hope of goodwill between them, it was the other five who made Parks' opinion clear: five marines, cared for and freed by the Leopard Seal, under the command of sergeant Poznatxen loped up in leather armor, shields slung across their backs and spears in hand. Unlike the boys, they had required no convincing.

For the rest of the journey, Polc was no more talkative than the girl Parks had dumped when he had to drive her back from Santa Cruz to L.A. The ice hissed at them and water trickled into their impressions. It had looked permanent and invincible to Parks, like a slab of concrete that would last the ages, yet its demise under the lengthening day now seemed immanent.

Parks blushed at his stupid trident every time he braced himself from falling off the sled. He was sure everyone snickered at it whenever a voice muttered just beneath his ear. The two loads carried wigwams, and three days of food. He stressed over sleeping arrangements, and whether it would be too much to post a guard overnight.

It came to nothing when a few hours into their patrol, they spotted a coal ship bobbing just off the pack among the shards.

"Hold it like this." Eskimo Joe extended his palms out from his chest, and Parks imitated the act with his trident for the figures on the deck to see. The old man nodded to the ice, and somehow Parks knew to set it down gently at his feet.

"Now do as you will, but do not jump naked and wave overhead." He added wryly.

There must have been discussions on board as to who they were, and what it meant. It was an hour before a skin boat launched. Two men picked their way, pushing ice as much as paddling. Their wary demeanor melted when they saw Parks standing a head above the rest. Shouts of joy skipped over the water, followed by "ooohs" of concern over his leg. He pretended to recognize the paddlers, as well.

"Just one. You." The man aft beckoned Parks into the boat.

"It'll be two, mate. The name's Captain Polc, and I treat on behalf of Assistant Viceroy and Fleet Admiral Alexicus."

Parks could offer only a reluctant confirmation. The Mattaka hearts skimmed along the bottom of the bilge at the realization that they had come so far only to be intercepted. Joe tried to climb in as well, but they stopped him.

"Too many. You wait here."

He rested a hand on Parks forearm, and held it long enough that it meant something. Polc maneuvered into the boat behind Parks, and shifted nervously before settling down distrustful of the hull.

"First time in leather, huh? Don't worry, these things are only made of the finest whale circumcisions." He joked to conceal his nerves at having the man at his back.

The ice nipped at the flesh in slow drafts and unexpected rotations. Parks pretended to survey the water side-to-side in order to take frequent glances at the man behind him. The Mattaka had cooled at the prospect of the extra visitor and all the complications he brought, but they made small talk with careful confidence.

"What happened to your leg, akjuru?"

"My leg? Oh my god! My *leg*!" Parks clutched his thigh and panicked as if he'd only just realized it was missing, to the paddlers' delight.

"And your mates? Are they whole?" The one in the bow asked. "Foster, and the red one. Gionn."

His stomach curdled, and Polc kept silent.

"Gone north, like all the good ones. My mates are here, now." Parks felt his security unravel from the frozen shore behind him.

Mattaka lined the deck to meet them. A boy shouted, "Leopard Seal!"

"Who's that," he squinted. "Blowhole?"

"I'm Grom, he is Blowhole."

"Damn right, you are!"

The ship let out a cheer at his arrival, shared by all except one who stood in the middle. They helped the guests onto the false deck, and men clapped him on the arms and conjectured about the strange object he carried.

"Is it a leg for walking on the ice?"

"It looks like a standard-staff, but the statue has fallen overboard!" One man teased.

Everyone on the ship had his turn looking them over, introducing himself and his voyage—"I am Werdatet and have come from the *Pallaia* by Yunoc, many miles,"—and asking of people on Drummoc. They insisted on sharing food and drink. A number of young men showed Parks and Polc weapons, trinkets, crafts of fish bones, interesting rocks they had gathered along the way that brought them...luck, or something. Some of these were offered in trade, and they wouldn't leave the guests alone until Polc finally handed over a pair of mittens for a vertebra the size of a fist. At last they were brought aft where six men waited to speak with them. Parks only recognized Lenet.

He wore the wispy strands of a beard like a bad disguise on a face hollowed by worry. The lines when he smiled seemed deeper, his skin more impermeable. A dozen little details had shifted almost beneath notice, and Parks sensed that the man had grown like trunk into the space he was given.

"I see our homecoming is spoiled. Do I need to ask by who?"

"I know it looks bad, but hear me out. I only told my boy Haraket so he could let your families at the hunting camp know you were OK. Then he told his old man, Satletaluk, and swore him to secrecy, but Satletaluk told my homey Carabiner, who in a surprising turn of events is now the admiral. "*But!* Nunoc thinks you're dead, thanks to me and Foster, not so much Gionn. And like I said, the admiral is my homey, so instead of killing you on sight, he's willing to hear your grievances against Ampos. He's starting what sounds like some kind of labor union, and everyone is going to get better working conditions and wages. There's no more bad guys, dude. You won, and you don't even have to fight."

Lenet and the others consulted through glances.

"'Tell one man, tell them all.' Your homies could not keep your secret. How can you trust this Carabiner to keep his word?"

"Because he's put it to parchment for all to see," Polc interjected. He unrolled a dirty sheet, scrawled with a skipping English cursive, and handed it to Parks. "Sorry, mate. Haven't got me letters."

"Homeschooled, eh?" Parks made no effort to hide his skepticism. He cleared his throat.

"'I, Assistant Viceroy and Fleet Admiral Alexicus, commanding officer of Drummoc, under the authority vested in me by the king of Ampos and by the sovereign Mattaka people, do upon signature of this treaty restore the signatories to their homes, occupations, and families with full amnesty from all crimes know or unknown and committed prior to the date of signature. I promise to do all in my power to shield them from acts of retribution by other parties, and shall attend to their complaints of unfair treatment and address them to full satisfaction at my earliest opportunity.

"'In the interest of amity and in good faith, the signatories hereby declare their allegiance foremost to Drummoc and the indigenous people thereof, and to their appointed leader, Assistant Viceroy and Fleet Admiral Alexicus, whose finger smells like butthole, and who alone can guarantee the terms of this contract, binding in the sight of Hawe.'

"Did I read that right?" He held it tauntingly under the nose of Polc. The captain snatched it away, and passed it to Lenet.

"Forgive me, I am but a rower. Perhaps my mates understand these words better than I?" Lenet said politely.

"We do not understand," one of the men confirmed.

"Can any trustworthy Mattaka, here or on shore, assure me it is written as he says?"

"I know of none," the same man answered.

Lenet returned the treaty. "To the Mattaka, a word is spoken. We do not know your letters, passed between men who will not look upon our faces. They tell us that speech cannot be trusted. That these words last longer. But my people have marked many parchments. We remember well what was told to us, but when we say the officials have broken their promises, they tell us that is not what was written.

"They say when I speak it does not last. Will you not remember my voice? This ship where I speak? There is only one. The Leopard Seal will not read my words in his voice in a room far from the people. If this man means to welcome us and restore to us what Ampos has taken, tell him to come to our ship. Speak to us. We will listen."

"Alexicus has much to do. If you want to speak with him, you'll have to come ashore," Polc said.

"How can we trust that if we come ashore we will not be harmed?"

"What choice do you have? Every man-at-arms knows you're comin'. You'll trust it if you want to come ashore, at all."

Lenet turned to the men and they murmured in soft Mattakatan.

"Leave us the parchment. We will speak to the crew and send word of our answer."

Polc rolled it crisply and passed it off with confident indifference.

While they waited for the Mattaka to get the boat ready in their own Mattaka time, Parks leaned against the mast and, to avoid having to make small talk with men he couldn't remember, regaled them with the story of his role in the battle, which drifted into rhyme on occasion. A thick crowd shielded off Polc, who wandered onto the false deck to oversee preparations. Only then did Lenet find him. He indicated for the crew to give them space, but not so much that Polc might see through the bodies.

"Tell me quick of your mate. If you do not say it, we will never know."

"Carabiner? I wouldn't call him my mate. More like a dude I keep running into."

"Braided. Like rope." Lenet said, and the Mattaka seemed to assign some gravity to the statement.

"He's your standard Annapolis bro. Has a thousand ideas of how to take the world by storm, and why he deserves to, and he's just waiting for someone to put him in charge of something. He's a windbag and a douchebag. But at the end of the day, I think he cares. Enough. For sure, more than anyone else who could end up running this place. He's too soft to do anything drastic. If he says he'll take care of you, I'd say you can trust him as long as you pretend to follow orders. That's assuming he doesn't piss off 'Polc,'" Parks made air quotes, "which he won't—the man has a Master's in ass-kissing from the Naval War College."

"What is…" Lenet imitated the finger gesture.

"It means—hm." Parks thought. "I'm only pretending that I believe what I said is true."

"Who is this Polc that an admiral must not 'piss him off?'"

Parks cringed at the need to tell another long story. But he checked that the man was out of earshot, and told Lenet all that he knew about the one Gionn had called Daldus, up through his bungled release.

"Carabiner says he doesn't buy a word of it. I wouldn't be surprised if he's got a spit-shake agreement that when that dude's navy comes to ream us, he'll hand over the colony in exchange for some title. King of Drummoc sounds a lot cleaner than Assistant Viceroy and Fleet Admiral." Deep concern stiffened over Lenet's face. "Don't worry, he won't leave you hanging. He has a five-year plan, he told me. Probably a fifty-year plan, too. He wants to make your people a great kingdom through lying and manipulating, without the need for bloodshed."

Lenet took a quick survey of the faces around him.

"My people once belonged to Atlantis. When Ampos came, our grandfathers thought they would be treated like men again, so they fought and won a great victory. Here is our prize," he swept his hand over the hijacked coal ship. "We came to give our people back to themselves, not to sweat and bleed for a different king. The farri murdered his own brother for spoils. How will he treat us?

"His son smiles because if we do not mark his parchment, he will return with many men to slaughter us. Perhaps we have not come so far for nothing, after all." Lenet looked Parks up and down, frustration and a little regret in his stiff mouth, and Parks wondered if he contemplated cutting his throat here and now.

"You have changed," Lenet said. "I do not mean your leg, but that is enough to bring a new man forth. I see you have endured many things you can't tell, as have I. You no longer follow after Foster. You speak for yourself, and you tell us a truth, even when your words invite danger from your enemies. I hope you see you can no more live among them than we can.

"I must ask the crew to stand for it, but if they do, you will hear our cries at dawn. We can't win unless the people rally to our side. You must make them ready."

"Whoa, whoa, whoa! I'm sure we can find some kind of compromise if that's what you need. I know how to talk to Carabiner. But you're asking me to wage war against my friend—my only ally other than a senile old man who talks to himself."

"We haven't come so far to compromise."

"*Hoy!*" Polc shouted and pushed through the men. "You comin', lad? The boat's in the water." He seemed to sense something in the air amidst the interrupted meeting, and frowned suspiciously. Parks rose with effort on his sorry trident. He glanced as long as he dared at Lenet, and parted the crew.

All the way back to the ice Parks felt Polc's eyes bore into the back of his head. He lurched on the sled, grimly fixed on the knot of a pant leg stretched before him and the ridiculous weapon on his lap. His modest guard picked their way over puddles, ice freezing their cuffs: a handful of orphaned POWs, including a man whose hair would never grow back from the burns that warped his face and scalp; the wavering dog drivers; a couple of grandpas. He noted every sticky stop and detour, and imagined that crew crossing the same stretch without any light to guide them, with mostly stone weapons, a few dozen men hellbent on picking a fight they couldn't win.

"How'd it go, sailors?" Carabiner greeted them at the launch with his pet officials and Satletaluk.

"Lenet heard us loud and clear," Parks seemed to boast. "They're voting. We'll have an answer tomorrow." He felt a small relief that he hadn't lied.

"Excellent. I want you with me when I meet them. Then afterwards, dinner: you, me, Sophia, Kjartke. We got some fresh seal in today, and I'm teaching Ratjuk how to grill steaks."

As the party broke their separate ways, he found the dog boys waiting expectantly.

"What of our coin?" Norwet spoke for them. To Parks' blank expression, he replied: "Tunguk said you will give us each a silver and a copper to go with you."

Parks glared at the old man, who spoke to the air, conveniently ignorant of the exchange. "Dude! That's all the change I got!" They didn't budge. He fished out the little pieces, cold and throbbing in his palm before he handed over the spoils of his labor at Drummoc.

He leaned heavier than usual on his trident as he hobbled up beside the prison and glimpsed a half-remembered escape, floating on the backs of others. There she waited for him, brooding and unsympathetic. Polc and Carabiner strolled past practically arm-in-arm on their way to the navy hall, and the captain saluted them politely. Nothing in his manner could explain the wave of fear that washed over Parks. He looked back to his lady friend, who had come ashore alone and found a way to get a captain arrested when Parks couldn't have done it himself. He saw a courage that she probably never bothered to notice. It issued from her when it was needed as naturally as a breath. She had no spear, no letters, no one trailing behind her to keep her safe. She wasn't strong, but there was a strength to her, and he felt it radiate against his skin when she was near.

He held those black eyes, and knew that his fear was not only for himself. Too many people had borne him here. Now he saw that if he couldn't lift them, too, none of them would stand much longer.

"Thank you," he said, his eyes welling, and she didn't understand why. If she felt contempt for his display, she concealed it. Kjartke slid under his armpit, and they hobbled ahead of the old man.

They came over the ice in the stars before dawn as a wave rears up at the shallows. The sixty men of the *Queen Taral* picked their way south since Autumn. They wintered hard. But every man stood for it, recalling the thrill of the mutiny, the bitter disputes at Yunoc that divided the camp, their responsibility to their families on shore. Lenet knew that the widest fetch brings the biggest swell, and there was much sea behind them.

He made no speech and no battle plan. Six remained with the ship. The others marched through the night without a word, each left to his own fears and dreams, until the torch of the watch flickered at the harbor. At the launch, they paused, and Lenet said to them:

"Let the people know you have come."

Their war cry woke the four marines on duty before the wave broke upon them. Urkuk himself heard the terrible sound and prepared his hearth.

Lenet could see no one. He knew his allies by their whooping, and they rushed about looking for an enemy. None came to meet them. In the torches beside the navy hall door, he spotted some sailors beating to be let in, terrified of the wail moving toward them. They turned as the war party rushed the steps and fell full of spears.

From the shouting inside, Lenet knew that a great force had slept in the hall and was making ready. The raiders formed a line on the landing to meet them. The doors seemed to beat like a man's chest but did not open. The men began to look with wonder at each other. The sky lightened, and from the buildings came a single Mattaka man.

"Quick! Arm yourselves! The army of Mennetungiliamuk returns to take what is ours!" The man hurried back into town. Many other faces appeared from every alley, old and young and women alike. Lenet grew unsettled, because there was no enemy, and the people were confused. He looked for Brother, who called himself Leopard Seal, but saw no sign. For so long he feared his death at the hands of this force, and now he worried he would not find them.

Soon the battle woke, slowly as men often do. A marine sergeant and some of his men ran out from the alleys, and Lenet recalled that their barracks were elsewhere. He told some of the crew to remain at the door, and with a group of men ran down to meet them. The marines did not seem to understand what they faced, and the sergeant told them to go back to their huts as if they had come to complain about rations. Lenet killed him before he could lift his weapon, and they drove the others back into the town.

Another bunch spilled from an alley. When they saw the Mattaka make a run for them, they fled for reinforcements.

"Come! We will be strong in the streets! Let us kill them while they put their boots on!" Munaponak shouted, and before Lenet could warn them to remain together, eleven men rallied after him into the tukits.

While these made off, more marines came on the other side of the navy hall—many more. Mattaka leapt off the stairs to meet them, and Lenet rushed over in support. Some of the crew had brought bows, and knowing how marines hate arrows, they fired from the landing. The first Mattaka fell ahead of Lenet. The dying man gripped the spear that slew him with all his might, and Lenet barreled over the marine while he tried to withdraw it, then thrust into the man behind him. He heard his crew killing the first man, yet he continued his run until the little force had split and Mattaka flowed between them like a gash in a hull. More men jumped from the stairs, and in moments the enemy once again retreated into the town.

But Lenet saw the toll, with three of his own dead. He knew they would not hold off the full might of Drummoc like this. So he called to the two boys among them, of only nine years and little good in a battle, to hurry through the tukits and rally the people.

They had not even taken the first step when the door to the hall swung inward and sailors flooded out. Too many had left the landing to meet the force on the ground. Those who remained either jumped into the snow or met their end on the spears. The two boys did not need encouragement to pull themselves out of the snow and hurry on their mission.

War cries mixed with loud curses at the foot of the stair. The rowers met them well. For every two that joined the battle another sailor turned the other way to shirk the fight. But the flood did not stop, and no one among the Mattaka knew what commands to give to an army. They ran in and out of the spears at will, confusing the enemy and little more. The crush of men drove them on their heels, and Lenet thought to fight into the town, where the narrow lanes would let them meet their foe one and two at a time.

As they moved for the buildings, the regrouped marines emerged to block their path with more men. Toward the harbor, he saw yet more hurry out ill-dressed but armed.

"Close the flank!" Someone ordered from the landing. Lenet dared a glance and saw Captain Polc waving at the oncoming marines. If these were allowed to reach their flank, they would be surrounded on three sides.

"Among the ships!" Lenet's men echoed his command. The Mattaka broke and ran away from the hall toward the shipyard, and sensing a rout, the enemy splintered into a wild chase. Lenet looked back for no man. His legs, stiff from the cold march, found life and put him among the derelicts. He rounded an old firestone ship sinking under rotten timbers and leaned against it, panting. On both sides, bodies flashed. Mattaka, Mattaka, Mattaka—at last, a sailor rushed around and Lenet slashed under his ribs. More followed close behind. They closed both ends of the path, trapping Lenet and four others between ships. He and his men scaled the ship where the false deck was missing and stabbed down to keep these marines at bay. From his vantage, he could see his crew darting between vessels in little pockets, fighting, running, unaware of what lay behind each turn.

Boots struck wood. He did not have to see to know they had mounted the ship on the other side. Lenet swiped to move the men below him back. He got a start, then launched his foot off the gunwale, vaulting over the enemy to the next ship, an open darraig. As his men landed after him, he knew it would not do, and jumped down the other side.

Two sailors cut his path in one direction. He went the other way, and nearly got the spear of a startled Mattaka who joined his party. The sailors who had chased him fled what was now a larger force. They headed for a nearby war cry and encountered a squad of marines. Lenet changed direction again. He paused when an arrow flew past the gap, then risked it anyway, darting into another little cluster. An ill-fated man peering after some other Mattaka earned Lenet's point in his back.

But Captain Polc and a healthy lot of mercenaries spotted him. Lenet's little force broke along three corridors. Lenet darted around a gutted docogon. Ahead, several marines charged them. He slipped into a hole in the hull and found another that led out the far side.

Arrows flew from a high place. Lenet hurried toward them without knowing the archer, and found a Mattaka atop a working docogon, scraped and nearly ready to sail. He and his companion scaled the ship, and from its high walls, he saw the chaos of the fight.

"Sons of Barduk! Rally to me!" His companions joined his shout, and soon more fleeing Mattaka climbed the ship. To port, some of his crew could not scale the side. They locked spears with the marines, too far down for Lenet to reach. The archer fired his last arrow.

Seeing the oar ports were open, Lenet dropped into the hold. He found the benches beside the marines, and his spear thrust into the ear of one. In the ebb, his men climbed aboard.

Across the shipyard they fought their way toward him. They ducked and twisted and climbed over the vessels. Mattaka jumped from deck to deck and their enemy followed. Sailors raised their spears in the gaps to stab at them. A man fell, but most made their leap.

Under cover of the raking spears from the docogon, his crew flung themselves one and two at a time, bloody upon the warship. Some could not reach them. A group of eight huddled inside a darraig, unable to move, driving back those marines who tried to board. The main force under Lenet fanned out to either side. The crew cut the rope ladders, and cleared the grappling hooks that snapped out now and then. They were eighteen—three sixes. It was a good number to have.

Late arrivals from Drummoc reinforced the sailors. Lenet found himself besieged on all sides, with a smaller force surrounding the other ship. Men called for torches. Captain Polc called for their surrender. At the edge of the buildings, the curious people sallied out to see what would happen to them, and were driven back in turn by miners who did not join the fight but carried steel and stood ready to put down a general uprising. To see his brothers join the officers of Ampos instead of his own band of raiders parted Lenet's flesh more sharply than any blade. A well-armed party of miners emerged with a halot at their center, a long blue coat brushing over the snow in the first rays of daybreak. They marched indignantly toward the shipyard.

"Surrender, or we'll burn you out!" Polc threatened.

"It is wise for a son of Atlantis to burn the only seaworthy docogon on Drummoc before his people attack," Lenet repulsed the bluff.

But the darraig had long been scrap. Fire sparked. Sailors brushed the hull with pitch and touched it off. Slow flames bled up the sides and flickered between Lenet and the concerned faces of the eight men aboard. His own band crouched beneath stray arrows. The attackers pelted them with taunts and vile promises. They numbered some hundreds now. Lenet knew his fate too well to fear. The courage of one who could no longer turn back filled him. He slammed the butt of his spear against the deck to the same rhythm he had often beat to give the oars the pace. Those who had not been on the *Queen Taral* that day had heard the tale of how the drummer drowned the sounds of mutiny, how he went first up the ladder. They had come far for this man, and all looked to him now.

"Brothers! It is a short walk to Urkuk!"

He raised the cadence to the fastest pace, but before they could stand, the air broke with a great roar from beyond.

Eskimo Joe wore an indecipherable smile as Parks informed him of the plan, conceived minutes prior and filled in as he rambled. Soon Ferrakut and Ulwet drove Kjartke out to the ships to stash her and plead for reinforcements. Norwet ran into town after some girl who he said would help him speak to the right Mattaka. He caught Poznatxen, who he called Hawk Bill to everyone but Poznatxen. The marine's debt of gratitude seemed near its end every time Parks encountered the stern warfighter, but he listened to the plot that Parks "had uncovered by chance," overhearing Polc and his officers on the ice. They argued over the timing of their plan to assassinate Carabiner and seize the colony from the inside, burning it to the last ember when their navy arrived in Spring.

Parks' gut told him that the marine wasn't fooled—he'd hardly left Parks' side, after all. But the ruse earned him a twinkle, and he promised to relay it to the captains who were most loyal to Ampos, who had doubted the mercenary even before his arrest.

Parks and Joe lay awake in the poorman's quarters, crowded with farting castaways.

"It will be a great victory," his ancient shadow said of the plot. "For who do you win it?"

"For the people of this fair land," Parks answered before the question rung in him with its full demand.

He finally drifted off, and dreamed he was in the prison again with a hairy creature, man-like but terrible, creeping always in his direction. A splitting cry spared him near dawn. Parks found himself upright as if raised by invisible hands, balanced entirely on one leg. Joe handed him his trident, and peeking through the door, he saw flickers of movement by the lights of the navy hall.

"Where's all my homies? Do you think they're coming?" He asked.

Eskimo Joe shrugged. "Perhaps these men wondered the same when they crossed the ice."

For some reason, Foster appeared to Parks in that moment. He had often forgotten his wayward friend, and the thought came as the answer to something he had never asked. Parks threw the door open and used his trident to pole himself out. The frigid breeze had barely nipped him when Joe slung him against the wall and pressed his back beside him. From both sides of the building, marines rushed toward the fight within feet of the two men in the last minutes they could have remained invisible.

Instead of following him into a rear assault on the marines, Joe led him back into town. They eddied through the tukits, avoiding the shouts that neared them from strange directions, until they came to the arranged place at the back of the prison, and found themselves alone.

Joe didn't have to say it. Parks felt the futility of their position as frantic grasping at air at the start of a fall. A heavy puff of steam escaped.

"How long should we wait?"

"Before what?"

A general shout from the local military gave him an idea of the battle. He considered a retreat to the poorman's quarters, where he could wait it out, and where he might continue to hide, slinking behind buildings, begging sleigh rides from boys while he avoided Carabiner's distrustful questions and the predatory eye of Polc that sent Gionn crawling at his feet what seemed a lifetime ago.

He put a hand against the wall for support and took the butt of his trident. The prongs reached up over the rim of the roof, and Parks poked it this way and that until it stuck. With some finagling, he caught a fold on the point and yanked down a sack, which burst on the ground at their feet. Stones spilled out—the kind that were used to build wigwams, or cell walls.

"There is another here." Norwet appeared with most of his cousins and some girl.

Parks fished down the next sack, this time into waiting arms, then a third, and a fourth. The boys filled their shirt tails until they sagged, pregnant with missiles.

"Is this all you could get?" He asked a little too desperately of the meager force.

Norwet shrugged. "I told many."

Shrill whoops carried from a nearby street. Another responded, nearly on top of them.

"Akjuru!" Parks shouted. He poled himself after the voice, rounded a wigwam, and came within feet of a trio of sailors standing over a Mattaka still writhing with a spear in his chest. The men's surprise turned to understanding when Joe and the dog boys bumped up behind him. The near sailor withdrew his weapon and stepped toward Parks, who fended at him with the trident. The man slapped it, and Parks lost his balance, tumbling onto the arced side of a wigwam. A rock flew over his shoulder and cut the sailor's lip. More followed in a barrage, driving the men out of sight.

"Death to Barrow Jak!" Norwet cried as he ran past after them, and his cousins echoed the call. Parks and Joe did their best to follow the boys' shouts. They caught sight of them again, then lost them; saw a rock skip over the top of a wigwam; collided with a man sprinting around a bend. The Mattaka rower raised himself, recognized Parks, and smiled.

"Munaponak! Leopard Seal has come!"

The man ripped him off the ground and from there he raced over a whitewater stream, pulled and pushed by a growing squad that split his ears with their high wails. Two marines blocked their path. Suddenly half their party appeared on the other side and men pressed against the warrior in front trying to sneak a thrust around in the narrow space. The marines went down. Another rock from parts unknown splintered across a wall ahead of a prepubescent curse. He knew without looking the palm on the small of his back was Joe's. A wider street opened, and sailors retreated under rock-fire, pursued by boys he didn't recognize and the little girl. Saunlauk and Siguvik crossed the path the opposite way, chased by marines. The native wails and English barks rose until they reached a long, rectangular wigwam with a pair of marines holding the door against Mattaka thrusts. A skirmish raged nearby from the sound of it. The arms set him down to join another fight.

A squad of marines nearly ran Parks over from behind. Joe spun to slash, but tangled his feet with Parks and knocked both of them down. He cut the achilles of the nearest man, then caught the shaft of a spear thrust that just missed him. The man above him whipped it until it pulled free. Joe up-kicked him in the balls. Parks, still flat on his back, slapped the man's face with the side of his trident. Joe stood at the wrong moment, and fell again from a two-seam fastball of a rock in his back. Norwet fired rocks as fast as he could pick them off the ground, and they began to come back from the enemy, causing both sides to take cover.

Parks and the old man got up again, and it was hard to tell who helped who.

"It is Ulwet! Tell the dead! It is Ulwet, your killer!" The little boy crouched atop a nearby wigwam, raising to pelt his enemy over a commanding web of lanes.

"Yo! What the fuck?" Parks got his attention. He thought the boy had been at the ships, but within moments, marines and stray sailors sprinted past the lanes on either side in full flight toward the open town. A dozen, two dozen, more Mattaka streamed in from all tributaries. Ostuk and Haraket and Attibatbarak arrived with spears. He heard frantic barking. Ferrakut trailed with two dogs on leashes, and brought them right to Parks. Winnie Cooper slunk from the chaos but Barbados Slim only paused from his ravenous fury to lick Parks face and nip at his arm.

"Leopard Seal! Get 'em off!" One of the marines holding the barracks door against the onslaught pleaded. Parks recognized him for the first time—Poznatxen, helmed and armored. He blocked off the combined force of rowers and miners.

"These are homies!"

The barracks emptied of the former POWs and the remainder of Costig's company, who led them to an empty provision building where more men were hiding: the crews of the Amposi captains Amachar and Rapana'ekunata, none of them pleased that a man of Atlantis had infiltrated their ranks.

"What orders, captain?" Ostuk asked, and it took Parks a second to realize that everyone was looking at him.

A host poured forth over the field. Munaponak led the pack, with many other Mattaka beside, but Lenet saw to his surprise that more than half were sailors and marines. The body formed a battle line across from the shipyard while those assaulting the docogon hurried to gather in response. This new force was perhaps only half the strength of their foe— one-hundred fifty, Lenet estimated, with more Mattaka running in from town. But it was enough to throw the command into confusion. The fleet admiral shouted and pointed, sent runners to the town for help, and shoved men into position. Already the shirkers drifted to the back of the line and lingered among the ships. In the flood, Lenet's brothers threw themselves out of the burning ship and slipped the encirclement. The docogon let out a renewed cry.

Stumbling up after the others, Lenet saw a towering man supported by an elder and flanked by a pair of dogs. The Leopard Seal had heard his plea.

"Parks! What the fuck, bro?" Carabiner stomped to the front of his men.

"We've known for months that Drummoc would be invaded," Parks shouted back. "What we didn't realize is that the enemy was already among us. These dudes behind are here to make a stand: Drummoc will never belong to Atlantis." As the words left his mouth, he frowned at the absurdity of what he'd just said. *Atlantis?*

"That was a rumor that *you* started. There's no evidence to support it, and even if it were true, I'm the commanding officer of this garrison. Everything I do is for these people—those behind you, too, whether they realize it or not. I lose sleep every night second-guessing myself to ensure that every word and every deed out of my body enriches our lives and makes us safe. I work for those who support me, and those who don't. I've kept you safe, too. You have no idea the things I've done. No one will invade us. There will be no war for the people of Drummoc, because I've already avoided it. Don't make these people slaughter one another because you're too goddamn shortsighted to recognize that."

"You're the only one who can stop this. Hand over the farri's son and his men." Norwet hissed something at his elbow. "And the criminal Barrow Jak," Parks added.

Carabiner stuttered in disbelief. "Did they cut out your fucking brain when they took your leg?"

"Gua!" Poznatxen stepped forward. "Have your forsaken your land and your service? Join us!" He implored the marine sergeant-at-arms.

"This man is appointed by the viceroy. I serve Ampos!" Gua replied.

Attibatbarak yelled something in Mattakatan, and Satletaluk answered from the other side. Men began to lob petitions to friends or the entire force confronting them.

"For Ampos!"

"Listen to the admiral!"

"Fuck Ampos!"

"For Costig!"

"Alexicus!"

"Leopard Seal!"

"Bastard squains! Cut 'em down!"

"Fuck 'em all!"

Up and down the ranks men bobbed forward as if hardly restrained by a slackening cord of elastic. Miners and even old women from the town pressed into their backs to add their shouts, jostling Parks. Eskimo Joe spoke in Mattakatan.

"Who's he talking to?" Parks asked Norwet.

"I don't know, but he say, 'Now you will see a battle.'"

The sailors on his right flank made last-ditch pleas to the opposing captains Korrel and Bruco to switch sides.

"Down with Polc! Give us Polc or die with him." Amachar shook his spear.

"We got twice your number!" One of Carabiner's Midshipmen replied.

Even Parks couldn't mistake the strained peace, held only by the frayed fears of what had to follow. He ordered out of the side of his mouth without taking his eyes off his blue-coated friend: "Nobody harms Carabiner."

Poznatxen shrugged. "Then get to him first, and don't harm him." The Eribath Islander had had enough flirtation. He jogged for the center of the line with a shout, his marines on his heels. All order collapsed. The rush knocked Parks from his feet, and when it had passed, he took comfort that Joe had also been flattened beside him. The two dogs dragged Ferrakut in the opposite direction. The rest of the men—and a handful of women—charged with such abandon that the greater force before them staggered ahead of the shock. The Midshipmen converged in front of Carabiner. An impressive number of cowards fled the field entirely, as though awaiting their cue.

Most of the venom ran for Polc and Carabiner, allowing the enemy to wrap around Parks' left flank. They knocked Munaponak's few warriors back then spilled among Rapana's crew. Immediately, the sailors wavered with confusion, swinging at friends and in one case, embracing a foe then escaping arm-in-arm from the fray.

Parks tried to hobble toward the fight, but a hand on his shirt tail slowed him—he couldn't help but think deliberately. Isolated behind the clash, a group of enemy sailors noticed him and peeled off at the free run. Barbados Slim shot in dragging a leash and latched onto the arm of the lead man. Ferrakut lunged at the second with a spear. He dodged easily, but it gave Joe's blade the opening it needed to nearly decapitate him. Sharp rocks flew in to stall the rest—the youngest boys, Ulwet and Arnake, stood with the girl over a full sack, and unarmed Mattaka helped themselves before scattering for the battle, back home, and everywhere in between. Winnie Cooper whined alone, too frightened to move.

"Do not go too far. Or too near," Joe warned while they inched in on the melee. Up ahead, Parks saw Carabiner being helped over the side of a ship where the heart of his line made a stand behind Polc and the Midshipmen. Beyond that pocket of intense fighting, it was impossible to tell the sides apart, most of all for the men involved. Marines shouted at one another instead of engaging, and sought out Mattaka; Mattaka from either side also shouted at one another, and sought out sailors. The formations disintegrated into little pockets of personal grudges, while townsfolk scurried back and forth between combatant and rabid spectator.

They followed the fight as it piled and streamed like snow against the ships. There were few dead to trip over. Most of the engagements amounted to wild exchanges of slapping wood, with one side retreating for support. Wounded hurried off the field, stopped, and settled in to watch like football players who'd reached the sideline. To Parks, the realities of battle were as bizarre as they were terrifying, and he didn't know whether to berate his team for cowardice or desert, himself.

By now some hundreds of Mattaka miners ran in from town, and in most cases, it was impossible to tell who they'd come for. Many of them threw punches or rocks at each other, ignoring the main fight. But a growing force rallied to Satletaluk and Carabiner, forcing a retreat by Poznatxen and Haraket. They fell back to Parks, swept around him, and flowed into the shipyard by another lane. He found himself carried and separated, then dropped like a pebble in the shallows among the wooden skeletons.

A group of eight sailors frowned at him in surprise from within a scrapped frame.

"Keep it up, boys!" He nodded valiantly, unsure of who they were. Not his, by their rush to raise their spears.

"Help! Joe! Slim!" He called. It was a company of Mattaka who responded, twenty-strong, and the mere sight drove the sailors to another hiding place. One of them gripped Parks' elbow. He squinted at the blood-washed face.

"Brother!" Lenet said. "If we wake tomorrow, I will make sure no one calls you anything but Leopard Seal."

More "armies" emerged as the battle wore on. One, mostly Mattaka, did its best to break up the clash between their friends and family. The other, also mostly Mattaka, took the opportunity to liberate scraps of wood and lumps of coal, nails and soapstone bowls from the colony. They greedily rushed, often with admirable courage, to remove the wounded and prepare the dead for burial—never mind if they left the world a little lighter than they had lived.

For the hundreds involved, though, the corpses were few. Most encounters remained confused and noncommittal. Not more than a few dozen men collided with any zest at one time, and that role shifted around a reluctant field. Allies hurried up, warning that someone was losing ground nearby, and rushed off with a few reinforcements, to be replaced by another dogged squad looking for a rest. Enemies milled among their own kind, argued, threw hands, and swatted away thieves.

By the early afternoon, Parks slumped against the side of a ship. Carabiner had managed to take the navy hall with a healthy company. Haraket led away almost half of their force after a rumor that marines had left to attack the people who remained on the ice. Women brought them food and water, and they watched the other side receive the same. Another skirmish broke out somewhere in the town, with both parties darting in then slinking back fifteen minutes later. He even saw a sailor call what could only be described as a "timeout" while surrounded by miners—only to have it honored.

Mattaka started back to their homes for the evening. Carabiner, as bewildered as Parks by the strange rhythm of the battle, sent out a last concerted effort to the shipyard. Parks' side, badly diminished, just climbed into the defensible ships until they went away. Fearing a night attack, Eskimo Joe had them set fire to a wreck. They slept in fits under the glare of the blaze, waking at every crackle and shadow.

All the next day, little groups of his men cured him of the illusion of command. Poznatxen set out with Amachar and Rapana to make another run at Carabiner without so much as inviting Parks. After a boy arrived from town with a tip, Norwet took the dog boys, Lenet, and most of his men to attack a building where the crew of Barrow Jak had spent the night.

While Parks huddled in the belly of a warship with Joe and a skeleton crew, the boys blockaded the barracks of their nemesis and began to take apart the masonry from the outside. Marines under Sergeant-at-Arms Gua came to the sailors' aid in what would turn out to be the fiercest and bloodiest action of the entire battle. Many miners, a number of whom had fought Lenet the day before, joined the boys in vengeance against the hated captain.

Parks would assemble the brutal details from snatches of conversation in the months that followed. The narrow streets piled them against one another in veins. The Mattaka wreaked havoc early with their knowledge of the layout, but once the battle clogged the streets, the superior training and tactics of the marines took its toll. They were pushed nearly off the building when a rock struck the temple of Gua, killing him. Ulwet lay claim to the throw, and in the resurgence, they finally opened the south wall of the barracks.

But the penetration only allowed Barrow Jak's men to rush into the fight. The Mattaka found themselves trapped between a reinforced enemy and a swell of townspeople who had crowded in to witness the event. Panicked fighters fled over the tops of wigwams to escape, and Barrow Jak led the marines on a blind slaughter.

Warriors entangled with old men. Children were crushed under their falling mothers. The snow vanished under leather and flesh as the men drove the people through the town. They pursued them over a few miles of open terrain, slashing at the stragglers, until they reached the ice, over which the people ran for the safety of the ships.

When Poznatxen returned with word of the other fight, they carried Parks to the dog camp to protect the boys' family from reprisal. Into the following morning, his men made personal sorties of every kind. An attempt to set fire to the docogon fizzled in the high winds. Poznatxen and his marines captured clothing from the dead Mattaka and dressed themselves so that no one would confuse them with the perpetrators of the slaughter. Several young rowers went searching for the snow-covered crevasse of Ingputka, intent on placing curses that would lead them to victory. All of it buzzed around a helpless and inert captain, incapable of moving himself anywhere meaningful: not to the icebound ships, which repelled a half-hearted attack from one crew in sloppy conditions; and not to Drummoc, where a riot raged into the night against Carabiner's forces.

It was on this news that a ragged council met over a lamp not far from the dogs that howled scoldingly at the night.

"Damn beasts! Can they give a dead man no quiet?" Rapana'ekunata sweated half-propped along the side of the wigwam, feverish from a pair of belly wounds.

"You're sure they don't encircle us as we speak?" Poznatxen asked.

"We have sent scouts twice, and the boys keep watch. Nothing stirs," Attibatbarak assured the marine, who for the first time, including his stint as a POW, appeared drawn and uncertain to Parks.

"Many travel this way tonight by the torch of Urkuk." Joe's remark met with a silence that made itself out to be skeptical to conceal its disquiet. Parks chilled at the memory of his own walk up that mountain, and the canine cacophony that somehow knew of his presence.

His skin rumpled with a chill in defiance of the fact that he knew better. Parks let the procession of ghosts form in his mind like a strand of lights under calm water. He wondered if they knew his presence, too— the man who dragged an island of people into a fight they didn't know they needed with a slap on the ass and a get-'em-young-hustle.

The others searched the faces around the wigwam the way a group of men empties their pockets to pool enough spare change for the tab.

"We may have to surrender." Amachar caved first.

"To speed our execution?" Poznatxen scoffed. "The squains have turned on Alexicus. Now is the time to press our advantage."

Attibatbarak nodded in support even as he bristled at being called a squain.

"Over who?" Parks spoke at last. Lenet shifted uncomfortably in the sling that held his fresh-set arm. Eskimo Joe appeared elsewhere. In the few strokes of action Parks had witnessed, the old man seemed a few squirts of WD-40 shy of a war machine. Compared to the first months of their friendship, his blade was slow, his balance off, his attention wandering. Meanwhile, Ostuk and Haraket lay at the ships, unwilling to travel for fear of losing them to the enemy or the melting ice. He didn't need to say any of it. Poznatxen, having barked his courage, left the question unanswered.

"We tried. Polc's still alive. Carabiner's still the admiral. They still hold Drummoc. We had a couple of hours to get it done. Now? Nobody wins. And it's too late to be forgiven." He felt the reproach fall on himself, and he threw back the flap like a suffocating blanket and burst into the swirling breeze.

His ribs and shoulder ached with every hop, unaccustomed to supporting the movement of the past days on the trident. As he set the butt into the snow, it slid out ahead, causing him to lurch forward. Parks' torso followed. The prongs, protruding from his panicked grip, rushed up at his face. He stiffened every muscle and closed his eyes as the whole of his body screamed in anticipation of his impalement.

His momentum slammed to a miraculous halt. One eye peeked open, then the other, to find the weapon inches from his nose, his torso inclined impossibly forward, but somehow still balanced on one quivering leg. He held the position, breathing in quick shallow gasps, unable to believe he'd caught himself. Boots shuffled through the snow. Soon a pair of hands righted him.

"I have come a long way. Do not spoil my labor." Eskimo Joe grinned.

"Yep. Smells just like I thought," Parks quipped as he removed his nose from the vicinity of his trident. They stood on the edge of camp and their eyes mounted the curving slope of the depression to the top where the stars peered over a black blanket.

Joe spoke in a thin voice that whistled from his throat from somewhere far away.

"Some men do not count the dead. These make good captains. For the man who feels every spear, it is brave to say to his brothers, 'There is the enemy. Let us go and fight them.' He would rather face the host himself than see one man fall at his side."

"Is that supposed to make me feel better?"

"I have never learned the trick to suppose before I speak," Joe admitted.

Parks vaulted a step forward, stuck the landing, and waited several seconds to be sure of it. Then he followed it with another. By careful groan, he reached the slope, and soon he slid harmlessly back and landed on his palms. Lacking the gymnastics to push his luck, he began to crawl by weighting his hands and jerking his right knee forward. Joe appeared at his side again.

"We will arrive faster if I do more than watch a lame dog drag himself." He reached down to lend a hand.

Parks regarded it, old and wavering, taken more often than it was extended.

"I need to feel like I can do it myself."

He expected an argument, but when he peeked under his armpit halfway up, Joe remained at the bottom watching him. Parks twitched with annoyance before he could remind himself that it was what he asked for. His hands numbed through his mittens. His knee burned, stiffening as it dragged a furrow. The piercing furor of the dogs dropped to a tinny crackle the second he cleared the top. Parks bellowed like an ancient man exiting his recliner when he stood.

The breeze washed past him like someone sweeping in broad strokes on either side with pauses between. Miles away he could see lights dancing by the harbor. They looked flat and near, but he blinked them into their proper distance. When he craned up at the moon lighting the field ahead, he saw sharp lines that made it seem too close as well, but this time, he realized he was picking out detail he hadn't managed in years. Within a silver ring of glare that broke along the little crystals in his lashes, he could *see*.

The three figures ahead dropped out of that satellite. They had already seen him, and stopped.

"Yo!" He hollered with false assurance. They leaned in to speak among themselves, then two of them turned back. The middle one headed toward him. Parks took his trident in both hands and let the points rest on the snow in front of him. His visitor's stride, artificially high for the shallow snow, betrayed the fatigue of the walk from Drummoc.

"Just the man I wanted to see," Parks greeted him.

"Single combat, to the death?"

Parks glanced over at the volcano, then rested the butt of his weapon and felt along Carabiner's shoulder and face.

"Just making sure I'm not hallucinating."

Carabiner looked around suspiciously. "You get here by yourself?"

"Just me and my salad fork," he stamped his trident.

They waited for some time, alternating looks over the other's shoulder for sneaking shadows.

"I came to apologize," Carabiner said at last. "You told me who you were all along, every step of the way. At Camne Drumlag, on the *Qarapara*, in the Navy. And I refused to believe you."

"Apology accepted. Now let's go off-script. I'm done bullshitting you. For real-sies this time. I would surrender, but I've seen what your bunch does to prisoners. And what would be the point? There are people here on this island that will never live together. Not in the same town, the same county, not within a whale's blow each other's second cousins. We can figure out whose fault that is, but it doesn't change the fact that my dudes and your dudes will never be dudes again."

Carabiner nodded in relief at the understatement.

"So what do you propose?"

Kjartke stood far from the men, and at her arrival, the other women gave her room. She had lived among the Kapadak, and it no longer grieved her to be treated so. She could have remained with Tunguk, or gone to the family of Sawipelagannapuk, but she preferred this distance. It was not because she feared a new battle. Many held weapons though Brother and Alexicus warned them to come unarmed. There was still much hatred between the two parties gathered on the harbor grounds where the dead had only just left on their journeys. Nor was she certain what would come.

She did not care if anyone thought she mingled with men. She did. Nor did she stand alone to avoid being thought to support those criminals. She had supported them. Kjartke stood apart as Alexicus savored the sound of his voice because though she shared many threads with these men, it was not she who lay them. They crossed waters and raised arms, told lies and truths, made their secret bargains, and asked bold favors. She lurched behind like a little boat on a tow rope, bumping into rocks, filling with seas. Even this peace was their choice, yet her fate. So she stood among the women, who had as much say.

Her young friend found her eye in the crowd, guarded by men at Alexicus' side. Brother and Alexicus went unheeded. It had taken Sophia to stop them—Sophia, who carried the hearts of many—and much silver for the families of the dead.

He read the names—she did not know if his memory was poor, or if he wanted to show everyone his skill with letters: "Parks. Lenet, and all his crew. Haraket." Haraket's father Sateltaluk withheld his grief if he felt it. "Sergeant Poznatxen. Ostuk. Attibatbarak. Amachar, and his crew. The crew of the late Rapana'ekunata, and the crew of the late Etan. Tunguk. *Kjartke*."

Kjartke shuddered with relief when Alexicus spoke her name. It seemed a flattery she had not earned. The women moved farther from her, but for one irritated girl, who she recognized as the cousin of Nuk.

"Why do you get named and not me?" She asked bitterly.

"…*Exiled* from Drummoc and Nunoc for all their days," Alexicus went on. Perhaps those nearby thought she hated the banishment, or rejoiced over the fear it would have been death. But Kjartke felt a heavy stone sink beneath clear water to a depth. She would never be a lady of Drummoc. If she had often convinced herself she wished it, now she was certain of the lie.

Other women wailed or wept, or shook with anger as he went on. The rest would be pardoned, but only if they swore an oath of loyalty to Alexicus, and despite many tender words of forgiveness, many could not. A battle for Drummoc had been fought, and those who could not take her, lost her forever. Those who could not be separate from these men also lost her. Many who would remain did so with uncertainty. They would mourn those driven forth as they mourned their dead, and wonder where they, too, would be towed behind these great men in Spring.

In the ripple of her relief, Kjartke glimpsed a new fear beneath those waters. For now, she was to be a wanderer—*tungutke*. There was nothing more hated to her people. No Jargadak spoke of those who sold themselves. But since she was a girl, they spat at the name "wanderer." These were the people who belonged to no land—no goddess. "They-who-hear-no-prayers," it was often said of the pitiless mothers who even the gods feared, but it was these who gave them the rock and the sea and the animals that kept them. To wander was to be orphaned. Without brother. Without sister. The consort of cruel strangers and the threads they pulled. Perhaps she had gone as such for some time, and only now recognized it.

Tunguk slouched among the others. Only he had escaped an evil course, for he had traveled it most of his days. But the old man did not look seaworthy, Kjartke thought. Nor did Brother, for that matter. Many would find banishment no kinder than the spear.

The great men left the crowd to its laments. He came to her moving on his silly weapon. She thought he took on a pathetic look to earn her sympathy, though she admitted he looked much better than before.

"Would it be insulting if I said, 'My bad?'"

"Yes," she used his word for *aye*. "It is bad to go with shame. A man always face his enemies. He do not always win."

Brother seemed to take some cheer in this. But he rode his moods like a young woman, and soon his face flattened as a coat laid on the rock when Alexicus led Sophia away.

"Do this mean no more date night?" Kjartke asked. Brother started to give a defense, then saw her grin. He laughed a little, as though to seek permission, and when she could not contain herself, he fell in. They braced on one another to keep their feet, and those around them stared as at a madman who cries his tricks to the moon.

At last Brother gathered himself, and rose again to some height. "Thank you for letting me pretend to be your atatapalatak."

"It is good we no more have to pretend." Kjartke forced a smile past many things, and left him bewildered upon the pitiless back of Drummoc.

Compared to his last visit, the reception at Nunoc looked to Foster like a damn homecoming parade. Lookouts spied the *Gairhle* as soon as she rounded the point. Several crews lined the quay, wide stance, left hand behind with the elbow neatly pointed. It seemed friendly enough, despite the spears that stood tall in the other hand. Just back, Foster recognized the little round helmets of the Marines. A squad of men worked with rope and block to lower a rotted mast from its base, where it had displayed the bird-picked corpse of the most recent soul to offend the viceroy, he assumed. The remains sagged against weathered bindings that gave in places as the post tilted, the tattered skeleton twisting in anticipation of his freedom.

Foster craned over shoulders for a glimpse of Barzos, ready to count every piece of lint on his beads, but the bureaucrat was absent. He imagined those wide eyes leaping from his skull when he saw the men he stole off the island had returned with a real ship, and wondered if either of them should be glad.

He might have had a more formidable crew this time, but his forty men had to be as cautious as they were hopeful. Foster knew the garrison outnumbered them by a hell of a margin, and it didn't take a number man to see it. By now, a few weeks since they last stuffed ice and dried seal in their barrels at Yunoc, there was no turning back. The ship's bilge swirled like a toilet from unseen leaks—wounds from a winter on the ice and a rough launch split and scraped around them. The watches bailed every minute of every hour. They pulled the last miles shin-deep in numbing water. A limping *Gairhle* drew along the quay, and though Foster had been briefed by Gionn and others about these proceedings, he knew that they couldn't even bluff the ability to turn around before a raw deal.

"Admiralty letter!" A captain demanded as they drew along shore.

"I got one better: a message from the admiral of Drummoc." Foster declared with optimism.

"No letter, no harbor. But perhaps we can work somethin' out."

Gionn pushed impatiently beside Foster and leaned out over the port side. "Hoy! Wanker! What if we give you our ship, and two of every three bollocks between our thighs? Fine! Four of five."

The sailors on shore chuckled while the captain floundered to regain his footing.

"No, we can do better," Gionn went on. "I'll throw in two of the three lads who stabbed your mates and fled on the dog ship. Aye, that'll be us," he draped an arm around Foster. "And if that's not enough, I'll see the viceroy spares your shit life when he learns you obstructed a dire message that will save every man of the garrison from certain destruction. Admiral Turrha's dead. Admiral Palqua's dead. We carry word from Admiral Costig and Tolba, himself. If you doubt it, send up a marine called Tasua, and I'll prove meself."

A murmur of irritation broke the order of the men. Foster cringed at the confession, and Gionn noticed. He answered in a hushed voice: "Would have made us eventually. Better that we choose the moment."

They didn't have to send for anyone, because the leader of the squad cutting down the dead man heard, and jostled to the front. He was an Amposi with a wide nose, turned up at the snout, and a long bowl cut spilling from under his helmet. The sailors recoiled from him with wary respect.

"What of Costig?" Tasua said.

"Nimaket lies faultless for the mutiny on the *Kawal-Atxl.* Costig knows the hand that held the rope." Gionn recited. Tasua might have blushed if his red-brown face had permitted it. He smiled to downplay his surprise. "Now heave us up, cunt!" Gionn called to the captain. Tasua nodded and returned to his men.

Foster hardly felt confident of their welcome. He left the twenty-four Mattaka from Yunoc at the ship with Pitras and Fergo to oversee repairs, and to make sure it didn't vanish without a fight. They met Tasua as he finished laying the mast on its side. Two marines lifted the narrow remains onto a shroud spread over the rock. A wooden sign rattled loose on the pole where it had hung beneath the victim, and it caught Foster's gaze, since he reckoned few enough here could read it. With a toe, he angled it for a look: CLERICAL ERROR.

He shot back to the forlorn figure, and for the first time noticed the soiled red trim along the pants and a mat of beads hanging broken from the neck of Barzos as they folded the shroud delicately around him. Foster staggered, and felt bile in his throat. There were no tears, or bursts of anger, as though his body understood his position and recomposed him. But his fear of this place turned to a hateful abandon. He remembered their naive visit to the viceroy's house and felt the tug of the lashes on his back. Foster shrank into a humbled specter of that man who tossed a spear into the viceroy's door to be heard. Visions of Parks' leg in the lamp-lit tent mingled with the frozen flesh of a kind and generous ally. He seemed to forget at intervals that the world was real and very consequential. At the same time, he despised it and wanted no part. Who was left for him to sail for? He wondered. Were there any besides these men around him?

Among this crew he may as well have come alone. There seemed little hope of success, but worse, no one to share it with. Who would believe him anyway if he made it home? And if he didn't, who here would thank him for trying? The last bitter breaths of his hope filled him with an unexpected courage as the familiar house loomed. He owed everyone, and could repay no one. There was no shore to gain that could forgive him. He returned free of the illusions that carried him this far. Maybe that meant he was free of the obligation to go any farther. There remained only Foster among strange company, and in the footprints of the place where he was whipped within an inch of his life, he no longer feared destruction.

Foster looked up at the shuttered window where the viceroy had appeared, and even caught himself searching the laundry line for the white cracked turtle that Barzos had mentioned, a trivial artifact of memory stirred up in the churn of regret. *Maybe I'll kill him myself,* he thought, fixed on the face of the two-story estate. He imagined his battle, as Parks and Tunguk once insisted: hordes of sailors rushing on him in revenge. He met them with his spear and cut them down, man after man, somehow surviving, somehow surviving, killing another and another, until the first point pierced him. He swung his weapon as a hundred blades broke his skin, without wanting to be anywhere else.

Tasua moved to knock on the door, but Foster stepped back and cupped his hands.

"Viceroy! Open up! The name's Foster, and I got a feelin' you'll remember my face!"

It was Gionn's turn to cringe. The crew looked on with reserve, sensing that something different had got into their captain. Foster gripped his spear in the long clatter of boards from above, unsure if he intended to deliver a message or hurl his weapon.

The bar lifted and the shutters parted. A woman of maybe forty with ebony wood hair past her shoulders hung out, her bead-studded dress spilling onto the sill. Dark eyes narrowed over the crook of a broken nose as her stern features softened into a mischievous smile.

"Didn't I hire you and your ship for something? I hope I'm getting a refund," the woman from the *Qarapara* said.

Foster wobbled. He covered her with an outstretched hand, then removed it. When she remained, he replied.

"I'm plumb broke right now, but if you don't mind, ma'am, I'd like another crack at it."

Sign up for the newsletter

to receive alerts about future installments in the series!

Visit www.ancientseakings.com

ROSTER OF THE GAIRHLE

Uldred	**STERN**	Bosc
Nakos		Banno
Palqua		Cormdran
Baghar		Dunn
Lozeder		Arthas
Ordacles		Hiren
Jonn		Mene
Dari		Mahal
Boot		Irilo
Aldan		Tawatu
Bale		Eckerd
Gewar	**MAST**	Jenneker
Nolan		Igonus
Tamarqan		Moipa
Chapa		Deowa
Casey		Fid
Tarvin		Otsander
Bubba		Imau'y
Pitras		Qawa
Fergo		Asdosa
K'sem		Horrio
Reed		Basa'u
Hogue		Gabol
Juru		Yuray
Bentos		Chirim
Foster		Gionn
Atalkut	**BOW**	Tunguk

GLOSSARY

A

â – *Mattakatan*. Yes.

Abalax – An angotak ship (abiama) patrolling the Attavaik Sea.

Aber – Youngest son of Farri Donn.

Adelate – A girl of the Mennegur family at Drummoc. Daughter of Satletaluk and Vatjate. Younger sister of Haraket, Muk, and Hiad.

adhu – a build of warship typical of Pone.

Adim – A sea god.

Aer – Farri, son of Mil, deposed by his brother Donn.

Aermon – Son of Aer.

Aftinoc – A small island off the coast of Fomorlann captured by Donn and Paladris.

Ainsome – One of the Bachla.

Ajatse – Mother of the Mattaka gods and name for the whole of the landmass on which they live.

Akawake – Mattaka god who beaches whales and foreigners on the shores of the people.

aklu – *Mattakatan*. A domed structure made of ice blocks.

akmanittak – *Mattakatan*. Brother.

Aku – Dog of Hawe, who led the people to Ajatse.

Aldan – A carpenter on the *Gairhle* who jumped from Captain Polc's crew.

Aleoatni – The people to which Pitshin belonged. Lost a fierce conflict with Atlantis.

Alexicus – Assistant Viceroy of Nunoc, on inspection at Drummoc.

Ama – Amposi goddess, twin sister of Lama, mother of Atxl.

Amachar – Captain of the abiama sent to pursue the *Juhketappat* as she fled from Nunoc.

Ampos – The kingdom of Tolba which rules over Hiade, especially Nunoc and Drummoc.

angotak – 1. *Mattakatan*. Orca. 2. Elite mercenary navy patrolling southern waters in service of Ampos.

Anseloc – An island of the upper peninsula of Hiade, just south of Breidoc.

Arhaid, (Battle of) – A Pyrrhic victory for Atlantis, known to many.

Ariatjate – Daughter of Onagnutulauk and Iniasep. Younger sister of Saunlauk, Siguvik, and older sister of Metkate.

Armenuk – *see Nuk.*

Arnake – A young dog driver of the Seleku family. Son of Sawipelagannapuk and Ebrakallite. Younger brother of Milak and Ravitak.

Arthas – A man of the *Gairhle*. Sailed to Drummoc under Cormdran.

Arwoset – A sailor of the *Juhketappat*.

Asdosa – A man of the *Gairhle*.

assistant viceroy – An officer under the Viceroy of Nunoc in service of Ampos.

Atalkut (Bucket) – A former blacksmith apprentice and man of the *Gairhle*.

Atl-Ceru – A little-known and humble fishing people who fell victim to raids of Paladris.

Attavaik Sea – The coastal waters of Hiade

Attibatbarak – A Mattaka miner and member of the Dawn Council in charge of Guests and Hospitality.

Atxl – Amposi god associated with battle and masculine virtue.

Aubatanes – An island group notorious for raids, unrest, and mutinies.

Awala – A sea god.

Aymos – An Amposi captain in the Drummoc Navy.

B

Bachla – The eight daughters of Nim, and the eight natures from which a man can be born.

Baghar – A man of the *Gairhle* and close associate of Palqua.

Baldrakut – Father of Ianate's first husband and grandfather of Uniatsate.

Bale – A man of the Gairhle. Sailed to Drummoc under Cormdran.

Banno – A man of the Gairhle.

Bannoc – An island of the upper peninsula of Hiade, just south of Breidoc.

Banugsep – Daughter of Senadak and Ianate. Younger sister of Uniatsate and Hattrakatsep.

Barduk – Legendary Mattaka warrior to threatened Atlantis.

Barereto River – An enormous river that empties into the Atlantic at Mabhan.

Barrow Jak – A captain in the Drummoc Navy.

Barzos – A bureaucrat stationed at Nunoc who helped Foster and Parks flee the island.

Basa'u – A man of the Gairhle.

Batadu – Small kingdom of Absha, where the *Gairhle* was built.

Bayochar - An Amposi captain in the Drummoc Navy.

Beithel's Breath – A sailor's song, thought to bring a favorable wind.

Bekiatven – A mine at Camne Drumlag tat translates as Bird's Mortar.

Belads – An Atlantean name for the aurora australis.

Bentos – A man of the Gairhle.

Berga – A woman named in a popular children's song.

Bernica – Kingdom of Donn prior to becoming farri.

Bilata – A many-eyed creature of myth.

Blowhole – Parks' nickname for a boy who helped him at Yunoc.

bluecoat – Nickname for Amposi Navy, especially officers who proudly dye their coats.

Boot – A man of the *Gairhle*. Sailed to Drummoc under Cormdran.

Bosc (Asahem) – A man of the *Gairhle*. Sailed to Drummoc under Cormdran.

Bragamil – City where Farri Mil relocated the capital of Atlantis after flooding.

Breidoc – A near-barren island of the Hiade peninsula, the last land before the Orin Sea.

Bronze of Eusk – A ship belonging to the Bronze Tongues

Bronze Tongues – The elite guard of the Farri.

Broom – A man who sailed down with Cormdran on the *Gairhle* but stayed on with the Navy.

Bruco – A captain in the Drummoc Navy.

Bubba (Bubua) – A man of the Gairhle.

Bucket – *see Atalkut*

C

Calda – A port near Bragamil.

Calm Harbor – A marginal landing place on the south side of Drummoc, typically becalmed.

Camne Drumlag – Mainland site of the mines operated from Drummoc.

Casey – A man of the *Gairhle*. Sailed to Drummoc under Cormdran.

Chaleda – An angotak.

Chapatawamiran (Chapa) – A man of the Gairhle.

Chatsikuy – An Amposi sea god.

Chirim – A man of the Gairhle.

Cleanthe – A darraig belonging to the Drummoc Navy.

Cormdran – Captain of the *Gairhle*.

Correscu – A kingdom traditionally using square rigs who later adopted the claw sail and outrigger.

Costig – Admiral of Drummoc, formerly a sergeant-at-arms in the Marines.

D

Dal – Ancestor of Mil. Legendary farri who reunited the kingdom after a major political crisis.

Daldus – One who belongs to the line of Dal.

Daloni – Site of a famous mutiny signaled by the song *Half by Hadal*.

Dannan – A demi-god hero of Atlantis.

Darfordlann – A site most famous for its offshore kelp forest, reputed to bring good fortune to sailors.

Dari – A man of the Gairhle.

Dasseder – A Marine sergeant under Gua at Drummoc.

Deana – One of the Bachla. Her kind are strong-willed and often rise to great roles, but are hampered by their vanity, selfish determination, and inability to inspire deep loyalties.

Debora – A figure of legendary beauty who appears in several songs.

Dedications – Huge monuments to the faces of Uinab located over a stretch of coast from Vequitan to Tsaba.

Delba – An Atlantean ship captained by the youngest brother of the wife of Farri Aer.

denankikumak – *Mattakatan*. Fire King grows weary. Refers to a period in which the sun lowers toward the horizon.

denuak – *Mattakatan*. Birth of the Fire King. Refers to a period in which the sun rises.

Deowa – A man of the Gairhle.

Donn (Donnab) - ("Little Donn" or "Young Donn.") Younger brother of Farri Aer who claimed the farriship.

Doran – An angotak.

Drummoc – An island and the southernmost settlement of Hiade. Site of a mining colony of Mattaka under the sovereignty of Ampos.

Dunn – A man of the Gairhle.

E

Ebrakallite – Wife of Sawipelagannapuk. Mother of Milak, Ravitak, and Arnake.

Eckerd – First mate on the *Gairhle*.

Edrasut – A Mattaka miner and member of the Dawn Council in charge of the weather report.

Eirgren – One of the Bachla. Her kin are peace-loving and kind, inspiring good relations among others.

Elward – A man who sailed down with Cormdran on the *Gairhle* but stayed on with the Navy.

Erdeshwe – A fishing people who sail by consensus rather than naming captains.

Etan – A captain in the Drummoc Navy.

Etsatep – A female relative of Vatjate living on Drummoc.

Etxe – An angotak.

Euskus – An Atlantean god popular among sailors and merchants.

Eye – Refers to the eye of a needle. A loop on Nunoc run by dog drivers for practice and initiation.

F

farri – The king of Atlantis, to whom other sea kings pay tribute.

feachle – A strategy board game.

Fergo – A man of the *Gairhle*. Sailed to Drummoc under Cormdran.

Ferrakut – A young dog driver of the Vjarku family. Son of Alakset, middle brother between Norwet and Ulwet.

Fid – A man of the Gairhle.

Fire Nose – A notorious unit of boarding marines under the farri.

Fomorlann – A land long-proven difficult to conquer for foreigners.

Fomraigh – A general name for the people who live in Fomorlann.

Foster – A contemporary sailor from North Carolina, marooned on the shores of the sea kings.

Foul Hand Waits – A sailor and sometimes recruiter in the Navy at Drummoc.

G

Gabol – A man of the Gairhle.

Gairhle – A whaler. The 60-oar ship of Cormdran.

Galichar – Served as admiral of Drummoc prior to Turrha.

Gaspar – A man who sailed down on the Gairhle with Corm.

Gerachay – An aide to the admiral of Drummoc.

Gerig – Father of Cormdran.

Geru – An Amposi household god.

getjar – One of eighteen bead shapes traditionally carved by the Mattaka.

Gewar – A man of the *Gairhle*. Sailed to Drummoc under Cormdran.

Gharnadil – A port south of Ampos.

Ghrane – Captain of the dog ship *Orin's Thief*.

Gionn – A whaler rescued by Foster and Parks.

Gjeplate – A crevasse field on the route around the Eye, a sledding passage on Nunoc.

Gjetsene – A Mattaka goddess who leaves a blanket of pure white snow behind.

Gjoraslag – Site of a number of funeral cairns for prominent individuals on Drummoc.

Good Korrel – Captain from which Cormdran purchased the *Gairhle*.

Greater Fahaile current – A strong current known to all sailors.

Grom – Parks' nickname for a boy who helped him at Yunoc.

Gua – A Marine sergeant-at-arms on Drummoc.

Guaracan – A jungle port once visited by Gionn.

Gunnlauk – Mattaka god, brother of Junnlauk. A quiet ruminator who weighs on men and causes them to hold back. Also brings daydreams and a wandering imagination.

H

Hadalis – Principal god of Atlantis and an important figure to many other peoples.

Hadalsbank – The elevated religious and civic center at Bragamil.

Hamarqeta – A people near Mabhan.

Haola – A sea king of old, minted on a series of unusually large copper coins.

Haraket – Originally called Mennetvattalatjatuk before changing his name to avoid legal troubles. A Mattaka miner and member of the Dawn Council reporting on foreign affairs and events on Drummoc. Son of Satletaluk and Vatjate, older brother to Muk, Hiad, and Adelate.

Harald – Royal tutor in service of Farri Aer.

Hastate – Granddaughter of the poye on Drummoc.

Hattrakatsep – Daughter of Senadak and Ianate. Middle sister of Uniatsate and Banugsep.

Haumak – A Mattaka clan of the peninsula who tattoo their faces.

Hautatlo – A place Gionn once claimed to have been born.

Hawe – The most-powerful Mattaka god, especially associated with the sea.

Hestens – An angotak.

Hiad (Mennethiadetartet) – Son of Satletaluk and Vatjate. Younger brother of Haraket and Muk, older brother of Adelate.

Hiade – Atlantean name for the southern continent.

Hiren – A man of the *Gairhle*. Sailed to Drummoc under Cormdran.

Hogue – A man of the *Gairhle*. Sailed to Drummoc under Cormdran.

Horrio – A man of the Gairhle.

Hup'atele's Cairn – A barren island far to the north of the Hiade peninsula.

Hupadak – An unconfirmed Mattaka clan.

Hurut-Atxlchar – Amposi viceroy at Nunoc.

I

Ianate – Sister of Sawipelagannapuk. Wife of Senadak. Mother of Uniatsate, Hattrakatsep, and Banugsep.

Icua, Battle of – Site of a battle and subject of a popular song.

Igonus – A carpenter on the *Gairhle* who jumped from Captain Polc's crew.

Iniasep – Wife of Onagnutulauk. Mother of Saunlauk, Siguvik, Ariatjate, and Metkate.

iqina – A gambling game that uses tokens.

Irilo – Spinnaker on the *Gairhle*.

Ithir – A captain in the Drummoc Navy.

J

Jalopong – A sea god of Jarrahil

Janten – An angotak with whom Costig briefly served as a youth.

Jargadak – A Mattaka clan of the Ajatse peninsula who tattoo their faces. Kjartke was stolen from this group.

Jenneker – A man of the Gairhle.

Jonn – A man of the *Gairhle*. Sailed to Drummoc under Cormdran.

Jordy – A sailor in Captain Folmon's crew.

Juhketappat – A dog ship captained by Ostuk.

Julea – A beautiful acquaintance of Gionn's.

Junnlauk – A Mattaka god, brother of Gunnlauk. He is a storyteller, and the route by which stories travel, as well as the performance or expression of words and songs.

Juru – A man of the Gairhle.

K

K'sem – A man of the Gairhle.

kaim – *Mattakatan*. A wide range of spirits that sometimes engage with the people. Can be helpful, devious, malign, or otherwise.

kaimatjuk – *Mattakatan*. A ceremonial arrow in which the owner lures a helpful kaim to take up residence via song.

Kammatuk – The Mattaka clan that occupies Drummoc.

Kapadak – A Mattaka clan of the Ajatse peninsula, among whom Tunguk once lived.

Katillike – A beautiful figure of Mattaka legend.

Ketklemak – A Mattaka god who returns with the sun to drive the children of Pautatse back to their ancestral grounds.

kjapadenalak – *Mattakatan*. Tide Queen steals from Fire King. Refers to a period in which the sun sinks below the horizon through peak darkness.

Kjartke – A member of the Jargadak clan taken to Drummoc by Parks and Foster.

kjatsensak - *Mattakatan*. Tide Queen flees the king's return. Refers to a period from peak darkness to the time the sun returns.

Korrel - A captain in the Drummoc Navy.

Ksit'hangi – The people of Asahem Bosc who dwell far to the north and inland.

Kullunuk – A Mattaka hunter and member of the Kapadak clan.

Kurrhatet – A Mattaka god associated with dogs.

Kurrhatetgiuk – A dog ship that routinely travels between Drummoc and Nunoc.

L

Laconos – A sea kingdom traditionally paying tribute to Mabhan.

Lama – Amposi god. Twin brother of Ama, Father of Atxl.

Lamachar – Amposi Minister of Coal at Drummoc.

Lanallike – A beautiful prostitute at Drummoc.

Lanasep – A Mattaka goddess who makes a bed of snow.

Lau – The port where Arthas and Jonn joined the *Gairhle*.

Leopard Seal – An epithet taken by Parks.

Liam – A captain in the Drummoc Navy.

Linikut – A Mattaka youth at Drummoc, sympathetic to the Mennegur family.

Lozeder – A man of the Gairhle.

M

Mabhan – A sea kingdom commanding the mouth of the Barereto River, traditionally the rival of Ampos.

Macuna – A sea kingdom near Bragamil, friendly to Atlantis.

Mag's Harbor – The main harbor at Taclann.

Mahal - A man of the Gairhle.

Manuclas – A whaler who sailed to Drummoc with Cormdran.

Maraigh – One of the coal ships seized by Mattaka rowers.

Marcans – An angotak.

Mattaka – "The people." A loose group of several clans isolated at Hiade.

Mattakatan – Language of the Mattaka.

Mawena – An Amposi household god depicted as a frog.

Mearfannan – A god and son of Uinab.

Mene – A man of the Gairhle.

Mennegur – A prominent Mattaka family on Drummoc known for making trouble.

Mennetarmenuk (Nuk) – *See Nuk.*

Mennethiadetartet (Hiad) – *See Hiad.*

Mennetsatletaluk (Satletaluk) – *See Satletaluk.*

Mennetungiliamuk (Muk) – *See Muk.*

Mennetvattalatjatuk (Haraket) – *See Haraket.*

Metkate – Daughter of Onag and Iniasep. Younger sister to Saunlauk, Siguvik, and Ariatjate.

Mil – A revered former farri who moved the capital across the Atlantic after a flood.

Miladus – One of the line of Mil.

Milak – A young dog driver of the Seleku family. Son of Sawipelagannapuk and Ebrakallite. Older brother to Ravitak and Arnake.

Mintalus – A sea god.

Moipa - A man of the Gairhle.

Muir - A whaler who sailed to Drummoc with Cormdran.

Muk – A rower on the *Queen Taral* who orchestrated the Mattaka mutiny. Son of Satletaluk. Middle brother to Haraket and Hiad.

Munaponak – A Mattaka rower who participated in the mutiny of three coal ships.

N

Nachreann – One of the Bachla. Her kind cause trouble, "strife, worms, and the unraveling of rope."

Nagal – An angotak on the *Abalax*.

Nakos – A man of the Gairhle.

Naopawi – A people known as excellent slingers.

Nawalte – Mother of Nuk, sister to Vatjate.

Neal – First mate to Captain Polc on the crew that delivered the warning of war from King Tolba.

Neferwet's Foot – A Mattaka hunting ground near Drummoc.

Neidis – An admiral of Farri Aer.

Nemas – A whaler who sailed to Drummoc with Cormdran.

Netsetone – A sea kingdom allied to Batadu, betrayed and sacked by Paladris with the help of Batadu.

Nim – Father of the Bachla.

Nolan – A man of the Gairhle. Sailed to Drummoc under Cormdran.

Norwet – A young dog driver of the Vjarku family. Son of Alakset. Older brother of Ferrakut and Ulwet.

Nuitatls – Mythical sea creatures who wreak much havoc.

Nuk (Mennetarmenuk) – A youth at Drummoc and member of the Mennegur family. Son of Nawalte.

Nunoc – An island of Hiade and the principal administrative seat of the colony.

Nurtas – The first captain of Cormdran.

Nutillen-Amalset – A Mattaka miner and member of the Dawn Council in charge of provisions.

O

Obdu Caran – Another world of legend.

Obrachar – A Marine sergeant-at-arms at Drummoc.

Oduy – A former captain of Gionn's on a whaler.

Oljarbaruk – A Jargadak and father of Kjartke.

Omera – An Amposi goddess associated with sea ice an icebergs.

Onadak – An unconfirmed Mattaka clan.

Onagnutulauk – Younger brother of Sawipelagannapuk. Husband of Iniasep. Father of Saunlauk, Siguvik, Ariatjate, and Metkate.

Onaster – Oldest brother of Farri Aer's wife.

onik – *Mattakatan.* Thread. Can refer to the fate a man lays for himself stitch-by-stitch.

Ordacles – A man of the Gairhle. Sailed to Drummoc under Cormdran.

Orin Sea – The violent belt of waters between Hiade and the lands to the north.

Oset – A Mattaka hospitality god.

Oterec – A whaler who sailed to Drummoc with Cormdran.

Otsander – A whaler who sailed to Drummoc with Cormdran.

Ottarbaghan – A port near Bragamil.

Ouretse – A Mattaka goddess related to snowstorms.

P - Q

Palchar – A marine at Drummoc.

Pallaia (-Akanoa) – An Amposi goddess, often called by epithets.

Pallaia – One of the coal ships seized by Mattaka rowers.

Palqua – A man of the *Gairhle* and an Amposi captain in the Navy at Drummoc.

Parks – A contemporary sailor from Santa Cruz, California, marooned on the shores of the sea kings.

Pattawa – An angotak.

Pautatse – A massive ice shelf south of Drummoc and one of the daughters of Ajatse, who births the ice.

Payaqura – A port just north of Ampos.

Perides – A prosperous group of islands.

petiuk – *Mattakatan*. Forge, or [it] forges.

Piktuk – A Mattaka god who favors male members of household, accord among men, and fertility and male children.

Pillars, The – Another world of legend.

Pitras – A man of the *Gairhle*. Sailed to Drummoc under Cormdran.

Pitshin – A slave of war belonging to Farri Aer who tutors his son in practical aspects of warfare.

Polc – A mercenary captain who delivers word of Tolba's revolt to Drummoc.

Ponotopl – An Amposi household god.

Potxl – An Amposi god who favors bead workers.

Poznatxen – An Eribath Islander and marine sergeant at Drummoc under Costig.

Qarapara – The Antarctic charter ship on which Foster and Parks worked until it sunk.

Queen Taral – One of the coal ships seized by Mattaka rowers.

R

Ralte – A legendary current believed by the Mattaka to run clear and cold and carry bold men who make their own choices.

Rampanatu – An Amposi holy place.

Rapana'ekunata – An Amposi captain in the Drummoc Navy.

Raratuk – The Mattaka man who broke his brother, the hero Vitjukvattajuk, out of prison.

Rasden – A mercenary in Captain Polc's crew.

Rat – An angotak.

Ravitak – A young dog driver of the Seleku family. Son of Sawipelagannapuk and Ebrakallite. Middle brother to Milak and Arnake.

Rald – A sailor in Captain Folmon's crew.

Reed – A man of the Gairhle.

Rixtan – A hard-nosed first mate in the Drummoc Navy known for his ability to train rowers.

Rolodarn – An angotak.

Rugarapay – An Amposi household god.

Rumit – A Mattaka hunter and member of the Kapadak clan.

S

Sagalak – A Mattaka miner and member of the Dawn Council who reports on internal affairs and the readiness of their forces.

Satletaluk (Mennetsatletaluk) – A Mattaka miner and member of the Dawn Council in charge of mining operations.

Saunlauk - A young dog driver of the Seleku family. Son of Onagnutulauk and Iniasep. Older brother of Siguvik, Ariatjate, and Metkate.

Sawipelagannapuk – Head of the Seleku family of dog drivers. Husband of Ebrakallite. Father of Milak, Ravitak, and Arnake.

sea king – A ruler of a coastal territory, usually subject to the farri.

Seander – A captain in the Drummoc Navy.

Senadak – A dog driver. Husband of Ianate. Father of Hattrakatsep and Banugsep.

setu – Face tattoos popular among Jargadak women.

Sewadkut – A Mattaka blacksmith at Drummoc.

Siguvik – A young dog driver of the Seleku family. Son of Onagnutulauk and Iniasep. Younger brother of Saunlauk, older brother of Ariatjate, and Metkate.

Sowe – A sailor at Drummoc, traded from the crew of Liam to that of Polc.

Sun Gate – A strait of water marking the passage between the Atlantic and the Orin.

Suyu – A shapeshifter god of the Hamarqeta, he has the head of a serpent, the wings of a bird, and the tail of a lion. He lures men away to distant shores under many guises.

T

Taclann – An island in the southern Atlantic known as a safe harbor for whalers.

Tair – A figure of myth whose head turns with the heavens.

takal – *Mattakatan.* Enemy.

Takka-tak – A derisive term for the babbling languages of remote people.

Tamarqan – A man of the *Gairhle*.

Tamash – A fire-spitting serpent.

Tannawauk – A Mattaka god who resides in the mountains of Camne Drumlag over Winter.

Tanset – A Mattaka god known for his rage.

Tarvin – A man of the *Gairhle*.

Tasua – A Marne sergeant-at-arms at Nunoc an a colleague of Costig's.

Tawatu – A caskip and man of the *Gairhle*.

Teague – An odd sailor who came to Drummoc with Captain Polc.

Temple of Omera – An iceberg.

Thachta – A goddess preferred by angotaks.

The Arm – The peninsula of the southern continent.

The Pillars - Another world of legend.

Timor - A whaler who sailed to Drummoc with Cormdran.

Tiril-Lama – An epithet for the Amposi god Lama, who took a wife from every kingdom and sent his seed out all at once in canoes so that no son would be held above the others.

tiriloy – A ship from the initiative of King Tolba to seed the colonies of Hiade with fine goods and the pleasures of home in order to lure more Amposi men and women to settle there.

Tlintaat – Another world where the dead cannot go.

Tolba – King of Ampos who recently declared himself farri.

Tsaba – A north-coastal kingdom, home to one of the Dedications.

Tuilapoy – Minister of Colony at Drummoc.

Tunguk – An old Mattaka who takes up with Foster and Parks as a guide.

Tunguk (whaler) - A former blacksmith apprentice and man of the *Gairhle*.

Turrha – A recent admiral of Drummoc.

U

Uinab – A prominent sea god waning in favor.

uitkalpate – *Mattakatan*. Lion seal.

Uldred – A man of the *Gairhle*. Sailed to Drummoc under Cormdran.

Ulmar – A Mattaka dog driver at Nunoc. Brother of Alakset and Sawipelagannapuk. Uncle of Norwet, Ferrakut, and Ulwet.

Ulwet - A young dog driver of the Vjarku family. Son of Alakset, younger brother of Norwet and Ferrakut.

Umatbarak – A dog driver at Drummoc and member of the Seleku family.

Unay – An Amposi carpenter at Drummoc, charged with building a landing ramp at the Calm Harbor.

Uniatsate – Daughter of Ianate and stepdaughter of Senadak. Older sister of Hattrakatsep and Banugsep.

Unniakattuk – *Mattakatan*. The night sailors. Winds that rush down from the mountains with tremendous speed as the sun sets.

Uppinikuanatuk – A Mattaka god who Tunguk names as his uncle.

Urkuk – The volcano near Drummoc; the Mattaka underworld; and its ruler.

Utrupanuk - A Mattaka miner and member of the Dawn Council who reports on injuries and the emotional state of men.

Utsetaret – A Mattaka fertility god said to be offended by Costig's mustache.

V

Vatjate – Wife of Satletaluk. Mother of Haraket, Muk, Nuk, and Adelate.

Vau-Patl – An antler trading ship on the Bragamil route.

Vekret – A Mattaka from the hunting camp who went north with the seized coal ships. Strong voice for the party who chose to remain at Yunoc over winter.

Vequitan – A north-coastal kingdom, home to one of the Dedications.

Vetkannar – A prominent Mattaka family in Drummoc, rival to the Mennegurs.

Vetravet – A miner at Camne Drumlag.

Vin – The family line to which Onaster belongs.

Vitjukvattajuk – A Mattaka hero who broke the prison at Drummoc and had many adventures in faraway places.

W - Z

Wakanat – A god named an uncle by Tunguk.

Wat – Amposi sun lands where the dead sail.

Wayranapan – An aide to the admiral of Drummoc.

Weiroc – A small island north of the Hiade peninsula where water and food can often be had.

Wendell – A Marine sergeant-at-arms at Drummoc. Serves independently of a company.

Werdatet – A Mattaka rower on the *Pallaia* involved in the mutiny.

Willakuy – An Amposi bead man and treasurer at Drummoc.

Wind of the Wide Fetch – An epithet for the farri.

Wisk – Another world of legend.

Yunoc – A large island along the Hiade peninsula where seals can be found in abundance.

Yuray - A man of the *Gairhle*.

Yurutpa - A legendary current believed by the Mattaka to run wide and warm, full of many boats and refuse. The current of the common fates that most men sail.

www.ingramcontent.com/pod-product-compliance
Lightning Source LLC
Chambersburg PA
CBHW022028120726
47901CB00003BA/727